MW01129813

BALANCE

A

DETECTIVE

LINDSTROM

STORY

For my wife,
Angela

For my children,
James, Anna, &
Evan

I love you all

BALANCE

A
DETECTIVE
LINDSTROM
STORY

DANIEL VAN DEEST

This is a work of fiction. All of the characters, locations, businesses, organizations, and events portrayed in this novel are either products of the author's imagination or are used fictitiously.

Copyright © 2018 by Daniel Van Deest

All rights reserved. No part of this book may be used or reproduced in whole or in part, distributed or transmitted in any form or by any means, or stored in a database or retrieval system, without the prior written permission from the author and publisher, except for a reviewer who wishes to use brief quotations for a review in newspapers, magazines, or other forms of broadcast.
For information, please contact:
danielvandeestauthor@gmail.com
www.danielvandeest.com

Editor:
Sion Lidster

Front Cover Photo & Design:
Matt Downing Photography

ISBN-13: 978-1986425032
ISBN-10: 1986425037

PART ONE:

ASUNDER

"Ridiculous! that happiness, justice, and love could survive in a cruel junkyard of second-hand crimes and first-rate animals."

- *__Prelude to Madness,__*

Daniel Van Deest, 1989

PROLOGUE

Detective Patricia "Tish" Lindstrom stood at the top of the embankment, her feet half on the asphalt of the curved trail. It was a cloudy morning, with a light breeze that offset the unusually warm early November temperature. She could hear the morning traffic coming from the interstate about a half mile away. Slowly, she surveyed the area around her.

A police cordon had been set up thirty yards to each side of where she stood, which meant any morning joggers or bikers would have to detour around the area. The bike trail that she stood on sat on a high embankment which lay parallel to Skunk Creek. The curve signaled a conflux, where the creek emptied into the Big Sioux River.

Her eyes watched the water flow, the current moving from the smaller waterway as it eventually merged into the Big Sioux. She then raised her gaze to the areas on the other sides of the water. To the east was a golf course that showed no signs of activity. To the north there was only tall grass and a few scattered trees. Vaguely, Lindstrom heard the voice of the witness that had called the police, and she shook her head ever so slightly. Granted, finding a dead body was upsetting. Perhaps it was nervousness, maybe even a mild case of shock.

Whatever it was, he didn't seem able, or capable, of shutting up.

"DETECTIVE!"

Lindstrom turned to face a uniformed officer jogging towards her, holding a walkie talkie. The officer clumsily stopped in front of her, almost as if he didn't know if he should come to attention or not. "The head examiner just radioed that they've started with the body and the area." He paused, then asked, "What do you want me to do with your witness?" The officer motioned with his head to where the witness was. He was sitting on a stack of building materials, presumably that were being used for renovations at the hotel behind her. Another uniformed officer stood next to the witness, keeping an eye on him, while the words continued to flow out of his mouth, talking a mile a minute.

"First, officer, um, Tisdale," Lindstrom said, looking at the badge on his jacket, "call me Tish. Second, tell him I'll chat with him in a minute. Third, if he isn't drinking decaf, don't give him any more coffee."

Lindstrom didn't like the fact that she hadn't remembered Officer Paul Tisdale's name. Yet, with close to three hundred police officers in the employment of the Sioux Falls Police Department, she didn't have the opportunity to work with every officer on a daily basis. Lindstrom remembered that Tisdale had only recently moved over from the graveyard shift. She quickly smiled at him.

"Yes ma'am, I mean, detective." Tisdale was visibly flustered. "I mean, Tish. Sorry." He turned and walked back down the embankment toward the witness.

Lindstrom pivoted back and looked down again, spotting Jerry, the head of forensics, and his three assistant examiners. Two additional officers stood several feet away, ready to assist if needed. She guessed that she was at least fifty feet above them, but no more than seventy-five feet. Multiple camera flashes started to go off as they began documenting the evidence. She turned three hundred and sixty degrees, taking everything in.

The grass on Lindstrom's side of the embankment had been cut recently, with large rows left behind. The grass showed no signs of tire tracks. The only foot prints were from the witness, but they stopped ten feet down. The examiners and officers had walked single-file down to the river's edge. The body must have been dumped upstream somewhere, floated down to this point, and become caught amongst the reeds and bulrushes.

Lindstrom took a deep breath of recently rain-soaked air. She remembered the rain starting at around eight last night, and it was still going ten minutes after midnight when the family cat had meowed his way onto her pillow. Nature wasn't really her thing, which was strange, since she had been born and raised on a farm. She had to admit, though, the fresh air felt good after the past two weeks on her last case. Thankfully, her hunch had been right, and the bastard was not only guilty of embezzling and money laundering, but, it turned out, he was also a wife beater. She had never felt so happy to slap a pair of handcuffs on someone in all her life. Her boss, Chief of Detectives Brad Engels, who was also the acting Chief of Police, had given her two days off. Now, here she stood, her first day back, not even eight thirty in the morning, and she had a dead body.

Lindstrom turned left, facing west, which was upstream for Skunk Creek. She looked along both embankments, yet she couldn't spot anything out of place. She whistled, and one of the officers standing at the police cordon turned and faced her. She waved for him. As he started briskly walking towards her, she walked up to meet him.

"Officer Tavon," Lindstrom said, smiling, "this isn't the best way to start a Wednesday morning, is it?"

Officer Tavon Aggers, who had been with the Sioux Falls Police Department for a little more than a year, shook his head. "Not really, Tish. But, put me to work, and let's make it right."

Lindstrom smiled a little bigger and nodded. She put a hand on his shoulder and turned him around, using her other hand to point along the banks of the creek upstream. "Grab a pair of binoculars and start walking the bike path. Look for anything that's out of place, on both sides of the creek. You find something, radio it back. If you get three miles up and nothing stands out, radio back and let me know."

"I'm on it!" Tavon grinned and darted off. Lindstrom had worked with him a few times, and she found him to be a smart and hard-working officer.

"TISH!"

Lindstrom turned and saw Officer Tisdale running up the incline toward her, almost slipping in the wet grass.

"Easy there, Tisdale, easy!" Lindstrom held up her hands to slow him down. "The witness is still yammering away, and the victim isn't any deader. Now, what's up? Oh, would you rather I call you Paul, instead?"

"Jerry's on the radio for you. Says it's urgent and that you're not going to like it. And Tisdale is fine. Honestly, I'm named after my father, and the name is about all I got from him. Thanks for asking, though."

Lindstrom took the walkie talkie from Tisdale's outstretched hand, and he proceeded back down the embankment to the witness. Interesting,

Lindstrom thought to herself. She didn't know why, but names were a curiosity for her. Some people liked being called by their last names, some by their first. For her, she preferred her nickname of "Tish". She briefly flashed back to the first day of second grade. Her teacher had asked if she would mind being called "Patty", instead of "Patricia". At the tender age of eight, Lindstrom had responded, "Patricia or Tish. Either one, I'll answer to." That was the end of it.

Snapping back to the present, Lindstrom put the radio to her mouth and spoke.

"Jerry! What've I told you about spooking the unis?" That was what she playfully called uniformed officers. "How will they ever get their big kid toys if you scare them off ordinary details like this?"

"Yeah, well, normally I'd agree with you," came Jerry's voice through the radio. "Pardon the current circumstances, but I'm going to rain on your parade."

"Cute, Jerry. Whatcha got?"

"Well, lots of cuts and bruises consistent with a fall. There doesn't seem to be any damage to the grass and weeds down here, so I'm guessing she floated to this point."

Lindstrom looked upstream again, and then watched the water flowing from the Big Sioux, north to south. She didn't see any vegetation that looked disturbed on that side of the river. "Jerry, considering where you're at, where do you think she floated from, Skunk Creek or the Big Sioux?"

"She got here from Skunk Creek. The water isn't moving fast, but the body couldn't have landed at this point. Even with last night's rain, I'd wager she didn't get here from the Big Sioux."

"Got it. What's next?"

"She's naked, with no immediate evidence of animal marks, claw or teeth."

"What about decomp? Can you tell how long she's been dead?"

"I'm not sure. It looks like the body has been bleached or been dipped in some kind of corrosive agent. And not a very effective one, either. That's going to make it difficult to ascertain the time of death. I'll know more when I get the body back for autopsy."

"Okay, nothing too strange yet, Jerry. Go on." Lindstrom seemed to sense that Jerry was building to a big reveal, so she would humor him.

Jerry's voice came through again. "She's been shaved. Hair, arms and pits, legs, and pubic area. Granted, this is just at first glance, but I'm not seeing any visible signs of hair."

Lindstrom was growing uncomfortable. "Jerry, normally, I enjoy these little back-and-forth revelations we have. Do me a favor, and just dump the rest on me. I can take it."

Jerry sighed into the radio. "Don't say I didn't warn you. She has extensive bruising around her cheeks, neck, nose, and forehead. It appears that someone wanted to make sure she couldn't be easily identified. Her face is caved in. I'll know more after I start the examination, but I'm going to guess there are no teeth in this mess. I'm also going to guess that, if the person who did this went to the trouble of shaving her, that there won't be any eyebrows or eyelashes, either. Also, her hands and feet have been removed, and not cleanly. It appears that they've been hacked off. Oh, and the cherry on top of all this misery? There is a pentagram carved into her abdomen. Over and out."

Lindstrom stood there, looking from the radio down to Jerry, and then she looked up and down the two waterways below her. She closed her eyes, and took another one of those deep, calming breaths. She forced out everything that Jerry had said, and also forced out the chattering of the witness. She opened her eyes, taking one last breath of this wonderfully fresh autumn air. She exhaled, turned around, and got to work.

ONE

THIRTY-SIX HOURS AGO

It was a strange sensation for Nathan Devlin, being in a bar and not holding an alcoholic beverage. Beer, wine, liquor, it really didn't matter. His mind would sometimes drift back, thinking about all the days when he had even a small taste of booze. When he compared that to the days when he had been alcohol-free, talk about tipping the scales. Were those days really, truly behind him? A twelve-step treatment program that Nathan's best friend, Andy Cole, had reluctantly sprung for was only the beginning. Nathan knew it was going to be a struggle, an every-day process to keep his demon in check. Considering everything that Nathan had put the people around him through, maybe grudgingly was the more appropriate word to describe how Nathan had gotten to this point.

Andy had been asked by Nathan's estranged wife, Allison, to stop by and check on him. Allison didn't want to divorce Nathan, though Andy's wife, Heidi Cole, had hired a family lawyer for Allison. The lawyer helped advise Allison on the legalities of separations, and the spouses' and parents' responsibilities. Nathan had been behind on child support payments for quite some time. Even though he could have seen his kids in supervised visitations, after some sporadic visits, Nathan couldn't even bring himself to be in the same building as his three kids, let alone look them in the eyes.

Andy had tried and tried to keep Nathan from spiraling, but to no avail.

From best friends in grade school, through high school, into adulthood, best men at each other's weddings, their friendship had been through everything. After everything that Nathan had put his family and friends through, it was amazing that Andy had stepped up and agreed to Allison's request to visit Nathan. Eighteen months is a long damn time to not see your best friend. Then again, maybe not, considering the overwhelmingly drunken asshole Nathan had become.

"Am I boring you?" The voice broke Nathan out of his memories.

"No," Nathan replied sheepishly. "This is just new to me."

"Oh?" The voice came from beautiful full lips attached to an attractive woman. "You don't normally lounge around in bars?"

"Let's just say that alcohol and I went our separate ways almost a year ago."

"Really?" She looked Nathan over with a quizzical look, like he had told a lie that she had caught him in. "You've been sitting in this booth for almost thirty minutes, nursing the same glass, and you expect me to believe that there's no alcohol in it?"

Nathan felt his cheeks blush. He had been grilled daily, in person, on the phone, via text and email, for eleven months. Different people, different races, different genders, but the one thing they had in common was to make sure Nathan was getting sober and staying sober. Now, coming up on one year, this strange woman that had sat down across from him was asking the same thing.

"It's true," Nathan said. "I stopped next door for dinner, and after an excellent piece of cherry pie for dessert, I decided to test myself."

"Test yourself?" Her voice. It seemed to slowly slide inside him, unnerving and relaxing him at the same time. "What do you mean?"

Nathan took in a deep breath. "I've done some bad things, I've made some terrible choices, and I live with that every day. Now, for almost a year, being sober, trying to put things right, I felt it was time to see if the alcohol controls me, or if I'm finally getting control."

She propped her elbows on the table, leaning in, chin resting on her folded hands, studying him with those soft, glowing eyes. Nathan felt like he was under a microscope. He tried to look her in the eyes, but he couldn't do it. She was so damn beautiful, and he knew she was out of his league. He sat there, his head hanging slightly down, trying to be brave, but feeling so small and insignificant.

"You're telling me the truth, aren't you?" Her voice dropped to a whisper.

"Yes," came Nathan's timid answer. After what seemed like an eternity, she spoke again.

"So, what's the verdict? Are you in control?"

Nathan pondered it for a minute, a minute that somehow stretched into hours and days. He brought his head up so that they were eye level, he straightened his posture, and he took a deep, soothing breath. "You know what? I am. I am in control." The words seemed like a vindication, like Nathan was on the right path. More importantly, he was staying on the right path.

"Interesting," came her reply.

The buzz of a vibrating cell phone on the table broke the mood open. Nathan was taken aback by the interruption, not realizing that the small jazz band that had been playing in the background and had taken a break had come back and were playing again. This beautiful, cryptic woman opposite him briefly displayed an annoyance with the phone, looked at the caller ID on the screen, and sighed.

"Please, excuse me for a moment." She glided out of the booth and stood up, walking slowly to the back of the bar by the restrooms while putting the phone to her ear. Nathan noticed that she had left her purse behind. Was that a good sign, that she wanted to come back and be with him?

Wait a second. What the hell was he thinking?! He hadn't been with another woman since he had first met Allison. The thought of being intimately physical with a woman after everything that had transpired in his life gave him such a bizarre feeling of elation and dread. Was he happy? Sad? Terrified? The one constant thing in Nathan's life had been alcohol. For the past eleven months, he had worked hard, trying to get that incredible weight off his back. And now, in a bar of all places, the same up and down feeling that had nearly destroyed him and everyone around him was back. Was sex with a stranger the answer to his need for a fix?

No! Good lord, absolutely not! Nathan had plans! Get clean and sober. Move out of that dingy basement charitably masquerading as a "furnished one-bedroom apartment". Keep the incredible job he had found as a janitor at Laura B. Anderson Elementary school. He needed to show legitimate progress so that he could see his kids. Would Allison ever welcome him back? Probably not. Maybe, over time, the best he could hope for was forgiveness. He did know that Allison wasn't dating, since she had to work three jobs to make ends meet. Nathan had been labeled a "dead-beat dad", after all. Being so far behind on child support tended to do that.

Nathan needed to remain focused, no matter what transpired for the rest of the night. A one-night stand, with such an attractive woman, might be fun for some cheap thrills. In the end, though, Nathan was willing to accept that, even if he and Allison never got back together, he would be willing to go without sex for the rest of his life. As long as he was part of his kids' lives, and maybe even in Allison's, even a little bit, that would be enough.

Nathan turned and looked back at the woman, as she was still on the phone. She stood, facing the dark wooden molding that framed the restroom area, her curves accentuated by the form-fitting slacks and black blouse. Nathan found it odd that, after sitting with this woman for the past thirty minutes, he was only now becoming aware of her. He allowed his eyes to wander over her one more time. As he slowly turned back to his table and his glass of strawberry lemonade, he began to take in the details of the bar itself.

The name of the place was Goldie's. Technically, it was a bar and a restaurant. It was one large building, yet if customers wanted to move from the bar to the restaurant and vice versa, they had to walk outside and enter through the designated entrance. It was a strange setup, but it seemed to work. Normally, Nathan would have been content to eat a cheap meal of fast food or whatever he felt like pulling together from the little corner grocery store five blocks from his basement apartment. Tonight, though, was different. Allison had agreed to let him see the kids for the first time in, well, in what felt like forever. Nathan's A.A. sponsor, Ben McKinley, had told Nathan the good news, that this Friday, it was all planned. Nathan had reacted with equal parts shock and dread. Ben told him, "Get out of that damn hole in the ground and have a nice meal!" Nathan hadn't been sure about it, especially since he felt so guilty about not being able to take care of Allison and the children. Ben insisted, telling him it would be good for his body and mind.

After the best meal Nathan had eaten in what also had felt like forever, he had left Goldie's restaurant. He was about to start the five-mile walk home, when he had stopped on the corner and stared at the entrance to Goldie's Bar. He had weighed the pros and cons, and then walked in. He wasn't anticipating staying long in the bar, so he had ordered his strawberry lemonade in a small glass with lots of ice. Either he would panic and waste a small drink at a large price, or he would be able to tell himself he had made the right decision and nurse the drink all the way until every drop was gone. He could then call it a night and walk out of this bar, feeling a great victory on his road to straightening out his life.

One of the advantages of not having the bar and restaurant connected on the inside was the ambience it created. Any noise from the bar would not interfere with the quieter restaurant setting. Conversely, there was no chance of any underage children strolling into the bar. Goldie's sat on the northeast corner of the block. The bar itself was in the middle of the room, with seats on both sides. Along the glass wall to the outside were high tables and chairs, with the small stage for live music nestled at the end of the row. The high booths, like the one Nathan was sitting on, were along the opposite wall. Four televisions hung above the beginning of the bar, but the volume was muted to allow the jazz band to play. The mood was inviting, dark enough for a feeling of intimacy, yet with enough light so that a person didn't feel suffocated. Having turned back to face his table, his drink, and the woman's purse, Nathan was starting to feel good about his current situation. He started replaying the day Andy showed up in that basement he was living in, more than a year ago.

Nathan hadn't slept in three days, let alone eaten. He had been curled up on the floor by that rickety old recliner that had doubled as his bed at the time. He hadn't acknowledged Andy when he came in, and barely moved when Andy squatted in front of him.

"Sweet Jesus, Nate," Andy muttered. "Is this how it's going to end?" Nathan had looked up at him, vaguely recalling the final bottle of cheap vodka he had finished off three days ago. He became aware that his jeans reeked of his own urine, since he had either been too drunk or too lazy to pee in the toilet. With an abruptness of speed and strength that he didn't think he had, Nathan had sat up on the floor in a flash, startling Andy so much that he lost his balance on his squatting knees, causing him to fall on his butt. Moving so fast wasn't without consequences, as Nathan felt a wave of nausea come over him. Determined to power through it, he willed

his body to respond and keep the bile in his stomach, closing his eyes, clenching his teeth, and forcing a deep calming breath, first into, and then out of, his lungs.

"Nate," came Andy's voice after a few minutes. "Allison asked me to stop by. I'm not sure what she thought I could do after all this time. I guess I felt I owed it to her and the kids to try to reach you, one last time." Nathan hadn't heard a word. It was all gibberish to him. His eyes shot open, and he considered Andy's dark brown eyes. He took in one more breath, and the words came falling out of a hoarse, alcohol-damaged mouth.

"I've hit rock bottom, buddy. Three days ago, I think, just when I thought I couldn't go lower, I did. I'm done. I'm tapped out. Please, get me outta here! No more of this! Any place that can help, any one that can help! This can't be their last memory of me." Nathan slowly opened his right hand, holding a picture of his three kids, his babies, his angels. The picture was worn and crumpled, frayed at the edges and with a semi-circle water stain from one of many bottles of beer. Fear and desperation were in Nathan's voice and on his face, like he was throwing the last Hail Mary pass of his retched, booze-filled life.

Andy looked at him, then took the picture out of his hand. His gaze went back and forth, from this disgusting abomination of humanity that was once his best friend, to the picture of his god-children in his hand. He had tried so many times to reach Nathan. As deep as their friendship had been, Andy had moved on some time ago. Allison had tried to be optimistic at times, but she had moved on, too, figuring Nathan was lost. But something had happened. Allison had called Andy out of the blue yesterday and had begged, nay, pleaded that this was it. One more checkup, one more visit. If Andy didn't see anything worth saving, then the door would be closed on the past. Nathan would be dead to everyone, at least in spirit, and, soon enough, in body, too.

Andy's words came soft and measured. "No more? The bottom has been hit? Nowhere to go but on to bigger and better things?"

"The only way I can make it better is to fix it. That starts with me, right now, this very second."

Andy eyed his best friend warily. "And this is Nate talking to me now? I need to know I'm hearing this from Nate, and not the cheap hooch you've been pouring down your pie hole."

"The last drop came in three days ago. I haven't eaten, haven't slept, haven't moved from this spot since I picked up the glass for the last swig. When I realized I put the glass down on that picture, I started laughing, but then I started crying. I bawled my eyes out for two days. I think I cried all the booze out of me. I'm ready to get started, with as much or as little help as you and Allison want to give."

"And the kids?" Andy eyed Nathan with caution.

Tears formed in Nathan's eyes as he said, "The kids can't see me like this! Too many mistakes. Too many people I've hurt." The sound of whimpering came out of his mouth, like a severely-injured animal that didn't want to be put down.

Andy weighed his options. When help had been offered in the past, it was always met with denial and anger. Never was there any kind of remorse or regret put forth. Something about the convergence of events, Allison's request, finding Nathan here in this state, the picture of the kids, and the suddenness of the words, it all seemed so heartfelt and authentic. Too good to be true? Hardly. They had been best of friends at one time for one simple reason. They cut through each other's bullshit and, as they both opined at each other's wedding, they had "kept it real, through the good and the bad."

Holding back a choked-up voice of relief, Andy helped Nathan to his feet and said, "Dude, it's about goddamn time."

Nathan's trip down memory lane stopped when one of the bartenders dropped a bottle of expensive tequila behind the bar, shattering it into a thousand pieces. He realized that the woman wasn't back from the phone call, but her purse was still there. He looked around, spotting her back by the restrooms, almost as if she hadn't moved at all. He allowed himself one more glance over her features, and then turned to resume staring at his drink. For some reason, he checked the clock on his cheap cellphone. It was almost ten-thirty. Nathan wasn't worried about getting home and getting to bed. One of the other janitors had asked him to switch shifts. Nathan's next shift was on Thursday, a few days away.

Nathan sat up a little straighter. Was there something wrong with the woman? Was she in trouble? How long had she been gone with her phone call? Jealous boyfriend? Irate husband? Hell, was the babysitter pissed about not being done yet? Nathan looked at his glass, realizing that only the melting ice cubes were left. He wasn't sure how long he had been in the bar, but he was feeling confident that he hadn't had any urge to indulge in alcohol. Even the smells of the various drinks weren't enough to start a craving in him. He gave himself a slight grin. He was going to make it. Things were turning around. He had a lot of collateral damage to clean up, a lot of bridges to rebuild, and a lot of trust to earn back. All things considered, the future was, most definitely, looking up.

Nathan was suddenly aware that he needed to use the restroom. The woman's purse was still there. While the bar wasn't Friday night busy, there were enough patrons milling about that he didn't feel comfortable leaving the purse unattended. November Monday nights in bars used to mean football and large, raucous crowds. He glanced up at the television. The Cleveland Browns were playing the Jacksonville Jaguars. No wonder the volume was muted, no one was watching the game, and the bar had a jazz band playing. Nathan swung his legs out of the high seated booth and turned his head to see if the woman was finished with her call. She was now leaning against an ATM machine, the right side of her body in full view. Nathan had to admit that, even though sex was the furthest thing from his mind in his current situation, she was awakening a desire in him. For so long, only Allison had gotten his libido going. Nathan began recalling the wonderful times he and Allison had made love. Their honeymoon, the first night in their new apartment, that thunderstorm on the Fourth of July. As quickly as those memories started creeping in, though, he pushed those desires out of his mind. Maybe it was a good sign that he was having these kinds of thoughts. He would have to call Ben tomorrow and discuss it.

Nathan raised his arm a few inches, hoping to get the woman's attention. What was her name? Had she even offered it? Then again, it didn't matter. He wouldn't see her again after he left the bar, so there was no sense in pursuing it. She saw him out of the corner of her eye and turned toward him. She started walking towards him, although it seemed more like gliding. Damnit, she wasn't making it easy to forget her. Then again, if he could fight off the urge to drink, he could fight off the urge for a one-night stand. As she got closer to the booth, she spoke into the phone, "Look, just hang on for a minute," then covered the phone with her free hand.

"I didn't want to leave your purse in the booth while I used the restroom," Nathan said, trying to sound more matter-of-fact than like an overeager gentleman. While the look on the woman's face had been playful and interested a few minutes ago, something about the phone call had turned her features to annoyance. She turned from Nathan to her purse and back again.

"Oh, that's so sweet of you," she responded, coming out a little forced. "Go ahead, and I'll try to be off the phone before you get back." She removed her hand from the phone and spoke into it, "Okay, I'm back. Can you wrap this up?" She sat down in the booth halfway, with her legs dangling off the seat into the aisle. Nathan stole one last glance at her before he turned and walked towards the back of the bar.

As he put his hand on the restroom door, he looked back towards the booth. She sat there in the same position, but with her head craned toward the front of the bar, as if she was trying to identify something or someone. Her legs were still lightly dangling off the edge of the seat. Nathan was about to walk into the restroom when he stopped, took a step back, and looked her way again. Was she wearing running shoes? He couldn't tell in the low light of the bar, especially with the brighter LED bulbs above him highlighting the restroom area. A quizzical look came over his face as he stepped inside and went to the first stall. As he proceeded to empty his bladder, something was bothering him.

Nathan had never considered himself an attractive man. Maybe he was being humble. While he had different girlfriends during his teens and twenties, nothing really stuck. When Allison had come along, that had all changed. Allison had been like something out of a romance novel, and Nathan had felt so lucky when she agreed to marry him. Which, of course, made his failings as a husband and a father even more glaring. So, why was this incredibly sexy woman spending even a minute of her time with him? And if she was out on the prowl, looking for a hookup, why wasn't she wearing heels?

Nathan shook his head, finished his business, and zipped up his pants. As he washed and dried his hands, he told himself that it didn't matter. He would return to the booth, thank her for her time, pay for his strawberry lemonade, and head for his basement apartment. The apartment wasn't much to speak of, considering it was an income-controlled studio apartment that was in a rundown Victorian home four blocks from the school he worked at. Considering the skid row-like basement that Andy

16

had found him in, his new digs were like a presidential suite in Las Vegas. It was only enough to get by on, merely another step-up on the road to a full, and lasting, recovery.

He walked out of the bathroom, expecting her to still be on the phone. He had hoped that was the case, so he could have quietly walked to the bar, paid the tab, and left without making a fuss. However, he was surprised to see her sitting in the booth, facing him, a disarming grin on her face. He smiled back, hoping the darkness of the bar had effectively hidden the look of shock and disappointment on his face. He walked a little slower, trying to compose himself for the conversation that lay ahead. As he slid into his side of the booth, he asked, "Is everything okay?"

She took a fleeting look at her phone, which she had laid face down on the table. "Oh, the usual. One minor little thing that got blown out of proportion." She looked back at Nathan. "Really, I am sorry for the call. And you've been honest with me, so I want to return the favor." She looked down at the table, as she seemed to be trying to find the words. Nathan took a slow, deep breath. He wanted to be understanding and thoughtful, but, frankly, his life was already a fractured mess. Having this woman unload on him wasn't going to help his situation, and he might end up making things worse for her.

"I haven't had the best track record with men and relationships," she stated. It came out with such a matter-of-fact tone that it almost sounded rehearsed. "I know it sounds corny, but it's the truth. The friends I was supposed to meet here tonight blew me off, because they knew that I'd end up ditching them for some random guy. The phone call was from what I guess you would call an ex booty call. When I saw the number, I panicked, but I also felt strangely relieved, like, after talking to you and hearing just the little bit of your story, I had a rush, just a surge, like maybe I could get away from my own demons and start making a change." The words were coming out of her like a tidal wave now, and Nathan wasn't sure what to do. He reached a hand across the table, but she stopped him.

"No, please don't." She looked at him with those piercing eyes of hers. He could tell she was fighting back tears. "Tonight, things are going to change. But, before that happens, I need you to do something for me."

Nathan was trying to remain neutral, his expressions not betraying how weirdly upsetting and exhilarating this whole thing was. In the span of an hour or so, had he really helped someone confront their own demons while confronting his own? He realized that the conversation with Ben tomorrow was going to be a lot longer and a lot more interesting than he previously thought.

"What do you need," Nathan asked.

"Just share one small drink with me," she said. "While you were gone, I asked the bartender for another of what you were drinking. Strawberry lemonade, right? Your two drinks are on me, since I paid your tab. And just so that we are on the same page, I ordered myself a 7Up. Nothing fancy, just a toast between two strangers."

He was taken aback. This wasn't what he was expecting. Then again, nothing ever seemed to go as expected. Nathan looked down, and only then realized that, sure enough, there was a fresh drink on the table just off to the side by the napkin dispenser. He carefully took the glass in his hands, mulling over what to do.

She seemed to sense his hesitance. "I'll understand if you don't trust me. I am a stranger that, only an hour ago, had designs on getting into your pants. But something in your honesty, your ability to be here, in this place, alone, fighting a private war, well, I'm ready to fight my own war now, and it starts right now." She raised her glass, which was the same size as his. Nathan could see the ice cubes floating in the clear, bubbly liquid. He looked down at his own glass, the ice cubes floating in the red liquid, which had no signs of carbonation. He glanced at the bartender, who seemed to have sensed what was going on. The bartender, a medium-sized woman who was almost six-foot, gave Nathan the thumbs up sign, a wink, and a smile. He turned back to the alluring woman sitting across from him, then raised his glass to hers.

"To new beginnings," Nathan said, lightly clinking his glass to hers. He downed all of the strawberry lemonade in one massive gulp, putting the glass down softly on the table. She had merely taken a sip of hers, but that was okay.

"Are you okay to drive home," Nathan asked, not sure why he had said it.

"Oh my, yes!" Her response was quick. "I barely had anything to drink. Besides, I took a taxi here. Too many bad choices taught me to never take your own car, or get into a stranger's, in case you have to get away fast." Her cheeks suddenly flushed, maybe realizing what kind of person that seemed to make her out to be. She set her glass down and

18

dropped her head.

"Listen," Nathan leaned in and whispered, "I'm not judging. God knows, I have no right to judge. I'm also in no position to give advice. You seem like a good person at heart. Just build on whatever happened tonight, and you can start making a positive change in your life." Her head came up, and her mood seemed to go from glum to glad in a heartbeat.

"Would you be willing to walk me to the door," she asked. "Hailing a taxi usually works better if there's a man with you. Besides, if I need to call for one, I don't want to be harassed by anyone."

"I'd be happy to," Nathan replied. Secretly, he was glad this night was coming to an end. There were too many things to process after such an amazing day of finding out he was going to see his kids in a few days, and to end the night almost getting picked up by a serial manhunter wasn't the way to end things.

As they both slid out of the booth to stand up, the woman's purse caught on the corner of the table, dropping some of the contents on the floor. "Damnit," the woman exclaimed.

"Please, allow me," Nathan said. He kneeled, quickly grabbing the loose contents of her purse that he could see in the darkness underneath the table. He handed the woman's cell phone, a tube of lipstick, a small appointment book, and a pen back up to her, and then crawled a little bit to fetch two more lipstick containers that had rolled underneath the table. He misjudged the height of the table and managed to hit the back of his head on the underside of the table. "Owww", he muttered.

"Oh, god, I'm so sorry for being so clumsy!"

Nathan stood up, rubbing the back of his head. "No, that was not your fault." He felt a little woozy, but he was probably just tired. "Let's get out of here and get you that taxi." They strolled past the multiple booths, some empty, some with other patrons. They reached the front door, and the woman held the door open for Nathan. Chivalry in reverse. The night seemed to be getting stranger.

Outside, the night air was unseasonably warm for November, with not even a hint of a breeze. The woman stood by the curb, looking up and down both streets that Goldie's was situated on. Realizing that traffic was minimal, she walked a few feet to a covered bus stop and sat down. Not really knowing what to do, Nathan followed her and stood next to the bench.

"You know," she said, "one of my friend's that ditched me tonight said that there's a twelve-step program for people like me." She chuckled a little bit. "I imagine there's probably a twelve-step program for every problem nowadays."

Nathan continued to feel uncomfortable, so he sat down next to her, but being careful to avoid any physical contact. He didn't want his actions to be misconstrued in any way. "Sometimes things happen. I don't know how or when or why I became an alcoholic. I can only be grateful that I never physically abused or killed anyone. Whatever started me on this path, I finally had enough, and I'm working to make things better. It isn't easy, but most things in life aren't easy."

She turned toward him, and the look in her eyes changed. Gone were the seductive, flirty glances. Her eyes looked like pools of sorrow, almost like they were trying to confess a multitude of sins. She reached her arm behind his shoulder and softly rubbed the back of his head. "What happened to you? I mean, what changed you?"

The questions seemed to be at odds with the look in her eyes, and the bewilderment on Nathan's face must have registered to her. She took her hand away and quickly stammered, "I'm sorry. That wasn't what I meant. I meant that, whatever has happened, I hope things can turn around for you." She folded her hands on her lap, but then looked down at them. She stood up suddenly, looking at her palms. She showed her palms to Nathan. Blood? Not a lot, but enough.

"My god, are you bleeding?" She seemed concerned, and Nathan put his hand to the back of his head. Sure enough, there was cut, and the blood was trickling down his neck. As he stood up, he felt his shirt sticking to his shoulders.

"I didn't think I hit my head that hard," Nathan said. He tried to arch his back, turning to see if he could catch his reflection in the reflective plastic of the bus stop. Stars crept into his field of vision, he felt lightheaded, and he stumbled backward, hitting the plastic wall and sliding down to one knee.

"What's wrong?"

Nathan glanced up at her, and even though she was only a few feet away, her words sounded like they traveled miles to reach him. He started to blink repeatedly, slowly reaching a now bloody hand out, grabbing hold of the back of the bench and pulling himself upright. He looked back where he had collapsed, seeing a smear of blood on the plastic wall. He tried to speak, but his words were slurred, like he had a mouth full of Novocain.

"Didn't think I hit head that hard," he stammered. "Please, help." His eyes locked with hers, and for an instance, it looked like fear had consumed her, like she was trying to decide whether to help or run for her life.

A few seconds later, she turned around and faced the street. She quickly scanned the area, and then stepped out onto the pavement. She pointed with one hand, whistled, and snapped her fingers with the other hand. Nathan could only stand in place, hunched over, trying to fight off whatever was happening to his body. He heard tires screech to a halt in front of him. Doors opened and closed. He tried to lift his head to see, but the effort only increased the disorientation he felt. As Nathan remained bent over, he heard voices.

"What the hell happened here?" A male voice.

"He hit his head." It was the woman speaking.

"Ya sure you didn't get cute and clock him, eh?"

"Just get it done."

"On your six. Let's rock." Another male voice, different from the first one.

"Sir, can you hear me?" Nathan lifted his head up as high as he could and forced his eyes open. A man in a paramedic suit stood in front of him. A bright patch on the left chest seemed to scream at Nathan. HealthStar Ambulatory Services. How long had he been struggling to remain conscious? Had she been able to call for an ambulance? Was time slowing down or speeding up?

"Sir," the paramedic said again, "you are bleeding and having trouble standing. We are going to get you on the gurney and get you taken care of." Nathan heard a loud clang and saw the gurney on the ground next to him. He felt hands reach under his armpits and try to move him down on the gurney. He tensed his muscles, trying to become dead weight, but the paramedics were strong, lifting and pushing Nathan with ease. Something wasn't right. Dread began to fill him, and anxiety began to fight through whatever was causing him to black out.

"No, I'm fine," Nathan blurted out, his legs feeling like they had dumbbells attached to them. "Get me up. I can get home, no problem."

"Sir," the paramedic said again. "You are in no condition to be on your own. Trust us, we'll take care of you."

Nathan vigorously shook his head, which only increased the dizzying effects. Those words, spoken by the paramedic, sounded like they were practiced. No care, no empathy. Only words. He felt the gurney move a little. He tried to get his body to react. He forced his body to shiver, as if he was outside in the dead of winter. His body began to shake, to get away, to scream for help.

"Hey guys!" Another voice, different, distant, but somehow inviting. "You need a hand? I'm a registered nurse."

The paramedic responded, "No, thanks anyway. Just a drunk that attacked this woman." He jammed a thumb, motioning behind him. "Luckily, she's stronger than she looks. Just getting him over to the hospital" he gestured with his head "to get his head checked out, and then down to detox."

"Lot of blood," said the nurse. "Ma'am, are you alright? Did he hurt you?"

"No," the woman said. "One punch I learned in self-defense class was all it took. Between all the booze and my one hit, that was it."

"Bullshit! Leave me alone! Ya damn liars!" Nathan thought he had managed to scream, but he was so groggy, he couldn't tell how much volume or conviction he had mustered, but he was hoping it had been enough.

The head paramedic looked at the nurse and shook his head. "See, a drunk. Thanks anyway, but we got this." He went to the foot of the gurney, while the other paramedic remained by Nathan's head. They quickly lifted the gurney off the sidewalk and onto the pavement, getting its legs and wheels down. Nathan felt like he only had one more chance of getting out of this, and with his last remaining effort, he thrashed with all his might. His left fist caught a glancing blow off the paramedic by his head. It didn't cause any major damage, but left a scratch along his cheek, ending under his eye, from Nathan's wedding ring that he had always refused to take off. Nathan's right foot barely caught the talking paramedic in his left elbow. Nathan's left foot, though, managed to strike the mystery woman, landing on her neck and ear. She spun to the ground from the hit, screeching in surprise and pain.

"Holy crap!" The nurse shouted, rushing to her aid. "Ma'am, please, let me help you!" As he moved toward her, Nathan tried to reach out and grab the back of the nurse's shirt. Unfortunately, all strength had evaporated from him, and Nathan could only slap the back of the shirt. His hand fell away, his arm hanging limply over the edge of the gurney.

In one fluid movement, the paramedics lifted and collapsed the gurney and pushed it inside the ambulance. The talkative paramedic reached underneath the woman's armpit, scooping her up, saying, "Don't worry, lady, we can get you taken care of, too." He lifted her into the back of the ambulance and slammed the doors shut. "Another lovely night out on patrol, huh?" He directed the comment at the nurse, dismissing him with a slight wave and saying as he half ran to the driver's door, "Well, night, buddy!"

"Hey, which hospital are you taking them to?" The nurse shouted as the ambulance roared to life, but no answer came back. The ambulance sped away, driving two blocks ahead before turning left and out of sight.

The nurse stood there. Not only had the paramedic not turned on his emergency lights and siren, but he had turned in the opposite direction of the closest hospital, which was Sanford Hospital. He noted the name on the back of the ambulance. HealthStar Ambulatory Services. A new outfit, maybe being tested out by Avera Hospital? Even so, the ambulance had headed south, away from both hospitals. He turned and looked at the bus stop. That seemed like a lot of blood from one lucky punch to a drunk.

"JASON!" The shout came from fifty feet away. The nurse turned and acknowledged his friend that was only now coming out of Goldie's.

"What the hell?"

"What?" Jason replied.

"Dude, you have blood on your back and, WHOA!" He stopped in his tracks, looking at the blood smear. "How did you get into a fight in the past ten minutes, and with no one around?"

Jason took off his shirt and examined it. He saw a bloody smear from where the drunk had slapped him. Another smear was on the shirt's arm, probably from where the woman's head had glanced off him. Jason stood there, shirtless, not saying anything, trying to process what he had witnessed.

"Jason," his friend said, a worried look on his face, "you alright, man? Seriously, what's the other guy look like?"

Jason looked from his shirt, to where the ambulance had peeled out, to the bus stop bench, to the plastic wall, and then to his friend. "The other guy? Or the woman? Or the two dipshit paramedics that were trying to get a fighting drunk on a gurney and into an ambulance without following protocol? Or the fact that the ambulance isn't heading toward the nearest hospital, which is Sanford, with no lights or sirens on?"

Jason's friend took in the scene, looking around to see if anyone else had seen or heard anything. "So, whaddaya think?"

"Got your cell," Jason asked.

"No, man," came the reply. "I left it in the car back at the bowling alley, remember?" His friend jammed his thumb over his shoulder, indicating where Jason and his friend had been before walking to Goldie's. "You wanna head back?"

"Yeah. There's something weird about this whole thing."

TWO

Detective Lindstrom stood in front of one of the refrigerators in the break room. She knew she shouldn't deviate from her routine, but after Jerry's revelations, she was famished, and getting her lunch out of the way now would help. She grabbed her lunch tote, which had a salad her daughter had made and a fruit smoothie that her oldest son had surprised her with that morning. Things had been tough ever since the two older kids had reached high school age, and sometimes it seemed they would only help when it best served them. However, since school had started at the end of August, things had been different. Both of them seemed to be taking more of an interest in their younger brother, too.

Lindstrom had gotten pregnant and married young. Trevor came first, followed by Bree, her daughter, only sixteen months later. True, in life, mistakes are made all the time. In Lindstrom's case, even with everything that had transpired between her and the ex-husband, she never once considered her two older children a mistake. She had fought through plenty, sending the bastard to jail when he became abusive. Once the trial was over, she decided that a career as a police officer was for her. Lindstrom wanted to make sure that no one - man, woman, or child - would ever have to go through what she went through.

Lindstrom's father had been of great support. Her mother had also approved of her decision. However, since her mother had been divorced and then remarried four times, the support wasn't always as strong as Lindstrom thought it could have been. Lindstrom seemed to fly through the academy and quickly found a rhythm on the force. She landed on the fast track to detective when her keen eye to detail had helped solve a homicide that, at first glance, looked like an easy cash grab, but had ended up being a revenge hit on a drug smuggling operation.

Even being a single mother with two kids, somehow, miraculously, Patricia found love. She had been shopping at the mall with the kids, Trevor was three and Bree was two. The double stroller had caught on a wire rack in a movie and music store, and the kids were getting cranky. Mark Walsh was the assistant manager of the store and had entertained the kids while the manager had worked to take the rack apart and get the stroller free. Patricia couldn't believe how quickly the kids had taken to Mark, and it seemed like Mark truly enjoyed making the kids happy. About an hour later, while entering the food court, Patricia and the kids spotted Mark sitting down at an empty table for lunch. Knowing what she was doing, but also not believing she was doing it, she went over to the table and asked if they could join him. For the next fifteen minutes, the four of them had a wonderful time. As Mark got up to head back to work, Patricia had stood up, looked him in the eyes, and said, "So, are you going to ask me out or not?" Mark then grinned, that stupid-funny-quirky grin that Patricia loved, and they exchanged numbers. A year later, they were married. For six years, all four of them had been a family, and when Patricia became pregnant, things changed a little bit, mostly because this was Mark's first marriage and his first child. Little Ryan was born, and life continued, through all its ups and downs.

Lindstrom sat at one of the empty tables. The time on the clock told her it was ten thirty-seven. No one else was in the break room, which was a little surprising. The Sioux Falls Police Department employed over two hundred and sixty-five officers, not counting detectives, support and administrative staff, or custodians. With so many bodies working various shifts, it was rare to walk into the break room and not find one person in it. The break room itself was nondescript, with neutral toned beige paint on the walls. Hanging on the walls, in various places, were a variety of different photos of the city from different eras of the past and to the present. A picture of the old police station, a newer picture of the state penitentiary that was located a mile away, a satellite picture of the city from the 1980's, which hung next to a satellite picture from 2015. Several round tables were in the break room, as well as two refrigerators, two

26

microwaves, and several vending machines. There were the standard Coke and Pepsi vending machines, as well as two recently installed machines that offered a wide range of teas, waters, and juices. Two vending machines had the standard chips, candy bars, and assorted junk food, while two other machines, also recently installed, offered healthier alternatives.

Lindstrom opened the lunch tote and started devouring her food. As she was finishing her last bite of salad, her boss, Brad Engels, came into the break room and sat down across from her. He opened his mouth, but Lindstrom shot up one finger to shush him. She quickly grabbed a small square of chocolate and mint from her tote, unwrapped it, and put it in her mouth. She chewed it slowly, savoring the taste for a whole minute. When she was done, she looked at her boss and said, "You were saying?"

Engels looked at her and said, "A goddamn pentagram? Are you kidding me?"

Lindstrom started collecting her dirty lunch items and repacked them into her tote. "That was fast. Were you on the phone, checking up on me? Or did Jerry feel the need to impress you with all of the gory details?"

"Tish, you aren't the least bit concerned?" Engels looked dubiously at her.

"No, I'm not." Lindstrom's reply was so calm, so matter-of-fact, that Engels decided to press his line of questioning.

"Murder investigations are difficult enough without throwing weird shit into it. Especially in a Midwest town like Sioux Falls."

"Chief, seriously, it's 2016."

Engels raised an eyebrow. "What's that supposed to mean?"

Lindstrom realized that her boss wasn't following her thought process. Normally, she wouldn't examine a case and reject anything without applying her due diligence. As usual, though, she had a gut feeling regarding the pentagram, and she was determined not to lose focus because of it. Rather than elaborate further, she decided to stop Engels' questions before his questions shifted her emphasis.

"Look, I'll admit it's a lot to process right off the bat. But I have more pressing things to consider first, without looking into alleged amateur devil worship."

"Oh? Things about this case, or are you referring to that letter on your desk?"

Lindstrom turned back from the refrigerator and her stare tore into her boss. "Ever heard of something called privacy? If I didn't need this job, I would seriously consider taking you out to the broken dumpster and kicking your ass."

"Wow, Tish, lighten up!" Engels tried to come off as lighthearted, but he knew he had crossed a line. "I wasn't snooping. It's a registered letter in a large envelope with South Dakota's state seal on it, plus an address from the state capitol in Pierre. And, in my defense, it's pretty damn hard to miss. You keep your desk cleaner than Jerry keeps the morgue, and that's saying something."

Lindstrom stared for a few more seconds, and then decided to back down a bit. Her boss wasn't the enemy. Stupid laws, an insipid bureaucracy that ran itself into loopholes, and elected officials that didn't seem to care about anything except kickbacks and getting reelected, those were the enemy. Her ex-husband had been in trouble with the law or in jail since she sent him to prison. This, of course, meant that he had accrued a large debt to her in the form of unpaid child support. She had sent a letter to a South Dakota senator, detailing the issues and looking for some kind of remedy. The response was basically "have a stiff upper lip and keep fighting".

Lindstrom was beyond furious with the reply, so much so that she had left the envelope with the letter inside on her desk last Friday. After closing the previous case, and taking a few days off, that meant the envelope had been on display for the past four days for anyone to snoop. Still, she had made it very clear on her first day on the force that she would never tolerate gossip and innuendo. To her credit, and everyone else's, there had never been any. She softened her gaze and said, "Sorry. I shouldn't have snapped."

"My fault," came Engels reply. "What's more pressing than a pentagram carved on a dead woman's stomach?"

"Is my witness here yet?"

Engels rolled his eyes. "If you're referring to a certain Walter Lowry, our witness that discovered the body and has been regaling everyone within earshot about his life and current circumstances, he has been in the interrogation room since everyone got back from the crime scene."

"Then I'd better get down there and see if he can help clarify a few things." Lindstrom got to the break room door and looked at her boss.

"Are you waiting for an invitation?"

Engels stood up and shook his head. "This is your case. However, let me know if I should alert the local faithful to be on the watch for any cult-level shenanigans."

"Will do," Lindstrom said. "Oh, can you track down Officer Tavon? Let him know I will go over what we found upstream after the interrogation? Thanks!" Without waiting for an answer, she turned and left the break room, making her way to meet Mr. Walter Lowry.

"You're telling me you've never heard of HealthStar Ambulatory Services?" Jason Iverson looked at his boss, not really believing her.

"I'm telling you, there are nine ambulance services that are contracted within a fifty-mile radius, and I've never heard of that one." Kara Reed was in her early fifties, but while the days and nights of tending to an emergency room had taken a toll, she still looked radiant, even in the worst of circumstances. "Jason, what the hell is this about? I've finally gotten control of my little corner of this hospital after a horrible morning. I don't need twenty questions before my lunch break."

Jason stood there at the nurse's station. Something about Monday night was bugging him, and now this little nugget wasn't helping.

"It doesn't make sense," Jason mumbled, more to himself than to Kara or to Evelyn Blok, the nurse standing next to them. Kara looked at Jason, who was clearly troubled. She then looked at Evelyn, who simply shrugged. Kara had learned a long time ago not to immediately dismiss small items and details. Doing so usually caused things to go from bad to deadly, especially in an ER. She looked at the wall clock, then grabbed her personal notebook from the nurse's station.

"Jason," Kara spoke calmly, putting a hand on his shoulder, "you have the day off anyway. Come have lunch with me in the cafeteria. You can explain what happened, and we'll see if we can find some answers."

Jason looked at her, and nodded, allowing himself to be led away from the nurse's station. Evelyn watched them leave, and then returned to her chair. The plastic bag that Jason had brought in was sitting further away on the desk. He had said he had put his blood-stained clothes from Monday night in the bag. Evelyn wasn't sure what was going on, but, better safe than sorry. She grabbed one of the medium garment bags that they used to store patient clothes in the ER, placing the plastic bag inside. She dutifully noted Jason's name on the log, along with the code on the bag, and then took the bag to the secure locker room down the hall. She placed the bag in a locker, locked it using the combination code, noted it on the log book, and went back to the nurse's station.

Lindstrom gazed through the one-way mirror, fascinated that Walter Lowry seemed to talk in one long sentence, never stopping, not even to breathe. The officer that had been assigned to him was clearly running out of patience. If weapons had been allowed in the interrogation room, Lindstrom was pretty sure either Walter Lowry or the officer, or maybe both, might be dead soon.

Lindstrom decided that she had waited long enough. She threw the door open, which surprised Walter enough to cause him to stop talking. The officer stood up, panic in his eyes, almost pleading for mercy. Lindstrom smiled. "Thank you, officer," she said. "Why don't you take five, hell, take a ten-minute break. You've earned it. And let Officer Tisdale know I want him to observe, please."

"Yes, absolutely, thank you!" The officer, who was new to the police force and hadn't been introduced to Lindstrom yet, practically tripped over himself as he flew out the door. Lindstrom shut the door and looked at Walter Lowry. He started to open his mouth, but Lindstrom quickly put one finger to her lips. Probably not accustomed to being quieted, Walter instead took a deep breath, getting ready to prepare his amazing story for the detective.

Lindstrom sat down in the chair that the officer had been sitting in. She set her notepad and pen in front of her, the preliminary police report file underneath. She folded her hands and placed them on top of the notepad. She studied Walter's features. According to Officer Tisdale, Walter Lowry was sixty-two. She could tell that Walter had never missed a meal. Put him in wire rim glasses and give him a long white beard, and he could probably pass as a mall Santa.

Walter was getting uncomfortable, as he shifted his weight in his chair. He started to open his mouth again, and again Lindstrom had to quiet him with a finger to her lips. This clearly irritated him, as his cheeks started to flush red. Another minute passed, and then a soft tap came from the one-way mirror. She looked back and gave a thumbs-up. Two taps this time. Officer Tisdale was now in position to watch.

Lindstrom looked back at Walter. She smiled at him. "Mr. Lowry," she said, "thank you for your time this morning, and thank you for coming down here to answer some questions."

Walter looked at her. "It's no problem. I am more than happy to help out this investigation, as I've told everyone that has been involved so far." His statement came with equal amounts of pride and contempt in his voice. Lindstrom was quietly impressed. Walter loved the sound of his own voice, and he seemed like the kind of individual that embellished a regular story to make it seem bigger and grander than it was.

Lindstrom opened her notepad, clicked her pen, and looked at Walter. "Walter, can you tell me when your last eye exam was?"

Walter looked confused. "I'm sorry?"

"Walter, according to your statement, you spotted something out of the ordinary in the river while you were over three hundred feet away. By the time you had closed within a hundred feet of the river's conflux, you say in your statement that you were sure it was a dead body. That is really, really amazing. When I stood at the edge of that drop off and looked down, the only way I knew there was a body in the water was because four forensic examiners and two police officers were there, and my vantage point was, at most, fifty feet away. Even then, I couldn't see the body among the reeds and bulrushes. So, Walter, tell me. When was your last eye exam? Because you must have eyes like an eagle."

The look on Walter's face went from perplexed to happy. "An eagle, you say!" Walter laughed, a little too loud for the small room. "As to your question, I had my eyes checked two months ago. Even in my advancing years, I have perfect eyes! Which is good, since I actually discovered the body from even further away!" He sat there, beaming with pride, arms folded across his chest.

Lindstrom accepted the pause as a good time to take a few notes. She looked at Walter again. She smiled at him. "You're a bird watcher, aren't you?"

Walter's expression changed from beaming to falsely pained. "My dear woman, you wound me! I am a nature watcher! Birds are only one of the many things I watch! Even though my waistline may beg to differ, I enjoy getting out of the house and seeing everything that life has to offer!"

Lindstrom wrote some notes in her notebook before she continued. "So, to be clear, you were able to see a dead body from more than, what, four hundred, five hundred feet away, partially submerged in water and caught up in tall grass, with no aid at all?"

Walter shook his head. "Oh, my dear girl, of course I had help!" He took in a deep breath, and Lindstrom prepared herself for what was coming next. "Before I retired two years ago, I had worked in retail for more than thirty-five years. In that time, a retail employee develops a keen eye for detail." Walter used his thumb and index finger to stretch the skin below his right eye and on his eyebrow. The affect, obviously, was to drive home his declaration that he had incredible eyes. "Wherever I go, I have an innate sense of when something is out of place. It drove my children crazy when they were young, because they couldn't get away with not picking up even the smallest thing. As for this morning, I knew the instant I started my stroll to the east that something was amiss. I have been walking your city's lovely bike trails for the past two weeks, and I have become acutely aware of all manner of little changes and imperfections! For instance, under the bridge that goes over the river at 41st street, did you know that a crack has begun to form in one of the supporting concrete columns?" Walter laughed, and Lindstrom couldn't tell if he was actually amused or used the laugh as an excuse to inhale more oxygen, so he could continue to talk. "So, you see, nothing gets past these eyes! I saw something that wasn't there before, and that's when I called 911!"

Lindstrom looked at Walter with a blank expression. This man seemed high-strung to a fault. She decided she needed to change things up a bit.

"And you never met the victim?"

Walter's expression instantly changed from jovial to perplexed. "Met? The victim? What are you, wait, you can't possibly be insinuating that I..."

"Mr. Lowry," Lindstrom interrupted as she held up a hand to break up a potential outburst. "I'm a police detective, and I wouldn't be doing my job if I didn't ask." She tried to convey a sense of urgency while not being rude.

Walter sighed deeply, as if he was insulted and didn't know why. "No, I have never met the victim, in any way, shape, or context." His tone indicated that he was hurt that he had to say the words.

Lindstrom jotted a few more notes, and then looked at him again. "Walter, I have a few more questions, but time is of the essence. I need you to answer with a yes or a no. Can you please do that for me?" Lindstrom tried to have the look of a child that was asking for a special toy for Christmas. Walter looked at her, clearly disappointed that he couldn't continue to talk for the sake of it, but also happy to continue to help.

"Very well," Walter replied with somber tone in his voice. "Ask away."

Realizing that this was going to be the lightning round, Lindstrom asked, "Walter, do you own a pair of binoculars?"

"Yes."

"Did you use your binoculars this morning?"

"No."

"Have you ever killed anyone?"

A look of shock swept over Walter's face, and he quickly replied, "NO!"

"Have you ever used your binoculars to look at something or someone you weren't supposed to?"

"NO!"

"Did you go down and inspect the body?"

"NO!"

"Did you help someone dispose of the body?"

"NO!"

"Are you a believer in the occult?"

Walter's face was becoming redder and redder by the second. His anger was growing, and Lindstrom could see the outline of a vein bulge at his temple.

"SERIOUSLY? NO! NO! NO!"

"Are you a Satanist?"

"NO!"

Lindstrom had seen and heard enough. Time to dial it back and wrap this up. She took a brief glance at her notes that she had written down while at the crime scene. "When is the wedding?"

Walter paused. He must have anticipated another outlandish question from Lindstrom. However, her inquiry seemed to take the air out of his outbursts, as the anger that he had expressed from the past few questions now seemed to subside. He slowly opened his mouth and said in a soft tone, "This Saturday."

"May I ask why you aren't staying in the hotel with the wedding party?" Lindstrom had talked to the officers that had been keeping an eye on Walter Lowry since they arrived at the crime scene. He had been talking constantly about the ceremony, his son, the plans, any little thing that he could bring up. Lindstrom figured that part of it was his nature of being chatty. However, she also surmised that Walter Lowry had been unnerved by discovering a dead body and was overcompensating and trying to cope the only way he could.

A hint of remorse appeared on Walter's face as he said, "My son and I haven't been on the best of terms in recent years." He sighed heavily before continuing. "Four years ago, my wonderful wife passed away suddenly. Three months after the funeral, I found out that she had been unhappy with our marriage and had started divorce proceedings. She had discussed this with my son and both of my daughters, and all three of them supported her decision." Walter paused, the breath that he took into his lungs sharp and painful to his soul.

"Two days before her death," Walter continued, "my wife sent my kids a letter, letting them know that she didn't want them to hold any kind of animosity towards me. That, no matter what happened going forward, I was still their father. When I found out about my wife's plans, I opened up to my daughters, who helped me understand my late wife's thoughts and reasons for her decision. My son, though, wasn't as forgiving. It was my future daughter-in-law's insistence that I be allowed to attend the wedding. But, by the time I was told, all of the rooms were already booked."

Lindstrom allowed the pause to hang in the air for a moment. "Walter, I am sorry. I know how difficult family issues can be."

A tear started to run down his cheek as Walter quietly said, "I'm not even allowed to come to the rehearsals or the pre-wedding dinners." He raised his hands, making a set of quotation marks in the air as he said, "'*Only the wedding, in the back, in and out, and don't even think about showing up at the reception.*'" Walter coughed, trying to clear his throat, and put his hands down. "Those were my son's explicit instructions to me, the rules I had to follow if I was going to attend."

"Is that why you booked yourself for a full four weeks at the

TownPlace Suites?" Before leaving the crime scene, Lindstrom had Officer Tisdale check on Walter's story. His hotel was a mile away from where the body was discovered, with easy access to the bike trails to the north, behind his hotel. Lowry's son's wedding party was booked at the ClubHouse Hotel and Suites, which happened to sit at the conflux point of Skunk Creek and the Big Sioux River. Cops hated coincidences, and Lindstrom had to be certain that this was only that, a coincidence, that circumstances had come together by pure chance.

Walter seemed to know what Lindstrom was implying. "Being retired does allow a person a certain flexibility when it comes to scheduling." A small grin appeared at the corner of his mouth, as he used his left hand to wipe away the tear. "Nicole, my future daughter-in-law, had hoped to convince my son to allow me to be a part of the festivities." Another short pause, before he added, "I guess there's still time before Saturday. At least I have been able to enjoy your city's bike trails and lovely scenic beauty!" His exuberance came out forced, though, and Lindstrom knew he was hiding his pain.

"Can I trust you to keep everything you have seen and heard today to yourself and not tell anyone?"

Walter looked sad. Lindstrom could tell he wanted to talk about it, to make it into a story worth telling, and he seemed to struggle with the question. He was also wrestling with the fact that he wasn't invited to his own son's wedding, and he had found a dead body only a few hundred feet from where his son and future daughter-in-law were staying. Finally, he said, "Yes, you can trust me. I won't tell anyone."

Lindstrom was quietly amazed. Walter Lowry was not a motor-mouth. She could tell he had a passion for nature and life that came off in a way that the vast majority of people couldn't begin to understand. She turned around and looked at the one-way mirror. She gave the thumbs up, and then flipped her fist between thumbs up and thumbs down. Two soft taps on the glass. Thumbs up.

Lindstrom looked back at Walter. "Mr. Lowry, Walter, I want to thank you for your time today. You have been very helpful. I may have more questions for you later. In the meantime, would you like Officer Tisdale to give you a ride back to your hotel?"

Walter looked at Lindstrom, and slowly stood up. He pressed his shirt flat against his chest and held out his hand. She also stood up and took his hand in hers. They shook hands as Walter said, "Officer Tisdale seems like a good man, and you seem like a good woman! While I appreciate the offer, I think I'll walk. I have nothing but time on my hands, and I think I could use the solitude." Walter smiled again, but no laugh came out of him. As Walter let go of Lindstrom's hand, Officer Tisdale opened the door.

"Officer Tisdale!" Walter bellowed. "Would you be so kind as to escort me to the front door?"

Officer Tisdale smiled politely, holding the door open for him as they walked down the hall. Lindstrom watched them walk away. Only a witness, she thought to herself, so she could mark one suspect off her list. With Walter Lowry's interview completed, it was time to find Officer Tavon. Six minutes later, Lindstrom was sitting with Tavon at her desk, going over the photos that he had taken after walking northwest on the bike trail.

"Excellent job," Lindstrom said to Tavon. Tavon smiled, looking at one of the photos.

"No big deal, really," he replied. "Anybody could see that something wasn't right about the area, if they knew what they were looking for."

After finishing the radio chat with Jerry at the crime scene, Tavon had called Lindstrom to meet him about a mile upstream on the bike trail. When Lindstrom arrived, they were standing at a culvert that emptied into Skunk Creek. With the ever-growing population of Sioux Falls, and the continual development of this particular section of the west side of the city, there had been issues with drainage over the past several years. The city's engineers had finally been given the green light to order necessary repairs and improvements along Skunk Creek. Those changes were scheduled to take place over the course of the next forty-eight months. This would help with drainage and water flow, as well as prevent possible flooding with the new housing and retail developments that were rapidly being built.

Lindstrom pointed at one of the enlarged photos, and asked Tavon, "Sure looks like the person had the right idea, doesn't it?"

"Yep," came Tavon's response. "Too bad he or she didn't know this culvert and drain didn't have the same wire mesh as the other culverts and drains along Skunk Creek have." Lindstrom grinned slightly. The fact that Tavon had not been gender-specific in describing the criminal was a good call. It meant that he was open to the possibility that the murdered could be either a man or a woman.

Lindstrom looked at another photo, this one of a manhole cover. There was a red X spray painted on the top of it, but the spray paint didn't line up with the spray paint outside of the manhole cover's edge. After documenting the area, Lindstrom had called for Jerry to send two of his forensic assistants to her location. They removed the manhole cover, seeing that the concrete tube that dropped down to the large concrete drain below had been disturbed. There were small streaks of red, most likely blood, all the way down. One of the assistants had climbed down, taking samples and photographing as she went. About ten feet from the bottom, it was visible that storm water had risen at different times into the concrete tube from severe storms or large water runoff. The concrete was not only discolored, but also had a noticeable film. However, the act of dropping a dismembered body had caused the film to be smeared along the concrete's surface.

Lindstrom organized the photos into what she considered was a chronological order, leaned back in her chair, and asked Tavon, "So, let's see if great minds think alike, shall we?"

Tavon smiled, raising an eyebrow, and responded jokingly, "Alright, great Jedi master! Go ahead!"

Lindstrom held up the first photo. "What do you see?"

"A manhole cover that has been disturbed. The red edges aren't lined up to the red X on the cover itself."

Lindstrom set down the photo and held up the next one. "How about now?"

"The inside of the tube down into the storm drain has been disturbed. The walls have red smears, likely blood, and", Tavon paused, waiting for Lindstrom to move on to the next photo, "you can see on this photo where the water marks and the oily film on the concrete, where that's been disrupted by something rubbing up against the concrete wall." Lindstrom went to the fourth photo, and Tavon continued.

"The bottom of the culvert as it empties into Skunk Creek. You can see on the concrete that something isn't right, like the constant stream of water was interrupted in some fashion."

Lindstrom smiled and set the pictures down. "So, if I'm a killer, trying to get rid of a body, I dump it down into a storm drain. I can see two culverts on the opposite sides of the creek, one upstream and one downstream. Both of those culverts, from my vantage point, have wire mesh and bars, in order to catch debris from going into the creek. I figure that I can put the body down there. The bike trails on the north side were removed last year, so no one should be able to see a body caught in this storm drain. Any rancid smell can be attributed to garbage resting in bad water. Besides, it will be winter in a month. By the time the body is discovered next spring or summer, in six to ten months-time, it will hopefully be too decomposed to yield any evidence." As Lindstrom paused to take a breath, Tavon continued.

"But, you didn't know that this culvert's wire mesh and bars were missing, so the body goes right into Skunk Creek. Add to that the rain from Tuesday night, and the water was moving fast enough to carry the body. If it hadn't been for those plants at the turn into the Big Sioux, the body might still be traveling downstream."

"See, I was right. Great minds do think alike." Lindstrom was beaming as Tavon accepted the compliment with a laugh.

"Anything else you need from me? If not, the chief wanted me to check with him after we were done here."

"Nope, we're good," Lindstrom replied as she stood up from her desk. "I need to get to Jerry. I'll talk to you later." Tavon nodded and started walking towards Engels' office. Lindstrom stepped away from her desk and pushed in her chair. She hadn't walked four paces when her cell phone vibrated. She fumbled for the phone, but it slipped out of her hand amongst the folders she was carrying. She knelt down, collecting the items she had dropped. A few seconds later, she stood up, looking at the caller ID. Her breath caught in her throat, and she felt her heart briefly skip a beat. Please, God, no, she screamed inside her head. Not this. Not now.

Kara looked at Jason, studying his facial expressions and his mannerisms. She could tell that he was frustrated and concerned about Monday night's events. His empathy and his ability to sense when something wasn't quite kosher were only two of the things she admired about his abilities as a nurse. Jason didn't stir up trouble, so he must be on to something.

"So?" Jason asked. "What do you think?"

"Jason," Kara started, "I'm not saying I don't believe you. But I need you to tell me straight up. How much did you have to drink Monday night?"

A fair question, Jason thought. Alcohol, in even small amounts, can dull the senses, and after a long stretch of nursing shifts and twelve to sixteen-hour days, alcohol could make things go haywire.

"I know what you're thinking," Jason replied. "Especially after what happened to that intern that we heard about in Omaha two years ago. After I got off work, I went home, showered, and changed. My buddy, Max, picked me up at six pm. We drove around for a bit, trying to decide where to go and what to do. We went bowling, and then we walked up to Goldie's to eat. Aside from the food, I only had water and 7Up to drink. Just after nine, we went next door to the bar, and watched some football, lord only knows why. The Browns and the Jaguars on a Monday night. Anyway, I ordered one beer, but I only drank half of it, so I didn't finish it. It was warm and tasted flat, so I went back to 7Up. Max started flirting with two girls in the booth next to us. He was trying to get me involved, but I'd been looking at the woman I told you about."

Kara nodded, "The stunner, right?"

"Yeah, wow," Jason said. Even thinking about her now caused him to lose his focus. He shook his head and continued. "Anyway, like I said, there was something about her. She had come into the bar and sat down. She wasn't there for more than a few minutes when she took her drink and sat with some guy that looked like he had seen better days. I think they sat together for about twenty, thirty minutes. Max was starting to strike out, the game was over, and I needed to stretch my legs. I got up and told Max I was going outside for a minute. I looked toward the woman again, but the booth was empty. When I stepped outside, I stretched and cracked my neck and back. I was looking down the block, to see if that arcade was still open, thinking maybe we could go play some skee ball or something. That's when I heard the whistle. I looked in the other direction, and up by the corner at the bus stop was the stunner and the guy she had sat with. He was down on a knee. Then the ambulance showed up, no lights, no siren, just out of the blue."

Kara listened to Jason, comparing what he was saying to her notes. She had made it clear when they sat down at the table in the cafeteria that she was going to take notes, so she could help him make sense of things. Too many times, patients came in, frantic and crazy, and talking so fast that important details and information got left out. It was only when going back over the events with properly taken notes that facts and, more importantly, the truth, took shape.

"I started to walk towards them," Jason continued, "but Max was at the bar's window, trying to get my attention and wave me back inside. I waved him off while walking towards them. I couldn't tell what the woman and the paramedics were saying from where I was. When I got to the bus stop, I asked them if they needed any help. The paramedics said no and gave some excuse about the guy being a drunk. As soon as he said 'drunk', the man from the bar threw a fit, swinging and kicking and yelling. But the fit didn't last long, only a few seconds, like he passed out. The paramedics seemed more concerned with getting the man and woman into the ambulance than taking vitals, assessing the situation, securing him on the gurney, anything that any properly trained medic or nurse would do in an emergency. The ambulance peeled out, no lights or sirens, and drove in the opposite directions of both Sanford Hospital and Avera Hospital."

Kara finished her examination of her notes and Jason going through the events a second time. "No cops," she whispered softly. She looked up at Jason, a perplexed look on her face.

"What?"

"They didn't wait for any kind of police to arrive," Kara said. "You were right, this whole thing is very strange."

"So, what do you think we should do?"

Kara looked at the wall clock in the cafeteria. She technically had three minutes left in her lunch break. She grabbed her phone and dialed the nurse's station in the ER. "Evelyn, it's Kara. How are things looking? Anybody arrive in the past thirty minutes or is anyone incoming that I need to be there for right this second?" A brief pause. "Okay, good. Listen, if something happens, call me immediately. Otherwise, I need to help Jason for a little while longer. Thanks." She ended the call, then looked at her phone for a few seconds.

"Are you okay?" Jason asked. He sensed that there was something wrong.

"I'm fine. I'm guessing you don't have any plans right now?"

"Nothing at all."

"Then give me a minute. I know someone that might be able to help." Kara unlocked her phone again and hit a contact number. She took a deep breath.

Lindstrom willed herself to be strong, as she accepted the call and put the phone to her ear. "Kara," she said. She tried to keep the tone in her voice positive, but it came across in such a matter-of-fact way that she immediately added, "What is this about?"

"Tish, relax, please," came Kara's voice on the other end. "This has nothing to do with Mark." Kara exhaled as softly as she could. Things were always going to be tense between them. Before Kara could lose her focus on details from the past, she shook her head and concentrated on the present.

Lindstrom felt her muscles loosen. Whenever Kara's number came across the caller ID, Lindstrom's head filled with despair. Not surprising, though, considering the past four years. "I'm kind of busy right now, so if you could..."

"Tish," Kara interrupted, "a situation has come up with regards to one of our nurses over here. You don't have a spare few minutes to talk or meet with him?"

"Normally, I would," Lindstrom said. "Unfortunately, a bad case fell into my lap this morning, and I'm on my way to forensics right now." She paused, not wanting to appear dismissive, but not wanting to sound vindictive, either. "Did your nurse do something wrong?"

"Oh lord, no," Kara exclaimed. "He witnessed something two days ago, and after hearing him tell me the story, I figured I'd better call in someone with more experience in these matters."

Lindstrom could tell from the tone of Kara's voice two things. One, she wouldn't have called her if it wasn't important, and two, that Kara was definitely concerned. Lindstrom sighed. "What does he think he saw?"

Kara's voice came through the phone again as she gave a brief rundown of the information Jason had relayed to her. Lindstrom had stopped in the hallway and scribbled down a few notes on a new page in her notebook. When Kara was done, Lindstrom asked, "And you believe him?"

"Jason Iverson is a first-rate nurse," Kara said, the conviction in her voice coming through loud and clear. "I have no reason to think he is making it up or misremembering."

First a gruesome murder, and now a possible missing person case that might turn into a kidnapping. This is what Lindstrom hated about being a detective. When it rains, it pours, and it always seemed like, no matter what she did, it would never be enough.

"Give me your nurse's name and number," Lindstrom instructed, "and I will have an officer get in touch with him as soon as I can."

"Thanks, Tish," Kara said. "I really appreciate it." Kara relayed Jason's information to Lindstrom, who wrote it down.

"Got it," Lindstrom said. "An officer will call him." Before Kara could say another word, Lindstrom ended the call without pleasantries. As she started walking to forensics again, she found Officer Tisdale's contact number in her phone and initiated a call. Two rings later, Tisdale answered. Lindstrom gave him Jason's information.

"I'm not sure what it's all about," Lindstrom told Tisdale, "but check it out and get back to me."

"You have no clue why I'm calling this nurse?" Tisdale sounded confused over the phone.

"I have some vague details, but I'm not going to share them with you." Lindstrom's voice came off as impatient, but that wasn't her intent. "I want you to talk to this Jason, find out his story, ask some questions, and figure out for yourself what the situation is. Once you finish, you can let me know what you find out, and then I can decide if the information links up. Understand?"

"Got it, and will do," Tisdale replied, and ended the call.

Hopefully, this was only a minor thing, maybe this Jason had his facts mixed up. Hopefully, things could be easily explained. Yeah, right, Lindstrom thought to herself. Kara called her on the same day Lindstrom gets a murder case. At least the phone call wasn't about Mark. THAT was something positive for the day.

THREE

Chief of Detectives Brad Engels sat at his desk, unsure of what to do next. He had been the de facto Chief of Police for nine months, and the stress was getting to him. He had gained thirty pounds, his hair was starting to thin on top and turn gray at the temples, and the one thing that he had been most noted for, his infinite patience, had dried up like a drop of water in the desert. Even his wife, Diane, as well as their adult children, had started taking him to task for all of his negative changes. Since he was, apparently, between tasks, he looked around his office, glancing at one certain picture that hung on his wall. The photo always brought up memories, and he allowed his mind to drift back to the events of the past.

It wasn't his fault, he thought. While Engels had technically been second in command of the department, his title as Chief of Detectives had allowed him to focus primarily on crimes. He had also hired an excellent support staff to make sure all of the minor details could be properly handled without his direct oversight. When an issue involving personnel requests or supplies or anything remotely trivial came up, he always instructed his three directors to work with the Chief of Police's liaison. When he had first gotten approval to hire the "directors" years ago, he made sure to call them "directors", not secretaries or clerks. He wanted these three people to feel empowered to solve problems, so that he could run his detectives efficiently and effectively.

It had definitely worked, too. Granted, being the Chief of Detectives in a Midwestern town like Sioux Falls, South Dakota, that was hovering around two hundred thousand souls may not seem that difficult. However, the world was getting smaller. This was not a knock-on immigration or terrorism, it was merely a fact. People moving away, people moving in, all states, all nations, all borders, everything was coming together, with lines becoming blurry. Of course, crime was always around, no matter where you were, which was the unfortunate truth. Hardly any homicides, but there were still drugs, sex crimes, violence, dead beats, and other law breakers to deal with. Engels and his team of cops and detectives worked hard to keep the city of Sioux Falls, South Dakota, as safe as possible. He had been so proud of the work they had done in the past. Unfortunately, every day was different, with a new challenge.

The photo on the wall that Engels had looked at featured the mayor at the time in the middle, Engels to his left, and to the mayor's right, Clive Gunvaldson, the now-former Chief of Police. Even as different mayors had been elected, Gunvaldson and Engels had continued to work as a great team. Clive had been great at motivating, logistics, and handling all of the day-to-day things that went into running a police department. He never interfered on Engels' side, unless it was absolutely necessary, and vice versa. Clive and Engels had sat down together years ago, along with their respective support personnel, and had outlined what they expected from their directors, clerks, etc. For twenty-one years, things had hummed along almost perfectly.

Then, a year and a half ago, two of Clive's three assistants had been killed in a freak car accident. What really hurt was one of the assistants was Clive's nephew, who had married two months prior to the accident. Four months after the accident, while interviewing candidates for the two open positions, it was discovered that the other assistant that had died had been skimming the books. The financial total wasn't really impressive, in the tens of thousands of dollars. Still, the damage that it could have done to the department would have been massive. As the embezzler had no husband or children, Clive and Engels had talked to the woman's only living relative, a brother who happened to be a staff sergeant in the Air Force. The brother was shocked at the revelation, but he had shared Clive's and Engels' concerns. As the sole beneficiary of his sister's estate, which wasn't much, he decided to gift the entire estate to the police department. This would allow the police department to quietly reabsorb

44

the missing funds, while also keeping the indiscretions from being discovered.

"I love my sister," the brother had said. "I don't know what caused her to make such a bad decision, but, hopefully, this will fix her mistake. Only the three of us will ever know." It had taken two months to close the estate and make things right.

One calamity had been avoided, but nothing prepared Engels for the next one. He had been driving to the station when he had received a phone call to meet at the mayor's office at city hall. That was unusual, but then he had remembered hearing about a puff piece that one of the local TV stations had wanted to run. When he walked into the mayor's office, he saw Clive Gunvaldson standing to the side of the mayor's desk. His face looked ashen, his eyes were bloodshot, and he was leaning slightly against a book case for support.

"Brad," the mayor said as he sat down, in a voice that was trying to sound calm. "There's no easy way to say this, so here it goes. Clive has tendered his resignation, effectively immediately. That means that you are now the acting Chief of Police. Until we can either hire or promote someone to either the Chief of Police or Chief of Detectives position, it is your show over the whole department."

Engels was stunned beyond on words. He sat there, jaw hanging open, looking from the mayor to Clive, back to the mayor, and then back to Clive.

"Clive," Engels stammered, "what the hell?"

"Easy, Brad, easy," the mayor hushed.

Clive quietly took a massive and deep breath. "Rebecca, well, she hasn't been feeling well, ever since after the funeral. Finally, she went into the doctor a few weeks ago. She got the results. Colon cancer, aggressive. Very, very aggressive. It's spreading. It's in her lymph nodes, too. The oncologist says that, even with a super-strong treatment regimen, odds are less than ten percent she survives a year. She doesn't want to be a burden, and she wants to die trying to live the rest of her life. She is going to put in for early retirement and roll all of her savings, 401K, investments, everything into as much cash as she can. I'm retiring, getting my pension and everything I can. We're selling the house, cars, all of it. The kids are grown up and have moved on. They are devastated, but they are supporting their parents. Rebecca wants to live, she wants to travel while she still can. And I need to be with her, to be with the woman I love, through all of it, right up to the end." The words fell from Clive's mouth, each one a hammer blow to Engels. Tears were welling up in everyone's eyes.

Engels stood up and went to Clive. This amazing man, who had been a partner, superior, and friend, all in equal measure, now looked like he had had his ass kicked in a UFC fight. Engels took him by the shoulders, straightened him up, and gave him a loving hug. "Go," Engels whispered in his ear. "Be with Rebecca." Engels let him go, and they locked eyes. They each gave a small smile to the other, a respectful nod, and Clive left without another word. By the time that Engels had made his way to the police station, the rumors had been flying. Clive's last remaining assistant, Michelle, had been called in early, with the unenviable task of quietly going through Clive's office and packing up all personal items. "Keep it quiet," the mayor had told her. "Don't ask questions, don't answer questions, don't speculate. Box up and tape up everything and stack it nicely in the office with the shades on the door shut." The same instructions had been given to Engels. "Don't ask questions, don't answer questions, don't speculate."

That day seemed to drag on forever, with the whispered words and hushed gossip consuming the police station. All three TV stations and the local newspaper got wind of something big brewing at the police station and set up camp outside the station and at city hall. Once Michelle had everything boxed up, the mayor called the TV stations and the paper and told them he would hold a press conference the next morning. At eight the next morning, Engels stood next to the mayor in front of a minor media circus.

The mayor was short and sweet, briefly explaining that, due to a matter of life and death, Chief of Police Clive Gunvaldson had resigned his position to be with his family. He would take no questions on the nature of the emergency, only that it was dire, and Clive had decided that he needed to be with his family. The mayor then said that Chief of Detectives Brad Engels was also assuming the job title and responsibilities of the Chief of Police. Further review of the police force would begin immediately, and any and all viable candidates for the Chief positions were encouraged to contact the mayor's office. The mayor then turned the podium over to Engels.

"Thank you, Mayor," Engels said. "I have a lot of work to do, so I'll

get right to the point. Clive made the best decision for himself and his family. We ask that you please respect his privacy in this personal, family matter. He leaves the police department in excellent hands. Thank you."

That had been nine months ago. Now, here he was. Older, heavier, somehow managing to keep the department running smoothly, although how was becoming lost on him. Gone were the days when he could delegate away the minutia, all of the minor details. Thank god he had talked Clive's third assistant, Michelle, into staying. With everything that happened over the past several months, culminating in Clive's departure, Michelle appeared like she was on the verge of a breakdown. After talking to the mayor, he had pulled his three directors and Michelle into a meeting and laid it out for all of them. Instead of taking on two salaries, Engels had convinced the mayor that it was an all hands-on deck affair. Clive's salary, therefore, would be equally divided among Michelle and the other three directors. "Each of you is integral to this police department, and the mayor and I need all four of you to be focused on the job going forward. We both feel that this revised salary package will help you navigate these challenges."

Even with four happy assistants, Engels felt like he was losing his love for the job, his love for why he became a cop. He had so much going on, with all police matters falling to him, it felt like a massive weight was on his shoulders. After nine months, the mayor seemed no closer to finding a new Chief of Police. Maybe he thought that with no signs of worry or issues coming from the department, there was no need to rush. Engels had a meeting set with the mayor for next month. He would lay it out for the mayor then, letting him know it was time to find someone else to take the load. As he played out that meeting in his head, a knock came from the door. He looked up.

"Boss, you look like hell." Lindstrom was standing in the doorway to Engels' office.

"Trust me, I look in the mirror every day. I know."

"So, do you want an update or not?"

"It's coming up on 5:30, and Jerry is still working on the body. I gave the news outlets some minor things that a body had been found in the river, but it was too early to say anything definitive. Unless you need anything else, I'm going to call it an early day. If anybody leaks anything about pentagrams overnight, I figure I'll need the extra rest to deal with the fallout tomorrow."

Lindstrom walked over to his desk and hit Engels in the back of the head with the manila folder she was carrying. Not too hard, only hard enough to get her point across.

"Okay, Tish, I'm ready to be enlightened."

"Boss, you really have been pulling double-duty too long," she said. "Like I told you earlier, this is 2016. Seriously? Pentagrams? Devil worship? I don't buy it, not for one second."

"Your reasoning behind that assumption?"

"Flip through the channels on cable or satellite TV. Check out the movies in the theater or on video at Best Buy. I'll guarantee that there's at least one show or one movie classified as horror that makes some mention of Satanism. If this woman was killed as some kind of sacrifice, her body wouldn't have been dumped. No, we would have found her in some elaborate manner, burned candles, blood, upside down crosses, and the typical signs of the occult. Whoever did this went to great lengths to mask her identity. The pentagram feels like an afterthought, like a deliberate attempt to throw us off the trail."

Engels leaned back in his chair and thought about what Lindstrom had just said. He closed his eyes, remembering some of the movies and shows that Lindstrom had alluded to. Hollywood had taken the concept of devil worship and the occult and given it a spin that was easy to spot, yet factually and historically incorrect. Engels also thought back to the "satanic panic" of the late 1980's and early 1990's. There had been numerous allegations of devil worship against multiple school teachers and day care providers, the majority of which that turned out to be false accusations. He looked at her again. Better to be safe than sorry, though. "You will keep an open-mind that devil worship might be involved, just in case?"

Lindstrom scolded her boss with a frown. "Of course, I will! Like you'd even have to ask."

Engels nodded, then continued the discussion. "For the sake of argument, let's say you're right, and the pentagram is a red herring. Which direction does the arrow now point?"

48

Lindstrom sat down on the edge of Engels' desk, looking out the window, but still talking to him. "Without reading Jerry's full report on the body, I can't say for certain. Someone did a number on that poor woman, for whatever reason." She became lost in her thoughts, trying to reconcile something she had seen out at the crime scene. The thread was there, and then gone. She tried to get it back, when her cell buzzed. Startled, she stood up and looked at the ID. Officer Tisdale. Damn, she had forgotten all about Kara and Jason, her nurse.

Engels craned his neck to see the ID. "Important?"

"Not sure yet," Lindstrom replied. She accepted the call and put the phone to her ear. "Tisdale, how did your meeting with the nurse go?" She winked at Engels, who looked back, frowning.

"Detective, I mean, Tish," Tisdale stuttered. "Sorry. We've just finished up. Where are you?" Lindstrom looked at the clock. 5:43pm. Even accounting for getting Walter Lowry out of the police station, plus anything else Tisdale had to do before tracking down Jason The Nurse, Lindstrom figured that an hour would have sufficed. Four plus hours?

"I'm in with the chief right now," she said. "Can't it wait?"

"I really don't think so," Tisdale blurted out. "Something feels wrong. I'm on my way back to the station. Please, just stay put." The line went dead. Lindstrom looked at her phone, then at Engels.

"Looks like you're going to be staying for a little while," Lindstrom told Engels. "Tisdale is on his way back and has something for us."

"Oh?" Engels said. "Has he broken the case wide open?"

"I wish," Lindstrom cracked. "No, I got a call earlier from Kara Reed over at Sanford Hospital. One of her nurses witnessed something Monday night that he couldn't wrap his head around. I told Tisdale to meet up with the nurse and get some information. I didn't realize it was going to take him so long, though."

"Kara Reed," Engels queried. "Isn't that the…"

"Seriously, you know better than that!" Lindstrom snapped. "It was hard enough seeing her name on the ID today."

"Okay, sorry. You have any idea what this is about?"

"Not a clue, just that he, Jason, this nurse, was a witness to something. Kara was supposed to call me back by four with some more information."

"Give her a call, then, and get it over with," Engels said.

Lindstrom sighed. She regretted not sneaking away when she had the chance. She pulled up Kara's contact and dialed. It went straight to voicemail. She was going to hang up, but the message got her attention.

"Tish, I had to turn off my phone. Jason was right. I'll call when I can." A beep, and then silence.

"Kara," Lindstrom said, "it's Tish. Touch base with me when you can." She ended the call.

"Is it going to be a long night," Engels asked.

"Let's sit tight and wait for Tisdale," Lindstrom said. "We'll get his report, and then we can decide how to proceed." She sat down in one of the chairs in the office. As she put her feet up on the edge of the desk, her phone rang again. HOME came up on the screen. She swiped the screen. "And which child do I have the pleasure of speaking to?"

"Oh, for Christ sakes, Mom!" Yep, it was Bree. "Can't you ever just answer the phone like a normal person?"

"Sorry, hon," Lindstrom replied. "My human form was replaced a long time ago with this battered husk of wit and wisdom. And I've told you to watch your mouth. You take the Lord's name in vain around your grandfather, and there'll be hell to pay."

"Yeah, okay, sure, whatever." Bree's typical response when she wasn't in the mood for being pandered to. "I thought you were going to be home with groceries by five. There's like nothing to eat in this whole house!"

Lindstrom quietly sighed. Raising three kids almost by herself had been hard enough, but when one of them was a teenaged daughter, sweet mother in heaven. A daughter that was sixteen, thought she was twenty-six, but acted like she was six at times. Bree was smart enough, but not smart like her older brother. Bree's problem was common sense, or the lack of it.

"Hello, can you hear me?" Bree's voice exploded from the phone.

"Easy there, girl. There's no need to shout. Where are your brothers?"

"I don't know. Isn't it one of little Ryan's taekwondo nights?" Bree had started referring to Ryan as "little Ryan", for some reason.

"Look, hon, after you left for school this morning, I was given a bad case. I knew I wouldn't be home in time, so look on the kitchen table. Do you see the envelope with your name on it?"

"Yeah, so?"

"I left you twenty dollars. Go out to eat, maybe see if one of your friends from cheerleading wants to go with you."

"Yeah, okay, sure, bye, whatever." The line went dead. Lindstrom looked at her phone. Another two and a half years before she was graduated and off to college. She loved her daughter, but sometimes, well, damn! Why was it so difficult raising daughters?

"Problems with Bree again?" Engels knew that Lindstrom was an excellent cop and detective. He and Diane had tried to help when and where they could with regards to her kids.

"Apparently, the imposition of a dead body had a negative effect on the ability to stock the cupboards." She took out her phone and sent Trevor a text, letting him know to take himself and Ryan out for dinner after taekwondo, and that she would pay him back.

Engels looked at the clock. A minute past six. "I'd say I'm getting hungry, but you might make light of the fact that I could lose a few pounds."

Lindstrom's face changed, her features displaying a mock-form of appearing heartbroken. She put a hand over heart, and with a sly, sarcastic town, she asked, "Boss, really, what kind of inhuman monster do you take me for?"

"Oh, shut up. Let's hope what Tisdale has to say is worth the wait."

It was the life of an emergency room nurse. Things could be so quiet for so long, and then everything happens at once. Kara had sent Jason on his way with Officer Tisdale's contact information, and she had started making her own calls. She talked to a few of her colleagues and left messages with others. The little bit of information she had written down didn't help clarify things. She was only able to spend another thirty minutes on this mystery when Evelyn had buzzed her. One heart attack, one stroke, one electrical fire in a new home construction, and a drunk driver that hit a tree that then crashed into a city bus, injuring seven people. As she made her way back to the ER, she had changed her voicemail message, so Tish would know something was up.

Things were quiet now, and she looked at the clock. A few minutes past seven. Kara thought about calling Tish. However, she decided against it. No, get your facts first, then call. Things had been awkward between the two of them, and she needed this to be professional. As Kara turned her cell back on and grabbed her notebook, she left some instructions with Evelyn. By the time she was out of the ER, her phone was powered up and, once service had been found, it had started pinging with message alerts, voicemails received, and assorted emails. She reached the cafeteria, bought a bottle of tea and three granola bars, and found a quiet corner away from some of the families that were seated in there. Some people were crying quietly, trying to come to terms with whatever news they had received. Otherwise, things were silent.

As she started snacking, Kara looked over the missed text messages first. After taking notes, she started listening to her voicemails. Fifteen minutes later, she set her phone down and looked over everything she had written about Jason's story. Kara had a sense of dread crawling up the back of her neck. She stood up, did some stretches, and cracked her back. She breathed, slowly and deliberately, inhaling, holding it, then exhaling. She walked four times around her table, then jogged in place for a minute. A few more stretches, and Kara felt reinvigorated. A few of the people sitting in the cafeteria had watched her but were now returning to their food. In times of stress or confusion, it was important to stay relaxed and refreshed.

Kara sat back down, looking over her notes one more time. She looked at the opposite wall. 7:34 is what the clock read. Realizing there was no denying it, she shook her head. She took her phone and dialed Tish's cell.

Engels spoke into the air since Lindstrom had transferred Kara Reed's call to Engels' speaker phone. "Kara, that was good work. Go home and get some rest, and we'll follow up with you tomorrow, okay?"

"Thanks. Let me know if you need anything else. Good night, Brad. Good night, Officer Tisdale. And good night, Tish." The line went dead as Kara ended the call on her end. Lindstrom picked up the phone's receiver and then put it back into the cradle. She looked at Tisdale and then to Engels. "Well? Any thoughts to add to this mess?"

Engels rubbed his eyes and face, then ran his fingers through his hair, massaging his scalp as he made his way to his neck. The day had started out bad enough with a dead body, but now was quickly slipping into bizarre, and that's not how he wanted the day to end. "Nope. None at all. Tisdale? Can I assume that you will have a full report ready by 9am tomorrow?"

Tisdale straightened up in the chair he had been sitting in next to Lindstrom. "Yes sir. First thing."

"Then I suggest we call it a night."

Lindstrom was mildly shocked. "You're kidding, right?"

Engels stood up to his full height, not bothering to try to hold in his expanding waistline. "Tish, we've known each other for a long time. Look at me. The last eighteen months has been one kidney punch after another. But even in my world-weary state, I know that things aren't adding up, on either case. It's now coming up on 8:30, and after the day that we've all had, I think it's best that we get some rest. Tisdale says that all of the evidence has been collected and is in lockup. Jerry has assured me that I'll have his initial report by the time I have to do my show for the cameras tomorrow morning at ten." He pointed a finger at Lindstrom. "You need to go home, hug your kids, and catch some winks. Both of you go home. Tisdale, call up Jason and have him work with you tomorrow morning at eight. Tish, do the same for Kara. I want the three of us in one of the conference rooms tomorrow morning at nine to go over everything we have on this ambulance crime. That will leave us," pointing at Lindstrom, "an hour before my presser to go over Jerry's findings with you."

"Understood," Tisdale said as he stood up.

Lindstrom wasn't prepared to let things end like this, but she knew she had no choice. Engels made a lot of sense, and after the initial shock of seeing Kara Reed's caller ID earlier in the day and not being home at a regular time as she had told the kids that morning, she wanted to spend even a little bit of time with them. "Understood," she said. "Who do you want as lead on this?"

"Tisdale can be primary on this," Engels said, as he turned from Lindstrom to Tisdale, "but, you run everything, and I do mean every last damn thing through Tish before you do anything. You read me?"

"Absolutely!" Tisdale snapped enthusiastically. "Detective Lindstrom, is there anything else you think I should do tonight?"

Lindstrom looked at him and sighed. "You can start by stopping the Detective Lindstrom salute. Call me Tish. Second, call Jason and set it up for tomorrow. And finally, get your report done and be ready for tomorrow. Now get out of here."

Tisdale started to open his mouth, then thought better of it. He dialed

Jason's number as he left the office. Lindstrom stood up, waiting a good two minutes as she looked at her boss, before she walked to the door.

"Something you wanted to add," Engels asked when she was at the threshold of the office.

Lindstrom turned back. "Nothing that needs to be said right now. If it's okay with you, I'm going to put out an all-points bulletin for the HealthStar Ambulatory Services vehicle, and then I'll get out of here. See you tomorrow." With that, she was gone.

FOUR

When Lindstrom had returned home the previous night, she had checked on all three children, making sure there were no issues that required her immediate attention. Trevor, surprisingly, wasn't playing video games. Instead, he was on the phone, talking to his grandfather about odd jobs to winterize the farm. Bree had been in her room, doing homework, while Ryan was in his room, building with LEGO's. She then told Bree and Ryan that she had to be at the police station early, so they needed to be ready early. Ryan was excited, because that meant breakfast at school. Bree complained until she heard the words "large iced mocha." That shut down the complaining.

The morning had come, and, after dropping Bree off at the high school first, she finished waving to Ryan as he opened one of the glass doors to the elementary school. As she turned the car in the parking lot, she thought about her children. Even with all three kids in the house, one a senior, one a sophomore, and one in third grade, mornings tended to be easy, which was amazing. Well, most of the time, at least. Trevor was graduating early and only had two classes. He slept in and got himself to school, no problem. Bree, being a teenage girl, sometimes had issues. Overall, though, she was getting better about getting herself up and ready. Of course, the time when she had been left behind at home, which caused her to be late for school because she had to walk, well, Bree never wanted a repeat of that "total and utter embarrassment!" Ryan did his part fine, well, for a soon to be nine-year old boy, anyway.

Yes, Lindstrom had good kids, but it was time to tuck those thoughts away and concentrate. Here she was, driving towards the police station, and she began mentally preparing for two case briefings. One case, a homicide with a mutilated corpse found in the river. The second case, a possible kidnapping. Lindstrom had gone to sleep almost immediately, because she wanted the morning to review her notes. When she had awoken at 5am, she was greeted to a secure email alert on her tablet. Jerry had finished his autopsy report and sent it to her on the police server. She had read over it, took some more notes, and was showered and dressed before Bree and Ryan were up. So, what was bothering her? Was it the case, or rather, the cases? Was it Kara Reed somehow coming back into her life? Lindstrom always knew there was a chance of that, but not in this way, not involving a case. Was it the way Brad Engels had been acting over the past few weeks, and then his reaction to a murder with supposed devil worship implications? Maybe it was nervousness, the fact that having two cases at the same time was going to put a strain on her family life. Strains on her family life were definitely not what she needed right now, being alone and raising three kids, even if one of them was two months away from being out the door. She sighed. Having one less child in the house would alleviate some stress and tension. However, she knew that she was going to miss her oldest son when he was gone.

Lindstrom was now stopped behind four cars, all of which were also stopped due to a train. She put her car into park and turned off the radio. Looking out the passenger window, she saw a billboard advertising a two-for-one sale on the buffet at Grand Falls Casino, which was only twelve miles from her house in Brandon. She thought about that. Maybe she could take the kids out this weekend. They hadn't been on any kind of family outing in what seemed like forever. Of course, part of that was because Trevor and Bree, being teenaged siblings, usually ended up yelling at each other and ruining the whole thing. Maybe it wasn't a good idea, no matter how great a two-for-one sale sounded. She had to admit, she had good kids, but they were still kids, especially to each other.

A honking horn from behind brought her back to the present. The train was gone, and the four cars ahead of her were already over the tracks. She shifted into drive and took off. Ten minutes later, she reached the police station. She was still having an issue with something, but she decided to push it aside for now. She parked her car and looked at the time. 7:42 displayed on the car radio. There was more than enough time to get inside and get situated.

Lindstrom made her way through various doors and checkpoints. The terrorist attacks of 9/11 had necessitated an overhaul on security, which, in some ways, was a good thing. It meant that no one was getting into a police station without jumping through a multitude of hoops. Ryan, bless his little soul, had once cried because he didn't want his mommy to get hurt. So, she had brought him to the station and shown him all the different security measures that kept all the police officers safe. Granted, that was only at the station, but she hadn't offered up that little nugget.

There were three conference rooms, with the larger, main conference room situated between the two smaller rooms. The door to the main conference room was open, with the lights already on. As she walked in, she saw that she was the first one there. She was relieved that she had arrived first. The digital clock that hung on the wall read 7:51 AM. Lindstrom walked into the room, noting that the only items on the conference room table were a phone and speaker, a remote control for using the digital projector, and a tray with a pitcher of ice water and some glasses. She continued walking around to the other side of the table. Lindstrom disliked having her back to the door. She had rolled out one of the chairs, when a uniformed officer appeared at the entrance to the conference room, motioning for someone to go in first. Kara Reed walked in and stopped when she saw Lindstrom.

"Good morning," Kara said to Lindstrom, smiling.

Lindstrom nodded and replied, "Morning", gesturing for Kara to take the chair opposite from hers. Kara obliged and sat down.

As Lindstrom opened her notebook and powered on her police-issued tablet, Kara surveyed the conference room. She was facing a large window that faced south. She could see the early morning traffic on Minnesota Avenue, as well as the various houses and businesses that dotted the several city blocks in view. To Kara's left was a large white dry erase board on the wall, and to her right was a large cabinet. The doors to the cabinet were collapsible, and Kara could see a flat-screen television inside. In the corner was a computer that wasn't turned on. Kara turned her attention back to Lindstrom. It was hard to hide the awkwardness between them, so Kara decided to try to nip it in the bud.

"Tish," Kara said softly, "I should thank you. I know things will never be easy between us. I wouldn't have called unless it was important."

"Well, looks like your instincts on this were right," Lindstrom said.

She wanted to keep her voice matter-of-fact. "So, let's get down to business. I have to meet with Engels and Tisdale as soon as we are done here."

Kara thought about trying to pry a little bit out of Lindstrom. Things didn't need to be like this. However, with time being short, she realized this wasn't the time or place to try to heal old wounds. Kara smiled and nodded, opened her notebook, and began.

"I talked to the head of the emergency room at Avera Hospital. They have no record of a man or woman being treated late Monday night or Tuesday morning for any injuries consistent with what Jason described."

As Lindstrom took notes without looking up, she asked, "Did you check with any other clinics in town?"

"Yes," Kara replied, nodding. "I called all six healthcare providers that would have been open after eleven at night on a Monday. No one admitted a man or woman, either."

"What about the ambulance?" Lindstrom remained focused on her note taking, trying to stay professional while not looking directly at Kara.

"Sanford and Avera have no record of a HealthStar Ambulatory being used by either hospital. I also called the Department of Health at the state capitol in Pierre. They also have no record of an ambulance company by that name requesting licensing in the state."

A brief pause hung in the air as Lindstrom continued her note taking. She skimmed a few lines from Tisdale's report, then asked, "What about Minnesota, Iowa, North Dakota, or Nebraska?"

Kara thought about the question. "It's possible that a company named HealthStar Ambulatory is licensed in a bordering state, but you would need to contact each state's department of health to know for sure. As it concerns Sanford and Avera, there are six ambulance services that are contracted and licensed within a seventy-mile radius." Kara stopped, and then added, "Since the alleged paramedic told Jason that the man was drunk, I also contacted the local chapter of Alcoholics Anonymous, as well as the three outpatient treatment centers. No one had either an ambulance drop-off a drunk or had someone walk in off the street in the past three days." Kara closed her notebook and looked at Lindstrom, who was still taking notes.

"Can you think of any other medical facilities in the area that might have had contact with the ambulance, the so-called paramedics, or the alleged victims," Lindstrom asked.

"Nothing that springs to mind," Kara replied. "Any clinics, from general practicing to specialty areas will advise patients in a crisis to contact 911. Even the voicemail for dentists and chiropractors inform callers to call 911 in the event of an emergency. And then, even if the victims demanded to be taken to a personal doctor, that doctor would have reported it to the authorities."

"Unless the doctor was paid off," Lindstrom offered.

Kara nodded. "Possible, but that seems a little far-fetched."

"As far-fetched as a phantom ambulance and paramedics abducting two people and not issuing any kind of ransom demands?"

Again, Kara nodded. "You got me there."

Lindstrom had pretty much all she needed. She should be able to get the system rolling on her next step of the investigation. She looked at Kara and asked, "Do you have anything to add?"

Kara looked over her notes one more time. She was trying to be thorough, but she was also trying to hide her annoyance. She hadn't expected such a quick Q&A. Then again, if that is all she had to offer, best to be finished and get on with the rest of her day.

"No," Kara said. "I think that pretty much covers it."

"Okay," Lindstrom said as she stood up and started walking around the table towards the door. "Good work. Thanks for coming in this morning. If you think of anything else, or you get any more info, let me know."

Kara stood up, sighing as she did. Lindstrom caught the sigh, though she didn't react to it.

"Tish, look," Kara began, "I know things have been, well, weird between us, and I wish they weren't. There really isn't..."

Lindstrom held up a hand and stopped her.

"Kara, really, not now. I have two major cases going right now, Trevor is graduating and leaving in two months, and," she briefly paused, not wanting to go into more details. Nobody else knew that Lindstrom was having financial problems, and the last thing she wanted was pity, especially from Kara Reed. Lindstrom would find a way to make it work, like she always did.

"Look," Lindstrom continued, "the point is I need to be focused right now. We need to be professional for the duration of this case. That's it."

Kara decided not to press the issue. She knew what kind of havoc work-related pressures could have on a person and their immediate circle of family and friends. Kara looked at Lindstrom, smiled and nodded, and said, "I'll let you know if anything else comes up, then." With that, she stepped out of the conference room and followed the uniformed officer who had been waiting outside of the conference room. The officer escorted her down to the lobby and outside to her car.

Lindstrom checked the time. She had about half an hour before she had to meet with Engels and Tisdale. She grabbed her notes, went to her desk, and picked up the phone.

Tisdale was finished interviewing Jason a second time, and went to one of the other, smaller conference rooms. Lindstrom was already inside, sitting at the table. The smaller conference rooms were similar to the main conference room, with the same basic layout, furniture, and paint. The only real difference was the number of people that each could hold comfortably. The smaller conference rooms could hold between fifteen to twenty, seated and standing, while the main conference room could fit thirty to forty.

"Where's the chief," Tisdale asked.

"Right behind you," came Engels booming voice. Tisdale was startled a bit, but quickly regained his composure. As Engels walked to the head of the table, he said, "First, good morning to both of you. So, let's get started and try to cut through it and get some handle on the events. Also, we are recording." Engels looked at Tisdale. "Officer Tisdale, you are up."

"Um," Tisdale stammered, "do you want me to stand up?"

Engels and Lindstrom chuckled softly. "Tisdale," Engels said reassuringly, "you don't need to stand on ceremony. Simply tell us what you found out."

Tisdale coughed and took a drink of water from the bottle he had brought. "Yes sir. Sorry sir. Okay, after meeting Jason at the corner of 32nd and Spring, I had Jason describe the events to me. As we approached the bus stop, we found that two of the plastic panels that partially enclose the area had been removed. No other panels had any blood on them. The bench showed some alteration, but only in a few spots on the back and shoulder area. The alteration looks recent, possibly from sanding or

60

cleaning with bleach. As for the street where the ambulance drove away, there were no visible tire tracks. Jason said that the ambulance 'peeled out', but where tracks should have been, there are two large smears of oil, most likely to obscure the tracks. And, since it rained Tuesday afternoon and night, any blood evidence was washed away. I contacted the city's transportation service, as they're responsible for all public bussing and maintenance of the bus stops. They have no record of anyone performing any form of maintenance or having any maintenance scheduled at that bus stop in the last six months. I had one of Jerry's team, Roger, come out to dust for prints and take pictures of the area. Not only were the areas around the missing plastic panels wiped clean, but all the other panels were thoroughly cleaned, too. Only four prints were found, but they were on the other side of the existing panels, away from where the so-called paramedics, the 'stunning woman', or the man were interacting."

Tisdale had used his fingers to make air quotation marks for affect. He took a long drink of his water, which allowed him to catch his breath. He was trying not to be overly impressive, but it wasn't every day that you were given an actual case and were working with a great detective like Patricia Lindstrom. Hell, it wasn't every day that you were giving the Chief a briefing, either.

"Is that all?" asked Lindstrom. She was amazed with what Tisdale had found. However, she attempted to hide her enthusiasm. Excited rookies can make mistakes, and she wanted to keep Tisdale level-headed.

"Actually, no!" Tisdale lit up. "I interviewed the bartender that was working Monday night, one Sarah Veld. She remembers a great deal about that night. She said that it was unusually slow since the Monday night football game was a dud."

Engels let out a heavy sigh. "Cleveland Browns versus the Jacksonville Jaguars." He shook his head. "Sorry, please continue."

"Yes, anyway, the man came in first, alone, and ordered a strawberry lemonade. She remembers that he seemed nervous. He took his drink and sat down. About twenty minutes later, the woman sat down at the bar. No alcohol, just flavored water. The bartender said that the woman took her water, looked around, and seemed to zero in on the man, and sat down across from him." Tisdale flipped a page on his notes. Before he could continue, Lindstrom looked at Engels, who nodded.

Tisdale continued. "Sarah states that for the next twenty minutes, they seemed to interact, but in a strange way. The woman came off as out of his league, and the man didn't really seem interested, focused more on his glass than anything else going on around him. When Sarah looked towards the booth again, only the man was sitting there. The woman was on her cell by the restroom doors. Sarah walked towards the end of the bar to retrieve a new box of bar napkins. Even though the woman was standing with her back to the rest of the bar, she seemed agitated on the phone. Next thing Sarah knows, the man is gone, and the woman is at the bar. The woman orders another small strawberry lemonade for him and a 7Up for herself. She sat back down in the booth with the drinks. Sarah was cleaning glasses when the man came back and sat down. The woman talked to him for a minute or two, and then the man looked at Sarah. Sarah smiled at him and nodded."

Tisdale paused to take another drink, which allowed Lindstrom to chime in with, "Sounds like a very attentive bartender."

Engels confirmed that. "Bartenders, certain sales clerks, basically anyone that has to deal with a seedier part of the public. They have to keep their head on the proverbial swivel, making sure that no trouble breaks out, things don't get stolen from under their nose. Being extra observant isn't just for nurses and detectives, you know." Lindstrom thought about that, remembering what Walter Lowry had told her. Being in retail for many years had given him the opportunity to train his eyes to spot the smallest of details.

Tisdale resumed. "Sarah had set some drinks down on the other side of the bar and looked back towards the booth. The woman's back was to her, but she couldn't see him. As she walked back to that side of the bar, she heard a small thud and saw the menus on the table fall over. The man had been on the ground and appeared to have hit his head on the table standing back up. They then walked out together. Jason and I reconstructed what he had observed in the bar with his friend, Max. Both stories match up." He took a breath and another drink.

"That's good work, Tisdale," Engels said. "Very thorough."

"But that's not everything!" Tisdale exclaimed, maybe a little too loud. In a calmer voice, he said, "The bartender says that the tables and booths are wiped clean every night. 'To preserve the bar's excellent rating with the health department', as Sarah said. I had Roger examine the underside of the table. He found a small blood smear with some hair attached to it!"

Engels and Lindstrom both sat up straighter. "You got DNA!", they both said in unison.

"Yes, but we already had the man's blood. Jason bagged his shirt in a sealed plastic bag at the emergency room. He gave me the sealed bag, and I logged it into evidence. No, this is where it gets better! I was trying to figure out why the man was under the table. There had to be a reason, right? Well, I figured that our mystery man is also a gentleman."

Lindstrom quickly connected the dots. "They get up to leave, but she drops the contents of her purse. He goes to the ground to retrieve any items, bumping his head on the way up."

Tisdale said, "But he didn't get all of the items! Roger and I also found an old-style flip open cell phone and a small plastic tube, about the size and shape of a tampon under the table."

"A tampon?" Engels asked.

"No sir. Not a tampon, but it's the size and shape of one. Inside the plastic tube are small, clear looking gel caps, like pills." Tisdale looked at Engels. "That's everything that I got." Tisdale sat down.

Engels stood up. Lindstrom could tell he was excited. "Okay, so let's lay this out. Tish, help me out if I miss anything." Lindstrom got up and went to one of the dry erase boards on the wall.

"Go ahead," Lindstrom said, marker in hand.

"We have a man in a bar that doesn't seem like he wants to be there. We have a 'stunning' woman who appears to try to pick up the man. Maybe she succeeds, maybe she doesn't. Somehow, they end up at the bus stop outside, with the man bleeding from the back of the head. The woman hails a fictitious ambulance and two supposed paramedics get a wounded man into the back of the ambulance and drive away from a hospital, but not before the man is able to injure the woman. Meanwhile, all trace evidence at the bus stop has either been removed or destroyed. However, we are lucky to get a blood and hair sample that should provide the man's DNA. We are also lucky enough to recover items that may or may not have belonged to the woman." Engels paused as Lindstrom finished writing. When she was done, he asked the room, "Can I get some thoughts on this?"

Lindstrom spoke up first. "The role-playing angle doesn't fit. Most couples that do role-playing have more intimate or intense methods. The black widow idea also doesn't really fit. Black widows work alone, and they are after more of a prize, men with money or power or both." Lindstrom looked at Tisdale and asked, "Are you sure that the items you found are the woman's? Maybe they are someone else's."

"It's possible," Tisdale said. "Here's the thing, though. Each booth is its own piece. You can't drop something in one booth and have it roll into the next. Whoever built them wanted each seat to be its own, probably so that you can't feel the next person over unless they move a great deal."

Lindstrom added, "We also have a man and woman that are injured that have not received medical attention. Either they can't get help, because of the situation, or they won't get help, for the same reason."

Engels looked at Tisdale. "Has Roger or Jerry ran a test on the gel caps from inside the tube yet?"

Tisdale shook his head. "Not yet. Jerry was working on the dead body, and Roger left right after we cataloged the evidence. His daughter was in a talent show last night."

"Odds are it's a roofie of some kind," Lindstrom interjected. "I've read about some of those effects from first-hand accounts in the ER." Roofies, otherwise known as date-rape drugs, were designed to leave a person incapacitated. "But why?" Her face contorted into a frown. "You are a beautiful woman, 'a stunner'. Don't you need to get the guy to a car, or to his house, before you drug him?"

Lindstrom looked at the clock. "Boss," she said, and motioned for Engels to look. They had been playing show and tell for almost an hour. If Engels wanted to be ready for the press, he needed to redirect and focus on the dead woman. She could see that he was conflicted. He wanted to stay working on this puzzle, but he also needed to look at the next puzzle, too.

"Tisdale," Engels said, "any chance there is video surveillance in that bar?"

"The cameras that are positioned around the bar are for show only," Tisdale responded. "The only cameras that actively transmit are behind the bar, and they are set up at the cash registers. They point straight down, like the cameras at blackjack tables, to make sure there's no funny business with the cash. Goldie's restaurant next door has cameras inside the front door, but after they finished a remodel two weeks ago, there's some issue with the wiring. The electrician isn't scheduled to come back and look at it for another two weeks. No go there, either."

Engels looked around the room, acknowledging both Tisdale and Lindstrom. "Tisdale, that's good work. Start following up on leads you can think of. Now, if you'll excuse us, Tish and I need to go over a few things. Tish, I need a minute in the restroom. I'll be right back." Engels then left the room.

Tisdale walked toward the door, and Lindstrom gave him a good squeeze on his shoulder. "Good job," she said to him. Tisdale smiled and walked out.

As he stood in front of the restroom mirror, washing his hands, Engels was trying to assimilate everything about this case. Sure, he had worked cases in the past where, eventually, everything came together. This one, though, he was having a hard time with. Tish was right. A couple involved with a role-playing gone wrong didn't even register. The black widow "she mates and then she kills" was interesting, but it also didn't play. Unless this was the woman's first time, in which case she had royally screwed it up. Add to that a fake ambulance and fake paramedics, and what did you get? As the kids would say, it was a hot mess.

Engels finished drying his hands and looked in the mirror. His wife had told him that morning that he looked good for the cameras. Now, after an hour on one case, he wasn't so sure. Maybe after he did a quick change into his blue uniform, he would look the part. He walked out of the restroom and back into the conference room. Lindstrom was looking out the window. He closed the door, to which she turned around, smiling like a cat with a mouse.

"I've seen that look before," Engels said. "Once again, would you like to share with the class?"

"Did we have Jason work with a sketch artist?"

A simple question, one that Engels hadn't even thought of. "Of course," Engels said. "We expect to have video of everything, of everyone, everywhere." Then the wave of revelation was met by a wave of defeat. "Unfortunately, Timmons moved to Phoenix last year, and we never replaced him. The closest sketch artist is four hours away." Engels thought for a minute. "I'll give her chief a call after the presser and see if we can get her up tomorrow or over the weekend."

"If we can get some sketches up on the news and on social media,"

Lindstrom said, "maybe we can get one or both of them to come to us. Right now, all we have is a something that may or may not be a crime, involving people that may or may not be hurt, and so on." She looked at her boss. She could tell the wheels were turning. "Are we sticking with this one, or shall we talk about a body that we actually have?"

Engels sat back down. "You read Jerry's report?"

"First thing this morning. All very preliminary, but an interesting read."

"Am I correct that we both have the same problem with it?"

"Problem? Boss, this is another case that makes no sense." Lindstrom sat down at the opposite end of the table, facing Engels. "Someone went to a lot of trouble to make it nearly impossible to identify this woman. In order to get us to look in a different direction, this person throws in a satanic symbol."

"Spell it out for me," Engels urged her on.

"Whoever did this wasn't expecting her to be found right away. You remove her teeth to eliminate dental records, and we know the teeth were removed before her face was caved in, since there weren't even tooth fragments in the stomach contents. Then the face is caved in. Next, let's hack off the hands, so no fingerprints. Now, let's really confuse the cops by cutting off the feet. The entire body is hair free, including the pubic and anal regions, and no eyebrows or eyelashes. Now you have this body that you are going to dispose of. But where? Dumping it down a storm drain makes sense. It's less likely to be discovered by someone, and you hope it will decompose faster when exposed in water. Plus, with fall ending and winter coming and the eventual thaw, the body should be jelly and bones by the time someone finds it. Unfortunately, you didn't know about the damaged storm drain, but that's another issue. If you wanted the body to waste away in the elements, then why in hell do you bleach the body?"

Engels listened intently, then he looked down at the photos of the dead body, both in the water and from the post mortem, with his gaze then moving on to the photos of the manhole cover, the drainage pipe, and the culvert. It was then that Engels realized what Lindstrom was getting at.

"Whoever did this is sloppy. This is the first time, and they panicked, to the point of over-compensation."

"More than likely, yes," Lindstrom explained. "And maybe not panicked, but they went out of their way to try to throw us off the track. This woman wasn't shot or stabbed or strangled. Jerry lists the cause of death as exsanguination. So, you're the killer, and I'm the victim. I've done something to piss you off, and you kill me. But now what? You don't want to get caught. You take all of these elaborate measures to hide the woman's identity, but you do a little too much. What animal would eat at a dead body in a storm drain that's been soaked in bleach? You are careful enough to remove the teeth but depraved enough to beat her face to a mess of blood and bone. You cut off her hands, but why the feet? And, to really try and mess with the police, you carve a pentagram on the body."

Engels was trying to reconcile what he was hearing with what he might be able to say in the presser. It was an ongoing investigation but saying too much would make it difficult for Lindstrom to do her job. "And there's not enough left to use any kind of facial recognition, correct"

"Not a chance," Lindstrom replied. "Jerry put her DNA into the national database, but who knows if we'll get a hit."

Engels could tell that she was frustrated about the contradictions in the case. However, he didn't push her. Lindstrom is an excellent detective, and she closed more than her share of cases. Just give her a wide berth, support as needed, questions when necessary, and things would get worked out. He looked at the clock and sighed.

"Wrapping up so soon?" Lindstrom asked.

"I think it's for the best, for right now," Engels said. "I need to call and get the sketch artist in the pipeline. I want to do a quick once over on my notes for the presser, and I want to grab a snack."

"Don't you think you should stop with the snacks? You aren't a spring chicken anymore, at least not since Clive left."

"That's for damn sure. Anyway, the Mrs. started making me homemade snacks that are supposed to be healthier for me. Granola, oats, chia seeds, honey, peanut butter, and some other stuff. It must be working, though. A month ago, I was eating almost five full meals a day to keep up with the demands of the job. I'm back to three squares a day, with one or two of these little snacks in between. Apparently, I am supposed to be around long enough to actually retire with her."

"I never knew you were such a romantic," Lindstrom replied sarcastically.

"Yeah, well, it's best to be prepared." A quiet pause, and then, quietly, "for anything."

Lindstrom snapped her attention away from the autopsy report and her stare bore down on Engels. "Boss, I swear, if you take a coward's way out with your meeting with the mayor next month, I can guarantee there will be a whole police force that will line up to knock some sense back into that overweight body of yours."

Engels stood up, making it known with his height and tone of voice that this was not the time. "Tish, I know you mean well, but right now, stay focused on these cases. Whatever happens will happen. Help Tisdale figure out a game plan for our phantom crime, and then go back over the autopsy report and see if Jerry missed anything. If he didn't, go over it again. Check with me after lunch." With that, Engels walked out of the conference room.

Good, Lindstrom thought. Her boss had no intention of bending over for the mayor. He was going to fight like hell for himself and for the entire police department. If Engels would have reacted differently, she would have known that things might play out differently. Then again, was it an act? Was he putting on a poker face for Lindstrom, to try to deflect the conversation? It didn't matter, Lindstrom thought to herself. Her boss loves his job, and no matter what issues he was facing, the entire police department would be willing to step up and help ameliorate the situation. For now, though, it was going to be Engels against the mayor, and she was sure the mayor was going to lose.

Tisdale arrived at Goldie's Restaurant twelve minutes after ten. Even though they didn't open for lunch until 11am, the doors were already unlocked, and they would gladly serve anyone who came in early. As he stood inside the entrance and coat check area, his cell went off. Detective Lindstrom. "Yes, ma'am, what's up?"

"Did you just call me 'ma'am'," came an annoyed voice from the other end. "Tisdale, I swear, this is your final warning. Start calling me Tish, or I'll have my friends over in SWAT put you through a whole week of obstacle courses in only twenty-four hours. You understand?"

Tisdale felt his cheeks flush. "Yes, I understand. Sorry, Tish. Too much academy training, proper discipline and respect. Besides, you and

Engels are such great cops."

"Lose the intimidation, Tisdale. You may be green, but I think you've shown you are a good cop. And stop with the brown nosing, too. Now, where are you?"

"I'm over at Goldie's. I wanted to talk to the staff again and see if they had any recollection of anyone acting strange on Monday night. Maybe something or someone stood out."

"Good idea. After that, talk to Roger again. Try to identify the gel caps you found, and then check that cell phone for any calls, texts, anything."

"Got it. I will let you know as soon as I have any updates. Talk to you soon. Bye." He ended the call. Tisdale knew the real reason he was clumsy around Lindstrom. She was attractive, but she was also damn smart. Unfortunately, he also knew that he didn't stand a chance of getting close to her in that way. Everyone knew that she had sent her first husband to prison for abuse. She had remarried and had another kid, Ryan, who was almost too adorable for his own good. It really was a shame about Mark, which meant that, no matter who came to call, no matter how many good and pure intentions there were, Tisdale doubted that Lindstrom would ever let anyone get close to her again.

"Officer Paul Tisdale!" The voice brought him back to reality. He turned away from the front door and saw Chad, the host, walking toward him. "Is this business or pleasure?"

"Chad, I wish it was pleasure. The surf'n'turf I had three weeks ago was amazing. Unfortunately, I need a bump in pay to afford coming here more often."

"Oh, come now. We have better food and better pricing than half of the restaurants in town, and you know it. But, enough about that. What can I do for you?"

"I was hoping I could talk to you again about Monday night. Anything or anyone that stood out, or maybe if any of your staff saw anything."

"Absolutely! By all means, let's sit down. Fortunately, with how we schedule our shifts, everyone that worked on Monday is working today, except for the four people that work the night hours. They will be in around 3:30." As Chad and Tisdale sat down, Tisdale's phone went off. He looked at the text message. Not good.

Tisdale quickly stood. "Sorry, Chad, but there's been an emergency, and all available officers need to respond. I will try to come back later tonight." With that, Tisdale bolted out of the restaurant to his police cruiser.

Normally, Lindstrom didn't go too far out of her way to help fix a mistake her daughter made. However, she was in no mood to deal with Bree's adolescent crap. After too many calls and texts from Bree, not only to Lindstrom's cell but to her desk phone, and then to the police station's switchboard, she had finally phoned the high school. Lindstrom told the secretary that she would meet the school bus at Augustana University's science center. Today was a field trip, and Bree practically shoved the permission slip into her mother's face a block from the high school that morning. As Lindstrom had pulled up to the commons entrance, she had hastily signed the slip. However, in Bree's mad rush to get out of the car with her purse, her backpack, and her large iced mocha, all while trying not to be seen by the other teenagers that weren't being dropped off by a parent, Bree had dropped the permission slip between the seat and the door. Of course, it was never Bree's fault, and she expected her mother to drop everything and get her the permission slip.

Bree had been equal parts livid and embarrassed that her "cop mom" was going to be seen in front of her class. Lindstrom had countered that it was either that or no permission slip, and Bree could stay at school, in the library, during freshmen study hall, and miss the field trip entirely. Bree grudgingly admitted to the less embarrassing of the two evils.

So, here Lindstrom was, sitting in her car, waiting for the school bus to arrive. Almost one o'clock. The day started out well, but then things had taken a turn. Lindstrom had hoped that talking with Tisdale, Jerry, and anyone else with a passing knowledge of the cases would help kick start her thought process. Unfortunately, right after talking to Tisdale, reports came in of a semi-trailer that jack-knifed in a construction zone. The accident had caused a chain reaction, which meant Tisdale had to assist in the response to the accident. At last report, eleven cars and the semi-trailer were damaged. Thankfully, word was that there were no fatalities, with the number of casualties only about thirty or so injuries.

A text alert came across her phone. It was from Engels. "GOOD NEWS! Sketch artist was already coming up here for a few days with his wife for anniversary. Will be here in the AM tomorrow. Jason will be here, maybe Max. Good luck with Bree."

Lindstrom re-read the text, and then smiled to herself. Once they had a sketch of either the woman or the man, or both, hopefully some more leads would open up. Lindstrom had planned on taking the morning off, anyway. She needed to meet Trevor's guidance counselor to go over the details for his early graduation, and then she had to go to Ryan's school. His class was putting on a performance, a collaboration of art and music classes. It was also a half school day, a teacher in-service. Trevor was going to be working after school, Bree had cheerleading, and Ryan was going to a birthday party. By the time she would be done tomorrow morning and get to the station, the sketch artist should be done with Jason and Max. If things went well, which was never certain when it came to police work, at least one of her cases would be moving forward.

Lindstrom saw the school bus turn into the parking lot. Time to act quickly and discreetly. The last thing Lindstrom needed was to do something "wrong" in front of Bree and her class. God, if that happened, Bree wouldn't stop bringing it up until the next travesty was committed. Lindstrom kept reminding herself, *I love my daughter, and my daughter loves me. Things are difficult, I'm a cop, she's a teenager.* A big breath in, and she got out of her car and walked toward the parked school bus.

Engels wasn't happy about having to put a high-profile case and a possible high-profile case on the back burner, but that was the way of the world sometimes. He was fortunate that the sketch artist was going to be in town anyway. He was unfortunate that a major car accident had diverted resources away from other cases. He was fortunate that no one had died. He was unfortunate that, during his press conference regarding the dead body, a reporter had broken the accident to him via the reporter's Twitter account. Engels knew it was all about balance, especially at this stage of his career.

As he finished some paperwork that Michelle had left on his desk before she had left for the day, he stopped for a minute. Balance, Engels thought to himself. He closed the folder of papers, straightened them by tapping the folder on his desk, and got up to put the folder on Michelle's desk. He turned off the light in his office, walked down the hallway, and stopped at the conference room they had used that morning. He unlocked the door, turned on the light, and surveyed each dry erase board.

Balance, Engels thought to himself again. He rubbed his eyes and shook his head. The thought was like a splinter, right under the skin, where you couldn't get it. Then it was gone again. Engels sighed, turned off the light, and locked the conference room again. Tomorrow was Friday. TGIF? Maybe. Engels left the police station, still thinking about balance.

FIVE

Considering everything that had transpired over the past two days, Lindstrom was hoping, probably needing, Friday to be better. Well, at least it had been interesting so far. As she drove to the police station, she reflected on the day.

Bree had woken up happy, got ready for school, and had been picked up by a friend. Trevor had been up early, at least early for him, and was out the door, telling his mother that he had an appointment with his Air Force recruiter before school. Lindstrom had decided to treat Ryan, so they left the house early and stopped by the local grocery store. Once inside, they made their way to the bakery department. Ryan got a roll with strawberry filling, vanilla frosting, and sprinkles to go with a pear and apple smoothie. She got a yogurt and granola bowl and a flavored tea. Ryan was so excited for his performance that morning, but he refused to rehearse in front of his mother.

"It's a surprise, Momma!" He had been saying that for three weeks. Alright, kiddo, she thought, you go ahead and surprise your Momma.

Lindstrom dropped him off at the elementary school, and then it was over to the high school. It was so great to live so close to everything. Well, except for work, but that was okay. The city of Sioux Falls, South Dakota was a city of around two hundred thousand. Brandon was a separate town. Would you call it a suburb? It took between seven and ten minutes to drive between the two, depending on the time of day and which road you decided to travel. There were some modest homes and some farmland between the two, and it seemed that, every year, a little bit more of the land between the two was developed. No matter. She was happy with the situation. Good schools, good people, and the right amount of businesses around to provide most of the essentials. Anything else, well, she could pick up in the "big city". As for the house, it wasn't fancy, but it was big enough to keep three kids happy, or at least content. Of course, once Trevor graduated in two months and moved out, the house would feel a little different. Then again, the house had felt different ever since Mark had been…

Lindstrom suddenly gripped the steering wheel tight, almost missing her turn. She put those thoughts out of her head. Now wasn't the time to think about Mark. She parked and went to the high school office and then to the guidance counselor's office. Twenty minutes later, she was back in her car. Not even 8:30 yet. Ryan's performance didn't start for another two hours. She drove back home, pulled into the driveway, and sat there. Lindstrom looked at the house that her and Mark had fallen in love with so many years ago, and her thoughts drifted into the past.

They had been bouncing around from apartments to rental houses for a few years, treading water with three kids in tow, waiting until their bankruptcy had cleared the books. They had decided to move, Mark having gotten a transfer and Lindstrom getting a job on the police force. Unfortunately, their previous house they were trying to sell in Medford, Minnesota, wouldn't sell. Of course, that was during the market crash at the tail end of 2007 and into 2008. Between a police officer's salary and Mark working retail, there hadn't been enough money coming in. Add to that her dirt bag ex-husband that didn't understand the concept of "child support", and things were grim.

Mark and Lindstrom decided that bankruptcy was the only way. It helped them unload the house that was six hours away and helped get rid of a lot of debt. They had figured that, while the next seven years would be lean, especially with three kids, it was necessary to correct things and move forward. Eventually, those seven years came and went, they got a letter of approval from a decent local bank, and they started house hunting. For a few months, nothing really came up. Everything was either too expensive, too rundown, or was off the market too soon.

Then, one Sunday afternoon, while driving back from the swimming pool, Mark had swerved to avoid hitting a dog. He turned the car down a different street, and halfway down the block, there it was. A for sale sign in the yard, and an "OPEN HOUSE, 1PM – 3PM" sign next to it. The car's clock read 2:50pm. Mark parked the car, and the five of them practically ran into the house. The house, the neighborhood, the location, the backyard, the price, it was beyond perfect. Mark had called their real estate agent from the kitchen, with the listing agent standing in front of him. An hour later, they were sitting with their agent at his office, filling out papers. Six weeks later, they were moving in.

Lindstrom got out of her car, walking around the lawn and into the backyard. She kicked one of Ryan's footballs towards his play area, and she picked up some small branches that had broken off the big oak tree. She went inside the house and walked from room to room. Their cat, Blonde, appeared out of nowhere, meowing as he rubbed up against her legs, wondering why she was home. She wasn't very sentimental. It wasn't a trait that worked well for a detective. After she spent a few minutes walking the house and picking up a few odds and ends, she sat down on one of the stools at the breakfast island in the kitchen. She briefly closed her eyes, contemplating about how so many things were changing in her family's lives.

As she sorted through a stack of papers on the island, Blonde jumped onto her lap and nuzzled his nose against her stomach. She scratched his ears and neck, and when she stopped, he stretched up, sniffed her nose, and jumped down. Lindstrom figured it was his version of a goodbye kiss. She went back to the papers. Had she really let things pile up like this? Lots of papers from Ryan's class, magazines on eating right and staying healthy, bulk mail from colleges with Trevor's name on the envelopes. Thank goodness recycling day was on Monday. She looked at the microwave's clock, which displayed 9:27. Only an hour until Ryan's performance. Lindstrom wasn't sure what she was feeling, but it was an odd mixture of happy, sad, contentment, and anxiousness. Somehow, she knew that her kids were each going to have a great day. She finished sorting the papers, recycling the bulk and junk, when she saw the envelope. It was the letter that she had brought home from the station on Wednesday. She looked at, staring at it, knowing full well what it said.

As usual, there was nothing that could be done. Between being incarcerated or having no job once he was out of jail, Lindstrom's ex-husband was unable to help support his children. The senator's office had appreciated that she had reached out to him, but he referred Lindstrom to other state agencies. She sighed heavily. Ever since she had sent her ex to prison and divorced him, getting full custody of Trevor and Bree in the process, she knew it might be difficult to get anything out of him. At least when he was in prison, the state sent her the little bit he made by working while incarcerated. When he was released, and the protection order was enforced, with supervised custodial visits, he had vowed to make things right. Two months later, he was arrested for assault. Charges were dropped, of course, but that was only the start.

Even though he had the right to see his kids, he never did. No cards, no calls, no gifts. Each month meant that the child support he wasn't paying got a little bit bigger. As time went by, Lindstrom eventually met Mark, and they married a year later. She would hear rumors from family members and friends in her hometown. *"The ex-husband had been arrested again." "He was into drugs again." "He was working, but they were paying him off the books, so he wouldn't have to pay her anything."* Even as a police officer and then a detective, she refused to use her connections to check up on him. That would have been an abuse of her authority. She simply had to use the avenues that were open to any law-abiding citizen, and she could only hope that, at some point in the future, everything would work out.

Lindstrom took the letter into her bedroom and locked it in her safe. Even though they were older, Trevor and Bree never asked about their biological father. They had been very young when she had met Mark, and Mark had treated them both as if they were his own children. She believed that Mark was imprinted on them, too, and nothing could change that. Oh, Mark, she thought, you should be here to see these three wonderful children.

Lindstrom locked up the house and got back in the car, heading toward the elementary school. Ryan's class performance was as good as advertised. She had used Bree's camera to film it on a flash card, and she used her cell to film only Ryan's part. These third graders were great. Rather than rehash some old play, the music and art teachers had helped the kids put together their own play, using their own favorite things. Each child had contributed art and lyrics, and the teachers had woven it all together. Each child had an equal part, and every parent was overjoyed at such a wonderful production.

Since it was early dismissal, the performance ended fifteen minutes before school was letting out. The parking lot was more chaotic than normal, even considering that it was Friday. As Lindstrom tried to find the two minivans that were going to take Ryan's friends to the birthday party for the afternoon, Ryan was excited, asking her if she had liked the show, what was her favorite part, he wanted to do it again, over and over. Lindstrom spotted the minivans, and started making her way over to them, holding Ryan's hand as they walked.

"Momma, will we be able to show Daddy how good I did in the show?"

The question caught her like a shotgun blast. She pulled him gently off the sidewalk and kneeled in front of him. She brushed his bangs across his forehead, thinking she needed to get this little cutie pie to the barber.

"Ryan," she said sweetly, "you did an outstanding job today! I have the whole thing taped, plus I recorded only your part on my phone. I think your Daddy would love to see your show. But, for right now, I want you to be happy that you made your Momma so proud today, and I want you to have all kinds of fun with your friends at this birthday party." She gave him a kiss on the cheek, picked him up, and said, "C'mon, you have a party to go to!" They both laughed as she ran along the sidewalk, weaving in and out of kids and parents, and got to the minivan. Ryan hugged her tight, told her he loved her, and jumped inside.

"Tish," one of the mothers said, "we should be done around six or seven. I'll call or text if something comes up."

That had been Lindstrom's morning and early afternoon, and all in all, she was happy. Even the sun seemed extra warm and bright for a season slipping into winter. Normally, when she drove, unless the kids were in the car, the radio was off, so she could focus on the road. Today, she had found a rock station and was tapping her fingers on the steering wheel to everything from classic Red Hot Chili Peppers to newer Metallica and back to some classic Led Zeppelin. Commercials had started when her phone buzzed. She turned off the radio and activated the hands-free mode.

"Were you planning on coming in today?" Tisdale's voice sounded distorted through the stereo speakers.

"You know," Lindstrom said, "I'm about five blocks away, I've had a wonderful morning, and if you have a problem with the hours I am keeping, I have a slightly overweight boss that would be happy to put you on meter maid detail."

Tisdale laughed, and it made the windows vibrate. "Damn, Tish, take it easy! Engels has been busy with the cleanup from the semi-truck accident yesterday, so I haven't talked to him. The sketch artist just finished with Jason and Max. Jason is dead sure on the woman, while Max is about eighty percent on the woman."

"What about the sketch of the man?"

"That gets a little dicey. Jason had been so focused on the stunner of a woman that he didn't pay that much attention to him. That is, until it was almost too late. Jason puts his recollection of the man at maybe sixty percent, but it could also be lower. Max only said maybe, maybe not."

"Okay, I'm pulling into the secure lot on the east side. I am coming in through the front lobby for a change."

"That's great," Tisdale exclaimed. "The four of us should be there in a few minutes, so just hang there. Bye!" Well, Tisdale sounded excited. If this kept up, there might be an epidemic of happy today.

Lindstrom walked into the lobby of the police station. She saw that Heather Gordon was working the receptionist area today. Heather had retired from the force three years ago. However, after her husband suddenly passed, she realized that she loved being a part of the police department so much that she had requested to come back as a "Jill-Of-All-Trades". Seeing her always made Lindstrom smile, and today was no different. As she made her way to Heather, three people, two men and one woman, were standing in front of Heather. From the look on Heather's face, she appeared to be frustrated. It took a lot to frustrate Heather, so it couldn't be good.

"Seriously, you don't have one goddamn cop that can take five minutes to get a statement?!" The taller of the two men was speaking in a raised voice. Lindstrom decided to take a position at the counter, only a few feet away from the trio. The woman seemed like she had been crying but was now trying to keep her emotions in check. The shorter of the two men had his arm over her shoulders, apparently trying to give her some support. The tall man who had spoken was tapping one foot fast. He looked like he was ready to explode.

"Heather, is everything alright?" Lindstrom asked, with an even tone that she hoped would help defuse the situation.

78

"I hope you're a cop, lady!" The tall man shouted loudly. He wasn't making any friends today.

"Detective Lindstrom, these folks are here…" Heather began, but the woman couldn't hold back any more. The tears came hard and fast.

"Ben, easy", the shorter man said. Ben looked at the woman, and made a step to help support her, too. Heather looked at Lindstrom, and was about to say something, when Lindstrom subtly shook her head. She wanted to observe their interaction for a minute.

Then, from behind Heather, through a set of double doors, out walked Tisdale, Jason, and two others. Lindstrom guessed that the man next to Jason must be Max, and the other man was more than likely the sketch artist. Tisdale was holding some large sheets of paper.

Tisdale saw Lindstrom and smiled. "Tish!"

The two men looked at Tisdale with venom in their eyes. Jesus, Lindstrom thought, we don't need a fight breaking out in the station lobby. She opened her eyes a little wider and tilted her head, hoping Tisdale would get the clue. Jason saw the look, as did Max, and they altered their walking direction to get out of the way. The sketch artist had ducked into a small, hidden alcove, to retrieve his jacket and backpack. Even the sketch artist seemed to be aware of the powder keg that was ready to go off. Tisdale, unfortunately, was amazingly unaware of what was happening. He walked around the receptionist, around the three people, and came up next to Lindstrom.

"This sketch artist is awesome! I think he did a great job. I have some copies upstairs, and once we…"

"CHRIST, I'M GOING TO LOSE IT!"

Ben's voice startled Tisdale, who whipped around, trying to assess what was wrong. "Sir, I'm sorry, but can we help you with something?"

That was the last straw, as, in one fluid move, he knocked the papers out of Tisdale's hands, grabbed him by the shirt collar, and pushed him against the receptionist counter. Tisdale wasn't in uniform, so Ben had no idea he was assaulting a police officer. Jason and Max backed away towards the wall. Heather looked at Lindstrom, and Lindstrom mouthed "no". She didn't want a bunch of uniforms with guns drawn making things worse.

"Ben," Lindstrom said calmly, "I'd like to apologize. OFFICER Tisdale is a good cop, but he's a little too excited today." She took a small step towards them, in case she needed to interject herself physically. Even though her secondary firearm was out of Ben's line of sight, she put her hands up at chest level, hoping to show him she wasn't a threat.

"As Heather said, my name is Detective Patricia Lindstrom. You can call me Tish, though." Lindstrom spoke soft and smooth, in a reassuring voice that she had used for all three of her kids at one time or another. "Please, what seems to be the problem?"

Ben continued to look at Tisdale, like he was debating whether to let him live or not. Lindstrom looked at Ben. He wasn't overly imposing, physically, but he had a passion that made him dangerous, like he had been through enough in his life that he was done taking shit from anyone that crossed him.

"Tish," the shorter man said, holding the woman against his chest, so she couldn't see what Ben was doing. "I'm sorry. Everyone is on edge. We're actually here for her." He nodded to the woman. "Ben, please, let Officer, I'm sorry, I didn't catch your name. Please, let the officer go. Let's just all calm down, okay?"

Ben looked from Tisdale to Lindstrom to Heather to the other man and then, finally, the woman. Ben slowly relaxed his grip on Tisdale until he had let go of him. Once he was released, Tisdale slowly dropped his hands.

"I'm very sorry, sir," Tisdale said meekly, realizing too late what the look on Lindstrom's face had meant.

Lindstrom inhaled. "Okay, now that we a little bit of order back, let's see what this is all about, alright? Tisdale, why don't you pick up your papers. Ma'am, as I said, you can call me Tish. How can we help?"

Tisdale knelt to collect the papers that Ben had knocked out of his hands. He was wary of taking his eyes off of him, so he was fumbling with his hands, grabbing at the ground and at the air, trying to find the papers blindly. As Tisdale was slowly collecting the papers, the woman turned away from the chest of the other man. Lindstrom could tell she was close to losing control of her emotions, so she let her take her time. She took a tissue from a box on the receptionist's counter and handed it to Ben. Ben stepped back from Tisdale and handed the tissue to the woman. The shorter man looked at Ben, visibly upset at him for the use of force.

The woman wiped her eyes and blew her nose. She appeared weak and frail. She looked at Lindstrom. She was about to speak, when Tisdale stood up. She looked at him, and her eyes opened wide in shock. She slapped her hands over her mouth and screamed. Everyone jumped with a start.

Trying to keep calm, Lindstrom asked, "Tisdale, what the hell did you do?"

Before he could answer, the woman screamed at Tisdale and Lindstrom, "WHAT THE HELL DID YOU DO TO HIM??" She must have reached her breaking point, because she fainted backward into the shorter man's arms. Ben rushed to help. Jason, being a nurse, also rushed to her side.

"Heather, get the first aid kit for Jason," Lindstrom said.

"Jason, do you want me to get your stuff from the car," Max shouted.

"Yeah, fast!" Jason replied.

Lindstrom looked at Tisdale. "Do you know this woman?"

Tisdale was in disbelief. "Tish, I've never seen or met this woman before! I swear to you!"

Lindstrom turned towards the woman and the two men. "Ben, I need some answers, fast. Who is she, and why is she here?"

Ben looked up at Lindstrom, but before he could speak, the shorter man said, "Ben, look!" He pointed to Tisdale.

Ben looked at Tisdale and the color left his face. "Sweet merciful God....", Ben said.

Lindstrom looked at Tisdale, who continued to stand there, holding the papers against his chest. Not realizing what he had done, Tisdale had picked up the papers backward, with the sketches facing out. Lindstrom looked back to the men, who were looking at each other.

"Gentlemen, answers, now." Lindstrom was growing impatient.

"My name is Andy," the shorter man said, cradling the unconscious woman's head in his lap. "We are here to file a missing person report on her estranged husband. But, you must know that."

"Why would you say that?" Lindstrom asked guardedly?

"Because," Ben said, "her estranged husband is the man in the sketch."

SIX

Kara was always preoccupied with doing her job. So much so, in fact, that she was able to block out any conversations that weren't medically relevant. She wasn't trying to be rude. It was necessary to remain focused, especially in the emergency room. When the ambulance had pulled up, with a cop car in front and one in back, all she knew was that a woman in her late thirties had collapsed at the police station and was unresponsive. She had a weak pulse and shallow breathing, with no obvious signs of trauma. When the back of the ambulance opened up, she was surprised when Jason jumped out. He had quickly told Kara the woman's vitals, as the two paramedics helped Jason and Kara get her in the ER. After running some basic tests, Kara consulted the ER doctor on duty. He ordered a head and chest x-ray, as well as a CT and MRI of the woman's head. Once the woman was being wheeled away to radiology, Kara had walked the paramedics out. The police cars were gone, but she could see that they were parked in the adjoining lot.

"Ms. Reed, how is she?" Kara turned to see Brad Engels behind her. What the hell was this about?

"Her vitals are starting to stabilize," Kara began, "but there are no overt signs of injury. She is heading to radiology for more tests." She paused briefly, and then added, "If I may, what are you doing here?"

Engels reached into his pocket and grabbed a cough drop, popping it into his mouth. "Whatever was going on is now more complicated." Engels turned around and walked back into the ER waiting room.

Kara followed, and was stunned to see Patricia Lindstrom and Officer Tisdale. Both were standing near two men. The two men were close in height, but they both wore completely different looks. One of the men kept looking down the corridor, as if he was trying to see someone. The other man was focused on Lindstrom and Tisdale, nodding deliberately. Engels stopped next to Tisdale, and Kara fell in beside him. Lindstrom spotted Kara out of the corner of her eye.

"Gentlemen," Lindstrom said, "this is Kara Reed, the head ER nurse here at Sanford Hospital. Kara, would you please inform these two men of Allison's condition?" Lindstrom's speech was even-toned, almost monotone. It relayed no emotion.

"I hate to be rude," Kara replied, "but may I ask what your relation is to her?" The calmer of the two men seemed to understand the reason for the question. Even with police involvement and the stress of the situation, you had to be mindful of patient confidentiality and HIPAA laws. Kara noticed that the other man shook his head violently and started to tap his foot. She had seen that kind of response many times before. The emergency room was a melting pot of emotions. Say the wrong thing, or even say the right thing but in the wrong way, and things could spiral out of control in the blink of an eye. Fortunately, there were always two security guards on duty, one at each end of the ER's waiting room. Kara glanced over the more agitated man again, and she made a mental note to be careful around him.

"My name is Andy Cole," the calmer man said. "The woman's name is Allison Devlin. She is the wife of my best friend, Nathan Devlin. This gentleman is Ben McKinley, and he is Nathan's A.A. sponsor. Nathan's kinda estranged from Allison."

"I'm sorry," Kara said, "but if you aren't direct relatives, there's nothing…"

"Ms. Reed," Engels interrupted, "Nathan Devlin appears to be the man that Jason…" Engels let the sentence hang in the air. Kara tried to keep the shock from registering on her face. She looked around the ER waiting room, realizing that some of the other people had started to take too much of an interest in what was going on. She heard the click of the ER security doors and saw Jason about to walk out to join them. Kara held up a hand, motioning him to stop.

"Perhaps it would be best if we continued this conversation in private,"

Kara said. "Andy, Ben, if you would please follow me. Officer Tisdale, Brad, Tish, you too." Kara turned and heard everyone fall in step behind her. As she got to the security doors that Jason was holding open for them, she looked at him without stopping and said, "C'mon. You started this ball rolling."

All seven people were now in a quiet room a few doors down the hallway from the main ER. Many hospitals had rooms like this, where family members could be taken with doctors and nurses, so that diagnoses, treatments, pretty much anything medically-related, could be discussed away from other patients and their families. The walls were painted a neutral blue, with a television monitor on both walls either side of the door. Engels stood off to the side by the door. The table was round, with Jason and Tisdale seated across from Andy and Ben. Kara stood behind Jason. Lindstrom stood between the two groups of men, essentially cutting the round table in half and acting as the de facto mediator.

"First off," Lindstrom began, "I must inform both of you", she pointed at Andy and Ben using two fingers, "that everything you see and hear going forward is confidential and privileged. We've been working this case for a few days now, and the last thing we need is for more surprises. Understood?"

Andy and Ben both nodded in silent agreement. The look on Andy's face seemed to relay that he understood that something bad was going on. Ben, on the other hand, seemed to be keeping his anger from erupting.

"Excellent," Lindstrom said. "Now, before I divulge any case details, I'd like to hear from the two of you. Andy, please, if you will start."

Andy looked around the room. "Nathan is my best friend. He's also a recovering alcoholic. While he never physically assaulted Allison or his kids, the booze pushed him further and further down. Allison had no choice but to leave him. But, she always held out hope that things could get better. It may seem naïve, but she loves Nathan, in spite of everything. Reconciliation was always her hope. After a few years, she called me pretty much out of the blue, and asked if I had heard from Nathan, and if I would check on him. When I found him, he had hit rock bottom. I mean, seriously, when I say rock bottom, I mean the absolute rock bottom, and he swore to turn his life around. I stayed in touch with him as best I could, which wasn't easy."

"Oh," Engels asked. "Why was that?"

"I would try to call or stop by, but he was never around. Sometimes, after I called, a day or two would go by, and my wife, Heidi, would tell me Nathan had called to say he didn't want any contact until he was a new man." Lindstrom had been watching Andy intently, but, at the mention of Heidi's name, she noticed that Ben rolled his eyes. Lindstrom made a mental note of that.

"I took that as a positive thing, I guess, figuring that Nathan wanted to get himself cleaned up before anyone saw him. Over the last month, Allison said that Nathan had been emailing and calling her. She said that Nathan had been very soft spoken about things, but, working with Ben and the others at A.A., he felt he was ready to show how far he had come." Andy paused, lightly coughing. "I'm sorry, could I have a drink?"

Kara stepped out of the room and returned a minute later with a pitcher of ice water and some disposable cups. She poured Andy a glass and handed it to him.

"Thank you," Andy said to Kara. He downed it quickly, and then continued. "So, Nathan had asked for a supervised visit with the kids. You know the Social Services Center downtown?" Lindstrom and Engels both nodded, but Jason, Tisdale, and Kara all shook their heads. "Well, they offer family play areas that are always monitored and recorded, where parents with questionable pasts can interact with their children, with very little chance of things getting out of control, for either the kids or the parents. The facility is secured, with no interaction allowed between the mother and the father. From what Allison told me, Nathan only wanted a little time with the kids, just to start things moving forward. The proverbial olive branch, so to speak. He wanted and needed the opportunity to express his remorse and show that he was capable of changing. Allison, Heidi, and I had talked quite a bit over the last month, and Allison, always hopeful but trying to be cautious, agreed." Andy stopped, and Lindstrom again noticed a slight tic in Ben's reaction to Heidi's name. Lindstrom looked at Andy. She could gather that seeing his best friend spiral out was bad enough. Now, with a sense of false hope fading into something that he couldn't figure out, that had to be equally as tough.

"Andy, why don't you take a minute to compose yourself," Lindstrom said. "Mr. McKinley?"

"Call me Ben."

"Very well," Lindstrom acknowledged. "How much can you corroborate?"

"All of it." Ben had been sitting up straight as Andy had talked. Now that the focus was on him, Ben seemed to sit up even straighter. "Nathan had been an absolute wreck when he came to his first A.A. meeting. As you may know, A.A. has ongoing partnerships with many local churches of different faiths and denominations. With the help of donations, they pay for detox for individuals that have no way of paying for it themselves. I could tell there was something different about Nathan. Most of the addicts I see are at meetings by court order, or looking to find new connections for a score, or whatever. That first meeting, he poured his soul out to everyone in the room. I knew he was going to have a hard time, so I introduced myself and told him I would be honored to be his sponsor. Nathan was desperate. He wanted to get clean for his family. He expressed such a deep love for Allison and for his kids, but addiction can be so overpowering. It takes control, and a person loses sight of everything else, like you have blinders on to the whole damn world. Anyway, I worked with him every day since that first meeting, and I do mean EVERY GODDAMN DAY!" Ben hit the table with his right index finger on every syllable, driving home the point that he wasn't exaggerating.

"I made sure that we talked at least once every day. I know you might find that hard to believe, but it's true. Every damn day, there was a phone call, or a face to face. No texting or tweeting or email or any of that crap. Phone or face to face." Ben allowed a small smile to creep up the corners of his mouth. "Nathan had worked so hard, he busted his ass getting himself clean, finding a janitorial job, getting a halfway livable apartment, every little step. Then, to have the courage to approach his wife, allowing himself to be patient and, more importantly, hopeful. When I talked to him over his lunch break on Monday, he started rambling. He was scared, he was having reservations, that he didn't know if Allison or the kids would accept him." Ben paused, taking in a breath, and then continued.

"I let him rant. I've seen it and heard it before. That last step for addicts, to see their loved ones again for the first time, that can be the most difficult mountain to climb and get over. When Nathan was done, he had talked his way out of the anxiety, and was focused again. He told me that

86

he had to do this for Allison and the kids." Ben stopped, pouring himself a drink of water. When he had finished drinking, he finished with, "And now, here we are."

"Excuse me?" Engels said. He walked from his position by the door to the open end of the table opposite Lindstrom. "That can't be all of it."

"No, that's not what I meant," Ben replied. "I mean that whatever happened after I talked to him on Monday can't be good."

"Forgive me," Lindstrom said to Ben, "but I need you to have no doubt at all. You said that Nathan and you have spoken at least once a day, every day for, what, a year or more? Even if you were on vacation, traveling with your family, home sick with the flu, there was communication at least once every single day?"

"I know how it sounds, but it is true," Ben said, leaning forward on the table, as if inviting Lindstrom to challenge him again. "Nathan was special. I have been a sponsor for close to twenty addicts in my life. Some got clean and sober, some couldn't come to grips with their demons, and three are dead." He pointed a finger at Kara. "I can see it in your eyes. That look. You've been keeping an eye on me, just like Tish here. Both of you aren't sure what to make of me. You see someone on edge, high strung, itching for a fight, right?" Ben slowly pushed back his chair and stood up. Everyone else in the room seemed to freeze in place, not sure what to expect. Everyone except for Andy. Andy started to grin, bowing his head down slightly. If Lindstrom hadn't known better, she could have sworn Andy was going to start giggling.

"Andy heard this little speech two days after I started sponsoring Nathan. So, let me explain it very simple. Alcohol and drugs nearly killed me, but alcohol and drugs did kill the family of seven that I crashed my pickup truck into more than thirty years ago. After my stretch in prison, I came out angry. Angry at anyone that can't pull their shit together and overcome their addictions. You see me on the street? Well, I'm good. You see me in meetings? I'm a cross between Mother Teresa and a SEAL team instructor. I am a mother hen and a drill sergeant for these people, because that's what they need. I will accept no excuses, because my addicts aren't alone in their fight. Now, here we are, four days since I have heard Nathan's voice. I'm worried as piss, so excuse me for losing my cool at the station. Every second we waste could be another nail in Nathan's coffin." Ben turned and looked at Lindstrom, his arms open at the sides, palms out, as if displaying he had laid all his cards on the table. "That good enough for you, Tish?"

Lindstrom leaned in, her fingertips on the table, facing Ben. Engels had seen her in this stance before while interrogating perps, and it always fascinated him. Like a mongoose staring down a cobra.

"Ben," Lindstrom said softly, "I believe every word you've said. Now, you need to believe me. I am going to do everything in my power to find out what happened to Nathan. You want to be angry, take it out on a bag at the gym. All of us in this room are plenty motivated to figure this out. That good enough for you, Ben?"

They stared at each other for a full minute, and the tension in the room was palpable. Engels didn't move, but he was secretly glad he had brought his Taser along. As the paramedics had been tending to Allison, Heather had called up to his office to give him a rundown of the situation. Jason and Kara had been holding their breath, and Officer Tisdale appeared frozen in place. Andy, to his credit, remained motionless, head down but still grinning.

Ben made the first move, relaxing slowly while offering out his hand. Lindstrom allowed herself to relax, too. She took his hand, and they shook. "Tish, when this is all over, I'd like to buy you and Officer Tisdale a steak to apologize."

"Tisdale enjoys Goldie's Restaurant," Lindstrom said. "As for me, let me do my job first."

"Goldie's?" Andy exclaimed. "Ben, isn't that where…"

Ben snapped from Lindstrom to Andy and back. "When Nathan and I talked on Monday, during his lunch break, I could tell that he needed a little perking up. Nathan had been so committed to the twelve steps and working and getting clean, I was worried that he might be wound up. I told him to get out and get some fresh air, go and enjoy life a little bit. Be out among people. See a movie, grab a bite to eat. Nathan said that he missed eating well cooked meals at restaurants, and that maybe he would try getting some pork chops at Goldie's." A pause filled the air as Lindstrom and Engels took stock of this.

There was a loud buzz, and Kara reached for her phone. "Excuse me," she said, "but I am needed. Jason, I could use your help." Jason got up and they both left the room.

As Ben sat down, Engels moved next to Lindstrom. "Ben, this one is going to be tough. In all the time that you worked with Nathan, did he ever fall off the wagon? Even once, maybe by accident?"

The look on Ben's face went from shock about Goldie's to pure hatred. He was about to jump out of his chair when Andy put his hand on his shoulder.

"Let me, Ben," Andy said. Ben turned to look at Andy, who locked eyes with Ben. Lindstrom watched the unspoken exchange. A few seconds passed, and Ben appeared to back down, with only an ever-so-slight nod to Andy.

"Chief Engels," Andy began, "I understand the need to ask the question, and the answer is no. This whole ordeal has been hard on everyone, seeing someone you love slip away, and then trying to climb out of the pit. Even though I didn't have direct contact with Nathan during his recovery, Ben kept me informed. I will personally vouch that Nathan didn't stray. That day that Nathan had decided to call it quits, when I was in that basement that he was living in, he was clutching a picture of his kids. He hadn't eaten in three days and hadn't had a drink in four. His place was empty of alcohol and food, he was lying on the floor, puke in his hair, and his clothes smelled of dried piss, and I'm pretty sure he didn't have running water to flush the toilet. Nathan looked at me like he never had before and vowed to get clean for his family. That's how I know that he has never had another drop of booze."

Engels looked at Andy and smiled with confirmation. He looked at Tisdale and said, "And you are sure, between Jason, Max, the staff at Goldie's, and the bartender, that he didn't order a drink?"

"Absolutely, chief," Tisdale said. He turned his attention to Andy and Ben. "Based on our evidence, Nathan left Goldie's and went to the bar next door. However, he only ordered strawberry lemonade."

Andy and Ben both smiled. Whatever motivated him to walk into a bar, he had resisted temptation and stayed clean. That was a victory for any addict.

"Was Nathan seeing anyone that you were aware of," Lindstrom asked.

Now it was Andy's turn to look insulted. "Nathan loves Allison! I don't care what he was battling or dealing with, the very idea that he would be out chasing someone else is preposterous! It's complete crap!" Now it was Ben's turn to calm someone down, quickly putting his hand on Andy's shoulder.

"My turn to vouch on this one," Ben said. "It may be a cliché, but alcohol and drugs are the addict's mistress. That's the way it is. As for Nathan, he had mentioned at different points in his recovery that he would be happy if his kids loved him and Allison was happy. One time, I was with him during a bad night of cold sweats and hot flashes. Nathan had called me, and I came over to his place at the time. I sat next to him as he was shaking on his bed. I remember Nathan actually joked that I could 'cut off his balls as long as he could make things right with Allison.' So, next question."

Lindstrom raced through her notes in her head. They had already ruled out the role-playing gone wrong scenario, but this confirmed it. The black widow scenario could still be a possibility, although that was looking less likely. A straight up kidnapping gone wrong?

"Am I correct in saying that the Devlin's don't have a lot, financially speaking?" Lindstrom continued to keep her voice at an even level.

"That's correct," Andy said. "They both had decent jobs back in the day, enough to support their family. When Nathan bottomed out, Allison waited as long as she could, but had no choice but to kick him out. That meant only one income. Of course, that meant that Nathan couldn't provide even a minimum of child support. Allison started working two jobs, and then three jobs, just trying to keep the kids warm and fed and clothed."

A sullen look came over Ben's face. He said, "Nathan was planning on surprising Allison with a check for five hundred dollars today. He had even rehearsed with me what he was going to say. 'No amount of money can make up for the misery I have put you and the kids through, but I promise to never put you through this again.' I know it sounds cheesy, but Nathan was trying."

So much for kidnapping, Lindstrom thought. She tried not to feel sorry for Allison Devlin. Lindstrom felt like she knew what Allison had gone through. Both had husbands that were addicts, which made it difficult or impossible to follow through on the commitments needed to support their respective families. At least Nathan Devlin had seen the light and was trying to work his way back to some form of reconciliation. Lindstrom's miserable ex had no such aspirations. She couldn't decide which was worse. Was it that her ex actively chose not to be a part of the lives he helped bring into the world? Or was that each day meant more money that he wasn't churning out to help support Trevor and Bree? Lindstrom felt a surge of adrenaline, and she looked at Engels.

"Boss, I think we need the press on this. It's getting late in the day. If you can get to the stations before their early additions and get Nathan's picture out there as a missing person, maybe we can get some leads on what the hell happened Monday night."

"Great idea," Engels responded. "Ben, Andy, we need some help. I need three or four pictures of Nathan. Two older ones, during happier times, and if there's anything recent, within the last six months, that would be great. Tisdale, get the pictures, and then meet me at the station ASAP. I will call the media and we'll get it going." As if in unison, Andy, Ben, and Tisdale quickly stood up from the chairs and were out the door of the room. Engels turned to Lindstrom.

"What are you thinking now?"

"That this case continues to be weird." Lindstrom started slowly walking around the table, pushing in the chairs and speaking to Engels. "A recovering alcoholic that goes to a bar five days before he is going to reunite with his family. He ends up disappearing, no body, no ransom, no evidence of a crime, other than the fact that whatever evidence there was has been removed." She stopped her pacing and paused. She shook her head. Something still didn't fit.

Engels sensed her frustration. "I know, I know."

A soft knock came from the door, and Kara Reed slowly opened the door. "What did I miss?"

"Questions were answered," Engels said.

"And it feels like we're no closer," Lindstrom said. "What was that about?"

"Well," Kara started, "the good news is Allison Devlin is stable and resting. Radiology is going over the tests. Based on what Andy and Ben said before I left, though, my money is on stress."

"Come again?" Engels asked.

"It actually makes sense," Lindstrom said before Kara could speak. "The man that you fell in love with, married, and had three kids with turns out to be an alcoholic. Sure, he never beat you or the kids, but being around someone like that can't be healthy. You kick him out, but now, like Andy said, you have to work three jobs to support your family, because your spouse can't help. Now, you have a ray of light that things will work out. For the sake of your kids, and maybe for your own state of mind, you allow yourself to hope, because if it doesn't work out, you've probably lost hope forever. Next thing you know, that hope seems to be dashed. You are standing in the police station, and you see a drawing of a missing person that turns out to be your estranged husband, the same estranged husband that you and your children were supposed to see for the first time in over a year that very day. As the saying goes, it was the straw that broke the camel's back."

Engels seemed to understand and accepted her analysis. "I'll tell you one thing, though. Nathan is lucky to have those two guys supporting him. He could have gone over the edge and taken everyone with him. He tipped it the other way, though." He sighed. "Andy and Ben. Those two guys."

"We will monitor Allison's condition closely," Kara said, "and if things go one way or the other, I will let both of you know."

"Wait, back up!" Lindstrom looked like the light had finally been turned on. "What did you say?"

"That we'll monitor…" Kara started to say.

"No! Boss, what did you say, about the edge?"

Engels looked confused. "That Nathan could have gone over the edge, but he tipped it back with those two guys." Engels and Kara were eyeing Lindstrom intently now.

"Kara, I'm sorry, but can you excuse us for a minute?" Lindstrom looked ecstatic, and Kara knew better than to press her for information. She nodded and left, shutting the door behind her. Engels watched Lindstrom, and he could tell the wheels were turning inside her head. As for Lindstrom, her mind raced back in time. Something about the past two days had bothered her, yet Engels' words seemed to bring clarity to the situation.

Before Engels could speak, Lindstrom asked, "How many cases do we get?"

"Tish, enough with the riddles. Spill it."

"Our case load comes and goes, some minor, some major. But there's always a balance, right?"

Engels perked up. Balance. It was about balance. "Go on."

"Remember the last case I worked, back in Minnesota, before Mark and I moved to Brandon in 2006?" Engels thought back, trying to remember the details that she had given him ten years ago. Lindstrom, in her mind's eye, was already there, reliving the details as if it happened yesterday.

There had been a break-in at the West Mall in Faribault, Minnesota, about ten miles from Medford. Many of the stores had been vandalized, some rather severely. It was initially thought to be the work of rambunctious teenagers. Two weeks had gone by, with Lindstrom and other officers conducting countless interviews with high school kids, numerous employees from the stores that had been damaged, as well as mall employees and service contractors. At the end of the third week of the investigation, the manager of the Faribault Farmers State Bank had called the police station. Somehow, the bank's ATM had been robbed four times in the past week, but the bank didn't know how. Since the bank was less than two hundred feet from the West Mall, Lindstrom's gut immediately told her there had to be a connection.

Sure enough, her instinct had been proven correct. Originally, the bank had been located inside the mall, but a standalone location was built in the late 1980's. For some reason, though, many of the bank's communications systems had never been moved from out of the mall's infrastructure. One of the empty tenant locations in the mall was being renovated for a new business. During that renovation, an I.T. technician had stumbled across the unassuming junction panel. After consulting the schematics for the building, as well as finding the original and updated blueprints for the mall and the bank, he decided to infiltrate the bank's systems. Unfortunately for the tech, the renovation had been completed ahead of schedule, and he no longer had access to the building.

He knew breaking in to the single store would be a dead giveaway. Instead, he found a group of kids out of Burnsville, Minnesota, and offered them a couple hundred bucks each to help him vandalize the mall. After easily defeating the mall's security system, the tech was able to get to the junction panel and finish his work to gain access to the bank's communication network. Meanwhile, the seven teenagers had been turned loose, doing enough damage so that no one knew that it had been a diversion the whole time.

The tech might have gotten away with it, too, if he hadn't been greedy. Most ATM's are capable of holding up to two hundred thousand dollars in cash. Of course, they usually don't, with banks only keeping fifteen to thirty thousand, depending on the day of the week, the amount of banking traffic at the location, and so on. The tech had been able to override the video surveillance for the ATM, as well as ordering and authorizing additional cash to be put into the ATM. He could have accessed the ATM slowly, over the course of many months, and the bank wouldn't have caught on. Instead, Lindstrom and the police arrested him a month after the bank manager had first called, and almost eight weeks after the initial vandalism at the mall.

"Like so many things in life, it's about balance."

Lindstrom had told Engels the story over lunch one afternoon in November of 2006. Now, here she was, ten years later, remembering why balance was so important.

"We aren't in New York or Boston or Los Angeles," Lindstrom said to Engels, as she reached for her cell. "Sure, we have two hundred thousand residents, but things never come at us like this." As she searched through her contacts and dialed, she said more to herself than to Engels, "Two-for-one sales. Two guys supporting him. Two, two, two. Balance." She put the phone to her ear and waited.

"Jerry, it's Tish. Have you gotten any hits on the dead woman's DNA?" A pause. "Has anyone started working on the tube with the gel tabs or the disposable cell phone from the other case?" Another pause. "Got it. Listen, the Boss and I are heading back to the station. I need you to go over that tube and the cell for anything that might have DNA, and then check it against the dead woman. Let me know as soon as you got something." She ended the call and looked at Engels, who looked back at her. A small smile started to creep in at the corners of his mouth.

"We've both said it, Boss. Balance. You put too much on one side or the other, you go over the edge. The odds of us getting two big, unrelated cases in the same week are slim. Let's get back to the station. Jerry can confirm, but I'd wager your pension that the dead woman is the same woman that tried to pick up Nathan Devlin at Goldie's on Monday night."

SEVEN

FRIDAY NIGHT, 10:49 PM

The driver was uncomfortable. The office that he was sitting in was cold, while the chair he was sitting in was awkward. He looked around the room, realizing that it seemed unusually bare. The desk in front of him looked like it hadn't been used in months. Two file cabinets stood behind the desk, but both were missing at least one drawer each. When he had been brought to the room, he had looked out the window, but to no avail. The window must have been tinted on both the outside and the inside. Even putting his face to the glass and covering his eyes, he could barely make out one or two faint points of light. The fluorescent light overhead flickered to the point of annoyance. He wasn't sure why he had been brought here, but he really didn't care. Aside from taking him away from his beer and the fact he had made over a hundred dollars playing pool and darts only a few hours ago, the driver figured that whoever was in charge had another job for him.

Before arriving in Sioux Falls, the driver had never heard of the place. Small town, big city, it had never really mattered to him where he was. Trouble had always followed him, even if he hadn't looked for it. One of the few rules he had been given by the guy that hired him for these jobs, though, was to stay out of trouble. *"When not on the job, stay inside."* Well, screw that.

Oh sure, the house that his employer put him in was decent enough.

Nice furniture, big screen ultra-high definition television with stereo surround sound, satellite channel package with over one thousand channels, four different video game consoles and a ton of video games, a jacuzzi hot tub, a delivery service that came by twice a week to make sure the kitchen was stocked, and a maid service came by twice a week to top off the whole package. The house even sat on a gorgeous acreage on the south side of town, so there was no chance of chatting with neighbors or being seen by anyone that might remember him. But he was sick of it. He was tired and bored. To hell with it, it was time to hit the town on a Friday night. He had driven around, and finally ended up at a little dive that was actually bigger on the inside than what it looked like on the outside. A couple of beers, some popcorn and peanuts, a few games of pool and darts, plus hustling some stupid college kids, it was all making this a fun Friday night.

Then came the tap on his shoulder. Somehow, he knew it was her before he had turned around. Sure enough, she was looming over him. If he was six feet tall, she was six four easy, maybe even six-five, with an athletic frame to match. The first time he had met her, he had laid on the charm, figuring he could get an easy hookup. Five seconds later, she had twisted his arm backward, pinning him face-first against the nearest wall. He couldn't move, and the pressure she had applied felt like his wrist, elbow, and shoulder were all about to explode at the same time. She had whispered into his ear, "Talk to me again about something other than the job we hired you for, and you'll have to learn to pick your nose with your knees." From that point on, the driver made sure to keep his mouth in check and to keep his eyes from lingering at her.

"Hey Doll," he had said. "Want a beer? Maybe a game of pool or darts?"

No emotion crossed her face. She had simply put a hand on his shoulder and started to turn him towards the door. As they started walking, the driver had shouted back to the strangers he had been shooting pool with, "You're just lucky that my better half showed up!" As they walked by the bar, she had stopped him so that the lanky bartender would see his face, and the woman dropped a hundred-dollar bill on the bar. They started walking again, with the man barely saying, "Keep the change," before the two of them were out the door. When they got to her car, she put him in the back seat, handcuffed him in secret restraints in between the leather cushions, put a hood over his head, and pushed him down on the seat so no one could see him.

The driver wasn't scared. He had been hired to do a job, and he had been successful, on multiple occasions. It was always the same job, but he had never had a problem. That is, until last Monday night. So, one little hiccup happened, and he had been forced to improvise. From what he could tell, the cops had nothing, so he had nothing to worry about. As they drove, he had tried to keep track of where they were going, but it was pointless. He wasn't familiar with Sioux Falls, and after five minutes of turns, he gave up. He guessed that they had driven for close to half an hour. The car was damn quiet, too, as he was barely able to hear anything on the outside of the car.

When the car had finally stopped, and he had been released, he looked around and found himself in an extremely dark underground garage. He could see what looked like black delivery vans, maybe two of them, and maybe something that looked like the ambulance that he had driven. Doll muscled him into the elevator. He didn't know what her name was, so he had nicknamed the woman, this tall amazon-like woman, "Doll". The elevator opened on the third floor, revealing cubicles galore. They didn't appear to be in use, though. No furniture, no computers, nothing that would suggest that any business was being conducted. Hell, no signs said anything about the building. The place looked and smelled abandoned.

Doll had put the driver in this office, shutting and locking the door. After a few minutes, he thought about testing the door, then decided against it. He went to the window, but the glass was so dark no light penetrated, either in or out. The glass must have been tinted, both on the inside and the outside. He pressed his forehead against the glass, cupping his hands at his temples, trying to block out the faint light from the flickering bulb in the ceiling. It was no use, though. He couldn't see anything, no moon, no stars, no lights, near or far.

Suddenly, he heard the door unlock and open. When he turned around, Doll was walking back into the room, holding two large briefcases. No, they were larger than briefcases, but they were solid, not like a duffle bag. She set the cases down, shut the door and locked it, then pointed to the chair and said, "Sit." The driver did as he was told, while Doll picked up the cases and set them against the far wall next to what looked like collapsible wooden TV trays.

Now here the driver sat, Doll standing behind him, guarding the door. On the desk in front of him was a flat-screen computer monitor, and the screen had been turned to face him. As the minutes ticked by and the chill was setting in, he was beginning to get anxious. Not scared. He could remember many times when he was in tougher situations, and with much angrier men all around him. No, he only wanted this over with, and quickly. He wanted to get back to his beer and his pool game.

The dark screen came to life. On the screen was a figure in silhouette, in front of an obviously fake backdrop of a beach view. The driver noticed that at the top of the monitor, a small green light had turned on. Must be a webcam, he thought. The silhouette began to speak.

"Please explain what happened," the silhouette said in an electronic voice. The driver guessed that the silhouette didn't want to use his real voice. The effect was odd, like a mix of Darth Vader, a Speak-And-Spell, and an automated answering machine. It also reminded him of the electronic voice of the man that had hired him months ago. Déjà vu, the driver thought to himself. He looked at the silhouette and started talking.

"Look, it's like I told Doll here yesterday. It started no different than the other times. We were waiting in the ambulance, me and Helen, and we hadn't gotten the signal." Helen was the name the driver had given to his partner, in mocking him as Helen Keller. The partner had barely spoke most of the time unless it was to ask about the job. He hadn't socialized or opened up, so the driver had started calling him Helen.

"All of the other times it was fast, in and out, no fuss," the driver continued. "After an hour, we still hadn't heard anything, so I called her. She was going on about how this one couldn't be the mark, it didn't feel right, she wasn't going to do it. I tried to talk to her, but she was ranting. I started yelling at her to do her job, but nothing was working. Helen grabbed the phone out of my hand and told her to calm down. 'Just get the mark outside, and if it was the wrong mark, we could always dump him where someone would find him.' That's what Helen had told her. Couple minutes later, they are both outside and she's flagging us down. We pull up, and the mark is bleeding and trying to resist. Then a goddamn good Samaritan has to show up. The mark tries to fight us off, ends up clocking her in the side of the head, and busted her open. Helen and I get them both in the ambulance, and away we go, another extraction done. End of story."

"End of story?" the silhouette said incredulously. "Hardly. Where is the woman?"

"She was freaking out," the driver continued. "The mark was out cold, and she's holding the guy's head, saying sorry over and over. When I told her to shut up and calm down, she snapped and started trying to hit me in the back of the head, while I'm driving the damn ambulance! She was raving like a lunatic, telling us to burn in hell, that she was going to the cops, that she wanted out, that this wasn't what she signed up for, going on and on. I pulled over and parked, and now she starts trying to wail away on Helen, who can't really do anything about it. I cracked her with my elbow, and she was out. When we got to the drop off, I checked on her. I didn't mean to hit her that hard, but I must've broken her nose and two of her teeth were laying on the floor of the ambulance. I pulled her out and put her in the back of my SUV. Doll shows up in the other ambulance a few minutes later, Helen and I put the gurney with the mark inside of her ambulance, and she leaves. No questions, no nothing. All in all, the job went as usual."

"Usual?" The silhouette had practically spit the word out. "There is nothing usual about this. Why has the woman not responded to communications?"

"Look, I parked the ambulance in the garage and locked it up, just like before, and told Helen to take off and call it a night. I stayed there and got the woman to wake up. She was pissed, like super pissed. She started again with the punching and kicking, yelling for the police. She ran a little bit but didn't get too far in her heels. I got a hold of her, but she was out of her mind, so I hit her. Knocked her out with one punch. When she hit the ground, her head bounced off a big rock on the gravel road. She didn't move. I checked on her, but that was it. So, I figured I'd help ya out and get rid of her. I've watched enough crime shows in my time, and I've talked to enough cons when I was locked up to know. I took the body into the garage, worked it over, and then dumped it. Trust me, she won't be found."

"Worked it over? Does that include carving a pentagram into her skin?"

The driver looked shocked. How could he know?

"I know," the silhouette said, "because the police know. Her body was discovered two days ago. And now, here we are, trying to ascertain the damage."

"Hey, wait a minute! Seriously, I did a major number on her! No hands, no feet, no teeth, no hair, bleach, and I beat her face completely in! I don't know how someone found her body, considering where I dumped it, but it shouldn't matter. There's nothing left of her to identify. Plus, the pentagram will have the cops thinking some punk kids listening to death metal did it!"

The silence that fell over the room was almost unbearable for the driver. He didn't know what Doll and this guy on the computer were up to, and he didn't really care. He was paid well for his services. It wasn't his fault that these two had hired a woman that couldn't cut it. Maybe it was time to move on from this. The driver figured he had enough cash stashed that he could make it south, maybe find someplace tropical with good food and cheap beers. This whole thing with Doll and her boss was twisted, even if he didn't know all of the details. Extractions, they called them. Well, whatever. Actually, the less he knew, the better. Time to start talking his way of this.

"Listen," the driver started to say, but was immediately cut off.

"SHUT UP!" the silhouette snapped at him. The silhouette's head moved, as if looking behind him. "What do the police know?"

"Nothing of consequence," Doll said from behind the driver. Somehow, she had moved up right behind him without him knowing it. "The police department has a lot going on right now. There are rumors of the police chief wanting out, there was a major car crash that required a lot of police involvement for a day and a half. My contact also said that someone had reported a possible crime, but nothing had turned up yet. Right now, they don't seem to realize that the extraction is tied to the woman. I will let you know."

"And the woman's body?"

Doll put her hand on the driver's shoulder and said, "I hate to say it, but he meant well. My contact said that he did enough to the body to make a visual identification impossible. Considering where he dumped the body, she shouldn't have been easily discovered. It was bad luck that we had such a downpour of rain on Tuesday, or that there was nothing to catch the body in the storm drain. From what I can gather, the city had been having issues with that culvert and the area around it for years. This driver may be an idiot, but he tried to help."

The driver was about to object, then decided to be quiet. The silhouette was silent, apparently assessing the situation from wherever he was. Seconds turned into minutes, while Doll's hand remained on his shoulder, holding a firm grip. Now he was starting to get worried. He quickly thought about trying to run, but knew he wouldn't be able to make it, not without knowing the layout of the building, how many others these two might have employed in the building, or even where the building was. The driver doubted that he could get the drop on the amazon-sized woman that was standing behind him, not after the way she had physically asserted herself during their initial meeting. Time for a different approach, the driver thought to himself. He decided to bluff and bargain.

"Look," he stammered, trying to keep a measure of control in his speech. "If you think I screwed up, I'm sorry. Whatever you need me to do to square things up, I will. Just know that, if you do anything to me, I've made sure that people will come looking for me."

The silhouette's head tilted a bit to the side, and then a chuckle came through the speaker. With the weird voice distortion, it would have sounded comical, if the situation didn't seem so dire.

"Really? Who might that be? Your sister? The sister that died tragically in the house fire last Christmas Eve? The police report said that the Christmas tree was too dry, and the lights started it on fire. Your brother? The two of you had a serious falling out at your sister's funeral, and then he deployed to Afghanistan. According to my vast resources, you have had no contact with him since the funeral. Did you know he died from an IED blast seven months ago? I thought not. You have no wife, no children, no girlfriend, no boyfriend, you have no friends and no living relatives. YOU HAVE NO ONE. When we discovered you, you were still looking at another five years in prison. You jumped at the offer of money, and we arranged for your release. You are a drifter and a criminal and I have no further use for you."

The driver was now visibly panicking. The cold office was now penetrating his clothes, and he was shivering. He could see his breath now. He didn't know what to do, and Doll seemed to sense he might do something stupid, as her grip on his shoulder tightened.

"However," said the silhouette, "we did have an agreement. I may be many things, but I am a man of my word. It was agreed that, should your services no longer be necessary, you would be given five hundred thousand dollars in cash and a plane ticket. Upon arrival at the destination of your choosing, one million dollars would then be deposited into a secret account at a bank of your choosing in your new location." The silhouette's head turned toward Doll. "If you would be so kind."

Doll released her grip on his shoulder, then placed one of the TV trays over his lap. She then placed one of the large cases on the tray. She opened it, revealing it to be full of money. The driver had seen a lot of money in his life, but never like this, all at once. In some of his other nefarious dealings, he would have insisted on counting the money. Not this time, though. Take the money and run, the driver thought to himself. He looked closer at the money. On top of the money he saw a plane ticket with no date, no time, no departure, and no arrival. It looked like an on-call ticket. Next to the ticket was a passport. The driver reached out, taking the passport and opening it. Sure enough, there was his picture, with a different name next to his. As he put the passport back, he saw a South Dakota driver's license laying where the passport had been. The license had his photo on it, with the same name on it as the passport.

"Please, feel free to count the money if you would like. The ticket can be validated and redeemed for any airline at any airport in the country. There is a code on the ticket that can be used either by phone or by computer. I am trusting you to take the money, keep your mouth shut, and disappear, forever." The silhouette paused, and then said, "In order to show there are no hard feelings, please accept this small token of my esteem." As if on cue, Doll walked to the desk and unlocked one of the drawers. She removed an oval-shaped bottle with a brown liquid inside of it, as well as a glass. She set the glass on the desk, opened the bottle, and poured the glass half-full. She then handed the glass to the driver. He reached out for the glass, cautiously, glancing from the glass to the silhouette on the computer monitor.

As if sensing the driver's apprehension, the silhouette elaborated. "What you have in your hand is a glass of Macallan Highland Single Malt Scotch Whiskey. That bottle on the desk is worth over twelve-thousand dollars. Forgive me if I am not there to share a drink with you, but I hope this will help assuage any fears you may have."

The driver wasn't sure what to make of the situation, but he decided to go with it. After all, it wasn't every day that you held a glass of whiskey worth twelve grand in your hands. He swirled the drink in the glass, sniffed it, and then took a sip. The fluid was warm and inviting as it slid down his throat. He grinned, raised the glass in a silent toast, and swallowed the rest of the drink in one large gulp. The driver was starting to relax a little, as the warmth of the alcohol seemed to counteract the chill in the room. The silhouette spoke again, seemingly looking beyond the driver.

"Where are we on prep?"

Doll spoke up. "He is sedated right now. When I was informed of a possible problem, I made sure that no further activity was done until you could be consulted. Unfortunately, the first protocol round had already been administered." A brief pause, and she continued. "You know better than I do the affects that the first protocol will have if the second round isn't administered, or if the remediation protocol isn't started in time."

"And do you know the source of the problem?"

"I have a pretty good idea, but I need to verify after I'm done here."

"Thank you," the silhouette said. The head moved again, seemingly looking at the driver. "You may go if you wish, but, as I previously stated, I believe there is one final way that you can help me if you are interested. I can definitely make it worth your while."

The driver weighed his options. Half a million, a clean passport and ID, and an open-ended plane ticket right in front of him. Couple that with the money he had already made, and, even if he got stiffed on the full million, this wouldn't be a terrible way to leave. He could also do some digging, maybe try to figure something out about Doll and her boss, the silhouette. Having blackmail material would help in case he needed insurance against them down the line.

As the driver considered his choices, Doll set another TV tray in front of him, next to the first one. She then placed the second case on the new table. The driver looked at the case, realizing that it was larger than the first case. Doll opened it, revealing it to be filled with more money. If the driver had to guess, he was looking at more than a million and a half in cash in front of him. He had to give it to his mystery employers, they definitely knew how to peak his curiosity, not to mention his greed. As he was mulling it over, the silhouette spoke again.

"Keep the sedation going until we make the swap. Then I will oversee the operation."

Doll seemed concerned. "You?"

"Yes. This is something that I feel needs my personal attention. I am hoping that this isn't our Waterloo. Nevertheless, it is vital that I am there to assist with all countermeasures." Another pause, and then the silhouette asked the driver, "So, have you made your decision?"

"I think I'll take door number two," the driver said, a smirk growing across his face, as he reached for the briefcases. He closed both of the cases at the same time, and then relaxed back into the chair. He looked at Doll, holding his empty glass in the air and lightly shaking it. "Doll, would you be a dear and top me off?"

The expression on Doll's face didn't waver, as she looked from the driver to the glass and then to the monitor. The silhouette nodded, and Doll poured the driver another drink into the glass, this time almost three-fourths full. The driver put his head back and drank the entire glass. He closed his eyes and savored the amazing taste, sitting there for almost a minute.

When he felt like he had stretched the moment out long enough, the driver opened his eyes and looked at the silhouette on the monitor. His vision was slightly blurry, as he blinked a few times to try to focus. He knew he could hold his liquor, but, then again, he had never had expensive hooch before. Maybe it was the added beers from earlier. No big deal, he thought.

Finally, the driver said, "So, how can I help you?"

The silhouette replied, "Oh, my, you have no idea how much help you will be providing."

Suddenly, the driver felt one of Doll's arms close around his neck, while a rag was put over his mouth and nose. He tried to twist away, but her hold was too strong. The smell on the rag was sweet, which he immediately recognized as chloroform. Years ago, he had done a job with a crew in Utah that liked to use chloroform when they stole cars. He was starting to see blackness at the corner of his vision. The cold had been sapping the strength from his muscles, and the awkward nature of the chair had made it impossible for him to be in a comfortable position to begin with. He tried to reach behind him, hoping to get some kind of contact with Doll's face or eyes, but she had the superior position. His mind raced as his body began to fail him.

The drink! These bastards must have spiked the drink, too! There's no way that he should have been down for the count so fast. He tried clawing at Doll's hands and arms, but she was wearing a jacket and had put on gloves. As the driver's arms slowly dropped, Doll leaned forward, placing her weight on his back. His vision was blurring, with stars intruding into the blackness. He tried to fight back against her, but it was useless.

The driver heard the silhouette softly say, "Yes, you will be able to help immensely." And with that, the driver's eyes closed, his body went limp, and the darkness completely took him.

EIGHT

Saturdays tended to be a mixed bag, depending on Lindstrom's case load and what the kids had going on. Fortunately, this particular Saturday was working out pretty well. Lindstrom had awoken at 7am to find Trevor gone with a note saying he was working on a farm and would be back late Sunday night. Bree was already up, frantically getting ready, as she had cheerleading all day, and then was planning on spending the night at a friend's house. That, of course, left little Ryan, who was still sawing logs after the birthday party he attended the previous afternoon and evening.

In fact, the morning flew by. Before Lindstrom knew it, it was almost one in the afternoon. Somehow, between making breakfast, Ryan getting up, and the occasional check for police-related emails on her secure tablet, the hours had melted away. It wasn't until Ryan asked, "Momma, what's for lunch", that Lindstrom realized that she had cleaned the kitchen, two bathrooms, done laundry, cleaned the fish tank, vacuumed five total rooms, and done a few other small household tasks. It wasn't that police work made her neglect the house, or that the kids didn't do their share. Sometimes, it felt cathartic to do even the most mundane of things.

Ryan was now fed for the second time that day and asked if he could bike up to the school playground with some neighborhood friends. Three minutes later, he was gone, leaving Lindstrom home in a quiet house. She checked her tablet. Still no secure emails. Now she was getting anxious. When she had told Engels her theory about the dead woman being the same woman that had tried to pick up Nathan Devlin, he had looked at her

106

like she had lost her mind. She instructed Jerry to go over the body again for anything out of the ordinary, and to check for DNA on the items that Tisdale had found at the bar. The more she had thought about it, it all added up to her.

In her years as a police officer and then as a detective, especially here in a decent sized city in the Midwest, she couldn't remember two cases like this happening at the same time. Maybe the city wasn't of sufficient size, but this wasn't New York City or Los Angeles, where you could guarantee multiple homicides, suicides, rapes, major car accidents, and the like, all happening on any given day. No, she knew that what looked like two separate cases were, in fact, one intertwined case.

Lindstrom thought about one of her favorite movies, "The Usual Suspects", with the great line from Kevin Spacey's character, "Verbal Kint", talking about police. *"If you got a dead body and you think his brother did it, you're going to find out you're right."* Damn, she loved watching that movie! She hadn't been that enthused at the time, but Mark had insisted, and wow, had she been impressed. And that had only been the start. Mark had been such a movie buff and had recommended so many films that she had questioned, but then she had been surprised. Mark, dear, sweet Mark. Lindstrom quickly shook her head. Nope, sorry, not happening right now. She was enjoying her day, and she wouldn't be going down that road.

A loud buzzing came from her cell, alerting her to an incoming text. She looked at the screen. Kara Reed. Really, this again? Why did it seem that, when she thought about Mark, Kara Reed had to come back into the picture? Were the three of them destined to be linked? She slid her finger across the screen to look at the message.

"No change in Allison Devlin's condition."

Well, no news is good news. Between her ex-husband and Mark, Lindstrom had had her fair share of marital issues, but she couldn't guess what Allison Devlin had gone through. From all accounts, Allison's husband, Nathan, had been a serious drunk. His actions had been a downward spiral that had left a lot of damage. She thought about Allison. What could it have been like, being in her shoes? The man you loved, the father of your children, slowly gone, one drink at a time. A ray of hope comes through the darkness. Then, that ray is snuffed out, in a police station, of all places. No wonder she finally collapsed under the pressure.

Her phone buzzed again. Another text, this one from Engels.

"No hits yet on Devlin's picture being up on the TV news, newspaper, or social media."

From no news is good news to no news is bad news. Tisdale had gotten photos of Nathan Devlin from Ben and Andy, and Tisdale was also able to confirm with Sarah and Chad, the bartender and host at Goldie's, respectively, that Devlin had, indeed, been in both places Monday night. Andy and his wife, Heidi, were taking care of the Devlin's kids while Allison was in the hospital, with Ben helping out as well.

Lindstrom looked at her phone, expecting another text, but after a few minutes, she gave up. Jerry, despite his flair sometimes, would let her know as soon as he had anything on forensics. She looked at the clock. Ryan had been gone for about half an hour, so she turned on the TV and grabbed a quick little snack from the kitchen. No sooner had she sat down then the landline rang. It was almost an afterthought, considering everybody carried their phone with them, yet she kept her landline active. She grabbed the phone off the cradle and looked at the caller ID. Private. Probably a telemarketer. She let it ring so that the answering machine would pick up. No message was left, so she returned her attention to the TV. A minute later, the phone rang again, still showing a private caller ID. Lindstrom wasn't in the mood to be pandered to, so she let it go to the machine again. For the second time, no message was left.

She channel-surfed for a few minutes, but nothing could grab her attention. Seventy-five channels of basic cable on the upstairs TV, and not a thing worth watching. Exactly why was she paying for this? She turned off the TV and laid down on the couch, looking out the front window. Lindstrom was trying not to get jittery, but it was difficult. Each passing minute meant that the odds grew worse that Nathan Devlin would be found alive. A botched kidnapping was bad enough, but if her suspicion was right about the dead woman being in on the kidnapping, then whoever had planned this wasn't about to leave loose ends.

Her cell phone rang. A call from Heather Gordon, the station receptionist. "Heather," Lindstrom said. "What can I do for you on a lazy Saturday?"

"Lazy for you, maybe," Heather's voice came over the phone. "I've been helping your two uni's compile the information from all area health systems." Lindstrom had sent out a mass alert to anyone remotely dealing with health care, from acupuncture to health supplies, asking for any information on HealthStar Ambulatory Services, or if anyone had seen or heard of Nathan Devlin.

"Any hits so far?" Lindstrom knew that it was a needle in a haystack, but if even a dentist or a secretary at a supply store selling bedpans had seen something, it was worth it.

"Based on our own information, and what you told me from interviewing Kara Reed regarding hospitals and ambulance services in the given radius, I would say that we have heard from maybe thirty to forty percent of anything related to the field of health. Still nothing."

Lindstrom sighed. Considering the alert had went out late Friday afternoon, the fact that they had heard back from at least thirty percent of health practitioners and suppliers was actually pretty good.

"Thanks for your help, Heather. I hope you're not being kept from anything more important."

"Not at all. One other thing. Someone called trying to find you. Caller ID was private, which is amazing, since the police switchboard and computer tracking should be able to identify any and all numbers."

"What did the person want?"

"The woman wouldn't say. She said they were looking for you, that it was important, and that they would try you at home."

Two private calls at home, now one at the station. Lindstrom sat up on the couch and was suddenly worried.

"Tish, are you there?"

"Yeah, I'm here. If you get another call, give them my direct line voicemail at the station."

"Got it. I'll let you know if anything comes up." With that, Heather hung up on her end.

Lindstrom didn't know what was setting off her radar, but better safe than sorry. She activated the family locator app on her cell phone. She didn't know whether some of these apps were a blessing or a curse, but, at times like this, the ability to immediately locate her family pushed her fears of Big Brother down the list of things to worry about. As she waited for the signal pings to return on the map, she got up and hurried to the garage. She thought about jumping on her bike and heading up to the school to check on Ryan, and then decided on the car. If something was wrong, it was better to be in a vehicle. As she fastened her seatbelt, the ping for Trevor's phone came back. She zoomed in on the map, and there was the little red dot, seemingly in the middle of nowhere. He must be out in a field, using a combine or a tractor. She swiped for Bree's phone. The ping came back, displaying the little blue dot at one of the high schools in Sioux Falls.

Lindstrom backed out of the garage quickly, wanting to get to the school, but not wanting to make a scene. A few turns here and there, and two minutes later she was pulling into one of the elementary school's parking lots. She could see the playground with the swings, rope ladders, and all the other equipment that was only about two years old. She saw Ryan's bike, but no Ryan. Actually, no kids at all. She parked and jumped out of the car.

"RYAN!" She screamed as loud as she could. She looked around frantically. There was no one else around. "RYAN!" She had run to his bike, and she knelt beside it, looking it over. It looked normal, no damage, no blood, no sign of anything wrong with it.

"RYAN!! RYAN WHERE ARE YOU!!!" Lindstrom was a decorated police detective, but she was also a mother of three children. Her patience was running out as she looked around, trying to see anything out of the ordinary. Everything looked like it belonged, the cars parked on the street, the fences surrounding the yards that sat next to the school property. Even the cars driving by weren't suspicious. A FedEx truck, two minivans with people visible, a tow truck, a black delivery van, a school bus, nothing seemed wrong, yet her intuition was telling her that something was askew.

"RYAN, IF YOU'RE HIDING FROM ME, YOU'RE IN BIG TROUBLE!" She stood there looking, turning around in circles, surveying the area, and then ran back to her car. As she threw the car into gear and started to turn her vehicle, she slammed on the brakes. Coming around the corner of the school was Ryan, along with four other kids. She recognized one as a girl in his class, and two of the boys as his friends on the block. The fourth girl she didn't know.

Ryan saw his mom's car, waved, and started running towards her. Lindstrom had never felt such elation. She also realized that she had to mask her emotions, and quickly. Within the few seconds it took him to reach her, she had calmed enough so as not to worry her boy. She hoped her face, voice, and body language wouldn't betray her.

Ryan's smile was replaced with a frown as he approached her, asking,

"Momma, what's wrong?" He seemed to have a sense when something was amiss.

"I was just a little worried is all," she said. She hated lying to him, but it was for the best. "Where were you, young man?"

"Oh, we played but then we got hungry, and Cassie," he turned and pointed at the girl Lindstrom didn't know, "well, Cassie said her dad was making cookies, and they live in the blue house on the other side of the school. We were only there for a few minutes. Cassie even has some drinks, see?" Sure enough, Cassie was carrying some kind of container. "Do you want to stay and play with us, Momma?"

"Oh, I'd love to," Lindstrom said, "but I wanted you to know that I needed to run up to the grocery store for a few things. I didn't want you to come back home and find me gone and have you worried that I was off doing police stuff. Remember, you made me promise to tell you where I am?"

"Yes, Momma!"

"Do you want to come to the store with me?"

"Can I stay and play some more?"

"Absolutely! And remember our rule about strangers and telling me everything?"

"Yes, Momma! And Cassie's mom is going to be here with Cassie's little sister in just a few minutes, too!"

Lindstrom gave Ryan a big hug and then let him run back to his friends. She sat in her car for a few minutes, watching the kids play. As she pulled away, she waved at Cassie's mom, who was now sitting on a bench next to the playground, a stroller parked next to the bench. Cassie's mom waved back. As Lindstrom drove back home, she tried to put her finger on what had triggered this kind of response from her.

Even when dealing with her piece of crap ex-husband, never had her maternal sensors gone off like this. Likewise, with every case that she had dealt with, nothing had alerted her to any sense of danger with her kids. Was it the pressure of two cases becoming one, assuming her hunch was correct? Was she projecting her situation with Allison Devlin's? Or was she merely anxious and frustrated with no leads coming forward? As she stopped at a red light, she realized that she had been driving aimlessly for about fifteen minutes. Not good, she told herself. That's how accidents happen.

Lindstrom made a few turns and started heading home. As she was stopped at a different red light for her street, she decided that she needed to unwind a little bit. Maybe a beer and a hot bath would help. A minute later, she turned the car into her driveway and saw a black delivery van turn the corner up the block. She pressed the remote for the garage door, but nothing happened. She pressed it harder this time, and still nothing. Damnit, she thought, didn't I fix this two weeks ago? She slapped the remote in her hand a few times and pressed the button a third time. Slowly, the garage door started to roll up. Great, one more thing to deal with.

She pulled into the garage, parked, and got out of her car. As she was shutting the car door, she saw a black delivery van drive by. Was it the same one, or a different one? She ran out of the garage to the driveway, but the van was already turning around the same corner again. And hadn't she seen a black delivery van among the vehicles driving by when she had been frantically looking for Ryan only twenty minutes ago?

Lindstrom had never considered herself paranoid, but her radar was going off again. The beer and hot bath would have to wait. It was time to call Engels and get his take. As she ran inside, she took her cell from her pocket. It was off. How did that happen? The battery was about thirty-five percent when she had left looking for Ryan. No matter. As she pressed the power button, a flash icon showed dead battery. Fine, the old-fashioned way, then. She plugged her cell into the charger, stretching the cable from the wall outlet, and set her cell down on the dining room table. Once she saw that the cell was charging, she turned it back on. It was always important to have her cell on, whether it was for police business or personal business. She took a few steps, walking back into the kitchen, and reached for the landline.

Before she could dial, Lindstrom saw that the digital readout was flashing one missed call. The caller ID showed private again. However, this time, a message had been left. Carefully, she reached out and pressed the play button on the answering machine. She stood there, listening as the message played, somehow awestruck and dumbfounded at the same time. When the message was done, Lindstrom felt light-headed, and she reached out to steady herself against the refrigerator door. What the hell was going to happen next?

"You're telling me," Engels said into his phone, "that someone wants to give you money?"

Engels was trying to process what Lindstrom had told him, but he was equally as amazed as she was. He had been raking leaves in his backyard when his wife, Diane, had shouted at him that Tish was on the phone. He was tired, strolling up to the sliding screen door that led into the kitchen, and he took the phone from Diane. When he had asked if Lindstrom had any information on the cases and she had responded with a very quick "no", he had stopped listening attentively. At that point, he was more interested in getting a refreshing drink out of the fridge and a slice of homemade cheesecake Diane had made earlier in the week.

"Boss, seriously, were you even hearing what I was saying?" Lindstrom's voice had changed from frantic to annoyed in a second, and Engels knew he needed to rebound quick.

"Sorry, Tish. I kinda tuned you out after you said it wasn't about the cases. Okay, I'm sitting down with a glass of orange juice. You now have my undivided attention." Engels took a few drinks and waited for Lindstrom to start over.

When Lindstrom had run through her story the first time, she had left out the parts of panicking about Ryan and seeing the same black delivery van two times, maybe even three times. Until she had a better handle on what had set her off, there was no reason to jumble up the issue at hand. She took a deep breath and started over.

"The landline phone rang twice over an hour ago. Each time it was a private number on the caller ID, each time I let the machine take it, and each time no message was left. Then Heather called me from the station to give me an update. She told me that a private number had called the station looking for me."

"No number showed in communications?" That got Engels attention. Even with blocked numbers, disposable cell phones, and apps that touted their ability to mask your number and location, the ability for law enforcement and the military to track phone numbers and where they were being used was hugely important. People sometimes criticized this kind of intrusion on privacy, but Engels hadn't waded into that argument.

"Not according to Heather. Anyway, after I hung up with her, I went to check on Ryan and his friends at the school playground. When I got back home, the message was waiting for me. I played it back three times, and then I called you."

"Put your phone next to the machine and let me hear the message," Engels instructed her. Lindstrom did as she was told, holding her landline's handset next to the answering machine's speaker. She pressed play.

A cheery female voice said, "Good afternoon. I am trying to reach a Patricia Lindstrom. This matter is regarding your ex-husband, who is currently incarcerated, and his delinquency in child support payments. I have some good news. I would like to inform you of the details regarding your ability to claim a large portion of the money that is due you and your children. Please contact us at 995-249-9939, extension 98969. The call is free. Thank you." The message ended, and the answering machine's computerized voice noted the date and time of the message.

"So?" Lindstrom asked Engels. "What do you think?"

"I think there's a lot of nines in that number," Engels joked.

"Brad, I swear," Lindstrom started, but Engels cut her off.

"I'm sorry, I couldn't resist. Have you tried calling the number yet?"

"No. I wanted to get your opinion on it."

"I don't think it could hurt. Maybe you should try running the number and see who or where it is registered."

Lindstrom was torn. For so many years, she had wished that she could have had the financial support from her ex. However, she had made peace with the fact that, if she never saw a dime of his money, she would live with the loss of income, as long as he never came near her children. It had been difficult at times, especially after everything with Mark, but she made things work and persevered. Now, like a lightning bolt out of the blue, someone was offering her money from her ex. Was it a joke? A trick, maybe? She didn't know if she could handle this not turning out to be true.

"Tish? Are you still there?"

"Yeah. I'm so conflicted about this."

"You know, Diane and I don't have anything going on tonight. We could be there in a few minutes and help you through it."

Lindstrom thought about it. "No. I need to face this. There's no sense in getting my hopes up." She took a breath, trying to calm her nerves. "For all I know, it could be a prank. I'll call them, and let you know."

Suddenly, her cell phone buzzed on the dining room table. Still holding the landline's headset to her ear, Lindstrom said to Engels, "Hold on, my cell is ringing." She walked back to the dining room table and pressed the power button to activate the screen.

Looking at the screen, Lindstrom said. "It's a text from Jerry." She swiped the screen to read the text to herself.

"I MISSED SOMETHING. CALL ME ASAP."

"Looks like Jerry has something. Sit tight, and I'll call you right back." She ended the call with Engels, and dialed Jerry's office number in forensics. The phone rang once, and a somber voice picked up.

"Tish, I'm sorry." Jerry's voice sounded somber and apologetic.

"Jerry, calm down. It can't be that bad. What did you find out?" Lindstrom heard a deep breath, and Jerry started in.

"Okay, first off, the obvious. You were right. I was able to lift DNA off the cell phone and compared it to DNA from the body. They match. I also examined Jason's bloody shirt from Monday night. There were two distinct blood patterns, and I tested both. One pattern matches the dead woman, and the other pattern matched Nathan Devlin. Looks like both victims are connected. The dead woman would appear to be the same woman that was in the booth that Nathan Devlin was in."

Lindstrom felt a surge of pride. She didn't express it openly, but she loved it when her hunches paid off. It was like solving a five-thousand-piece puzzle, only to find out that the puzzle you had completed was part of an even larger puzzle. "Alright, that's excellent news! What else did you find?"

Another deep breath, and then Jerry said, "So, here's where my apology comes from. I did what you asked and went back over the body. I did more x-rays, this time from different angles, and I found something. It looks like she must have had some kind of stomach trouble at one time. My guess is that it was acid reflux brought on by a hiatal hernia."

Lindstrom's heart dropped. That was the same thing that Mark had gone into the hospital for. She steeled herself, and asked, "What makes you think that?"

"Well, there are the tell-tale staples in the diaphragm that a surgeon would use to reinforce the muscle. The stomach has also been folded and stapled to prevent it from being forced up through the diaphragm again."

Lindstrom knew all about the procedure, unfortunately. Why was it that so many things over the last few days had somehow circled back to

Mark? She took a quiet breath, and then said, "Right. I've heard about the procedure. How does that pertain to the case?"

"Because she must have had more damage than what the doctor or surgeon had anticipated. The sphincter connecting the esophagus to the stomach had a large amount of degradation. The surgeon decided to support this area by using a stent. This way, if the muscle ever failed, the stent would remain. It's the same procedure that heart specialists use to guard against aortic aneurysms."

Lindstrom was trying to stay focused, to listen to Jerry and correctly process what he was saying. It was incredibly difficult, though. Her mind kept trying to take her back to the past, to think about Mark's visits to his doctor regarding his own hiatal hernia.

"Tish, are you still there?" Jerry's voice sounded perplexed.

"Yeah, sorry," Lindstrom stammered. Okay, I understand. A stent for the esophagus, similar to one for the aorta. Once again, how does it help us?"

"Because the stent was designed to be permanent, it has a serial number on it, in case of a medical recall."

Lindstrom's eyes lit up. "Jerry, that's awesome!"

"I've already put out the information. I'm not sure if we'll get anything with Saturday almost gone and tomorrow being Sunday. At least it's in the system."

"Great work, Jerry! And don't beat yourself up. What matters is you found us a solid lead. Wrap it up in a report, and I'll let Brad know. Bye!"

Lindstrom ended the call. She immediately entered Engels' number to give him the news, but then paused, not pressing the "talk" button on the phone to dial the number. She looked at the phone for a few seconds. Her gaze then went to the front window and the sunny fall day outside. She then turned her head and looked out the kitchen window to the backyard. After a few minutes, she leaned against the dining room table. She tried to come to grips with the events of the last ninety minutes.

It started with a woman's mutilated body on Wednesday morning, with a missing or kidnapped man showing up on Friday. Her hunch, that the two cases were connected in some way, had been confirmed by DNA analysis. Over the course of the last three days, Kara Reed had come back into her life. This meant more time thinking about Mark, which had been amplified by Ryan's request to show Mark the video of Ryan's school

116

performance. The mutilated woman had, at some point, the same medical procedure that Mark had undergone. Finally, a stranger had called, informing Lindstrom that her ex-husband was ready to fork over some money.

Lindstrom snapped back to reality and pressed "talk" on the handset, readying herself to inform Engels of Jerry's discovery. Now wasn't the time to try to sort out her personal involvements. She had two connected cases to solve. She put the handset to her ear and waited for Engels to pick up, suddenly anxious to give her boss some good news.

NINE

SATURDAY NIGHT, 9:15PM

The driver was suddenly wide awake, eyes open, fully aware. He tried to sit up, but he couldn't. He craned his neck as best he could, but nothing was working. He then realized that his head was strapped down. As he regained his senses, he could feel his arms and legs were also strapped down. It seemed like every part of him was strapped down. He couldn't move, not even a millimeter.

The driver tried using his eyes, but his field of vision was limited. All he could see was the dull gray of the ceiling and lights, lights on a movable arm, maybe. He thought they looked like the lights that a dentist would use, although he wasn't sure why. That's when he started to panic. His breathing came hard and fast, and he felt like his heart was going to jump out of his chest. He tried to talk, but a strap across his chin meant he could only whimper and whine and make guttural sounds.

"BE QUIET!"

The voice seemed familiar in some way. Even though the driver's mind was going crazy about his situation, he decided not to anger whomever had shouted the order, and he tried to relax. It took a few minutes, but he managed to bring his breathing down to a normal level. He laid there, silent and still.

"There, much better. You see, you can do what you're told, without deviating from the strictest of orders."

The driver tried not to think about his predicament, but it was difficult. His mind was racing, and he couldn't focus on a coherent thought. His muscles twitched. He needed to move, but he was bound so tight that it was nearly impossible.

"You are struggling with calm," the voice spoke again, "with your thoughts, with your emotions. Yet your muscles, your joints, your sinews, they are betraying you, doubling over again in your body and into your brain. It's like a horrible closed loop."

The words that the voice spoke, they hung in the air, permeating into the driver's consciousness. Before the driver could gather the words into thoughts that would formulate questions, the voice said, "Oh, yes, I know what's happening."

If only the voice would shut up, the driver thought. He tried taking deep breaths, inhaling deep, holding it deep and long for as much time as he could, then exhaled, then repeated.

"That's right, keep breathing."

Why did the voice continue to talk? And why was it so familiar? The voice's tone, the register, it had an authority to it, yet it was strangely inviting. The driver's thoughts drifted back, his memories opening up, like a door to an attic that hadn't been touched in years.

Suddenly, the driver was seven years old again, playing in his grandfather's backyard. The only happy memories from his childhood came from his time at his grandparents Victorian-style home. The backyard was fenced in and massive, and he remembered running around and playing. His grandfather, watching him from the porch, while rocking back and forth in his rocking chair, the driver recalled those being the best of days.

His grandfather's voice had had the same kind of pitch and inflection that the voice that was speaking had. Authoritarian, yet with a warmth to it. Like a farmer that had been working the same earth for fifty years. Or, perhaps, a country doctor. The speech patterns always came across the same way, the driver thought to himself. "You listen to me, young man, and everything will be alright." The driver was brought back from his happy memories to the present, as the voice spoke again.

"Breathing is always the key, you see. Women in labor, people experiencing heart attacks, those in shock after a terrible accident, it's all a matter of breath. Keep breathing, slow the pace, rhythmic, almost hypnotic, and you'll find that spot, that point of Zen." The voice paused. When it spoke again, this time, the timbre and cadence was different.

"Then again, maybe you won't, hmm? You are a criminal, after all. You are filth to me. Unfortunately, for my goals to come to fruition, you were a necessary evil."

The words, they came out with a hint of anger, even a touch of sadness. The driver was back in the past.

The driver remembered his grandfather's warning from one particular summer afternoon.

"Be nice to your sister and stay away from her while she is in the sandbox. You can have the rest of the yard."

Of course, the driver hadn't listened, resulting in a huge fight between him and his sister. Some of the rocks from the sandbox ended up breaking two windows, and the two of them had tussled into his grandmother's garden, ruining almost the entire crop.

"You didn't listen, did you? Why didn't you listen?" The words came out of his grandfather's mouth, with the exact same sound, timbre, and cadence that the voice was speaking with.

On the entire ride home, the driver had been read the riot act from his father. The driver had never really cared for his father. However, his mother and his grandparents, especially his grandfather, that was a different story. He practically worshipped his grandfather and he loved his grandmother. He had begged his mother to let him go with her to see them the following weekend. The answer had been a resounding no. She was going to help out with a church picnic. A return visit to his grandparents, along with his father, sister, and brother, had already been planned in two weeks, at which time the driver would be expected to offer a full and sincere apology and offer any kind of restitution to his grandparents. The driver remembered he had been so desperate to atone for his mistake and make things right. He didn't know whether he would be able to make it two weeks.

Unfortunately, it wasn't to be.

That next weekend, his mother and both grandparents were dead. A series of thunderstorms had hit the area around Sumner, Illinois, where his grandparents lived. The storms had gone through the area hard and fast, seemingly out of nowhere, and during the church picnic. When it was all over, almost seventy people had died when the church's roof had collapsed after several trees had been ripped out of the ground and thrown against the sides of the church. The driver never had the chance to apologize, to hear his grandfather's voice change from anger back to that world-weary drawl.

After the funerals, the gulf only widened between the driver and his father. The disapproval grew and grew. The driver had no one to try to make happy, no one to try to impress. His hatred for his father grew with each passing day. The only thing that stopped him from getting rid of his old man was that, for reasons he couldn't comprehend, his sister and brother both dearly loved their father. The driver never understood why his father never loved his first-born, his first son, his first heir. As time had gone by, the driver realized it didn't matter.

Finally, at the age of fifteen, the driver reached his limit, telling his siblings that he loved them both and that he would try to stay in touch. He ran away, and never saw his father again. The driver's trip down memory lane stopped, as the voice spoke again.

"Oh my, have I been boring you? For a minute, the look in your eyes told me you were focused. Hmm, could it be that you were actually paying attention to me?" The voice let out a small chuckle. "Well, as I was saying, your existence and your use to me lasted as long as you obeyed the orders and didn't stray. Now, because of you, I have questions being asked."

The voice's inflection changed. It wasn't only anger being directed at the driver, but something more. It was something that, in many ways, is even worse for any person, child or grown up, to hear. Disappointment, with a hint of pity. He ruminated on his past, the course of events, the choices made and those left alone. From not having a father that he could've called "Dad", to his unresolved feelings about his grandparents and mother, his loss of contact with his siblings, the multiple crimes that he'd gotten away with, and the crimes where he'd been caught, all of it was magnified and made worse with the tone that the voice was speaking with. The driver, who had never been repentant in his life, suddenly had a swell of melancholy wash over him. His emotions were betraying him, as every terrible thing in his life crashed into him at once. The voice continued, the same sound of disapproval raining down on the driver.

"You have brought shame upon my house. Was my word not good enough for you? What about the house that I provided? Or was it greed, the need for more of my money?" A heavy sigh, and then, "No matter. Even in these most trying of times, I will persevere." There were sounds, like papers being looked through, followed by, "And you, dear fellow, whether you like it or not, you will have a part. Granted, it will not be the part that I originally envisioned for you. Yet, maybe it's for the best, yes? The money that was intended as payment for your fulfilled extraction contracts, that will be reabsorbed. Oh, the help that you will provide, though," the voice whistled softly, almost satisfyingly, "that help will be wonderful."

What the holy hell was the voice droning on about? If only the voice would stop, if only the driver could have quiet. He wasn't sure it would have mattered, though. The driver was immobilized, his only company a voice that seemed to be judgmental and preachy, compounded by all of the memories of everything rotten he had ever done in his past. The driver couldn't decide which was worse. Then, he heard a soft clicking, rhythmic, which he quickly identified as someone walking. The voice spoke again.

"Ah, my lady, judging by the look on your face, you are not the bringer of joyful news."

"The cops know that the woman he killed is part of it." A small pause, and then, "What would you like me to do?"

The driver listened to what the new voice had said. He recognized it, but, from where? From when? If only he could slow down his thoughts, shut out the past, and close off the resentful voice, maybe he would have a chance to…wait, is that…?

"Don't keep our guest in suspense, my lady. If he hasn't figured it out by now, I'm sure he will be delighted to see you."

The driver stared up when a shadow came over him, then a head blocked his view of the lights and the ceiling. It took his eyes a moment to adjust, and when he opened his eyes again, he could see Doll's face above him. His mind suddenly focused into white-hot rage, rage that he tried to focus into something tangible. The driver felt, no, he knew, that if tried hard enough, all of this anger would shoot from his eyes and kill Doll where she stood over him. Doll, that amazon-like bitch, simply stood over him. The look on her face was disinterested, almost bored. Her eyes looked over him, and the driver thought he saw the faintest sign of a grin. Doll then straightened up and was gone from the driver's line of sight.

"What do you think?" The driver heard Doll's voice again.

"The fact that this miserable cretin has made such a mess is unfortunate. However, I think I have the perfect corrective actions that will rectify these events. Now, tell me, what is the status of Mr. Devlin?"

"Per your instructions, the second protocol was never administered. The remediation protocol has been initiated. He's being treated in room five."

"Please increase the remediation to double the usual dose."

"Is that wise, considering the circumstances?" Doll's voice seemed concerned, and the driver was trying to figure out what this was all about.

"I know it is not standard procedure for us. Considering how I want to bring this matter to a close, though, it is necessary. I am sure Mr. Devlin's system will be able to handle it."

"Very well."

"Good. And the partner?"

"Exactly where he was ordered to be."

The driver caught the air of condescension and disapproval in Doll's voice. His grandfather's tone, first woven among the words from the voice, now was layered onto Doll's last sentence. Doll continued speaking.

"I made contact and brought him in. As you advised, I told him the exact situation and your plans to resolve things, his role, and his benefit. He was surprisingly accepting. In fact, I didn't need to explain the penalties if he refused." Doll paused, then resumed by saying, "However, there is something."

"Oh?" The voice was curious. "What might that be?"

"The only thing he asked was to meet you in person. He wants to know that he can trust you." There was apprehension in Doll's voice.

The voice chuckled. "Honor among criminals? Very well. Where is he?"

"Waiting outside. Are you sure about this?"

"Then by all means, bring the man in."

The driver heard the soft clicking of Doll's feet as they walked away.

No sooner had they faded away then they returned. This time, the driver could hear another set of footprints, likely sneakers, considering the number of squeaks coming from each step.

"Ah, Ronald," the voice announced, the authoritarian sound returning with a hint of swagger to it. The tone came across clear, that the voice was in charge.

"Sir, I understand what happened was wrong. I accept my role in it, and I accept my fate. Please, give me your word, and I will do anything you require of me."

The driver's eyes grew wide with astonishment.

It was the familiar voice of his partner, "Helen". What had the voice called him? Ronald? The three of them, including the woman he had killed, had been hired separately, only meeting when a job was given to them. No names, no personal information, nothing exchanged between the three of them, ever. So, his partner's real name was Ronald. The driver briefly wondered what the woman's name was. Yet, as quickly as he had thought it, he pushed that thought out of his mind.

The driver was trying to keep it together, trying not to struggle, trying not to make noise, but he was so close to snapping. He had done what he was told, and, when things got a little messy, he had made the decision to clean it up. Now everybody was getting their panties in a bunch because of one dead body. If these miserable slugs would give him an inch, he could make them see that everything would work out fine.

"I appreciate your directness," the driver heard the voice say, "as well as your repentance. Yes, you have my absolute word. Carry out the plan, and everything will be resolved most favorably."

"Thank you, sir", came "Helen's", or rather, Ronald's voice, and the driver listened to his squeaky sneaker footsteps walk away.

"You may release Mr. Devlin to his care," the voice said. "Please make sure that everything is done to the letter. Put it in motion quickly."

"Yes," the driver heard Doll say, and then her footsteps were gone.

"Now, for you," the voice said. "I'm not sure if you have been able to keep up with what has been going on, especially in your current situation. However, if you have yet to figure it out, I am the man you spoke to via the computer the other night."

Of course, it was the voice of the silhouette! The driver now had three people he wanted to tear apart. His rage continued to grow, exponentially, as if the restraints would melt away with the white-hot anger he had towards these three, the silhouette, Doll, and Ronald.

"I imagine you have a great many questions," the voice said, with a hint of reflection. "Perhaps you also have a great many regrets, yes? If I were a betting man, I would wager you would like a go at me, yes? You would like to hurt me, yes? You would like to kill me, yes? And maybe take out evil upon Ronald and my lovely associate, as well?" The voice sighed heavily. "As I said, I consider you scum, but you were necessary. I thought it was made crystal clear to you when you were brought into this that there would be no deviation, no improvising. Do and report, at all times. Now, see what you have come to." Another silent pause, and then the driver heard two hands clap together.

"Did you really and truly, in that microscopic criminal brain, believe that you would have gotten away with this? That I would be unaware of your divergence?"

There it was again, the driver hearing it plain as day. The sound of disappointment, of pity, of regret, the cadence of his grandfather's disapproval from the grave, coming through the silhouette's voice. The driver's anger morphed back into sadness, into knowing that somehow, he had screwed up again, all because he didn't listen. He fought the urge to whine, to show any emotions to the silhouette, to give him any kind of satisfaction.

"Well, as I told you, there are still ways you can help. Oh, my yes, you won't believe how you will be able to help!"

The silhouette sounded happy, almost blissful, and the driver saw the silhouette's hands clap several times. The driver's emotions were a jumbled mess, rising in anger, falling in shame, rising again in humor for some reason, and falling in despair. His thoughts were a confluence of history, of choices and actions made, and of future scenarios, of what may happen and what might have been. What the hell was the silhouette up to? What possible help could the driver be if he was strapped down? He couldn't hold back any more. His muscles were twitching to the point of exploding, he started making guttural noises again, and his eyes flared at the silhouette.

"My, my, Mr. Utecht, you seem to be in distress."

The driver froze, his eyes growing large. Hearing his last name, his real last name, scared him, and he knew why. Ever since he started in with the silhouette and Doll, with Ronald and the woman he had killed, he hadn't used his real name for anything, never, not once. That was a condition of the work, of the extractions. No names, no personal information exchanged between the three of them. To hear his name, the sound of it, sliding off the silhouette's tongue, struck the driver. Fear, mortification, terror, he wasn't sure those words could do justice to how he felt as he lay there, looking at the silhouette. Instead of his anger allowing him to explode out of his restraints, it seemed far more likely that he would melt away, that his body would liquefy, and his remains would drip-off the table he was strapped to, leaving nothing left of him.

"Mr. Utecht," the silhouette said again. "Mr. Charles Utecht. Or would you rather be referred to as Charlie?" Each time he heard his name, it was another ice-cold dagger shoved into his brain. "Please, be assured that I am not a monster. I have a plan, a mission, actually. You could even call it a vision. Even though you can't see my plan, my mission, my vision, for yourself, I need you to remain calm. You are going to be very helpful in the achieving of my goal. Now, shall we start the second protocols?"

The driver, Charles Utecht, lay on the table, restrained and immobilized. He had no family left in the world, his mother and grandparents dead long ago. He didn't know when his father had died, while his sister had died last Christmas. Apparently, his brother was gone earlier this year. Charles Utecht had no friends that would remember him or welcome him with open arms. He had screwed up, more so than at any other point in his life. He closed his eyes, hearing the disappointing last words his grandfather ever spoke to him. The words continued, ringing over and over inside his head, an endless loop of disappointment.

"You didn't listen, did you? Why didn't you listen?"

TEN

Lindstrom always tried to make Sunday mornings special for her family. Mostly, it involved a massive breakfast to properly feed three ravenous children. This particular Sunday, with the two teenagers out of the house, she could focus on Ryan. She had made pancakes with chocolate chips in the form of a smiley face, with bacon and fresh pineapple. As she was making his plate, Ryan walked into the dining room, sat down at the table, and said through a yawn, "Morning, Momma." Lindstrom smiled. What a wonderful way to start a day!

After serving up breakfast for the both of them, Ryan changed out of his pajamas into clothes and settled onto the couch to watch some television. Lindstrom took a shower and dressed casual for the day. She was looking forward to spending the morning with Ryan, before Mark's niece, Amy, would be coming by to pick him up for an afternoon of playtime and maybe a movie. Lindstrom wasn't expecting Bree to be home from cheerleading until after seven, and Trevor probably wouldn't be home until ten that night.

A little bit after eleven that morning, Ryan had been bundled off with Amy, leaving Lindstrom at home alone again. She was glad that Jerry had called yesterday and distracted her from the answering machine message. After talking to Jerry and relaying the information to Engels, it was made quite clear from Engels to enjoy the night with Ryan. Not one to argue about her little boy, they had had a great Saturday night. Now, with the house quiet, she was preparing herself for what might be a very important phone call.

She sat at the dining room table, but she didn't dial the number right away. She found herself paralyzed. These past four days had been something, and maybe they were taking their toll on her. A dismembered female body, a botched kidnapping or something, a victim's wife possibly comatose, that major traffic accident which actually hadn't impacted her too much, typical teenager drama, a near panic-attack involving her eight-year old son, and a mysterious van that she witnessed in her neighborhood three times in twenty minutes. Now, here she was, house empty except for the cat, trying to get the courage to find out if the message was too good to be true. She must have sat there for fifteen minutes, building up the fortitude to dial the number. She looked at her cell phone for the time. Almost eleven-thirty. Finally, after a few deep breaths, she got a piece of paper and a pen, dialed the number, and put the phone on speaker.

After two rings, the other line picked up. A man's automated voice said, "Thank you for calling R.T.A. Your call is very important to us. If you know your party's extension, you may enter it at any time." Silence. Normally, an automated system gave you a list of basic extensions to help direct you to whom you needed to talk to. She waited for a full two minutes. The voice picked up again. "Thank you for calling R.T.A. Your call is very important to us. If you know your party's extension, you may enter it at any time." Well, no sense in waiting. She dialed the extension.

After another two rings, the line picked up and a woman said, "R.T.A., customer relations, Veronica speaking."

Lindstrom cleared her throat and said, "Yes, I, well, I received a message on my answering machine regarding possible restitution from my ex-husband." She was trying to stay calm, but the butterflies were creeping in.

"Absolutely!" Veronica's voice perked up, the tone changing from mildly happy to Christmas morning thrilled. "May I please have your name?"

"Lindstrom. Patricia Lindstrom." She spelled out both her first and last names. It was habit on her part, especially since part of her job in taking witness statements was to verify the correct information had been relayed and written down.

"Okay, give me a moment." The sound of typing in the background. "Ah, yes! Here we go! How would you like your payment dispersed?"

"Payment dispersed?" Lindstrom was stunned. "I'm sorry, forgive me, but I really don't know what is going on. My ex has been out of our lives for fifteen years. After the first three years in jail, I never bothered to follow his movements, his jobs, anything. The only thing I had heard about him was about seven years ago. I had gotten word that he had violated a protection order from a woman he had been seeing. So, I don't know what he's been up to or what he's gotten himself in to, but I have moved on, and I don't think I can take it if this is a scam or pipe dream." She suddenly realized that she had been ranting louder and louder. She immediately stopped, lowering her voice while saying, "I'm sorry, I didn't mean to unload on you."

"Ma'am, I completely understand your concerns," Veronica said. The tone of her voice had changed again, this time to a concerned mother hen. "Rest assured, I can answer all of your questions. But first, let me give you a little background. R.T.A. has been working with law enforcement agencies at the local, state, and federal levels. Our goal is to work with these agencies to identify those individuals that are currently incarcerated in the prison system that are in debt to their spouses and, more importantly, to their children. R.T.A. then works with these agencies to bring these indebted individuals into our care system. They are put to work in strictly supervised settings, and all pay that is received on their part is then put into escrow. In addition, the money in escrow accumulates interest. One of two conditions must then be met. Either the money in escrow reaches a predetermined amount as to represent a sizable payment against the debt owed, or the amount is enough to bring the account sufficiently into the black as to wipe the debt clean and provide an amount of extra financial restitution for the spouse and children."

Lindstrom was trying to fathom what she had been told. "So, you're telling me that my ex has actually worked while in prison, and has made some money, and that I now have the rights to?"

"First, we don't like to use the word prison," Veronica corrected in a slightly snotty tone. Lindstrom could imagine this woman making quotation marks in the air when she said the word "prison". Her tone changed again, this time to helpful nurse. "These indebted individuals are transferred to us. We work with various agencies to make sure that each indebted individual is assigned an area of expertise best suited to the indebted individual. The indebted individual works hard and is rewarded, and all financial earnings go to the spouse and children of the indebted individual."

Lindstrom didn't know whether she was listening to a sales pitch from an infomercial, or a public service announcement on Saturday morning TV. Plus, Veronica's continued use of the words "indebted individual" was beginning to annoy her.

"I'm sorry," Lindstrom said, "but I find this to be a little bit too much. Forgive me, but isn't this where you say, 'April Fool's' or something?"

Veronica's tone changed again. "I understand your confusion and your disbelief." Holy crap, Lindstrom thought, the way this woman changes her tone and attitude, she would be amazing on Broadway. "This whole process can be overwhelming, especially considering the situation R.T.A. has, unfortunately, put you in."

"I'm sorry?" Lindstrom asked, incredulously. "Your company put ME in a situation regarding my ex?" She heard Veronica clear her throat slightly.

"According to my records, we should have contacted you over three years ago. Apparently, when R.T.A. did some computer modifications, some client files were lost, mislabeled, or misappropriated. On behalf of everyone at R.T.A., you have our fullest apologies! Fortunately, the only thing that you have lost is time, as your indebted individual's earnings have accrued interest. Once again, you are entitled to all the earnings, plus interest." A slight pause, and then, "Now, Ms. Lindstrom, if there are no further questions, may I ask how you would like your payment dispersed?"

"Indebted individuals," Lindstrom said to herself, shaking her head. She must have said it loud enough to be heard, as Veronica's voice came through the telephone's speaker again.

"Yes, I know it can sound repetitive. It's our way of letting the spouse or guardian or children know that they are owed. They are the victims in these unfortunate situations, and it is vital that they accept the recompense that R.T.A. has managed to broker for them."

Lindstrom's head was spinning. It had been so long since she had received any amount of child support. She didn't even know how far behind her ex was in payments. Five thousand? Seven? Ten? More? It didn't matter. She had been young and in love, but she always knew that Trevor and Bree were never mistakes. She had given birth to and raised two wonderful children, and no amount of financial ineptitude was going to stop her from loving them. A small cough came through the speaker, as if Veronica was clearing her throat, trying to get attention.

"Ms. Lindstrom? Are you still there?"

"Yes, yes," Lindstrom replied. "I'm sorry. Caught up in my memories." Maybe this is all on the up and up, Lindstrom thought to herself, but better to play it safe. There was no guarantee that this was legitimate, so she inquired, "Would it be too much to ask for a check?"

"Oh my, not at all! We offer the use of a secure online payment service. However, some customers don't like to put their banking information on the internet or divulging their information over the phone. We also offer direct deposit, prepaid credit cards, and bank to bank transfers with accredited and verified institutions. Now, would you like the check sent to your home or to your place of employment? Please be aware that a person at least eighteen years of age or older will need to be available to sign for it, as we send it via registered mail and courier."

"You can send it to my place of employment. Here is the address." As Lindstrom recited the police station's address, she figured that, if this was a gag, having backup around her would help keep her anger in check. She would make sure she got to the station early, and if she gathered a support team of Engels, Heather, and maybe even Tisdale, at the front reception desk, that would help take the sting out of a possible hoax.

"Okay, thank you, give me one moment." More typing in the background. "Ah, I see! You work at a police station. I am surprised that you never bothered to check up on your ex. However, I understand that every spouse has their reasons. Anyway, if you ever have any questions, please feel free to contact us, any time, day or night. You can expect your check to arrive on Monday morning between eight and nine in the morning. Is there anything else I can assist you with?"

Lindstrom realized that she hadn't asked the most important question in this whole situation. "I hate to be rude or unappreciative, but how much is this check?"

The tone of Veronica's voice moved to one of apology. "I am sorry, Ms. Lindstrom, but I do not have access to that information. For security and privacy reasons, the amount that an indebted individual owes, and the amounts that the family receives, are not shared openly. Only the financial and restitution department has access to that information." Her tone changed again with, "Will that be all today?"

Lindstrom felt the call was rapidly coming to an end, so she quickly grabbed at the one thing that was bothering her. "Yes, Veronica, I have one last, quick question. What does R.T.A. stand for?"

The tone went to chipper in the morning. "Why, R.T.A. stands for Rehabilitation Therapies and Associates. Now, you have a pleasant afternoon, and try not to spend your check all in one place! Goodbye!" With that, Veronica and her ever-changing vocal tones were gone. The line was dead.

Lindstrom sat there for a few minutes, and she thought about what she had just been told. She figured that the likelihood of this being a farce was about eighty to ninety percent. Still, she allowed herself a little fantasy about this whole thing being true. Veronica had said that this R.T.A. should have contacted her three years ago. So, Lindstrom figured that her ex had maybe been in this program for a year before that. How much could a felon realistically earn in prison? On top of that, whatever he earned had been sitting there, accruing interest? She didn't know what the current interest rates for savings was, but, coupled with a felon's meager earnings, there probably wasn't that much waiting for her. A couple hundred bucks, probably. No more than a thousand, though. For a single parent of three kids, though, a thousand dollars could go a long way.

Lindstrom grabbed her cell phone and called Engels. She gave him a rundown of the call, before asking if both Tisdale and Engels could be in early to be at reception with her. Engels said no problem.

"Also, I talked to Jerry," Engels said. "Still no word on the serial number on the stent, but it is the weekend. Enjoy the rest of your Sunday, Tish!" The call ended.

Lindstrom looked at the clock and tried to figure how much time she would have until the kids started coming home. She decided to get up and finish as much housework as possible. As she walked downstairs to the laundry room, she stopped. She sat down on a step, looking out the sliding door to the backyard. It was Sunday afternoon. Veronica had said to expect the check to arrive on Monday, via registered courier, between eight and nine in the morning. She had no idea where R.T.A. was based out of, so how would it be possible?

She glanced at the clock on the wall by the fireplace. It was ten minutes after noon. Would she really have a check in her hands nineteen hours from now? She shook her head. Doubtful. Maybe Veronica meant the following Monday, or maybe Veronica didn't realize it was a Sunday afternoon. Either way, Lindstrom realized it was out of her control. She stood up from the stair and finished her walk to the laundry room.

Money or not, police detective or not, she was still a wife and mother, and she had a house to tend to.

Lindstrom's eyes slowly opened. How long had she been asleep? She remembered putting Ryan down a little early, since Amy had brought him back happy but tired. She had vaguely heard Trevor around 11pm. Normally, he would have been up playing a video game for a few hours, but after hearing the doors open and close, it had been quiet. Bree had gotten home as Lindstrom had closed Ryan's bedroom door. She had asked Bree about her day, with a simple, "It was fine". Bree had grabbed a large cup, poured some juice from the refrigerator, and gone right into her room.

Wait a second. Why was she awake? Then the cobwebs started to clear. Her cell phone was buzzing. She grabbed the phone, but it slipped out of her hand. She was finally able to get it unwrapped from the power cord and swiped the screen active. She rubbed her eyes, trying to get them to focus on the bright screen in the dark of the bedroom. A few seconds later, she was able to read the cellphone's clock. It was 2:47 in the morning. Trying to focus, she quickly scrolled through all manner of alerts on the phone, until she found her messaging app. She selected the newest message from Engels and read it. She sat up in bed, mouth open in shock. After a minute, the cell phone went dark into power saving mode. She activated the phone again, re-reading the message. Still in amazement, she read it one more time, not sure what her emotions should be.

"ANONYMOUS TIP REPORTED A SUSPICIOUS MAN BY OLD SHELL GAS STATION AT 26th AND CLIFF. OFFICERS RESPONDED. PERP WAS HOLED UP, CLAIMING HE HAD A HOSTAGE. TWENTY MINUTES LATER, PERP TOOK HIS LIFE. UPON ENTRY INTO THE BACKROOM, THEY DISCOVERED A CAUCASIAN MALE, BOUND TO A BED IN SERIOUS DISTRESS. MALE IS ON HIS WAY TO SANFORD HOSPITAL. GET SOME REST, YOU'RE GOING TO NEED IT. MALE HAS BEEN ID'D AS NATHAN DEVLIN."

ELEVEN

A quiet weekend had been completely obliterated by one phone call. Engels had had a restful weekend, finishing a few projects around the house, and enjoying a night out with Diane. He even watched a little football on Sunday, for a change. When Tish had relayed the information about her possible check, he decided to retire early so he would be rested and ready for Monday. Normally, it took him a long time to fall asleep, with his mind constantly wandering about different things, including his job, his officers, and their caseloads. Tonight, he seemed to drift right off, feeling positive about how things were progressing. Now, here he was, at a crime scene at three in the morning, trying to make sense of what happened.

Engels looked at the officers, a young woman and a young man that had only been with the force for a year. The man, Officer Eli Clemens, was visibly shaken. The woman, Officer Fiona Gilbride, was the complete opposite. If she was upset, she wasn't showing it. Clemens was sitting on the tailgate of a police SUV, with Gilbride standing a few feet away. Clemens was holding a cup of hot coffee, the steam rising into the cool air. Gilbride was surveying the area, watching the paramedics come and go, observing the fire and rescue unit pack up, and slowly, methodically, turning her head back and forth. She appeared to be on alert, looking for anything out of the ordinary.

"Okay, I need a deep breath from both of you," Engels said. He nodded at Tisdale, who, after hearing the call, had rushed over from his apartment

134

to help out. Tisdale held out a miniature voice recorder and pressed the record button. "Clemens, you start. What happened?"

Clemens drank from his cup before beginning his statement. "I was on patrol when I saw six kids playing around in a front yard about six blocks southeast. I stopped and told them they were out past curfew, and they should get home. As I watched them walk in several different directions, a call came in from dispatch. An unidentified caller reported a suspicious white male walking around the abandoned Shell station. I responded, as did Officer Gilbride here. We parked at opposite sides of the station. Just as I reached for my radio to update dispatch, the front door opened, and a man walked out. He was surprised, reached for a weapon, and shot at Gilbride's car. We took cover and I radioed for backup. Within two minutes, three more squad cars surrounded the back of the building. I got on the bullhorn and informed the perp that the station was surrounded, and that he should give himself up before things got worse. About a minute later, his arm came out, waving a white flag on a pole of some kind." Clemens took another deep drink. The night air was cold, and he was shivering while recounting the events. His face was ashen, and he seemed to be collecting his thoughts.

"It's okay, Clemens," Engels said. "Take your time and get it right."

"Yes sir," Clemens said after a few seconds. He cleared his throat and continued. "The perp stepped out of the door halfway, with the left side of his body exposed and his left hand holding the white flag. I instructed him to come out and lie down on the ground. 'But I didn't do anything', he said. 'It was all the other guy's idea. I didn't hurt anybody. I thought we were just robbing someone. I didn't know nothing about no kidnapping. I don't want to go back to prison.' He kept rambling about how it wasn't his plan, it wasn't his fault. I asked him if there was anybody else in there. 'Just the guy.' I asked him where his partner was. 'He's been gone for days now. This wasn't right, this whole job, this whole idea of getting rich off a kidnapping. I should have known it was bullshit!' I asked him to calm down, and I wanted to help him, but he needed to surrender so we could help the man inside. He just stood there for a minute or two, looking down at the ground. He dropped the white flag and said, 'Officer, do me a favor? Tell my daughter that I'm sorry I wasn't a better dad, and that no matter what happens, I am sorry.' He took four steps sideways out of the front door, and that's when we saw the gun pointed at his head. I yelled for him not to do it, but he pulled the trigger and went down."

Clemens stopped and closed his eyes, clearly shaken. Violent encounters were a fact of life when it came to police officers, and Engels could see that this was going to stay with Clemens for a long time. Engels was also aware that, if any of the facts weren't correct, the media might call this a "suicide by cop". Of course, it was easy to label things after the fact. Based on Clemens' account, though, Engels wasn't buying into that notion.

"It's okay, son, take a minute," Engels said, putting a hand on his shoulder. Engels turned to Gilbride and asked, "Can you corroborate Clemens statement?"

"Word for word, Chief," Gilbride said matter-of-factly. "After the perp went down, I approached him with my weapon drawn. I kicked the gun away, while yelling for backup. Stevens," Gilbride turned slightly, pointing a quick finger at an officer helping one of the firemen twenty yards away, "came around the corner of the building, and we proceeded to enter the station. We found no other active perps, and in the back cold storage room, we found the victim tied up on a cot, unconscious. While we waited for the paramedics and Stevens checked his vitals, Officer Fisher joined us inside. He looked at the victim, and said 'Isn't that him?' He ran out to his squad car and grabbed a sheet of pictures from that night's meeting breakdown. The pictures matched your kidnapping victim, Nathan Devlin."

Engels looked at Tisdale and nodded, and Tisdale stopped recording. He gave the recorder to Engels, who said, "Tisdale, head over to Sanford. Make sure Kara Reed is notified, and get in touch with Andy Cole and Ben McKinley, Devlin's friends. Let them know Devlin has been found and is headed to the hospital."

"On it, chief!" Tisdale took off and was gone.

"FISHER!" Engels shouted and waved. Officer Fisher saw Engels and hightailed it over to the chief.

"Yes sir?"

"I want you to hang here with Clemens. Get one of the EMT's over here to check Clemens out."

"But," Clemens started to say, "the EMT's already checked me out."

Engels turned to Clemens and said, "You did good work tonight, son.

136

Now, let us get you checked out a second time. Sit tight, and do exactly what the EMT's tell you, understand?"

Clemens looked up into his boss's eyes and, with as much resolve as he could muster, he said, "Yes sir."

Engels looked at Gilbride and said, "Walk with me." As Engels walked toward the station, Gilbride fell into step next to him. Most of the station's windows had been boarded up with plywood, including the front doors. Engels saw Jerry and Roger dusting for finger prints on the padlocks that were kept in place to keep the large garage doors from being opened. Engels walked inside with Gilbride right behind him, being careful to avoid the taped areas on the ground. The dead body had already been marked, removed, and transported to the morgue. They were inside the cash register area. Dusty shelves, cracked or missing linoleum tiles, the stale smell of a building that hadn't been in use for years. Everything was stripped down, no candy bars, no cigarettes, nothing to show that this place was in business. With plywood boarding up the windows, both Engels and Gilbride were using flashlights to look around. They were out of the line of sight of the news vans that had converged half a block away. Engels turned and looked at Gilbride.

"Okay, Gilbride, spill it."

"Chief?" she responded.

"I've been on this job for a long damn time. One of the things I have learned is how to read people. I can tell that this little incident is going to affect Clemens. Hopefully, though, it won't be too bad, because he has the makings of a good cop. You, on the other hand, are different. Is this the first time you've ever had to pull your weapon?"

Gilbride looked Engels in the eye and replied, "Yes."

"Is this your first shooting that you've been involved with?"

"Yes sir."

"Is this the first time you've watched someone kill themselves? The first time you've seen a body go from alive to dead in millisecond? The first time you've seen a fresh, dead body?"

"Yes sir, on all counts, sir. If I may, what is your point?"

"I'm not trying to provoke you, Gilbride. Every officer, hell, every person handles situations differently, and that's okay. There's no right or wrong way to deal with someone putting their brains all over the pavement. But I can tell you have something else going on. So, once again, spill it."

Gilbride was taken aback by her boss's observational skills. "Alright. The whole thing stinks to high heaven."

"Explain."

"Dispatch said an anonymous tip. Okay, from where? Look at where we are right now." Gilbride started pointing. "We are on the corner lot of a busy intersection during the day. At night, though, it's quiet. Across the street is a cemetery. Unless a ghost figured out how to dial a phone, that's a no go. On that corner is another gas station, but they're closed after ten on Sunday nights. While we waited for the ambulance, I ran across the street and knocked on the station's doors. No one answered, no one was working. Then we have the other corner. The building has been under renovation for a year. The church next door is remodeling it into a youth center. Now, here we are, at our crime scene. The house next to this station is vacant, with signs saying it is undergoing a mold and asbestos abatement. Behind the station, we have a big parking lot belonging to the First Credit Union. Assuming someone was using the ATM drive thru, well, it's on the opposite side of the building, with no clear view of the back of the station."

Engels considered what she was saying. "Interesting. So, putting our location aside for a minute, let's assume a concerned citizen was driving, walking, or riding a bike by and saw our perp messing around and called it in. What else are you thinking?"

Gilbride continued. "This guy's actions don't add up. If he got mixed up into something and felt abandoned, why not try to negotiate your way out? If you were only watching the body for whoever is in charge, you can probably plead out after you turn evidence and roll on the one that started this whole shit-show." Gilbride shook her head and continued, "This whole thing happened way too fast, and it wraps up way too easy."

Engels was surprised. It was almost like listening to Tish. Gilbride seemed to be onto something. As much as he would love a quick and easy exit out of this case, he knew it wasn't going to happen. "You have some good points, Gilbride. Anything else?"

"Who watches the watchers?" As soon as Gilbride said it, she stared at Engels.

It took a second, but then it clicked. Sometimes, people that commit crimes would hide in plain sight, observing what the responders were doing. While many people were only rubbernecking, trying to see a dead body or waiting for something to post on their social media accounts in a vain attempt to say to the world, "Hey, look at me, I was nearby when this happened", it was always worth it to take note of the crowd.

"Anybody in particular set off your warning flares?" Engels asked.

"There's a large tree towards the northeast on the opposite corner." Gilbride pointed in the direction of the tree, even though Engels couldn't see it from inside the station. "The person was there when I came out of the station. As people began to come out of their houses or stop in their cars, that person hasn't moved. With the dark, I can't tell if it's a man or woman, but you can't miss them. At least six-foot five, easy."

Engels thought about it. "There's a backdoor out of here, correct? And it's been opened for us?"

"Yes sir," Gilbride said, nodding affirmatively.

"Get Fisher and Clemens in here, then tell the fire team to put a ladder up against the west wall. After that, get back in here." Gilbride turned and left. Engels moved around the door and, making sure he couldn't be seen from the northeast, looked northwest, out into the corner intersection. The intersection had been cordoned off in all directions, and even with the cold fall temperatures, there were enough people milling around, trying to find out what was going on. And there was what he was looking for, diagonally across the street, parked next to the closed gas station. Engels pulled his cell from his coat pocket and swiped the internet icon. He pressed the favorites tab and found the website for the local news station that owned that van. Sure enough, a "breaking story" was already being announced on their main page. He pressed the play button for the video, and Kendra's voice could be heard over the moving images. He closed out of the internet and dialed Kendra's cell in his contacts.

One ring, and then, "Chief Engels, what a pleasant surprise!"

"Kendra, enough already. I need your help. You do for me, I do for you, like always. Deal?"

Kendra immediately dropped the act and said, "I am in the van with two of my camera people, and I'm putting you on speaker. Go for it."

"I need your camera people to shoot as much of the crowd as possible. Do some panning around, not ignoring any areas. Get on top of the van if you can. Then filter out and get up to the cordon line. Go in opposite directions. At some point, I need a sustained focus area of the northeast direction. As much as you can give me. Get the tapes to me by noon. If there's something useful on them, you'll have the first information leak by your early edition. Deal?"

"Deal." The line went dead. As Engels put the cell phone back in his pocket, the three officers came into the station.

"Gilbride, do we have any more officers in the area that aren't in uniform?"

"I think I saw, um, what's his name, Officer Jefferson, helping out one of the fire rescue units."

"Good," Engels said. "Clemens, I need to know you have it together. Do you?" Engels hoped this would play out.

Clemens nodded and said, "I'll be fine."

"Okay! Here's the plan. Clemens, I want you to climb the ladder with one of the firemen. Take some flashlights and make a sweep of the roof. Nothing fancy, and if you find anything, great, but it has to be convincing. When you see me come out, be positioned by the east edge of the building, shout for me in a way to get my attention but not to cause a panic. When I come over to you, point at the house next door, and pretend you have found something. Understood?"

"Understood," and Clemens turned and left.

Engels looked at Gilbride and Fisher. "You two are going out the backdoor. Fisher, you follow Gilbride's lead. Work your way around the block so that you can have a better view of that northeast corner. Get going." Gilbride and Fisher walked into the garage area so that they could reach the backdoor. Engels grabbed his cell again and found Jefferson's number and dialed.

"What's up, Boss?" Jefferson answered.

"There's a chance we might have a voyeur out there. I need you to quickly and quietly get to your car. There is a tree at the northeast corner from this station, with a witness that's about six-foot five, not sure on the sex yet. I want you to park a block north and sit tight. Whenever and wherever the witness goes, follow discreetly. Questions?"

"None," Jefferson said. "I'm on it."

Engels gave everyone five minutes to position themselves. He walked out the front again, and went up to Jerry and Roger, who were still collecting forensic evidence. He kept his back to the northeast corner, not wanting to spook the possible witness that Gilbride had seen. Another few

140

minutes passed as he observed Jerry and Roger when he heard Clemens shout from somewhere above him. Pretending to be startled, he made his way to the east wall of the station and looked up. "Find something, Clemens?"

"Not sure, chief," Clemens spoke loud enough to be heard by those in the immediate vicinity. Anyone in the crowd across the street would only hear noise. Clemens then pointed his flashlight toward the west wall of the house next door to the station. Engels made his way to that side of the property, turning on his flashlight, and pretended to examine the wall. He then swept the light up to the roof of the station that Clemens was standing on.

"Clemens, move your flashlight slowly up and down the wall, and then focus your light on the northwest corner of the house." Once Clemens had focused his light there, Engels moved in with his flashlight, first straight toward the corner, then moving south along the property line. He stayed out of sight of the northeast corner long enough to see Kendra's camerawoman moving along the police line. She was doing a good job of taping the front of the station, then doing slow sweeping shots of the crowd, moving further east, and repeating. As she made another easterly move, Engels moved back along the property line.

As he cleared the house, he had a full view of the street and the northeast corner and the spot that Clemens held his light on. Engels then turned around and faced northwest and took a few steps away. As he turned around to face the house again, he made sure to turn to the right, so that he could get a look at the northeast corner. As he completed his turn, he could see the shadowy figure that Gilbride had spotted. Gilbride was correct. The possible witness was easily six-foot five and standing by the tree. Engels completed his turn back towards the property and waved for Clemens and the officers to come down.

Out of the corner of his eye, Engels saw Gilbride and Fisher slowly come into view and cross the street towards the northeast corner. Engels moved towards the corner of the house again, hoping to keep the potential witness preoccupied with what he had found. All they needed was a minute or two for the camerawoman to be close enough to get good film, or for Gilbride and Fisher to box in the witness from escaping, or both. Clemens had made his way down the ladder and taken up position to the right of Engels.

"What's going on, chief?" Clemens was trying to keep it together, but it was difficult. As with Gilbride, this was the first time he had drawn his weapon as an officer, his first dead body, and the first time witnessing someone put a bullet in their head. A night of firsts, and not in a good way.

"We are playing a little game of misdirection," Engels said, still focused and pretending to point at an area of the house. "Keep your head down and look at where I'm pointing. Gilbride thinks that she has a bead on someone that might be involved in Devlin's abduction, and that the person is watching what's going on." Having two cases merge into one with no real explanation was hard enough, yet Engels took comfort in the fact that he had good officers working for him. He desperately wanted to get this case in the books, so that he could focus on the mayor and his future.

Engels felt his cell phone vibrate. He looked at the caller ID. Jefferson. He swiped the screen to accept the call. "Talk to me."

"I'm parked one block down, and I saw the figure that you were concerned with. I wasn't here for two minutes when the person turned around and started walking down the block. I can't be one hundred percent, but I'm guessing it's a woman. She walked about three houses down, looked back, stretched, and went into a house. A light on the main floor turned on for a minute, then turned off. Another light came on upstairs for a few seconds, then turned off."

"Thanks for the update," Engels said. "Stay put and watch the house until we have everything wrapped up and the crowd disperses. Once everyone is gone, call me back." Engels ended the call, just as Gilbride and Fisher were walking across the street towards him. "Did you spook her?"

Gilbride looked at Engels quizzically and said, "I don't think so. We started crossing the street when the light from the camerawoman panned through the crowd. Before the light hit the tree, the woman turned and left. We reached the tree, but there was no sign of her."

"You think it's a woman," Engels inquired.

"Ninety percent sure. Why?"

"Jefferson is parked up the block and guessed that your witness is a woman. She walked halfway down the block and entered a house. Jefferson says lights came on, and then lights went off. I'm going to have

142

him sit on the house until things clear out."

"Brad," Jerry said as he was walking toward him.

"Anything to report," Engels asked him.

"I think we have everything we need for now. Roger and I will go over the area one more time with Officers Clemens and Gilbride. If you want to keep two extra officers here until we wrap up completely, I think you can start shutting down the carnival."

"Will do," Engels said. Jerry walked away, motioning for Clemens and Gilbride to follow. Engels looked at Fisher and said, "I want you to stay here. Pick three other officers, and each of you take a corner of the lot. When Jerry says so, tape off the station."

"Understood," Fisher said, and walked away.

Engels took his cell and texted Kendra. "THANKS FOR YOUR HELP. SHOW IS OVER FOR NOW. GET ME YOUR TAPES BEFORE NOON IF YOU CAN." Engels whistled at the captain of the fire and rescue team that was present at the scene. The captain turned, and Engels gave him a corkscrew motion with his finger. The captain nodded and started barking orders at his team to pack up. Some of the crowd seemed to sense that, as the old saying used to go, "There was nothing to see here." Cell phones were being turned off or put away, which meant no more amateur videos were being shot and posted onto Facebook and Twitter. Engels could hear different groups of people chattering and speculating about what had happened or what was going on. He was tempted to walk up to the corner and peer down the block at the house the woman had walked into, but he refrained. Sure, someone had been acting suspiciously, but considering the person hadn't gone that far, and had apparently went back home, now was not the time to make a mistake.

Engels checked the time. It was past four in the morning. He decided to head over to Sanford Hospital and check on Nathan Devlin. Could this be the end to the case, Engels thought to himself. Then he chuckled.

"Sure, Brad," he whispered to himself, "that will be the day."

TWELVE

Lindstrom had been surprised she was able to fall back to sleep after Engels' text. She figured with Engels on site, nothing was going to get overlooked. Nathan Devlin would need medical attention anyway, so the best thing she could do is get as much rest as possible. She got up when her alarm went off and showered quickly. Monday mornings Bree had to be at school early for choir, so Lindstrom had made sure to be ready and out of her way before she got up.

As she was making herself breakfast, her cell phone buzzed. It was a text from Tisdale. "NATHAN DEVLIN IS IN STABLE CONDITION, BUT HE HASN'T REGAINED CONSCIOUSNESS. HIS FRIENDS ANDY AND BEN ARE AT THE HOSPITAL. I WILL BE AT THE STATION BY 8." Engels must have gotten him involved last night, or Tisdale responded on his own. Either way, he was pulling his weight on the case.

Lindstrom finished eating and could hear Bree thundering around between her bedroom and the bathroom. When the commotion was only heard in Bree's bedroom, Lindstrom figured it was safe to get Ryan up. She gently tousled his hair, whispering "Good morning, star shine!" Ryan stretched and yawned, sleepily opened his eyes, and murmured "Morning, Momma." Lindstrom picked him up and held him close, with his head resting on her shoulder. She told him that she needed to leave for work early, so he needed to get ready for breakfast at school.

He said softly into her ear, "Not yet." He put both arms around her and

144

gave her a big squeeze. "You need morning hugs first!" After thirty seconds, Ryan let go and seemed to be wide awake. He jumped down and ran into the bathroom. Lindstrom got his clothes for the day, cracked the bathroom door, dropped the clothes on the floor, and walked back out to the kitchen. For a soon-to-be nine-year-old, Ryan was getting pretty good at doing things for himself. Lindstrom heard the toilet flush, the laundry chute open and shut, a couple of gurgles and spits letting her know that he had brushed his teeth, and the shower turned on.

As Lindstrom started cleaning up her small breakfast mess, Bree's door opened and slammed shut. "Yeah, I'm out the door like right now." Before Lindstrom could say one word, Bree, her cell phone pressed to her ear, had walked through the kitchen, into the garage, and was gone. She let out a deep, heavy sigh. She remembered being a handful for her own mother. However, with cell phones, the internet, all of the technology made the disconnect seem like a universe separated them at times.

Lindstrom also knew that Bree, being the typical teenaged girl that she is, was still upset about her "worst birthday ever." As always, money had been tight. Lindstrom had tried to explain that a roof over their heads, food on the table, and clothes on their backs was what she worked for every day. Anything after that, as the saying went, was icing on the cake. Unfortunately, it didn't seem to register with Bree. Lindstrom wasn't going to get her hopes up. However, if an actual check from her ex-husband appeared in her hands this morning, she would try to make it up to Bree this coming weekend. No, wait, she thought, quickly checking the calendar on the refrigerator door. Bree was going to be out of town for a cheerleading competition. Okay, no sense in getting anyone's hopes up. Get the check first, and details can be worked out later.

"Momma, did you hear me? Whatcha thinking about?" Ryan was standing there, with an odd look on his face.

"Oh, nothing special, sweetie!"

Ryan looked at his mother quizzically, as if she was hiding something. He walked up to her, placed a hand on her hip, and said, "Are you sure it's nothin', Momma?"

Lindstrom smiled, kneeling down so she was at his eye level, and said, "You caught me! I was thinking how I have such a little cutie pie for a son!" She reached out and started tickling him, and they both laughed for a couple of minutes, with a big hug and kiss to end the happiness. They finished helping each other get ready, and they were out the door and in the car in a flash. Ryan was in a good mood, and they sang and goofed around. Ryan gave her an extra big hug in the car before he got out. He was about to shut the door when he stopped. Normally, the school wanted the cars not to wait too long at the drop off, but since it was early, there weren't any cars behind her.

"What's wrong, honey?" Lindstrom could tell that something had changed.

"When can we show Daddy my video from last week?" The question caught her off-guard.

She looked her youngest son in the eyes and said as sweetly as she could, "You remind me when I get home tonight, and we will figure something out together. Deal?"

"Deal! Love you, Momma!" The car door was shut, and Ryan shuffled into school. That little angel was something else.

Lindstrom had hoped that, with a busy weekend, Ryan would have forgotten the request. Well, maybe "forgotten" was the wrong word. It was difficult for her to deal with Mark, given the present circumstances. Despite it all, though, Lindstrom knew deep down in her heart that she couldn't avoid this anymore. Maybe that's why Kara Reed had kept creeping into the picture. Well, as usual, first things first. Lindstrom needed to focus on her day. She would work things out with Ryan tonight.

Lindstrom arrived at the police station, parked in the parking garage, and bypassed the main reception area. By the time she got up to her desk, she could see the light on in Engels' office. Reaching his door, she poked her head inside, and found Engels laying on the floor behind his desk. His head was cradled between two pillows, with only his mouth and nose visible. Lindstrom remembered a conversation that she had had with Diane, Engels' wife, years ago. They had purchased one of those beds that allowed each person to control the level of support the person wanted. Diane had preferred a softer mattress, whereas Engels needed something stronger. This was not an uncommon sight in the police station, if Engels needed a quick power nap. Lindstrom giggled to herself. Two years ago, a rookie had sounded the alarm, having come into Engels' other office at the time and thinking he was dead or had been the victim of an attack. Engels had laughed it off and made sure that no one gave the rookie a hard time after that.

146

"Boss," Lindstrom said. "Are you dreaming about something happy?"

"Actually," Engels said as he started to sit up, "I was dreaming of Diane and I sipping champagne on a cruise ship at sunset."

"I thought both of you hated the ocean?"

"We do, which is why I have no idea why I was dreaming about it." Engels stood up, stretched and cracked his back. "I went to the hospital after we wrapped up at the old Shell station, but Devlin was still being worked on, so I came back here for a nap. So, what's the word?"

Lindstrom said, "Nothing to report. You want to give me a breakdown of what happened with Nathan Devlin last night?"

As Engels finished stretching out his arms, legs, neck, and back, he started recounting the events of the early morning. Lindstrom sat in one of the chairs in his office, listening intently as everything was laid out. After a twenty-minute synopsis, Engels reached for his coffee mug and walked to his coffee maker in the corner. As he put the cup under the dispenser, he said to Lindstrom, "Alright. Get started on the third degree."

"Any idea on who phoned in the tip?"

"The operator that took the call said that it was a male, elderly-sounding. Hold on, I have the audio here." Engels stepped back to the desk and played the audio of the 911 call that had been sent up from the communications center.

"911, what is the nature of the emergency?"

"Yes, I think there's something going on at the old filling station at 26th and Cliff. I was stopped at the red light, and I saw someone pulling back the plywood on the door and sneaking inside."

"Sir, can you still see the gentleman?"

"I drive by here every Sunday night after bingo at First Presbyterian Church. I remember one of my old friends used to do general maintenance at that station before it went out of business."

"Sir, I understand. Are you still at the red light? Can you describe the individual?"

"It's just a shame that it had to close. Hello? Are you still there?"

"Sir, I can hear you. Do you hear me?"

"Hello? Goddamn phone. My nephew told me I should get one of those fancy smartphones, and I can't barely make this one work. Hello? 911? Are you still there?"

"Sir, I can hear you just fine. Hello? Sir? Sir?"

Engels pressed stop and looked at Lindstrom. She was trying not to laugh, but she couldn't help it. Seeing Lindstrom laugh made Engels burst out laughing. They must have laughed together for five minutes. Engels wiped his eyes of tears and said, "Well?"

Lindstrom answered, mimicking an old man's voice, "Ah, this goddamn phone! And where the hell is my cane? Has anyone seen my teeth? I can't eat this pudding! You little whippersnappers get off of my lawn!" That brought another laughing fit out of both of them. Finally, after another couple of minutes of laughing off the tension of the last several days, Engels reclaimed a measure of composure and spoke.

"Alright, all kidding aside, what do you think?"

"Does the story check out?" Lindstrom asked.

"Tisdale should be calling the church soon to verify that they had bingo last night. According to the church's website, they do have senior functions on the weekends, including bingo that runs to ten at night on Sundays. If we're lucky, someone may remember something."

"Do we know anything on the perp that killed himself?"

"His name is Ronald Vance. Mostly petty crimes, a few breaking and entering, never more than six months in jail, but it looks like he's kept himself clean for almost a year. No outstanding warrants. We're trying to get more information."

Lindstrom was thinking. If this Ronald Vance had felt cornered, that there was no other way out, why kill himself? He wasn't the mastermind behind this. Shooting himself in the head seemed like a pretty harsh extreme to end a situation that he was only involved with peripherally. She would circle back to that. "What about this supposed woman that Gilbride and Jefferson saw?"

"When I checked with Jefferson, he said that no one had come or gone since just after four. He said the lights came on around seven thirty, but then went off again an hour later. I figured, once you got in, we would head over there with Gilbride, and have Jefferson serve as backup."

Lindstrom looked at the clock. 8:41am. She wanted to take a look at the crime scene and check out this supposed "watcher", but she also wanted to wait until nine to see if this R.T.A. company came through or not. As if on cue, the speaker phone on Engels' desk beeped. It was Heather the receptionist. "Chief Engels?"

Engels pressed the open intercom button. "I'm here."

148

"Have you seen Tish?"

Lindstrom answered, "I'm here, Heather. What's going on?"

"You've received a message from Speed-E Courier Service. They regret to inform you that they are running behind, but you can rest assured that they will be here between eleven-thirty and noon today. Those were the exact words."

"Okay, thanks Heather." A beep, and the intercom was silent as the connection was closed. "Well, boss," Lindstrom said to Engels, "shall we take a drive and meet up with Gilbride and Jefferson?"

Engels pulled up in front of the house that Jefferson had identified the suspect entering almost five hours earlier. Engels was driving his unmarked police car, with Lindstrom hitching along with Gilbride in her police cruiser. Jefferson parked across the street in his unmarked car. As the four of them got out of their vehicles, Engels looked up and down the block. It was two minutes after nine on Monday morning. No traffic, no people outside tending to any kind of fall lawn maintenance. He assessed the situation. From the outside, the lights were still off. The lawn looked well taken care of, with only a few scattered leaves. The house looked like it had recently been painted, with a new front door as well.

"Jefferson, you stay back with your vehicle. Be ready in case there's trouble. Lindstrom, you run point with Gilbride. Gilbride, look and listen. Once you're inside, I'll take a look around the driveway, garage, and backyard. Everyone clear?" Everyone nodded. "Okay, let's go."

Jefferson stood by his car, Engels stayed on the sidewalk by the driveway, and Lindstrom walked up to the front door with Gilbride right behind. Lindstrom reached the front door and pressed the doorbell. She could hear the faint ring from inside the house. No answer. Lindstrom rang the doorbell again, following that up with a hard knock. Still no answer. Lindstrom looked at Engels and waved him to go around toward the back of the house. Engels nodded, slowly walking the driveway until he disappeared around the side of the house. Lindstrom rang the doorbell twice in quick succession and then knocked hard again. After another minute, she looked at Gilbride. Gilbride raised an eyebrow, shrugged her shoulders, and said, "You know, I thought I heard someone call out for help."

Lindstrom smiled and nodded. She hadn't met Officer Gilbride until today, but she liked her already. Lindstrom slipped a latex glove on, took hold of the door knob gingerly, and tested it. The door opened easily, as the deadbolt wasn't engaged. They walked into the living room. "Hello? Is there anyone here? We are police officers." Lindstrom waited and listened for a response. Nothing. She didn't like this at all. She drew her service weapon, and she heard Gilbride do the same thing behind her. For an older house, the main floor had an open concept, so she could see through the living room, dining room, and kitchen. Lindstrom saw the top of Engels head walk past the door in the kitchen to the backyard. Keeping her weapon drawn but pointed down, finger off the trigger, she made her way to the back door. Gilbride checked out the only two doors on the main level. One was a closet, and the other was a powder room, both of which were empty. Lindstrom opened the back door and said, "Boss, come on in."

As Gilbride walked upstairs, Engels walked up the small set of stairs and came into the kitchen. He looked around, turned to Lindstrom, and asked, "Did you find anyone?"

"Not yet," Lindstrom responded. "I'll check the downstairs. You watch the main level while Gilbride takes the upstairs." Lindstrom disappeared down the stairs behind the kitchen cabinets, leaving Engels to survey the main floor. There was something off about the setup. As he looked at the kitchen table, he saw a car pull up into the driveway. A middle-aged woman with slightly graying hair got out of the car. As Engels moved to get a closer look, he saw Jefferson walk across the street and intercept her. He watched the conversation, and then turned around as he heard Gilbride, and then Lindstrom, re-enter the kitchen.

"The downstairs is clean," Lindstrom said. "And I do mean clean. No boxes, no furniture, it is empty."

"No one upstairs," Gilbride said. "There's some furniture, but nothing else. There are no clothes in the closets, either. There is a frame for a bed, but no box spring or mattress."

Engels could see Jefferson following the woman up to the front of the house. As they entered, Jefferson said, "Everyone, this is Mrs. Leslie Arndt."

Before anyone else could speak up, Engels stepped forward, offering out his hand, and said, "Mrs. Arndt, my apologies. My name is Brad

Engels, and I am the Chief of Detectives. Forgive me, but have you had an issue with squatters here?" The other officers in the room, although surprised by what Engels had said, maintained poker faces. Leslie Arndt, on the other hand, displayed genuine surprise.

"Why yes," she exclaimed. "This house has been on the market for almost fifteen months, with no concrete offers. The seller has the house priced so far over market value, but he is adamant on getting his money out of it. He inherited the house from his grandmother when she died. He lives in Kansas City, and is trying to apply market prices there to this house." Leslie Arndt shook her head slightly, as if she caught herself getting off the subject. "Anyway, yes, I have had some squatters. Nothing has been damaged, but I have had the neighbors call and say that someone is snooping around, or the same person has been here a few days in a row." While Mrs. Arndt was speaking, Lindstrom and Gilbride had each holstered their weapons discreetly.

"Is that why you furnished the house?" Engels walked to the refrigerator and opened it. It had power, but it was set to the warmest temperature, with a box of baking soda on the shelf.

"Yes, I picked up some inexpensive furniture at the reclamation store on the north end of town. You know, to give it a lived-in look. I also have the lights programmed to go on and off at certain times."

"Excuse me," Lindstrom said, stepping forward. "Detective Lindstrom, but you can call me Tish. Where is the for-sale sign for the property?"

"Oh, that," Leslie started. "One of the neighbors that keeps an eye on things said that it had blown away last week. You know, the night that we had that big rain storm. Last Tuesday night, I believe. I was delivering a new one this morning when the neighbor called me telling me there was a police car out front." As if realizing that she was standing in a half-furnished house with four cops, Arndt inquired, "If I may ask, why are you here?"

While Arndt had been talking, Jefferson and Gilbride had switched positions. Gilbride was still looking around, this time at the front of the house, examining the furniture and the windows. Jefferson had walked past Lindstrom and Engels, through the kitchen, and was now surveying the backyard.

Lindstrom looked at Engels, and Engels turned to Arndt and said,

"There was an incident last night at the old Shell station around the corner. We had reason to believe that a witness came into this house." Arndt was about to speak, but Engels held up a hand in a reassuring gesture. "I'm sure there was no danger. More than likely, someone had been crashing here and got spooked with the police so close by. If you don't mind, would you do a quick walkthrough and tell me if you see anything out of place?"

"Oh, absolutely! It'll only take me a minute or two." With that, Arndt went upstairs. Lindstrom quietly leaned into Engels.

"Do you buy what you're selling, Boss?"

"Not in the least," Engels whispered back, "but until we have some concrete evidence that the person that Gilbride and Jefferson saw had any involvement, there's no sense in scaring Mrs. Arndt." Jefferson reappeared at the backdoor and came back into the kitchen. He had a frustrated look on his face, like he had missed something obvious.

"No wonder I didn't see anyone leave," Jefferson said. "The backyard opens up to a closed alleyway. She could have turned on the lights, turned them off, and waited until the time was right. Walk out the back door to the alley, and then make her way out of the neighborhood without me knowing, since the alley opens on the other side of the block from where I was parked. Damnit!"

"Hey, calm down," Lindstrom said. "No one is at fault. Right now, we have two possibilities. One, a real squatter checked out the commotion last night, then got scared with all the cops, and bailed. Second, the witness you and Gilbride saw knew what he or she was doing, and…"

"She," Gilbride interjected. "That witness or whatever you want to call her, it was a she. I'd stake real money on it."

"Me too," confirmed Jefferson. "It might have looked like shadows, but even at better than six feet tall, men and women walk different. This was a woman, graceful, walking with a purpose."

Lindstrom conceded. "Very well, the woman knew what she was doing, she had checked out the area, and found a viable exit strategy, if she needed one."

Arndt's footsteps grew louder as she descended the stairs, and she came back into the kitchen.

"Everything looks to be in place."

Lindstrom looked at Arndt and asked, "Leslie, if I may, I have three questions. First, when was the last time a realtor showed the house?"

152

Lindstrom knew that all realtors had to use a special key code specific to each realtor to gain access to any vacant house.

"Almost a month ago," Arndt replied. "The price isn't bringing in any potential buyers."

"Okay. Second, where is the lockbox for the house key?"

"It is on the backdoor," Arndt continued. "I left specific instructions for any realtors to use the back door. When the new front door was installed last year as part of the remodel, the deadbolt lock is different than the lock in the door handle, and I didn't want to have more than one key in the lock box. Also, removing the first few squatters made it easier for neighbors to identify actual potential buyers and realtors. If they came in the front door, they weren't on the up-and-up."

"Excellent thinking," Lindstrom said. "Lastly, do you have a cleaning crew come through the house on a regular basis?"

Arndt said, "I had the house cleaned a month ago, a day before the most recent showing. They are actually scheduled for a final winter cleaning on Wednesday, the day after tomorrow." Lindstrom looked at Engels.

"Mrs. Arndt," Engels said, "We appreciate your time and patience this morning. More than likely, this is nothing to worry about. However, I am going to have one of my forensics people come over and dust the house for prints. If no one has been in the house in over a month, it should be easy to find any trace evidence."

Arndt had a look of relief, which quickly changed to a smile, and said, "Absolutely! It will be no trouble at all. This might be the situation I need to finally convince the grandson to come down in price and get this place sold!" Although her face didn't show it, Lindstrom was surprised with the realtor's reaction. Today's society was all about speed and convenience. Whenever a situation might have a negative impact on the flow of a person's day, the reaction could get cold and ugly, especially if the police were involved.

Engels was relieved to hear that. "Jefferson, I know you are running into overtime here, so you are dismissed. And don't beat yourself up. You did good work. Go home and get some rest."

"Yes sir," Jefferson said as he walked past everyone and left.

"Gilbride, that goes for you, too. Get some rest, and if you need to add anything to your report, do it when you report for your shift tonight. Understood?"

"Understood," Gilbride said. She walked up to Lindstrom, held out her hand, and said, "It was a pleasure meeting you, Tish." There was sparkle in Gilbride's eyes as she shook Lindstrom's hand.

"The feeling is mutual, Gilbride," Lindstrom said. "Excellent work on your part. Now go home and get some sleep. I've been on the night shift before, and I know what it can do to a body."

"Thanks," Gilbride released Lindstrom's hand and walked out the front door.

Engels was on his cell, requesting a uniform and someone from Jerry's team to come out to the house. As he was talking, Leslie Arndt stepped up to Lindstrom and asked, "So, dear, are you happy with where you're living right now? I have a lovely five-bedroom ranch on the southwest part of town by the new middle school that would be perfect for you and your family."

Lindstrom and Engels waited until backup arrived. A uniformed officer, a male officer that Lindstrom hadn't met yet since transferring off the night shift, and one of Jerry's new techs, Samantha, pulled into the driveway. Lindstrom had done her best to deflect Leslie Arndt's prodding real estate questions. Finally, Engels stepped in, gave Arndt his business card, telling her that he and Diane weren't going to be looking until after the first of the year. "You call me on January the third, and not a day before, okay?" That seemed to pull Arndt's focus away from Lindstrom. Having the chief of detectives buy a house from her would be a great feather in her cap.

"Thanks for that," Lindstrom whispered out the corner of her mouth as they walked to Engels' car.

Lindstrom hitched a ride back to the station with Engels. On the way, Engels called Tisdale. Engels had told Tisdale earlier that morning to stay at Sanford Hospital, at least until Engels told him otherwise. Now, Engels wanted any updates on the Devlin's. Considering what had happened at this house, Engels hoped for some good news.

Tisdale said, "Both Nathan and Allison Devlin's conditions hadn't changed. They're both still unconscious but in stable condition. Nathan's friends, Andy and Ben, are still here."

While Engels was hoping for a witness to talk to, as long as neither

154

Nathan or Allison took a turn for the worse, that was a positive sign.

"Tisdale," Engels said, "let Andy and Ben know that you need to come back to the station, but to call us as soon as something changes. Got it?"

"Got it, chief," Tisdale said, and the call ended. Engels and Lindstrom finished the ride back to the station in silence.

After Engels parked the car in the garage, they both got out and started walking. "You're awfully quiet over there," Engels said.

"Sorry. I have a lot on my mind," Lindstrom said.

"Is it something about the case?"

Lindstrom sighed. "It's everything, it seems. Two cases becoming one case, Trevor graduating in eight weeks, Bree being Bree, this crap with R.T.A., the black van, Ryan asking to see Mark, things seem twisted together but oddly separate. It's difficult to explain."

Engels stopped walking, which made Lindstrom stop. "Ryan wants to see Mark, so let him see Mark. And what black van?"

Lindstrom realized that she had said a little too much, but there was nothing she could do about it now. "Let's get up to your office and I will fill you in." As they made their way through the station, they got pulled into different directions by different people. Lindstrom looked at Engels and said, "Half an hour, in your office." Engels nodded, and they went off to their separate business.

Officer Tavon had spotted Lindstrom and had come up to her first. "Here's more of the follow-up on the clinics, doctor's offices, dentists, everything you wanted us to look for regarding HealthStar Ambulatory Services. Now that the weekend is over, we're getting more of a response. So far, I would say almost seventy-five percent of the area's medical community has never heard of HealthStar Ambulatory Services."

"Good job," Lindstrom said. "Keep going. Either way, we're going to find what we need."

"How do you figure that?"

"Easy. If one clinic or doctor had an interaction with them, we can pull on that thread and see what it unravels. If no one has heard of them, we know that whoever worked with our dead kidnapper somehow got their hands on an ambulance."

"I got it," Tavon replied, and hurried off. Meanwhile, Lindstrom stopped by her desk and sat down. She closed her eyes, stretched, and massaged the back of her neck. My God, she thought, when was the last time I went to the chiropractor for a massage and an adjustment? Obviously, it had been too long, if she couldn't remember. As always, the kids and work came first. She let her mind wander for a few minutes. She felt she had done well for a woman raising three kids on her own, especially considering her chosen profession. She still wasn't getting her hopes up regarding the phone call with R.T.A. A check was supposed to show up, and then someone calls and says it's been delayed? Yep, she was ready to call shenanigans on the whole damn thing.

On the positive side, Nathan Devlin had been found. Was it really a botched kidnapping? If so, how did the dead woman fit in? More importantly, who had started the ball rolling on the plan? It should have been obvious that the Devlin's had no money, no assets, nothing that was of financial interest. It would have been easy to dismiss the whole thing as a kind of Three Stooges operation. Still, something felt off about the whole setup. Lindstrom hated the idea of a conspiracy, but when things wrapped up too neatly, it was important to re-examine everything.

Her cell phone buzzed, and she looked at the text message. "Office. Now." It was from Engels. She must have drifted off a little bit. She thought about what she was going to say, then realized there was no sense in lying to her direct superior. She got up and walked to his office. She walked in without knocking and sat down in the same chair she always sat in. She was about to put her feet on the edge of his desk when he put up his hand in a stop motion.

"This is no time for our usual witty back and forth, Tish. We made a deal a long time ago when you got promoted to detective. It's the same deal I make with everyone under my command. I don't tolerate bullshit or omissions. I don't care how trivial you think it might be, I need my people to be focused on the job. If you're not focused on the job, you end up dead or worse." Engels leaned forward in his chair, folding his hands on the desk. "Now, as far as Ryan and Mark, we can talk about that later. If you want Diane and I to help you sit down with Ryan, we can do that. But you drop something like a mysterious black van? Are you ready to be straight with me?"

Lindstrom knew Engels meant well. Even with the added pressures of running the entire department and the physical toll it was obviously taking on him, Engels was loved and respected by everyone at every level of law enforcement in the area. She realized that she had screwed up, so it was time to come clean.

"Look," Lindstrom started, "before you get all pissy, you need to realize that I don't even really know what happened. You can call it a sixth sense, my motherly instincts getting out of control, a bad case of indigestion, but something happened on Saturday afternoon that made me think that Ryan was in danger. When I went up to the school to look for him and he wasn't there, I did the one thing I've never done before, okay? I panicked! In those frantic few moments, I saw a black delivery van drive by on the road. After I found Ryan safe with his friends, I drove around for a few minutes. When I got home, a black delivery van was turning at the corner of the block. I pulled into the driveway, and the garage door stuck again. It finally went up, I pulled in and parked, and I saw a black delivery van drive by again." She took in a deep breath and exhaled. "Look, I should have told you, and I'm sorry. I can't understand it or explain it, so I didn't tell you." She thought about trying to justify it out loud, but then realized that would be a mistake.

Engels looked at her, stood up, and walked to the window. The pause between them seemed to stretch on for days. Finally, Engels turned around and leaned against the window. "Tish, I know you have a lot going on. I can appreciate why you didn't tell me, but you of all people should know that even the littlest thing can make the biggest difference. You're a good cop and detective because of your attention to the details. You've helped other officers look at those same small details. Hell, you help me re-evaluate situations, too. So, once again, no more bullshit. I don't care if Bree has a hangnail, you tell me, and we'll decide if it is relevant or not. You hear me?"

Lindstrom looked at her boss and smiled. "Absolutely." She stole a glance at the clock. It was a quarter past eleven. "What do you say I buy you an early lunch down in the break room?"

Engels smiled back at her and said, "Sounds great. And while we eat, we can talk about Ryan and Mark." They walked out of the office and headed toward the elevators when they heard someone call after them.

"Tish!" It was Tisdale. Both Engels and Lindstrom turned towards him.

"What's up?" Lindstrom asked.

"Nathan's friend, Andy, called. Allison has regained consciousness. Her doctor says that nothing came up on her x-rays or on the CT scan.

Most of the blood work looks clean. They are chalking it up to exhaustion and stress." The elevator doors opened, and they all got in.

Engels asked, "Have they told her that Nathan has been found?"

"Not yet," Tisdale replied. "The doctor wants to make sure she is out of the woods before we put that on her."

Lindstrom nodded, "That makes sense. Do we have the medical report on Nathan yet?"

"Nope," Tisdale said. "The doctor is still waiting for the radiologist to confirm the results of the x-rays and CT scan." The elevator door opened, and the three of them stepped out. They hadn't walked two paces when a ring came over the in-ceiling speaker, letting everyone know to listen up.

"Detective Lindstrom to reception, please." It was Heather. "Detective Lindstrom, please come to reception. Thank you."

Engels looked at Lindstrom and said, "You want us to come along?"

"If you don't mind," Lindstrom said.

As Engels and Lindstrom turned away from the direction of the break room to walk towards the front entrance and reception, Tisdale fell in step, walking behind them, and asked, "Tish, what's going on?"

"Supposedly, I am getting a check for delinquent child support."

"Really," Tisdale asked, somewhat shocked. "How much are you getting?"

Lindstrom said quietly, "I really don't know. I wasn't expecting anything. Considering how much he has been behind, and for so long, I can't imagine it's any amount that's going to make a dent in the family budget."

"How much does he owe you," Tisdale inquired.

"No idea," came Lindstrom's curt response. "I haven't looked in years, and I haven't cared in longer."

Engels said, "Well, even a few bucks are better than nothing, right?" He tried to sound optimistic, knowing how much of a sore spot this topic was for Lindstrom.

"I guess," Lindstrom said. "Look, this is all new to me. All I know is what this woman told me in a fifteen-minute phone conversation. If it is legit, I would be happy with a hundred-dollar bill."

"And if it's not legit," Tisdale asked as they had reached the doors to the front lobby and Heather's receptionist counter.

"Then make sure I don't shoot the messenger," Lindstrom cracked.

She opened the double door and walked out first.

Before Engels could follow her, Tisdale put a hand on his arm and whispered, "She's joking, right?"

Engels whispered back, "It's probably best if we don't dwell on it." Engels walked through the slowly closing double doors, with Tisdale quickly following. Lindstrom was already on the other side of the receptionist counter, so Engels stood at the end of the counter, but behind Lindstrom. Tisdale took up position to Heather's right. While it was important to provide Tish with moral support, Engels wanted to ready for anything, in case this turned out to be a cruel hoax.

Heather looked at Lindstrom and said, "Detective Lindstrom, this gentleman has something for you.

"Good morning, ma'am", the messenger said. He was young, in his early twenties, wearing black knee-length shorts, a black polo, and a black hat that read "Speed-E Courier". The name and logo were also on the polo in smaller print. "We at Speed-E are sorry for the delay. We hope this won't reflect negatively in your review of our service."

Lindstrom looked back at Engels, who had a bemused look on his face. It was always interesting to see how different people reacted to doing their jobs. Some people, Engels thought, you could tell that their heart wasn't in it, or they were having a bad day, or the passion for their work had died long ago. This delivery driver, on the other hand, seemed to really enjoy what he was doing, and really wanted to make sure that Lindstrom wasn't upset. Engels appreciated those people. No matter your job or your lot in life, Engels had been told by his father long ago, do your job with as much passion and energy as you can muster. If you can't, everyone around you will know it.

Lindstrom returned her attention to the messenger mustered a smile and said to the him, "No harm done. I'm sure you've had a busy Monday morning."

"Oh, thank you, ma'am! Now, if I can just get your signature here...", the messenger said as he held out a clipboard and pointed to the fifth line. Lindstrom signed it, and the messenger put the clipboard on a hook on his waist. "Excellent, and now give me one second...", and the messenger used a key to unlock the zipper on a satchel that was hanging over his shoulder. He removed a large envelope and handed it to Lindstrom. "There we go! I apologize again for the delay! I hope you have a great rest of your Monday! Thank you again!" With that, the messenger pivoted on his heel, turning around, and strolled briskly out of the police station.

Lindstrom stared at the envelope in her hands. After a few minutes, Tisdale gently asked, "Tish, are you alright?"

Lindstrom turned around and looked at Engels, then Heather, then Tisdale. "You know, I think the world of all three of you," she said, "but if this is a prank or gag, I swear, I am going to open up the gates of hell, right here and now."

Engels looked at her and said, "Tish, I think there's enough love and respect for you among the entire police force that no one, and I do mean NO ONE, would even dare to think about pulling some kind of bone-headed stunt like that."

Tisdale chimed in with, "Tish, I agree with the chief. We're all here for you."

"Besides," Heather added, "I would have suggested better looking male strippers to pose as delivery men."

Everyone looked at Heather, and Engels responded with a sarcastic, "Really, Heather?"

"Now now, Brad," Heather taunted, "you know that, without me, this police station would grind to a halt."

Trying to stay focused and avoid their banter, Lindstrom walked back behind the reception counter, still holding the envelope. She set it down on Heather's desk, staring at it.

"Alright," Tisdale said, "Heather might be onto something. I think we need to lighten the mood a bit. I want the four of us to believe that Tish has money in that envelope. Having said that, Heather, how much do you think she received?"

"Really?" Lindstrom looked at Tisdale. "You want to put a wager on how much child support is in here?" Lindstrom tapped a finger against the large envelope.

"Why not? I will bet you one dollar that you have, um, three hundred dollars." Tisdale looked at Engels. "Chief? What do you think?"

Engels thought for a second, rubbing his jaw with his hand, then saying, "I will wager one dollar that Tish got five hundred." He looked down at Heather, who was still sitting in her chair. "Your turn, Heather."

"I will bet one dollar that Tish has a check for six hundred," Heather said.

160

Strangely enough, this was helping buoy Lindstrom's mood about the whole situation. She kept staring at the envelope, seeing her name and the station's address. The return address simply read "R.T.A.", with no physical address, no city or state, no zip code.

As Lindstrom continued to look at the envelope, Tisdale asked, "Forgive my ignorance, but are child support payments taxed? You know, like income tax?"

Engels replied, "Nope, not at all. Whatever money is paid to the spouse and the children is completely theirs. The government takes no piece of it for themselves."

Another few moments passed, with Engels finally saying, "Tish, I know this is difficult for you, but I'm getting damn hungry, so let's get this show going."

Lindstrom chuckled. She looked at Heather, who was holding a letter opener for her. "No need," Lindstrom replied, as she found the perforating seal on the back of the envelope. She pinched the tab between her thumb and forefinger and ripped the envelope open in one move. She removed the contents, which included a tri-folded letter with a check inside the letter. She carefully set the check face side down, unfolded the letter, and read it aloud for the three of them to hear.

"Dear Ms. Lindstrom,

We at R.T.A. are pleased to present you with this check regarding your ex-husband's delinquent child support payments. We understand how difficult life can be for spouses, guardians, and children of indebted individuals. Please be assured that we take every measure to make sure that proper restitution is given to those individuals that are owed it and deserve it. Indebted individuals are encouraged to work hard to make sure that their debts are resolved and that their spouses and children can move forward in a more fitting environment.

As I explained to you over the phone, you should have been made aware of your account several years ago, which was a mistake on our part. While the delay in contacting you was an error that falls completely on us, all restitution owed you continued to accumulate interest. However, we realize the addition of the interest payment isn't enough to offset our error. For that, we can only apologize again. R.T.A. truly hopes that this payment from the indebted individual helps you and your children.

Sincerely,

Veronica K., Victim and Restitution Coordinator, R.T.A."

Engels, Heather, and Tisdale looked at Lindstrom, not saying a word. Lindstrom looked at the letter again. It was amazing to her how this company, this R.T.A., could gloss over the wretched actions of these deadbeat moms and dads and paint them as people that had seen the error of their ways, that wanted to now do right by their families. Whatever, she thought to herself. I have a check in my possession, and if it means I can restock the kitchen cupboards on my way home, fill the car with gas, and maybe buy an early Christmas present or two, then I'll be happy.

Lindstrom let all three of them take a turn and read the letter. When they were all done, she said, "Well, I guess this is it. Are you ready?" All three of them nodded excitedly at her. She picked up the check and turned it over. It was dated from the previous day, Sunday, when she had first talked to Veronica at R.T.A. The "Pay to the order of" line had her name typed out. She then looked at the amount, and froze. She couldn't move. She was finding it difficult to breathe. She looked at the amount again, and her hands began to tremble.

Heather stood up, putting a hand on Lindstrom's shoulder. "Tish, what's wrong? Are you okay?" Lindstrom slowly turned, looking into Heather's eyes. Her arms started to drop, and the check fell out of her hands, landing face down on the floor.

"I, um," Lindstrom stuttered, but she found her mouth dry. Her knees were buckling. "I need to sit." Heather helped her sit down.

"Is there some water?" Lindstrom felt her strength draining out of her limbs. Heather moved fast, reaching into a smaller cooler she kept under her desk and retrieved a fresh water bottle. Heather opened the bottle and helped Lindstrom take a drink. Engels and Tisdale were looking on with concerned expressions on their faces.

"Tish," Engels started, kneeling next to her, "what's wrong? Is it bad?"

Lindstrom looked at him, but she couldn't speak. She looked toward the floor, slowly raising her hand, and pointed at the check.

"May I?" Engels asked softly. Lindstrom gently nodded her head. Engels slowly reached for the check, picking it up off the floor, and turned it over. His eyes grew bigger, losing any appearance of a poker face. Heather moved behind Engels to get a look.

Heather shrieked in excitement and gave Lindstrom a big hug. "Oh my god, Tish, that's beyond amazing! I am so happy for you!"

With a perplexed look, Tisdale asked, "Well, who wins the bet?"

Engels looked up at him and chuckled. "Nobody wins the bet. Here," Engels said, handing the check over. "Have a look for yourself."

Tisdale took the check and looked at. Utterly stunned, he said, "Does this mean Tish is buying lunch?" Engels and Heather looked at him and laughed.

Engels looked again at Lindstrom as she sat in Heather's chair. Lindstrom appeared almost catatonic. "Tish," he said while patting her hands, "don't act like someone died. You should be ecstatic. It's not every day that you get a check for fifty-two thousand dollars."

THIRTEEN

Engels had never seen Lindstrom in such a state before. The reception area had been quiet for a Monday morning before lunch, so, with Tisdale's help, they helped Lindstrom to her feet and took her to Engels' office. Some of the other officers saw them and asked what was going on, expressing genuine concern for Lindstrom.

"Oh," Engels replied, "she's feeling a little faint. Typical Tish, working too hard and she skipped breakfast this morning."

Everybody bought the little white lie. They also added to let them know if she needed help. Before heading upstairs, Engels had instructed Heather to put the letter, the check, and the envelope in an evidence bag, seal it, and then have Officer Tavon bring it up to Engels' office.

Now, here they were, Engels sitting at his desk, Lindstrom sitting in her usual chair while holding an ice pack to her forehead, and Tisdale standing by the closed door to the office. Tavon delivered the evidence bag to Engels and left the office. Now, the three of them stared at the bag on Engels' desk. No one said anything. It seemed like no one was even breathing, like the smallest disturbance would cause the contents in the bag to evaporate into thin air. After what seemed like an eternity, Engels stood up, fished his wallet out of his pocket, and pulled out ten one-dollar bills. He walked over to Tisdale, handed him the cash, and said, "Go grab us some snacks from the breakroom. I don't know about you, but I'm starved, and I need something." Tisdale nodded and left quietly, closing the door behind him. Engels sat back down at his desk and looked at

Lindstrom.

Lindstrom looked at Engels, "Sorry about this, Boss." She had a resigned look on her face.

"Oh, Tish," Engels said as he shook his head slightly. "You can cut the tough guy act. You are one of the best cops in the department. You are also a role model for the next generation like Gilbride and Tisdale. You have nothing to apologize for. The only thing you need to do is decide what's next."

Lindstrom looked from the bag to Engels and then back. "Is it me, or does this seem unbelievable?"

"Do you know how much your ex owes you in child support?"

"I really don't. I stopped keeping track years ago. His parents had sent me a check for, I think, three hundred dollars more than eleven years ago, but that was it. If I had to venture a guess, probably around nine thousand, maybe less than nine."

Engels thought about that, and then took the evidence bag. He re-read the letter through the plastic. "Okay, for the sake of discussion, let's round it up to ten thousand. Without knowing anything about R.T.A., how its run or mission statement or financials, or how R.T.A. puts these guys to work, it might be conceivable that this is legit."

Lindstrom took the ice pack from her head and stared at Engels. "You can't be serious right now, can you?" Her frustration was rising, like a teapot slowly boiling. "He goes from owing the kids and I ten thousand, and now, eleven years later, he is flush with fifty-two grand? And as a guest of the goddamn state of Nebraska, or whichever state he ended up in? Do you hear how ridiculous that sounds!?"

"I admit, it does seem like a stretch. It's not like he got rich playing the ponies or hitting it big in Vegas. And didn't you say that you should have had this money three years ago? A chunk of this could be interest." Engels was trying to play devil's advocate, mostly because he realized how much this could help Lindstrom and her family. "I know it's a lot of money, all at one shot, and it does seem to be a little too good to be true. Seriously, though, what do you have to lose?"

Lindstrom stood up, put the ice pack down on Engels' desk, and stretched. She rubbed her temples, her shoulders, her arms, and bent over, trying to get the blood flowing. As she was doing some light running in place, a soft knock came from the door, which then opened to show

Tisdale, his arms holding bags of chips, some nutrition bars, and three different bottles of pop from the vending machines downstairs. He walked to the desk and gingerly set everything down.

"I'm not your usual waiter," Tisdale joked, "so I guessed as best I could for you."

"Thanks," Lindstrom said, "you did fine." She grabbed a nutrition bar and scarfed it down in three bites. She finished off the bottle of water that Heather had given her downstairs, and then took the off-brand lemon/lime soda. She continued to drink while she walked around the office, trying to collect her thoughts. Tisdale looked at Engels, and Engels shook his head, signaling Tisdale to keep his mouth shut. Tisdale sat down and quietly ate. Engels also snacked away, letting Lindstrom figure out whatever was going on in her head.

Lindstrom, for her part, was wrestling with the situation. She realized her biggest objection to the whole thing wasn't that a check had shown up. It wasn't that the amount of the check seemed to be off the charts nuts. No, Lindstrom thought. The thing that had really crawled under her skin and stayed there was the fact that now she had to make a choice. Does she accept this money from her scumbag of an ex-husband? Or does she rip up the check, telling her ex-husband to burn in hell because he hasn't given a rat's ass since the kids were brought into the world? She had more questions. Before she decided on her course of action, she needed those questions answered. She turned around and faced Engels.

"Boss," Lindstrom said, "would you mind if I made a phone call?"

Engels smiled. "Not at all. Do you want us to leave?"

"Actually, I'd like it if you would stay, as long as both of you are quiet." Lindstrom looked at Engels and Tisdale. Engels smiled and turned the speaker phone towards her. Tisdale finished crunching a handful of chips, and then chugged the rest of his Coke. He stood up and moved to a different chair by the window.

Lindstrom activated the dial tone on the phone and dialed the R.T.A. number. After two rings, the automated greeting came on. She let it play, and then dialed Veronica's extension. Two rings, and a woman's voice answered. "R.T.A., Veronica speaking. How may I help you?"

"Yes, hello. This is Patricia Lindstrom again."

"Ah, yes, Ms. Lindstrom! I hope everything is going well for you." Her tone changed from pleasant to concerned. "Did you not receive your funds?"

"Um, no, I received the check a little while ago. I have a few questions for you, though. The amount of the check is, quite frankly, staggering."

"Yes, I can see how receiving such a windfall can be troubling." The tone had changed again, and Lindstrom looked at Engels with a look on her face that screamed, *WAS I LYING?* Lindstrom had told Engels about how Veronica's tone of voice was constantly changing, trying to keep the conversation smooth and even. "You have the full support of everyone here at R.T.A. However, if you'd like to hold, I could put you in touch with one of our counselors. They are excellent at helping spouses, guardians, and children work through these difficult times and coming up with a solid financial plan for the future."

"I'm sure your counselors are very good," Lindstrom said, trying to keep her irritation from intruding into her voice, "but I really need to have my questions answered."

"I understand completely. I'm actually on another line with another spouse of an indebted individual, but I think I'm almost done. May I put you on hold for a few minutes?"

"Yes, that would be fine." There was a click, and smooth jazz started playing softly through the speaker.

"Wow," Engels said, "you weren't exaggerating about this Veronica and the tone of her voice."

"If only all customer service agents were this helpful," Tisdale said.

Engels was about to speak when the music abruptly ended. There was a click as the line picked up and Veronica's voice came through the speaker. "Okay, thank you for your patience! Now, Ms. Lindstrom, I believe you said that you have some questions regarding your funds?"

Lindstrom cleared her throat and said, "Yes, Veronica. To be completely blunt, this doesn't seem right. I haven't kept track of how much my ex-husband owes us, but I guessed it was around nine thousand dollars. Now, today, I receive a check for fifty-two thousand dollars. It's overwhelming, to put it mildly."

"Oh, yes, I imagine it is," Veronica said reassuringly. "We here at R.T.A. work very hard to make sure that these indebted individuals are placed in the environment best suited for them. That way, as they work, they are maximizing their efforts and, in return, maximizing the financial dues that go back to the families."

Lindstrom's patience was wearing thin. "Veronica, let me put it to you another way. How in the hell was my ex-husband able to earn fifty-two grand working in prison? There's no way anyone could motivate him enough to help anyone except himself."

A deep sigh came through the speaker as Veronica said, "Ms. Lindstrom, everyone here at R.T.A. works very hard to make sure that every indebted individual, both men and women, are motivated to make sure they make a positive contribution to the families that they have injured by their actions." There was a brief pause, as a crackling noise came through the speaker. A few seconds passed, and then silence. Lindstrom and Engels exchanged glances.

"Veronica, are you there?" Lindstrom asked.

A cough came through the speaker, and Veronica said, "I wish I could answer all your questions right now, but my assistant has informed me that I have a family emergency I need to attend to." A sound like someone taking a drink was heard, another cough, and then, "Ms. Lindstrom, I apologize for the awkwardness of the last three days. I can personally vouch that the check you received today is valid. While the amount may seem excessive, I promise you that every dime of it came from your ex-husband's work and sacrifice while in our system. And, as I discussed with you on Sunday, the funds also include accumulated interest, since it was R.T.A.'s error that kept you from receiving the funds when you should have." Veronica coughed again, followed by another sound of drinking. "If you have any more immediate questions, you can access our website at www.R-T-A.org. Otherwise, I am afraid I really need to go." Her tone had changed from frantic to decisive, and then, finally, to heartfelt, as Veronica asked, "Will you be alright, Ms. Lindstrom?"

Lindstrom had more questions than answers, but she realized that she wasn't going to get them now. "Yes, I think I'll be okay. I will check out the website. Thank you, Veronica, and I hope everything is alright with your family."

"Thank you, Ms. Lindstrom. Take care!" A click, and the line went dead.

A pause filled the office, no one knowing what to say or even where to begin. Lindstrom walked to the window and looked outside, watching the noon rush hour go by below her. Tisdale sat in the chair. Finally, Engels was the first to speak up.

"Veronica sure knows how to talk. I'll give her that much."

Tisdale glanced at his boss with questioning look on his face. "What do you mean?"

"It's like they are empathic, anticipating how the conversation is going. They keep their tones, inflections, and cadence changing, depending on the emotions that are being displayed. I can only imagine how the first conversation with Veronica went. It was almost hypnotic." Engels rubbed the bridge of his nose with his right thumb and index finger.

"Look, I don't mean to be an ass," Tisdale said, looking from Engels to Lindstrom, "but what does it matter? You have been working hard raising three wonderful kids with absolutely no support. Now, someone comes along. They give you a large amount of money that they got out of your ex-husband. Not to sound petty, but if I was in your shoes, I'm thinking ka-ching! You know what they say about looking a gift horse in the mouth."

Lindstrom looked at Tisdale. "Look, I realize the money is heaven sent." She paused, let out a weary sigh, and continued. "The thing that bothers me the most is that I am going to cash that check and find out that the S.O.B. was behind this, that he somehow came into money and this is his way of sticking it to me." Tisdale frowned and opened his mouth to speak, but was cut off.

"Tish," Engels interjected, "if he wanted to stick it to you, he would have sent you a postcard from the Bahamas to rub it in your face. Even if he won a five-hundred million-dollar Powerball, why would he bother giving you fifty-two cents, much less fifty-two thousand?"

"Exactly," Tisdale exclaimed. "You're giving him way too much credit. You told me that you sent him to prison for abuse. Didn't you also tell me that he got out, shacked up with someone, and went right back to jail for violating his probation because he beat her, too? After that, you stopped keeping track. He's not some kind of master criminal. You're trying to paint him as George Clooney from 'Ocean's Eleven', when he's only a two-bit thug."

"I agree," Engels said. "Tisdale, I want you to pull up the jacket on her ex. Read only the highlights of his criminal history, incarcerations, and the like. Be back in fifteen minutes. Go."

"On it," Tisdale said, jumping out of the chair. He quickly left before Lindstrom could object. As Lindstrom turned to rage at Engels, he held up one hand to stop her and waved her behind his desk with the other.

"Before you get your Irish up, come over here and see what I've found," Engels said to her. Lindstrom walked to his side and looked at the website that Engels had pulled up. It was the homepage for R.T.A. It had rotating pictures of families playing outside, having dinner at a table, doing laundry, shoveling snow, and other family-friendly things that would make Norman Rockwell proud. Engels motioned for her to take the mouse, which she did. As she moved the mouse, a drop-down menu appeared. The options listed were HISTORY/ABOUT US, CONTACT US, and REPORT AN INDEBTED INDIVIDUAL. Lindstrom clicked on the CONTACT US link, and was brought to a standard email form. She backed out and clicked the link titled REPORT AN INDEBTED INDIVIDUAL. Another standard email form appeared, so she backed out again. Finally, she clicked on the HISTORY/ABOUT US link, and was brought to another beautiful webpage. Across the top of the page, the scroll read, "THANK YOU FOR INQUIRING ABOUT R.T.A.! ALL OF YOUR QUESTIONS WILL BE ANSWERED!" Lindstrom scrolled down, and they read the information together.

"R.T.A. stands for Rehabilitation Therapies and Associates. Our company was founded on the premise that indebted individuals have an obligation, not only to society in general, but to the families they left behind. We are a privately-owned company. Our sole focus is to take these individuals and nurture them in an environment where they can achieve the highest positive impact back to their families and the community. R.T.A. works with local, state, and national agencies to identify those indebted individuals that have the most potential to successfully make that positive impact. We at R.T.A. are proud of our history in turning around the lives of these indebted individuals and of the many positive effects that have been felt by the families and communities. If you would like more information on our history, our areas of expertise, or our areas of service, please click on the CONTACT US link on our home page."

Lindstrom had been hunched over, so she stood up and put her hands on her hips. "Not much to go on, is it?"

"Maybe not," Engels said, "but it hits some of the same talking points that you said Veronica laid out for you over the weekend." A knock came at the door, and Tisdale came in with one of the station's secure tablets.

"Here's what I pulled up," Tisdale said, handing the tablet to Engels. He saw the webpage for RTA was up and asked Engels and Lindstrom, "Mind if I look?"

"Go ahead," Lindstrom said. She walked back to the window, having no desire to take even a passing glance at her ex-husband's rap sheet. Her mind drifted back to the first time he had hit her.

It had been such a shock to Lindstrom. She had looked at him with a questioning terror in her eyes as she held her jaw. The look in his eyes immediately conveyed remorse, apology, and fear that it didn't even register with her at the time that this might happen again. He had backed away from her, dropped to his knees, and started whimpering, begging for her forgiveness. They both sat there on the floor for the longest time. She was trying to process the situation. What had she done? What should she do? She was thankful that Trevor, who was only three months old, was with Lindstrom's mother. Somehow, he had convinced her that it was a mistake, and that it would never happen again.

It wasn't until a few days after that first incident that he had started in with little comments, passive-aggressive statements, that were meant to shift the blame away from him. He insinuated that it had been her fault all along. She hadn't thought much of it at the time. Upon reflection, though, she realized that he said these things to make her believe that, if she "stepped out of line" again, he was within his right to "discipline" her. It was his prerogative to set her straight. Soon enough, she was pregnant again, this time with Bree, so she made every effort to be the young, dutiful wife.

Two months after Bree was born, Lindstrom had been cleaning and found a shoebox. When she opened it, she was shocked by what was inside. A Glock 9MM handgun, two wads of rolled-up fifty-dollar bills, and various bags and bottles containing pills, powders, and syringes. Using the computer that was in the living room, she typed in physical descriptions of what she found. Percocet, heroin, Adderall, Klonopin, Ecstasy, meth, and heroin all appeared to be present. And those were only the drugs she could describe into the computer's internet search engine.

Since he was at work, she hurriedly drove Trevor and Bree to her mother's and was back at home before he returned. She confronted him, and he snapped. He screamed at her, telling her it was none of her business what he did, and that she needed to remember her place, or else. His face was flush with rage, and he proceeded to break a lamp, several cupboards full of dishes, and the TV in the living room. When she tried to leave, he grabbed her by the arm, twisted her backwards, and pushed her hard, causing her to tumble over the kitchen table. She could feel where the glass from the broken dishes on the floor cut her arms, cheeks, and hands. As she struggled to stand up, he reached into the refrigerator, opened a bottle of beer, and drank half the bottle in one gulp. He glared at her, a sneer growing across his face.

"Remember your place, or next time it'll be you AND those fucking brats." He practically spat the words at her, his voice a mixture of daring and malevolence.

Something inside her exploded, and she knew what needed to be done. There were only two good things about the situation she was currently in. One was that he was on the other side of the kitchen, meaning she was two steps from the door to the backyard. She gave him a look unlike any other, and he openly mocked her.

"What? You think you're going to get tough with me, you stupid bitch? I'll do what I want, when I want, to whoever I want, and there's nothing you can do about it. Now start cleaning up this mess you made!" He finished his beer and threw the empty bottle at her, just as she turned for the back door. The bottle hit her in the back of the head and shattered, lodging glass in her head and hair. As she jumped off the small steps, she could hear him yelling after her. She heard what sounded like the kitchen table being thrown and broken. She took five giant steps, turned around, and fell to her knees. As he came flying out of the backdoor to give chase, he stopped, slipping backward and landing on his ass on the top step.

"FREEZE!", two voices had yelled at the same time.

The other good thing about the situation was she had the foresight to call the police. She had asked for a patrol car to be on standby, in case the situation deteriorated out of control. The officers parked down the block, saw him pull into the detached garage and walk into the house. Once he was inside, they had walked up to the house to watch and listen. They radioed for backup when they heard dishes breaking, and ran towards the back of the house, arriving as Lindstrom cleared the back door. Both officers had their weapons drawn and pointed.

172

"Tish," Engels said. Lindstrom immediately came back to the present and turned to look at her boss.

"Yeah?"

"I know your feelings about knowing his history. Considering what I've read, it isn't possible that your ex-husband somehow came up with an elaborate plan to trick you into getting fifty-two thousand dollars. Looking at all of this, I doubt he could figure out how to come up with fifty bucks."

"Besides," Tisdale interjected, "if he was giving you what he owed, plus extra, don't you think he would have brought the check himself? Or had a lawyer deliver it with something about how he wanted to get back into their lives and make up for lost time?"

Engels smiled and nodded at the observation. "That's a very good point, Tisdale."

Engels' opinion made Lindstrom feel a little better, because she didn't want to fall for some generosity scheme. She'd done so well with her children up to this point. Considering what she had been through on that fateful night, she would rather be living in a homeless shelter than take a dime that he freely gave to her. Was she being too proud? Maybe, but so what? She had done everything in her power to make sure Trevor and Bree had turned out to be decent human beings. She would be damned if one penny made its way into their lives that was part of a scheme, some kind of master plan on his part to worm his way back into their lives.

"Tish," Tisdale started, "I agree with the chief. The website looks on the up and up. There isn't much content to it, but it was created by Vectrom Utilities, which is well known for its web design and hosting. My guess is that R.T.A. wants to keep a low profile, considering the stigma surrounding for-profit prisons."

"Come again?" Engels asked Tisdale. "That's quite a leap you're making there."

"But Chief, it makes sense," Tisdale countered. "How else is someone that is in prison supposed to work the equivalent of a forty-hour work week while being paid white collar wages? To amass that kind of money while behind bars is unheard of. The only thing that makes sense is that R.T.A. is working as a for-profit prison. It seems to me that the only difference is that the actual profit is going towards a good cause. In these cases, to pay off delinquent child support."

Engels considered what Tisdale was saying, and it did make sense.

"The woman on the phone said as much, that this company works to maximize what each individual can offer." There was a buzzing, and Engels reached for his cell phone.

"Well," Lindstrom said, "what do I do now?"

Engels looked at her and said, "You grab your purse and that check, and we'll stop by your bank on the way to Sanford Hospital." Lindstrom and Tisdale looked at Engels, a measure of happiness in their eyes. "That's right. Nathan Devlin is conscious. Andy's text says to drive slow, so he can be ready for questions when we get there."

FOURTEEN

Lindstrom tried talking her way out of going to the bank, but Engels wasn't listening. A check for fifty-two thousand dollars doesn't show up every day. Besides, Engels reasoned, Andy's text had specifically said to take some time getting to the hospital. Before Engels and Lindstrom left the station, Engels told Tisdale to remain. Tisdale started to protest, but Engels told him to work the background on Ronald Vance. It was imperative to establish any connection to Nathan or Allison Devlin. Tisdale looked disappointed, but he did as he was instructed.

Engels drove Lindstrom to the federal credit union that was associated with the police department, which was located only six blocks from the police station. He parked, and they walked in together. For early afternoon on a Monday, there was only one other customer in the lobby.

"They look pretty busy," Lindstrom said. "We'd better come back."

Engels looked at her with amusement. "If it wouldn't work on you with your kids, it's not going to work with me. Now, quit stalling and pick a window."

Lindstrom walked up to a window with a teller she didn't know. She didn't want any small talk, considering she was cashing a check of such large proportions. She looked behind her, and saw Engels sit in a chair, shooing her forward while he reached for a magazine. Lindstrom turned back toward the teller's window and stepped forward.

"Good afternoon, my name is Paige! How can I help you today?"

Lindstrom set her purse down on the floor, pulling out her wallet in the process. "Yes, I have a check that I would like to deposit." She took her driver's license, debit card, and the check from her wallet, placing them on the counter in front of Paige. She also took out her police ID, setting it on the counter as well. Paige smiled at her.

"I can absolutely help you with that," Paige said as she examined the identification that was in front of her. Lindstrom signed the back of the check, trying to keep her hands from shaking. She slid the check across to Paige, face down. Paige had finished typing on her keyboard, and, as she picked up the check, she said to Lindstrom, "Can you verify your information on the keypad, please?"

Lindstrom took the attached stylus and started tapping the prompts on the keypad. When she was done, she looked at Paige, who had the check in her hand. Paige seemed to be frozen in place as she was looking at the check. When she realized that she wasn't doing anything, Paige recovered and looked at Lindstrom. "Um, if you'll excuse me for a moment. Due to the size amount of the check, I need to get my manager's approval."

"No, I completely understand," Lindstrom said, trying not to sound annoyed. She knew that the check would need to be approved, but Lindstrom didn't want the added attention. She watched Paige walk away and turned to see Engels still sitting in the chair in the open lobby. He was pretending to read a magazine. However, Lindstrom could tell he was trying to suppress his laughter. "What the hell is so funny," Lindstrom asked, probably a little too loudly.

"It's a good thing that the police are here," Engels said, pointing at his chest, "because if you're going to get arrested for trying to cash that check, the response time will be nothing flat!"

Lindstrom didn't want to give Engels the satisfaction, so she scowled at him and said, "You make a move, porky, and I'll out-draw, out-gun, and out-fight you every step of the way. You'll go home and have to explain to Diane how I kicked your ass." That was too much, as Engels erupted, laughing out loud, as heads started turning toward him, trying to figure out what was going on.

Lindstrom was trying not to join in, so she said, "Good god, I can't take you anywhere," turning back to the teller's window. Engels was still chuckling away behind her.

Lindstrom looked down the counter to see Paige standing in the manager's doorway. The manager, whose name she couldn't remember, was standing behind his desk, and looking at the check. He looked it over, then put it into a check reader on his desk. After the check went through, the manager typed a few things on his keyboard, and looked at his screen. He took the check, looked it over again, looked at his screen, gave the check back to Paige, and said something as he sat back down. Paige turned around and came back to her window, smiling.

"Okay," Paige said, "I'm sorry for the delay! We had to verify it was an authentic cashier's check, and that the funds were available." Paige put the check through her own reader, and asked, "Will you need any cash back today?"

Lindstrom pondered the question, not knowing what to say. This whole situation felt like a dream. From the beginning, a mere forty-eight hours ago, discovering she had this money, to having the money show up, finding out the amount of the money, and now, the check was good. This bank teller was now asking if she wanted any money back. Lindstrom closed her eyes, rubbing them with her palms. She was still feeling conflicted about the whole thing. Her thoughts and emotion about this predicament were starting to affect her. She felt like she was going to hyperventilate.

"Detective, are you alright?" Paige looked concerned. Lindstrom stood there, her hands still over her eyes. She then realized that someone was standing behind her. A large hand was on her shoulder.

"Tish, it's okay." It was Engels.

Lindstrom took her hands away, looked at Paige, and said, "Yes, I'm sorry." She cleared her throat with a small cough, and asked, "Um, yes, can you give me a thousand dollars? Five one hundred-dollar bills, eight fifty-dollar bills, and the rest in twenties." Paige, still with a concerned look on her face, opened her cash drawer and started counting out the money that Lindstrom had requested. Once she had everything, Paige counted the money back to Lindstrom, and then put the bills into a self-sealing envelope.

"Okay, here is your cash, as well as your driver's license, your police ID, and your debit card," Paige said, trying to sound cheerful, but still with an uneasy look on her face. "Is there anything else I can help you with today?"

"No, thank you, though," Lindstrom said. She put the envelope, her cards, and her wallet in her purse, turned, and started walking out of the bank. Engels removed his hand from her shoulder as she walked away. Once she was through the lobby doors and outside, Engels turned to Paige and smiled.

"Thank you," Engels said to Paige. "It's been a rough couple of days for her."

With that, Engels turned and followed Lindstrom out the door. She was waiting at the car, and Engels clicked the unlock button on his key fob, so she could get in. Once they were both in the car and buckled up, Engels looked straight ahead and asked, "You okay?"

"I guess I'm as good as any person that cashed a fifty-two thousand-dollar check. Now let's go see the Devlin's." As Engels turned the key in the ignition, Lindstrom had opened her purse, putting her cards back in order inside her wallet. She then opened up the envelope that Paige had given her, shoved two twenties into her pants pocket, and put the rest of the cash in her wallet. She closed her wallet, put it inside her purse, and set her purse on the floor between her feet. By the time Lindstrom had finished organizing her belongs, Engels had driven them two blocks away from the credit union.

They were silent all the way to Sanford Hospital. There wasn't really anything to say at this point, so Engels turned on the radio and let the all-80's station fill the void. It took about thirty minutes to get from the credit union, through midtown traffic, then through the road construction between Tenth and Fourteenth streets, which was concerned with relocating train tracks and the expansion of the bridge over those train tracks. Finally, they reached Sanford Hospital.

They parked in the large four-story garage, with Lindstrom securing her purse in the car's trunk. It took them another fifteen minutes to navigate their way from the parking garage, through multiple hallways and doors, into the hospital's main lobby, where they approached the receptionist's desk. There was a large group of people, both women and men, standing around the reception area. Some had tablets or phones out, three were standing next to hand carts that had plastic toolboxes, while two more were climbing ladders.

Engels waited until a receptionist freed herself from the confusion, when he identified himself with his police badge, and politely asked for Nathan Devlin's room number. The receptionist didn't flinch, typing in the name while looking at the badge. She wrote down the room number and wished them a great day.

"Busy morning," Lindstrom queried the receptionist.

"Something happened with the construction at the cancer center across the street. Certain areas of the hospital have limited or no WIFI coverage." The receptionist smiled, looking past Engels and Lindstrom to the couple that was waiting behind them. Not missing the cue, they made their way to the elevators.

Almost fifty minutes since they had left the police station, the elevator doors opened onto the third floor. Both Nathan and Allison Devlin, somehow, were on the same floor, only a few rooms apart and across the hall from each other.

As Engels and Lindstrom turned the corner from the elevators and entered that floor's waiting area, they immediately spotted Ben McKinley and Andy Cole, Nathan's friends. Ben and Andy stood up and moved to intercept Engels and Lindstrom. This can't be good, Engels thought to himself.

"Gentlemen," Lindstrom said, "I take it you have some bad news?"

"In a way," Andy said. "I tried calling you, but my cell phone and WIFI reception haven't been working very well in the hospital. I called Officer Tisdale on a courtesy phone, but I guess he didn't reach you before you got here."

Engels and Lindstrom both took out their cell phones and looked at them. Neither phone had a signal, either to a cell tower or to a WIFI connection. Lindstrom put her cell back in her pocket and said, "Well, we didn't get the memo, but no harm done. Now, what's going on?"

"Nathan's doctor wants to keep him calm until his body stabilizes."

"Stabilizes?" Engels looked confused. "I thought he had regained consciousness?"

"Look, I don't get it either," Ben snapped. "Sit tight, and I'll get the nurse or the doctor or whomever is in charge around here to explain it." He stormed off briskly, leaving Andy to stand in front of Engels and Lindstrom, shaking his head.

"You look upset," Lindstrom whispered to Andy, loud enough for only the three of them to hear. Andy stood there, a twisted, almost bizarre expression on his face. Lindstrom couldn't determine what emotions were on Andy's face. Perhaps he was feeling a strong cocktail of many emotions, all at the same time. It was strange, to say the least.

"The doctor doesn't even want Nathan to know that Allison is here," Andy replied to both Lindstrom and Engels."

"What?" Engels sounded irritated, his voice louder than he meant it to be.

"The doctor says he doesn't think Nathan's system can take it."

"The man is awake, but he can't even see his wife?"

A voice from behind Engels said, "His wife, his kids, even these two endearing gentlemen haven't seen him. Even when this big one here threatened to send me through that window to your left, I still told them absolutely no visitors."

Engels and Lindstrom turned around to see Ben standing next to an older-looking gentleman, possibly in his fifties.

"You're just lucky I don't want to spend the night in jail, doc," Ben said, walking past him and sitting down on one of the couches next to everyone.

"You must be Nathan Devlin's doctor," Lindstrom chimed in.

"Doctor," Engels began, "my name is Brad Engels, and I'm the Chief of Police. Can you please tell me what's going on with our victim?"

Lindstrom noticed that Engels said, "Chief of Police", instead of his usual "Chief of Detectives" title. Only a few hours ago, he introduced himself to Leslie Arndt as the chief of detectives. She made a mental note of it.

"Chief Engels," the doctor started, "I am Dr. Preston. I appreciate that you need to talk to Mr. Devlin, especially considering the circumstances from early this morning. My concern is what's still in his body."

"Go on. What are we looking at?"

"Officer Tisdale told the admitting doctor that there was a good chance Mr. Devlin had ingested flunitrazepam, or what is commonly called a roofie or a date rape drug."

"That's correct."

"Let me ask you, when do you think Mr. Devlin went missing?"

Lindstrom said, "The evidence suggests he was taken last Monday evening."

"Then we have a serious problem," the doctor said. "Drugs, like rohypnol, aka roofies, are like most any other drug. After it enters the body, the drug does what it was designed to do. Eventually, the body breaks it down, the affects wear off, and the body removes the drug's properties in the form of waste. After we did our first blood panel, we found some of the components still in his body."

"After a week, he still has roofies in his system?" Engels asked, shocked.

"The components of the drug, yes," the doctor continued. "But it's more complicated than that. Mr. Devlin also has components of an anesthetic, a paralytic, antibiotics, morphine, an antiviral, and even antipsychotics. Strangely enough, he also has diuretics and masking agents in his system."

Andy had sat back down next to Ben, his head in his hands. Ben put his arm around him and rubbed his shoulders gently, trying to be supportive.

Engels' gaze went from Dr. Preston to Lindstrom and back again. "Doc," he started slowly, "you're telling me that whoever kidnapped Nathan Devlin pumped him full of drugs, and then tried to get them cleared out?"

"It would seem so," Dr. Preston replied.

"Alright, so what happens now?" Engels needed to move this along. Under most circumstances, he was a patient man. Regrettably, with everything that had occurred since the previous Wednesday, his tolerance was wearing thin.

"You don't seem to understand, or even appreciate, the gravity of this situation. I've never seen anything like this in any medical context. If you've ever talked to your pharmacist when you pick up a prescription, they tell you not to mix certain drugs with certain foods or drinks, or even with other drugs, because of the potential side effects. Frankly, I'm surprised Mr. Devlin is still breathing after having this kind of pharmaceutical cocktail in his system."

"When can we talk to him," Lindstrom asked. "I don't want to put undue pressure on you, but we have a victim that was kidnapped for no ransom, two dead bodies directly linked to Devlin, and the person behind this is still out there."

Dr. Preston sighed. "The dire nature of the situation is not lost on me. I also appreciate your duties here, officers. Under ordinary circumstances, we would start him on dialysis and get his system flushed out. The thing that worries me is the presence of antipsychotics. These can have lasting effects on the body and, more importantly, the mind. When Mr. Devlin first regained consciousness, he was instantly on edge, agitated, like he was being pumped full of adrenaline. We had to sedate him and secure him in restraints, so he wouldn't hurt himself or anyone else." The doctor paused to let that information sink in. The silence seemed to consume everyone in the room at once. Preston glanced around to all four of them, and then continued.

"Please, give us the night to monitor his condition and get a handle on what we're dealing with. From what Mr. Devlin's friends have told me," Preston motioned towards Andy and Ben, "he is a recovering alcoholic. We have to be careful as we attempt to clean out his system. If we push things too hard, his liver might fail, or he might go into renal shock from all the waste being shunted through his kidneys. We are going to do the very best we can for Mr. Devlin. I will let you know immediately if anything changes. Otherwise, you will be my first call at nine tomorrow morning. Now, if you'll excuse me." Dr. Preston turned around, walking back down the hall, and disappeared around the corner.

Engels headed to the hospital's lobby to use a courtesy phone to call the police station. Meanwhile, Lindstrom had taken Ben and Andy to the hospital's cafeteria. She figured the two of them needed some time to decompress. She bought them lunch, trying to change the subject. Ben ate his food in a ravenous manner. Andy, though, sat there, solemn, picking around the food on his plate. People dealt with dire situations differently, and while Ben seemed to be an overly-aggressive optimist, Andy looked like this was one more piece of bad news that he didn't know how to deal with. Hopefully, Lindstrom thought, he'll be able to work through this and get over it.

As they sat there, a woman came into the cafeteria, saw Andy, and ran up to him. "Oh, honey, I'm so sorry! Are you okay?" She threw her arms around him and held him tight.

Lindstrom looked at them, and once he was free from her grip, Andy said, "Yes, I'm fine. Dear, this is Detective Lindstrom. Detective Lindstrom, this is my wife, Heidi Cole."

Lindstrom stood up, held out her hand, and said, "Please, call me Tish. It's a pleasure to meet you."

Heidi shook Lindstrom's hand in a deliberate, one stroke movement.

She then said in a curt, almost cold, manner, "Likewise." She then returned her attention to Andy. "Does Allison know yet?"

"I doubt it, considering that doctor up there," Ben said sarcastically. Lindstrom could tell that Ben wasn't endearing himself to anyone, and that it was probably time to make an exit.

"I hate to pay for lunch and run," Lindstrom said as she stood up from the cafeteria table, "but I need to get back to the station. Ben, Andy, please let us know if anything happens overnight. And please, try to get some rest. I will see you both tomorrow. Heidi, take care of them both."

Lindstrom pushed in her chair and bussed her tray. As she set her tray on top of a stack of other dirty trays, Lindstrom glanced back towards the table. What she saw was odd. Ben had moved, now sitting at the table next to Heidi and Andy. Heidi was now seated next to Andy yet positioned in such a way that her back was to Ben. Essentially, from Lindstrom's perspective, it had the appearance of Heidi acting as a wall between her husband and Ben. Lindstrom turned back and made her way to the lobby. Engels was sitting on one of the big couches in the entry, looking at his cell. When he saw Lindstrom walking up to him, he stood up.

"How are they doing," Engels asked.

"Ben is holding up like a slab of granite. Andy is another story, though. At least Andy's wife is here to help."

"Andy's wife, what was her name again? Heidi, right?"

"Yes sir. Heidi is her name. C'mon, let's get back to the station."

They walked back to the parking garage in silence. Both Engels and Lindstrom were lost in their respective thoughts. It wasn't until Engels had them almost halfway back to the station that one of them broke the silence.

"Are we missing something," Engels wondered aloud as he slowed the car to a stop at a red light.

"You're damn right we are," Lindstrom confirmed. "In fact, we're missing a lot of somethings." She rubbed her temples, followed by moving her head in a circular motion. Her neck cracked several times, which helped ease the pressure she was feeling.

"The problem is," Lindstrom continued, "until we can talk to Nathan Devlin and get a better idea of what was going on from his perspective, we're going to have to keep working this puzzle without knowing what the final picture is supposed to be."

Tisdale was disappointed that the chief had ordered him to stay behind. However, he also realized that, on a case like this, with multiple threads, each one of those threads needed to be pulled. He had spent the better part of the afternoon working on the history of Ronald Vance, the man that had committed suicide rather than be arrested for the kidnapping of Nathan Devlin. So far, his history read like any other petty criminal. His life had been filled with too many mistakes and bad choices. He was reaching for the telephone to call Engels, when he spotted him walking towards his office.

"Chief!", Tisdale shouted towards him as he stood up from his desk.

Engels acknowledged the shout, pointing towards his office, and replied, "Ten minutes."

Tisdale nodded, sat back down, and began gathering the file that he had worked on. Meanwhile, Engels went into his office, walking straight to the windows that faced south. He began a slow process of stretching his arms, neck, and back. Suddenly, he was aware that he needed to use the restroom. Once he returned to his office, he sat down at his desk, rubbing his eyes, temples, and neck. A soft knock interrupted his attempt to unwind.

Tisdale was standing in the entrance to the office. He had been standing there for a minute, not really knowing how to approach his boss. Finally, he had knocked softly. Once Engels opened his eyes and peered at him, Tisdale spoke.

"Everything okay, chief?"

"Sometimes, with this job, there seems to be more bad than good."

Tisdale didn't know how to respond, so he repeated himself. "Um, I'm not sure you answered the question. Is everything okay?"

Engels didn't need a counseling session. As he continued rubbing his head and neck, he posed a question. "I take it that, since you aren't bursting forth with information to break the case wide open, that the life of Ronald Vance has yielded nothing but dead ends and false hope?"

"I'm sorry to say it, chief, but he was just a crook." He set the file down on Engels' desk. "Lots of priors, mostly B&E, one armed robbery, grand theft, the usual. He was a loner, though, so how he factors into an elaborate kidnapping is anyone's guess."

"Any outstanding warrants?" Engels was done massaging the various parts of his head and was now looking at the file Tisdale had placed on his desk, not sure if he wanted to open it or not.

"For the last three plus years, Mr. Vance had been clean. Up until eighteen months ago, he even had a job as a delivery man. I talked to his boss, and she said Vance had never missed a day and never caused any problems. Then, one day, he came in and said he needed to quit. No explanation, just up and left." Tisdale looked at Engels. He merely sat there, staring at the folder. "Chief, seriously. For the third time, is everything okay?"

Engels looked up at Tisdale and smiled wearily.

He stood up, tapped the folder lightly with his fingers, and said, "Everything will be better after I get a good night's sleep. If there is nothing earth shattering in here, I am going to leave it for tomorrow." As he walked around the desk towards the door, he waved for Tisdale to lead the way. "I already sent Tish home early, so why don't you take off. Relax, grab a bite to eat, and come back tomorrow refreshed." As Engels turned off the light in his office and locked the door, he said, "Oh, by the way, Tish wanted me to give you this." Engels reached into his pocket, pulled out something, and put it in Tisdale's hand. Tisdale looked at a hundred-dollar bill, folded twice. He looked at Engels.

"Chief," Tisdale started, "you know I can't…"

Engels held up a hand. "Tish said if you refused, that I was supposed to shoot you, and trust me, that's not how I want to end my day. She insisted I take one, too, so that I could take Diane out for a nice meal this weekend. Spend it, don't spend it, I don't care. In her own words, 'shut up, take it, and be happy'." Engels patted Tisdale on the shoulder and said, "Good night," and walked away.

Tisdale stood there, unfolding the hundred-dollar bill. He examined it, admiring the anti-counterfeiting measures, the details on Andrew Jackson's portrait, the texture of the bill itself. It felt odd to accept money in this way, especially knowing some of Lindstrom's history and current circumstances. Maybe this was Tish's way of dealing with this strange situation. He re-folded the bill twice, took out his wallet, and put the bill between his library card and his dental insurance card. If he ever needed it, he had it.

As he walked back to the desk to collect his things for the night, Tisdale wondered if he should call Tish. No, that would be awkward. They weren't friends. They were barely colleagues at this point. He was an officer, she was a detective, and Engels was their superior. The chief was right. It was better to get some rest and continue to hammer away at this thing tomorrow.

"Tisdale!" The voice startled him, and he turned to see Officer Tavon coming towards him.

"I'm heading out. What's up?"

"Have you seen Lindstrom anywhere," Tavon asked.

"Chief Engels said he let her go home early, before he bailed for the day, too." Tisdale quickly added, "Anything I can help you with?"

"No, I was going to give her an update. And you said the chief left already?"

"Yep, you just missed him."

"Okay, well, that hot reporter chick, Kendra, had some video sent over from Devlin's escape, or whatever it was. What should I do with them?"

"Bag them as evidence and get them secured. Engels and Tish can look at them tomorrow."

"All right." With that, Tavon was gone, and Tisdale headed home for the night.

FIFTEEN

Lindstrom was surprised that neither Trevor or Bree were at home. She had pulled up to the garage to find Trevor's vehicle gone. Upon entering the house, she found it to be empty, except for the cat. She looked at her phone. No text messages from either of her oldest children. She shook her head. Typical teenagers, she sighed to herself. Then again, she thought to herself, maybe I shouldn't be too hasty. She checked her calendar on her phone to see if she had missed something. Trevor should have taken Ryan to martial arts, and, judging from the time on the car's dashboard, class would be starting in two minutes. Bree had oral interpretation after school, with cheerleading practice to follow. She wouldn't be home until much later.

Lindstrom left the car in the driveway and walked into the house through the garage. She took in the silence of the house for a few minutes. She set her purse down on a kitchen counter and looked out the window to the backyard. Even with everything that had happened with regards to the case since the early morning, her thoughts kept moving back to one thing. More precisely, to fifty-two thousand things. She couldn't decide whether she should feel elated or pissed. Her mind couldn't figure out how a convicted, violent felon, in prison for how many years, would be able to work enough to make that much money, and in such a short amount of time. Should she have vetted this R.T.A. more before accepting the check? Should she have declined the check? Maybe she should have ripped up the letter, with the check inside, without ever looking inside?

Lindstrom shook her head. This was getting her nowhere. She grabbed the cordless phone and started dialing Veronica's number at R.T.A.

The line rang three times, and after the usual call routing, Lindstrom was treated to the sound of Veronica's voice. "Ms. Lindstrom, what an unexpected pleasure this fine evening! How can I help you?"

"Wow, I wasn't expecting you to pick up. Don't you ever go home?"

"To be truthful, due to the nature of R.T.A.'s business, and the clientele we strive to serve, even if I am not in the office, the call will be routed to my mobile device."

Lindstrom was impressed. "Doesn't that get a little awkward, with calls coming in at unwanted times?" Lindstrom heard something that sounded like a "tsk, tsk" come through the phone.

"Now, Ms. Lindstrom, I'm sure you didn't call to inquire about me." The ease with which Veronica changed her vocal patterns continued to amaze Lindstrom. Engels was right. Veronica must have been trained to adjust her voice as each situation warranted. "Am I correct in assuming that you are still having reservations regarding your payment?"

"The payment, the letter, the whole situation." Lindstrom cleared her voice. "Quite honestly, I am in utter shock at the amount of the check. Let me be frank with you, Veronica. After I sent my ex-husband to jail, I never once followed up on where he was or what he was doing. I made sure that I had a protection order against him. Sure, I would've loved to have had the financial support, but I gave up on that dream a long time ago. Somehow, I fell in love again, re-married, and had another child. Through everything, through the ups and downs of raising three children on a police officer's salary, I made it work. Suddenly, boom, like a thunder blast out of nowhere, you call and tell me that my ex has been put to work behind bars. On top of that, the money he made is coming to me. Now, here I am, two days later, and I have a check for fifty-two thousand dollars. Forgive me for being blunt, but I deal with bullshit in my job every day. I can't even begin to believe that any of this is possible."

"Ms. Lindstrom," Veronica began in a very matter-of-fact tone, "rest assured, we deal with this kind of thing all the time. You are not the first spouse or guardian, if I may paraphrase your own words, 'to call bullshit on this situation'. R.T.A. works hard, at all levels of the organization, to make sure that all of the indebted individuals in its care are tasked appropriately to make proper restitutions to any and all parties involved."

"But how is that even possible? Even if my ex started working with R.T.A. from his first day in jail, and even with accumulated interest, a check for fifty-two thousand dollars after fifteen plus years is damn near impossible to comprehend!" Lindstrom felt like screaming. She kept asking the same question, but Veronica or R.T.A. didn't give any kind of concrete response. It was all words, repackaged and told back to the person that was asking. Like a smooth-talking politician, it was a non-answer answer, designed to assuage fear and put the mind at ease. It was infuriating to Lindstrom.

"That would be true," Veronica countered, calm and cool, "if they were being paid by the state, or even being told the truth."

Lindstrom was stunned into silence. Had she heard correctly? "I'm sorry," Lindstrom said. "You're telling me that R.T.A. is lying to these men?"

"And women, Ms. Lindstrom."

Lindstrom was taken aback by those last four words. They had come out a little too hasty, with a hint of sarcasm. It was the first time that Veronica's speech pattern slipped, even a little bit. "Fine, whatever. R.T.A. is lying to men AND women, trying to make a few dollars?"

A deep sigh came through the phone. "Ms. Lindstrom," Veronica began, "we here at R.T.A. are not ignorant to the ways of the world." The tone of her voice was back to changing as she needed it to change. "For that matter, we also realize that these indebted individuals, mostly male and yes, some female as well, we recognize them for who, and what, they are. Felons. Criminals. The overwhelming majority of them would not, as you have said in the past, work hard for anyone but themselves. As a police officer, are you familiar with for-profit prisons?"

"Yes I am." Lindstrom knew that there were two major companies that operated about one hundred and thirty for-profit prisons in the United States. She had heard the debates about these institutions, the pros and cons from all sides. However, she tried not to wade into it. Her job was catching the bad guys. After that, it was up to the lawyers, the judges, and the juries.

"Well, R.T.A. was founded on the same principle of for-profit prisons, but with a twist. What good would it be to have these individuals make money for themselves? For that matter, why should a felon work hard to make a corporation money? R.T.A. identifies individuals that are incarcerated or about to be incarcerated, that have an outstanding debt to a spouse and or child. R.T.A. arranges a private interview with the indebted individual. During this interview, the individual is given a choice. He or she can choose to go to a state-run prison facility or be incarcerated at an R.T.A. facility. R.T.A. is portrayed as an alternative. Why not make an honest living, only without the temptations of everyday life? They are promised better living conditions, with the only stipulations being that they don't cause problems and work hard. They are promised that all the money they make will be set aside in interest-bearing accounts, stocks, bonds, anything that can maximize their effectiveness. Finally, upon completion of their full prison term, they are told that all the money they have earned, with interest, will be waiting for them. To my knowledge, we've never had an individual that didn't accept R.T.A.'s offer."

Lindstrom was feeling equal parts amazement and befuddlement. "And what happens on the day when one of these felons get out and find out that they have been lied to? What does R.T.A. do then?"

"Absolutely nothing. You see, even though R.T.A. has been in business for around twenty-five years, no indebted individual has ever been released. A few violate the terms of their contract with R.T.A., at which point they are sent back to standard correctional facilities. However, most have such long prison sentences ahead of them that they will be with us for the duration of their terms. It is made quite clear to them that there is no parole, no release for good behavior. You may find it cruel, maybe even inhumane, but we don't. Considering what these people have done, we feel that our way is the best way to turn around a bad situation."

This was getting too much for Lindstrom to process. What was her responsibility here? If her ex had worked for this money, she had every right to a share of it. On a deeper level, it felt incredibly wrong. She should only be entitled to the amount owed her and the kids, maybe with a little bit of interest. This wasn't like a cop show on television, where the detective fudged the truth to get a confession. Then again, she had never been put in a situation where she had to make that kind of choice. Maybe she was feeling some pangs of her church upbringing. This felt like "an-eye-for-an-eye", and she wasn't sure if she wanted to be a part of this.

"Ms. Lindstrom, are you still there?"

Lindstrom snapped back to reality. "I wasn't expecting all of this, the size of the check, the reality behind R.T.A., it's all a lot to take in and process."

There were a few seconds of silence, and Veronica started speaking, slowly and softly, like she was trying to reassure an injured animal to come out of a hiding place.

"Ms. Lindstrom, I understand how you must feel. Believe me, I was once on the other end of this phone call." Lindstrom heard Veronica take in a deep breath. "My mother was a piece of work. My father, though, was a good man, an honest man, and he tried his best when it came to me and my siblings. Unfortunately, for every good thing he tried to do, my mother would do five bad things. Somehow, through the late-night police raids, the trials, the divorce, the brutal custody battles, incredibly, I came through it. I started working at victim's shelters. I worked with law offices dedicated to family issues. Anywhere that I felt I could make a positive difference with families, I was there. One day, many years ago, I happened across my mother. She didn't recognize me, and for that, I am grateful. What we do at R.T.A. has nothing to do with vindictiveness or spite. We do this because, for every criminal that has done something wrong, it's not only the victim that they have wronged, but those closest to him or her as well. Family and friends feel these burdens, too. As I said earlier, if we at R.T.A. can turn a negative into a positive, that is what is important."

Lindstrom thought about what Veronica had said. Lindstrom had taken some beatings and vowed to never be in that position again. Veronica had lived through this kind of thing from an early age, apparently. Who knows how many more mothers and fathers out there could use this kind of help to keep their families going. She was about to say something, when she heard a car pull into the driveway, and saw Trevor parking his car next to her's. The parking lights had barely gone off when Ryan had jumped out of the backseat, ran into the house, yelling.

"Momma, you're home!" He jumped into her arms, almost causing her to drop the phone. "I missed you today, Momma!"

Veronica's voice came through the phone. "Is that your littlest one?"

"That is a solid affirmative," Lindstrom said, wondering if Veronica could see or hear the smile that was across her face with Ryan in her arms.

"Ms. Lindstrom, I can't tell you what to do or how to feel. From personal experience with other spouses, guardians, and children I have had the pleasure to encounter, I can safely say that the vast majority of people make some kind of peace with their situation. I can tell you that, whether you accept or use the money or not, that is entirely up to you. I am sure you have a lovely family. It is unfortunate what happened in your life. You have turned negatives into positives. Keep loving your family and working hard for them, and everything will work out. Might I suggest you take them out for dinner tonight?"

"That sounds like a great idea," Lindstrom said, as Trevor walked into the kitchen. "Anybody want to go out to eat tonight?" Ryan and Trevor both exploded with delight, as Ryan wiggled out of his mother's arms and ran off to change out of his martial arts clothes.

"I hope I've helped, Ms. Lindstrom," Veronica said. "You have a great night." Lindstrom heard a click, and the line went dead.

"Who was that," Trevor asked.

"I'm not really sure," Lindstrom responded. She looked at the phone for a moment before Trevor spoke again.

"So, where're we eating?"

"Really? That's the most I get? No 'hi Mom', no 'how was your day, Mom'?"

"Look Mom," Trevor said, an exasperated look on his face. "I'm starving. Can't we just get going to wherever we're going?"

Lindstrom knew her son meant well. He was intelligent and had grown taller than she was. The only downside were his emotions, or lack thereof. She figured that, as a teenager, graduating early and joining the Air Force, he needed to get out of the house to turn him into a well-rounded young man.

"Fine, but I'm expecting at least one 'please', 'thank you', and 'I love you' before the night is over."

"Jeez, Mom, or else what?"

Lindstrom let a smirk come over her face. "Or else, we won't be talking about this different vehicle you've been pestering me about."

Trevor's eyebrows perked up, a rare grin coming across his face. "Mom, you'd better not be playing around here."

He had been working hard, driving tractor and combines at a few local farms. He had also been hired to drive a snowplow when the winter season eventually hit. All of his money went into his savings, but he was still short of what he needed to buy a different vehicle. The truck Trevor was currently driving had been Mark's, but it had seen better days, even before Mark's, well, "situation". It was his goal to be able to work enough and have enough money saved that, when he found the truck he wanted, he would be able to trade in Mark's old truck and payoff the rest. For a seventeen-year old that would be going out into the world in a matter of months, he wanted nothing to do with a car loan. Lindstrom had always admired his son's drive and initiative.

Lindstrom smiled, grabbed her purse, and, as Ryan came running out of his room, said, "How about we talk about the extra money you need over dinner?"

SIXTEEN

Engels was surprisingly refreshed after getting an excellent night's sleep. His day began when he was wide awake at six. He decided to make breakfast for Diane before she woke up. He was feeling good about what the day would bring, arriving at the police station and being in his office before seven-thirty. Engels quickly went through his messages, as they were mostly minor items. He had been reading the file on Ronald Vance for about fifteen minutes when everyone seemed to show up at once.

"Come on in," Engels said, doing a head count. Good, everyone was here. "I hope everybody got some rest last night, because we are going to hammer this thing hard and fast today." He looked to his right. "Tish, I want you to go over Officer Tavon's findings regarding any medical outfit that might have heard of HealthStar Ambulatory Services." Lindstrom nodded at Tavon, and they left the office. "Officers Gilbride and Jefferson, the videos from the television crews are set up in Conference Room Three. Start going over them and see if anything or anyone catches your eye." Gilbride and Jefferson turned and left. "Jerry, work your forensic mojo. Go over everything related to the dead woman, Ronald Vance, the empty house, whatever you can think of. Anything that seems out of place, get it down on a report." Jerry left the office. "Tisdale, have a seat." Tisdale sat down.

"What's up, chief," Tisdale asked.

"Have you tracked down any of Ronald Vance's next of kin?"

Tisdale shook his head. "According to his file, Vance was an only child. His mother died in labor. His father died of pneumonia when Vance was ten. There were no relatives to take guardianship, so Vance became a foster child. In and out of trouble, juvenile detentions, mostly petty stuff, all things considered. He was never married, but he did have a daughter with a woman by the name of Natalie Gaines. Since Vance was in and out of jail, delinquent child support became another line on his rap sheet. Gaines died in a car accident when Vance's daughter was seven. The courts ordered the daughter to be raised by Gaines' sister."

Engels continued looking through the file. "Any history of violence?"

"None at all. Vance's criminal history seems strangely subdued. Burglary, theft, breaking and entering. As far as I can tell, though, he never pulled a gun or raised a fist."

"A criminal that's a pacifist?" Engels was thinking out loud, comparing what he had been reading in Vance's file to what Tisdale had told him.

"It would explain why he kept on getting out of jail early due to good behavior. Vance wasn't violent, maybe only troubled."

"What about his most recent job, as a delivery driver?"

"For a company called VMS. It stands for Visceral Medical Supplies. The company buys and sells all kinds of medical parts and supplies, from bed pans and tongue depressors to advanced diagnostic computers and scanners. According to the company, there were never any issues with missing inventory or fudged numbers while Vance was employed there. He kept to himself, never caused a problem. Apparently, it was quite a shock when he came in and quit."

Engels set the file down, leaned back in his chair, and rubbed his chin. "So, how does a low-key criminal like Ronald Vance go from being in and out of jail, to finding a steady job, to quitting that same job, and then killing himself in front of the police in a busted kidnapping scheme?" Engels gazed out the window of his office, looking at how the sun was rising over the rooftops. "Do we have his last known address?"

"Vance listed an apartment in the industrial park, but the manager said he hadn't lived there in over a year. Whatever Vance got mixed up in, he quit his job and moved out at the same time. He hasn't been seen or heard from until yesterday." Tisdale shifted in his seat. He felt he had put together a pretty comprehensive jacket on Ronald Vance.

"What about Vance's family? You said he had a daughter?"

"That's correct," Tisdale replied. "I called the aunt in Greeley, Colorado. After the sister's death, and with the court's help, the aunt tracked Vance down in Kentucky. Vance took the news that he had not only fathered a child but that the mother was dead incredibly matter-of-factly. Vance signed over all his parental rights to the aunt, never once asking to see his own daughter."

"What about child support? Surely, the aunt wouldn't have let him off the hook so easy."

"Vance must have felt some kind of responsibility. The aunt said that the court established a bank account for the girl, with the aunt as a trustee. Every so often, a deposit would be made. The deposits came via Western Union, or cashier's check, or via a deposit from another bank branch. A hundred here, fifty there, no amount earth shattering. The aunt figured it was pointless to try to get more out of Vance, and the amount due kept getting larger."

Even though he was the de facto Chief of Police, Engels wasn't that familiar with family law. He made sure that some of his officers were well schooled in those areas, since family issues tended to bring out a lot of passion in people.

"If Vance signed over his parental rights," Engels began to muse.

Tisdale interrupted him. "Giving up your parental rights doesn't absolve you from any financial duties to a child. Based on my preliminary research, most courts are extremely clear cut on those matters. The thinking is, even if you don't want to be associated with the child, that doesn't mean you can't help financially for the child growing up and developing. Raising a child in today's modern world is damn expensive, after all."

Engels nodded. "Did VMS garnish his wages?"

"From what I can tell, no. In whatever way Vance earned his income, before and during his employment with VMS, Vance would make uneven and erratic payments. This went on from the time the daughter's trust was established until about a year ago, when he quit."

"How much did he owe at the time?"

"According to the state of Colorado, he owes a little under eighteen thousand dollars."

Engels considered that amount. Eighteen thousand dollars is a lot of money to owe someone. If Vance had been pulled into a scheme, one that

196

had the added carrot of a big payday, it might have given Vance the incentive to move away from his comfort zone. "Interesting."

"That's not where it ends, though," Tisdale said. Engels looked at him, raising an eyebrow. "As of the most recent filing, he owes around eighteen thousand. When he quit VMS a year ago, though, he owed closer to twenty-five-thousand. Somehow, even after he quit, Vance was still paying the back-child support."

"This is getting more fascinating," Engels said. "We obviously don't know how Vance was getting the money to pay. In the last year, do we know in what manner Vance was paying?"

"From what the aunt told me, the payments were larger than before, but usually less than two thousand dollars. As before, the issuing bank would vary, but a cashier's check would be generated, or the money would be deposited via Western Union. Since he was only dealing with small amounts, they went undetected under the banking provisions of the Patriot Act. The aunt also said that the payments became more frequent, almost on a regular basis."

"When was the last payment deposited into the account?"

Tisdale flipped through his notes, stopped at a page, and said, "The aunt told me a deposit for five hundred dollars was made two weeks ago."

Engels smiled at Tisdale and said, "You did good work here. I want you to go over every page of it, one more time. Look for anything or anyone that might be a connection to whoever is behind this."

Tisdale stood up and said, "Will do, chief." He turned and was out the door.

Engels stood up and walked to the window. Ronald Vance, for all his petty crimes, seemed like a decent enough guy, trying to get by in the world. According to the file that Tisdale put together, Vance was also trying to make amends for a life spent making the wrong kinds of decisions. As Engels watched the traffic below, he felt a tinge of sadness. He had arrested and helped convict many criminals in his life. How many of them felt genuine remorse for what they had done? How many would do anything to try to make things right?

Engels shook off the soul-searching. The question was, how had Ronald Vance gotten mixed up in such a situation that he felt he had no other option than to take his own life?

Lindstrom and Officer Tavon were sitting in the cubicle that Tavon had been using for his search. It was a tight fit to have two people at the desk at one time, but they were making it work. Lindstrom was impressed with the work Tavon had done and would make sure to let Engels know.

Lindstrom pointed to the computer screen, which displayed a database that Tavon had built, and said, "You're telling me that, out of more than three hundred plus clinics in a seventy-mile radius, no one has ever heard of HealthStar Ambulatory Services?"

Tavon nodded affirmatively. "That's right. I checked hospitals, clinics, dental offices, specialty fields, labs that offer drug screenings for employers. No one has ever heard of HealthStar. I also did several web searches through different search engines, and nothing came back."

"How difficult is it to buy an ambulance," Lindstrom asked. "They have to be pretty hard to come by, right?"

Tavon shook his head. "Not at all. Ambulances are like most vehicles. If there is a demand for it, a market will present itself. You can find them on eBay and Craigslist. There are even websites that have a full inventory of all different models of ambulances for sale."

"Different models? You mean there's more than one kind of ambulance?"

"Absolutely. Judging from the websites I looked at, there are at least eight different models, if not more. Here, see for yourself." Tavon opened a web browser on the desk's computer, and immediately opened a bookmarked webpage that he had already researched. The new webpage opened, and Lindstrom was greeted with a website that touted itself as having the largest selection of used ambulances. Nine photos of different ambulances appeared, each one parked in some kind of car lot. She looked closer at the webpage and saw that those nine ambulances were only the beginning. Another seven pages were available to scroll through.

"Used ambulances for sale," Lindstrom muttered, more to herself than to Tavon. "Like you said, if someone wants it, someone else will provide it."

Lindstrom stood up, shook her head, and stretched. Even though it was still early in the morning, sitting hunched over in the cubicle was giving her a pain in her back. She leaned over, minimized the web browser with the ambulances on it, shifting her gaze over the database that was on the screen, and then looked at Tavon.

"How about pharmacies or drug stores? Did you check those out?"

Tavon looked at her. "No, I guess I didn't." He spoke with a hint of disappointment, as if chastising himself for making an obvious error. He recovered fast, with an upbeat tone, by adding, "I will expand my search and see if I can come up with anything." Tavon turned back towards the computer and started typing away.

"Get creative," Lindstrom said. "Any company that might have even a passing interest in an ambulance needs to be looked at."

"I'm on it," Tavon said, furiously moving his fingers across the keyboard. As Lindstrom stood behind him, watching him work, her cell phone buzzed. She swiped the screen active. It was from Jerry in forensics. COME TO MY OFFICE ASAP.

"Keep working, Tavon, and let me know when you find something." Lindstrom left the cubicle and made her way to the elevators. A minute later, she was standing in Jerry's office. "I hope you have good news for me, Jerry."

"Indeed, I do," Jerry said, smiling. "The victim's name is Olivia Sherman."

Lindstrom's eyes lit up. "How did you figure that out?"

"The serial number came back. It wasn't a piece of mesh to support the esophageal sphincter into the stomach. It was an actual artificial sphincter. I have read about artificial sphincters being used in the rectal and vaginal areas, but I haven't heard of one being used in a way that is autonomous from being controlled."

"So," Lindstrom began, "this is cutting edge bio-tech?"

"Well, yes and no. From my examination, it was clear that she had stomach and diaphragm issues at some time that required surgery. I'm not sure if the nature of the artificial sphincter is important at this point."

Lindstrom thought about it. She was familiar with the surgical procedure that was designed to help fix an issue with the stomach and diaphragm. It was called a lap nissen. The problem started with the stomach pushing up and through the diaphragm. That condition was known as a hiatal hernia. This caused the opening into the stomach not to close properly, or at all. This resulted in acid reflux. The procedure for the lap nissen involved the surgeon pulling the stomach down, suturing the enlarged hole in the diaphragm, and then wrapping the stomach around itself and stapling it. Ideally, this would prevent the stomach from herniating the diaphragm again, while insuring that the sphincter connecting the esophagus to the stomach would open and close normally.

"Tish," Jerry asked, "did you hear me?" He knew that Lindstrom understood the basics of the procedure. She appeared lost in her memories. He tried to shake her out of her respite. "Tish, hello?"

Lindstrom snapped back to the present. "Yes, Jerry, I heard you. I think you're right. At this point, we need to focus on who Olivia Sherman is. The fact that she had the procedure is probably inconsequential to the investigation. Is there anything else you can update me on?"

Jerry looked over his notes. "According to the results from the house you visited yesterday morning, there were no prints or fibers. The house was clean. Whoever went into that house didn't stay long enough to leave a mark."

"I will let Engels know," Lindstrom said. "Good work, Jerry. Let me know if you come up with anything else." Lindstrom left and headed back upstairs to her desk to find out who Olivia Sherman was.

"How goes the search?" Engels was standing in the doorway of Conference Room Three. Officers Gilbride and Jefferson were using two separate computer monitors to look over the tapes that the television crews had sent over.

"Well," Jefferson started, "it's a good news, bad news situation."

"Give it to me straight, then," Engels said, walking into the room and taking up a position behind them.

"The good news," Gilbride said, "is that we both agree that this person…" pointing to the frozen image on one of the monitors, "this is the person that was watching what we were doing. The bad news is that there is no shot that doesn't have the person in shadow, or with the face obscured."

Engels leaned forward, examining the frozen image. Even with state of the art high definition television cameras, with everything being recorded in digital and replayed in 1080p resolution, he was basically looking at a shadow. "This is the absolute best image you have found?"

"Unfortunately, yes," Jefferson said. "We played through the recording from the camera that went away from this area on a fast forward,

200

and at no time did that camera person get even a glimpse of this area."

Gilbride continued, "By eliminating that entire tape, we were able to focus on this one. We have zoomed in and out, moved forward and back, and this person didn't want to be seen. As soon as she,"

"Hold on," Engels interrupted. Gilbride looked at him, as he pointed a finger to the shadowy figure on the monitor. "Even with no face, no reference points, no discernible features, you are certain that this person is female?"

"Call it what you want, chief," Gilbride retorted, "but this is a female. Call it a hunch, gut feeling, intuition, whatever, but this shadow is a woman." Gilbride was standing firm, which Engels admired. Jefferson sat in his chair, wondering if he would have had the guts to stand up to Engels like Gilbride had done.

"Very well, Gilbride. Continue."

"As I was saying, as soon as she realized that there was a chance of being recorded, the suspect left the scene. By the time I got there, the person was long gone."

Engels looked at Jefferson. "And you weren't able to see anything from where you were parked at the end of the block?"

"Nothing at all. The person was either in shadow or was silhouetted by the street light from the corner. I remember thinking that the person walked like a woman, but I'm feeling less certain, maybe down to a seventy percent chance."

Using his right thumb, Engels applied pressure to a sore spot on his neck. "Is there a silver lining here?"

"Based on the shadow's position and the other people around the shadow," Gilbride said, "the person is probably in the six-foot-two to six-foot-four range. There is a chance the shadow is a male, but something about this says it's a woman."

Engels processed what they were saying. He looked from Jefferson to Gilbride to the frozen image on the screen. "Any chance that the tech boys could clean this up?"

"It's possible," Gilbride said, "but I doubt it. There isn't a frame where the figure isn't in darkness, but we'll take it to them." A knock came from the door, and all three of them looked to see Lindstrom standing there.

"Any news on the mystery person," Lindstrom asked the group.

"The news," Engels said, "is that the mystery person is tall, is always in shadow, and there's between a seventy percent chance," he pointed at Jefferson, then to Gilbride, "to a one hundred percent chance that the person is female. Other than that, there's not much to go on. What have you come up with?"

"Forensics on the house came back clean," Lindstrom said, "so whoever this person is, they got in and out without leaving anything behind. On the plus side, Jerry identified our female victim as Olivia Sherman. I'm going to get started on her history right now."

With that, Lindstrom turned around and left the doorway, heading for her desk to start working on a file for Olivia Sherman. While it was disappointing that they couldn't get a lead off the videos that the television crews provided, it still provided a valuable clue. It meant that there was, at a bare minimum, one more person involved with Nathan Devlin's abduction.

Lindstrom sat down at her desk and started typing over the keyboard, pulling up multiple windows and tabs, getting as much information on her dead victim, or dead accomplice, as she could. She was reading and printing, placing everything into a jacket, when Tisdale came up to her.

"I hear we have an ID on the dead woman," Tisdale said.

"Yes. Yes, we do," Lindstrom responded happily, keeping her eyes on her computer screen and her fingers typing on the keyboard. "Do you need something, because I'm kind of busy here."

"Actually, the chief wants you to head over to Sanford Hospital. Dr. Preston, Nathan Devlin's doctor, called. Devlin is conscious and can field questions."

Lindstrom's face lit up, and she clapped her hands together in joy. To hear Preston talk, she figured that it would have been days before Devlin would be ready to chat. As much as she wanted and needed to talk to Devlin, she needed to keep investigating Olivia Sherman. "Are you working on anything," Lindstrom asked Tisdale.

"I can take over for you," Tisdale said. "I've already gone over everything on Ronald Vance twice, per the chief's instructions. Engels hasn't given me any follow-up to do yet."

Lindstrom stood up, grabbed her purse and her jacket, and pushed her chair out so Tisdale could sit down. "Alright, get to it. I expect to have a nice history to read by the time I get back." As Tisdale sat down, Lindstrom looked at him and said, "And Tisdale, you are only allowed to have one of the cookies I keep stashed in my filing cabinet."

"Understood," Tisdale said, turning his attention to the computer screen. Lindstrom hurried away, wanting to talk to Nathan Devlin before something else happened.

SEVENTEEN

Nathan Devlin was sitting up in a hospital bed, the television turned off above him, staring out the window to his right. He had spent the last two hours being poked and prodded, the same questions being asked from every nurse and doctor that came into his room. Finally, after what seemed like an eternity, Andy Cole and Ben McKinley had strolled in, huge smiles of relief on both their faces, and they had each given him a soft hug. The only questions they asked were how he was feeling. After a few minutes, Dr. Preston had come back into his room.

"Mr. Devlin," Preston began, "you have obviously been through a lot. However, the police do need to ask you some questions. If you feel up to it, I'll contact the detective heading up the investigation and have her stop by. Is that alright with you?"

Devlin nodded slowly and said softly, "Yeah, that's fine."

"You sure, buddy?" Andy had a concerned look on his face. "If you need more time, that's your right, you know."

"Andy is right," Ben chimed in. "The cops can wait until you're up for it."

Devlin smiled. "Thanks, guys, but I'll be fine. Besides, with you two here, I think things will be okay." Devlin looked at Dr. Preston. "Go ahead and call. I just want to rest until the police get here, okay?"

Everybody nodded and quietly left the room, leaving Devlin to continue gazing out the window. He was glad that he was wearing a condom catheter. One of the nurses had said that his system had been

204

bombarded with all manner of drugs. To counteract their affects, his system had been equally flooded with IV fluids to flush out his body. This, of course, meant that his kidneys were producing urine at an ungodly rate. He was only vaguely aware of it, but he could tell that he was basically peeing, non-stop, into a bag.

Devlin didn't know how long he had been engrossed with the view out of his hospital room, until he heard something. It was a soft knock at the door. "Come in" Devlin murmured, loud enough to be heard. The door opened, and Dr. Preston walked in, followed by a nurse, Andy, Ben, and a woman he didn't know.

"Nathan," Dr. Preston said, motioning to the unknown woman, "this is Detective Patricia Lindstrom. She is investigating your case."

"Mr. Devlin," Lindstrom said, stepping forward and offering her hand, "you can call me Tish. I'd like to ask you some questions about what happened to you. If at any time you need a break, say so, and we can stop. Is that okay?"

Devlin nodded his head, "Sure, but what time is it?" Devlin looked at Dr. Preston. "Didn't you just leave?"

Dr. Preston took out a pen light and approached the bed. "It's been about forty-five minutes since we left your room." He checked Devlin's pupillary reflexes, which reacted normal. "Rachel?" The nurse moved quickly and efficiently, checking Devlin's vitals on the monitor, verifying the flow rate of the IV drip, and making sure there was no obstruction in the catheter line.

"Everything is good," Rachel replied.

"Maybe we should wait." Preston put away his pen light, glancing from Andy to Ben, until his gaze fell upon Nathan.

Devlin shook his head and said, "No, I'll be fine. I must have dozed off." He waved the doctor away. Andy and Ben sat on a small love seat in the corner, while Dr. Preston and the nurse stood by the diagnostic machines, keeping track of Devlin's vitals. "Detective, go ahead with your questions."

Lindstrom smiled. She opened her notebook and said, "Can you remember anything about your abduction?"

Devlin took in a deep breath. "It was Monday night. I had gone out to eat. I had been feeling uneasy about meeting Allison and the kids later that week. Ben had insisted I go out, get some fresh air, have a decent meal, and keep my head clear." He looked at Andy and Ben. "With everything that I had put people through, I wasn't sure if I was ready. After I left the restaurant, I felt like I needed to test myself, so I went into a bar. I ordered a strawberry lemonade and found a booth to sit in." He looked at Lindstrom, who was jotting down notes. He waited until she was done, and she looked at him. "Detective, have you ever screwed up so unbelievably that you thought you'd never get things fixed?" As Devlin peered into Lindstrom's eyes, he thought he saw something, like a connection to what he had done to his wife, to his family, to his friends, hell, basically to everyone he had ever met.

"Mr. Devlin," Lindstrom said, calm and cool, "Nathan, we all make mistakes. I'm not here to judge you. What happened to you was not your fault. Someone did this to you. I want to find out who and why, and make sure that this never, ever, happens again. Take it slowly, nice and easy, and tell me what happened." There was a reassuring tone in her voice that made him feel at ease.

"I'm not sure how long I was sitting by myself," Devlin continued, "but a woman approached me and asked if she could sit with me. I remember the bar being maybe half-empty, but I didn't want to be rude, so I let her sit down. I was so lost in my own thoughts that I don't really remember what she talked about."

"Do you remember what she looked like?"

"Maybe five-foot eight, but I'm pretty sure she was my height."

"Do you remember her hair or eye color, or any distinguishing characteristics?"

Devlin struggled to pick up the details in his memory. He closed his eyes, trying to visualize the woman in his mind. "I'm sorry, Detective. The only thing I remember is that she was very, very attractive. I remember thinking to myself, why does this stunning woman want to sit with me?" Lindstrom looked back through her notes. The nurse, Jason, had used that exact same word to describe the woman. "A stunner." Unfortunately, she would have to wait to see a picture of her to see if they were telling the truth. The mutilated corpse in the morgue wouldn't do the woman justice.

"What else do you remember about that night," Lindstrom asked.

Devlin took a breath and closed his eyes. "My memories aren't solid. I have bits and pieces."

"Take your time," Lindstrom said. "Don't rush it. I don't want you endangering your well-being getting frustrated." Lindstrom could see out of the corner of her eye that Andy and Ben had concerned looks on their respective faces. She didn't want Devlin's health to take a turn for the worse in this interview.

"I remember thinking how much I had hurt Allison and the kids," Devlin said, still with his eyes closed, "and that, if this woman was trying to pick me up in the same week that I was going to try to reconnect with my kids, I wasn't going to let it happen." Another breath, and he continued, "I think I told her why I wasn't interested. She seemed to understand, but she also seemed puzzled by it. Like it wasn't what she had expected or planned." He was trying to put the images back together in his head, but things seemed somehow detached in his mind.

"She got a phone call." Still with his eyes closed, Devlin spoke deliberately, as if he was trying to meticulously narrate a movie that was playing inside his head. "I think the call upset her. I waited until she came back from the call, then, um, yeah, I used the bathroom. When I got back, she had gotten us both drinks. I was worried, but the bartender gave me a thumbs-up, I think."

Lindstrom paused in her note taking and she looked at Dr. Preston. He gave a slight nod, indicating that Devlin's vitals were good. She then looked at Andy and Ben. They both nodded, approving of the interview so far. She didn't prod any further. Rather, she wanted Devlin to continue when he was ready. Besides, everything appeared to lineup with what Tisdale had discovered in his interviews with Jason Iverson and Sarah the bartender. Two minutes ticked by, when Devlin, his eyes still closed, continued.

"She dropped some things. I went under the table to help pick them up. I bumped my head. We got outside, and then, then, um…" His voice trailed off. His eyes were still closed, but his face was turning into a frown.

"Nathan," Dr. Preston asked, "are you okay?"

Devlin coughed a little bit. "Can I have some water, please?" Rachel walked to the counter area and poured him a fresh glass of ice water and gave it to him. Devlin took a long drink, and then rested back against his pillows. He opened his eyes and looked at Andy and Ben. "It's all such a blur after I got outside."

"We think that she drugged you," Lindstrom said, "and Dr. Preston would probably vouch for me on that opinion."

There was a change in the soft beeping of the diagnostic machines that were tracking Devlin's vitals. "Nathan," Dr. Preston said, "maybe we should stop here."

Devlin shook his head. "No, that's not it. I remember little bits and pieces, but it's more about how I was feeling. I remember feeling betrayed, for some reason. I remember feeling helpless. I remember feeling angry." His eyes squinted, and he tilted his head slightly to the left, like he was trying to solve a puzzle. "I think I hit someone, somehow, and then I was moving. There was yelling, a woman's voice." He closed his eyes again, taking some more deep breaths. "She said something about this not being right. This wasn't part of the plan. Someone screwed up." He closed his eyes, rolling his head on his shoulders. Several seconds later, he opened his eyes and looked at Lindstrom. "After that, I think I remember bright lights and shadows looking at me. I couldn't move, I couldn't even speak." He tried to pull more memories from the darkness, but it was no good. He shook his head. "And now I'm here, in this hospital room."

Lindstrom smiled at him and patted his hand. "That was extremely helpful, Nathan. That corroborates our witness's details of your abduction." Now it was time for Lindstrom to take a deep breath. "Nathan, I know you've been through a very traumatic experience. The last thing I want is for your health to be put in jeopardy, and not only your physical health. I'm talking about your mental and emotional health, as well. I also don't need your amazing friends getting angry with me. However, I need to ask you a simple question. Take as much time as you need." She looked from Andy to Ben to Dr. Preston. Andy had a quizzical look on his face, while Ben looked like he was going to tell Lindstrom off if she crossed a line. Dr. Preston seemed to understand where this was going, so he directed Rachel to watch Devlin's vitals extremely close.

Lindstrom looked back at Devlin and asked, "Why would anyone go through all of this trouble to kidnap you?" She hadn't meant the question to hang in the air like that, as if she was judging him, but there wasn't any alternative. Trying to sugarcoat the situation would only make it seem insignificant, and nothing about this case was insignificant.

Devlin looked at her for a minute, and then looked at Andy and Ben. He contemplated the question, pursing his lips together. After a minute, he smiled at both of his friends, and the smile assuaged their fears, and they both smiled back. His gaze went back to Lindstrom, and he said, "Detective, I think I know where you're going. I'm sure you've talked to those guys over there, and maybe you've had a chance to talk to Allison." Lindstrom's facial expression remained stoic, not wanting to reveal that she hadn't, as yet, spoken to his wife. "The fact is I have no idea why someone would want to kidnap me. Aside from a mountain of debt that I owe Allison and the kids, I've never been arrested or committed any kind of crime. I've hurt a lot of people, but never in violence. I have no great inheritance. Whatever money I had when my parents died is long gone in the form of liquor that I drank and pissed away. If someone thought they could get rich off me, they were grossly mistaken." He smiled at her, took a drink of water, and said, "And no, I'm not mad at you for asking the question. You've got a job to do."

Lindstrom smiled back at Devlin, finishing a few more notes. If this was a kidnapping gone wrong because of some bad intel, that begged the question if there would be another attempt on the correct target. She put the thought out of her mind. With two collaborators dead, the chances of another kidnapping happening so soon after a botched one were slim. Whoever was behind this would have to hire a new crew, get the facts correct, and maybe lie in wait until the heat died down. She looked at Andy and Ben. "I hope I wasn't too hard on your friend."

Andy smiled and said, "I can't speak for Ben, but I think that went fine."

"I agree," Ben added, with his face in what could charitably be described as a grin.

Dr. Preston was about to speak, when a knock came at the door. "Come in," Dr. Preston called. The door opened, and Andy's wife, Heidi, came into the room.

"I'm sorry to interrupt," Heidi began, but she seemed to stop dead in her tracks with a fearful look on her face when she recognized Lindstrom sitting next to Devlin on the bed.

"Heidi," Andy said as he got up from his part of the love seat, "is everything okay?"

"Why, yes, of course, why wouldn't it be?" Heidi tried to regain her composure, walking around the end of the hospital bed to Andy. "I didn't realize that you had a convention going on in here." Her smile and laugh were awkward, but maybe that was to be expected, considering the events of the last week.

Ben stood up and said, "No offense, Tish, but if there's nothing else for right now, let's give Nathan some peace to rest up."

"That sounds like an excellent idea," Lindstrom said. She stood up from the chair next to the bed and gave Devlin's shoulder a soft squeeze. "I'm glad you're feeling better. If you think of anything else, I'll leave my card on the counter." She placed her card next to the hospital's phone, then started looking around the room. "Dr. Preston, you know how to get in touch with me if something comes up. Andy, Ben, thanks for your time, and I'm sure I'll be back. Heidi, if anything comes up with Allison, please let me know." Andy and Ben had relieved expressions on their faces, while Heidi's expression remained mildly apprehensive. Lindstrom turned and left the room. Once she was in the hallway, she re-opened her notebook and wrote "Heidi Cole" in the sidebar with a question mark.

Lindstrom started walking down the hospital corridor. As she reached one of the nurse's stations, she felt her cell phone vibrate. She swiped the screen active. She had a message from Tisdale that was copied to Engels. "HERE IS A PICTURE OF OLIVIA SHERMAN". She pressed the paperclip icon to pull up the attachment and looked at the photo. She immediately frowned. Lindstrom was expecting a woman with supermodel good looks, but the face staring back at her was, well, ordinary. Olivia Sherman was pretty, only in a plain sort of way. She looked up from her phone and back down the corridor. She thought about returning to show Devlin the picture. No, not yet, she thought. He had been through enough for one day. Then she remembered where she was.

Lindstrom got in the elevators and pressed the ground floor button. It took a few minutes to navigate the hospital, but she finally arrived at the emergency room. One of the nurses at the front desk looked at Lindstrom and said, "May I help you?"

"Yes, my name is Detective Lindstrom. Is Jason working today?"

"Tish!" Lindstrom turned around and saw Jason pushing an empty wheelchair down the hall. He walked a bit faster and set the wheelchair against the wall where two other wheelchairs were already sitting. "What's going on?"

"I was upstairs interviewing Nathan Devlin, and I wanted to talk to you. Do you have a minute?"

"Sure. Give me one second." Jason turned to the nurse and said, "ER five is empty now, the room just needs sanitizing. And have building maintenance look at the wall outlets. I think one of them caused the ventilator to short out." Jason turned back to Lindstrom and asked, "What do you need?"

Lindstrom motioned for him to walk with her. They walked a few feet and found a quiet corner. She swiped her phone and pulled up the picture that Tisdale had sent. "Is this the woman that you saw at the bar?" She handed the phone to Jason, who looked at the picture on the screen. He seemed puzzled, not really knowing what to say.

"It is, but it isn't," Jason replied. He set the phone down on a cart and pointed to the picture. "Her eyes are right, but the cheekbones are off. Her hair should be darker. The nose in the picture is too flat."

"You're suggesting that the woman in this picture had plastic surgery?"

Jason nodded his head. "Some of this woman's features are the same, but some are different from the woman I saw. I wouldn't go so far as to say she has a completely new face, but judging from this picture, she had just enough work done to move her from a six to a nine, maybe a ten."

Lindstrom looked at the picture and asked Jason, "What kind of certainty are you talking here?"

Jason thought about it for a minute. "I'd say eighty to ninety percent certain. I've seen my share of wounds to the human body. As an extra credit assignment in anatomy class, I was part of a project to reconstruct a face from only a skull. The professor only gave us a sixty percent. She showed us, through computer modeling, how even small changes in how the muscles are attached to the bone can cause differences in the final product."

Lindstrom smiled, picked up her phone, and said, "Thank you. That's very helpful."

"Do you know who she is," Jason asked.

"We have an ID, and we're getting background right now."

"Well, let me know if you need any more help." With that, Jason turned and walked back towards the nurse's station.

Lindstrom walked out of the emergency room into the waiting area. She had parked in the garage, but that was on the other side of the hospital. She didn't feel like walking through the many twists and turns of the hospital, so she decided to walk around the outside of the hospital. It would take longer, but it was an unusually warm fall day, and the fresh air would do her good. She walked outside and got to the end of the driveway that the ambulances used to pull up to the ER entrance. In the distance, she heard a siren getting louder. Realizing that an ambulance was coming around the corner, Lindstrom quickened her pace so that she was to the corner as the ambulance was turning in.

As she continued walking, Lindstrom looked at many of the cars that had pulled over to make room for the ambulance. That's when she saw it. A black delivery van, unmarked, almost up on the curb. It hadn't started moving yet, as there were three cars in front of it, and the lead car was waiting for the red light to change.

Lindstrom started walking faster, hoping to get a better look at the driver, maybe even a license plate number. The light changed to green, and the cars started rolling ahead. Lindstrom broke into a run, pulling out her cell phone and activating the camera. There were other pedestrians walking on the sidewalk, and she started bumping into them. "POLICE," she yelled, "MAKE A PATH!" Some of the people looked around in confusion, but they got out of her way as she was running. She took several pictures as the cars started picking up speed. By the time she had reached the corner with the stop lights, the van was too far away to continue the chase, especially with more cars now blocking her view of the van.

Lindstrom stood at the corner and turned so her back was to the sun. She pulled up the camera gallery. She had snapped thirty pictures. She looked at each one. Most were out of focus and blurry or had something in the way. No picture of the driver. Fortunately, three of the pictures appeared to be good quality, displaying the back of the van. She zoomed in on the license plate and frowned. There was no plate. Instead of an actual license plate, there was a plate that advertised where the van had been purchased. She looked at the name. "Best Auto Sales". She pulled up a directory assistance app on her phone and typed in "Best Auto Sales". No such business was listed in a fifty-mile radius. She expanded to two hundred miles, which was the limit for the app. Still no business was listed. She closed the app, opened the internet on her phone and typed in "Best Auto Sales" in a yellow pages' directory. "No such business" was the result in a fifty-mile search radius, with numerous "*Did you mean*" search results. She changed the search parameters to one thousand miles.

"No such business". She changed it to the entire United States. "No such business".

Lindstrom put her phone back in her pocket, looked around to get her bearings, and started walking towards the hospital's garage again. If it wasn't the exact same van that she had seen by Ryan's school and that had driven by her house on Saturday, it was a carbon copy. She reached the hospital's parking garage and found her car. As she started the engine, she looked at the time. 12:40pm. It was time to grab some lunch and get back to the station.

As she started driving back to the station, Lindstrom's cell phone rang. She activated the hands-free calling from the steering wheel and said, "Detective Lindstrom."

"Hi, Tish! It's Sherry at the elementary school!" Sherry was the school's secretary. It was pretty much a given that every child that ever attended the elementary school loved Sherry. It was also abundantly clear, from anyone that had ever met Sherry, that she knew the name of every single child in the building.

"Hey Sherry. What's going on?"

"Ryan wasn't feeling well after lunch. From what his teacher said, he sat down on one of the outside benches during recess. After recess, his teacher brought him down to the office. He's looking pale and doesn't have any kind of energy."

Leave it to a sick child to spoil an investigation. "I will head back into town and pick him up. Give me about twenty minutes, okay?"

"Thanks, Tish! See you soon!" The line went dead.

Lindstrom dialed Engels' cell. After two rings, Engels picked up. "If you think, because you are awash with new found riches, that you can take the rest of the day off whenever you feel like it, you have been misinformed."

"Very funny, wise ass." Lindstrom laughed. "Ryan is sick, so I'm heading to the school to get him. In the meantime, here's what I learned from Nathan and from Jason." She proceeded to go over everything from the interview, as well as showing Olivia Sherman's photo to Jason. She didn't mention Heidi Cole or Heidi's reaction to seeing Lindstrom in the hospital room.

"Well, where does that leave everything," Engels asked.

"For now, have Tisdale keep working background on Olivia Sherman.

Tavon should keep researching the HealthStar Ambulatory angle. If Ryan is okay tomorrow, I'll be in bright and early to look over everything."

"Sounds like a solid plan to me. Give Ryan a hug for me."

"Hold up there, boss. I have a job for you."

"Oh? Is this regarding Devlin, Vance, or Sherman?"

"I'm not sure. Check with the DMV for any black delivery vans that have been purchased, registered, or are in use. Limit the search to Ford models."

"Want to share with the rest of the class?"

"I don't like coincidences. Like we talked about the other day, on Saturday, I saw a black delivery van drive by Ryan's school, and then later either the same van or a similar one drove by the house twice. About half an hour ago, I saw the same exact kind of van in front of the hospital. I got some pictures, but there were no plates on it, and no distinguishing marks or logos on the side of the van. The advertised name on the plate was for an auto sales company that doesn't exist."

Engels sighed. "Things keep getting stranger. Anything else?"

Lindstrom thought about it for a second, and then said, "Check with our tech guys and see if anyone would be able to work on facial manipulation. If not, I may have to put a call in to Mitch at the F.B.I.'s field office." Mitch was a friend of Mark's. Or, more accurately, he was a friend of a friend of Mark's, one of those "small world" instances. Years ago, Mitch had requested Lindstrom's help on a case he was working. Her help led to evidence and a conviction, and Mitch told her he owed her one.

"I'll talk to the techs. Get Ryan squared away, and I'll see you tomorrow morning." Engels ended the call on his end, and Lindstrom continued driving to Ryan's elementary school.

EIGHTEEN

It had been an interesting night. Somehow, though, everyone had made their way through it. Ryan definitely looked the part of a sick child when Lindstrom had picked him up. After lots of water to drink, some chicken noodle soup and crackers for dinner, a warm bath, and lots of cuddle time on the couch, Ryan had woken up happy and alert with all kinds of energy to start his day.

Bree, on the other hand, had been her usual self, alternating from happy to sad, then mad, and circling back to happy. Lindstrom had pretty much ignored her for the night, finally putting a lid on her attitude by telling her daughter that if Bree didn't settle down, Bree could forget about the cheerleading competition and sleepover that weekend. When Bree started to argue, Lindstrom pulled out her cellphone, pulled up the cheerleading coach's phone number in her contacts list, and let her thumb hover over the screen. "If I dial," Lindstrom had threatened, "you are done with cheerleading for the rest of the school year." Bree had started to object, thought better of it, and went to her room. She banged around and talked to herself for about ten minutes, then things went quiet for the rest of the night.

Unfortunately, even Trevor had acted up, poking and prodding Ryan on the couch, asking him if he wanted to play, and, basically, being an older brother bully. Before Lindstrom could chastise her oldest son, Ryan, to his credit, looked up at his brother and said, "If you don't leave me alone, I'm going to go downstairs and puke on your X-Box." Trevor had started laughing, still sitting next to Ryan on the couch, but when Ryan got up and started walking towards the stairs, horror had filled Trevor's eyes. Trevor leapt off the couch and basically jumped over Ryan to get to the stairs first. Seconds later, they heard the door to Trevor's room slam shut. Lindstrom watched Ryan turn around, walk back to the couch, and lay back down. That was impressive for an eight-year old boy, Lindstrom had thought.

Now it was Wednesday morning, and Lindstrom was on her way to work after getting Ryan and Bree to school. As she was driving, she received a text message from Engels. Diane's car had a flat tire, and Engels needed to help get her situated, so he would be late. Lindstrom thought about it, then decided to make a detour away from the police station. She started driving towards Sanford Hospital. With any luck, Nathan Devlin would be awake and would be able to ID the picture of Olivia Sherman. She was also hoping that she might be able to ask Allison Devlin a question or two, away from Andy, Ben, and Nathan. Dr. Preston had called Lindstrom last night to update her on the condition of both Devlin's. Things were looking up for both of them.

Lindstrom had called Dr. Preston on the drive in, to make sure it was okay for her to come. He didn't think there would be any harm in a few questions. "Keep it brief," had been his only request. It took Lindstrom an extra fifteen minutes to get to the hospital, but she was hoping it would be worth it. As she rounded the corner, she was about to turn into the parking garage, and then stopped. Sanford Hospital had undergone extensive renovations, one of the drawbacks being that the parking garage was on one side of the hospital, with the lobby and main entrance in the middle, and then the majority of the hospital with the patients' rooms on the other side. That meant a lot of walking, doors, and corridors, before you even got to the elevators. She normally wouldn't have done it, but she decided that, for once, valet parking was going to be her choice. She pulled up, got out of her car, grabbed her purse, and took the valet ticket from the attendant.

As Lindstrom walked through the waiting room area and down the hall towards Nathan Devlin's room, she noticed that neither Andy nor Ben were visible. She reached Nathan's door, knocked softly, and waited until she heard a voice say, "Come in." She walked in and saw Nathan laying in his bed, with the head of the bed at a forty-five-degree angle. No one else was in the room. "Detective Lindstrom, I wasn't expecting you today." He smiled faintly.

"I apologize for bothering you today," Lindstrom said, "but I wanted to show you something. Would that be okay?"

Nathan used the bed controls and brought himself up to a near sitting position. "Absolutely. What is it?"

Lindstrom took out her phone and activated the photo gallery. She pulled up the picture of Olivia Sherman that Tisdale had sent her, the same picture that she had shown Jason. She gave the phone to Nathan and asked, "Is this the woman that sat down with you at Goldies?"

Nathan held the phone and stared at the picture. As he studied the picture, Lindstrom studied him, looking for any facial tic or tell that might tell her if he was lying. While Devlin was a victim, Lindstrom was still trying to figure out why he had been singled out as a target for a kidnapping. Something wasn't adding up, and for her to crack this case open, she needed to figure out why the bulls-eye, mistakenly or otherwise, had been painted on Nathan Devlin's head.

Nathan opened his mouth to speak, and then stopped. His smile turned into a frown. He took a finger from his free hand and double-tapped the screen. He zoomed the picture in, then moved the picture so that the focus went from the lips to the nose, then to the eyes, back to the lips, and then to the cheeks. "I think it could be her, but this picture is definitely NOT her."

"How do you mean," Lindstrom inquired.

"The woman in this picture might be the same woman that sat with me, but only if you changed a few things. The cheeks, the lips, the nose, they just need to be tweaked a little bit. Add a bit, just a little bit, of makeup, and I'd say you have the identity of the woman." Nathan handed her the phone and asked, "Is that her?"

Lindstrom nodded. "We believe so. This woman's body was found a week ago." She stopped, not wanting to go into details.

Nathan sensed her unease, asking, "Can't you tell me anything more?"

Lindstrom had played this kind of chess match before, trying to decide how much information to give, without divulging too much. Her mind raced, calculating pros and cons. She figured it was almost impossible that Devlin could have orchestrated his own abduction. There was no winning endgame to it, for himself or for his family. However, if someone close to him knew something, giving Devlin a full sit-rep could torpedo the entire investigation. Lindstrom decided to play it safe. She hadn't seen one newspaper from the hospital lobby to his room, so she would only give out the same information that Engels had given the media outlets.

"Her body was dumped into Skunk Creek. It rained heavily last Tuesday night, which caused her body to be swept downstream. A morning walker spotted the body, stuck in some reeds and bulrushes where the creek merges with the Big Sioux River. It was only by a miracle that we identified her. A witness to your abduction from ten days ago has said the same thing about the picture. That she must have had some plastic surgery done, but it could definitely be the same woman." She had left out the mutilation, as well as the location of the dump site and the storm drains.

Nathan closed his eyes and sighed. Lindstrom stood there, looking from Nathan to the diagnostic machines that were tracking his vitals. The numbers didn't seem to be changing. She didn't want to put him in distress, but she wasn't getting enough information. She decided to push it a little bit.

"Nathan," Lindstrom said softly, "from what Andy and Ben have told me, you have been through a lot in the past several years. I realize that you have been through hell over the past week and half. I also realize that I asked you this question yesterday, but I need to ask again. Can you think of any reason why anyone would think that you would be a viable option for kidnapping?"

Nathan continued to lay there, his breathing steady, his eyes closed. The numbers on the machine weren't changing, which was good. Lindstrom didn't want Nathan to have a heart attack or stroke out while answering her questions.

Nathan opened his eyes and looked at her. "After you left yesterday, and after Andy and Heidi and Ben took off, I laid here thinking about it. I wish I could tell you that I've got a secret account in Switzerland, lots of drug money stashed in the Cayman Islands, and I've won the lottery multiple times. It would make so much of this easier. Unfortunately, I don't have any financial secrets. I drank away whatever money I had. Honestly, sometimes I wonder how I survived as long as I did with hardly anything going into our bank account. Like I told you yesterday, I owe so much more than I'll probably ever be able to repay. Yes, I owe Allison

218

and the kids a lot of back financial support. But I'm more worried about repaying my family and friends for all of the mental and emotional bullshit I have put them through."

Lindstrom stared Nathan in his eyes, trying to find something that was betraying his honesty, but there was nothing there. His vitals hadn't moved, his eyes weren't darting around the room. He seemed at peace with everything he had done and was trying to bring it full circle and make amends to everyone he had hurt. She was trying to hide her pride and amazement at this man, who realized he had screwed up and was trying to bring his life and family back together. Of course, she had dealt with the opposite side of that spectrum, with her ex being part of, what seemed like, an ever-growing fraternity of deadbeat dads and abusive husbands the world over. And, as Veronica had mentioned, being an absentee parent wasn't gender specific. Women weren't immune to being worthless parents, either.

Lindstrom smiled at Nathan and said, "Look, you focus on what's important. Get healthy, improving your mind and body, and getting your family back together. I appreciate your help this morning. Get some rest, and if I need anything else, I'll let you know."

Nathan smiled and said, "Thank you, Detective." He lowered his bed back down and closed his eyes. Lindstrom quietly let herself out of his room and looked up and down the hallway. Nurses were calmly walking around, and it looked like breakfast was being delivered further down the hall. According to Dr. Preston, Allison Devlin had come out of her fatigue and stress-induced coma two days ago, around the same time that Nathan Devlin had been "found". Lindstrom didn't want to think about any kind of romantic connotations that her recovery implied. Dr. Preston was adamant that any questions be short, sweet, and to the point, because Allison was still in a fragile state of mind and body. Considering what Lindstrom had witnessed at the police station, she doubted that Allison had anything to do with her husband's abduction. However, she was hoping that Allison could help confirm one thing for her.

Lindstrom turned away from the direction of the nurses' station and walked past two more hospital room doors, stopping at a third. The handwritten name on the plate underneath the room number read "A. Devlin". She knocked, and a soft voice replied, "Come in". Lindstrom pushed the door open, and saw Allison Devlin laying on her hospital bed.

While she looked better than she had last Friday at the police station, Lindstrom figured it would be some time before Allison regained her full strength. She looked small and frail, probably from having to deal with so much stress involving her estranged husband and raising three children.

"Mrs. Devlin," Lindstrom started, "I'm not sure if you remember me. My name is Detective Patricia Lindstrom. We met briefly last Friday at the police station." Allison nodded her head slightly, so Lindstrom continued. "I am leading the investigation into your husband's disappearance, and I wanted to ask you one question. Would that be alright?"

Allison adjusted her bed slightly, reached for a glass of water, took a drink, and replied, "Sure, go ahead. What do you want to know?" The voice was hoarse, with a raspy tone that suggested she was still recovering from her breakdown.

"Can you think of any reason why your ex-husband would be a target for a possible kidnapping?" Lindstrom knew that the Devlin's were estranged from each other. From what she had gathered, though, neither Nathan or Allison had been seeing other people. By calling Nathan her ex, Lindstrom was hoping to get an idea into Allison's mindset about the whole situation.

"I don't know," Allison replied, with words spoken softly. Allison's eyes were locked on to Lindstrom's, and even though there wasn't a lot of fire in the stare, this told Lindstrom that Allison wasn't fumbling for a lie. "Nathan's parents were gone before we met, and they didn't have a lot, so there was no massive inheritance. When things were good between us, we lived paycheck to paycheck. It was hard, but we made it work. When things started to go bad with his drinking, he would pawn things to pay for his alcohol." Allison took another drink to cool her parched throat, and then continued.

"And Nathan is not my ex-husband, detective. Even with everything he has put the kids and myself through, I still love him like I could never love anyone else. When I asked Andy to check on him one last time, over a year ago, I had had a feeling that something had happened to Nathan, and that this might be my last chance to get my husband back. I tried not getting my hopes up, especially in front of the kids, but I wanted my husband home, healthy and healed." Another pause, as Allison closed her eyes and took in a deep breath. Lindstrom noted that Allison's vitals had

220

risen a little bit, though nothing that would suggest that she was either lying or was about to have a stroke from this line of questioning. Allison opened her eyes after about thirty seconds and continued.

"Whoever thought Nathan, or I, had any kind of money to try and get their hands on definitely didn't do their homework. For all the bad choices Nathan made when it came to his drinking, borrowing or stealing from someone probably wasn't one of them." Allison looked out the window at the morning coming over the treetops. "Maybe I am a fool to think that Nathan could or would change, Detective. Maybe I was a fool not to divorce him at the first sign of trouble. Maybe I was a fool not to sue him for every last penny that he owes the kids and I over the last several years. But the man gave me three absolutely precious gifts. While I have tried to be strong for my family, I realize that I was relying too much on hope and not enough on being strong. This last week has shown me that I can be stronger, AND that I NEED to be stronger. Not just for myself and my kids, but for Nathan, too." Allison turned back to Lindstrom and said, "I love Nathan, and I love my children. I don't know who or why this happened. I do hope you find who is responsible."

Lindstrom found it odd that Allison ended her sentence like that. She raised an eyebrow and asked, "No offense, Mrs. Devlin, but is that it? You want me to find out who is responsible, and nothing else?"

Allison grinned sheepishly, almost as if she was embarrassed. "Were you expecting me to say that I want you to make them pay?" She lightly chuckled, then continued. "Detective, what you do to the person or persons responsible is your business. My only prerogative, from this day forward and every day after, is to bring my family back together."

Lindstrom stood there, looking at Allison Devlin. Her opinion of her had changed, in the past few minutes. She remained motionless, silently admiring everything that Allison had been through and how Allison was determined to bring everything back together, stronger than ever. Lindstrom knew that every relationship had its ups and downs, triumphs and tragedies. Yes, her first husband had turned out be a worthless piece of slime, but she still loved Trevor and Bree with all her heart. Yes, she still loved Mark, and wished more than anything that things could be different, but she still loved Ryan with all her heart. She thought about Ryan's request from last week, to let Mark see the video of his performance. Maybe it was time to try to do some healing in her own life.

"I am sorry that I had to ask," Lindstrom said to Allison, a smile of gratitude coming across her face. "I appreciate your candor. I'll make sure we do our very best to find out what happened and why." She was about to ask one last question, and then decided against it. She could find the answer with a quick search through public records. "Thank you for your time this morning. Get some rest, and if you think of anything that might be helpful or useful in our investigation, please call me." She placed one of her business cards next to the hospital phone.

Allison returned Lindstrom's smile and said, "Thank you, Detective."

"Please, call me Tish." Lindstrom turned and tiptoed out of the room, while Allison took another drink of water, lowered her bed, and turned to look out the window again. Lindstrom quietly shut the door behind her. She stood there for a moment, her hand on the door. Even with everything Allison Devlin had been through, her recent medical crisis had, apparently, been a turning point for her. Whatever concerns or doubts she had were now gone, replaced with resolve and determination. Her goal was to heal her family, bring the fractured pieces back together, and become whole again, stronger than before. Good for her, Lindstrom thought. Now it was up to Lindstrom to help Allison with that, by solving this case and bringing the Devlin's closure.

Lindstrom turned to walk down the hallway but came face-to-face with a large rolling cart that the kitchen staff used to deliver meals. As she sidestepped the cart and could see down the hallway again, she caught sight of Heidi Cole coming around the corner by the nurses' station. Heidi also caught sight of Lindstrom and seemed to freeze for the briefest of moments. The moment passed, with Heidi stepping backwards, now out of sight around the corner. Lindstrom started walking, making her footsteps slow and deliberate.

The first time Lindstrom had met Heidi Cole, she had come off as a pain in the ass. That could be excused because of the situation regarding the Devlin's, and the fact that she had found Lindstrom, Ben, and her husband in the cafeteria. The second time, when Heidi had interrupted Lindstrom interviewing Nathan, she had a look in her eyes. Was it fear? Panic? Dislike or hatred? There was something going on, that was for sure. Now, Heidi had to know that Lindstrom had spotted her, and rather than confronting her, she had chosen to retreat. Nice, slow steps, Lindstrom thought.

As she approached the corner, rather than turning left to head toward that floor's waiting room and the elevators, Lindstrom moved to the right and went to the nurses' station. "Good morning," she said to the nurse sitting behind the counter. "Can you let Dr. Preston know that Detective Lindstrom talked to both of the Devlin's this morning, and that everything went fine."

"Absolutely," the male nurse replied. He wrote the information down and attached the note to a file.

"Thank you," Lindstrom said, and turned and walked down the small hallway to the waiting room. As she came out of the hallway to the open area, she saw Heidi Cole sitting in a chair by a window, looking at Lindstrom. The way Heidi was seated, directly facing the nurses' station, gave her the effect that she had been waiting for Lindstrom the whole time. Lindstrom thought to herself, is she hiding in plain sight, waiting in ambush?

"Detective Lindstrom," Heidi said, trying to mask whatever emotions she was having. "Is everything alright?" Her voice betrayed her, like a child that had been caught red-handed, yet still insisted on trying to lie their way out of the consequences. Lindstrom decided to let it slide, taking a more direct approach.

"I had a few questions for Nathan this morning, and I decided to speak with Allison for a moment," Lindstrom said. "I wasn't planning on stopping by until this afternoon, but I decided to get it done right away. I gave Dr. Preston my guarantee that the questions wouldn't bother either of the Devlin's." She looked at the clock hanging in the waiting room. "What brings you here so early on a Wednesday morning?"

"Allison is my best friend in this world," Heidi responded, with a mixture of derision and annoyance. "Someone had to help her and the kids when that piece of," she caught herself, and said, "when Nathan went into his selfish downward spiral. I've been there for Allison as best as I can, and I will continue to be there for her, no matter how many bad decisions continue to be made."

Lindstrom was intrigued. She sat down in a chair opposite from Heidi and said, "I take it you don't approve of Nathan?"

Heidi leaned in and said, "Look, I love Allison and I love her kids. But I don't think she can hold out hope that Nathan can turn it around and make this story into a happy, fairy tale ending."

"Based on what I have heard from your husband and from Ben, it sounds like Nathan was making some pretty good strides in getting cleaned up. Moving on from, as you said, the downward spiral."

"Ben is a head case, a glorified football coach that makes any little step of progress feel like they've climbed Mount Everest or landed on the moon or some other nonsense. As for my husband, I love him, too. But I've never thought he had the best taste in friends." Heidi's words were laced with equal parts sarcasm and cynicism.

The picture was starting to come into focus, but Lindstrom needed a little more. "So, in your opinion, Nathan Devlin deserves what happened to him?"

The question surprised Heidi, as she immediately sat back with a shocked look on her face. "Wait, no, that's not what I'm...," then she caught herself and looked at Lindstrom. "What the hell are you implying?"

Gotcha, Lindstrom thought. The reaction, the look on her face, the body language, it all fell into place. Lindstrom stood up from the chair and said, "I'm not implying anything, Mrs. Cole. Now, if you'll excuse me, I really need to get to the police station." She walked out of the waiting room, right into an open elevator car. As the elevator descended, she was trying to put the puzzle pieces together in her head.

If Heidi Cole was trying to protect her best friend and the kids, why come up with some convoluted kidnapping? Even with a minimal life insurance policy in place, Heidi could have easily found an ex-convict to run Nathan Devlin over. Hell, if Heidi was involved, why wait until Nathan was clean and sober and on track to reconnect with his family? Heidi could have forced the issue months ago with a mixture of drugs and alcohol. The autopsy would have shown an overdose, and no questions would have been asked. Sure, Allison probably wouldn't have gotten any money from insurance, but at least Nathan would be out of the picture.

The elevator doors opened, and Lindstrom walked across the hospital's atrium to the valet's desk. She gave the attendant her ticket, and he left to get her car. She stood by the sliding doors, trying to figure out what she was missing. HealthStar Ambulatory Services, Nathan Devlin, Olivia Sherman, Ronald Vance, and now, quite possibly, Heidi Cole. Lindstrom was still missing something, and she was determined to figure out what it was.

Being the Chief of Detectives and now, by default, the Chief of Police, Brad Engels was used to things not going his way. After all, crime was an unfortunate fact of life. Engels was used to late night phone calls and texts, rushing out to deal with emergencies, and other things that were simply a part of the job. When it came to his home life, though, he and Diane had worked hard to make sure that surprises didn't happen. From the furnace to the water heater to regular car maintenance, both of them made every effort to make sure that things were taken care of before they became a problem.

So, when Diane had walked out to the garage and found two flat tires, she was stunned. Not only was this a surprise but having two flat tires on one side of the car was a shock, too. At first, both Brad and Diane had been angry, each of them even throwing out a swear word or three. They then looked at each other, started laughing, shared a hug, and then kissed. Sometimes, the frivolity of life had to be acknowledged.

After calling for a tow truck, Engels, with Diane in the passenger seat, followed the tow truck to the garage. The mechanic quoted a price for both tires, to which Engels had countered, "Just put four new tires on the car. It'll be easier that way." Diane said she was fine waiting by herself, so Engels kissed his wife and left for the police station. Now, here he was, more than two hours late, feeling like his whole day was wasted. He sat down at his desk and started looking through messages and listening to voicemails. He didn't like the term "anal-retentive", but he had a set way of doing things. Even in the chaos of running a police department, Engels felt he had a good system in place. Oh well, he thought, it had been a very long time since something like a flat tire had disrupted his routine. He needed to get over it and move along with whatever the day put in his path.

Engels grabbed his phone and dialed Officer Tisdale. After two rings, a voice came over the line.

"Yes, Chief?"

"Where are you and what are you working on?"

"I am standing here with Officer Tavon. We were collecting our files and coming to see you."

"Is Tish in yet?"

"She's walking towards us now."

"I'll meet the three of you in Conference Room Two in ten minutes." Engels hung up the phone, stood up from his desk, and headed toward the conference room.

Lindstrom walked into the conference room behind Officers Tisdale and Tavon and took a seat. She was still trying to process her conversation with Heidi Cole as Engels walked in and sat down. "Okay," Engels said, "who wants to start? And, I've had a bad morning, so let's keep it short, sweet, and to the point." The other three officers looked at each other. After a few awkward seconds, Tisdale coughed and moved toward the file he had brought into the conference. He gave the file to Lindstrom, who started going through it.

"Well," Tisdale started, "here's what we know about Olivia Sherman." Tisdale positioned himself, so he could easily pivot between looking at Lindstrom and at Engels. "She was in and out of foster care for most of her early years. When she was finally adopted at age twelve, things were good for about two years. At age fourteen, her adoptive parents were killed in a traffic accident while driving to watch Olivia perform in a school play. She lived with an adoptive aunt for two years, but she had started having issues in school. By age seventeen, she dropped out of school and left the aunt's house. She worked a lot of minimum wage jobs and had a few minor dustups with various police precincts in different states. At age twenty-four, she had gotten pregnant. She didn't marry the father, but they stayed together for about a year. She left him and the son she gave birth to, and then continued to drift around the country. She only showed up when she got on the wrong side of the law."

"Did she serve any time," Engels asked.

"Nothing of consequence," Tisdale answered. "A night here, a night there, maybe a week waiting for arraignment, but she would skip town."

"How about her last known address," Lindstrom asked.

Tisdale said, "It's from more than two years ago, an apartment complex on the northwest side of Sioux Falls. I called the manager yesterday. He wasn't available, but his wife said that she vaguely remembered her. Unfortunately, she hadn't lived there in almost nineteen months."

"Any employment history to speak of," Engels asked.

"If she was working," Tisdale replied, "it was most likely with cash

226

under the table. Her last job that we can find was as a research liaison, whatever that is. It was for some company called All Things Medical."

Lindstrom suddenly sat up straight. "You're sure it was All Things Medical?"

Tisdale looked at her with a surprised look. "Absolutely, but I don't see the connection."

Lindstrom stood up and started shifting through the many folders that were laying on the conference table. She found the file she was looking for, opened it up, and flipped through pages, stopping when she found what she was looking for. She leaned over and handed the file to Engels. "Ronald Vance worked as a delivery driver for VMS, Visceral Medical Supplies."

As Engels read the page in Ronald Vance's file, he held out his hand. Lindstrom gave him the file on Olivia Sherman, which was opened to her employment history. Engels compared the pages side by side, and then looked at Lindstrom with a slight grin. Lindstrom smiled back at him.

"Hey," Tisdale said, "I hate to interrupt your telepathic communication thing, but I don't see what one has to do with the other."

"That's because you haven't lived in Sioux Falls long enough," Lindstrom said. "All Things Medical was a family-owned business since the late forties. Twenty years ago, they partnered with another family-owned business from out of state, I can't remember where. Then, about two years ago, the two companies finally merged entirely, renaming the company Visceral Medical Supplies. Most people call them VMS for short."

Engels set the folders down and leaned back in his chair, his hands folded behind his neck. "So, we have a decent case that Olivia Sherman and Ronald Vance knew each other through mutual employment at VMS. Have we looked into VMS at all? What do we know about the company or its owners?"

This time, Officer Tavon stood up and took the floor. "We would have to start an investigation, but we do know one thing about them."

"Oh," asked Engels.

"VMS is the only health-related company in a three hundred-mile radius that has heard of HealthStar Ambulatory Services."

Lindstrom's jaw dropped. "Are you kidding me, Tavon?"

Tavon smiled at her. "Not at all. When I got in this morning, I finished checking every last drug store, holistic medicine shop, anything that I could think of that would have use for an ambulance. The email was in my inbox this morning. Visceral Medical Supplies has dealt with HealthStar in the past."

"Tavon, Tisdale," Engels said, pointing to the two officers, "go and start pulling all records we have on VMS. Find out how easy or hard the sale involving the original family was. I want to know what VMS does, and how well they do it. Go!" Tavon and Tisdale both nodded and left the conference room. Engels stood up, looking at the files of Ronald Vance and Olivia Sherman. He shook his head. "We're missing another piece."

"Actually," Lindstrom corrected, "we're missing three pieces." She walked to the white board, grabbed a dry erase marker, and started writing. "Piece one, who started this whole thing in motion? Piece two, who is the third person from the night Nathan Devlin was abducted, the man that helped load him into the back of the ambulance? Piece three, why did this happen in the first place?"

Engels looked at the white board and then at Lindstrom. "Three very important pieces. You want to venture a guess?"

Lindstrom gave Engels a wry grin. "Let me bring you up to speed about my interviews with both Nathan and Allison Devlin this morning, and an interesting conversation with Heidi Cole."

NINETEEN

Engels had listened to Lindstrom's recap of the interviews with the Devlin's and the face-to-face with Heidi Cole. While he was intrigued, they would need a lot more than a gut feeling and Lindstrom's intuition. However, from the prior cases that Lindstrom had worked, Engels knew that her intuition and gut usually proved correct. Unfortunately, they needed proof to justify any kind of search warrants for anything related to Heidi Cole. He told Lindstrom to keep her suspicions on the back burner, and to focus on the All Things Medical, Visceral Medical Supplies, and HealthStar Ambulatory angles.

Lindstrom stood there for a moment, looking at the various folders and papers that were on the conference table. She turned to the white board with the three-piece puzzle that she had written earlier. She took another dry erase marker and drew a long line down the middle of the board, essentially cutting the board into two halves. On the blank half, she wrote Nathan Devlin, Olivia Sherman, and Ronald Vance. She stepped back and stared at the board.

"Now what are you thinking," Engels inquired.

"There's something else here," Lindstrom said, in a far-off tone. "Something else that connects the three of them."

Engels stood up. "Go ahead and work on it. I'm going to…" His cell phone started to ring. He took it from his pocket and looked at the ID. It was Officer Jefferson. He swiped to accept the call. "Jefferson, what's going on?" As Engels listened, he held up an index finger to Lindstrom.

She was still looking at the dry erase board, lost in thought, so she couldn't see his gesture. "Okay, sit tight, and I'll head over with forensics and see for myself. Make yourself as invisible as you can in case the driver comes back." Engels ended the call. "Tish?"

Lindstrom turned around and looked at him. "Who was that?"

"It was Jefferson. One of the meter maids radioed for backup. They found a black delivery van matching the description and picture you gave. It's parked in a metered portion of the downtown library."

Lindstrom looked perplexed. "How long has it been there?"

"At least since before five yesterday afternoon."

"Let me grab my coat and we can head over."

Engels held up his hands. "Whoa there. I'll check it out with forensics. You stay here and work on this problem." He made a sweeping gesture from the dry erase board to the conference room table. He walked out of the room, went to his office to grab his coat, and headed down to forensics to get Jerry.

Lindstrom had been reading through the files on Ronald Vance and Olivia Sherman, trying to find a common thread that would link one or both to Nathan Devlin, Allison Devlin, or Heidi Cole. After two hours, she was no closer to it. There were no commonalities to link any of them together. They were born in different cities and different states, they attended different schools, there were no links between parents or siblings, they didn't share the same jobs, and they had never been incarcerated together. The only links were Vance and Sherman, who, maybe, possibly, knew each other through working at VMS. And, obviously, Nathan and Allison were married, and Nathan's best friend's wife had become best friends with Allison.

Lindstrom stood up from her chair and stretched, and as she let her muscles relax, she felt light headed. Dammit, she thought to herself, she had missed lunch. She left the conference room and headed to her desk to retrieve her lunch tote. She opened the tote and found that half of her lunch was gone. Her container of carrots, snap peas, and broccoli was gone, as was her protein and fiber bar. Worst of all, the reusable ice pack was also gone. The only things left were a bottle of tea, the salad she had made last night, and a small container of dressing. Of course, without the ice pack to keep everything cold, the salad and dressing were essentially garbage now. She shook her head and closed the tote. Bree had a habit of late night snacking. While Lindstrom tried to keep healthy alternatives in the house, Bree had done this before, pilfering from her mom's lunch tote.

Lindstrom had approached Bree about this a few months ago, and Bree, in typical teenage drama mode, had blown up about the whole thing. After that, Lindstrom had started packing her lunch in the morning. However, once school started and the weather started changing, it was easier to pack her lunch at night, usually using leftovers from dinner. This was the first time Bree had done this since that initial argument. Lindstrom put her lunch tote back under her desk and headed down to the break room. She hated eating out of the vending machines, but she needed something in her stomach.

A few minutes later, she walked into the break room. There were a few uniformed officers milling around, and two other detectives in the department were sitting at a table watching something on a cellphone.

"Tish!" Lindstrom turned toward the voice, and saw Heather Gordon, the receptionist, eating by herself. Lindstrom smiled and walked over to her. "Taking a late lunch today," Heather asked. "Or, should I rephrase that? Taking a late lunch again?" Heather smiled.

"Kind of," Lindstrom replied. "I got wrapped up in my investigation, and when I grabbed my lunch, turns out Bree helped herself to half of it last night."

Heather laughed and pulled out the chair next to her. "Well, sit down and stay away from the vending machine. Your misfortune is actually a blessing." Heather reached into a paper bag next to her and pulled out a plastic plate, fork, and spoon. She took hold of a different paper bag and slid it over to Lindstrom.

"What's all this," Lindstrom asked.

"Some of the uniformed officers and I ordered from the new Oriental place that opened a few months ago. As a thank you for catching the kid that had broken the front window and spray painted the tables, they sent a ton of extra food. There should be crab rangoon, egg rolls, and shrimp lo mein in that bag."

Lindstrom realized she was more famished than she had initially thought, as she devoured two egg rolls almost in one bite. Heather looked at her and laughed. Lindstrom started chuckling as she scooped the lo mein onto her plate. "Give me a break, Heather."

"Sorry, sorry! You reminded of Trevor for a minute. Remember? When you had that picnic at your place last summer? I don't think I've ever seen anyone that wasn't a competitive eater consume that much food that fast!"

Lindstrom laughed as she went to one of the community refrigerators, grabbed a bottle of water, and came back to Heather's table. "I know! As much as I love him, I can't wait until he's graduated and moved out. My grocery budget will be very happy!"

"The kids are doing okay, then?"

"I guess as well as can be expected for having a mom on the police force. The secret is the refrigerator and kitchen cabinets. Keep food in the house, and the teenagers are okay. Trevor helps with Ryan, and Bree is Bree, I guess."

"Well, I'm sure things aren't all that bad. This is a different time to grow up in, with the internet, cell phones, Facebook, Twitter, reality TV, there's so much to have to balance to try to keep kids grounded and to grow up to be decent human beings. Considering everything you've been through, I'm sure your children are turning out fine."

Lindstrom smiled. Heather had been an outstanding police woman in her own right, taking it upon herself to be equal parts guidance counselor, pastor, and mama bear to the rest of the police force. Whether it was a compliment or a critique, Heather told it like it needed to be told.

"Thanks, Heather, that means a lot."

Heather smiled back. "You're most welcome. Besides, with the extra money you got this week, that should help with some bills and keeping things chugging along, right?"

Lindstrom realized that she hadn't thought about the check from R.T.A. since dinner with the boys the other night, when she had talked to Trevor about that different pickup he wanted. "Yeah, I guess. Honestly, I haven't thought about it. It seems too unreal to even try to contemplate."

Heather was wiping her mouth after taking the last bite from her plate and put the napkin down. "Oh, come now. It's an absolute godsend! Sure, it would have been nice to have that money coming in along the way, but at least it is here now, for you and for the kids! I mean, Tish, think about how many wives and husbands, parents and children, are all owed alimony and child support. I'm sure the figures have to be staggering."

Lindstrom suddenly looked up from her plate, a noodle dangling out of her mouth. She quickly slurped it up, and some sauce slapped against her chin. Heather looked at her with a bemused look on her face. Lindstrom grabbed a napkin and wiped her mouth and chin, looked at Heather, and smiled. "You're right, the figures have to be staggering!"

Heather's face now turned into one of puzzlement. "I don't understand, Tish. What are you getting at?"

Lindstrom's smile grew as she stood up from the table, grabbed her bottle of water, and gave Heather a hug. "I think I know how it all fits together! Thanks Heather!" Lindstrom let her go and flew out of the break room. She didn't want to wait for the elevator, instead taking the stairs two at a time. She ran into the conference room and started looking through each file. Lindstrom's smile grew bigger and bigger. She grabbed a dry erase marker and started writing down the information from each file.

After fifteen minutes, Lindstrom had finished writing on the board and stepped back. She looked at everything on both sides of the dry erase board. There were still questions that needed to be answered, but the overall picture seemed to be coming into focus. She reached for her cell phone, but it wasn't in her pocket. She looked on the conference room table, and found it buried under some crime scene pictures of Ronald Vance's dead body. She must have been hungrier than she thought, because she kept her cell with her always, in case the kids called.

Lindstrom swiped the phone on. She had missed a call from Engels twenty minutes ago. No message was left. She pressed the icon to call him. After three rings, Engels came on the line.

"I hope you're having better luck than me."

"I think so," Lindstrom said, "but you first. What's going on?"

"The library is having a big book fair for grades preschool through four today. The parking lot still has a few school buses left, and I don't want to go in with police cars and a forensics crew until the kids have left." That was logical, Lindstrom thought. No sense in scaring school kids, teachers, and parents if you didn't have to. "How come you didn't answer your phone?"

"I forgot to have lunch," Lindstrom replied, "and I was so hungry I left it in the conference room. How much longer until you make a move on the van?"

"I checked the library's website, and they should be done in the next ten minutes. I can see another bus leaving the parking lot now, and more kids are getting onto a different bus. But enough about my mini-stakeout. Did you find something?"

Lindstrom hoped her smile was coming through the phone. "I think so. It makes a lot of sense. You finish up out there. I'm going to check on Tisdale and Tavon, and I'll see you when you get back to the station." Lindstrom ended the call. She knew that teasing Engels would upset him, but she didn't care. He needed to focus on the van, and it would be easier for Engels to understand if he saw it with his eyes. Lindstrom put her phone in her pocket and went to find Tisdale and Tavon.

Engels was definitely not having one of his better days. While the revelation that Ronald Vance and Olivia Sherman might be connected through being employed by the same company was good news, Engels was still frustrated with the early morning flat tires. Now here he was, on a mini-stakeout for a couple of hours. His patience was waning, and whatever Lindstrom had discovered, she was keeping to herself. Great, he thought, just great. This was a kidnapping and murder investigation, not trying to hide who a Secret Santa was.

Engels closed his eyes and took a deep breath. Lindstrom wasn't usually like this, so she must have a reason for the subterfuge. He opened his eyes and saw the last bus leave the library parking lot. He motioned to Jefferson in the patrol car behind him, and Jefferson gave him a thumbs-up. Engels started his car, navigating the parking ramp until he was on the street, quickly turning into the library's parking lot. He parked a good hundred feet away.

Even with all the buses that had been at the library, none had parked near the black delivery van, and with good reason. The small parking area would have been a bottleneck for a bus to get in and out of, with no exit from that area of the parking lot. If someone was in the van and tried to make a getaway in the vehicle, the only realistic way out was to plow through Engels' car, Jefferson's squad car, Jerry's forensics van, and the tow truck that Engels had called for.

Engels was out of his car, with Jefferson about ten yards to his right. Engels looked beyond the van, past the wall that closed off the parking lot, to the street on the other side. Officer Clemens was on the sidewalk and nodded. Engels motioned toward the van, and all three of them walked forward, hands on their individual weapons, ready for anything. When they were within twenty-five feet of the van, Engels put up his fist. Jefferson and Clemens stopped, each taking out their weapons, ready to act if necessary.

Engels hadn't been on this end of police duty in many years, but he was relieved that his instincts and his reflexes hadn't dulled with age. He didn't know if this was a fool's errand or not, but Lindstrom deserved the benefit of the doubt. If she suspected that there was something going on, it was worth a few hours of his time to check it out. He signaled the two officers to be ready, and that he was going in. They both nodded and stood at the ready.

Engels walked slowly towards the van, trying to get an indication if someone was hiding inside. The van was solid black, waxed to a high shine, and the windows were tinted. Even the windshield had some form of tinting to it, which, of course, was illegal. He had reached the passenger door, and carefully put his hand around the door handle. He slowly tried the handle, but the door wouldn't open. He carefully put his face close to the glass, trying to see inside past the tinting without touching the window. He figured Jerry would give him hell by not wearing a glove when trying the door handle. Oh well, Jerry would have to be upset.

As Engels looked in the window, he realized that he couldn't see the driver's side window. Even with the darkest tint, he should be able to see through the cab and see the other window, especially since it was a sunny afternoon. Something must be blocking the window. He made his way to the back of the van. He looked down where the license plate should be. As Lindstrom had said, there was a plate that read "Best Auto Sales". Engels looked through the back window, but again saw nothing. The windows were blocked or covered.

Engels took a few steps backward, then looked to the right and left. Clemens and Jefferson were still in position. Engels took a quick assessment of the situation. He decided to be more direct. He signaled for both to be ready. Engels took a position at the corner of the vehicle and banged his fist on one of the back doors.

"POLICE!" Engels yelled. "COME OUT WITH YOUR HANDS UP!" No answer came from inside. In fact, there was no noise at all. He banged again, harder and louder this time, and shouted again. "POLICE, OPEN UP, THIS IS YOUR LAST WARNING!" A few seconds and still nothing, so Engels holstered his weapon and took out his billy club. He swung it back to extend it fully, and then swung it forward, shattering the window. As he used the club to finish knocking the rest of the glass out, he stole a quick glance around. At this time of the afternoon, there were no pedestrians, no one stopping with their cell phones out, recording video to post to the internet. Even the cars that were driving by didn't seem to notice that anything was going on. As he turned back towards the back of the van, he was hit with an incredibly putrid smell. He suppressed his gag reflex and covered his mouth and nose with his arm.

Engels looked through the area where the glass used to be, and he was face-to-face with a clear plastic bag full of garbage. He put his arm through the open window, reaching down and trying to find a door knob or release. He did, and he pulled the back door open. With the back doors open, more plastic bags of garbage spilled out of the back of the van, causing Engels to stumble and then fall on the ground.

"CHIEF!" Jefferson shouted, as he pointed to Clemens to stay put. He ran towards Engels. He put his free hand under Engels armpit and helped him to his feet. "What the hell is all this," Jefferson asked, astonished.

Engels collapsed his billy club and put it in his pocket. He walked around the back of the van to the other side, surveying all the garbage bags, looking into the van, and then looking at Clemens. "I think you can relax," Engels yelled to Clemens. "I don't think anyone is home." Clemens holstered his weapon and walked toward the front of the van. Engels looked at Jefferson, who also holstered his weapon. Engels put up his arm and waved. Jerry opened the door of his van and got out, walking toward the officers.

As Jerry walked up and stood next to Engels, he said, "Yeah, I don't know what you expect me to do about this, but I'm not going through every bag of garbage."

Jefferson had stepped closer to the bags, taking a closer look. "You don't have to. Looks like all these bags came from the food court at the mall."

Engels looked at the bags, peering past the clear plastic of the garbage liners to the contents inside. He saw wrappers and containers for Taco Johns, Culvers, Subway, and Dairy Queen. There were a lot of those places in town, but only one place where they were all together. Then Engels spotted a box for a pretzel shop and the very distinct red, green, and white cup for the pizzeria that was only in the mall's food court. Engels looked at Jerry and confirmed the obvious, saying, "Jefferson is right. This is all from the food court."

Clemens had now joined the rest of them at the back of the van. "This doesn't make any sense."

Engels disagreed. He looked at Jerry and said, "I'm going to call in one of the waste disposal companies and have them bring a truck out. My guess is you won't find anything useful on any of these bags. Try to verify that every bag came from the mall food court, which shouldn't be difficult if they are all clear plastic. Once the van is clear, tow it back to the station and start your forensics on it. When everything comes back negative, let me know."

Jerry was looking over the van, yet he spoke directly to Engels. "You must be thinking what I'm thinking, then"

Engels nodded. "You better believe it." He looked at Jefferson and Clemens. "You two sit tight with Jerry. Help with anything he needs." Engels took out his cell and found the contact info for the waste company that the city used for public buildings. After he finished getting a truck authorized to get to the library on the double, he told the tow truck driver to wait until Jerry was ready for him.

Engels stood by his car and looked back at Jerry, Clemens, and Jefferson. He looked around the area, from the library to the parking ramp to the various office buildings and parking lots. No one was taking a particular interest in what was going on. His day had been a rollercoaster, starting out bad, getting slightly better, then got worse, and now was much worse. He got into his car, slammed the door hard, and sat there. This wasn't what he was expecting. He took out his cellphone and called Lindstrom. After two rings, she answered.

"How did the stakeout go," Lindstrom asked.

"It's a good thing I'm not a hard-drinking man, Tish." Engels gave her a rundown on the events involving the black delivery van, trying to keep his composure while he did so.

"I'm sorry, boss," Lindstrom said in a conciliatory tone. "What are you going to do now?"

"Where are we at with Visceral Medical Supplies?"

"I'm standing here with Tisdale and Tavon right now. They've got some information, but I'm not sure how it fits into the investigation. I was going to head over there and talk to someone, maybe get some ideas regarding Vance and Sherman."

"Speaking of those two," Engels said, "did anything come up between them and the Devlin's?"

"I've got a pretty good idea, but I need to do a little more checking."

"Okay," Engels said. "You head over to VMS and snoop around. I will be back at the station in a little while." He ended the call, started his car, and peeled out of the parking lot. He was driving angrier than he meant to, and he immediately slowed down. He was pissed, and he should have known better than to let his emotions show, especially in front of his officers.

"I'm telling you, from what we've found, there was no animosity between the two companies." Tisdale was sitting in front of a computer screen, with Tavon leaning on the desk next to him. Tavon was rubbing his eyes. Lindstrom was standing behind Tisdale, hovering over him.

Lindstrom replied, "It's not that I don't believe you, but don't you find it odd that a big company buying up a little family-owned company didn't generate any kind of negativity?"

"Not in this case," Tavon said. "Paul, pull it up."

Tisdale clicked the mouse and found the file, a copy of an article from the local chamber of commerce newsletter dated from three years ago. He stood up so that Lindstrom could sit down and read it off the screen.

"The article runs about two pages, but I can summarize it for you," Tisdale said.

"Go ahead," came Lindstrom's answer. "I'll read it off the screen while you're talking."

"Raymond Mobley had taken over the company from his father in the fifties. It wasn't the most successful, but for a family-owned business competing in medical sales and supplies, All Things Medical did okay. Mobley's wife died of uterine cancer in 1975. They had one daughter, but she had no interest in the company. She became a missionary in Central America and died during a hurricane in 1993. With no wife and no heirs to try to divide the company between, Mobley was approached in 1996 by

238

someone named Edward Kirkham. They formed a partnership that lasted past Mobley's retirement in 1998, and then his death in 2004. Upon his death, Mobley bequeathed his estate to numerous charities across the country. The only thing that wasn't part of the estate was All Things Medical. Two years ago, Kirkham changed the name of the company to Visceral Medical Supplies."

"What do we know about VMS, then," Lindstrom asked.

"Nothing," Tisdale answered. "They have one website. It is privately owned, apparently by Edward Kirkham. No board of directors, no CEO or COO or CFO. There are no criminal or civil complaints against them, no tax liens, absolutely nothing that indicates they are involved in anything nefarious."

Lindstrom stood there, dumbfounded. They had a credible link between Ronald Vance and Olivia Sherman and their place of employment. Now here were three cops, standing around a computer monitor that was displaying information that she found hard to believe. Unbelievable, she thought sarcastically, that the company both suspects had worked for was the only company in the world not involved in any form of litigation or malfeasance. As everything else with this case, something wasn't adding up.

"Okay," Lindstrom said quickly to both Tavon and Tisdale. "You two keep working on the company angle, anything you can think of. I'm going to head over to VMS and dig a little bit." She grabbed the mouse, minimizing the window with the article she had finished reading, and pulled up VMS's website. She clicked on the location link, and two addresses appeared on the computer screen. She pointed to the addresses, asking both Tavon and Tisdale, "Which one should I be going to?"

Tisdale pointed to the first one. "This is the company's address here in town. It must be an office location, maybe a distribution center, or some form of public contact area. The other address is a warehouse north of Sioux Falls."

Lindstrom wrote down the address. "Alright, get back to it, and call me if you find out anything else that you think I might be able to use."

"Definitely," Tavon said.

Lindstrom headed down to the police garage and got into her car. As she headed to the office of Visceral Medical Supplies, she was trying to process what Engels had told her about the black delivery van. Maybe it didn't have any connection to the Devlin case. Still, she couldn't shake the weirdness of it. At least she felt confident about what she had pieced together about Nathan Devlin, Ronald Vance, and Olivia Sherman. Sure, it may seem thin. Sometimes, however, that's how real life worked.

It took Lindstrom almost half an hour to drive across town to the VMS office. She pulled into the parking lot and found an empty space. The office occupied one spot in a strip mall. The other tenants included a coffee shop, a second-hand children's clothing store, a gourmet popcorn shop, and two empty spots that looked to be under renovations. There were no signs that advertised what was coming soon, only the name of the construction company that was doing the work.

Lindstrom got out of her car, walked across the parking lot, and entered the front door of Visceral Medical Supplies. It was fairly nondescript, with a high counter area for part of the front, a lower counter area for anyone in a wheelchair, and a small swinging gate to the back. On the wall to the right was a large painting of a caduceus, on the wall to the left was a painting of a sunset in the mountains, and on the wall behind the counter area was a large black and white print by Ansel Adams. She recognized the print as being from Yellowstone National Park. Lindstrom remembered because a year ago, her sister had taken Bree on a vacation to the Black Hills, Yellowstone, and the Rocky Mountains. On that trip, Bree had purchased a journal detailing all the national parks, with the intention of, one day, visiting every single national park. Bree had also taken a copious number of photos.

A door chime had sounded when she walked in, and Lindstrom heard a voice say, "Good afternoon! How can I help you today?" Lindstrom walked up to the counter area, and saw a woman sitting at a desk that was hidden behind the high counter. As the women made eye contact, she said to Lindstrom, "Hi there! Sorry about that. I'm always asking to have the counter lowered so people can see me when they come in. Anyway, welcome to VMS, also known as Visceral Medical Supplies! How can I help?"

Lindstrom had her badge out and showed it to her. "Hello, my name is Detective Patricia Lindstrom. I need to ask you a few questions."

The woman stood up and walked to the counter. She looked at Lindstrom's badge and said, "So, you found it, then?"

"I'm sorry," Lindstrom replied, "but what was I supposed to find?"

"Our stolen delivery van, of course. The warehouse reported it stolen over the weekend. I was told that one of our delivery drivers became disgruntled, and when he was relieved of his duties, he left with one of the vans." This was news to Lindstrom. Maybe she could use that to her advantage.

"Actually," Lindstrom began, "I will get to that in a minute. I need some information regarding two of your employees, Ronald Vance and Olivia Sherman. But first, I didn't catch your name."

"Oh, forgive me" the woman said. "My name is Cassie, Cassie Butler. I am the receptionist here at the VMS retail site."

"So, Ms. Butler, did you know either Ronald Vance or Olivia Sherman?"

"Well, I don't really know any of the employees. I only work here, and most of the action, you could say, happens at the warehouse. If anyone comes in here, the best I can do is offer them a catalog, help them place an online order, or schedule a time to come back and speak with a sales rep."

"That sounds pretty dull for you," Lindstrom said.

Cassie nodded. "Yes, it can be most days. I remember my second interview, when they offered me this job. The woman with human resources said that I'll be bored and lonely most days of the week. However, as long as I did my job well and never had any complaints from customers, I was free to read, play on my phone, or whatever."

Must be rough to have a job like that, Lindstrom thought to herself. "So, you never met either Ronald Vance or Olivia Sherman?"

"I'm sorry, Detective, but no, I never met Ronald or Olivia. I did hear some gossip about a year ago that they were seeing each other, which was a strict breach of company policy. Absolutely no fraternizing is allowed between co-workers. I believe they were both let go because of it." She paused for a moment, and then added, "I think that's why the other driver got fired last week."

"Do you know the driver's name," Lindstrom asked, all while taking notes on what Cassie Butler was saying.

"Charles. Charles Utecht."

"So, this Charles Utecht was seeing someone at the warehouse?"

"Actually," Cassie said, "hold on. Human resources called me with the information on Monday. It was a big deal. Give me a minute to find the note." Cassie walked back to her desk and started looking through a small stack of papers.

Lindstrom was looking around the office, and it was sparse. There was a chair at the lower counter area, and one more in the corner by the window. There were no magazines, no pamphlets, no plants, nothing that made the area seem warm or cozy. On the lower counter area was a computer monitor with a pen lying next to it. Lindstrom could see a hallway that ended with a door that read "EMERGENCY EXIT, ALARM WILL SOUND". The hallway had two doors on the left and two doors on the right. All the doors were open with no lights on in any of them. Even Cassie's desk seemed devoid of activity. There was a computer monitor that was on a screen saver, a cell phone, a calendar, and a small plastic riser with three shelves. Each shelf had a few papers in each, but nothing that screamed bustling activity. The only thing that looked busy was an electronic tablet on the desk that was paused on split screen. It looked like Cassie had been playing Sudoku and Words with Friends when Lindstrom had arrived.

"Ah," Cassie said, pulling out a piece of paper. She walked back to the counter and read to Lindstrom, "Charles Utecht was fired over the weekend when it was discovered he had been trying to have a relationship with a co-worker. He was going to be relieved of his duties. However, he didn't report for work over the weekend. We have terminated his employment, and we have also contacted the police to report that he has stolen the delivery van he used." Cassie finished reading and showed the paper to Lindstrom. It was hand-written.

"Did you write this," Lindstrom asked.

"Yes, I did. Even when something big comes up, I don't warrant a visit from the higher ups. They called me first thing Monday morning when I opened the doors, and I wrote it down word for word. I even had to read it back, so they knew I got it right."

Lindstrom would need to verify that a report had been filed. A stolen vehicle wouldn't have come across her desk, but she could check with the switchboard operators. She looked up from her notes and asked Cassie, "So, you have never met Ronald Vance, Olivia Sherman, or Charles Utecht?"

Cassie shook her head. "I'm sorry, Detective, but I never met any of them. I wish I could be of more help to you. Heck, I wish I could say that if I hear anything, I will let you know. But, as you can see," Cassie held out her arms and spun in a circle, "I don't think I'll be hearing anything anytime soon."

"Do you think that the three of them knew each other?"

Cassie shrugged her shoulders. "It's possible, but I really couldn't say for certain. This is where I work. I've never been to the warehouse, and the company isn't really about being social. No Christmas parties, no get-togethers, in fact, the last time that someone from the warehouse came here was maybe two months ago."

Lindstrom looked over her notes, and then asked, "Have you ever heard of HealthStar Ambulatory Services?"

Cassie thought about it for a minute, grabbed a sheet of paper from one of the risers on her desk, and then answered, "Yes, but vaguely. I received this email from the woman in human resources. It says that VMS had been contacted more than a year ago from a company called HealthStar. They were looking at trying to establish a presence in the Sioux Falls market. VMS told them they weren't interested." Cassie handed the sheet to Lindstrom, who stopped writing and, taking the printed email in her hands, read it over.

"When did you receive this?"

"Just this morning," came Cassie's response. "H.R. said that they received an inquiry from the police about HealthStar, and, in case the police stopped by to ask questions, to have this information available."

Lindstrom gave the sheet back to Cassie, closed her notebook, and looked at her cellphone for the time. It was almost three fifty in the afternoon. She looked at Cassie Butler, smiled, and said, "Thank you for your time, Ms. Butler. Here is my card, and if you think of anything that might be relevant, please don't hesitate to call." She handed her a card, which Cassie took.

"I will, Detective, and you have a great afternoon!" Cassie stood at the counter, smiling, as Lindstrom turned around and left the office. She got into her car, left the parking lot, but then pulled into the parking lot of a Taco Bell five blocks away. Lindstrom had been hoping for more from her visit to VMS, but not in this manner. Not only was she no closer to finding out about Ronald Vance and Olivia Sherman, but now it appeared that the whole delivery van angle might be completely separate from the initial investigation. She glanced around, realizing the parking lot was practically empty. She turned off the engine and decided to run inside the

Taco Bell and get an iced tea to go.

A few minutes later, Lindstrom was back in her car, heading towards the police station. Unfortunately, with all the schools in town dismissed for the day, the last remnants of the summer construction season around, and people getting an early jump on getting home, it would take even longer to get back there. Before she had left the Taco Bell parking lot, Lindstrom had texted Officer Tavon to check if Visceral Medical Supplies had filed a stolen vehicle report in the last month. Tavon had responded that he would check and let her know ASAP.

Lindstrom decided to try to separate the two cases, at least for the moment. If Charles Utecht had indeed quit before getting fired, he had come up with a pretty unique way of getting revenge on the company. Parking his delivery van and filling it completely full of garbage was inspired, if ultimately stupid. Not only would he be unemployed, but the charges would be grand theft auto, vandalism, destruction of property, and, considering garbage was involved on public property, the district attorney might even throw in some health code violations. The D.A. could also get the owners of the mall involved and the various businesses that had had their garbage "stolen".

Of course, it still didn't explain how she had seen the same van in her neighborhood over the weekend. Then again, Lindstrom hadn't actually seen a license plate on that delivery van. For all she knew, that van, or those vans, had been making actual deliveries that day, and she had happened to see the van that Utecht was driving yesterday outside of the hospital. Lindstrom thought about that for a minute, and then frowned. While she acknowledged they could happen, she absolutely hated coincidences. This one, though, was pushing her ability to suspend her disbelief.

Finally, Lindstrom was closing in on the police station when her cell phone rang. She was still deep in rush hour traffic, so she pressed the hands-free button on the steering wheel. "Lindstrom," she said.

"Tish," Engels' voice came over the car speakers. "Where are you?"

"I'm about three blocks away. Why?"

"Tavon checked for a stolen vehicle report. Looks like VMS did file a report on a stolen vehicle on late Monday afternoon. The human resources director called the station's main line instead of calling 911. Apparently, she didn't want to cause a panic or bring any bad press to the company."

That would absolve Visceral Medical of any potential misconduct. It was also convenient, Lindstrom thought. Almost as convenient as having an email ready that said the only company in town that had heard of HealthStar wasn't interested in doing business with them, and that that had happened over a year ago.

"Are you planning on heading home," Lindstrom asked.

"Not yet," Engels said. "Diane said she was running late, but she was going to bring dinner home for us."

"I'll be turning into the police garage in thirty seconds. I'll meet you in the conference room." Lindstrom ended the call. She parked and made her way upstairs. On the way, she bumped into Tisdale, who looked like he was collecting his things to head home. "Calling it a night?" she asked.

"Yes, I am," Tisdale said. "Tavon and I didn't find anything else amazing, outstanding, or dirty about Visceral Medical or All Things Medical. From a family-owned business to a privately-owned business, no one has ever leveled a complaint against them, either as customers or as employees. We brainstormed a few other avenues, but they all came up empty."

"When you get in tomorrow, I want you to start looking into a Charles Utecht."

Tisdale took a piece of paper, wrote down the name as Lindstrom spelled it out, and taped the note to the keyboard.

"You got it," Tisdale said. Lindstrom started walking away, when Tisdale caught her. "Hey, I know you're in a hurry, but can I steal one minute?"

Lindstrom stopped and pivoted back towards Tisdale. "What's up?"

"Look, I haven't asked the chief about this, but how long do you think this is going to last?"

Lindstrom looked at him curiously. "What do you mean?"

Tisdale took a step closer so that any other officers or detectives wouldn't hear him. "I mean I've really enjoyed being on this case. I've learned a lot, and I want to see it through. I guess I'm wondering if I'm going back to a squad car and regular patrols after this, or if I'll be working out of the station, or exactly where I'm sitting at."

Lindstrom smiled. "You've done good work on this case, Tisdale. Believe me, Engels always makes sure that his officers, check that, he makes sure that everyone involved with the department is taken care of.

When the case is over, I'd guarantee that he will call you into his office and talk to you about your performance on the case, and your options going forward."

Tisdale smiled. "I guess I just wanted to know where I stand for the future. Not only for me but, well, for someone else, too."

Lindstrom raised an eyebrow. "My, my, my, Officer Tisdale, I didn't know."

Tisdale blushed a little bit. "It's been a little on again, off again, but this last month has been more of a whirlwind. I'm feeling kind of confident about things moving ahead, and it would be nice to give her a hint that I might be in line for moving up."

"Don't overplay your hand, be positive and keep doing good work around here, and things will work out for the best."

"Thanks, Tish. Have a good night!" With that, Tisdale headed towards the elevators, and Lindstrom walked to Conference Room Two. As she walked in, Engels looked up from the chair he was sitting in.

"What kept you," Engels asked. "Couldn't find a decent place to park?"

"Well, we can't all get the prime spots like you and the mayor," Lindstrom retorted with a mock-sarcasm. "Actually, I had a chat with Tisdale. He's hoping you have noticed his hard work on the case."

Engels smiled while shaking his head. "He's done some good work, I will say that. Whether it's me or the next chief, Tisdale will get his."

"Really, are you going to start in with this crap right now?"

"I'm not having this argument with you again, Tish. You know my feelings about this department, and if I could make a clone of Clive and put him back in charge of the overall force, I would. I wasn't meant to be behind a desk, managing overtimes, budgets, and prepping for TV interviews."

Lindstrom was going to counter back, then thought better of it. There were more important things to deal with, and Engels' meeting with the mayor wasn't for another two weeks.

"You win, for now, so let's talk about the case," Lindstrom said. She sat down and gave him a rundown of what she had learned at VMS from Cassie Butler.

"Let me guess," Engels began, "your BS alert went off, because you don't like coincidences?"

246

"Well, there is that. But I'm also thinking about what Cassie told me and what Tisdale told me. Imagine a company that fired two people because they might have come together in a relationship. A third employee, apparently disgruntled, steals a company vehicle, either before he gets fired, or right after he's terminated. Yet, somehow, there are no complaints or litigation against the company. It doesn't seem to track, does it?"

Engels thought about it. "Well, you're right, but I've seen non-disclosure agreements that are ironclad and completely immobilize someone from taking any kind of action, public or private." Engels took a handful of peanuts out of the bag he had on the table, ate them quick, and then took a drink from his glass. "Let's move on for now. I see you have Nathan, Ronald, and Olivia on the big board there. Walk me through what you think you have."

Lindstrom stood up and walked to the dry erase board. She pointed to the first section she had written and said, "Nathan Devlin is a recovering alcoholic, separated from his wife and three children, with no income, no savings, and no known criminal past." She took a step to her left and pointed to the next section, saying, "Ronald Vance is a petty criminal, never married but has a child, has never been known to engage in violent crimes, and who gets mixed up in a kidnapping plot gone wrong and kills himself." She took one more step to her left and pointed to the final section, saying, "Olivia Sherman had a pretty tough life, has a child but skips out, leaving the child with the father, keeps getting into minor trouble with the law, somehow gets plastic surgery, but ends up dead, horribly disfigured and mutilated, and dumped in a storm drain." She stopped and looked at Engels. Engels looked at all three sections, then at Lindstrom. He shrugged his shoulders.

"Okay, you have me stumped, Tish."

Lindstrom took a dry erase marker. Above Nathan Devlin, she wrote $7,000. Above Ronald Vance, she wrote $18,000. Above Olivia Sherman, she wrote $16,000. She set the marker down and looked at Engels. Engels looked at the numbers, and then back to Lindstrom.

"Tish, spell it out for me! What am I, wait a second, what are you suggesting?"

Lindstrom smiled. "Each person involved in this has at least one child, and each owes back child support in these amounts."

Engels leaned forward, eating the peanuts from the bag. He stood up and walked toward the white board. He examined each section, processing what Lindstrom had said.

"Don't you think that's a little flimsy, Tish? Lots of people have kids, and lots of people get divorced or leave their spouses and kids behind."

"True. And you're right, it may seem flimsy, but look at what we know. All three of them owed child support, two of them more than likely knew each other, and those two are now dead."

Engels had to admit that it was definitely a link, but he wasn't sure it was strong enough. "Okay, let's assume that Vance and Sherman met at VMS. They bemoan that they owe so much, especially after they both lose their jobs. So, they come up with the kidnapping scheme. The problem is they pick a guy that is basically in the same boat as they are."

Lindstrom shook her head. "Don't even go down that road right now. All I'm saying is that there is definitely a link between the three of them. All three of them have kids and all three of them owe money to those kids." She took the dry erase marker again and made a fourth section out of some empty space on the board and wrote a big question mark. "We need to find the fourth person. This person helped load Nathan Devlin into the ambulance and was the driver, too. If we find him, then we'll know if that's where the case stops, or if there is more to it."

Engels looked at her. "Any idea on how you hope to find the fourth person?"

Lindstrom looked at the board. "Not yet, but I have all night to think of something."

"I take it you are calling it quits for the day?"

"Standing here looking at the dry erase board isn't going to get me any closer to the fourth person." Lindstrom stepped back and looked at Engels. "Besides, I've been doing some thinking today, and I think it's time to move forward on a few things." She started walking toward the door and said, "Go home and have a good night with Diane. I will see you in the morning." With that, Lindstrom left the police station, a smile on her face and an added spring in her step.

INTERMISSION:

AMELIORATE

"I leave this façade,

this reality of falsehoods…

Escape the Pain; escape the power;

Escape myself…"

- **_Prelude to Madness,_**

Daniel Van Deest, 1989

INTERMISSION

"Mom, seriously, do I have to go with the two of you?" Trevor was dressed in his pajamas, which was part of his daily routine. Get up late, go to school for his only two classes, leave early, come home, put on his pajamas, and do nothing except play on his computer or his Xbox or his phone. Oh, and try to eat as much food as possible.

Lindstrom looked at her oldest son. On the drive home, she had played out the different scenarios in her head of how the two older kids would react to her invite. Each scenario ended exactly the same, with Trevor and Bree whining, complaining, and generally throwing a fit. It was more of a courtesy that she had invited them in the first place. She didn't want to have an argument with either of them. As their mother, she had invited, and they had said no.

"No, Trevor," Lindstrom said, "you don't have to go. I thought I would invite you. Bree is studying at a friend's house and didn't want to go, either." Ryan came running out of his room, so excited that it looked like he was celebrating Halloween, Christmas, and his birthday all at once.

"BYE BRO-BRO!" Ryan shot between his mother and brother and was in the garage before Trevor could respond. Lindstrom smiled, looked at Trevor, and started walking after Ryan.

"We'll be back later," Lindstrom said to her oldest son and closed the door between the kitchen and the garage. She got into the car, and as she was buckling her seatbelt, she looked at Ryan. He was smiling ear to ear, buckled up in the back seat, bursting with excitement. She slowly backed out of the garage, and once the car was clear, she looked back at the house to close the garage door. As she reached for the remote on her visor, Trevor ran out of the house and came up to the driver's side. Lindstrom put the car in park and rolled down her window.

"Mom, listen, um," Trevor started to say, stammering and trying to find the words. "It's not that I don't want to go. I'm just, um, well, I just don't know." Lindstrom looked at her oldest son. In some ways, he was a typical teenager, but in other ways, he wasn't. She waved him down to the window, and as he leaned in, she softly rubbed his cheek.

"Trevor, I know we haven't done this in a very long time," Lindstrom said. "I've been thinking a lot about it for the past week, and I think it's time I start making a stronger effort, not only for your little brother, but for myself, too. If you need some time, I understand. You have a vehicle of your own and more free time after school. I trust you to make the right decision. The best decision." With that, Trevor stood up and stepped back from the car. Lindstrom put the car back into gear and left the house.

Thirty minutes later, Lindstrom pulled into their destination. At this time of night, there weren't many cars in the parking lot, so she was able to pick a parking spot with ease. She turned off the engine, but she didn't move. It had been almost a year and a half since she was last here. She had tried to justify to herself the reasons why she couldn't or wouldn't go. However, after everything that had happened over the last week, Lindstrom knew that she had been a coward. Seeing Allison Devlin that morning had lit a fire in Lindstrom, and she vowed to change, not only for herself, but for Trevor, Bree, and, probably most importantly, for Ryan.

"Momma, c'mon, let's go!" Ryan was unbuckled and climbing out of the car as he spoke. Lindstrom smiled and got out of the car, locking it, and taking Ryan by his hand. They both ran to the building and through the front doors as they automatically slid open. It was closing in on seven at night, so most of the night shift personnel were already on duty. Other people were coming and going, and while there was a front desk with attendants on duty, most people that came here knew where they were going.

The one drawback to doing this on a Wednesday night was that Ryan and Lindstrom wouldn't be able to stay very long. However, when Lindstrom had made her decision to begin this healing process tonight, she had done a little checking via a phone call on her way home. The information that she received made her feel confident that this was the perfect time to do this.

Lindstrom stopped and had to hold Ryan back. "Momma, what's wrong? Let's go, let's go!"

"Hold on for a second there, big man! Mommy has to do one thing. You stand right here and don't move, understand?"

"Yes Momma!" Ryan practically froze in place, which must have been difficult, considering how excited he was for this. Lindstrom walked to the front desk and pulled a folded note out of her pocket. One of the attendants looked at her and smiled.

"Yes ma'am, can I help you," he asked.

"Would you be kind enough to contact this person," Lindstrom said, pointing to the name she had written on the note, "and give her this note as soon as possible?" She handed the note to the attendant, who looked at the name. He smiled at Lindstrom.

"Absolutely," he said. He reached for a telephone, and Lindstrom went back to Ryan.

"Well there, little man," Lindstrom said, "are you ready?"

"You betcha, Momma!" They held hands and started skipping down the hallway together, navigating their way through different twists and turns of the halls until they arrived at their destination.

Lindstrom stood at the door and looked down at Ryan. "Do you remember the rules?"

Ryan nodded with great enthusiasm. "Keep my voice down and be very careful!"

Lindstrom was smiling, brimming with unimaginable love and pride at this little boy that she had brought into the world. "Well, what are you waiting for? Knock on the door!" Ryan's eyes grew to the size of saucers as he knocked on the door. He then reached for the handle, pushed it down, and slowly opened the door into the room. Ryan held the door open with one hand while holding his mother's hand with the other, pulling her into the room. They walked in, with Lindstrom helping the door close quietly. A small entryway greeted them, maybe five feet long, and it only took them about six steps to emerge into the room. Ryan let go of her hand and he went to the left side of the bed. Ryan put his hands on the hand of the man who was laying there. Using his foot, he was able to move a small step stool out from underneath the bed, stepped on top of it, and leaned over the edge of the bed so he could give the man a kiss on the cheek.

"Hi Daddy! I've missed you so much!"

Lindstrom stepped to the edge of the bed, looking at Mark Walsh, her second husband, and watching Ryan interact with him. Even in Mark's current condition, Lindstrom had to admit that he looked handsome. One of the things that she had insisted from the hospice workers was that Mark should be groomed. Mark enjoyed going from a goatee to a five o'clock shadow to a partial beard. She had always loved his little "salt and pepper" in the facial hair on his chin, and when Mark sometimes shaved it off, she had always joked with him that she couldn't look at him until it grew back. Mark would never grow a full beard, though, because the facial hair always caused his neck to itch like crazy. That was why he always changed his look with regards to his facial hair, and Lindstrom had always found it sexy.

"Momma, aren't you going to say hi?"

Lindstrom moved around to the other side of the bed, carefully sitting down next to Mark's motionless body. She looked at him carefully. He had good color to his skin, and it looked like he had been shaved within the last day. Apart from the oxygen tube beneath his nose and wrapped around both of his ears and the small collection of wires that was coming out of his gown by his neck, anyone would have thought that Mark was only sleeping. Maybe, in some vague way, that's what he was doing, only sleeping, waiting for the right time to wake up and rejoin his family. She took one of his hands and put it in her's, while taking her other hand and slowly caressing his cheek.

"Hello, my sweet Mark," Lindstrom said. "I'm sorry I haven't come to see you in so long. I could make excuses, but that wouldn't be fair to you. I'm so sorry. I want you to know that I'll get better at coming here and spending time with you." She was trying to hold back her tears, because she knew if she started to cry, Ryan would start crying, too. Mark had always been a big softie, which was one of the things that Lindstrom had loved about him. Ryan shared some of those same emotional qualities. Sometimes, seemingly out of nowhere, Ryan might be sad or come up to his mom and give her a hug, saying that he had thought about something sad or that he missed his "Papa", which was the name he had given to Mark's father.

"Momma really missed you last Friday, Daddy! I was in a performance at school, and Momma got it on video! Do you want to see?" Ryan was already reaching into Lindstrom's purse, grabbing her cellphone and pulling up the video.

"Mark, you would have been so proud of your little boy," Lindstrom said to him. "He was absolutely amazing!" Ryan found the video and pressed the play icon. He fast-forwarded it until the video was at Ryan's first part. Ryan held the phone up so that, if Mark were to open his eyes, he could easily see the video. Ryan's little arms never got tired, even after holding the phone in the same position for all fifteen minutes of the video. Lindstrom sat there, looking from Mark to Ryan to the video and back again. She was on an emotional overload, her love for both of these two threatening to explode out of her in tears of joy and sadness.

After Ryan was done with the video, he started talking about any little thing he could think of. He was talking to Mark as if Mark could respond, and it was wonderful. Lindstrom would chime in here and there, trying to keep the happiness going. This kept going for fifteen minutes, and then Lindstrom heard a knock at the door. Before she could say anything, Ryan was up off the bed and said, "Come in!" The door slowly opened, and in walked Kara Reed.

Kara smiled when she saw Ryan, but when she looked at Lindstrom, she froze in place, a worried expression growing across her face. The note she had been given only stated she needed to stop by Mark Walsh's room when she was available. No reason had been written down, and she hadn't expected to see Lindstrom.

"Hi there," Ryan said. "Are you here to help my Daddy with something?"

Kara looked at Ryan, and then looked to Lindstrom. She was unsure of how to answer.

"As a matter of fact," Lindstrom said, "I asked Kara to stop by, because I needed to talk to her. Hey, I have an idea! Why don't you grab the remote for the TV and try to find one of those cartoons or cooking shows that you and Daddy liked to watch, okay? You cuddle right up next to Daddy but be careful, so you don't hurt him. We're going to be right outside the door, okay?"

"Okay Momma!" Ryan found the remote on a small table and started pressing buttons. Lindstrom stood up and walked toward Kara. Kara still had a perplexed look on her face, not knowing what was going to happen.

"Kara," Lindstrom said, using her arm to steer Kara towards the door, "I need to talk to you for a minute." Lindstrom walked past her, opened the door to Mark's room, and stepped out, holding the door for her. Kara looked at Lindstrom, still not sure what was happening, and walked out after Lindstrom. She turned around, watching the door slowly close.

"Um, Tish, I don't know," Kara started to say, but Lindstrom held up both of her hands to pause her.

"Kara," Lindstrom said, in a tone that was humble and conciliatory, "things have been difficult for me and the kids. But, over the last week, with everything I've had going on with the Devlin case, I've had some time to think about a lot of things." She took a deep breath, then continued. "It's time to move on. I'm not sure why things happened the way they did, but at this point, it doesn't matter anymore. I love my husband and I love my kids. For what it's worth, I'm sorry for how I treated you."

Kara stood there, thunderstruck, not really sure how to react.

"Tish, I really, I mean, I don't." Kara was flustered, and, trying to regain her composure, she cleared her throat and said, "I really don't know what to say."

"You don't need to say anything. I wanted to start clearing the air between us." Lindstrom smiled at Kara and put her hand out. Kara looked at her and a smile started to replace her frown. She took Lindstrom's hand, and they shook.

"Tish, I'm just, I am so, so," Kara stammered.

Lindstrom shook her head. "Kara, I'm going to go back in and be with Mark and Ryan before we have to go home." Lindstrom let go of Kara's hand, smiled, and went back into Mark's room. Kara watched her go, flabbergasted by what had happened. This was completely out of the blue. She only volunteered at the hospice center one night a week. This wasn't what she was expecting for tonight. Either way, Kara felt like an incredible weight was starting to be lifted off of her. She looked at the door to Mark's room for another minute, and then headed back to work, with a little more spring in her step.

Lindstrom was looking at Ryan cuddled up to Mark, watching the TV. Ryan had brought Mark's arm over his shoulder, so that it looked like Mark was holding him. Lindstrom was still suppressing her tears, so she walked up to the bed and gently tousled Ryan's hair. Ryan looked at his mother and whispered, "Is it time to go?"

"Oh, I think we can stay for a little bit more," Lindstrom said. Ryan smiled, and laid his head on Mark's chest. Lindstrom walked back around to the other side of the bed and sat down in a chair. She hoped that, by talking to Kara face to face, here, in a safe place, that it would be the start of a rejuvenation. Not only for Lindstrom, but for everyone that might have been affected by Mark's situation. She bore much of that yolk, if she was being honest with herself. Lindstrom's thoughts drifted back, back to how this unpleasantness had started.

Mark had been diagnosed with acid reflux as a result of a hiatal hernia. After a few doctor visits, Mark decided he wanted to get the lap nissen surgery. His doctor, the surgeon, the nurses, multiple internet searches, people that Mark talked to that had gone through with the surgery, everything and everyone said that it was a simple, routine procedure. He had grown tired of taking over-the-counter acid reducers and prescription acid neutralizers, so much so that he decided it was time to stop treating the symptoms and fix the problem.

Lindstrom had been sitting in the waiting room, all three of the kids in school. After two hours, Kara Reed, who was a head surgical nurse at the time, came out and told Lindstrom that the surgery was completed, everything looked good, and that the surgeon would be out to talk to her soon.

An hour later, a different nurse appeared in the waiting room and asked Lindstrom to follow her. Lindstrom had assumed that the nurse was taking her to see Mark in recovery. Instead, she was brought to a room that was marked "Consultation" on the door. Perplexed, Lindstrom walked in, and the nurse asked her to sit down. Before Lindstrom could ask what was going on, the nurse had shut the door and was gone. A minute later, Mark's surgeon walked in with Kara Reed and three other people walking right behind him. Kara's face was devoid of color, her head turned down, averting Lindstrom's eyes.

"Mrs. Lindstrom," the surgeon began, "I'm afraid there's been a complication with Mark's surgery."

Lindstrom felt her heart stop. Her mouth went dry. Her hands started to quiver. Her eyes went from the surgeon to Kara, and she said, "But you said that everything looked good." Kara lifted her head slightly, looked at Lindstrom for a second, and then turned away, wiping a tear from her eye.

"Mrs. Lindstrom," the surgeon continued, "we're not sure what happened yet, but..."

Lindstrom stood up from her chair slowly, made her hands into fists, and leaned forward on the table, her fists supporting her weight on the table. "Where is my husband?"

The surgeon replied, "Mark is currently in the intensive care unit. We need to run tests to determine..."

Lindstrom straightened up and held up a hand, motioning for the surgeon to stop talking. "Take me to my husband, now." She walked around the table towards the door, with everyone in the room stepping out of her way. The surgeon opened the door and held it for Lindstrom. Before she left the room, Lindstrom stopped in front of Kara. Kara looked up, embarrassment on her face.

Through clenched teeth, Lindstrom said to Kara, "YOU told me everything looked good." The words came out of her mouth in a low, guttural rage. Looking back on that moment now, Lindstrom knew that it had taken every last ounce of will power and control she had not to have wrapped her fingers around each of their throats and choked the life out of each of them.

Over the next few days, every test came back negative or inconclusive. Basically, the doctors had no idea why Mark had slipped into a coma. The best guesses the doctors could come up with was that Mark had been allergic to something used during the surgery, and had gone into anaphylactic shock, which resulted in the coma. Lindstrom had immediately contacted one of Mark's best friends, who knew an excellent lawyer. After three weeks of looking over medical charts, interviewing the surgical staff, and getting a solid idea of what happened, the lawyer had given Lindstrom the news.

There was no case for medical malpractice or negligence. The entire staff and board of directors at the Outpatient Surgical Center had been extremely forthcoming about the situation. Lindstrom had often wondered if they would have been as open if the victim wasn't married to a police officer. As her lawyer had told her, though, it really didn't matter. A lawsuit would accomplish nothing. The lawyer had told Lindstrom that she needed to focus on her family moving forward.

Between their combined health and life insurance policies, once it was determined that there was nothing more that the doctors at the hospital could do for him, Lindstrom had Mark moved to this hospice facility. A multitude of different doctors from across the country had been contacted and consulted about Mark's case at various times. Unfortunately, the answers were always the same. They didn't know what had happened, they didn't know why it had happened, and they didn't know how to fix what had happened.

Trevor and Bree took the news in a strange way, with a mixture of shock and "oh well", as if they were saying, "Yes, it's sad that he is in a coma, but there's nothing we can do about it." Mark had gone out of his way to be a father to both of them, and he had succeeded. Even if he wasn't able to make it legal, for all intents and purposes, Mark was their dad, their father in every way except biologically. That's what mattered the most.

Ryan, on the other hand, had taken the news hard. Being so young, he couldn't really process that his Daddy wasn't coming home. Lindstrom didn't know it was possible for one little boy to cry so much. Through it all, though, the four of them had soldiered forward, and they had come together to help support each other.

The worst part of it, though, was remembering the look on Kara Reed's face as she had spoken those three words. "Everything looked good," Kara had said. Then, an hour later, Lindstrom's life had been shattered, broken apart by three words. Over the course of the first year of Mark's coma, Kara had tried to apologize on at least half a dozen different occasions. Every time, Lindstrom had rejected Kara's attempts with a hatred that Lindstrom thought was only reserved for Lindstrom's ex-husband. As time had gone on, Lindstrom had bumped into Kara only a handful of times. No words had been exchanged, only uncomfortable glances or quick movement to avoid each other.

Was the animosity towards Kara justified? In hindsight, probably not. Lindstrom was a detective, rational, and attentive to details. She was able to balance that side of her personality with strong emotions for her family and an uncanny intuition when it came to certain matters. Everything had changed in the course of one hour, and that balance had shifted inside of her. Logical or not, she had latched on to that imbalance for the past eighteen months. After all, it was human nature to assign blame. She had been hanging onto the anger for so long, it had become a crutch and a blindfold.

When Lindstrom had decided to start repairing the situation, memories of her ex-husband had creeped in. When his abuse had upset her balance so many years ago, she had an easy remedy to fix things. Have him arrested, take him to trial, send him to jail, and start a new career in law enforcement. It was physical, it was tangible, and it made sense. With Mark's predicament, it hadn't been as simple to know how to restore order to the chaos. She loved Mark so much, but she had found it so difficult to be with his comatose body and not think of Kara's words. That was in the past, though. She needed it to be, and to start anew, with Mark.

Now, the Nathan Devlin case was upon her. Plus, the interview with Allison Devlin that morning had awakened something inside of Lindstrom. A renewed sense of closure had washed over her, in order that a new chapter could be set in motion. Add to that the introduction of a large check from R.T.A. for her and the kids, and Lindstrom could move forward, to bring the balance back into her family's lives. What had happened to Mark hadn't been Kara Reed's fault. It was as simple as that. Lindstrom hoped that her words had reached Kara, and that things would get better, not only between them, but for everyone else involved.

A quiet knock came from the door. Lindstrom called softly, "Come in." The door opened slowly, and Trevor walked in. Lindstrom smiled a smile like she never had before. She stood up, went to her oldest child, and gave him a hug. She took his face in her hands, gazing into his eyes, and said, "You are a good kid and a great son. Don't you ever forget that." Trevor smiled sheepishly and looked at the bed. Lindstrom looked, too, and saw Ryan sleeping, his little head rising and falling against Mark's chest as Mark breathed in and out. Lindstrom looked at the time. It was after 8:30.

"I'd better get Ryan home," Lindstrom said.

"If it's okay with you," Trevor said, "I think I'm going to stay for a little while. I'd like to spend some time and talk to Dad."

"You stay as long as you want, Trevor." Lindstrom gave Trevor another quick hug, and then walked to the bed. Trevor carefully lifted Mark's arm, and Lindstrom scooped up Ryan. Ryan woke up a little bit and looked at his mom.

"Is it time to go, Momma?"

"I'm afraid so, pumpkin. Do you want to say night-night to Daddy?"

Lindstrom leaned down, and Ryan kissed his father's forehead and said, "Nighty-night, Daddy. I love you." He shifted his weight in his mother's arms, so his head was resting on her shoulder. "Hi bro-bro," Ryan said to Trevor. "Take good care of Daddy."

Trevor smiled and patted Ryan's head. "I will, little buddy." He looked at his mother and said, "Night, mom." He sat down on the bed, looking at Mark.

Lindstrom bent over slightly, kissing Mark's forehead, and said, "Good night, my love." Carrying Ryan in her arms, she quietly left Mark's room and headed for home.

PART TWO:

APOLOGIST

"Innocence believed...innocence tested...

innocence fallen...blessed innocence...

Philosophical wonders, intellectual ponders,

the trail stretches on,

a confused path."

- <u>*Variations on a Theme (Parts II & V),*</u>

- Daniel Van Deest, 1989

TWENTY

THURSDAY MORNING, 3:49 A.M.

Charles Utecht was aware, although he wasn't sure why. That seemed strange, and he couldn't understand it. Time had merged, blending from one moment into another. He had no concept of minutes, hours, or days. He hadn't seen the sun or the moon since, since, since, was it when the amazon had come for him in the bar? Utecht struggled through his mind, trying to place it. Friday night, yes, he was almost certain it had been Friday night. His mind was suddenly on point.

The amazon, Utecht thought, the one he liked to call "Doll", what had she done to him? Even with the haze he was fighting through, he could remember Doll and, and, what had happened? It was a double-cross, yes, that's what happened! He should have taken the money and left. Suddenly, he became keenly aware that it wouldn't have been that simple. The voice, that computer-generated voice, the voice had belonged to the silhouette. The silhouette had done this to him, with the help of Doll.

Charles Utecht's thoughts suddenly froze, trying to register exactly what they had done to him. It was dark, but why? He tried to open his eyes, but they wouldn't move. Was he in a dark room with his eyes open? Was he unable to open his eyes? He started to panic, unsure of where he was, frightened by the uncertainty that was swirling around him. He was drowning in futility, and he had no way out.

Keep it together, he thought to himself. You've figured your way out of other tight spots before. Just take a minute. Okay, it's dark, for whatever reason. Think about it, where are you? Are you hot or are you cold? Utecht tried to detect some hint of temperature, but it was no use. He couldn't tell if he was shivering in cold or sweating from excess heat. He couldn't tell if he was breathing or, no, wait, he had to be breathing. After all, he was alive, right? Right? Okay, let's stay positive here. You are alive.

Somehow, he knew he was alive, because he knew he was breathing. How, though, how did he know? Then he felt it. Barely, but it was there. Something, like a soft wind, across his nose and his lips, that's what he could detect. Wait, there was something else, too. Was it sticky, touching his skin, or was it itchy? Why wouldn't his arms move? Why couldn't he open his eyes? What was happening to him? Why was this happening?

"You didn't listen, did you? Why didn't you listen?"

His grandfather's voice began to murmur, to stir, repeating those same nine words. No, wait, they weren't repeating. The words were a whisper, echoing inside his cranium, reverberating, growing louder and louder, until the words became a shockwave, threatening to crush him from the inside of his own memories.

"Are you paying attention?"

The voice, it wasn't his grandfather's. The shockwave ended, his brain now focused on the sensory input his ears had fed him.

"I take it that you are trying to figure out why you don't have control over your body. Am I right?"

The voice, where was it coming from? Wait, wait, Utecht knew that voice! The goddamn silhouette, that's who was talking to him!

"My, my, my, Mr. Utecht, does the sound of my voice upset you? Well, I guess that is understandable. After all, you thought you were getting away clean. Now, here you are, outwitted by an old man and his daughter."

What the hell was he talking about, "old man and his daughter"? Doll was his daughter?

"Oh, Mr. Utecht, if only you had listened and done what you were told, things could have worked out much, much differently for you."

"You didn't listen, did you? Why didn't you listen?"

His grandfather's voice, a whisper, driving home the despair of his situation, like a hammer drives home a nail.

"When you were brought in to my employ, it was made incredibly simple for you. You don't deviate from the plan. Any change, no matter how seemingly insignificant, was to be reported. You were not to think for yourself. You were to do as you were told. You were to stay at the house, the more than generous accommodations I provided. You would be taken care of, both regards to the work, as well as your time between extractions. Was that too much for you to understand?"

This old man, the silhouette, was getting on Utecht's nerves. He wanted to bust out of this place, throw this senile old goat from the tallest bridge he could find, and tear apart his daughter. Just give me a chance, a few seconds, that's all I'd need, Utecht thought to himself.

"Why do you insist on torturing him like this?"

That voice, it was the amazon! It was Doll! If only he could open his eyes, he knew that his unbridled fury would explode from him, a supernova of hatred that would burn down the silhouette and his daughter, utterly destroying both of them where they stood!

"My dear, whatever do you mean?"

"Father, please, spare me. This is the same soliloquy that you spouted at him days ago. He's been through all three protocols. He is ready. And yet here we are. You are delaying, and I have other matters to attend to. There is no point to this."

"Maybe you're right, my child." Utecht heard the old man sigh. "Things have been going so well, for so long, for us. Yet now, I can see the end." The old man paused, a pregnant space that spoke volumes of the situation. "The future, THIS future, it frightens me."

"Father, don't say that. This is merely a test. Despite what he did, everything will work itself out."

Utecht was trying to follow what they were saying. It was difficult, so difficult, and it was growing more difficult as each second passed. He couldn't fathom why, though. Was it because of his rage at the both of them? Was it because of his limited sensory input? Or was something else interfering with his train of thought?

"Oh, my dear child, I truly hope you are correct. Now, where are we at with the corrections?"

"Everything is in place. If we need to act quickly, the pieces will come together, and it will all be sorted out. For the most part, anyway."

The silhouette heard the veiled hint of discontent. "I take it you don't approve of my final notation, should I decide to use it?"

"Father, please. I think it's a waste of time, resources, and, in the unlikely event your final notation should be used, I think it would draw even more scrutiny upon us."

"Have faith, dear child. While you have always been there to ground me when my vision seemed to consume me, I believe that, in this specific situation, should the worst come to fruition, my final notation will not be rebuked."

Charles Utecht didn't know whether he wanted to puke, to punch, or to cry. Maybe he wanted to do all three at once. This back and forth between the silhouette and his amazon-sized daughter was like listening to fingernails on a chalkboard. Utecht was unsure of how much more of this he could stand.

"Very well, father. Are you ready to proceed with Mr. Utecht, then?"

Proceed? What the hell did she mean by that? Yeah, honey, you can proceed by letting me go and never bothering me again. God knows I don't want anything to do with either of you, that's for damn sure.

"Soon, my child, soon. I require a little more time with Mr. Utecht. Please, allow your father a little catharsis in this hour of tribulation."

"As long as you stop with your grand speeches, father. I will see you at supper time, then." Doll's voice was gone, and Utecht was sure that he had heard footsteps fade away, followed by silence.

Silence. Sweet Jesus, the silence was truly unbearable. Utecht was left with a sense of longing, a sense of emptiness, like all the choices he had made up to this point hadn't been the right ones.

"You didn't listen, did you? Why didn't you listen?"

His grandfather's tone, the disappointment in those nine words. The last nine words Utecht heard from his grandfather.

He had never felt this way before, never considered the path not taken. His life had been a lump of coal, pretty much from the beginning. He didn't have time to dwell on crap like that. He had to keep pushing forward, every minute and every day, if only to survive. Now, here he was, if only he could figure out where he was and how to get out. Yet, his grandfather's words wouldn't stop haunting him.

"My apologies, Mr. Utecht," the old man's voice said, "but I had a few things to take care of. I am sure you have many questions. I am also sure that, if it were up to you, you would take out your hostility on me and my wonderful daughter. Fortunately, that choice is not up to you. Instead, allow me to set the record straight for you."

Suddenly, Utecht was flooded with blinding light. It took him time for his eye to adjust. When he could see clearly, there he was, the silhouette, now an old man, looking at him. He was definitely old, but Utecht couldn't venture a guess as to how old. The old man seemed to be hovering over him, somehow, for some reason. Utecht could see part of the old man's hand and fingers. It was as if the old man was holding his eyelid open.

"Considering your current predicament, Mr. Utecht, I am sure you have many questions. For what it is worth to you, I fully intended on living up to my side of the agreement. I like to think of myself as an honorable man. Maybe that is misplaced in this day and age, but, as I have heard the younger generation say, that is how I roll."

Utecht could see the hand move, and he plunged back into darkness. His emotions were again all over the place, fluctuating in a multitude of incarnations and scenarios. The problem, of course, was that he couldn't manifest his emotions physically, which meant he couldn't fight back, let alone escape.

"Perhaps my daughter is right. I am torturing you." There was a slight pause. "Am I torturing you? That is not what I wanted or intended. However, you need to understand that this is on you, and you alone. You deviated from the instructions, from the plan, and now two people are dead. A penance must be exacted, Mr. Utecht. So, having said that, I want to take a little time to tell you what this has all been about. Think of yourself as Dorothy, and I am the Wizard, pulling back the curtain, allowing you to see the machinations of the great Oz."

Charles Utecht had many faults, but fear had never been one of them. Yet, in this moment, at this time, with this old man, the fear had started to set in. Within the first few sentences that this man had spoken, Utecht's fear had started. It had started as a drop in a bucket. As the man continued to talk, to pull back the layers, explaining his plan to Utecht, the drop of fear had soon multiplied so that it filled the bucket. Soon, the bucket of fear was overflowing, washing over, around, and through him. Utecht couldn't believe what he was hearing. It was nonsensical, bizarre, insane. Yet here he was, Charles Utecht, listening to this old man, growing more fearful by the second.

After what seemed like an eternity, the old man had stopped talking. The old man had opened one of Utecht's eyelids again, and he saw him smile at him, almost tenderly. The old man's face grew bigger, until Utecht realized that he had leaned in to give him a kiss. A kiss on the forehead, of all things!

"Rest assured, Mr. Utecht, you will be happy to know that this will all work out for the best." With that, Utecht's eyelid was closed again. He could only lay there, trapped in his own mind.

"You didn't listen, did you? Why didn't you listen?"

There was no way out. There would be no grand escape, at least not in the traditional sense. Utecht, now knowing what the old man and his daughter had been up to all along, since before Charles had become involved, resigned himself to his fate. He let the fear wash over him until he had drowned in it. The only thing left to do was wait. Wait for the end to come, and maybe, just maybe, the plan that the old man had spoken of would lead to something greater. However, considering everything that had happened to Utecht in his life, he realized that was merely wishful thinking.

Death was coming to Charles Utecht. The only question was when.

TWENTY-ONE

Tisdale was at the police station early. He wanted to get a head start on the day, having the file regarding Charles Utecht ready for Engels and Lindstrom when they got in. He had set his alarm early, not only because of work, though. He had wanted to surprise his girlfriend with breakfast. However, as usual, she was gone. The relationship felt strange, yet it was also oddly rewarding. She took a genuine interest in his job as a police officer. Was it because she was self-employed as a fitness instructor, and would sometimes go for days or weeks without appointments? Tisdale figured it didn't matter. Sure, they had been on again, off again for about ten months, but the last three weeks she had been calling more often and spending more time with him.

Even after ten months, their relationship hadn't progressed much physically. However, Tisdale didn't really mind. Obviously, she was attractive as hell, but she had made it clear from the very beginning her beliefs and views on sex. They weren't old-fashioned, rather very logical and pragmatic. Tisdale had honored her views, and, even though they slept in the same bed at times, intercourse never happened. Over the last three weeks, she had opened up more about her plans, the future, changes she was thinking of making. In each discussion, Tisdale was always mentioned, which seemed to suggest that she was laying the groundwork for a stronger relationship between the two of them. Hearing her talk like that had allowed Tisdale to focus more, not only on her and a possible future, but also to focus on work. He wasn't really into the dating scene, thankfully.

While he did harbor secret feelings toward Lindstrom, Tisdale knew that there wasn't anything to it, not really. Yes, Lindstrom was attractive, and smart, and strong. After thinking it through, Tisdale had reached the realization that his feelings toward Lindstrom weren't anything of a romantic nature. Rather, he concluded that his feelings were protective, like a sibling trying to help out in a bad situation. Nothing more, nothing less, and nothing could change that. It was best to keep those feelings to himself, focus on the fact that she was his superior on the police force, and work at being the best officer he could be.

Now, here he was, at the police station, pulling up everything he could find on Charles Utecht. Tisdale had only been working on the guy's bio for half an hour, and it was already thick. He didn't know how this Utecht character factored into Lindstrom's investigation. Considering Utecht's criminal history, though, it was a safe guess that he was a player in this convoluted investigation.

Tisdale finished putting the entire file together, standing up from the empty desk he had been using during the investigation, when Engels walked in. Tisdale looked at the time. 7:28 displayed on one of the clocks. Tisdale guessed that the chief was in early to atone for his tardiness yesterday.

"Tisdale," Engels called as he weaved his way amongst the desks to get to Tisdale. "You did go home last night, right? I'm not paying you overtime just to kiss up, you know."

"Yes, chief, I did go home last night," Tisdale said. "Tish had asked me to gather some info on a possible person of interest, so I came in early to get a head start."

Engels smiled. He liked the initiative that Tisdale had been showing on the case. "Anything worth mentioning to the boss?"

Tisdale responded, "I'm not really sure how he fits into the case. Vance and Sherman were, to coin a phrase, two-bit crooks. This one," Tisdale patted the outside of the folder that held Utecht's history, "he's on the other end of the spectrum. Card-carrying member in the career criminal section. I can go over it with you if you want."

Engels shook his head. "Unless there's something actionable right now, sit tight until Tish gets here. Go over the file with her, and we can take it from there. I'll be in my office." Engels walked away, and Tisdale walked over to Lindstrom's desk and left the file in front of her computer where she would see it right away. He then went to see if Officer Tavon was in.

Engels spent the first few hours of his Thursday morning working on all matters of police department business. He answered messages, signed papers, did follow-up on cases, talked to the district attorney and the mayor, and generally got caught up on a lot of minute details. Before he knew it, he received a text from Jerry in forensics.

"STILL WORKING ON THE DELIVERY VAN. FOUND SOME WORKABLE PRINTS. RUNNING THEM THROUGH THE SYSTEM. WILL UPDATE AS I FIND OUT MORE."

Jerry could be long-winded in casual settings, but when it came to work, he was short, sweet, and to the point. Engels appreciated that, especially on complex cases. He still wasn't sure what to make of Lindstrom's story involving the delivery van, but it was worth following up. Engels didn't like coincidences, either. He was hoping that, in this case, it would turn out to be a simple matter with a simple explanation, and that would put an end to it.

Engels got up from his desk and stretched. He walked to the window of his office, which faced south and overlooked the public area of the parking lot. Beyond the parking lot he watched the morning traffic on Minnesota Avenue, one of the busier streets in Sioux Falls. He glanced over the trees before his eyes wandered to the few scattered houses and some of the businesses that were dotted along the avenue. A strip mall with a newly-renovated laundromat, an old Victorian-style home that was now a historical landmark and museum, an appliance store that was still owned and operated by the same family going on seventy years. Pedestrians seemed to hustle out of the parking garage two blocks away, hurrying to get to their jobs. Morning joggers, power walkers, and some cyclists were making their way along the sidewalks, across the streets and avenues. Engels watched the scene, observing how chaotic and how orderly everything seemed to be, often at the exact same time. He closed his eyes, taking in a deep breath. As he slowly exhaled and opened his eyes, his mind started down a path that had become all too familiar over the past few months.

Was he really willing to give up his chosen profession over more responsibilities? He thought about how great the department had been running when he had the police end of things and Clive Gundvaldson had the bureaucracy. Was the department slipping away from him, as he had been feeling recently? Or, maybe, things weren't as bad as he thought they were. Engels shook his head. His meeting with the mayor was coming up soon, so he had time to try to flesh out all his emotions about the job. A knock came from his door. Engels turned around and saw Lindstrom standing there, a perturbed look on her face.

"I know that look," Engels said. "Give me the bad news gently."

Lindstrom held up the file on Charles Utecht that Tisdale had put together. "Have you read this?"

Engels shook his head. "Not yet. I told Tisdale to leave it for you, and that you would bring it to me when you had anything to go over. So, what seems to be the problem?"

Lindstrom walked into the office and set the file down on Engels' desk. "The problem is Charles Utecht doesn't fit. He's a square peg being forced into a round hole. His rap sheet is extensive, with burglary, armed robbery, assault and battery, destruction of property, aiding and abetting, grand theft, and extortion." Engels walked back to his chair and opened the file as Lindstrom continued to talk.

"Of course, those are only the crimes that the various police departments and DA's could make stick. He was also charged with murder, attempted murder, manslaughter, and kidnapping. In those cases, though, they couldn't make the charges stick, he pled out, or he turned state's evidence and flipped on his criminal cohorts."

As Engels perused the file, he asked, "Okay, so he's a bad guy. What's the problem?"

"The PROBLEMS," Lindstrom replied, emphasizing the word, "as in plural, chief, are that he disappeared three years ago. As in literally, poof, gone. He walks into a courtroom in Santa Fe, New Mexico, accepts a plea deal for an assault with a deadly weapon charge, and, for some reason, walks out of the courtroom a free man. No one has seen or heard from Charles Utecht since then. Now, three years later, he shows up in our neck of the woods. He's working as a delivery driver for a medical supply company, gets fired, allegedly steals a company vehicle, leaves it brimming with trash, and is gone again. Oh, and the vehicle he maybe

276

steals looks like a van that I saw drive by my house two times and was driving by Sanford Hospital as I was walking to my car."

Engels looked up from the file and stared at Lindstrom. He could see that she was upset. Her neck was turning red, the blood rushing to her head in anger. Combined with the red in her hair, it made Engels think that Lindstrom looked like an old-style thermometer that was about to pop. He tried to take a different approach with his next question.

"Are you saying that you don't think that Utecht had anything to do with Nathan Devlin's kidnapping?"

"On the contrary. Judging from his criminal history, Utecht sounds like the kind of guy to pull off a kidnapping and ransom." The words hung in the air, Lindstrom biting her lower lip.

Engels knew she was working on her thought process. He tried to give her leeway to follow the thread, but the pause was becoming untenable. He waved his hand in a circular motion, trying to get Lindstrom to continue. "Go on, what's the issue, then?"

"It makes too much sense, and it doesn't make any sense," Lindstrom said.

Engels frowned while Lindstrom sighed. She moved her head left and right, letting her neck crack. She then leaned forward in her chair and continued.

"Let's assume that Charles Utecht met Ronald Vance and Olivia Sherman at Visceral Medical Supplies. At some point, Vance and Sherman both left the company, possibly because they were involved with each other. Utecht has kept in touch with them, maybe even knows the financial situations they are both in and comes up with this kidnapping scheme. They put the kidnapping plan in motion, but something happens that night. Olivia has cold feet and ends up arguing on her cell phone. Somehow, she gets Devlin outside, but he doesn't go quietly, eventually injuring Olivia. Ronald stays quiet, just doing his part. They also don't count on witnesses, which is where our nurse, Jason, comes in. The kidnappers realize they have the wrong guy. This causes the plan to fall apart, Utecht kills Olivia, somehow setting up Ronald to get picked up."

Lindstrom paused, looked down at the floor, and frowned. Engels started to open his mouth when her stare moved back up to her boss, resuming her thought process out loud.

"If Utecht was the driver and the engineer, how does he get an ambulance? Based on what I looked at last night, a cheap used one starts at about fifteen grand. How does Utecht set up Vance to be discovered and to kill himself when cornered? After all the trouble of a kidnapping, why draw more attention to yourself by stealing a delivery van from the company you've been fired from, and then leave it in a public place filled with garbage? And, if this was a kidnapping gone wrong, why not even attempt to get something from the family?"

Engels looked at Lindstrom and then at Utecht's file. "Do you think Charles Utecht is the fourth person, the mastermind behind this?"

Lindstrom leaned back in the chair and looked out the window, trying to put the pieces together in her mind. "I think he's involved, but not in the way that would wrap up this whole thing."

Engels also leaned back in his chair. "What's the next step, then?"

"I think we need to tie off the small pieces. I want to take Scott from forensics to see Jason and Nathan. After we had to bring in the sketch artist last week, Scott got a facial recognition program from a friend of his at the NSA. He can take the photo we have of Olivia Sherman and alter it, like a sketch artist would. Once we have confirmation that Jason and Nathan can ID the same picture of Olivia Sherman, we can safely say she was there the night of Devlin's kidnapping."

Engels nodded in agreement. "Sounds good. What else?"

"I'll also show Utecht's and Vance's mug shots to Jason. If he can ID either or both men, then we know that they were there that Monday night when Devlin was abducted." Lindstrom stood up from the chair, adding, "I need to talk to someone in charge at Visceral Medical and get a handle on Utecht, Vance, and Sherman, as well as their knowledge of HealthStar Ambulatory Services." Lindstrom paused, then said, "And, of course, there's…" Lindstrom's voice trailed off, her right eyebrow rising in a curious way, like she was asking for special permission.

Engels seemed to sense where she was going. "Are you out of your mind?"

"Whether you want to believe me or not," Lindstrom said emphatically, "Heidi Cole knows something about this case, either directly or indirectly. Trust me on this one, Heidi Cole is involved."

Engels sighed again. "I will take your word for it." He leaned forward, put his elbows on his desk, and pointed a finger at Lindstrom in an almost threatening manner, saying, "But you'd better be damn right, you'd better be damn discreet, and you'd better be damn careful. You understand me, Tish?"

Lindstrom smiled at her boss. "I'm always damn careful, you know that." She turned and left Engels' office.

"Yeah, but what about the first two?" Engels shouted after Lindstrom, but she was already through the door of his office and gone.

Lindstrom had phoned ahead to the hospital to make sure that both Jason and Nathan were available. Jason was on a lunch break but would be available by the time Lindstrom and Scott had arrived. Nathan had a physical therapy session in the afternoon, but he was also available to work with Scott. Lindstrom looked in her rearview mirror, making sure Scott was still behind her in an unmarked police car. Sure enough, there he was, trailing a car behind Lindstrom's. Lindstrom smiled to herself. One of the things that made the police department work so well was the diversity. Not only when it came to race and gender and the like, but also when it came to individual personalities.

Lindstrom tried to know everybody in the department at least by first name. Unfortunately, there were never enough hours in the day to know everyone inside and out. Scott had been anxious to help when she approached him, but he would have to drive them to the hospital, either in Lindstrom's car, in a squad car, or in separate cars.

"Um, I guess that's okay," Lindstrom had said, "but, if you don't mind my asking, is there a problem?"

Scott looked at her with an embarrassed look on his face. "No, no problem, nope, none at all." Lindstrom stared at him, and he knew that she wasn't buying it. He sighed and said, "My daughter is fourteen, and my son turns thirteen in two months. My wife thought it would be a good idea to get them a head start on driver's ed next summer, so I've been taking them out to the convention center parking lot to teach them how to drive." Scott paused and closed his eyes.

Lindstrom could easily connect the dots. Trevor had picked up driving with no problems. Bree, on the other hand, hadn't taken instructions from her "cop mom" so easily. Lindstrom had tried on two different occasions to help give Bree some tutoring. After the second one had ended with Bree in tears because she "couldn't understand what the hell the rules of the road are", Lindstrom had decided that Bree would be better off with the actual driving education teachers.

"Let me guess," Lindstrom offered, "you would feel safer if you were doing the driving right now?"

Scott opened his eyes, and he had joyful look on his face, like a puppy that was done being scared of a storm. "If it's okay with you," Scott had said, "yes, I'd really like to drive." A quick requisition, and they had left the police station in separate vehicles.

Lindstrom had tried to call the main office of Visceral Medical to talk to someone in charge, but she had been bounced around between departments, never once talking to an actual person. The automated phone system had been annoying. As she pulled her car into the parking garage of Sanford Hospital, she tried the retail office of Visceral that was serviced by Cassie Butler. Once again, Lindstrom had only heard automated recordings for different departments. She hung up without leaving any messages.

As Lindstrom and Scott entered the ER, Jason was approaching from out of the security doors. Lindstrom introduced Scott to Jason and vice versa, and Jason brought them into and through the ER into one of the consultation rooms. As they walked in, Lindstrom spotted Kara Reed out of the corner of her eye.

"Gentlemen," Lindstrom said to Scott and Jason, "why don't the two of you get started. I will be back in a few minutes." She closed the door and walked toward Kara. Kara was finishing some papers and giving them to a nurse that Lindstrom didn't recognize, when Kara saw Lindstrom walking toward her and smiled.

As Kara held out her hand, she said, "Are you here looking for me again?"

Lindstrom shook her hand and said, "Not this time, actually. I have one of my forensic tech guys working with Jason on a computer model of the female victim's face. I'm going to have him do the same thing with Nathan Devlin. In the meantime, would you mind if I asked you a question?"

Kara beamed and said, "Go right ahead and ask away." It had been less than a day since Lindstrom had offered her apologies to Kara, and already there seemed to be a healing between them. This is good, Lindstrom thought. Life was too short to hold meaningless grudges.

"How much business does Sanford Hospital do with Visceral Medical Supplies?"

"None that I'm aware of," Kara replied almost immediately. "I mean, not any more. Not since the buyout and the change in ownership."

"Oh," Lindstrom said. "Was there an issue of some kind?"

"I'm not really sure. As a big hospital, there are a lot of moving parts, and a lot of departments that need all kinds of supplies." Kara paused and looked around. "I'm not only talking about medical supplies, either. Whether we're talking about disposable silverware or pop and candy for the vending machines or toilet paper, hospitals buy a lot of supplies. It's almost impossible to have one vendor supply everything."

"I'm guessing the hospital has a lot of competition to get them to buy from particular vendors."

"You don't know the half of it. Discounts on buying in bulk, free samples for hospital staff, kickbacks for doctors that endorse products, you name it and my guess is that a vendor has offered it to get the hospital's business." Another nurse walked up to the two of them, holding out a clipboard towards Kara. "Excuse me for one second." Kara quickly inspected the sheet on the clipboard, took a pen from her pocket, signed the paper, and handed the clipboard back to the nurse. The nurse strolled past Kara and Lindstrom, leaving them alone again.

"Then what happened with Visceral?" Lindstrom had taken out her notebook by now and was jotting down notes.

Kara leaned against the counter and massaged her neck as she spoke. "Before VMS came into the picture, it was All Things Medical, and Sanford Hospital, then going by Sioux Valley Hospital, did a fair share of business with All Things Medical and its owner, Raymond Mobley. After Mobley died and All Things became VMS, contracts weren't renewed, and Sanford moved on to other vendors."

Lindstrom thought about it for a minute. "Was a reason ever given?"

"Not that I was ever told about," Kara said. "I mean, I could speculate, but since there wasn't any gossip about it or any kind of acrimony in the papers or on the news, there wasn't anything to talk about."

"Don't you find that a little odd?"

Kara thought about it and then said, "Not really. The healthcare industry has changed and evolved so much over the last ten, twenty, even thirty years, and it's changing by the minute. Think about when you were a kid. If you weren't feeling well and your parents took you to the doctor, it was the doctor that diagnosed you and prescribed a treatment." She paused again and pointed at four separate rooms of the ER that had curtains closed, indicating they were occupied. "Today, even in an accident, I would guess that each one of the patients in those rooms could be on the internet with their cell phones in seconds, look up their symptoms, find a diagnosis, and prescribe their treatment options. Hell, go out to the lobby and turn on the TV and start channel surfing. Do that for thirty minutes, and you could come back in here and list at least fifteen drugs that were advertised during the commercials."

"What you're saying," Lindstrom countered, "is that one little company didn't even register as important?"

"It sounds cold, but yes. All Things Medical became Visceral Medical Supplies, and the hospital was informed that VMS would not renew any vending contracts upon expiration. Visceral gave the hospital a six-month window, which allowed Sanford to have other vendors in place well ahead of the expiration." Lindstrom pondered what Kara had told her. As she looked at her notes, Kara asked, "Would you mind if I asked why you are interested in Visceral?"

"Oh, just following up on something for Chief Engels." Lindstrom didn't want to spread word that Visceral Medical or any of their employees may or may not be involved. She figured it was best to keep it low key for now. "He helped out on something yesterday, and, as I long as I was here, asked me to get a little information. No big deal, really."

That seemed to satisfy Kara, who nodded and then said, "Tish, about last night, I want to thank you. It really means a lot to me."

Lindstrom put her hand on Kara's arm and gave it a friendly squeeze. "Kara, I should be apologizing to you. And, frankly, we should both be thanking Allison Devlin. After interviewing her and listening to what she had to say and how strong her feelings are for her husband and her family, well, it made me realize that it was time to move on." Lindstrom smiled at Kara, who returned the smile.

"Tish, I think we're done here." Lindstrom turned around and saw Scott and Jason standing at the door to the consultation room. She walked towards them, Scott holding out the tablet that had a dual image on it. On the left of the screen was the last known ID photo of Olivia Sherman, and, on the right, was the digitally altered image that Scott had made, based on

Jason's recollections.

Kara had walked up to the two men with Lindstrom, and when Kara saw the images, she whistled softly. "Wow, Jason," Kara said, "if that is her, you weren't kidding. She is definitely a stunner, as you called her."

Jason had a conflicted look on his face. "Are you sure that she is dead?"

Lindstrom looked at Jason with a solemn but determined expression, and said, "We don't know for sure, but this will go a long way to helping us out." She took out her phone, and, pulling up the photo gallery, added, "Jason, one last thing. Do you recognize any of these men?" She handed the phone to Jason, which showed six different males.

Jason looked at the picture, zoomed in on each photo that was being displayed and replied. "Hell yes! That's the driver of the ambulance and his buddy! You found them?"

Lindstrom took back her phone, saying, "We have an idea of who they are and how they fit into the situation." She smiled and continued by saying, "Thank you so much, Jason."

"Well," Kara interrupted, "if you are done with this young man, I need to put him back to work. Tish, thank you again, and if you need anything, give me a call."

"I will," Lindstrom replied, "and thanks again." Kara and Jason walked off, leaving Lindstrom standing there with Scott. Lindstrom put a hand on Scott's shoulder and nudged him towards the back of the ER, where they could exit and get to a set of elevators. Excellent, she thought. Jason had positively identified Charles Utecht and Ronald Vance as being at the scene outside Goldie's. Now, she needed to shift her focus to the next order of business.

As they walked, Lindstrom asked Scott, "How accurate is that program? Did Jason really transform the woman on the left into a realistic version of the woman on the right?"

"Definitely," Scott answered. "This isn't like one of those photoshop-style programs where you can morph a face into Godzilla or something silly. The program is designed to analyze the face and manipulate it only within the realistic limits of plastic surgery."

"How was Jason able to come up with this so quickly?"

Scott pointed to the original picture of Olivia Sherman on the left. "Because we had a starting point. This isn't like making a sketch of someone and then altering it." Lindstrom nodded and thought to herself, that makes sense. They left the ER through a set of large security doors and made their way through a set of hallways and turns to a set of elevators. Lindstrom pushed for an elevator going up. A minute later, the doors pinged open, and an empty car was revealed. Good, Lindstrom thought.

As they got into the elevators, Lindstrom pressed for the floor that Nathan Devlin was on, turned to Scott, and said, "While you are working with Mr. Devlin, I want you to keep your eyes open for anything that might be suspicious."

Scott looked at her with a raised eyebrow. "Is there anyone or anything in particular I should be focused on?"

"No, but I want you to be observant of anyone or anything that might be odd. Okay?"

"I'll do my best," Scott replied as the elevator doors opened.

As they navigated the floor to get to the patient rooms, Lindstrom was playing out how best to broach her suspicions about Heidi Cole. This case had grown from one dead body to two dead bodies, a botched kidnapping, and now maybe a missing delivery driver with a now recovered delivery van. Purely from a conjecture standpoint, if Heidi Cole had somehow hired people to kidnap Nathan Devlin, what was the point? Allison Devlin had no access to money, and, based on the financials that Tisdale and Tavon had pulled, the life insurance policy on Nathan had lapsed, so there was no way to cash in on his death.

Even though Engels had shot down her instinct, or at least tried to muffle it, Lindstrom couldn't shake the feeling that Heidi was, in some way, involved. It wasn't only the way she had reacted, but it was the changing look in her eyes. Lindstrom had seen that look many times before, from criminals that had been caught in a lie. Hell, she had seen it in the eyes of her own kids. One minute they are so confident that they are getting away with something, and the next they realize they've messed up and are about to get caught.

After fifteen minutes of walking, Lindstrom and Scott finally reached Nathan Devlin's room. She raised her hand to knock on the door, then stopped. Lindstrom looked at Allison Devlin's room, and saw the door was open.

"Follow me," Lindstrom said, and went to Allison's room. With the door open, a person could see into the room, but not get a full view.

Immediately inside the room was a door that opened into a bathroom, and further in, Lindstrom could see the foot of the bed. The blankets were pointed up, showing that someone, most likely Allison, was laying in bed. Lindstrom knocked on the open door, and she heard Allison's voice call out.

"Come in."

Lindstrom and Scott walked in and saw Allison Devlin sitting up in bed, with Heidi Cole sitting in a chair next to her, a laptop computer sitting on a small table in front of Heidi. Allison gave them both a warm and inviting smile, which Lindstrom returned. "Detective Lindstrom, it's a pleasure to see you again. And you are?", Allison asked, looking at Scott.

"Mrs. Devlin," Lindstrom said, "this is Scott. He's one of our forensics investigators. He's going to ask your husband some questions if that's okay with you." She didn't need to ask for Allison's permission. Rather, this was a chance for Lindstrom to mildly provoke Heidi Cole, to see if she would betray some measure of emotion.

Allison smiled. "Absolutely, but please, try not to upset him. Dr. Preston says he needs as much rest as possible to get all of those horrible drugs out of his system."

Lindstrom nodded her head and said, "I understand." She then turned to Heidi Cole and said, "Mrs. Cole, I hope everything is okay."

"Everything is fine," Heidi responded, immediately turning her attention back to her laptop. Lindstrom could tell that Heidi was trying to hide her true emotions, so she left it at that. Lindstrom looked back to Allison.

"This won't take too long," Lindstrom said, "and I will stop back when it's done. Okay?"

"That would be fine. Thank you, Detective, and thank you, Scott." Allison closed her eyes and lowered her bed a little bit. Lindstrom and Scott turned around and walked back to Nathan Devlin's room.

Before Lindstrom could knock, Scott whispered, "The other woman in the room, Mrs. Cole, definitely doesn't like you."

Lindstrom grinned and whispered back to Scott, "That's why I need you to keep your eyes open." She knocked, and heard a muffled voice inside invite them in. Lindstrom opened the door. She and Scott walked in to see Nathan Devlin laying in his bed and Andy Cole sitting in a chair to Nathan's right.

"Nathan, Andy," Lindstrom began, "this is Scott, one of our forensics investigators. Scott, this is Andy Cole, Nathan's best friend, and this is Nathan Devlin, our kidnapping victim." Lindstrom waited for the men to exchange handshakes and greetings before continuing. "Mr. Devlin, Scott needs your help. He is going to ask you some questions regarding the woman from the bar. Based on your responses, he is going to digitally alter the picture we have. This will help us make a final identification and continue with the case. Are you up to that?"

Nathan nodded his head in agreement. "Whatever I can do to help you out."

Lindstrom smiled and motioned towards Andy Cole. "Mr. Cole, would you mind stepping out into the hall with me, so that they can get to work?"

Andy stood up and said, "Absolutely, and if you need anything, buddy, holler for me, okay?"

Nathan smiled at his friend. "I'll be fine, buddy." Andy walked around the bed and followed Lindstrom out of the room. They moved to the side of the door, away from Nathan's and Allison's rooms. Andy leaned against the wall, looking up and down the hall.

Lindstrom asked Andy, "Where's Ben today?"

"Oh, he'll be here later. He was here this morning but decided to do a few things at the halfway house." Andy's voice was quiet, and Lindstrom noticed that he glanced a little too frequently at the door to Allison's room.

"How about you," Lindstrom asked, trying to keep the dialogue going. "Are you okay?"

Andy shrugged his shoulders. "It's tough, trying to be here for Nathan and his family. The kids have been going to school and are staying at our place at night. We've had them up here to see Allison a few times, but Allison, Ben, Nathan, and I all agreed it was better if the kids not see Nathan. At least, not just yet."

Lindstrom looked at him carefully. "The four of you decided that?"

"I know, it sounds cruel," Andy said, "but this isn't how Nathan wanted to re-enter their lives. Dr. Preston agreed, too, that Nathan needs to get better first before this kind of emotional jackhammer hits everyone."

"What about your wife, Heidi? Does she not agree with the rest of you?"

Andy looked sheepishly down at the floor. "Yeah, she agrees with us, too."

Lindstrom could tell Andy wasn't being straight with her. "Mr. Cole? Andy? Is everything alright?"

Andy was still looking at the floor, opened his mouth to answer, when a voice behind her said, "He's fine."

Lindstrom half turned and saw Heidi Cole walking up to her, holding her closed laptop by her side. She walked up to her husband and Lindstrom, a look of defiance on her face. She positioned herself so that she was standing closer to Andy, yet in such a way that Andy seemed to shrink in stature. Lindstrom could see it was a power play on Heidi's part, to make it appear that she was in control of the situation and the people around her. Now that Heidi had made her presence known, she continued speaking.

"Everyone in my family AND in Allison's family would be better if you and your cop buddies would leave us alone. Our families need to heal, not to have you swooping in here whenever you want."

"Look, Mrs. Cole, we're here to," Lindstrom started to explain before she was cut off.

"NO, YOU LOOK, DETECTIVE," Heidi retorted, purposely sounding out each syllable, as if she was speaking to someone hard of hearing. "I don't know what you think you know or don't know. But my best friend has been through a living hell over the past few years, and it needs to stop, right here and now!"

"I understand how you feel," Lindstrom said, but couldn't get out any more before Heidi interrupted again.

"You understand nothing, DETECTIVE!" Heidi's voice was rising in volume and anger. "You're lucky that I don't report you and your smug, arrogant attitude to your bosses at the police station. I've had it up to here with cops, nurses, doctors, even family and friends who think they know what's best! What's best is if everyone not directly connected to Allison and her children would leave them alone!"

Lindstrom was instantly aware that Heidi had neglected to mention Nathan in her little tirade. She was about to speak when a nurse, who had been in a patient's room two doors away from Nathan Devlin's room, came out and said, "Excuse me, but is there a problem here?"

"No, ma'am," Andy said, looking up from the floor, clearly startled that this scene was attracting attention.

"Honey, just stand there and be quiet," Heidi said to Andy, with a great deal of venom in her voice. Heidi turned to the nurse and said, "Actually, can you call security and have this woman removed from the hospital?"

The nurse looked at Lindstrom. Before the nurse could speak, Lindstrom smiled, pulled out her badge, and showed it to her. "I'm sorry. My name is Detective Patricia Lindstrom. One of my colleagues is working with Mr. Devlin, and our conversation got a little loud. We will keep it down."

Heidi snapped at Lindstrom. "Don't you dare presume to speak for me!" The words came out as a hiss, as if Heidi was trying to drive Lindstrom off.

Before anyone else could speak, the door to Nathan's room opened and Scott appeared at the door. "Sorry to interrupt," Scott said, "but my tablet died. I have a charging cable, but I must have left my adapter at the station. We'll have to come back later."

Lindstrom looked at Scott with murder in her eyes. "Scott, seriously? Mr. Devlin needs his rest, and I don't think…"

"Oh, great!" It was Heidi Cole talking over Lindstrom again. "We've gone from one inept cop to two! Jesus, both of you, get out of here!"

Lindstrom was about to say something, when Scott said, "Look, I apologize, okay? It was an oversight on my part. We can plan on being here tomorrow, at say…"

"You don't get it," Heidi practically yelled, "you two aren't coming back here!"

"Ma'am," the nurse said to Heidi, trying to diffuse the situation. "I think you need to calm down. I will page Dr. Preston and see about working something out."

"Heidi," Andy said, looking at his wife with puppy dog eyes, pleading with her to take her attitude down a few notices. "It's only a day. I think we should…"

"Stop trying to think!" Heidi was raging right now, and Lindstrom could tell that this was spiraling now. It was only a matter of time before things went bad.

"Look here," the nurse interjected, "either calm down and quiet down, or I'll have security remove all of you from the building."

Before Heidi could respond, Lindstrom looked at Scott and said, "What exactly do you need to get this done right now?"

"I need to either charge my tablet or get an adapter to charge it with my cable. Look, I'm very sorry about this. I guess I should have grabbed one of the tablets that was fully charged."

"Heidi," Andy said to his wife, "if it gets them out of here faster, let him borrow the laptop. He can use the laptop as a battery, long enough to do his job and then both officers can leave."

"That sounds like a good idea," the nurse said. "And while he is doing whatever he needs to do, you," the nurse pointed to Lindstrom, "you could wait in the visitor's lounge by the elevators." The nurse looked at Heidi, conveying to her that she either accepts the situation, or she can risk the consequences of getting security involved.

"Fine!" Heidi thrust out the laptop towards Scott. "Do your job and leave!" Scott took the laptop and mumbled a quiet thank you. As Scott went back into Nathan's room, Heidi turned away and stormed off to the end of the hallway, which was a massive pane of glass to the outside. She stood there, her back to everyone, like a petulant child that was throwing a tantrum because she hadn't gotten her way.

"I am sorry about all that," Lindstrom said quietly to the nurse, as she turned and walked to the visitor's lounge. Before Lindstrom turned the corner by the nurse's station, she looked back. The nurse was gone, Heidi was still facing the window, and Andy had sat down on the floor by Nathan Devlin's door. Very curious, she thought to herself, continuing to walk and finding an empty chair. Maybe curious wasn't the right word. Sad, perhaps?

As Lindstrom sat there, she cleared her head, checking her phone for any messages. There was nothing waiting for her, so she closed her eyes, thinking about what Kara Reed had said about Visceral Medical Supplies. She would have to go over the file that Tisdale and Tavon had worked on about Visceral, to make sure she hadn't missed anything.

"I hear you are upsetting a lot of people?" Lindstrom opened her eyes, and Dr. Preston was standing in front of her. She checked the time, and she realized she had been napping for about fifteen minutes.

Lindstrom looked at the doctor and smiled. "Actually, it was only one person. And trust me, she didn't need any help from me to get upset."

"She? I take it you've interacted with Mrs. Cole?"

"So, it's not only the police she doesn't tolerate?"

"Let's say that my life will be considerably easier when she is no longer in the hospital," replied Dr. Preston.

Before Lindstrom could delve any deeper, Scott appeared from around the corner and walked up to Lindstrom and Dr. Preston.

"Sorry about that," Scott said. "I gave back the laptop to Mrs. Cole, and the picture that Mr. Devlin made is an almost identical match to the one that Nurse Jason made."

Dr. Preston seemed satisfied. He looked from Scott to Lindstrom and said, "I hope there won't be any more distractions?" Lindstrom stood up and shook the doctor's hand.

"Doctor, you have my sincerest apologies. Come on, Scott, let's get back to the station."

Lindstrom and Scott rode in the elevator and walked in silence for several minutes. Finally, in a long and empty hallway leading towards the ER, Lindstrom said in a tone that was equal parts irritation and anger, "Scott, I am truly pissed at you."

"I know," Scott responded humbly. "It was a dumb thing to do, and I'm really very sorry."

"I'm half-tempted to report this near fiasco to Engels."

Scott huffed. "That's your decision, but maybe this will make you feel better." He held out his hand while they were walking. Lindstrom reached out her hand, and Scott dropped a small piece of plastic with two metal prongs in it. It was a wall adapter for charging electronic devices.

"You're telling me that you had a charger this whole time?" Lindstrom stopped at a corner section of the hallway. About another hundred feet, and they would be at the walkway connecting the parking garage to the hospital. "Why the hell would you do that?"

Scott held out his other hand, dropping a small USB flash drive in her hand. "Give me back my power adapter, and you can have that."

Lindstrom looked at it and then looked at Scott. "So, you made a copy of Nathan's and Jason's digital alterations?"

Scott was grinning ear-to-ear. "Even better. You have a ghost in your hand."

Lindstrom wasn't in the mood for riddles. "A ghost? A ghost of whom?"

"Not of whom," Scott corrected, "but of what. I knew something was up the second I saw how Heidi Cole reacted to you. When I heard her yelling in the hallway, I made up a story about my tablet being dead. While I was working with Nathan, I was able to copy her entire laptop over to that flash drive in your hand."

Lindstrom was stunned. "You did what?"

"It's a good thing her laptop was almost brand new," Scott happily said. "If it had been an older laptop with a standard hard drive, I couldn't have done it. Fortunately, it's a newer model with a solid state hard drive, meaning it reads and writes and copies faster. Otherwise, my little stunt wouldn't have worked."

Lindstrom couldn't tell if she wanted to hug Scott for his ingenuity, or if she should kick him hard for almost blowing the interview with Nathan. Before Lindstrom could talk, Scott sounded a word of caution.

"Granted, anything you find in there can't be used in court. If there's something in there that ties Mrs. Cole to any of this, you'll have to find a different avenue of discovery."

Lindstrom looked at the flash drive. As she put it safely in her pocket, she started to walk again towards the parking garage. "You know what," she said, "I don't think I'll tell Engels about what happened up there. In fact, the last half hour is suddenly a little hazy."

Scott smiled again and said, "I only hope it helps."

I hope so, Lindstrom thought to herself, I really hope so.

TWENTY-TWO

Lindstrom had parted ways with Scott in the parking garage of Sanford Hospital, though she hadn't moved since he had driven away. In fact, she hadn't even started her car. She had taken the flash drive that Scott had given her and locked it in her gun case underneath the driver's seat. She sat there for close to twenty minutes, trying to ignore the sounds coming from her stomach that she needed to eat. Instead, she was focused on the conflict of emotions she was now feeling. Scott's heart had been in the right place. Regrettably, she was left to deal with the ramifications.

Lindstrom prided herself on being a good cop. Fortunately, in her entire career in law enforcement up to the moment that Scott dropped the USB flash drive in her hand, there was only one instance when she had been on the wrong side of her duties. Now, here she was, sitting in her car, the key not even in the ignition, her memories taking her back to that fateful night.

Lindstrom was still a beat cop, a uniformed officer. She and her partner, a cop fifteen-years her senior, had responded to a domestic disturbance. Other officers had arrived as well, and the whole scene was like something out of a Jerry Springer special. Thirteen individuals were involved, and it was a circus, to say the least. There was the husband, the wife, six children, three neighbors, and two mistresses of the husband. Depending on the person, they had been separated from the others and were either being treated for minor injuries or being interviewed.

Lindstrom, her partner, and two other officers were checking the inside of the house for any other suspects and witnesses.

Once they entered the house, Lindstrom had flashbacks to her own time with domestic abuse. The place was in absolute shambles. Furniture overturned, pictures smashed and barely hanging from the walls, sporadic holes in the drywall, cupboards ripped apart and the contents strewn everywhere. The only room that wasn't in complete ruin was one of the kids' bedrooms. When the melee had started, the oldest of the kids had gathered up her siblings and barricaded themselves in her room. She had also called 911 when the sounds of things being broken had been replaced by two gunshots. Thank heavens, no one had been hit by gunfire, or even a ricochet. By the time the police had arrived, the house looked like some combination of bomb going off and a tornado ripping through it.

As Lindstrom and the other officers had spread out, each calling a room clear, Lindstrom stepped carefully through the large kitchen. She was trying to avoid stepping on cereal, pasta, and broken jars of alfredo sauce on the floor. Her partner had walked into the kitchen from the opposite side and, not paying attention, suddenly slipped on ice cubes that had fallen out of the freezer. When he landed on his butt, the fall had kicked up food debris, lightly covering his stomach and legs. As he reached for the counter to pull himself up, he inadvertently knocked over a ceramic jar that read "FLOUR" on the outside. The jar crashed to the floor, exploding into small pieces, revealing four large bundles of hundred-dollar bills, lightly covered in flour.

"Everything okay?" came a shout from one of the other officers deeper in the house.

Lindstrom's partner shouted back, "Yeah, I just slipped on some of this crap is all! I'm fine, though!" Lindstrom and her partner were staring at the money.

"Are you thinking what I'm thinking," the partner had asked Lindstrom in a hushed voice.

"That this is about much more than a simple domestic disturbance?"

The partner shook his head. "C'mon kid, don't be naïve. This isn't time to play things by-the-book. You know what I'm talking about here." Lindstrom had been partnered with him for a little over two months, and he never called her by her name. It was always "kid". At least he hadn't started in with sexist nicknames. He had been a bit of a whiner and complainer, how he hadn't made detective, he had been a beat cop for too long, life wasn't fair, blah blah blah.

Lindstrom looked her partner dead in the eye and said with no hesitation in her voice, "Not now, not ever, it's not happening." She half turned away to start walking out of the kitchen. From her vantage point, she could see through the front window of the house and the front door. The yellow police tape was up at the property line, with fire trucks, ambulances, police cars, and now, teams of television news setting up shop.

As she walked away, Lindstrom heard her partner say, "Well, your loss then, kid." She turned back to see him bending down to retrieve one of the bundles of cash.

"You're a cop," Lindstrom said in a raised voice. "Act like it! You so much as touch one of those bills, and I walk out of here and let the camera crews know that you're dirty!"

Her partner straightened up, a look of amazement and rage on his face. "Kid, hold on now," the partner had started to plead, but Lindstrom decided to end this before it could escalate.

"TIM! SHANNON! COME TO THE KITCHEN! WE FOUND SOMETHING!" Lindstrom had shouted to the other officers still checking the house. As they made their way to the kitchen, Lindstrom quickly walked to the front door and yelled from the threshold, "I NEED THE DETECTIVE IN CHARGE IN HERE, NOW!" Lindstrom turned and walked back to the edge of the kitchen. By the time Lindstrom had reached the kitchen, Officers Tim and Shannon had come around opposite corners.

"What's up," Officer Shannon asked. Lindstrom stared at her partner, whose gaze went from Lindstrom's eyes to the floor. He meekly pointed down to the broken flour jar. Nothing had been moved, and all four bundles were still in place.

Officer Tim whistled softly, and Officer Shannon said, "You bet your ass, Tim!"

The detective in charge came into the house and said, "Okay, I'm here. What did you find?"

Lindstrom waved him over and pointed to the broken flour jar and money. "My partner found it," she said.

The detective in charge looked from the money to Lindstrom's partner and said, "Good work! If the house is clear, you four officers can head outside and help out. I want to get forensics in here to start tagging and bagging." Lindstrom and the other officers left. When it was time to leave, Lindstrom and her partner didn't speak a word. No words were exchanged in the car back to the police station. No words were spoken until their shift ended. They went their separate ways, with nothing left to say.

The next day, her partner had requested a leave of absence, his reason being that, after witnessing the carnage from last night, he needed to evaluate his role on the force. He never did return, opting to cash in his pension early and move out of state with his wife.

Whenever Lindstrom felt puzzled or conflicted about something relating to her duties as a police officer, she would often times think about that night. It had never once crossed her mind to take one of those cash bundles. Now, here she was, years removed from her first moral quandary as a cop, with a new one to deal with. Yes, there had been a few other morally-dubious scenarios pop up, but those could have been counted on one hand, and nothing of this potential magnitude.

Scott, bless his heart, was only trying to help. After all, Lindstrom had told him specifically to keep an eye out for anything unusual. He had done what she asked him to do, identified Heidi Cole as a possible suspect, and worked the situation to gain an advantage.

Unfortunately, the instant Lindstrom would open up that flash drive and start poking around, anything she discovered was tainted and would be thrown out in court. She remembered back to a day of guest lecturing at the police academy. A lawyer, a woman, had been asked to give a lecture to the trainees. Instead, she had opted to open up the floor for questions regarding hypotheticals, cases, and anything the officers-in-training could come up with. One of the members of Lindstrom's class had asked a question similar to the situation she now faced. The lawyer had been intrigued and had spent almost twenty minutes on the question. The lawyer had flipped the question around, starting out in court and, basically, reverse-engineering the scenario, back to the trainee's question.

"Now," the lawyer had said, "is it worth jeopardizing your career AND the integrity of our offices to try to find a short-cut to true justice?"

Those words had struck Lindstrom, and she found comfort in them during those few moral quandaries she had found herself in. Now, here was another one. Was it different because this case was so complex and unnerving? Like she had said to Engels that morning in his office, *"It makes too much sense, and it doesn't make any sense."* If she found Charles Utecht, and it went to court, and it was determined that she had used nefarious means to convict, indict, or even arrest him, it would be game over for her career as a detective. Lindstrom and Scott would both be brought up to Internal Affairs, definitely reprimanded, maybe even fired. Worse, of course, was that the bad guy would go free. Was it worth it? Lindstrom had tried to raise her three kids with a strong sense of right and wrong. Yes, areas of gray sometimes emerged, but if the person had a strong moral compass, things could be navigated with a strong sense of certainty.

Why had Lindstrom accepted the flash drive in the first place? She should have dropped it on the ground and smashed it, admonishing Scott and walking away. But she hadn't, and now she had the proverbial Pandora's Box locked away, underneath her car seat. Suddenly, she inexplicably did something that she never, ever did. She allowed her anger at the case to come to the surface, and she punched her fist on the steering wheel. The impact caused the car horn to go off for a split-second, the noise jolting her thoughts to exit her mind and focusing her attention on the stupid thing she had done.

"Anger isn't a weapon, and it isn't an excuse." She couldn't remember where she heard those words before, but they were good words to remember when things got tough.

The rumblings from Lindstrom's stomach were now too loud to ignore. She knew she needed food. The flash drive could stay locked away, safe and sound. She turned the key in the ignition, starting the car. There were good people working on this case, Lindstrom thought to herself. We will make this work. If the case ground to a halt, she would re-visit this dilemma. She looked at the time. Almost two in the afternoon. Holy crap, she thought, and headed over to a little Oriental place she liked to go. Fifteen minutes later, she was sitting in the restaurant at her favorite booth. She could see the beautiful fish tank and watch the traffic go by. She had also called ahead with her order. Within another two minutes of sitting down, Lindstrom had her food and was devouring it down. As she ate, she pondered what her next move should be.

Both Nathan and Jason had altered the image of Olivia Sherman to near identical levels. While it was good to close off that part of the investigation, there were still so many unanswered questions. How had Olivia Sherman paid for plastic surgery when she owed so much in child support? Why did she get plastic surgery in the first place? What was her connection to Ronald Vance? Was Charles Utecht also involved? Suddenly, her cell phone buzzed. She swiped the screen active and read a text from Engels.

"PRINTS FROM THE DELIVERY VAN MATCH CHARLES UTECHT. NEXT MOVE?"

Lindstrom thought about it for a few minutes. Without more leads, she didn't know how much further they could proceed. She wanted to take a run at Andy Cole. He had looked like a man conflicted, like he was being forced to choose between his best friend and his wife. Could Lindstrom push the right buttons and get him to open up about his wife? It would be difficult, especially since Lindstrom had no evidence and only a gut feeling about Heidi Cole's possible involvement. There was really only one realistic course of action at this point. She used a napkin to wipe off her fingers and started texting Engels.

"LET'S RUN PHOTOS ON THE NEWS CHANNELS. KEEP VANCE AND SHERMAN SEPARATE FROM UTECHT. POLICE ARE SEEKING ANY INFO REGARDING VANCE AND SHERMAN. LATER, POLICE ARE SEEKING INFO REGARDING UTECHT AND HIS POSSIBLE WHEREBOUTS."

Lindstrom sent the text, and then went back to finishing her late lunch. Two of the stations had early editions at five, with the standard news at six and ten. If they were lucky, they might generate a lead. She finished her fortune cookie, paid the bill, and got into her car. She pulled out her phone and tried Visceral Medical again and was once again greeted with voicemail from the retail site and the warehouse. From where she was, it would be about a twenty-minute drive, but she didn't want to waste her time if she couldn't speak to Cassie Butler. She could call the station and have a patrol car near Visceral's retail store check it out, but that seemed like a waste of time, too. There's probably a logical explanation, so she called each location again, leaving the same voicemail message.

"Hello, this is Detective Patricia Lindstrom. I am trying to reach someone regarding the stolen delivery vehicle that Visceral Medical reported. You can contact me at the following number," which Lindstrom then gave. After she was finished leaving the message on both the Visceral warehouse number and the Visceral retail number, she ended each call. There wasn't anything left to do except head back to the police station.

As she put her car into gear and pulled out of the parking lot, she had an idea. She pulled over quickly, scrolling through her contact list, until she found the name. She pressed the talk icon and merged back into traffic. It was a long shot, but maybe someone else could give her an idea of what was happening in Andy Cole's life.

Engels hung up the phone, satisfied that the local news stations would give the investigations a boost. He had put together an impromptu conference call with all three stations, sending them photos of Ronald Vance and Olivia Sherman, and then a photo of Charlies Utecht. He made it very clear that the stories needed to be aired separately, since they were two different cases. Fortunately, even though he didn't like being in front of the camera, Engels had developed a solid relationship with the editors and most reporters at all of the local TV stations, as well as with the local newspaper. He felt confident that taking the cases public, as Lindstrom had suggested, would yield some solid results.

Since Lindstrom wasn't back yet, Engels decided it was a good time to do some more paperwork. His assistant, Michelle, had set a large stack of forms and folders on his desk during his conference call. Strangely, he was feeling invigorated, and he tore into the stack, reading and signing as he went. He didn't even realize that his phone was ringing for several minutes. It wasn't until Michelle knocked on his door.

"Brad," Michelle said, "are you going to answer that? It's been ringing for a while."

Engels looked from the phone to Michelle.

"Sorry," he said as he reached for the receiver, "I was really focused on getting caught up." Michelle smiled and shook her head, walking back to her desk. He put the receiver to his ear and said, "Chief of Police Brad Engels."

"Um, hello," a female voice said. "I was trying to reach a Detective Patricia Lindstrom. Did I dial the wrong number?"

"Not at all," Engels replied. "Detective Lindstrom is currently away from the police station. As I said, my name is Brad Engels, and I'm the

Chief of Police. How can I help you today?"

"Oh, well, I guess it's okay to talk to you. My name is Cassie Butler. I'm the receptionist at Visceral Medical's retail store. Detective Lindstrom stopped by yesterday to ask me some questions."

"Yes, Ms. Butler. Did you have anything to add to your interview?"

"Actually, Detective Lindstrom had left a message on our voicemail. Apparently, the main computer systems for Visceral crashed overnight. I was getting ready for work this morning, but Veronica from the main office called me and told me to stay home. I wasn't told exactly what the issues were, only that several key systems failed overnight, and I was told there was no reason for me to go into work yet, but I should call back before noon. I called the warehouse, and I was told there was nothing to do until the tech guys could fix the system. They told me to stay home but to check the voicemail every hour."

That would explain why no one had answered the phone at the retail store, Engels thought. "How bad is the computer outage?"

"I was told it's pretty bad, with no orders coming in or going out. I don't even know if I can go into work tomorrow."

Before Engels could respond, Lindstrom appeared in his door. He put a finger to his lips, letting Lindstrom know to be quiet.

"I'm sorry to hear that," Engels said. "I'm guessing it's an inconvenience to you, not knowing if you're going to be able to go to work and make a paycheck."

"Oh, it's not that bad," Cassie Butler said happily. "Visceral takes really good care of their employees. They sent me home with a full day's pay, and they said that if I can't work tomorrow, they will pay for that day, too."

Engels had remembered reading good things about the previous company, All Things Medical, before they became Visceral Medical. Maybe they carried a lot of the good things over after the merger, or buyout, or whatever it was that had happened between the owners and the companies.

"I appreciate the phone call," Engels said, "and I'll let Detective Lindstrom know what the situation is."

"Thank you so much!" Cassie Butler ended the call. Engels slowly set the receiver back into the phone's cradle as he looked at Lindstrom.

"Screening my calls now, boss?" Lindstrom walked into Engels' office and stood in front of his desk.

"That's what happens when you take a three-hour lunch. I end up being your personal secretary."

"Yeah, sorry about that," Lindstrom said apologetically. "Seriously, though, who was that?"

"Ms. Cassie Butler was calling for you. She said that the computer systems at Visceral crashed overnight, and that's why you weren't able to reach anyone."

Lindstrom stood there, thinking about that. Her eyes moved over the stacks of paperwork on Engels' desk, then to his phone, and then she sat down, looking out the window. "The computer systems that Visceral Medical uses are down, huh?" Lindstrom tapped a finger to her lip. "Computers crashed last night, hmm? Very interesting." The inflection of her voice suggested to Engels that Lindstrom wasn't buying it.

Engels looked at Lindstrom. "It would explain why no one is answering the phones." He was trying to play devil's advocate, since he hadn't questioned the information from Cassie Butler, or the overall situation. Like most things, computers were great, except when they didn't work.

Lindstrom continue to think about it, and then pulled out her cell phone. She activated the internet browser and typed in the web address for Visceral Medical. She was immediately met with a white page with solid black letters in the middle.

**"THIS WEBSITE IS UNAVAILABLE AT THIS TIME.
PLEASE TRY AGAIN LATER."**

Lindstrom handed Engels her phone. Engels didn't like it, either, but sometimes it was best to work suspicions from the other side. "Let it out, Tish. What are you thinking?"

"We start looking for a delivery van, and one just so happens to go missing and is reported as stolen. I stop by and start asking questions about two former employees that are both dead in our morgue, and now they can't answer their phones. The employee that allegedly stole the van is still unaccounted for, and Visceral Medical's computer network has crashed."

"The question is," Engels asked, "are these things one giant coincidence, or is this a pattern for a cover-up?"

Lindstrom rubbed her temples. "Boss, I keep saying it with these cases.

I hate coincidences. I want to say that this is merely a company trying to stay out of the spotlight. Three employees have run afoul, and now the company is doing whatever it can to distance itself from them." Lindstrom stood up and walked to the window. "It makes sense, it's logical, and…" Her voice trailed off.

Engels waited for a few seconds. "And, what?"

"And it's too convenient. It's too perfect."

"Perfect? I wouldn't say that. Two people are dead, a kidnapping victim has been recovered, only two doors away from his estranged wife, who had a breakdown in the police station lobby. And we still don't have reasons for any of it to be connected. I'd say that's pretty far from perfect."

"You know what I mean, boss."

Engels was about to say something, when Lindstrom's phone beeped. He swiped the screen, and the internet browser was still up. The hourglass icon was up, indicating that the browser was trying to refresh. "Tish, come and take a look at this." Lindstrom walked to the desk and looked at her phone. A few seconds later, the main website page was showing, but it was badly pixelated. A few more seconds, and the white page reappeared with the "website down" warning appeared.

Lindstrom took her phone and closed the browser. "Try pulling it up on your computer," Lindstrom said, "and let's see what happens."

Engels slid his keyboard out from the desk drawer and pulled the computer out of sleep mode. A minute later, the monitor came to life. He clicked on the secure web browser that the police station used and typed in the web address for Visceral Medical Supplies. For ninety-seconds, the screen showed a progress bar with the hourglass icon. Finally, a full webpage was displayed, with a banner that read "WELCOME TO VISCERAL MEDICAL SUPPLIES." As Engels tried to scroll down, the page pixelated and turned a solid blue. Within the blue, though, the black letters warning of the website being unavailable could be seen.

"Maybe it's legit," Engels said.

"Maybe," Lindstrom said, sitting back down in the chair. "There's still something fishy about the whole VMS angle."

"It's possible, but there's nothing more you can do tonight. Your work with Scott gave us a solid ID for Olivia Sherman. Let the TV news do its job, and hopefully we'll have some leads to work with tomorrow. Why don't you take off and surprise Ryan with an early pickup? Maybe watch him at martial arts for a change?"

Lindstrom smiled. "That sounds like a good idea. I have one stop to make first." Lindstrom stood up and walked out of Engels' office. "Have a good night, Boss," she said as she left.

By the time Lindstrom arrived at the little coffee shop across the street from the nondescript halfway house, Ben McKinley was already finishing his smoothie. "You took your damn time getting here, Detective."

"Sorry, but traffic is a real pain this time of day. And are you always this happy, or is it just for me that you put on this tough-guy act?"

McKinley offered no apologies. "It's no act, and you knew that the second we met. When you deal with men and women that are trying to turn their lives around and get off of the booze and the drugs and the gambling, hell, trying to get off all the shit, one of the things I stress is keeping your word. That includes punctuality. You say you're going to meet at five fourteen in the morning, it had better be five fourteen or earlier. Even one minute late, to me, is a lie."

Lindstrom wasn't sure if she should be impressed or embarrassed. Ben McKinley came across as crass, arrogant, and borderline violent. "You subscribe to the tough love motto?"

McKinley shrugged. "Call it what you want. Most of the people I have helped need to have their asses kicked, and in more ways than one. If they want to end up on the wrong side of a gravedigger's shovel, that's their choice. When that choice affects others around them, that's when I get truly pissed off. That's when I need to drag them back to reality and teach them the error of their ways."

"Do you work only with the person that is trying to get clean and sober, or do you work with the family as well?" Lindstrom was trying to ask valid questions, slowly working her way to what she really wanted to know.

"It really depends on what I see from the individual," McKinley replied. "Some people need all the support they can get. Others, like Nathan, want to do it on their own, so that when they get back with their families, the family won't be reminded of the crap. Instead, they'll see the new person. Now, before you ask another question, it's my turn. What's with this little visit? I'm guessing you're not in need of a twelve-step

302

program. I haven't heard anything negative about you from Nathan or Allison, otherwise I would have been calling you for a friendly chit-chat."

Lindstrom realized she couldn't pull the wool over McKinley's eyes. "Before I get to the point, I need to ask you for full discretion. What I'm going to ask you needs to be held in the strictest of confidence." She looked at him with a laser focus and asked, "So, this stays right here, between the two of us, right?"

McKinley smiled an evil-looking smile, which came across only half of his face. "Tish, even if you broke my kneecaps, I wouldn't spill all of the BS I've heard from people over the years. Now go ahead, why are we here?"

Here goes nothing, Lindstrom thought. "Andy Cole and his wife, Heidi." She didn't go any further, only looking McKinley in the eyes. There was silence for a minute, until McKinley broke away from Lindstrom's gaze and looked at his empty cup. He raised the cup towards the teenager behind the counter, who nodded and started working on a refill.

"Which end of the shit-show did you get caught on," McKinley asked.

"Let's say I get the feeling that Heidi Cole isn't exactly the easiest person to live with."

The look on McKinley's face changed from one of intensity to one of sadness. Or was it one of pity? Lindstrom couldn't tell.

"Your order's ready, sir." McKinley turned and saw the teenager wave at him. He got up from his seat and brought back two cups and placed one in front of Lindstrom. She picked it up and took a drink. It was delicious, a mixture of different berries and a subtle hint of chocolate.

"Thank you," Lindstrom said, motioning to the drink. "It's excellent."

"I love little places like this," McKinley said, showing a softer side. "They really know how to take care of a customer." He took a large drink from his cup and then looked at Lindstrom. "Andy Cole introduced me to Nathan. After the initial intro, though, I didn't have much interaction with Andy. Nathan wanted to, no, I take that back, I think Nathan NEEDED to get clean on his own, with no outside support. Nathan gave me the green light to share his progress with Andy, but not to sugarcoat anything." McKinley rolled his eyes. "Like I would EVER sugarcoat anything for anyone."

Lindstrom chuckled. "Yes, I think I've noticed a directness with your personal interactions."

"Yeah, well, it's what gets the best results. Anyway, the few times I've been around Heidi, I could tell that something had crawled up her ass. Andy invited me over to their home one night to give him an update on Nathan's recovery. I wasn't in the house two minutes when Heidi goes off on me. *'ANYONE THAT THINKS THAT WORTHLESS DRUNK WILL EVER BE GOOD ENOUGH FOR MY BEST FRIEND CAN GET THE HELL OUT OF MY HOUSE!'* Andy turned red with embarrassment, not really knowing what to do. I looked her right in the eye and said, *'I am here to talk to your husband, lady. If you don't like it, go dig a hole in the backyard and stick your head in it until I'm done."* The look on her face was priceless. I don't think Heidi had ever been talked to that way before, and I don't think she knew what to do." McKinley smiled, as if the thought of Heidi being flustered gave him a perverse pleasure.

"Anyway," McKinley continued, "she stood there for a few seconds, huffed a little, and then stormed off. I asked Andy if everything was all right. He nodded like a little kid that was in trouble and told me that Heidi doesn't like Nathan. *'Doesn't like,'* I asked, *'or hates?'* Andy didn't answer, so I gave him a quick report and left."

Everything that McKinley was saying was tracking with what Lindstrom had experienced first-hand with Heidi Cole. "Have you had any other confrontations with Heidi," Lindstrom asked.

"Two other times stick out. The first was when I called Andy to let him know that Nathan hadn't called me in two days. I heard Heidi in the background ask who was on the phone, and when Andy told her what I'd just said, I distinctly heard Heidi reply, *'Good riddance! For everyone's benefit, he's probably dead somewhere, and we can all move on with our lives!'* The other time was this past Monday morning. This time, Heidi had answered the phone. After a few seconds of mild insults, I told her that I needed to talk to Andy because the police had found Nathan. *'Jesus, why can't the piece of shit just die?'* If Heidi has to set foot in Nathan's hospital room, it's to get Andy out of there. I've overheard her berate Andy in the hallway or in the cafeteria, but I think she knows better to try anything with me."

Lindstrom didn't know what to make of what McKinley had told her. Assuming Heidi Cole may have been involved, these conversations were conjecture and hearsay. It was a typical he-said/she-said situation. She took another drink of her smoothie, trying to find a way to connect Heidi to Nathan's abduction.

"Come on, Detective," McKinley prodded, "what's going on in that cop brain of yours?"

"Do you think Heidi could be involved in Nathan's disappearance?"

McKinley's face registered minor shock. He definitely had not expected that question. "You don't think that…"

Lindstrom cut him off. "Right now, I'm asking YOU what you think."

McKinley looked at his cup before chugging the rest of his smoothie. He wiped his lips with a napkin, and then looked out the window. Lindstrom could tell he was working through it in his mind, seeing if everything added up. He was quiet for a few minutes, then turned slowly back to Lindstrom.

"If I was a betting man, I would say that the odds are fifty-fifty. Heidi has an absolute hatred for Nathan, and for reasons that I don't know and don't want to know. Whether she has the means to pull it off is another question." McKinley paused. "You don't have any proof, do you?"

Lindstrom shook her head. "No, I don't. All that I have is a kidnapping victim, two dead kidnappers, at least three people that are one hundred and ten percent on Nathan's side, and one person that hates him beyond all reason." She took another drink. "My gut tells me that Heidi is involved with this whole mess, in some way, shape, or form."

McKinley also shook his head. "There is definitely something wrong with Heidi. I've seen things like this before with other recovering addicts. Anger, hurt, betrayal, the emotions can be misdirected at the wrong thing. Heidi sees what Nathan's actions did to her best friend, Allison, and her family, and blames Nathan. Like I said, the emotion and intent are there. Whether Heidi acted on it, that's another story."

Lindstrom finished her drink. She wasn't exactly back at square one, but at least she had some validation for her gut feeling. She looked at the clock. There was nothing left to accomplish here.

"Thank you, Ben," Lindstrom said, standing up from the table. "I really appreciate your candor and discretion about this."

McKinley stood up and offered his hand, which Lindstrom shook. "Nathan made bad choices, but he was working damn hard to make amends. No one deserves this, and if Heidi is involved, all she did was drag everyone through hell."

"You're right about that," Lindstrom said. "Thanks again." She walked toward the door.

"Detective," McKinley called as she reached the door. "You need anything, you let me know." Lindstrom smiled and went to her car.

TWENTY-THREE

Heather Gordon didn't mind helping out at the police station. She had been a police woman for thirty-five years. Even though she had been offered numerous promotions in the department, she always felt she could do the most good in a squad car, helping the community in a hands-on environment. When school principals had called asking for someone on the force to visit, they always asked for Heather. When she retired, several schools got together and threw her a retirement party. It had been kept under wraps, and when her husband had brought her to the old convention center downtown and surprised her with so many school kids, parents, teachers, and police officers, she had broken down and wept. It had been a truly moving and humbling experience.

A year into her retirement, Heather's husband was dead. No warning, no sickness. She got up early one morning and made a quick run to the grocery store to get a few things. When she returned home, she had found her husband on the living room floor, still in his pajamas. The ambulance arrived within minutes of her 911 call, along with several squad cars and a fire truck, but there was nothing that could have been done. The coroner's report had determined a massive stroke was the cause of death. Heather had kept the funeral a small affair. However, the outpouring of flowers, cards, and gifts from the community was almost too much to bear. A week after the funeral, she cleaned up the house, packed a bag, took some money out of the bank, and went to the airport. She bought a plane ticket to the first city that was departing from the first airline that she walked up to.

Two weeks later, Heather returned after several more airline-hopping trips around the country. She came back home, refreshed and over her grief. She put her husband's estate in order, making several gifts in his name to various local charities. Due to numerous fertility issues, they never had children.

Exactly three months to the day after her husband's death, Heather had walked into the police station and asked if she could help out in any way. Clive Gundvaldson, who was still Chief of Police at the time, had asked her, "Would you mind being one of the police station's receptionists?" Heather's smile had said it all, and there she was, back with the police department. Over the years, she had mostly worked the day shift, but she didn't mind an evening or even an overnight shift if she was asked. It had been common knowledge over the years that, whenever an officer left the department, for whatever reason, when the officer was asked in the exit interview, "What will you miss most about the Sioux Falls Police Department", the answer was almost always "Heather Gordon".

Which would explain why Heather was at the police station's receptionist desk at 11:52pm on a Thursday night. One of the overnight receptionists had asked for a few shifts during the day, as she had family passing through. "Not a problem," Heather had responded, "but you owe me." Of course, Heather said that to anyone that asked for her help on something, but Heather never tried to collect the debt. Deep down, Heather always wanted to help and to feel useful. That had been her overriding desire to be a police officer, all those years ago.

Heather had run out of paperwork to process and file, so she had found the login and codes for the department's crime tip hotline and had started filtering through the messages left. She had seen the six o'clock news with the different segments asking the public for any information regarding Ronald Vance, Olivia Sherman, and, finally, Charles Utecht. Heather figured she could get a head start for Tish and Engels before they arrived in the morning.

Heather was expecting more messages. Then again, how many people actually watched the news anymore? Well, maybe there would be something that would help. She had started listening and cataloging the messages around 11:30pm, stopping only to answer a phone call or direct someone that came into the station's main lobby. Most of the messages were vague. *"She looks familiar." "I think I might have seen him." "I'm not sure where I know him from."* There were a few prank messages, to be sure, but that was to be expected. One message, though, did seem promising. The caller was a bartender, and he was almost positive that Charles Utecht had been in the bar last week. The bartender remembered because the woman that was with Utecht was extremely tall and had paid Utecht's ten-dollar bar tab with a hundred before walking out with him. Heather took down the information carefully, then replayed the message, making sure it was saved and copied.

Twenty minutes later, Officer Tina Williams came through the lobby. She had only been with the department for ten months, but those that had worked with her spoke well of her. She saw that Heather was working and came up to the receptionist's counter.

"Heather, why are you here so late?"

Heather looked up at her and smiled. "Oh, I'm here helping out, as usual. Karen asked to swap a few shifts this week, because she had family stopping by for a day or three. No big deal." Heather ended the playback on the most recent message and took off her headset. "And how are you, Officer Williams? Life on the swing shifts working okay for you?" It was standard policy for new officers to work a variety of shifts at different times. The reason being that it was important to get a feeling for what you might run into as an officer at any time of the day and night.

"It took a little getting used to at first," Williams said, "but I think I have the hang of it now. You just have to get your body to respond to all the ups and downs."

"Well, if you ever need help with something, don't hesitate to let me know. Everyone in the department depends on everyone else." Heather gave Williams a warm smile. Bless her heart, Williams thought. Her first day on the force, Williams had been told that Heather Gordon was a combination of mother hen, school counselor, crisis manager, and matriarch. After she had talked to Heather a few times, Williams had come to realize that description didn't do Heather justice.

"Oh, I know, Heather," Williams said. "The minute I get into trouble, I will be speed dialing you!"

Heather grinned that wonderful grin of hers. "You stay out of trouble first, and then call me anyway!"

"I will," Williams said, starting to walk off, before she turned and came back to the counter. "Actually, would you mind if I asked you something?"

"Absolutely, dear. What is it?" Heather leaned in close, even though there were no other people in the lobby.

"I don't mean to gossip," Williams began, clearly shy about what she was about to ask, "but, well, Detective Lindstrom?"

"Yes," Heather said, a mild look of concern on her face now, "what about her?"

"Is it really true that she received a check on Monday for a hundred thousand dollars, right here at the police station?"

Heather started to laugh. She figured that, like most places of employment, there was going to be small talk and water cooler chatter. "Yes and no, Tina. Yes, Detective Lindstrom did receive a check on Monday, but no, it was definitely NOT for a hundred thousand dollars!" Heather shook her head light-heartedly. "It was a payment for delinquent child support from her ex-husband."

A confused look came over Williams face. "So, the check was real? I mean, it wasn't some kind of practical joke?"

"Heavens no, dear!" Heather looked concerned. "Why would you say that?"

Williams was quiet for a few seconds, and then said, "I guess I figured it was a prank that went too far, since the truck the delivery guy was driving is downstairs in lockup."

"I'm sorry, but what truck are you talking about?" Heather slid her chair down the desk a few feet so that she could access the security monitor that displayed the camera feeds throughout the station. Even though she was fully trained on their use, she had rarely had a reason to access the feed. As she cycled through the various cameras, Williams continued to talk.

"Um, it's a black truck, I guess it's a van, actually. It's in the property lockup. There are signs and police barricade tape up letting everyone know that forensics is still processing it for evidence."

Heather found the feed for that part of property lockup. Obviously, the delivery van was too big to store, so Jerry had gotten creative with the small loading area between the police garage and the secure lockup. Heather zoomed in on the truck and waved for Williams to come around the counter to look.

310

"You're saying that the man that delivered Detective Lindstrom's check was driving this truck?" Heather was looking at Williams while pointing at the screen.

"I'm not sure if it is the exact same truck," Williams said, "but it's definitely the same make, the same model, and the same color."

"Tina, forgive me for asking," Heather started, "but how do you know?"

"I was outside the station on Monday, talking to Officer Jefferson. I was going to be his partner this week, but I had to take a few days off to help my father get situated at an assisted living center in Minneapolis. We were talking, and his cell phone rang. He excused himself for a minute to take the call, and I was leaning against the stone wall. A black delivery van pulled up and parked with the hazard lights on. The delivery driver got out fast and started running up the steps. I shouted to him that he couldn't park there for security reasons, but he shouted back, saying he had to deliver something important. Jefferson had walked away with his back to me, so he didn't see what was going on. I didn't know what to do. Before I really knew it, the driver was back out, yelled sorry, and drove off. Oh, and the truck had no license plates, just some red plates that advertised a car lot. Jefferson finished his call a minute later, and then I left to go pack. I didn't get back to town until late last night. Before I went home, I stopped to check out my schedule for the rest of the week, and I heard the rumor about Detective Lindstrom. When I was walking through the garage on my way up here, I saw the van, so I thought something bad happened to her."

Heather looked from Williams to the monitor, trying to comprehend what she had been told. A few minutes of silence passed, as time seemed to stop.

"Heather," Williams said, "did I do something wrong?"

"Not at all," Heather said, moving her gaze from the monitor to Williams. Heather smiled at her. "Why don't you have a seat. I have a phone call to make."

Lindstrom had returned home to find one child gone and two children getting ready to leave. Due to a teacher in-service day and multiple school activities, there was no school tomorrow or Monday, which meant a four-day weekend for the kids. Bree was dismissed early, as there was a large, state-wide cheerleading competition taking place all weekend in Rapid City, which was five hours away. Trevor had taken Ryan to martial arts, and, upon coming home, had started packing.

"Where are you off to?" Lindstrom had asked her oldest son.

"Grandpa called," Trevor had said. "He needs some help with combining and hauling corn this weekend, and, since there's no school, I figured I'd take Ryan along, so he can play on the farm."

Lindstrom had quickly made her boys some sandwiches for the road, got a hug from both of them, and they were out the door by 6:30. Trevor was an excellent driver, so Lindstrom figured she'd get a phone call that they had arrived safely by nine o'clock at the latest. Having the house to herself, Lindstrom made a light dinner, and then unwound with a beer and some TV. Normally, she wouldn't have had alcohol. But, considering she couldn't tell whether the cases were stalled, she decided to let her hair down, in a manner of speaking, and try to give her brain a rest. She figured there was zero chance of getting called in. Now, in hindsight, she should have known better.

Normally, Lindstrom would have snapped awake at the first sound of her cell phone going off. However, she was feeling unusually tired. Lindstrom rubbed her eyes and dreamily reached for her phone. It was still ringing and vibrating, and as she accepted the call, she saw that she had missed three calls, all from the police station. The call she was accepting was from Heather Gordon's personal cell. She put the phone to her face, but she was so tired she didn't realize that the phone was upside down. It wasn't until she heard Heather yelling that Lindstrom figured out the problem. She turned the phone the right way and spoke.

"Sorry, Heather. All of the kids are out of the house for the weekend, and I must have been more tired than I thought."

"Dear, sweet Tish," Heather's voice said, "you need to wake up and listen."

Lindstrom yawned loudly. "Go ahead, Heather, I'm listening."

"No, you're not listening." The tone of Heather's voice was that of a mother scolding a child that wasn't paying attention to a much-needed lecture. "You are going to get up, walk to the bathroom, splash cold water on your face, and then come back. I WILL WAIT."

The tone in Heather's voice told Lindstrom that it was pointless to argue, so she yawned again and said, "Okay, hold on." She set the phone down and stumbled to the bathroom. The bright lights above the mirror started getting the fog to lift from her brain. A few splashes of cold water did the rest. She was still tired, but at least she was awake enough to function. Lindstrom walked back to the bedroom, almost tripping over Blonde the cat, who was probably wondering why she was awake. She picked up the phone.

"Okay, Heather, I'm back. What's going on?"

"First off, good morning to you," Heather said. "Second, I wouldn't have called if it wasn't important. Third, I think there's a reliable tip regarding Charles Utecht from the news story that ran tonight. It came from a bartender."

Lindstrom yawned, trying to muffle the sound as not to alert Heather that she still wasn't fully awake. "Well, first, good morning to you, too. Second, it must be important for you to call. Third, that's great news about the tip. Now, what's the payoff here? You didn't rouse me out of bed for a reliable tip."

"There is more to the delivery van than it only being stolen and filled with trash."

"Okay, I'll play along. What is it?"

"Allow me to put Officer Tina Williams on the phone." There was a bit of noise, as the phone was being transferred from one person to another.

"Hello, Detective Lindstrom." It was Officer Williams. Lindstrom had only come in passing contact with her twice since she joined the force, but Lindstrom had heard good things about her from her squad captain and from Engels.

"Morning, Williams." Lindstrom didn't know her well enough to call her Tina, and she hated the protocol involved with referring to her as officer. "Before you tell me what you must tell me, cut to the chase. I'll only get mad if you draw out the suspense, okay?"

"I am ninety-five percent sure that the black delivery van that is currently in forensics is the same delivery van that brought you the child support check on Monday."

Whatever trace of sleepiness instantly evaporated. Lindstrom was sitting up straight on the edge of her bed. How did Officer Williams know about her child support check? Heather probably told her, she thought, now, focus on what's important. At first, she wasn't sure if she had heard correctly, but the silence on the other end of the line was deafening. She felt her heart start to race, suddenly frozen with equal parts elation and dread. All the evidence and clues, the dead bodies, the cases coming together, it was all slamming into her, like waves crashing against the shore. Lindstrom took a deep breath. She needed to slow her brain down and take it slowly.

"Officer Williams, I know we've only met twice, but may I call you Tina?"

"Yeah, absolutely, no problem."

"Good." Lindstrom took another deep breath. "Now, Tina, I want you to tell me exactly why you think the vans are the same." Lindstrom listened to Williams recall the story of this past Monday that Williams had told Heather Gordon. With each syllable, Lindstrom was more awake. She had started to get dressed. There was no way she could go back to sleep now, and she needed to get to the police station. Lindstrom quickly fed Blonde, considering she didn't know when she would be home. By the time Williams was done, Lindstrom was pulling out of the driveway and closing the garage door.

"That's the story, Detective," Williams said. The last several minutes had left her slightly rattled, so she continued. "I asked Heather, and I'll ask you. Am I in trouble for this? Should I have reported this sooner?"

"Absolutely not, Tina," Lindstrom said, having enabled hands free speaking in her car. "You didn't know that there was anything to be suspicious of. I'm not even sure how this fits into place yet. For now, you don't tell anyone, not your partner, not your squad captain, not even Chief Engels, you don't repeat this story to anyone. Do I make myself clear?" Lindstrom didn't like keeping secrets, but the investigation had slowed to a snail's crawl. She needed some time to ask some questions and do some digging, and then, when the picture was clearer, she would present the case to Engels.

"Yes, I understand. Only you, Heather, and myself know the story." Williams was relieved she wasn't in trouble. While she hated keeping secrets from her superiors, if it helped Detective Lindstrom solve her case, she would have to oblige.

"Tina, thank you so much. Can you give the phone back to Heather, please?" A few seconds of muffled noise, and Heather was back on.

"I take it you are wide awake now?" Heather was being coy, of course, which was her prerogative. Lindstrom also detected a hint of a giggle in her voice, too.

"Before you start patting yourself on the back for dragging my butt out of bed," Lindstrom said, "I want you to send me the information regarding Charles Utecht from the tip line."

"Now? Tish, it's almost one in the morning."

"I'm driving in as we speak. I can get to the bar before closing time and talk to him. Send me the audio, as well as the bartender's name and where he works. I will call when I'm done. Thanks, Heather!"

"Be careful, Tish." A beep came through the speakers, indicating that Heather had ended the call.

A few minutes passed by, with Lindstrom focusing on the dark road. Even though she was awake, she had both front windows cracked to let in the cool night air. The radio DJ was teasing upcoming music from Bon Jovi and Soundgarden after the commercial break. Lindstrom had so many conflicting thoughts that she was trying to keep things separated. Finally, she decided it was best to not get her hopes up. The last thing she needed was her emotions getting the best of her. Like she did with the flash drive that contained a duplicate copy of Heidi Cole's hard drive, she locked her feelings away. It was time to focus.

Lindstrom's phone buzzed, and she carefully swiped the phone active. She was out of the country road areas and gradually driving into the city. With the bright light being cast from a near full moon and the passing street lamps, she would be able to see the cell phone's screen without much danger of having to correct her eyes back to the road. This went against everything she preached to Trevor and Bree about the dangers of cell phone activity while driving, but she needed to know where she was going. The text read, "BARTENDER'S NAME IS MONGO(?), WORKS AT JOE'S HOLE ACROSS FROM THE PAWN SHOP THAT BURNED DOWN IN JULY."

Lindstrom knew the place. Joe's Hole was a dive bar, but it had enough of a loyal client base with a great owner and wait staff that it continued to thrive. When Mark and Lindstrom had first started dating, they decided to try going somewhere different, and they decided to try Joe's Hole. The mixture of people and atmosphere that normally wouldn't come together was impressive. A group of bikers had been shooting pool with some college kids, tattooed goth girls had been playing darts with a group of what looked like bankers, various couples were at different tables and booths, and all this while the jukebox would cycle from country to rap to metal to top 40 and back again. It had definitely been an experience, and a great night out with Mark.

It took her another fifteen minutes to get to the bar, and, even though last call was still ten minutes away, with the bar closing fifteen minutes after that, it looked like a lot of customers were already heading home. Fortunately, that meant that Lindstrom was able to get a decent parking spot. She grabbed her cell phone and her notebook, locked her car, and walked briskly into Joe's Hole. She had to navigate a large group that was leaving. From the looks of them, it was a bachelor party, probably trying to get loaded into the party bus she had spotted outside and get across town to the strip club for last call.

A member of the bachelor party stepped in front of Lindstrom, a drunken smile on his face. As Lindstrom tried to sidestep him, he blocked her way.

"Hey sweetheart," he said, his breath reeking of beer and pretzels. "Where ya goin' in such a hurry? Wanna come and party with us?"

Lindstrom smiled at the man. He was almost six inches shorter than her, but she figured he was overflowing with liquid courage.

"I can't tonight, shorty." She showed him her badge. "Police business. You behave yourself at the strip club, or I'll make sure you find out what police brutality is all about. Deal?"

She was able to walk around him and, as she walked to the bar, he called back, "Yes ma'am!" How adorable, she thought to herself. Lindstrom made it to the bar and looked around. There was still a generous number of patrons inside, but only about half of the barstools were currently occupied. There were three bartenders, two women and one man. Lindstrom motioned for the woman closest to her, a brunette. The bartender walked over.

"This is last call, hon. What can I get ya?"

"Actually, I need to talk to Mongo, if he isn't busy," Lindstrom said. The bartender nodded and walked towards the other end of the bar. She whispered something and motioned behind her with her thumb. The male bartender set down the glass he had been drying, threw the towel over his shoulder, and started walking toward Lindstrom, putting a smile on his face by the time he got to her.

"I'm Mongo," he said. "What's up?"

"You don't look like you were in 'Blazing Saddles'," Lindstrom said with a smile. Thank goodness for Mark and his love of movies, or she never would have gotten the connection with his name, or nickname, as it were. He smiled back.

"Yeah, I wish. It was my favorite movie growing up. Eventually, my friends started calling me Mongo, and the name stuck. So, what do you need? We're starting to close down."

"My name is Detective Lindstrom," she said, showing him her badge. "I understand you left a tip on the police hotline involving a suspect."

Mongo looked at the badge, nodding with approval, and then looked at Lindstrom. "Wow, that was only a few hours ago that I made that call. He must be pretty important."

"Let's say he has the answers to some very important questions. Now, what do you remember?"

Mongo whistled towards the end of the bar. The second female bartender, a woman with dark auburn tied in a bun, looked back at Mongo. He gestured towards Lindstrom, and when the bartender shifted her glance from Mongo to Lindstrom, she held up her badge. The bartender gave him a thumbs-up, but also tapped her wrist. Obviously, she wanted Mongo to hurry.

"It was last Friday night, and we were busy, like packed to the rafters busy. The only reason why I remember him is because of who he left with."

"And who was that," Lindstrom asked.

"No idea. I've never seen her before or since. But I won't forget her, that's for damn sure."

"Oh? Why is that?"

"Detective, I'm almost six feet, and this woman was like something out of a comic book. She had to have been six-foot four, easy, but she wasn't just tall. You could tell she worked out. The way she walked, her arms and hands, she had a look that screamed 'don't even think about messing with me'. She was attractive, but she looked pissed as hell."

"Did they come in together," Lindstrom queried while taking furious notes, ignoring the cacophony of sounds around her.

"Nope. He came in by himself, ordered a beer and asked to start a tab. He only ordered one more beer before he left. One of the waitresses said he was acting like a complete tool, trying to act like a hustler while throwing darts or playing pool. In fact, he told the waitress that the next time she came for his drink order, he was going to give her a slap on her curvy ass."

Lindstrom half-chuckled. "I'm sure that didn't curry any favors."

"Not in the least," Mongo said, nodding in agreement. "She told him that if he did, she'd kick him in his tiny balls and have him thrown out, puking up blood." Mongo smiled. "Our waitresses can take care of themselves."

"What happened after that?"

"Nothing. We let the bouncers and other waitresses know to be careful around him, but he was quiet and didn't order another drink. I figured he did enough hustling between pool and darts to get an extra drink or two out of his opponents. Next thing I know, he's being dragged out by that tall drink of water."

Lindstrom perked up. "Dragged out?"

"Not literally, but anyone looking at the two of them could tell it wasn't like they were leaving so they could have a good time."

Lindstrom thought about it, trying to figure out where this new player fit on the field. Wait, it wasn't a new player, was it? The mystery woman from Ronald Vance's suicide? Like most police officers, she tried not to believe in coincidence. She re-focused her attention to Mongo. "Did she say anything to you?"

"Not one sound. He got my attention, she dropped a hundred-dollar bill on the bar, and he told me to keep the change. Then they left, her hand on his shoulder, and I mean ON his shoulder, not on his back, almost like she wanted to make sure he didn't try to run."

"Can I arrange a time for you to sit down with a sketch artist?"

"I talked to the owner before I called the tip line.

We looked at the tapes for that night, and she made a copy of every camera recording, fifteen minutes before the guy walked in, to fifteen minutes after he left with the woman."

"Mongo, if I wasn't on duty and married, I would give you a kiss!"

Mongo gave Lindstrom a wry smile. "I appreciate that, Detective, but I don't think my husband would like that too much. If you can wait until the bar is closed, I will get the owner down here to give you the videos."

"No problem. While I wait, can I trouble you for a pineapple juice and a small bag of chips?" Lindstrom was pointing at a rack behind the counter.

"Sure thing." Mongo walked a few feet and was back with Lindstrom's order a minute later. As she enjoyed her snack, Lindstrom was trying to figure out how this new piece of information fit into the bigger picture. When Charles Utecht had entered the picture, it appeared that he was probably the mastermind. Of course, she was using the word "mastermind" loosely. Nathan Devlin wasn't a viable financial asset worthy of being kidnapped. However, if Utecht was only muscle, whose job it was to coordinate with Ronald Vance and Olivia Sherman, that would mean that Lindstrom had not yet reached the top of the pyramid, so to speak.

Lindstrom was finished with her chips and drank the last of her pineapple juice when the house lights came up to full brightness, which meant the bar was closing and everyone needed to head for the exit. Most bars had issues with stragglers not wanting to leave until they had finished their drink or their pool game. The patrons of Joe's Hole, however, filed out in a calm and orderly fashion, thanking the employees and not causing any problems. Five minutes later, Mongo returned with the video.

"The owner was too busy to come down, and she didn't know which format the police would prefer," he said to Lindstrom, handing her a large, padded envelope, "so she made a copy on a flash drive and on a DVD. Sorry, no VHS."

Lindstrom took the envelope, smiling, and said, "This will work, no problem." She put out her hand and shook his. "Thanks again for your help!" When Mongo had turned away, she put a ten-dollar bill underneath her empty glass, left Joe's Hole, and got into her car. Before she started the engine, Lindstrom called the station's main line. Heather Gordon answered on the first ring.

"Heather, it's Tish."

"Thank heavens," Heather said. "Is everything okay?"

"Everything is great," Lindstrom replied. "Do you know where Officer Williams is?"

"Not at the moment, but I can find out. Why?"

"It'll take me about fifteen minutes to get back to the station. I'd like her to meet me by the delivery van. Can you do that for me?"

"I'll see what I can do. Tish, about the van, I was thinking…"

Lindstrom cut her off. "Heather, I know what you're going to say. For right now, I want to talk to Officer Williams first. After that, I will stop by and chat with you. Okay?"

"Sounds good. I will track down Officer Williams for you. Bye." Heather ended the call while Lindstrom started her car and headed to the police station.

TWENTY-FOUR

"I'm not trying to pressure you, but I need you to be very, VERY clear."

Lindstrom was standing in the loading area where Jerry had taped off the black delivery van that had been impounded from the library parking lot. Even though the doors and windows were shut, there was still a faint smell from the garbage that had been put in the van. Officer Williams was standing a few feet away, looking at the delivery van, inspecting it while being careful not to touch the police tape that cordoned off the area.

It had taken Lindstrom about fifteen minutes to get from Joe's Hole to the police station, and another ten minutes for Officer Williams to show up. Her partner for the next few weeks, Officer Jefferson, took the time to walk across the street and grab a cup of coffee from the gas station. In the meantime, Lindstrom was going over Officer Williams' story with her.

Williams had walked around the truck several times, kneeling, standing up, using a flashlight to illuminate the area, since the loading area didn't have adequate lighting. Finally, Williams backed away and stood next to Lindstrom.

"Like I said on the phone," Williams began, "I am ninety-five percent certain it is the same van. It looks like a lot of other delivery vans that Ford makes, the body style, the color, all before they are detailed with a company's logo. The black van that pulled up didn't have any kind of logo or identifying markings, just like this one. But, here's the thing, I remember those red ads where the license plates should be. That's what makes me so sure."

Lindstrom looked from Williams to the delivery van. She hadn't had a reason to come and inspect the van. At first, the van had been an anomaly, a curiosity that needed to be checked out. Somehow, it had become an ancillary part of the investigation. Now, thanks to Officer Williams' revelation, it might be a part of something much larger. Lindstrom was trying to remain focused on the task, and the case, at hand. If she allowed herself to go off on tangents that involved Visceral Medical Supplies, R.T.A., her ex-husband, her cashing of a fifty-two-thousand-dollar check, she would never keep things together. First things first, she kept telling herself.

Lindstrom looked back at Williams and said, "Ninety-five percent is fine by me." She smiled at the younger officer. "Jefferson should be back soon. If he asks, you mentioned the van to Heather, and Heather was already on the phone with me. You saw it on Monday, and you saw it here. No other details, nothing else to say about it." She paused, realizing what she was asking of Williams. "Look, I know it's not good to keep secrets from your partner and your bosses. Until I can finish connecting the dots on this, I don't want anyone else gossiping or interfering. Can I count on you to keep this between us for the time being?"

Williams looked at Lindstrom and gave her a hearty smile. "Detective, you can absolutely count on me," she said, with no sense of trepidation in her voice. Lindstrom smiled back. As if on cue, the door to the loading area opened, and Officer Jefferson walked in, holding two cups.

"I hope I was gone long enough," Jefferson said, handing one of the cups to Williams. He looked at Lindstrom. "Are you done with my partner yet? It's time she learns about the seedy underbelly of this town." He glanced at Williams. "We're going to be doing a lot of patrolling tonight around the college campuses."

"Yes, Officer Williams was a great help with the investigation," Lindstrom said. "I'll put your findings in my report. Jefferson, take good care of Williams. And Williams, you do the same for Jefferson. Good luck patrolling tonight!" Lindstrom walked back into the police station as Jefferson and Williams said goodbye to her. Jefferson and Williams walked to their squad car, with Williams hoping that Lindstrom's case would work out.

As she had made her way from the loading area to her desk, Lindstrom had checked the time on her cell phone. It was closing in on three in the morning. Engels would be to the station by 8am, giving Lindstrom at least four hours to dig up as much as she could on Visceral. Fortunately, she had the research that Tisdale and Tavon had worked on. She had thought about working on the video from Joe's Hole, but she decided to put that on hold for the moment. She could let Tisdale and Tavon look at it. Right now, she wanted, no, she needed to focus on Visceral Medical Supplies and the delivery van.

Once she was at her desk, Lindstrom called down to Heather. "If you're not busy, can I get your help?"

"Like you have to ask, dear," Heather responded. "What do you need?"

"Pull up any video from outside the building and in the lobby from Monday. I want to get a picture of the delivery driver and see if he's a match to either of our male suspects."

"Where are you at?"

"I'm at my desk, working some other leads."

"I'll send up the video as soon as I can." Heather disconnected.

Lindstrom started looking through the information that Tisdale and Tavon had pulled together on Visceral Medical. Before Visceral was in the picture, Raymond Mobley, who had inherited All Things Medical, ran the company well. The company hadn't been big or flashy, but they were rooted in the community and had done well. When Edward Kirkham and his private equity firm showed up, All Things Medical remained. What exactly the partnership included wasn't a matter of public record. After Mobley passed, All Things Medical continued, until finally being renamed Visceral Medical Supplies. There were no details regarding how the partnership started, why it started, or why the company was renamed, all of which was odd.

Another thing that was odd was, for a company that dealt with buying and selling medical supplies, there wasn't a lot of information. It was a privately-owned and operated company. As such, they weren't required to file quarterly earnings sheets, discuss P&L, or put forth any kind of public information. Add to that the fact that it had been locally-owned and operated for the better part of a century, and there weren't any hard facts regarding its current business.

The file had only mentioned the partner-turned-owner, Edward

Kirkham, in passing, almost as if he was an afterthought. Lindstrom clicked her computer's mouse, pulling it out of sleep mode. A quick internet search turned out to be uneventful. It was one page, with no follow up links or page shortcuts. On a pastel blue background, the text simply read:

THANK YOU FOR VISITING THE OFFICIAL SITE OF THE KIRKHAM FAMILY. PLEASE CHECK BACK WHEN OUR PAGE IS COMPLETED.

Lindstrom scrolled to the bottom of the webpage. In small print, a line of text read *"Last updated 2006"*. The website hadn't been touched in almost a decade. Lindstrom sat back for a moment. She opened a new tab and typed in Visceral's official website. It was still on the fritz. She typed in the website for All Things Medical and was greeted with an error page that the site was no longer in operation. Lindstrom continued to look through what little files there were. Not only was there no pending litigation against Visceral Medical, apparently, no litigation had ever been filed against them. She chuckled to herself. It was a testament to the sad state of civil litigation when there was a company being run that wasn't being sued and that had never been sued.

Lindstrom closed out of the Visceral website tab and opened a new search window. She typed in Visceral Medical Supplies and limited her search to only entries that had all three words and hit enter. She quickly checked each link, and almost all of them were local stories involving the name change from All Things Medical. Only one of the search results provided a link to something new. The local newspaper had published a story regarding Avera Health, the other hospital in Sioux Falls. The hospital had received a large charitable donation many years ago from an entrepreneur that had died in a plane crash. The story was about many of the changes that Avera was implementing across all of their health care platforms. After reading through what seemed like an eternity, Lindstrom finally found the reference to Visceral.

"The donation also will allow Avera Health administrators to leverage competing bids for many of the medical supplies and equipment that the facilities will use. This is because the hospital's current supplier, Visceral Medical Supplies, has informed the hospital that their current contract will not be renewed when the contract expires."

The article then continued on to other areas. Lindstrom read the two

324

sentences again, a second time, and then a third time. She remembered what Kara Reed had told her regarding Visceral not renewing their contract with Sanford Hospital.

The phone on Lindstrom's desk rang. It must be Heather, she thought. She picked up the receiver. "Lindstrom," she said.

"It's Heather," came the response. "I pulled the video and I put it on a flash drive for you. Do you want me to bring it up to you?"

"Not yet. I'm working a few other things right now. I'm sure I'll need a walk in a little bit, and I'll swing down."

"Anything else I can help you with," Heather inquired.

"Not yet, but I'll let you know. Thanks." Lindstrom hung up the phone. She opened a desk drawer and found a directory of important phone numbers that was updated yearly and provided to all city departments. She looked through the list and found the number for the emergency room at Avera's main Hospital. She dialed the number and waited. Two rings later, the call was answered by a male voice.

"Avera ER, Phillip speaking."

"Good morning, Phillip. My name is Detective Patricia Lindstrom. I apologize for calling so early in the morning, but I need to speak to someone in charge."

"I'm the closest you're going to get right now, Detective. We're running short-staffed tonight and are directing all emergencies to go to Sanford or the outlying acute care centers. No offense, but please make it quick."

"Okay. Hopefully you'll be able to help me," Lindstrom said. "Do you know if Avera Health purchases any of their medical supplies from Visceral Medical Supplies?"

"Not anymore," Phillip replied. "I remember the head of our ER at the time, Dr. Randall, was beyond furious that VMS didn't renew the contract. Avera Hospital and All Things Medical were like brothers in business for, like, fifty years or something. Back then, Avera was known as McKennan Hospital, with most of the clinics under the McKennan umbrella being known as McGreevy Clinics. Anyway, from what Dr. Randall told me, the contract was an unusually long one, which Visceral honored for its duration. Six months before it was going to expire, VMS sent a letter that the contract wasn't going to be renewed. There was quite a bit of drama among the board members about it, but there was nothing they could do.

Avera now gets most of its medical supplies from large distributors out of Kansas City and Chicago."

"I'm not sure you would know, but was there a reason given why the contract wasn't renewed?"

"Nothing concrete or substantial, from what I heard. The only thing that was ever really told was that Visceral needed to re-focus and re-align their buying, retailing, and shipping priorities. That was seven years ago."

"Thank you, Phillip, you've been a great help! If you think of anything else that might be useful, you can contact me at the station." Lindstrom spelled out her name and gave him her direct line number.

"Will do, detective. Bye." The line went dead. Lindstrom hung up the phone on her end, and then looked up the information for the new acute care center that had opened last year on the southwest side of Sioux Falls, Plains Peace. She dialed the center's direct line, and, after being routed through a computerized message board, she finally heard the line ringing.

Three rings, and the line connected. A woman's voice said, "Plains Peace Acute Care Center, this is Julie. How can I assist you?"

"Good morning, Julie. My name is Detective Patricia Lindstrom. I need to talk to someone in charge regarding a police matter."

"Hmmm, I think Dr. Martinson is available. One moment, please." There was a click, and some kind of jazz started playing over the headset. A minute later, the line reconnected.

"This is Dr. Martinson." The voice was definitely older, which should help.

"Good morning, doctor. My name is Detective Patricia Lindstrom. I apologize for the early morning call, but I need to ask you a few questions. Do you have a moment?"

"You will need to be brief, detective," Dr. Martinson responded. "I am expecting test results for a patient any minute."

"Then I'll be quick. Do you know if Plains Peace purchases any medical supplies from Visceral Medical?"

"None whatsoever. As you may or may not know, Plains Peace is the newest healthcare provider in the city. Plains Peace was founded in early 1986 and has slowly expanded to various market cities ever since. Anyway, Plains Peace is contracted exclusively to a medical warehouse out of Salt Lake City, Utah, and that contract has been in place since the hospital opened."

"Two businesses operating under the same contract for thirty years?" Lindstrom paused for a brief moment. "Isn't that a little unusual?"

"Not when the founder of the hospital is the daughter of the woman who founded the medical supply company." Dr. Martinson let out a chuckle. "Sometimes, nepotism is a good thing. It helps Plains Peace keep our operating expenses lower by not being gouged when it comes to the cost of our supplies and equipment."

"That actually sounds like an excellent deal. Dr. Martinson, I appreciate you taking the time to answer my questions this morning. If you think of anything else, don't hesitate to call me at the police station." Lindstrom gave Dr. Martinson her name and number.

"Absolutely. Good morning, detective." Dr. Martinson ended the call, and Lindstrom hung up her phone. She looked at the receiver for a moment, and then stood up and stretched her arms, legs, and back. She wasn't tired. On the contrary, she was wide awake, and now she was trying to process this new information. A medical supply company that doesn't supply anything? What is the point of partnering with a company, and then eventually taking it over and renaming it, if you're not using it for its intended purpose? It was now confirmed that three healthcare organizations didn't currently do any kind of business with Visceral Medical Supplies. Lindstrom looked down at her desk, with her open notebook, the computer screen showing different open web browsers, and the files regarding Visceral. She figured it was a good time to take a quick break.

Lindstrom made her way to the lobby. As she came through the set of security doors, Heather Gordon turned around in her chair and smiled. "I was wondering when you'd be getting down here."

Lindstrom returned the smile. "Just needed to finish up on a little research. So, can I see our delivery driver?"

Heather minimized a few open windows on the computer screen, and a frozen video image displayed. The police station had upgraded to high-definition cameras last year, so the image was crisp and clear. Lindstrom leaned in and looked at the delivery driver.

"Can you play the video from when he comes in until he leaves," Lindstrom asked. As a police detective, she needed to be good with details, especially faces. When she had asked Heather to pull up the video of the delivery driver, it must have been strange. However, Lindstrom's thoughts four days ago had been the receipt of the check. She couldn't believe that she hadn't remembered a single thing about the person that delivered her check. No matter. She leaned in to watch the computer monitor.

Heather clicked the mouse, and the video started over. The driver entering the lobby, Lindstrom signing for the envelope, and the driver leaving. Heather paused the video and looked at Lindstrom.

"It's not Charles Utecht or Ronald Vance," Lindstrom said. While it was disappointing that the driver in the video wasn't Utecht or Vance, it was also a relief. It meant that the case wasn't at an end, especially since Lindstrom had an unidentified woman to find. "Can you pull up the outside cameras from the same time? I want to see if Officer Williams' story matches."

Heather typed a new command, clicked the mouse a few times, and a new video player window opened on the computer screen. The video was a split-screen, showing the front of the police station and the parking lot, with a shared view of the front door. Heather started the video. At the edge of one of the screens, Officers Williams and Jefferson could be seen, engaging in a conversation. Jefferson looks down, grabs his cell, and holds up an index finger to Williams and then walks a few feet away. Williams watches him go, while on the other half of the screen the delivery van pulls up and pops the curb. Williams turns and appears to shout something to the driver. The driver lifts the pouch partially off his hip and his clipboard while taking the front steps two at a time. Williams takes a few steps forward, looking at the van, then looking at the front door, and then turning towards Jefferson. It was apparent that Williams didn't know what to do. The driver comes bounding out of the front doors and waves at Williams, gets in the van, and drives away. Williams watches the van drive away. Heather stopped the video.

"Well?" Heather looked at Lindstrom, who was now standing upright after leaning over Heather's shoulder.

"Officer Williams' story checks out, too." Lindstrom stared at the computer screen, frozen on the split screen.

"You know what you have to do now, right?" Heather gave Lindstrom a knowing glance, but Lindstrom shook her head.

"I know where you're going," Lindstrom said, "but I have one more thing to check out. Can I have the flash drive with the videos, please?"

328

Heather moved the computer's mouse, double-clicking the USB icon in the system tray. Two seconds later, the computer instructed that it was safe to remove the drive from the computer's USB port. Heather slid the drive out of the port, handing it to Lindstrom, who gently took it from Heather.

"Are you stalling on the obvious angle here?" Heather had a concerned look on her face.

"Not at all. As soon as Williams gave me her story over the phone, I knew I'd have to take a closer look at R.T.A. I was hoping that I could find the connection from this end. Unless my last lead pans out, I'll have to go from the other end." Lindstrom put a hand on Heather's shoulder, and Heather patted her hand.

"I know this is going to be tough for you," Heather started to say, but Lindstrom stopped her.

"What's tough for me is a company that has at least two former employees involved in a kidnapping gone awry, with both of those employees now dead. A third absconds with a stolen vehicle, but the vehicle, or a similar vehicle, is used to deliver a member of the police department a delinquent child support check. The vehicle is driven by someone who is not currently a suspect, and then the vehicle is found stuffed with trash. The only remaining suspect is missing, but a video shows him leaving a bar with an unknown woman. Add to that the company that the three suspects worked for is looking more and more like a shell, well, you can see it for yourself." Lindstrom stretched and cracked her neck. She thought about her three children, and then she thought about Mark. It had felt so good to see him again the other night.

"You're in a maze right now," Heather offered softly. "Go back over the trail, and you'll find your way." She stood up and gave Lindstrom a motherly-like hug. "Now get back to work." Heather let her go and sat back down at the receptionist's desk.

"Thank you," Lindstrom said, turning around and heading back upstairs to her desk. She had one last lead to check on. Once she sat down at her desk, Lindstrom started looking into Cassie Butler, the receptionist at Visceral's retail store that she had met. After twenty minutes, Cassie Butler turned out to be a dead end. Cassie had been born and raised in Hurley, South Dakota, a small town thirty-five miles away. After she graduated from high school, she bounced around to different jobs, and had been working at Visceral for less than a year. One speeding ticket, which had been paid two days later, but no outstanding warrants.

Lindstrom looked at the files on her desk. Was she missing something? Then she looked at the flash drive. She quickly plugged it into her computer and pulled up the video of the delivery driver. She froze the image and zoomed in on his uniform. The logo on his uniform and his hat read "Speed-E Courier". Lindstrom did several internet services, and, surprise, there was no delivery company named "Speed-E Courier". In fact, there was no company specifically named "Speed-E Courier". Several companies had similar names, but nothing that matched.

Lindstrom didn't know whether she should be disappointed, pissed, paranoid, or a little bit of all three. She looked at the time. It was almost 4:40am. This case wasn't adding up, and each new thread that she pulled didn't unravel the larger picture. She stood up from her desk. What did she know? Really, what did she know about any of this? Well, Lindstrom thought to herself, like Heather Gordon had said, this is a maze. So, I'll start over and hope I don't get lost again.

A woman's body was found floating in the river. A recovering alcoholic is abducted and then recovered. One of his abductors kills himself rather than being arrested. The woman, though terribly mutilated, is identified and was, allegedly, in a relationship with the man that killed himself. They also worked for the same company, as did another man, who is now missing. That missing man reportedly stole a delivery van, maybe filled it with garbage, and left it in a library parking lot days after it was stolen, but not before a third unidentified man used it to deliver an envelope to Lindstrom at police headquarters. The company that three of the suspects worked for apparently no longer does business in the medical field, which is what the company is supposed to be about. The man that was abducted was trying to turn his life around and reconnect to his wife and family. His wife's best friend has a real hatred for the victim. And, to top it off, a mystery woman, tall, barely visible at a suicide, who may or may not be connected to the missing delivery van thief.

Lindstrom was frustrated. She had many of the pieces, but things were still missing. She walked from her desk to one of the conferences rooms. She unlocked the door, and saw her dry erase board was still intact, with Nathan Devlin, Ronald Vance, and Olivia Sherman's names and information still there. She stood at the other end of the room, looking at all of the information that she had written down regarding all three of them. Aside from an alleged relationship between Vance and Sherman, there were no common areas where they could have come into contact. Even though Engels hadn't put much stock into it, the common thread between the three of them was the unpaid child support that all three of them....

No, all FOUR of them! All four of them had the common thread!

"DAMNIT!" Lindstrom shouted. Why hadn't she seen it sooner? She raced back to her desk and pulled up R.T.A.'s website. As the hourglass turned, indicating that the webpage was being loaded, Lindstrom opened another browser and tried to pull up Visceral's website. Sure enough, the Visceral website was still experiencing difficulties, only this time the webpage that displayed was more detailed. Against a white background, the following message read:

**THE WEBSITE YOU ARE TRYING TO REACH IS
UNAVAILABLE AT THIS TIME. PLEASE CONSULT THE
FOLLOWING HTTP STATUS CODES: 400, 402, 403, 404,
405, 407, 408, 409, 411, 412, 414, 415, 416, 421, 423, 424, 426,
429, 451, 500, 501, 502, 503, 505, 507, 511,
VARIOUS SUBSET CODES.
WE APOLOGIZE.
PLEASE TRY AGAIN LATER.**

Lindstrom didn't know enough about computers to fully understand, so she did another internet search for HTTP status codes. There were a lot of numerical codes assigned for why a webpage might have an error, dependent on a preset of five overall error labels. Each error label was assigned a possible one hundred codes, which meant there were a possible five hundred status codes that could be assigned, though not every numerical code had been assigned. She counted seventy-seven that were currently active and in use. She counted the codes listed on the Visceral webpage. Twenty-six codes were specifically listed, and that didn't factor in the "various subset codes". Lindstrom took a screen capture of the Visceral webpage, so she could add it to her file. She closed the browser and returned to the previous browser that was displaying R.T.A.'s webpage. It looked the same as the main webpage that Engels had pulled up on Monday. Lindstrom systematically went over every part of every page connected to R.T.A.'s website. Nothing had changed since Monday. The "CONTACT US" and "REPORT AN INDEBTED INDIVIDUAL" links went to an email submission page, while the "HISTORY/ABOUT US" page was the same.

Leaving the R.T.A. page for the moment, she opened a new tab and did a search for R.T.A. Only the main webpage came up. She tried searching for Rehabilitation Therapies and Associates and was rewarded with the same results. Lindstrom thought about it. If R.T.A.'s goal was to help families recover delinquent child or spousal support, people had to talk about it. After all, this is the age of social media. Everyone's most mundane activities had to be posted and shared with the world. It stood to reason that someone, somewhere had posted or tweeted about receiving money from R.T.A. She refined her search to R.T.A. reviews. Nothing. She conducted multiple searches with R.T.A. and different variations, including feedback, results, child support, spousal support, issues positive and negative, Facebook, and Twitter. Everything came back empty, with only the main R.T.A. webpage being the primary search result. So, Visceral Medical and R.T.A. were both closed-loops. How was that possible?

Lindstrom shook her head. There had to be a way to crack through this. She decided to search in a broader way, hoping to narrow down her search gradually. She started with a search "requesting child support", which resulted in page after page of links for different states, different laws, and different avenues to pursue. She clicked through several links, but everything looked legitimate. She kept going, determined to find some way to connect everything together. Before Lindstrom knew it, her cell phone alarm was going off. It was 6:30am, which meant it was time for her to get up and get ready for work.

Lindstrom stood up and stretched, rubbing her eyes, and trying to decide on her next course of action. Maybe she was approaching this incorrectly. After all, she was basically a single mother who had never tried to collect the delinquent child support that she was owed. On top of that, she was also a police officer, so the thought of breaking the law to get the support owed to her would never cross her mind. Any web search through a valid search engine, like Google or Yahoo, would most likely only result in links to safe, verified webpages. Every link she had clicked on over the last two hours had a green and white checkmark next to it, meaning it was safe from viruses, malware, and other internet hazards.

Lindstrom stood there, thinking about what R.T.A.'s website had read. It seemed to mesh with her conversations with Veronica from R.T.A. The people at R.T.A. supposedly worked with law enforcement agencies to identify "dead-beat" parents and get them to pay up. So, if I wanted to report someone, what would I do, Lindstrom thought. What's more, what if I wanted to report my best friend's husband to try to help her out? She sat back down and typed in "Heidi C child support help". She was greeted with several links for different attorneys named Heidi that dealt with family law in various states around the country, so she refined her search again. "Heidi C child support help for a friend", which narrowed the search results down. Lindstrom refined the search again to "Heidi C child support help for a friend alternate results." The search results shrunk from millions of hits to only a few thousand. On the first page of results, she found a link to a blog forum. The blog forum was part of a website called SupportingBrokenFamilies.org. She clicked on the link. The webpage loaded, and she read the blog that was shown. She re-read it, making sure she wasn't missing anything. She screen-captured the link, and also saved it as a favorite in her computer. Lindstrom then printed the blog entry and read it a third time. A small grin came over her face. The internet never forgets. She read it one more time.

"I'm hoping someone can help me! My best friend is going through an extremely difficult time, and I don't know where to turn! Her husband is a drunk and a loser, and he owes her a lot of money in child support! She seems to be holding out hope that he can get his shit together, but I don't see it EVER happening, and I don't want her or her kids to continue to live this way! Can someone help me, since my friend can't/won't see the light, and she hasn't taken him to court? PLEASE, SHE NEEDS RESOLUTION!! Signed, Heidi C. in S.D."

TWENTY-FIVE

Lindstrom wasn't sure if a blog entry with a first name, last name initial, and the initials of a state would be enough to convince Engels of Heidi Cole's possible involvement. However, like any complicated criminal case, it was another piece to the overall puzzle. She was looking through her notes and interviews regarding the case. She had briefly considered calling Veronica at R.T.A., but quickly decided against it. If R.T.A. was involved with Visceral Medical, and if there were issues involving current and former employees, the last thing she wanted to do was tip them off to a police investigation. No, it would be better to wait until she had a stronger case that there was a link between R.T.A. and Visceral Medical Supplies. She needed to keep digging, getting more pieces to fit together.

As Lindstrom re-read the officer statements regarding Ronald Vance's death, her cell phone rang. The caller ID showed a local number, but no name was attached to it. She checked the time. It was almost seven-thirty in the morning. She hoped it wasn't about the kids. She swiped the phone and put it to her ear.

"Detective Lindstrom", she said.

"Detective, hi there," came a female voice. "I'm not sure if you remember me, but my name is Cassie Butler. We talked on Wednesday." Lindstrom sat up a little straighter. This was a surprise.

"Yes, Ms. Butler. How can I help you this Friday morning?"

"Well, I'm not sure if it's important or not, but I was let go this morning."

"Let go? As in, you were fired?"

"Um, well, yeah, I guess so," Cassie replied. "I got a phone call about ten minutes ago from the woman in human resources that hired me. She said that Visceral Medical was no longer going to have a retail store presence, effectively immediately."

"Did this woman say why?" Lindstrom checked the Visceral website again. It was still showing the multiple error codes, even after several refreshes.

"Nothing that really made sense. Visceral was looking into different markets and marketing platforms, a brick and mortar store was no longer viable, and they have the added issue of ongoing computer and network problems." Cassie sighed heavily. A job where you didn't really do anything and got paid for it was a shame to lose.

"I'm so sorry, Cassie," Lindstrom said sympathetically. "Do you know what you're going to do now?"

"Well, I'll have to find another job, although the woman suggested I look into colleges, especially with my termination package." Lindstrom frowned at what Cassie had said. A full-time employee getting vacation and health benefits was one thing. However, having some form of termination package as a glorified secretary was something else altogether.

"What does your termination package include," Lindstrom asked.

"I guess I don't know," Cassie responded. "When I asked that same question, the woman said that one of the parts of the nondisclosure contract I signed includes a termination agreement, with some kind of package of benefits. She was going to send me the particulars via a company courier."

Lindstrom shot out of her chair like a bullet from a gun. "Did you say a company courier?" She started looking for her purse and car keys.

"Um, yeah. I'm supposed to meet him at the store at 8:15 to turn over my key."

Lindstrom figured with early morning traffic she could be there in twenty minutes, right around eight. "Cassie, go ahead and get to the store, but take your time. I'm at the police station right now, but I will meet you there." She didn't want to spook Cassie, so Lindstrom added, "You aren't in trouble, but if Visceral is having computer issues, I need to find out if they are relevant to my investigation."

"Oh, okay. I live about twenty minutes away. See you there." Cassie ended the call.

Lindstrom put her cell phone in her purse, saved all of her information on the computer by putting it into sleep mode, and quickly grabbed a few items of the various files on her desk. She turned around and saw Engels coming off the elevator. Engels saw Lindstrom, and looked at his watch, being careful not to spill his coffee.

"Did you forget something at home?" Engels asked as he walked up to Lindstrom.

"Nope. I've actually been working since after midnight, and I've been here since two." Before Engels could ask, Lindstrom put up a hand and walked by him. "I'd love to stay and chat, but I have another lead to follow up on. I will give you an update soon." As she caught the elevator, she yelled back to Engels, "Oh, and when Tisdale gets in, have him call me!" With that, the elevator doors closed.

Lindstrom was stopped at a red light, five blocks away from the strip mall that had Visceral's retail store, when her cell phone rang. The caller ID showed that it was Tisdale. She swiped the phone active. "About time you get to work, Tisdale."

"Yeah, well," Tisdale countered, "unlike you, I'm not trying to milk overtime out of the chief."

"It's not polite to kiss the chief's ass when you're standing right next to him."

"Then it defeats the purpose of kissing his ass. Now, what do you need?"

The light turned green, and the semi-truck ahead of Lindstrom started to rumble forward. "In my top right desk drawer, there's a padded envelope that has a DVD and a flash drive. They both contain the same video, so it doesn't matter which one you use. The video is surveillance footage from Joe's Hole from last Friday night. It shows Charles Utecht leaving or being escorted out of the bar by an unknown female. I haven't looked at the footage yet, so see if you can get a clear image of her so we can try to track her down."

"Okay. Engels wants to talk to me first, but then I'll get right on it."

"I'm in the middle of something right now," Lindstrom said, "so I will call you when I'm done with this lead. Good luck." Lindstrom ended the call as she pulled into the strip mall's parking lot. She parked in the exact same spot as she had on Wednesday. The other stores in the strip mall

336

wouldn't be open until at least ten, and there were no other cars in the parking lot yet. Lindstrom looked in her rearview mirror at Visceral Medical Supplies' retail spot, then she turned around, looking through the back window of her car. She quickly got out of her car and looked at the retail spot for a third time. Frowning, she thought to herself, what the hell is going on?

The large plexiglass sign that had advertised Visceral's retail store was gone, with only the back plexiglass remaining to protect the fluorescent light bulbs. The door and the front windows were covered from the inside with white paper. She looked back towards the street, near the curb. There, in a grassy section by the public sidewalk, was a monument sign, maybe seven feet tall, that advertised the businesses in the strip mall. Sure enough, there was an empty spot. Had the sign been there when she was here on Wednesday? Lindstrom couldn't remember, but, either way, this was unusual.

Lindstrom surveyed the rest of the area in her immediate view. The small office building to the north of the strip mall didn't appear to be busy. Across the street, a local hardware store was already open for the day. Three pickup trucks were parked by the front entrance of the store, and one car was parked on the other side of the lot, facing the strip mall that, apparently, used to house Visceral's retail store. To the southwest, diagonally from Lindstrom, was a gas station and convenience store, which was doing healthy business this Friday morning.

As Lindstrom turned back toward the building, she heard a car horn. She turned, seeing Cassie Butler wave at her as she turned her car into an empty spot next to Lindstrom's car. Cassie got out of her car slowly, looking at the place that used to employ her.

"Detective," Cassie asked, a concerned look on her face, "what happened?" She pointed to Visceral's store front. "What's going on?"

"I was actually going to ask you the same thing."

"I have no idea! I haven't been here since I locked up on Wednesday."

"Cassie, I need you to be very clear and specific with me. Did you discuss our interview with anybody?"

Cassie gave Lindstrom a sad look. "Look, things haven't been great lately, okay? I found out that my boyfriend was cheating on me and we broke up, but that was a month ago. My mom and dad are visiting relatives in Phoenix. I come to work, I go home. That's been my routine for the past three weeks. I wanted this job, because I thought a retail job would help me be more social and meet more people. Don't get me wrong, the money is really good for basically doing nothing, but I'm not meeting anyone." Cassie raised her right hand towards Lindstrom, palm open, motioning towards her. "You were the first person that came into the store in probably two months."

"So, no tweets, no Facebook updates, nothing?" Lindstrom eyed her warily.

Cassie lowered her head and shook it slowly side to side. "Nothing at all."

Lindstrom was about to say something when another car pulled into the parking lot. It turned and parked next to Cassie's car. A man with a silver and black goatee got out and looked at the two women.

"Um, is there something I can help you ladies with?" The voice registered at a higher pitch, not a typical voice from a male that, if Lindstrom had to guess, was in his fifties.

Lindstrom took out her badge, walking towards the man. "Detective Patricia Lindstrom. I am assisting this young woman to receive her final paycheck from Visceral Medical. And who might you be?"

"Call me Billy," the man said, putting out his hand as he looked at Lindstrom's badge. They shook hands, and then Billy said, "I am a property manager for the owner of the strip mall. He called me early this morning and asked me to meet someone named Cassie here at eight. Said she'd be handing over the key to the store."

"I'm Cassie," Cassie said, pointing to herself, "but I wasn't told any of that!"

"Cassie," Lindstrom said in a smooth, even voice. She could tell Cassie was upset, and Lindstrom didn't want her making a scene. "I need to talk to Billy for a minute. Would you do me a favor? On the backseat of my car is a manila folder with some photos. Can you take a look at them and tell me if you recognize anyone?" Lindstrom had brought along pictures of Olivia Sherman before her plastic surgery and the digitized alterations of Olivia after surgery, as well as pictures of Ronald Vance, Charles Utecht, and the delivery driver that had dropped off her check from R.T.A. on Monday. It was a long shot, but maybe Cassie would recognize someone.

As Cassie walked to Lindstrom's car, Lindstrom turned back to Billy.

"Do you know why Visceral is no longer going to be renting here?"

"Not a clue, ma'am," Billy said. "I go where I'm told and keep things looking nice, neat, and tidy."

"Can you call the owner, so I can talk to him?"

Billy took out his cell phone and pressed a button. Five seconds later, he spoke into the phone. "David, it's Billy. I'm here at VMS. Someone, a police detective, wants to chat for a second. Yeah, hold on." Billy handed his phone to Lindstrom.

"Hello, David, my name is Detective Patricia Lindstrom. Do you know why Visceral is leaving your strip mall?"

The voice that came over the line sounded young and energetic. "Not a clue, but it doesn't matter to me, because I'm not out any money. In fact, the sooner I can get it rented, I'll be making even more money."

"Oh? May I ask how?"

"You see the empty spot next to Visceral?" Lindstrom looked as David talked. "That spot and Visceral spot used to be one. When All Things Medical was still around, they leased that area. Then, during the period that All Things became Visceral, they informed me of their desire to downsize. I reconfigured the area and was able to get more rent out of the other spot, since it sits on the end of the mall. Visceral also wanted a new, rolling lease, which was a sweet deal for me. Basically, Visceral paid for their spot a year at a time, including a flat fee for any and all common maintenance charges. In return, Visceral could terminate the lease and vacate at any time, for any reason, and I could keep all money from any unused months. They were only three months into the new year, so I have nine months of free money."

Lindstrom stood there in mild shock. That was one hell of a deal for the owner. "Okay, thank you, David. If I have any further questions, can I get your number, please?" Lindstrom quickly wrote the number down in her notebook. "Thanks again. I'm giving the phone back to Billy." She handed the phone over and looked at the blank store front that used to house Visceral retail. Was Visceral a victim of bad timing, with unhappy employees involved with felonies, a possible cyber-attack on the company, and a lack of business? Or was Visceral involved with something deeper, and they were eliminating their footprint while they could?

"Detective, is this some kind of joke?" Lindstrom turned and looked at Cassie, who was holding up one of the photos in her hand. Because Cassie was waving her arm, Lindstrom couldn't tell what picture she was holding. Before she could speak to Cassie, another car pulled in and parked perpendicular to Lindstrom's car, turning off the engine. Both Cassie and Lindstrom looked at the driver, and then at each other as both of their faces lit up. The driver was suddenly aware that this wasn't where he wanted to be, making a move to restart his car. Lindstrom reached for her weapon, dropping her notebook and the ground, and pointed it at the driver.

"DON'T MOVE! HANDS WHERE I CAN SEE THEM!"

Lindstrom was now walking slowly towards the driver's door. The driver looked scared, with both of his hands shaking above the steering wheel. Lindstrom opened the door.

"GET OUT! KEEP YOUR HANDS UP WHERE I CAN SEE THEM!"

The driver did as he was told, still shaking from head to toe. Lindstrom could tell the driver wasn't a threat to run, but she still needed him secure.

"GET DOWN ON YOUR KNEES, HANDS BEHIND YOUR HEAD, FINGERS LOCKED, AND DO IT NOW!"

The driver dropped to his knees in front of the driver's side tire, almost hitting his head on the car as he dropped. Lindstrom lowered her weapon but kept it ready as she stepped backward towards her car. She reached into the panel in the driver's door and pulled out a pair of handcuffs. She holstered her weapon as she handcuffed the driver, and then frisked him for weapons. Finding nothing, she helped him turn around and sat him down against the car's wheel. Lindstrom stood up and looked at the driver.

"Long time no see, huh? The last time was, when, Monday, when you were at the police station to make a delivery, right?" Lindstrom was amazed that this scared looking kid was the same one that had delivered her package from R.T.A.

"You know him, too?" Cassie had stepped up next to Lindstrom, still holding the picture. Lindstrom could see Cassie was holding the picture of the delivery driver.

"And how do you know this little messenger, Cassie?"

"THIS is my ex-boyfriend!"

Lindstrom looked at Cassie, stunned. She looked down at the driver, his head down. Lindstrom couldn't tell if he was embarrassed or crying, or possibly both.

"Your ex-boyfriend?"

"Yeah, look, you know what I told you about Visceral having a strict policy about employees dating? Well, every now and then, NOAH, that's his name, he would show up with some papers for me to file or to pick up some paperwork. One time, he asked me out. I told him employees couldn't date, but," Cassie paused, kicking Noah in the knee, "NOAH here said that it was cool, because he was only a driver and didn't actually work for Visceral. Two months later, I find out NOAH has been sleeping with one of my friends." Cassie's constant emphasis on Noah's name made it abundantly clear that she loathed him.

"Billy, Cassie, I need both of you to sit tight. Don't go near the store." Lindstrom's head was spinning. The situation was getting weird and out of control. She needed some help. She reached for her cell phone and dialed the station's switchboard.

"Dispatch, this is Carol."

Lindstrom gave Carol her name and badge number and requested one squad car with uniformed officers at the strip mall's location. Lindstrom made it clear that no lights or sirens were to be used. She didn't need more attention, especially since there were so many moving parts to these cases. She hung up and looked down at Noah, who hadn't moved or reacted at all. Lindstrom knelt in front of him, making sure she had a safe distance, in case he tried to do something stupid.

"So, Noah, is it?" He looked up at Lindstrom. She guessed him to be in his early twenties. He was wearing the same uniform as he had worn on Monday. "Would you mind telling me what you're doing here on this lovely Friday morning?"

"Well, ma'am, I, um," he stammered, his voice cracking. "It's like this, see. Um, I got a call last night that my job delivering odds and ends for Visceral was ending. But I was told I had one last delivery to make, and to be here by eight-thirty in the morning. I was to deliver a package to Cassie. When I tried to explain that it wasn't a good idea, she said that the company knew about Cassie and I."

"ARE YOU TELLING ME I'M OUT OF A JOB BECAUSE OF YOUR UNFAITHFUL ASS?!"

Cassie had been eavesdropping, and she took a few steps toward Noah. Lindstrom held out her arm, motioning her to stop. Cassie did, but she wasn't happy, turning back and kicking the bumper of Noah's car, instead.

Lindstrom looked back at Noah, who was clearly afraid of Cassie's wrath. "Keep going, Noah," Lindstrom said reassuringly.

"She said that our relationship wasn't why we were being let go. I was to deliver the package to Cassie. After Cassie opened it, there would be something in there for me, and that would end my employment."

"Whose car are you driving today?" It was a beat-up Chevy Malibu, a faded red with dents and some light rust.

"Ma'am?"

"When you were at the police station on Monday," Lindstrom began, "you were driving a black Ford delivery van. Today, you are driving a Chevy. So, I'll ask again, whose car are you driving?"

"This is my car," Noah said.

"And what happened to that delivery van?"

Noah looked down, his face blushing with embarrassment. "After I made my delivery to you, I went back home. I played video games for most of the afternoon, and when I was going to leave and go to the movies with some friends, the van was gone."

Lindstrom looked at him, trying to determine if he was lying, but it didn't look like it. He was genuinely upset and scared. "That van was reported stolen on Monday afternoon. Did you report it?"

"Are you kidding me?!" A look of shock registered across Noah's face. "Look, I did errands in that van so rarely that I let my friends borrow it. I told them not to wreck it and fill it with gas, but to always have it back the next day. When it didn't show up by Wednesday night, I started making calls, but all of my buddies said they didn't have it."

"Did you tell your bosses that the van was missing?"

Noah dropped his head again. "All I said was I was having some problems with the van. She said they knew that the van was gone, and to use my car and not to screw up. 'Be there at eight-thirty Friday morning,' and she hung up. Two minutes later, my doorbell rings, and the package is sitting against my front door."

"Where is the package now?"

"It's on my front seat," Noah said, motioning with his head to his car. Lindstrom stood up, looked, and saw a large brown envelope. She looked at Cassie and Billy. Both seemed anxious to get things moving along. Then the squad car pulled into the parking lot. Lindstrom motioned the squad car to park behind the Chevy Malibu. After the squad car parked, Lindstrom was surprised to see Officers Jefferson and Williams climb out.

"Aren't you two supposed to be off-duty by now?"

"We were closest," Jefferson said, "so we decided to make this our last stop for the night. What do you need?"

"If you would kindly put Noah in the back of your cruiser and keep an eye open out here, that would be great." Lindstrom paused and looked at Noah as Jefferson helped him to his feet. "Noah, I want you to behave yourself and sit in the back of the cruiser. Can you do that for me?"

Noah looked at Lindstrom, nodded, and said, "Yes ma'am." Jefferson walked Noah over the squad car and put him in the back, shutting the door.

"Officer Williams, will you do a quick recon to the back? Stay away from the second door, just in case."

"You got it," Williams said, and she walked around the corner of the building and was out of sight.

"Cassie, may I have your key, please?" Lindstrom held out her hand, and Cassie handed her the key. "Cassie, Billy, stay out by your vehicles until I say so. Jefferson, be ready. Are we all good?" Lindstrom looked around at all three of them, and they all nodded. Lindstrom took out her weapon with her right hand, carefully walking up to the front door. She used her left hand to insert the key into the door's lock, unlocked the door, and carefully opened the door. As she waited for a minute while her eyes adjusted to the dark, she began to smell something. The scent was strong, and it was everywhere. She saw a light switch on the wall to her left, which she turned on, letting the front door close behind her. As the overhead lights came on, Lindstrom saw that the front area was empty. Both sections of counter area, the one chair, the two hanging pictures, the desk that Cassie had used, everything was gone. As she started walking down the hallway, she started coughing. The air was thick with the smell of bleach, paint, and something else that she couldn't identify. She turned on the light in each office, finding each office empty.

Lindstrom holstered her weapon and walked back to the front door. She opened it slowly, putting a hand out and yelling, "ALL CLEAR!" She opened the door the rest of the way, and saw Jefferson holstering his weapon. Cassie and Billy came out of hiding and walked up to join Lindstrom at the front.

"JEFFERSON," Lindstrom yelled. "Go around back with Williams and see if there's anything out of place, then both of you come join us." Jefferson nodded and walked behind the building. Lindstrom glanced at Noah, who was sitting like a statue. Looking at the other two, Lindstrom said, "The building is empty, but please don't touch anything. Billy, why don't you take the key from the lock." Billy did as he was told, and Lindstrom held the door open for Cassie and Billy, and the three of them went inside.

"WOW!" Cassie said, whistling, and then she started to cough from the pungent mix of odors.

"I guess I don't have to worry about any kind of cleanup," Billy said.

"Cassie," Lindstrom asked, "was there ever anything in those offices?"

Cassie started pointing at the offices in succession as she spoke. "Um, that office had three boxes of computer paper and one box of printer cartridges, that one had a desk until two months ago, same with that one. The last office had a spare chair and a box with an extra computer monitor."

"A real bare-bones operation, huh?" Billy walked around, looking in each office, examining the doors, door frames, walls, and floors. "Detective, may I have your permission to open the door to the bathroom?"

Lindstrom looked from Billy to Cassie. "You have a bathroom here?"

"Yeah, it's just a toilet and sink in that office over there," Cassie said, pointing.

When Lindstrom had been her on Wednesday, she hadn't thought of the spot having a restroom. Lindstrom walked up to Billy, putting her hand back on her weapon. She walked to the office that Cassie had pointed at, and, sure enough, there was another door there. Lindstrom realized that the office next to this one was smaller, obviously to accommodate the restroom.

Lindstrom walked in and carefully opened the door. The third smell came rushing out like a toxic cloud. Lindstrom's eyes started to water, and she backed away, covering her mouth and nose with her arm. Billy, who must have been used to these kinds of odors, turned on the light and looked inside.

"Definitely clean enough to eat off of," Billy said.

They both walked back up to the front, with Lindstrom opening the front door and inhaling as much of the outside air as she could. She was joined by Cassie, who also took in some deep breaths. Billy came up behind them, pushed the front door open as far it would go, and reached up to activate the locking mechanism in the pneumatic hinge, which kept the door from closing.

Lindstrom looked at Billy through watering eyes and said through a cough, "I take it you are used to smells like that?"

"I've seen a lot of property torn apart and destroyed with every substance under the sun." Billy jammed a thumb behind him. "To me, that's a bouquet of roses. Fresh paint, bleach, industrial drain opener, hell, all I need to do is write 'for rent' on this paper and she's ready to go!"

Cassie and Lindstrom were still coughing when Jefferson and Williams came around the corners. When they saw the two women bent over and coughing, they rushed up with Williams asking, "What the hell happened?"

"No appreciation for the smells of a clean building," Billy said.

Lindstrom looked up, snorted and coughed, and spit on the ground. "Billy, get your boss on the phone. Ask if I could please get a copy of his rental agreement with Visceral." As he took out his cell phone and went back into the building, Lindstrom looked at Williams. "What's the word in back?"

"Clean as a whistle," Williams said. "There's no trash or furniture laying around, and, judging from some of the weeds growing out of the cracks, that backdoor hasn't been opened in a long time."

"When I was hired," Cassie said, "I was told not to use the backdoor because of a wiring issue with the alarm. I had to walk around the building to take out what little trash I had."

Lindstrom's head was spinning. Between only a few hours of sleep, the adrenaline of the past seven hours, and now having her lungs burning with the smell of chemicals, she was having trouble focusing.

"Tish, are you alright?" It was Jefferson, stepping forward and putting a hand on her shoulder.

Lindstrom took in a deep breath, held it as long as she could, and exhaled. She walked to her car and leaned against the trunk. Everyone except Billy and Noah circled around her. Lindstrom looked around, spotting the convenience store and gas station.

"Williams," Lindstrom said, "I need you to run over there and get Cassie and I a couple of bottles of water, each. And I haven't eaten since our phone call, so grab me something healthy. I have money in my purse."

With a concerned look, Williams hustled to the front seat, grabbed Lindstrom's wallet, and ran across the street, deftly dodging traffic as she did. Jefferson looked at Lindstrom and asked, "You want me to call a bus for you two? Neither of you look to good right now."

Lindstrom shook her head. She needed some time to air out, and she had no need of an ambulance. At least, she hoped she didn't have the need. "Not yet, anyway." She looked at Cassie. While her eyes were red, and she wasn't coughing anymore, Cassie was doing better than Lindstrom. "Let me have some water and some food first. If I'm not better after that, we'll leave my car here and you can take me to Sanford. Deal?"

Jefferson nodded. He wasn't trying to be chivalrous, only making sure that a fellow cop wasn't endangering herself. As they waited for Williams to return, Billy came out of the open front door, his cell phone held out in his hand. He walked up to Lindstrom and said, "The boss wants to talk to you." He handed the phone to Lindstrom, who took it.

"David, it's Detective Lindstrom."

"Detective, may I ask why you need to see our confidential lease agreement?"

Lindstrom didn't have time for this. She walked gingerly to the front of her car, so she wouldn't be overheard. "David, let me speak to you about something confidential. I am investigating kidnapping, extortion, grand theft, fraud, and murder. Now that you know what I am confidentially investigating, let me take a look at that confidential lease agreement."

"You don't think any of that happened in my building, do you?" The shock in David's voice was apparent.

"I think you can help yourself by making sure you are cooperating with this investigation. And, if it makes you feel any better, I'm not concerned with any of the language, details, or financials of the agreement. Are we clear?" Lindstrom couldn't care less about the document itself or any of the myriad details of the lease. She wanted to see whose name and signature were on the final sheet.

David must have gotten the message, because he said, "I will have it scanned and emailed to you immediately. What is your email address?" Lindstrom gave him her police email, and David said, "It will be in your inbox by the time you get back to the station." A click, and the line went dead. Lindstrom walked back to the group, handing Billy his phone as

Williams returned with two plastic bags.

"I hope you don't mind," Williams said, "but I bought something for everyone, just in case."

Lindstrom smiled at her, and Williams winked back. Lindstrom figured that Williams saw the multiple hundreds in her wallet from her check from R.T.A. She was glad that Williams had shown some initiative.

"Well, you heard the lady," Lindstrom said to everyone standing around. "Don't be shy. Grab something and dig in." After drinking half of a bottle of water in one gulp, Lindstrom looked at Williams and asked, "Did you get something for our guest in your cruiser?"

"Absolutely," Williams said.

Lindstrom motioned for Jefferson, and the three officers walked to the back of the squad car. Jefferson opened up the door, and Lindstrom looked in at Noah, who looked at her.

"Are you alright, ma'am?" Noah looked genuinely concerned, which Lindstrom thought was sweet.

"I'm feeling better," Lindstrom said. "There were a lot of nasty smells in the building. Now, Officer Williams was nice enough to get you something to drink and something to snack on. If I take off your cuffs so you can eat, will you answer some more questions for me?"

"Yes ma'am, whatever you need."

Lindstrom gave her keys to Jefferson, who leaned in and took the hand cuffs off Noah. Williams leaned in and gave him a bottle of pop and a small bag of crackers. After a minute of letting Noah eat and drink, Lindstrom leaned in.

"So, is there anything you want to tell me?" Lindstrom was looking at Noah, hoping some time stewing in the back of the squad car in handcuffs had given him a chance to consider his options.

"Ma'am, I don't know what's going on." Noah looked from Lindstrom to Williams to Jefferson and back. "I've worked as a delivery driver for Visceral for almost two years. Visceral calls, tells me where to go or what to get, and I do it."

"How often do they call," Lindstrom asked.

"It depends. Sometimes once a month, sometimes three times a week. I would go out to the Visceral warehouse, pick up my packages, deliver them to the airport, and that was it."

"Did you ever bring anything back from the airport?"

"No ma'am, not once."

Interesting, Lindstrom thought.

"Hey, Detective," Billy shouted from his car. "If you don't need me for anything else, I have some other things to do. Can I lock up and get out of here?"

Lindstrom thought about having forensics come through, but she figured it would be a waste of time. All of the cleaning and chemical in there would have destroyed any trace evidence.

"Go ahead and go," Lindstrom said to Billy. "And thanks for your help." As Billy walked to the building, Lindstrom looked at Cassie. It was time to cut her loose, too. Lindstrom looked into the squad car again.

"Noah, do I have your permission to get the package from your car?"

"Yes ma'am."

Lindstrom walked to Noah's Malibu, opened the door, and retrieved the package, which was basically a large padded envelope with nothing written on the outside. She walked over to Cassie and handed her the envelope. "Cassie, why don't you see what's inside, so you can get on with your day."

Cassie took the envelope and looked at it. She turned it over and ripped the easy open seal. She reached inside and took out two sheets of paper that were stapled together and another envelope. Cassie read the first sheet of paper, with her face turning from a blank expression to one of bewilderment. She turned the paper over at the staple, so she could see the second sheet. Her eyes went wide with amazement.

"Cassie, are you okay?" Lindstrom looked at her with concern.

Cassie handed her the papers and said, "See for yourself." Lindstrom took the papers and read the first page.

Ms. Cassie Butler,

We at Visceral Medical appreciate your work and effort during your employment. Unfortunately, we are terminating your position. Attached you will find your final paycheck, including your unused vacation time, as well as your termination package, in accordance with the non-disclosure agreement you signed upon your hiring. In addition, we feel you have something positive to offer this world. Please put the extra money towards improving yourself. By improving yourself, improve those around you.

Sincerely,

V.K., Visceral Medical Human Resources

Lindstrom turned the paper over, and attached to the sheet was a check, made out to Cassie Butler, in the amount of thirty-five thousand dollars. Lindstrom couldn't believe it. That was one hell of a termination package, Lindstrom thought. She re-read the letter and then looked at the check. Lindstrom regretted not examining the check she had received from R.T.A. more closely, but she had been in shock at the time. This time, Lindstrom noted the name of the issuing bank on the check. First Federated United Trust. She would have to check with her bank and see if they could verify if her check was drawn from the same bank. Lindstrom handed the papers back to Cassie, who took them in her quivering hand.

"Cassie," Lindstrom said softly. "I think you're a good person. Take those words in the letter to heart. Do something with your life. I think you can go home now."

Cassie handed Lindstrom the other envelope, smiled, and then hugged Lindstrom. "Thank you so much!" Cassie got in her car and drove away. As Lindstrom watched Cassie drive away, Billy had finished locking up the building, got into his own car, and drove off. Lindstrom walked back to rejoin the other officers and Noah. She handed Noah the envelope.

"I believe this is for you, Noah. Go ahead and open it."

Noah did as he was told, opening the envelope and taking out two sheets of paper. He read the first paper, then looked at the second sheet, a stunned look shooting across his face. He looked at Lindstrom and handed her the papers to read. Lindstrom took the papers, reading the first sheet.

Mr. Noah Jacobs,

We at Visceral Medical appreciate your work during your employment. Unfortunately, we are terminating your position. Attached you will find your final paycheck. In addition, we feel you can learn from your mistakes and make something of yourself. Please put the extra money towards improving yourself. By improving yourself, improve those around you.

Sincerely,

V.K., Visceral Medical Human Resources

The letter was similar to the one Cassie had received, but Lindstrom noted the differences in the tone and the implications to Noah's performance. She turned the paper to look at the other sheet. Sure enough,

Noah had a check, only his was made out for fifteen thousand dollars. Lindstrom looked at the check, and it was also drawn on the same bank, First Federated United Trust. She gave the papers back to Noah.

"I hope you understand what that letter is trying to tell you, Noah." Lindstrom gave Noah her best stern mother look, and Noah seemed to acknowledge that something good had happened to him. "Officers, let's get him out of the squad car." After Noah got out, Lindstrom turned to a blank page in her notebook, handing the notebook and a pen to him. "Please write down your contact information in case I have any additional questions." Noah did as he was told, returning the notebook and pen when he was done. Lindstrom looked at him, adding, "Don't go too far, though, in case I have some more questions for you. Understand?"

"No ma'am, I won't." Noah's smile was ear-to-ear. "I mean, yes ma'am, I understand! I think I'm going to go home and call my mom! Wow! I never knew Veronica thought that much of me!"

Lindstrom walked to her car, getting one of her business cards, and giving it to Noah. "If you think of anything you need to add, you give me a call immediately. Understand?"

"Yes ma'am!" As Noah got into his car, Officer Jefferson moved the squad car, allowing Noah to drive away in his Malibu. Noah waved goodbye and left.

"Do you think that was a good idea, letting everyone go?" Williams had walked up to Lindstrom and was standing beside her.

"Cassie has never been in trouble in her life," Lindstrom started, "so I'm not worried with her. As for Noah, I can run background on him when I get back to the station. Something tells me, though, that his days of doing stupid things are over."

"Are you feeling well enough to drive?" Jefferson was walking up to Williams and Lindstrom, obviously still concerned with Lindstrom's health.

"I'm feeling much better, thanks. You can follow me back to the station if you want." Lindstrom smiled at Jefferson and Williams.

"That sounds good," Williams said. Everyone got into their vehicles, and as Lindstrom started her car, she heard a dull vibrating. She looked around, finding her cell phone under her purse. She looked at the screen, and the caller ID showed it was Engels. She activated the screen, not moving her car.

"What's up, chief?"

"What the hell are you up to?!" Engels was not happy.

"I've finished with this lead at Visceral's retail site, and I'm heading back to the station right now. Why? What's going on?" Lindstrom was concerned. What had happened? Was her boss yelling at her, or conveying a genuine sense of urgency?

"How fast can you get back here?"

"I called for backup, so I have a squad car here with me."

"As soon as you can, got it?!" Engels hung up. Whatever it was, it wasn't good. Lindstrom got out of her car and ran up to Jefferson on the driver's side.

"Change of plans. The chief needs me back at the station ASAP. You escort me, okay?"

"Roger that," Jefferson said.

Lindstrom got back into her car and pulled in behind Jefferson's squad car. Once they were at the driveway into the parking lot, the squad car's lights and sirens came on, and Jefferson got into traffic with Lindstrom right behind. It was a little after nine, and the morning commuters had died off, leaving most of the streets nearly empty. With the squad car alerting motorists to get out of the way, Jefferson, Williams, and Lindstrom were back at the station in twelve minutes. Jefferson and Williams went to the motor pool to relinquish the squad car, while Lindstrom parked in the garage and raced upstairs. She took the stairs instead of the elevator, and, by the time she reached Engels' office, she was gasping for air.

Even with three bottles of water and two nutrition bars, Lindstrom could tell her body wasn't responding like it should. Her muscles were tired from not getting a full night's sleep, her eyes were still irritated from the chemicals at the now-former Visceral retail store, and her lungs were burning from the combination of inhaling those chemicals and racing into the police station. The door to the office was open, and Engels was sitting at his desk with Tisdale in a chair to his side. From Lindstrom's perspective, it appeared that Tisdale was looking at the Engels' computer, but his eyes were closed, with his head resting in one hand.

"Good lord, Tish," Engels said with surprise. "What the hell have you been doing?"

"Long story, boss," Lindstrom responded, her voice hoarse.

As Engels stood up and walked toward Lindstrom, he said, "Why don't you sit down for a minute?"

Lindstrom was going to object, then decided against it. As she walked towards one of the chairs in front of the desk, she asked, "What's so important?"

Engels looked at Tisdale, but he hadn't moved. "Tisdale did as you asked, and he went over the video footage from Joe's Hole. First things first, the man in the video is Charles Utecht. A little older than his last mug shot, but it is him." Engels stopped talking, turned, and looked down at Tisdale again. An awkward pause hung in the air, which bothered Lindstrom.

"Okay," Lindstrom pressed, "I'm waiting for the other shoe to drop here, guys. What am I missing? What's wrong?"

"What's wrong," Tisdale said as he slowly lifted his head and locked eyes with Lindstrom, "is that whoever is behind this knows what's been going on."

Lindstrom studied Tisdale. She could tell he was physically upset. It didn't appear that he had been crying, but something had turned him from his usual happy self to this. Lindstrom looked at Engels. Engels simply stood there, a frown on his face, his left arm across his midsection while he rubbed his head and neck with his right hand.

"Guys, seriously, you know I hate this kind of suspense. Spell it out for me. What is it?" Lindstrom stood up, and even in her physically exhausted state, she hoped that this would be enough to snap Engels and Tisdale out of it.

Engels sighed and said, "We think we know..."

"Damnit, chief, I screwed up!" Tisdale stood up, knocking over the chair he had been sitting in. He looked at Lindstrom and said, "The woman that was in the bar, the woman that took Charles Utecht out. She's the one I told you about the other day. She's my girlfriend!"

TWENTY-SIX

Tisdale sat in the conference room, his back to the white board that had Lindstrom's handwriting on it, the white board detailing a possible connection between Nathan Devlin, Ronald Vance, and Olivia Sherman. He was waiting for Lindstrom and Engels. As he sat, his mind thought back to his younger years. Tisdale had always wanted to be a cop, all the way back to elementary school. He had always waved at police officers as they drove by, and he always loved to talk to any of the officers that came to his school. He worked hard and studied hard to become a police officer. And now? Would it be taken away from him? Would he be charged with a crime? Could he be charged with a crime? Internal affairs? A grand jury indictment? Tisdale shook his head. There was a very real chance that everything was going to be taken away from him.

The door opened, and Engels and Lindstrom walked in. Lindstrom shut the door behind her. Engels sat down, while Lindstrom stood by the door. Engels started first.

"How long have you been seeing this woman?"

Clearing his throat, Tisdale replied, "Ten, maybe eleven months, sir. Like I told Tish the other day, we've been on-again, off-again. She's always asked me questions about cases, police gossip, things like that." He sighed, then continued. "She told me she was a fitness instructor and personal trainer. I figured that, since she didn't have a regular job and didn't have, I guess, normal everyday interactions, that she was living vicariously through me."

Engels looked at Tisdale, carefully examining him. He was obviously distraught, but what was the endgame here? There was no harm in dating a police officer, but that was the problem. Tisdale was only an officer. If this woman wanted intel, why start so low on the command structure. He glanced at Lindstrom, and Engels could tell she was about ready to explode. She shifted her head down, ever so slightly, and raised an eyebrow, as if trying to prompt Engels. Engels returned her gaze with a look of exasperation, as if to say he couldn't read her mind. That was enough to push Lindstrom into the fray.

"Are you done with the pity party?"

Tisdale looked at Lindstrom, who had an anger flashing in her eyes that he had never seen before.

"Come again?" Tisdale wasn't quite sure how to react.

"Life sucks sometimes, and believe me, I should know." She had walked from the door, and now was standing in front but to the side of Engels. "I have no intention of letting this case slip away because this woman plucked at your heart. It wasn't your fault, and you have no reason to think otherwise. Ten months is a long time for her to string you along, and any amount of supposedly-damning information over that time is negligible. This case is your first participation in something major. My guess is she was hanging around, on the off-chance that she would need information. So, it's time to focus on the here and now." She slapped her hands together, rubbing them vigorously, as if preparing for an arduous task.

"What are you thinking?", Tisdale asked, not sure what Lindstrom was planning.

"Do you know where she is right now?"

Tisdale took some comfort in Lindstrom's pep talk, so he sat up a little straighter. "The last time I saw her was Wednesday night. We had a late dinner at my place, watched some TV, then went to bed. In ten months, we never had sex, though. When I got up, she was already gone. I tried calling her last night, but she texted that she was busy."

"Do you know where she lives," Engels asked.

"Yes," Tisdale replied.

"Then let's go," Lindstrom said. "You drive."

Lindstrom turned, walking back to and then opening the door, and walked out of the conference room before either of them could object.

Tisdale looked at Engels, who merely motioned with his head that Tisdale better follow her. By the time Tisdale walked out of the conference room, Lindstrom was walking away from her desk, purse over her shoulder, making her way to the elevators. Tisdale sprinted quickly to his temporary desk, grabbed his keys and sunglasses, and met Lindstrom as the elevator door was opening. They rode the elevator to the garage and walked to Tisdale's car without a single word. The silence between them continued for another ten minutes. Finally, while they were at a red light, Tisdale looked over at Lindstrom. She had reclined the seat back and had her eyes closed.

"What do you think is going to happen to me?" Tisdale didn't want to lose his job.

"Nothing," Lindstrom said without opening her eyes. "You're a good cop, and, in this day and age, with stories all over the country about the militarization of the police force, viral videos of police brutality, and corruption in departments from top to bottom, well, we need all of the good cops we can get. Engels and I both know that. You weren't being manipulated by some Mata Hari, trying to get nuclear codes or anything. Maybe she got enough out of you to help her stay ahead of our investigation. Whatever the case may be, you're not going anywhere, so stay focused on catching her."

Tisdale was still seething, and the fact that they were stuck behind what seemed to be a convoy of semi-trucks wasn't helping matters. They had been at this same red light for two cycles already, and they had barely moved. He clenched his hands tight around the steering wheel and muttered, "Damn you, Veronica."

"What?" Lindstrom hadn't heard what Tisdale had said.

Speaking louder, Tisdale said, "I said 'Damn you, Veronica'. That's her name, Veronica."

Lindstrom immediately opened her eyes, sitting up, and staring at Tisdale. "Her name is Veronica?"

Tisdale looked confused. "Yeah, so?"

Lindstrom reached for her cell phone and her notebook. She found the most recent entry from earlier that morning, and punched Noah Jacobs' number into her phone. It rang three times before the call connected.

"Um, hello?" It was Noah's voice.

"Noah, it's Detective Lindstrom. I hope you haven't spent all that money yet."

"No ma'am! Actually, I am going to have lunch with my mom in a little while, so we can talk about colleges."

Lindstrom smiled. Good for him, but she had more pressing business to deal with. "Noah, I have some questions for you. Do you have a minute?"

"Yes ma'am. Go ahead."

Normally, Lindstrom would have told him to call her Tish, but she didn't have time for niceties at the moment.

"What did you say the name of the woman in Visceral's HR department was?"

"Oh, you mean Veronica. Yeah, she's the one that hired me."

"Could you describe her to me?"

"Um, she's like really tall, like six-foot four or so. Kind of attractive, but she also looks like she works out and always gave off a vibe to not mess with her."

The description matched the video from Joe's Hole, or at least the parts that showed a decent view.

"One more question, Noah. Do you know her last name?" Tisdale looked at Lindstrom and was about to say something, but Lindstrom put a finger to her lips, telling him to shut up.

"Um, well, I know it started with a k. Um, Kingman, maybe, or was it Killian?"

"How about Kirkham," Lindstrom asked, looking at Tisdale, whose eyes opened like saucers.

"Yeah, that's it! Veronica Kirkham!"

"Okay. Thanks Noah. Remember to stick around and don't go crazy with that money. And tell your mother I said hello." Lindstrom ended the call before Noah could reply.

"How the hell do you know..." Tisdale started to say, but Lindstrom cut him off.

"Not yet. Hold on." Lindstrom dialed Cassie Butler's number. It rang twice, and the phone connected.

"Hello?"

"Cassie, it's Detective Lindstrom." Before Cassie could get a word in, Lindstrom kept going. "I have a quick question for you. The person that signed your termination letter. The initials were V.K. Do you know who

356

that is?"

"Oh, that's Ms. Kirkham. Veronica Kirkham. She's the one that hired me. I always thought she didn't seem like a human resources person, considering how tall and athletic she is. I guess I pictured HR people to be more like an overweight mom who's also a principal at a kindergarten school or something."

"Thanks Cassie, you've been a big help. I have to go now. Get that money deposited so it's safe. Bye." Lindstrom hung up and looked at Tisdale. "So, are you still interested in continuing your relationship with Veronica Kirkham?"

Tisdale was stunned. "Wow, you've been busy since midnight, haven't you?"

Traffic was finally starting to move at a decent pace, with Tisdale saying that the apartment complex Veronica lived in was only a mile away.

"She won't be there," Lindstrom said. "How many times did you actually go to her apartment?"

"Maybe a dozen, I guess, but nothing in the last two months, probably."

Tisdale pulled the car into the apartment's general parking lot, which was separate from the tenants' lot. He found a parking space close to the front door. They stopped in the small entryway, as the apartment had a security door. Tisdale found the button for Veronica's apartment and pressed it. After a few seconds, the intercom came to life.

"Yeah? Who's this?" The voice was female, but with a deep inflection and a thick rasp. Lindstrom guessed the person belonging to the voice was a smoker. Tisdale looked at Lindstrom and shook his head, indicating that it wasn't Veronica's voice.

"Yes, I'm sorry to bother you, but is Veronica home?" Tisdale felt like an idiot, but he needed to say something.

"No one by that name lives here, son. Just me and my two birds."

"Are you sure?" Tisdale regretted saying it the moment it came across his lips.

"Son, it's just me here. I've been on disability for two months now. There's something wrong with my phone line, and it hurts to come across the living room and answer the intercom. Goodbye."

Lindstrom stepped up and activated the intercom again. "Ma'am, I'm a detective with the police department. The young man you were speaking to has been robbed by his ex-girlfriend, and your apartment is her last known address. I hate to be a burden, but would you mind terribly if I came up? I promise to be quick and gone."

There were a few seconds of silence, and then a loud buzzing indicated that the door was unlocked. Lindstrom and Tisdale opened the door and bounded up the stairs two at a time. They went to apartment twenty-nine, and the door was cracked open. Lindstrom knocked, and the raspy voice said, "C'mon in."

Sure enough, as soon as Lindstrom pushed the door open, the stale smell of cigarettes came out of the apartment. A quick glance showed very little for furniture. A folding table, a recliner, and a small entertainment center with a decent television and a Blu-Ray player comprised the living area. The curtains to the balcony were drawn, and a hallway and a kitchen were the only other parts of the apartment that could be seen.

"So," Lindstrom said to Tisdale, "I take it that this is not your girlfriend?"

The woman with the raspy voice laughed, although it sounded more like a cough. "Honey, I swore off men after I found my husband sleeping with the next-door neighbor after I got hurt at work."

"I'm sorry, ma'am," Tisdale said. Tisdale had moved his badge and weapon behind his back to appear like a civilian. "Officer, I mean, detective, she isn't here, and I don't see any of her furniture, or mine, for that matter."

Lindstrom smiled on the inside. Tisdale was playing along with the act very well. "Ma'am, you said you've lived here for two months?"

"Yeah. My sister helped me find this place. It's close to where I go for physical therapy."

Lindstrom pressed for more information. "Were you or your sister aware of the previous occupant? Did you ever see her, or was anything left behind?"

The woman eyed Lindstrom curiously. "Not that I know of. Like I said, my sister did all the apartment searching for me."

"Well," Lindstrom began speaking to Tisdale, while opening her notebook, "looks like your ex left you high and dry." Turning toward the woman, she said, "I apologize for the intrusion. Might I have your name and number, as well as your sister's? Just in case I have any more questions." The woman nodded, with an understanding smile. She gave Lindstrom the information, which Lindstrom wrote down in her notebook, and then read back to her.

"I appreciate your time, ma'am. Have a good rest of your day," Lindstrom said.

As Lindstrom and Tisdale backed out of the apartment and closed the door, the woman shouted to Tisdale, "Don't you worry, son! Take it from me, if she hurt you, you'll find someone better!"

Lindstrom and Tisdale walked back to his car, getting in and buckling seatbelts before Tisdale spoke.

"What now?"

Lindstrom looked at Tisdale. "Call her."

"What? Are you nuts?" Tisdale's facial expression was utter shock.

"Call her, say that you were hoping to take her to lunch, since the two of you couldn't have dinner last night." Tisdale gave her a look of disdain, so she explained it. "Look, this is going to go one of two ways. If you play it right, Veronica is none the wiser, and we can either tail her or arrest her. Or, it goes the other way, she says that she can't meet you, and isn't sure if she wants the relationship right now."

Tisdale sighed, and figured there was nothing to lose in trying it this way. He pulled out his cell phone, dialed Veronica's number, and put it on speaker. It went to an automated voicemail.

"Keep trying," Lindstrom said. As Tisdale tried again, she leaned back in the seat and closed her eyes. Her body was starting to rebel again. The surge of adrenaline from racing back to the police station and then coming to this apartment building, combined with the water and snacks that Officer Williams had brought her, it was all fading away. She needed some sleep, maybe not a full eight hours, but an hour-long power nap would do her wonders. Lindstrom's mind was all over the place, thinking about all of the leads, the victims, the motives, everything was an avalanche in her brain, and she couldn't separate everything. She also realized that she hadn't received a good morning phone call from Ryan yet, and it was after ten-thirty, and, and, and…she snapped awake.

"You alright?" Tisdale looked at her, surprised by her sudden motion.

"Yeah, fine, just need a little rest is all. Keep dialing." Tisdale did as he was told. He had already tried five times, but he would try a sixth time. This time, the phone started to ring. After three rings, the line connected.

"Hey. I wasn't expecting you to call during your work hours." There was some kind of distortion coming through the speaker, but Lindstrom couldn't tell if it was from Veronica's end or from Tisdale's phone.

"Actually, things are a little slow right now, and I was kind of hoping I could treat you to a nice lunch."

There was an awkward pause, and then Veronica's voice came through. "Yeah, that sounds great, but things are a little crazy right now." She took a deep breath, and then continued. "Look, I don't want to scare you or anything, but I moved a few months back. I didn't tell you, because I didn't want to alarm you. I had this crazy stalker, and he followed me home, so I packed up quietly and moved. I like to do things on my own, and I didn't want my cop boyfriend coming to my rescue. I really need some space right now. You can call, and we can talk, but I want to make sure that I am safe. I had to change some of my clients, which really sucks, so I hope you understand."

Tisdale looked at Lindstrom, who looked like she was sleeping.

"Yeah, okay, I get it. Well, take care, and I guess we'll talk when we talk, then." Tisdale hoped that he had struck the right tone.

"Thanks, babe. You're the best." The call ended from Veronica's phone.

"Did you get all that," Tisdale asked Lindstrom.

"Every word," Lindstrom replied. "She seems like a pro. She might need you again, so she's stringing you along. Stay back, but be ready, in case I come back." Lindstrom paused, her mouth open, trying to articulate her thoughts into spoken words.

"Yeah?" Tisdale asked. "What is it?"

"There was something else, though."

"What? What else was there? I didn't pick up on anything."

"I don't know. Something, I can't put my finger on." Finally, after everything she'd been through in the last almost twelve hours, Lindstrom yawned. "Maybe I'm just tired. Let's head back to the station." Tisdale started the car, pulled out of the parking lot, and merged into traffic, driving them back to the police station.

From a Lewis Drug parking lot two blocks away, a woman lowered a pair of binoculars. She watched Tisdale and Lindstrom drive away, then turned her attention to the cell phone she had just used. Putting the phone into sleep mode, she placed it in a carrier with several other cell phones. She waited a minute, then left the parking lot, following several blocks behind the car that was carrying Officer Tisdale and Detective Lindstrom.

TWENTY-SEVEN

A buzzing noise greeted Lindstrom as she almost rolled off the fold-up cot. She caught her balance, reached her cell phone, and turned off the alarm. It was one-thirty in the afternoon. She rubbed her eyes, and then stretched. Upon returning to the police station, Lindstrom wasn't sure what to do next. Not because she was out of leads and ideas. No, it was because fatigue was setting in, and she was close to the end. Engels was gone for the rest of the day. He had a fundraising luncheon to attend with various civic leaders, followed by a visit to a local daycare, and then ending with assorted meetings with various business interests in the area. That was actually a good thing, as Lindstrom wouldn't have to give him an update on her activities since midnight.

Tisdale had been off in his own world, deciding to get an early lunch, driving away after leaving Lindstrom in the police garage. She had considered giving him instructions about a report on Veronica, then thought better of it. After some solid police work on this case, he had been blindsided by the revelation that his girlfriend was involved. Probably worse, he was realizing that she had never been his girlfriend. No, the best thing for Tisdale was to give him a little time. Let him sort through his emotions first.

Lindstrom decided not to drive home. It would be too dangerous to drive in her fatigued-state. Besides, she still had things to do. Instead, she had gone upstairs and found one of the storage rooms on the third floor. She had unfolded the cot, put a "Do Not Disturb" sign on the door handle, and crashed. It was common knowledge that, if an officer needed a break, the storage rooms were available. Some laymen might scoff at the idea, but hospitals offered their staff lounges for long shifts, so Gundvaldson and Engels had purchased the cots out of their own pocket and told the police force to use them, if necessary.

Lindstrom swung her legs off the cot and stood up. Was a two-hour power nap going to be enough to recharge her batteries? She didn't know, but she was feeling better, so that was a good sign. The next step was food. She put the cot and the "Do Not Disturb" sign away and headed downstairs to the breakroom. The room was empty. Fortunately, the refrigerator was full, with several pizza boxes left over from lunch and a sign inviting anyone to help themselves. Lindstrom pulled four slices out of one of the boxes, warmed them up in the microwave, and devoured them quickly while chugging down a Pepsi. She didn't normally drink soda, but she was hoping a shot of caffeine would help. Besides, her favorite flavor of tea was sold out in the other vending machine.

After her lunch, Lindstrom did a quick self-assessment. After stretching, rubbing and cracking her neck, and doing a few quick jumping jacks, she figured that she was functioning at about eighty percent, which was good enough for her. She cleaned up her lunch and headed back to her desk. Everything looked as she had left it earlier that morning, before her trip to Visceral's retail store. So, what was her play? She glanced at the door to the conference room, deciding that a fresh perspective might help. She used her cell phone camera to take pictures of the dry erase board with the information that she had written about Nathan Devlin, Ronald Vance, and Olivia Sherman. She then gathered up all of the physical files and put them in a plastic tote. She quickly made backups of everything related to the cases and copied them over to two separate flash drives. She put one in her top desk drawer and put the other one in the plastic tote, which she then closed and locked. Turning off her computer, Lindstrom gathered her purse and the tote and headed to her car.

As she drove out of the police garage, Lindstrom dialed Ben McKinley's number and put the phone on hands-free talking. After four rings, the line picked up.

"Detective," Ben's voice came through, "I hope you're not calling for another smoothie date."

"Unfortunately, no," Lindstrom said, smiling. "Are you with Nathan at the hospital right now?"

"Not yet. Andy and I were going to head up there after his kids and Nathan's kids get out of school. I guess Allison was supposed to get discharged today, but she said she wanted to wait until Nathan gets discharged, too."

"Have they talked yet? Allison and Nathan?"

"Not that I'm aware of. Nathan knows that Allison had a mini-breakdown, and it really depressed him. Allison wrote him a note saying that she plans on walking out of the hospital at the same time as Nathan, and that she refuses to let him fall back into the darkness. Allison wants to go home to their kids, with Nathan right beside her, and start the healing together."

Astonishing, Lindstrom thought. It would seem that Allison Devlin definitely had some kind of epiphany during her recovery.

"How about Heidi?"

"I'm pretty sure she is up there with Allison right now. I think she works in the mornings, and then takes Andy's laptop to the hospital and works from there."

Good. Everybody will be there. "I have a few things to check out, but I will be joining your merry group in a couple of hours. Don't mention it to anyone, and I hope you have a good poker face."

McKinley laughed and said, "I don't need a poker face. I don't suffer bullshit kindly. See ya soon." McKinley ended the call on his end. Lindstrom checked her contacts and dialed Scott from computer forensics.

"Hey Tish. What's up?"

"I need you to check on a website called Supporting Broken Families dot org. Try to find out who owns it, what it does, whatever. Then see if you can find anything that links that website to either Visceral Medical Supplies, R.T.A., or First Federated United Trust. Call me once you have something."

"You got it." Scott hung up.

A few minutes later, Lindstrom slowed down and turned into the federal credit union parking lot. She parked and quickly went into the bank. She looked at the multiple teller windows and found the window that was being used by Paige, the teller that had assisted Lindstrom with her check from R.T.A on Monday. Another customer was thanking Paige and walked away, and Lindstrom quickly went to Paige's window.

"Good afternoon! How can I help you today?"

Paige had a standard retail smile on her face, but something about the tone of her voice was extra happy, probably due to the fact that it was Friday.

"I'm not sure if you remember me, but I cashed a large check on Monday. Detective Patricia Lindstrom is the name." Lindstrom produced her badge, her driver's license, and her debit card.

"Yes, of course, Detective!" Paige looked at all three forms of ID, and then looked at Lindstrom. A quick look of concern came across Paige's face. "Is there a problem?"

"Actually, I was curious about something. Can you tell me the name of the bank that the check was drawn on?"

Paige turned to her computer screen, swiping Lindstrom's debit card through a magnetic reader.

"If you would enter your PIN number, please," Paige asked, pointing to the keypad in front of Lindstrom. She entered her PIN and waited while Paige worked her computer's keyboard and mouse. "Okay, let me check here, yes, okay, and how is your day going?"

Lindstrom had little patience for small talk, and bank tellers seemed to be the worst. She needed Paige to be focused and efficient.

"A typical Friday, with A LOT to do and not enough time." Lindstrom made sure she stressed her words, letting Paige know to get this moving forward, and fast.

Paige got the hint, because she typed and clicked a little faster. After what seemed like forever but was only about another minute, Paige said, "Yes, here we go. The check was drawn on an account from First Federated United Trust."

Exactly what Lindstrom surmised. Visceral Medical and R.T.A. having the same bank wasn't a coincidence. Lindstrom gathered up her ID's and her debit card.

"Thank you, Paige. Have a great weekend." Lindstrom could hear Paige's voice behind her, the words lost in her hasty exit. She was out the door, in her car, and heading to her next destination. As Lindstrom pulled into traffic, a woman finished sending an encrypted text message via a secure cell phone from her car in the credit union's parking lot. She started her car and proceeded to follow Detective Lindstrom's car from a discreet distance.

It took around thirty minutes for Lindstrom to drive through city traffic, get through the industrial park, and make her way to the developing west side of the city. The way the investigation was going, it was time to finally take a trip out to the warehouse for Visceral Medical Supplies. She had typed the company name into the Maps app on her cell phone, and she was getting directions from a computer voice. She was now on 60th Street North, which had been newly renovated to be a four-lane highway. The renovations had been completed to accommodate the growing traffic from the commercial and residential developments that seemed to be popping up overnight. The computer voice continued guiding her, eventually telling her to turn onto a two-lane road, which she drove on for at least two miles. Another turn, this time onto a gravel road, for another two miles. The computer voice spoke again, saying, "Your destination is on your right."

Lindstrom stopped her car and looked around. There was nothing but farmland all around her. She looked at her phone, and the Map app had a blinking red dot, letting her know that she was at the warehouse for Visceral Medical Supplies. She got out of her car, stepping onto the back bumper, gingerly climbing on top of the car's trunk, and then, finally, onto the top of her car. She shielded her eyes by putting her hands to her forehead, and looked around, covering all three hundred and sixty degrees. There was nothing out here. She climbed down and got back into her car. She entered "Visceral" into the information line for a Google Earth search, and was rewarded with a single picture that could be rotated three hundred and sixty degrees. According to the picture, if you were looking directly at the Visceral building and turned around, there was a dead tree in the opposite field. Lindstrom didn't see the tree, but she was stopped on a moderate incline, with the crest of the hill the length of at least two city blocks away. She drove forward slowly, finally cresting the small hill and going down a moderate slope. On her left, at the bottom where the road began to level out again, was the dead tree. She pulled up parallel to the tree and looked to her right. Sure enough, there was a road, although maybe the word "road" was too generous. It looked like some kind of service ramp that a farmer used sparingly to gain access to a field.

About two hundred yards in, Lindstrom could see a gate, so she turned her car and drove until she had to stop. The gate was rather unassuming, faded black paint covering the façade. The gate was on wheels, with the wheels in metal tracks in the ground. It reminded her of a backward train track. The gate was at least twelve feet high, yet it didn't have anything on the top to prevent someone from climbing over it. Along either side, for about fifty yards, was chain link fence, at least ten feet tall, but, like the gate, there was no razor or barbed wire on the top to keep anyone out. There was an intercom for anyone to contact the main building, with a video camera pointing down at the general area.

Lindstrom pressed the intercom and waited. No response. She pressed the intercom again and held the button for a few extra seconds. Still no response. She looked at the camera, noticing that the light that would indicate whether it was working was actually off. She walked up to the gate and noticed that a sign was laying down on the ground. It was attached to the gate via a chain, but it must have fallen down. She picked it up and turned it over. The sign read, "DUE TO UNFORESEEN CIRCUMSTANCES, VISCERAL MEDICAL SUPPLIES IS CLOSED. PLEASE CONTACT YOUR DIRECT SUPPLIER FOR ALTERNATIVE DELIVERY OPTIONS". Whoever attached the sign didn't do a very good job of attaching it, so it could be seen.

Which was probably the point, Lindstrom thought. She went back to her car, opened the trunk, and retrieved binoculars from an emergency duffel bag she kept. She closed the trunk, retrieved her cell phone, and locked her car. She walked to the gate and inspected where the gate ended, and the chain link fence began. Lindstrom figured the support poles in the ground should be sturdy enough to allow her to climb over. She moved carefully, trying not to fall, or to damage the fence or gate. She swung over, landed, and rolled. Yes, she was trespassing. The moral implication started needling at the back of her brain, but she needed answers.

As Lindstrom started walking, the "road" slowly morphed from a barely recognizable tract for two wheels to a gravel road. Unfortunately, she had to walk up another slow incline. After maybe three hundred yards, the hill crested. Lindstrom stopped and saw a large, three-story building off in the distance. She put the binoculars to her eyes, surveying the area. The building was at least a mile away, maybe two. While she was surrounded with knee high grass in the fields around her, the building's grass was cut short. Around the building ran chain link fence that was stronger, with razor wire running along the top. The fence surrounded the building by at least two hundred yards in every direction. The gravel road ran up to the only gate Lindstrom could see. After the gate, the road turned into asphalt. Beyond the building, there was more open field with tall grass. In the extreme distance, barely visible, was Interstate 90, which ran east-to-west.

Lindstrom examined the building as best she could with the binoculars, but there were no defining characteristics. No logos, no lights, no parking that she could see. She didn't want to press her luck by being discovered, so she tried walking into the tall grass, essentially putting herself in an orbit around the building. After a hundred yards, she was able to see a bit around the corner of the building. The back of an ambulance. She tried to adjust the binoculars for a clearer view, but it was no good. She was too far away, but she had no doubt that it was an ambulance. It was solid white, with no discernible color or logo that she could tell from her vantage point.

Lindstrom considered moving further, then decided against it. She had no warrant, no probable cause, and she was trespassing. She started back the way she came but working her way further away from the building. She stayed in the tall grass until she was over the crest of the hill, and then sprinted as quickly as she dared on the rough and uneven ground. She reached the pseudo fence and gate, climbing back over. A quick glance at the camera and intercom showed that they still were non-functional. She got back into her car, backing slowly away from the gate, until she was able to turn around on the other gravel road with the dead tree. Lindstrom began retracing her journey.

Meanwhile, the woman that had been following Lindstrom was able to keep track of every one of her movements. She had watched Lindstrom initially stop and climb on her car, every step until Lindstrom had retreated to her car and drove away. She quickly recalled her drone, with its amazing 4K Ultra HD camera. By the time she had landed the drone and packed it away in her trunk, she could see Lindstrom's car coming over a hill about a mile away. She got in her car, sent another encrypted text, and waited for Lindstrom to pass. So far, she had anticipated every one of Lindstrom's moves on this Friday. She had watched her from across the street at the Visceral retail store, earlier that morning. She had waited patiently in the Lewis Drug parking lot. It had been a simple matter to wait until she left the police station, knowing that Lindstrom would, eventually, go to her credit union and make her way out to Visceral's warehouse.

So far, the only thing the woman hadn't accounted for was Lindstrom jumping the fence to try and get a closer look at the VMS warehouse. For whatever reason, Lindstrom had aborted her search and retreated to her car, rather than risk being discovered approaching the building. Not that approaching the building would have done Lindstrom any good. Yes, the building had secrets, like an ancient adytum. However, those secrets couldn't be discovered so easily. The woman considered what had happened over the last several hours and her discreet reconnaissance of Lindstrom. Everything, up to that point, had been calculated by the woman.

Now, however, was a different story. Where was Lindstrom going? The woman had guessed back to the police station, but that wasn't Lindstrom's current direction. No matter, she thought to herself. She started her car and began following Lindstrom again.

TWENTY-EIGHT

It was almost four o'clock. Looking from the view outside her car window, to the clock on the radio and back again, Lindstrom was reminded of why she hated this time of day, especially on a Friday. Everyone was trying to get a head start on the commute home, which meant lots of people leaving work early to avoid traffic, which, of course, caused even more traffic. She was trying to get across town to Sanford Hospital, but it was slow going. She had made the mistake of turning onto a street that was still under construction, and she was plotting where she could leave it and work through some of the residential side streets. Her cell phone rang as she cut in front of a tow truck and got onto a side street. She checked the caller ID, and it was Scott from computer forensics. She activated her phone.

"Scott," Lindstrom spoke happily, "tell me you have something interesting."

"Well, the company that designed the R.T.A. website also designed the Visceral website, as well as the Supporting Broken Families website. That really isn't that surprising, though. The website designer, Vectrom Utilities, is a pretty big deal as far as website design goes. They are expanding daily into mobile apps, online security packages, and things like that. I did a quick look at their client list on their website, and they have over six hundred companies that they work with. I don't see a major connection between Vectrom and the three companies you are looking at."

"Do you have the client list for Vectrom in front of you," Lindstrom

369

asked.

"Yes, I do."

"How about First Federated United Trust? Is that bank listed as one of Vectrom's clients?"

"Yes, it is. How do they fit in?"

"R.T.A. and Visceral Medical Supplies use First Federated United Trust as their bank."

"Okay, so you have Vectrom designing websites for four companies. I still don't see a connection for you, Tish."

Lindstrom was about to speak, when she received an email alert on her phone. She was stopped in a school zone, so she said "Scott, hold on a second", and then pressed the alert icon. The secure email servers weren't supposed to link into unsecured phones, but Scott had worked on Lindstrom's phone months ago to make sure it was secured and encrypted. The email was from David, the owner of the strip mall. She was still stopped, with traffic waiting for multiple school buses to depart the school's parking lot. She opened the email.

"Detective, I am sorry this email is late getting to you. It kept getting returned because it wouldn't accept the .pdf file through the police's email security. I have scanned the five pages of the lease agreement and pasted them below. Thank you for your discretion. David."

Lindstrom looked through the lease agreement, and David had been right. It was a sweet deal for him. Visceral had arranged it so that, if the company ever wanted out quick and clean, they could be gone in a heartbeat, with no questions asked, and David getting quite the financial payoff. Lindstrom looked up from the email and thought about that.

"Scott," Lindstrom said, "I need to make a call, and I will call you back in a few minutes." She disconnected from Scott before he could say anything, scrolled through her contacts, and found David's number. As she dialed, she tried to process how David or Billy possibly fit into the investigation. Quickly, though, she dismissed the thread. At this point, the likelihood of either of them being involved, other than in a peripheral way, were slim. After three rings, the line connected.

"This is David," came the voice from the other end.

"David, this is Detective Lindstrom."

"Detective, did you receive my email?"

"Yes, I did, and thank you. Actually, I have one quick question for you."

"Go ahead," David replied.

"Would you happen to know which bank Visceral Medical Supplies paid their lease payments to you from?"

"Um, let me take a quick look here, hold on." There was a click, and some form of elevator music came over the line. The cars ahead of her had started to roll slowly forward, and Lindstrom's eyes refocused to the road. Five minutes passed by before the elevator music ended, and David was back on the line.

"Detective, thanks for holding. Looks like it was direct deposit into our account from some place called First Federated United Trust."

"Okay, thank you, David. Have a great weekend." Lindstrom ended the call, putting this information into the overall picture. Not only was David getting a financial payoff, but so was Cassie and Noah. Of course, the bigger question for Lindstrom was wondering if her check for fifty-two thousand was a preemptive payoff, or if it was only a massive coincidence. She shook her head. Nothing about this case had been a coincidence yet. The more likely scenario was that the check was actually a diversion, a way for R.T.A. or Visceral or whomever was actually behind this whole business with Nathan Devlin to keep Lindstrom distracted. If Lindstrom got too close to the truth, whatever the truth was, then the check could be used as leverage against Lindstrom.

Lindstrom pushed that out of her mind for the moment, and she re-dialed Scott's number.

"Sorry about that, Scott," Lindstrom said. "Is there anything else you found out?"

"Well," Scott began, "there's not a lot I can do with Visceral's website. Whatever is going on with them, it must be massive." Lindstrom thought about all of the error codes that had popped up on her computer screen.

"Is it possible that Visceral took down their site and manufactured all of those error messages?"

Scott was silent for a moment, then said, "I guess it is possible, but I don't know what purpose it would serve. It would be easier to take the site offline." Unless, Lindstrom thought, you were using your website being down as another diversion.

"What about the websites for the other two, R.T.A. and Supporting Broken Families?"

"There wasn't a lot I could do from an official capacity," Scott began, "but…", and his voice trailed off.

"I understand," Lindstrom said. "Let's speculate, off the record."

Lindstrom had always prided herself on being a good cop, always being on the straight and narrow, but this case was pushing her to the edge. She had already committed a crime by trespassing on private property earlier, and, even though she hadn't done anything with it yet, the fact that she had a ghost drive of Andy and Heidi Cole's laptop underneath her car seat was another crime that she had allowed. Was the check she had received another crime, a preemptive bribe on behalf of the party or parties behind all this?

With every case she had ever worked on, things were cut and dry, with the "bad guys" clearly marked. This case, though, was something else. Two dead bodies, one victim that she knew of, and at least one if not two shady companies dealing in who-knows-what. Lindstrom would proceed cautiously, and hope that any information and evidence would be circular, and she could argue it as discovery after the fact. She drifted back, momentarily, to that guest lecture. *"Reverse-engineering a case is never a solution."* The words still rang out in her ears all these years later. Was Lindstrom becoming cynical in her advancing police career? Or was it simply trying like hell to finish the puzzle, getting the bad guys off the street, and letting the chips fall where they may? A brief honk brought Lindstrom back to reality.

"I did some poking around with someone that has, shall we say, the same skill set as I do," Scott said. "There actually wasn't much to find, as R.T.A.'s website and security protocols are strong, as is the website for Supporting Broken Families. The only thing that we could find was that, for both sites, their online email forms both dump into the same website."

Lindstrom thought about that. "So, if I went to R.T.A.'s website and submitted an email to R.T.A., that email would be sent to the same website as an email submitted on Supporting Broken Families' website?"

"That is correct," Scott said.

"And what website do those emails go to," Lindstrom asked.

"Visceral's website."

Lindstrom started to think that it was unbelievable, but then shook her head. Nope, she was starting to believe a lot of things where this case was concerned.

"Scott, you did good work," Lindstrom said.

"No problem at all," Scott replied. "Let me know if you need anything else." The call ended.

There was still one other thing Lindstrom needed to check in David's email, but it wasn't a good idea to take her eyes off the road. It took another fifteen minutes, but she finally arrived at Sanford Hospital. She pulled into the parking garage and pulled up the email again. She glanced through the first four scanned images, making sure she hadn't missed anything, which she hadn't. Moving to the fifth and final page of the lease agreement, Lindstrom inspected the scanned image carefully. There it was, plain as day. David's signature and printed name was written on the "Landlord" lines. On the "Tenant" lines, the signature and printed name of Visceral Medical's apparent head of human resources, Veronica Kirkham.

TWENTY-NINE

As Lindstrom walked briskly towards Allison Devlin's room, she had made a brief stop to talk to Dr. Preston. She wanted to make sure that Allison's health, both physical and mental, were strong enough for what she had planned.

"Allison is improving rapidly," Dr. Preston had told Lindstrom. "Her vitals are strong, and her cognitive functions aren't impaired. She had some issues when we put her through physical therapy, though, which is why I am concerned with some of her blood work. The stress on her system has caused her to have imbalances when it comes to vitamins, nutrients, and the like. I want to make sure she is strong enough when she leaves the hospital. I'm hoping that, after the weekend, she will be able to leave with her husband." Dr. Preston then paused, and said, "Actually, she insists on leaving the hospital with her husband. Allison told me she views the two of them walking out of the hospital together as a renewing of their marital vows and a chance to start over."

Lindstrom then asked Dr. Preston one last thing. Dr. Preston thought about it before agreeing. Lindstrom thanked Dr. Preston for his time and, as Dr. Preston walked away, she made a quick phone call. Two minutes later, after ending the call, she started toward Allison's room. Lindstrom had texted Ben McKinley, asking him to meet her in Allison's room, and to bring Andy Cole as well. She was turning the corner at the nurse's station when she saw Ben and Andy leaving Nathan's room and walking across the hall to Allison's room. They didn't see her, which allowed her a few extra seconds to get herself mentally prepared. She was taking an enormous gamble, but she was hoping it would pay off.

Lindstrom arrived at the door to Allison's hospital room, took a deep breath, and knocked softly. A woman's voice told her to come in, which she did. Sitting up in the hospital bed was Allison Devlin, with Ben standing to Allison's left, by Allison's heart monitor. Heidi Cole was seated in the same chair she always sat in to Allison's right, the laptop open and resting on her legs as she typed. Andy stood against the wall by the foot of the hospital bed, almost in the exact middle of the other three individuals. From what Lindstrom was able to observe about Andy, it appeared to her that he was trying to appease everybody by staying an equal distance from Ben, Allison, and Heidi, all at once.

"Good afternoon," Lindstrom said. "Allison, how are you feeling?"

"I am feeling incredible, Detective. Thank you for asking." Allison seemed positively radiant, as if nothing could possibly bring her down. Lindstrom hoped she wasn't about to destroy this poor woman that had been through so much.

"Ben, Andy, Heidi, thank you all for taking a few minutes to be here." Lindstrom looked at each individual as she said their names. Ben smiled warmly. Andy smiled and nodded, but it was a half-hearted gesture, probably designed to seem polite while not offending his wife. As for Heidi, she gave Lindstrom an icy stare. The only other time she had felt that much hostility towards her was when she testified against her ex-husband in court about the spousal abuse she had endured. Lindstrom chuckled inside her head, thinking to herself that it was going to take more than a nasty glare to rattle her. Meanwhile, Lindstrom positioned herself so that she could easily see all four people.

"Allison," Lindstrom began, "I wanted to let you know that we are making excellent headway in Nathan's case. Two of the suspects are dead, a third suspect has been positively identified and the police are searching for him as we speak. We also had a break in the case late last night, and we now have a positive ID on a fourth suspect, whom we are also searching for."

Allison smiled and said, "Detective, that is excellent news! Thank you so much for all of your hard work in trying to bring Nathan's kidnappers to justice."

As if on cue, Ben said, "I don't mean to rain on the parade, but why the hell was Nathan kidnapped in the first place? It doesn't make any goddamn sense."

Before Lindstrom could answer, Andy spoke up. "Ben is right. Nathan and Allison don't have any kind of financial assets to justify a kidnapping." From her vantage point, Lindstrom could see Heidi roll her eyes and shake her head, if ever so slightly.

"Actually," Lindstrom said, "we have solid evidence to believe that this wasn't a simple kidnapping." She looked from Ben to Andy to Heidi to Allison.

"What are you saying, Detective?" Allison was genuinely shocked, with Ben and Andy displaying similar expressions. Only Heidi's face remained the same, with equal parts disdain and hatred.

"Allison," Lindstrom said, "it makes no sense that a group of criminals would kidnap your husband and hold him for ransom. Your family is in dire financial straits, with the very real possibility that you will lose your home soon, and that's even with you working three jobs. The only logical conclusion is that someone orchestrated this whole scenario to eventually kill your husband." She let that hang in the air for a minute. Allison's face started to pale, with her heart rate going up.

"You didn't bring us here for a guessing game," Ben stated with fury in his voice. "Do you know who did this?" Lindstrom couldn't tell if Ben was acting or was genuinely mad, but she guessed it was probably both. She turned to Andy.

"Andy," Lindstrom said, "I'm afraid I'm going to need you to come down to the station and answer some questions for me."

Andy's posture, the look on his face, his whole demeanor changed in a heartbeat. "You can't possibly be serious?! Nathan is my best friend, and I would never, EVER, do anything to hurt him or his family!"

"If you're that confident in your innocence, will you permit my forensics team to search your computer?"

"Yes, absolutely, anything you need!" Andy moved toward Heidi to get the laptop, when suddenly Heidi closed the computer and stood up.

"THE HELL YOU'RE LOOKING AT MY COMPUTER!", Heidi shouted, fixing another intense stare at Lindstrom. "You have no evidence that anyone in this room was involved, and you're just trying to get everyone upset and give Allison some kind of false hope of closure!" Andy had only taken a few steps toward his wife, and now he was frozen in place. Lindstrom guessed this wasn't the first time that one of Heidi's outbursts had stopped Andy dead in his tracks.

Lindstrom kept her tone level and measured. "That is certainly your opinion, Heidi, misguided as it is."

"DON'T YOU CALL ME HEIDI, YOU BITCH!" Heidi's face was red, her eyes narrowing like daggers. "YOU DON'T KNOW ANYTHING! IT'S BAD ENOUGH THAT SONOFABITCH ACROSS THE HALL NEARLY DESTROYED MY BEST FRIEND, AND NOW YOU'RE TRYING TO TAKE OUT EVERYONE AROUND HER!"

"If you're so sure that your husband is innocent," Lindstrom said calmly, pointing at the laptop Heidi was now clutching against her stomach and chest, "a quick search of his computer's internet history and emails is all it will take to clear his name and prove me wrong."

"THERE IS NO WAY IN HELL YOU'RE LAYING ONE OF YOUR FILTHY FINGERS ON MY COMPUTER!" The words dripped from Heidi's mouth, like venom from a poisonous snake.

"Heidi," Andy said, taking one cautious step toward his wife, "what are you doing? I have nothing to hide. Just let her take a quick look and…"

Heidi stepped toward her husband and, with her free hand, shoved him in his chest, pushing him backward. "DON'T YOU DARE TAKE SOMEONE ELSE'S SIDE OVER MINE! SINCE THE DAY WE MET, I'VE HAD TO PLAY SECOND FIDDLE TO THAT PIECE OF SHIT YOU CALL A FRIEND, AND I'M SICK TO DEATH OF IT!" Heidi turned from Andy to Lindstrom, yelling, "THIS IS MY COMPUTER, AND YOU CAN'T HAVE IT!"

Lindstrom stared at Heidi for a few seconds, letting everyone in the room take in what had happened. She looked at Ben. Considering the kind of man that Ben appeared to be, Lindstrom would never have thought he was capable of having a look of shock on his face, but there it was. Lindstrom looked at Allison. While Allison's face also registered some form of surprise, there was also annoyance, possibly even boredom. It seemed to Lindstrom that Allison had been down a similar road with Heidi before, and Allison's patience with her supposed-best friend was coming to an end. Lindstrom moved her attention to Andy, who had recovered and was unsure of how to proceed.

"Andy," Lindstrom said, getting his attention while keeping her tone even, "did you purchase that computer?"

"Yes," Andy said, meekly looking at Lindstrom.

Before Heidi could say anything, Lindstrom asked, "And did you give that computer to your wife?"

"No, it wasn't a gift. It was purchased on my credit card, and it was set up with my name, my username, and my password. The warranty, the internet security, Microsoft Office, every program and app is registered under my name." The words poured out of Andy, born from the combined fears that he might be implicated in the kidnapping and attempted murder of his best friend while also angering his wife.

"ANDY, SHUT THE HELL UP! THIS BITCH HAS NO REASON TO THINK YOU COULD EVER PULL OFF SOMETHING AS COMPLICATED AS KIDNAPPING AND MURDERING NATHAN! NOW KEEP YOUR MOUTH SHUT!"

Lindstrom knew all too well the signs of abuse, and it definitely wasn't gender-specific.

"Andy, it is your decision," Lindstrom stated. "With the evidence we have, I just have a few questions. Let me look at your internet history and your email inbox and sent folders. If you are innocent, you shouldn't have anything to hide. Five minutes, ten at most, is all it will take to clear your name."

"She's right, man," Ben said from his position behind Lindstrom. His voice was positive, as if trying to cheer on Andy to making the right decision. "Everybody knows you couldn't hurt Nathan, so let her look at the damn laptop."

"Andy, look at me."

The sound of Allison's calming voice shocked everyone, as all eyes turned toward her. Andy shifted his gaze to Allison, and she continued speaking.

"You and Nathan go back a long way. The two of you are as close as two people can be without being related or married. I want this whole situation to be resolved. Please, let the police look at the computer, put an end to it, and let's move on so that the police can eliminate you as a suspect and focus on who is responsible." Lindstrom noticed that Allison's head and eyes changed direction slightly, moving in Heidi's general area.

"ANDY!" Heidi's shrill voice cut through the air, and Andy's eyes went from Allison to his wife. "I WON'T LET YOU RUIN OUR LIVES OR ALLISON'S LIFE! SHOW SOME SPINE FOR ONCE IN YOUR

GODDAMN LIFE AND LISTEN TO ME!!"

Andy looked at Heidi for several seconds. "Detective," he said, still looking at his wife but talking to Lindstrom with specific emphasis, "you have MY permission to examine MY laptop and use any evidence you find to clear MY name." Andy's posture straightened. Lindstrom recognized what had happened, because it was the same thing she went through that fateful night with her ex-husband. It was the moment when someone realizes that they are through being pushed around. A sense of pride filled Lindstrom, knowing that Andy had taken a very important first step.

The look on Heidi's face, however, was a different story. It was a combination of hatred and terror, and Lindstrom knew that the next few minutes would determine the outcome of this little gamble of hers. She took a few steps around the corner of Allison's hospital bed, stepping slowly as if trying not to spook a cornered animal. She held out her right hand, once again speaking to Heidi in a level tone.

"Heidi, please give me the laptop." Lindstrom stood there, her hand and arm outstretched. Time slowed to a crawl, everyone in the room unsure of what was going to happen.

Heidi's eyes moved from her husband and focused on Lindstrom. If looks could kill, Lindstrom thought, but, fortunately, they couldn't. When Heidi finally spoke, the words came out in a low, guttural growl.

"YOU!" Heidi stared at Lindstrom and her outstretched hand. "JUST BECAUSE MY HUSBAND ISN'T SMART ENOUGH TO SEE WHAT'S GOING ON AND DOESN'T HAVE THE BALLS TO STAND UP TO YOUR BULLSHIT, I WON'T LET YOU DESTROY MY FAMILY! Heidi stood there, both hands now clutching the laptop. She took a step backward away from Lindstrom.

"Heidi, for God's sake, stop it!" Allison seemingly had enough, as she moved to free herself from the blankets that covered her lower body.

"HEIDI," Andy yelled at his wife, "that's MY computer, now give it to me, NOW!" He took a few steps toward his wife, but Heidi lashed out, swinging the laptop towards her husband. The blow hit Andy on the left side of his head. Andy dropped to the floor, clutching at his head and calling out in pain. Allison had stopped moving, unsure if Heidi would attack her. Ben had seen enough, and looked to get involved, but Lindstrom waved him off without looking at him. She put her left hand out and moved her right hand to her holstered weapon.

"Heidi," Lindstrom said, "that's enough! Set the computer down and back away, now!" She hadn't raised her voice, but Lindstrom put enough inflection behind her words that Heidi was running out of options.

"I TOLD YOU, BITCH, DON'T CALL ME HEIDI!" With those words, in one swift movement, Heidi raised her arms and threw the laptop onto the floor. The two halves broke apart, and, while smaller parts flew in all different directions, Heidi tried stomping on part of the broken laptop, while also landing a kick to her husband.

"OFFICERS," Lindstrom yelled as she moved toward Andy's body on the floor, "GET IN HERE!"

The door to the hospital room flew open and two uniformed officers came racing in. One of the officers quickly squared up, bringing her right arm up while yelling, "FREEZE!" Heidi didn't stop, throwing another kick at her husband, which Lindstrom was able to block.

"DO IT!" Lindstrom's shout was all the officer needed to here, and she pulled the trigger on her stun gun. The two probes shot out, striking Heidi in the chest and sending sixty-thousand volts into her body. Heidi simultaneously froze and shook, and then dropped to the floor. As the two officers stepped around the mess on the floor and proceeded to handcuff Heidi Cole, Lindstrom looked at Ben and shouted, "Get some nurses and a doctor in here!" Ben moved fast, running out of the room. Lindstrom looked up at Allison and asked, "Are you alright?"

Allison let out a sigh. She closed her eyes for a moment, and then looked at Lindstrom. "I always knew Heidi hated Nathan, but I could never figure out why." The words poured out of Allison, like a faucet being turned on. "I would let her go on her rants, and then I would try to forget about them. While Nathan and I were apart, she tried to set me up with other men. After my little incident at the police station, when I regained consciousness and heard about what happened to Nathan, I resolved to be a better wife, mother, and person. When Heidi started in again, I told her in no uncertain terms that, if she valued our friendship, she would never say another unkind word about Nathan in my presence." Allison stopped, looking from her friend to Andy, who was lying semi-conscious on the floor, Lindstrom holding his head against her leg. "I don't understand what Nathan could have done to Heidi, or why Heidi held such resentment against him. It doesn't make any sense." Allison took in a breath, while two nurses, two orderlies, and Dr. Preston were now attending to Andy.

As the hospital staff took Andy out of Allison's room on a gurney, Lindstrom stood up and looked at the uniformed officers. She knew Officer Gilbride from Engels' report, but she hadn't met her current partner. After putting away her stun gun and handcuffing Heidi, Gilbride and her partner had picked her up off the floor and sat her down in the hospital room's small recliner. Gilbride was standing watch over Heidi.

"Officer, um,", Lindstrom said, looking at his badge, "Adams. We haven't been introduced. Detective Patricia Lindstrom, but everybody calls me Tish. Please get the forensics kit I told you to bring. Take pictures of the damage, and then collect all of the computer pieces and get them to Scott in forensics back at the station."

"Yes, Detective, I mean, Tish," Adams said. "Will we need to take witness statements?" Adams looked at Ben and Allison.

Lindstrom looked at Ben, who took a few steps back. He reached up, took his cell phone off the shelf, popped the memory card out of its slot, and handed it to Adams. "You can get my statement off the video. In the meantime, I'm going to go check on Nathan. He was napping when Andy and I came over here, and I want to make sure he isn't awake and worried."

"Thank you," Allison said, giving Ben's forearm a gentle squeeze. Ben smiled back, and then left the room, with Officer Adams following closely behind.

"Gilbride," Lindstrom said, "call in another car and have Heidi Cole taken to the station. I want you and Adams to process the scene."

As Gilbride reached for her radio at the shoulder, a voice started to speak. "You, you can't arrest me, you stupid little cow." Heidi's words may have been slow, but they were spoken with clarity and contempt.

"Actually, Mrs. Cole, I can. I have you for assaulting your husband, assaulting a police officer, resisting arrest, and destruction of property." Lindstrom paused, adding, "That's only the beginning of the charges."

"It'll be your word against me, my husband, and my best friend." A smug look came over Heidi's face, as if nothing could touch her.

"Detective," Gilbride said, "two more officers are on their way up from the ER. We'll have her out of here in a few minutes."

"The hell you will, you cow!" Heidi practically spat the words at Gilbride. She looked at Allison and said, "Please help me out here! You saw how they attacked me! I was just trying to protect my husband! And you! I was trying to protect you too, Allison!"

Allison looked at Heidi for a long time. Silence hung in the air, no one moving. Gilbride was watching Heidi intently, her hand resting above the stun gun, muscles ready at the first sign of trouble. Lindstrom's eyes moved back and forth between Allison and Heidi, as if watching an invisible tennis match. This continued, no one saying a word, making a sound, or moving an inch. Finally, after what seemed like an age but, in fact, was only a few minutes, two more officers came into the room.

"Officers," Allison said, still looking at Heidi, "I believe you are here for her. Please escort her from my room."

"NO!! ALLISON, DON'T DO THIS!! HELP ME!!" Heidi began to struggle as Lindstrom mirandized her, but the other two officers were strong, being able to keep Heidi from hurting herself or lashing out at anyone else. As they made their way past Allison's hospital bed, Lindstrom stepped out of the way, being careful not to step on the large pieces of the broken laptop that were still together.

"FINE, GO AHEAD, ARREST ME! WHEN YOU FIND NOTHING ON THAT COMPUTER AGAINST MY HUSBAND, I'LL MAKE SURE YOU ARE ALL FIRED!!   I'LL SUE THE ENTIRE DEPARTMENT, AND YOU'LL ALL ANSWER TO ME!!   MY HUSBAND IS INNOCENT!!"

"Officers," Lindstrom said, and they stopped, turning around so that Heidi and Lindstrom could see each other. "You are probably right, that Andy is innocent. You, on the other hand, definitely aren't innocent in all of this."

"KEEP TALKING, YOU BITCH! I'M GOING TO OWN YOUR ASS! YOU HAVE NO PROOF THAT I HAD ANYTHING TO DO WITH NATHAN!"

"No proof? Then why destroy the laptop?"

Heidi's eyes were almost slits, her face contorted with a look of malevolence, aimed solely at Lindstrom. "You have nothing. You never did. And now, you never will." Each word came with pure evil, emphasized through gritting teeth.

Lindstrom took a few steps toward Heidi and the officers, and then stopped. She was now close enough so that only Heidi and the officers could hear, but far enough away so that Heidi couldn't lash out with a kick or a headbutt.

"Remember, HEIDI," Lindstrom said, rubbing in the fact that she was still saying her first name, "the internet never forgets."

Heidi raised an eyebrow, questioning what the hell Lindstrom meant.

"What's that supposed to mean, bitch?"

"I have five words for you, HEIDI. Supporting Broken Families Dot Org." Lindstrom watched the color drain from Heidi's face, the tension in her muscles evaporating. The officers, realizing that she wasn't resisting, had to adjust their balance and grip. Lindstrom nodded at them, and they turned around and walked Heidi Cole out of Allison Devlin's hospital room.

THIRTY

It was after six-thirty before Lindstrom had felt comfortable leaving Sanford Hospital. Allison Devlin had assured both Lindstrom and Dr. Preston that she was fine. Her vitals checked out, and she was more concerned about whether Nathan had heard any of the commotion, as well as Andy's condition. After Gilbride and Adams had finished taking photographs of the broken laptop and then collecting them, Lindstrom gave them their instructions again. A nurse had come in to take Allison for some physical therapy, which was only a ruse to allow the janitorial staff an opportunity to clean her room.

Ben had checked on Nathan. Surprisingly, he had slept through everything. Ben was in Nathan's room, waiting to find out what room Andy was going to be admitted to. Early word was that Andy had a hairline fracture in his jaw, his cheekbone was broken, and he had a severe laceration that was going to require at least thirty stitches. In the meantime, Ben had reached out to one of his contacts at the halfway house and arranged for a pair of nannies to head over to the Cole house and relieve the babysitter of watching the Devlin kids and the Cole kids. When the pair arrived, the babysitter called Andy's cell phone, which Ben was holding at the time. Ben explained the situation, telling the babysitter not to inform the kids. Allison would phone them soon enough with instructions.

Lindstrom had thought about calling Engels to give him an update, but there was too much to go over. Besides, she still had too many unanswered questions. Adding to her situation was the fact that she was teetering on the verge of exhaustion, and this wasn't the time to get Engels involved. The confrontation in Allison's hospital room had not gone as she had anticipated. Lindstrom had figured a bait-and-switch between Andy and Heidi would get Heidi to admit to her culpability in Nathan's abduction. Unfortunately, Lindstrom hadn't known what a raving psychotic Heidi could turn into, and now Andy was in surgery and there were two sets of children that wouldn't have their parents tonight. Allison had mentioned to Lindstrom that, while she always loved the friendship between Heidi and herself, she was aware of her mood swings. However, she had never seen them manifest like they had.

Now here Lindstrom was, riding the elevator down to the cafeteria. She decided that she was too tired to try to make it home. Instead, she would eat dinner at the hospital, and then head back to the station. With no kids to worry about, she could pursue more leads and try to get a clearer picture of what she knew. She piled her tray high with food, considering what her body and mind had been through since midnight. The cafeteria was almost deserted, with only three other people sitting at one table, so Lindstrom picked a table on the other side of the room for privacy. She sat down, and as she started to eat, she started processing everything she knew about the case

Nathan Devlin, Olivia Sherman, Ronald Vance, Charles Utecht, R.T.A., Visceral Medical Supplies, Supporting Broken Families Dot Com, First Federated United Trust, Heidi Cole, and Veronica Kirkham. Somehow, everything was connected, but Lindstrom couldn't see how. Why was Nathan Devlin targeted in a kidnapping? Why would Visceral partner with and eventually take over a successful, locally-owned medical supply warehouse, only to close it off from its actual business? If employees of VMS were involved in a kidnapping, why close down the business and leave? Why would Veronica Kirkham pretend to date a police officer for almost a year? Why was Visceral paying out money to low-level employees like Cassie Butler? Were R.T.A. and Visceral innocent bystanders in all this, or were they running some bizarre murder-for-hire business?

Try as she might to get the connections to come together, Lindstrom's thoughts kept gravitating towards Heidi Cole. It had begun with observations, little tics, subtle movements, changes in tone and mood.

Every interaction she had with Heidi had led to an escalation, almost like a hand of poker. A raise, a re-raise, and a re-raise right back, until everything blew up. Now, Andy was in surgery and Heidi was in cuffs. Why was still the question that needed to be answered. Lindstrom was in no position to diagnosis, yet she saw elements of her ex-husband in Heidi. Abusers and those they abused were gender blind. As it pertained to Heidi, though, it seemed strange. She seemed to love Allison and, Lindstrom would assume, Allison's children. But the pure malice, the invective, could there be a reason for it, beyond Nathan's alcoholism?

Sensing what she was struggling with, Lindstrom's mind plucked another memory from her past, helping to fill in the logic gap and provide her with something tangible to work with, a foundation of sorts, so that she could move on.

It was mid-December 2004. Lindstrom and Mark were at a Christmas gala event being hosted at the Washington Pavilion. It had been a beautiful night, cold enough for thick, heavy snowflakes to fall, but not so cold as to put a damper on everyone's holiday spirit. They rarely went in for such get-togethers, but tickets had been for a good cause, and they had needed a break from little Trevor and Bree. Mark had bumped into various people he knew through different associations. A friend here, a co-worker there, a friend of an acquaintance he had met in passing, and, of course, lots of fantasy football league players.

They had been having a wonderful time, enjoying all of the holiday exhibits, the various musicians that were placed in different performance rooms, the festive mood that everyone seemed to have. Then, it happened, one chance encounter, and Lindstrom's happy emotions had almost flatlined.

Mark and Lindstrom had circled back to one of the bars when a woman turned around, holding a drink. "Oh, hey, Tessa," Mark had said, smooth enough to come off as polite. "Great night for a holiday celebration, isn't it?"

The look on Tessa's face relayed one of disdain and boredom, as if she had grown weary of the interaction before Mark had finished speaking. "Yes, just lovely," had come the cool, detached, almost sarcastic response. Lindstrom sized up the woman in front of her. Tessa was dressed in a stunning manner, makeup done in a meticulous fashion to accentuate her features, not a single hair out of place, and her clothes screamed expensive sophistication.

"Tessa, this is my wife, Patricia." Mark placed his hand gently on Lindstrom's shoulder, his face radiating a smile that she had always cherished. Mark had always loved to announce, "his wife", as his way of saying that he loved her. It was sweet and simple, and Lindstrom blushed a little every time he did.

"Nice to meet you, Tessa," Lindstrom had said. Tessa's face changed in an instant, betraying an expression of animosity that Lindstrom hadn't anticipated.

"Yes, if you'll both excuse me," Tessa practically snarled, taking her glass from the bartender and walking away by cutting through them both. Lindstrom couldn't believe the sheer rudeness of the act, and was about to say something, when Mark immediately closed the gap between them and whispered in her ear.

"Don't bother."

Upset by her husband's reaction, or lack thereof, Lindstrom had replied, "Are you serious? What the hell was that all about?"

"I don't know," came Mark's reply. "All I know is that she seems to hate everyone and everything. No one seems to know her that well at work. All they do know is to keep it professional around her".

Lindstrom observed her from a distance for a few minutes. Tessa seemed to slice through the throng of holiday revelers, never really stopping. Her face betrayed only a negativity, a complete antithesis to the joy and companionship happening all around her.

"And you have no idea what you said or did to her?" Lindstrom had asked Mark as they made their way to the car twenty minutes later.

"Honey, I can't explain it. Whether there's a reason or not, whether it's rationale or not, sometimes, one person just doesn't like another person." That ended the discussion of Tessa.

Lindstrom tried to apply that night twelve years ago to what she had seen from Heidi. She knew there had to be backstory, a reason behind her utter loathing towards Nathan. Until she could get more to go on, she would have to file Heidi's motivations under "nuts" and move on.

The other three people in the cafeteria got up to leave, bussing their trays as they left, leaving Lindstrom alone. She pulled out her cell phone, made sure she was connected to the hospital's WIFI, and opened an internet window. She typed in a search "What is R.T.A.?" The results with exact matches were links back to R.T.A.'s official site. Further results started going off topic, with many of the links concerned with different uses of the acronym R.T.A. She adjusted her search to "How has R.T.A. helped you?" Again, most of the search results were bare-bones.

Lindstrom opened a new tab in her internet window and typed in the web address for R.T.A. She was greeted with a gray background and the words "**R.T.A. IS UNAVAILABLE AT THIS TIME.**" She quickly typed in Visceral's website, and was greeted to the same page as before, with all of the http codes listed. She typed in the website addresses for both Supporting Broken Families and First Federated United Trust. Both pages were blank, stating they were unavailable. Lindstrom sat in her chair, trying to figure out what it all meant.

Visceral Medical Supplies supposedly dealt in the buying and selling of medical supplies. Yet they no longer had contracts with hospitals or clinics in the region. Plus, their retail store, which actually wasn't a retail store, was now closed. As for the VMS warehouse, she hadn't seen any kind of discernible activity from her all-too-brief excursion there earlier in the day. Supporting Broken Families appeared to be a website devoted to helping broken families, but Lindstrom hadn't followed up enough to know exactly how they operated. A check written out to Lindstrom from R.T.A. and two checks written out to employees of Visceral were all drawn on an account from a mystery bank named First Federated United Trust. Finally, R.T.A. was in the business of employing convicts and somehow the money they earned was given back to the convict's family. Restitution, apparently, for delinquent and unpaid child support.

Lindstrom thought about that. What would a company like R.T.A. have to gain? It was all well and good to have altruistic goals, but the majority of companies were all about bottom lines and the almighty dollar. If R.T.A. was working in some kind of capacity as a for-profit prison, taking criminals out of the penal system, what was the end game? Lindstrom looked at her tray on the table, which was almost empty, and she rubbed her neck. This case was like a splinter, and the more you tried to extract it, the deeper it went under the skin. She was so tempted to call Veronica at R.T.A. and start demanding answers, but she knew if….

"DAMNIT!" Lindstrom yelled so loud in the empty cafeteria that the sound reverberated back at her. How the hell had she missed something so obvious? She closed her eyes, looking back in her memory, making sure she wasn't trying to manufacture a lead that wasn't there. She thought back a mere five days, when she had received her little package from R.T.A. The letter, giving vague explanations about why she had received such a large check, would be in her memory forever. She tracked down to the signature line. There it was, fresh in her mind's eye, the letter was signed Veronica K. Everything was connected! But why? What were R.T.A. and Visceral really about?

Lindstrom looked at her cell phone, Veronica's contact information automatically saved as the result of two phone calls. She looked around and found the cafeteria was still empty. She could hear noise coming from the kitchen, and she saw the cashier wiping down the outside of several coolers. Lindstrom cleaned up her table and bussed her tray, walking out of the cafeteria. As she walked through the hospital, she kept her hand on her cell phone. Should she call Veronica and confront her? Maybe Lindstrom could call on the pretense of some other issue? If the Veronica she had talked to ended up being the same Veronica that had been dating Tisdale, had hired Noah and Cassie, and was now cleaning up the mess left over by Olivia, Ronald, and Charles, would Veronica see right through a blatant phone call?

At this point, with so many unanswered questions, Lindstrom felt like taking a swing for the fences. Her instincts had proven correct about Olivia Sherman's dead body and Nathan Devlin's kidnapping being linked, as well as Heidi Cole's involvement in this whole mess. If Lindstrom played along, overstated the strength of her evidence, and did some well-placed name-dropping, it was possible that Veronica would give up more on the whole situation.

"No," Lindstrom said to herself. "Not yet." She put her cell phone away and headed toward her car in the parking garage. She needed more information on R.T.A. and Visceral before she would attempt a phone call to Veronica. A few minutes later, she was sitting in her car, deciding on her next move. Go home and get some rest, or head back to the station? No kids to worry about at home, which meant peace and quiet to work and think. Then again, she wouldn't have access to the case files at home, while she would be tempted by a hot bath, a beer, and ten hours of uninterrupted sleep. The decision was easy. The police station it was.

Upon arriving back at the police station and sitting down at her desk, Lindstrom logged into the state of South Dakota's Department of Corrections server. She thought back to one of her conversations with Veronica, regarding how R.T.A. employed prisoners. Lindstrom was hoping to find some of these prisoners and talk to them about their "employment" with R.T.A. She started looking through the records of prisoner transfers in the state, but no prisoners were shown as being removed from the state's corrections system. She searched for any mention of R.T.A. through the state's computer files. Once again, she found nothing. She searched again, only this time looking for any mention of Visceral. Like before, the search came up empty. Since her divorce and subsequent custody trials had taken place in Nebraska, her ex-husband's information wouldn't show up in South Dakota's D.O.C. system.

If R.T.A. and Visceral were one and the same, how were they getting these prisoners? It was possible that no prisoners in the state of South Dakota had ever been moved into R.T.A.'s system, which meant Lindstrom would have to start checking other states. That was going to take a lot of time. Unless, of course, she asked for a favor. She pulled out her cell phone, looked through her contacts, and found the number for Mitch Slausen, a member of the F.B.I.'s local field office that she had helped on a case two years prior. She dialed his number from her landline, waiting through four rings before the call was answered.

"Tish," Mitch said, "most people are out having a good time on a Friday night."

"True, but I'm not most people, Mitch. I'm working a case, and I'm calling in the favor that you said you owed me. Any chance you can lend me some help? And are you still dating that U.S. Marshall?"

"Yes, I can help," Mitch answered. "And if you are referring to Stephanie, actually, she proposed to me last month, and the wedding is set for next summer."

"Wow!" Lindstrom didn't know what she found more shocking, that an F.B.I. agent was marrying a U.S. Marshall, or that she had proposed to him. "That is great! Congratulations!"

"Thanks, and you will be getting an invitation. Now, what's going on?"

"I need to ask Stephanie a few questions regarding JPATS. Any chance

I could steal a few minutes of her time?" JPATS stood for Justice Prisoner and Alien Transportation System, and it was one of the many things that the U.S. Marshall service handled.

"She's in Kansas City right now," Mitch said, "but I will call her and give her your number. Is that okay?"

"That would be great! Thanks Mitch, and congratulations again!" Lindstrom hung up, waiting for Stephanie to call. Ten minutes later, her landline rang. She picked up the receiver.

"Detective Lindstrom."

"Tish, this is Stephanie. Mitch said you had some questions regarding JPATS?"

Lindstrom had never talked to Stephanie before, let alone met her, so she decided to keep things short, sweet, and all business.

"As a U.S. Marshall, have you ever worked with transferring prisoners to a company called R.T.A. or Visceral?"

"Hmmm, can't say that I have. Are they for-profit prisons?"

"I can't say for sure," Lindstrom answered. "I'm working on a case, and every answer leads to three more questions. R.T.A. and Visceral sound like they are in the for-profit prison business, but I'm not finding anything substantial or actionable on my side."

"Give me a minute, and I'll see if they show up in any of my databases." There was a brief pause, and Lindstrom could hear the familiar sound of typing on a keyboard. "I'm not showing anything on my end. It doesn't appear that JPATS has done any kind of prisoner transfers to R.T.A. or Visceral. My guess is that R.T.A. or Visceral didn't want to jump through all of the hoops of getting on board with a federal agency."

"Well, it was worth a shot," Lindstrom replied. "Thanks for your time, Stephanie. I owe you one."

"Have a good night, Tish. I've heard good things about you, and I can't wait to meet you." Before Lindstrom could respond, Stephanie disconnected the call on her end.

Lindstrom hung up her landline and leaned back, thinking about what Stephanie had said. True, it was possible that R.T.A. didn't want to deal with the logistics of getting involved with a federal agency. Of course, that presumed that R.T.A. was on the up-and-up to begin with. Lindstrom knew that the U.S. Marshalls moved tens of thousands of prisoners every year, probably even more. Taking JPATS out of the equation, how the hell was R.T.A. getting prisoners to work for them?

Lindstrom looked at the time. It was a little after 9:30, and all she had to show for her return to the station was another dead end. Between two hours of sleep on Thursday night and a ninety-minute power nap earlier that afternoon, Lindstrom was closing in on thirty-eight hours of being awake. She could tell her body and mind weren't as sharp as they usually were. She entertained the idea of heading upstairs with a cot and taking another power nap but decided against it. Go home, feed the cat, take a hot bath, get a solid night's sleep, and get back in here bright and early tomorrow. Lindstrom put her desk and computer back in order, hoping that tomorrow everything would come together.

As she navigated her way to the parking garage and her car, Lindstrom thought about calling Veronica at R.T.A. again. She weighed the pros and cons of making such a bold move. True, she had talked herself out of it a few hours before as she left Sanford Hospital. Maybe Lindstrom could use the U.S. Marshalls and JPATS against Veronica and get some answers. Lindstrom mulled over the many different avenues that a conversation with Veronica could take, before she realized that she did have an ace up her sleeve, even if she didn't want to use it. Lindstrom shook her head and cursed under her breath. It made her angry, and she resisted the urge to slam her fist into the nearest wall. She had worked so hard for herself and her kids, in spite of everything that had happened in her past. This case, though, this case had brought her past into the present, even into the future, and Lindstrom hated it.

For eleven years, Lindstrom hadn't received one single penny from her ex-husband. He hadn't called to talk to Trevor or Bree, no birthday or Christmas cards, nothing since that one check from his parents more than a decade ago. Now, for whatever reason, in the midst of a baffling kidnapping and murder investigation, Lindstrom had received a check. That check had been made out to Lindstrom for more than fifty-thousand dollars. It was money supposedly made by the miserable bastard, but distributed by a company, or companies, that appeared to be involved, in some way, with her investigation. She hated the idea of having to use her ex-husband to further her case. She had to admit, though, that calling Veronica and asking to speak to her ex-husband would definitely rattle Veronica's cage.

Lindstrom activated her cell phone, scrolled through her contacts, and pressed the dial icon next to Veronica's name. If Engels were there, he would have been enraged. The more she thought about it, though, she doubted Veronica would answer. Veronica was cleaning house, getting rid of loose ends, and closing-up shop. Seeing Lindstrom's number on her caller ID probably would amount to blocking the call. Strangely, the phone kept ringing and ringing. Most voicemails pick up after a maximum of five rings. Lindstrom had gotten into her car and was a good mile away from the station before she realized that she had let the phone ring for a few minutes. She looked at the cell phone and ended the call. She would try again once she got home.

A few minutes later, her cell phone rang. The caller ID listed "PRIVATE". Lindstrom thought about it. It could be Veronica, calling from a different number. Either way, she couldn't avoid the phone call. She swiped the screen active.

"Detective Lindstrom," she said.

"Oh, hello," a jittery female responded. "This is Detective Patricia Lindstrom, correct?"

"Yes, it is, and to whom am I speaking?"

"Oh, I am Cynthia Isaacson, and I am a nurse at Sanford Hospital. Andy Cole asked me to call you. He needs to see you, immediately."

Lindstrom frowned. To get back to the hospital, she would have to do a one-eighty, driving back into the heart of Sioux Falls. Not a problem, she thought to herself, and she could be there quick. Wait a second, though. She was surprised that Andy Cole would be awake, considering the beating he got from Heidi several hours beforehand. She moved into a turning lane, adjusting her course away from Brandon and towards the hospital.

"Andy is conscious? I didn't expect him to be able to see anyone until tomorrow."

"I know," Nurse Isaacson replied, "but I was in his room only a few moments ago. He wrote a note on a piece of paper that he needed to talk to you ASAP, and that no one else was to know. I am actually calling you from a hospital telephone in a doctor's lounge. What should I tell him?"

"Tell him I am on my way, and I should be there within the next thirty minutes."

"Okay. He is on the third floor, room 3-227. Bye!' Nurse Isaacson hung up.

Lindstrom thought that, whatever Andy Cole had to say, it must be very important. As she drove, she assessed the events of the last few hours. Should she call Engels? No, that could wait until tomorrow. Lindstrom would find out what was going on with Andy. She doubted that he had any information that could be acted upon immediately. Talk to Andy and find out what was so important. Then back to her original plan when she had left the station. Home, feed the cat, relax in hot bath, and got some much-needed rest. Her thoughts went over the events of the afternoon in Allison Devlin's hospital room. Seeing Heidi smash the laptop on the floor, followed by her stomping on it, had been shocking. However, even if the laptop was thoroughly destroyed, the ghost that Scott had made on the flash drive would allow them access to whatever they needed. Lindstrom pulled back from that thought quickly. Hope and pray the hard drive can be recovered, she told herself. Don't take the easy way because you lucked your way into it, she told herself.

Almost twenty minutes later, she was pulling back into the parking garage of Sanford Hospital, driving up multiple ramps until she was on the designated third floor level. Even though it was after visiting hours, there were still multiple cars parked in the structure. She found a parking spot about ten yards from a set of double-doors that led into the hospital.

As she got out of her car and looked around, Lindstrom realized that the parking garage seemed darker than when she had left earlier, and that the air also seemed heavier, with the smell of car exhaust thicker than before. She shut her car door and locked it, and that's when she heard it, a cry for help. Lindstrom's instincts kicked in, and she looked around frantically, not seeing anyone. She heard the cry for help again, to which she responded, "WHERE ARE YOU?"

"By the minivan with the flashing lights," the voice shouted. Lindstrom looked toward the double-doors, and the taillights of a minivan were flashing. She ran quickly and found an old man in a wheelchair between the minivan and a pickup truck. It looked like the wheelchair had started to tip over but had become caught between the open side door of the minivan and the pickup's running board.

"Please, is someone there, help!", the man shouted, but the sound of his voice was washed out in the concrete vacuum of the parking garage.

"Sir, try not to move," Lindstrom said, trying to figure out what to do. It looked like the driver of the pickup had parked too close to the minivan, not allowing enough clearance for anyone in a wheelchair to get in and out of their vehicle. "What happened to you?"

"I came out to my van," the old man said, "and some ne'er-do-well decided to park right on top of me. I thought if I could get in, I could then back up and retrieve my wheelchair, but I didn't have the strength to work my way from the chair into the van, and I almost toppled over."

Lindstrom was standing behind the man and the wheelchair, trying to figure out how to help. "Okay, sir," she began, "I'm going to brace the back of the wheelchair and start pushing it forward slowly. Try to climb to the edge of the minivan's floor, if you can, and then I will get your wheelchair free." She bent at her knees, bracing her right arm and shoulder against the back of the wheelchair. There was no acceptable way to get leverage, and, as she started pushing, the muscles in her legs, arms, and back screamed in protest at this kind of exertion, especially after being awake for so long. Her head began to pound, the beginning of a major headache setting in.

As Lindstrom pushed the wheelchair up and forward, the old man said, "Please, young lady, don't take it easy on my account. If you should scratch the fiend's truck, I won't tell." Even in the midst of the situation, Lindstrom found his choice of words and his articulation interesting, not that she was mocking him for it.

"Sir," Lindstrom responded through grunts and heavy breathing, "I am a police officer, so I won't be scratching the truck."

"Good thinking, officer. Shoot the tires instead. I like your train of thought." The man's humor caught Lindstrom off guard, and she had to struggle not to burst out laughing, which probably would have meant the wheelchair would fall backward, pinning her under the weight of the chair and the old man.

"Sir, I think you need to hold off on the jokes until we're both in a better situation."

"Very well, officer. Back to the task at hand. Another inch, and I shall be able to reach the support rod in the van." Lindstrom heard the old man grunt, and, after a few more seconds, the intense weight in the chair was gone.

Lindstrom was squatted down on the ground and looked over the back of the wheelchair to see the old man sitting on the edge of the minivan. She could see part of the lift mechanism for the wheelchair to his side.

"Are you alright, sir?" Lindstrom was out of breath, her muscles on fire, her head feeling like it was inside of a drum kit.

"My dear officer, I am more embarrassed than anything." He put his hand to his heart and said, "Granted, I am not embarrassed by the idea of being rescued by you. In all my life, I have never been the damsel that was in distress. No, heaven forbid, it was the utter silliness of the whole situation." Lindstrom couldn't get over the old man's voice and his vocabulary. He seemed like he came out of England in the 1960's, only without the accent. "Now then, officer, if you are still up for it, shall we commence with shooting out the rascal's tires?"

The old man was too much, and Lindstrom started to laugh, but her throat was parched. The laugh came out like an angry cackle. Her muscles began to spasm, and she started coughing. After a few seconds, it started to subside.

"My goodness, officer, I should be asking YOU if you are alright."

Lindstrom looked up again, wiping tears from her eyes. She was down on her knees now, and, while she thought about standing, she didn't think she had the strength left in her body.

"I'll be okay," Lindstrom said, her voice raspy and irritated. "I've just had an incredibly long day, and I desperately need some sleep."

The old man strained to look at Lindstrom over the back of the wheelchair, and then said, "Well, I think I see another kind soul walking over here. Perhaps we can get you taken care of." The old man whistled. It wasn't terribly loud, Lindstrom thought, but enough to be heard. Oh well, she thought, at least it hadn't aggravated her headache.

"Ah, yes, you there! Nurse...?" The old man's voice trailed off.

"Isaacson. Nurse Isaacson. What happened?" Through strained breathing, Lindstrom could faintly recognize the nurse's voice.

"We've had a bit of trouble," the old man said. "Would you mind helping this poor officer to her feet?" As Lindstrom heard footsteps coming up behind her, her cell phone rang. In the concrete tomb of the parking garage, the sound of the ring tone turned into a cacophony of hideous noise. She reached for her cell phone and looked at the caller ID. Lindstrom's eyes grew large, not sure what do. It was Veronica! She wanted to talk to her, but she was on her knees between two vehicles with an old man sitting less than three feet from her. A shadow came over Lindstrom, but she was too tired to turn and look at Nurse Isaacson.

Lindstrom accepted the call and put the phone to her ear.

"Hello, this is Detective Lindstrom." The words came out coarse, her throat exceedingly dry. She felt a hand on her shoulder, and she was about to say something when another coughing fit took hold. While she coughed, Lindstrom could feel the other hand gently patting her back between her shoulder blades.

After she had stopped coughing, the old man said, "Oh my, where are my manners? Dear officer, what is your name?"

"Patricia. Detective Patricia Lindstrom." Lindstrom was still on her knees, the grooved concrete now digging into her knees. She looked at the phone, and the call had disconnected. Nurse Isaacson's helping hand was still on her left shoulder, but the other hand was no longer patting her back. Lindstrom's eyes were burning, her mouth and throat were dry, her brain felt like it was about to split in two, and it seemed like every muscle fiber was a five-alarm blaze. Just get me up and inside the hospital, she thought to herself.

"Detective Patricia Lindstrom, it is an honor to make your acquaintance." Lindstrom's head was down, her eyes looking at the ground, but she saw a shadow move over the wheelchair. She looked up, and saw the old man was now standing in front of the wheelchair. "You have given me your name, now allow me to extend to you the same courtesy. My name is Edward. Edward Kirkham. Doctor Edward Kirkham, to be precise."

Before Lindstrom could react, the hand on her shoulder grabbed Lindstrom by the back of the neck, and a wet rag was suddenly clamped over Lindstrom's mouth and nose. Each breath was an exercise in futility, as the sickly-sweet substance on the rag was causing Lindstrom to lose consciousness. Even if she had her strength and reflexes, Lindstrom was at a decided disadvantage. She was on her knees, between two large vehicles, with no room to maneuver or fight. Nurse Isaacson had her entire weight on her back and shoulders. Through the fog that was closing in on her, Lindstrom wondered why Nurse Isaacson was doing this. Lindstrom tried to reach behind her, to grab for an eye or a nostril or a clump of hair, or for her fingers to touch something to use as a weapon, but it was no use. She had no strength before this had started, and there was nothing Lindstrom could do.

"Now, before you fade away," Edward Kirkham said, "I would like to apologize that Nurse Isaacson played a trick on you. In fact, Nurse Isaacson is fictitious, an imaginary form, born out of necessity." Lindstrom could see a sly grin roll over Edward Kirkham's face. He gestured with his hand, pointing a finger behind Lindstrom, and said, "I believe you know Nurse Isaacson more accurately as my daughter, Veronica Kirkham."

Even with her consciousness rapidly dissolving into nothingness, Lindstrom's eyes exploded wide. The name. She tried pushing through her physical and mental impairments, thrusting the fog in her brain to the edges. Kirkham. The name behind it all. First, the daughter, and now, the father. Was he the missing piece?

Stars popped at the sides of Lindstrom's vision. Her body and her mind were spent. Moments before the darkness came over her, Lindstrom heard Edward Kirkham whisper to her, almost intimately, "Don't worry, Detective. Everything will become clear to you very, very soon."

THIRTY-ONE

The water was warm and soothing as the current slowly carried Lindstrom and Ryan away. Lindstrom glanced back over her shoulder and saw Bree, sitting in a lounge chair under an umbrella, sunglasses on, a Shirley Temple on a table next to her. Ryan squirmed in his seat, giggling, and when Lindstrom faced forward again, she saw Trevor hurriedly climbing the stairs, an innertube under his arm, trying to get to the tallest waterslide in the park. She smiled at all three of her children, each one having fun in their own way, while she enjoyed floating on the lazy river.

Lindstrom had wanted to take the kids on a big family vacation for so long, but it never seemed to work out. Whether it was because of Mark's health, or her job on the police force, or the growing challenges of managing two teenagers, she was never able to plan something like this before. Fortunately, things had changed for the better, and here they were, enjoying all of the benefits of this massive resort and indoor waterpark.

"Honey, have I told you lately how beautiful you look?"

Lindstrom turned and saw Mark floating in an innertube next to hers. She smiled mischievously at him.

"Hey now, you naughty old man. You stop talking like that in front of your children."

Mark's face turned into a playful look of hurt and shock. "Why, whatever do you mean? I'm nothing but an honest gentleman, who would never even think of such things!" He gave her a little wink, adding, "Obviously, though, we both know where your mind is wandering towards."

Lindstrom looked at Mark's features, the features that she loved so much about him. The facial hair with the slight hint of salt and pepper color, the off-blue eyes with a touch of green, his inviting smile, and those hands, oh, those wonderful hands. Whether his hands were rubbing the tension out of her neck after a hard day or tickling Ryan or doing the dishes, for some reason, Lindstrom had always loved Mark's hands. Looking at his left hand, with his wedding band glistening in the sun that was coming through the high glass ceiling, it made her love him even more.

"You told me this morning at breakfast how beautiful I look," Lindstrom said as she kicked a little water at Mark, "but don't let that stop you from saying it again."

"Well, maybe later. I don't want you to get some strange idea that I like you or anything." Mark smiled like the little devil he could be. "Besides, being scared of a waterslide isn't very beautiful, now is it?"

Lindstrom had been through a lot in her life and had overcome a lot of fears. There was something about a waterslide that still bothered her, though. Even with Mark and the kids begging her to go, "just once, only once, please please just one time", she had refused, instead opting for the lazy river, the hot tub, and the lap lane.

"You love me, you think I'm beautiful, and don't try to deny it," Lindstrom whispered to Mark as their innertubes bumped together and she held them together.

"Yeah, maybe, but only a little bit, a very little bit," Mark whispered softly back. "I'd love you more if you trusted me with the waterslide." With that, Mark rolled off his innertube, stood up in the lazy river, and said, "Ryan, wanna go down one of the waterslides with your Dad?"

"Let's go, Daddy!" Somehow, Ryan jumped from the two-seated innertube that he was sharing with Lindstrom into his father's arms, and they were out of the lazy river and climbing the stairs before Lindstrom could say anything. As they made it to the first turn of stairs, Ryan looked back and shouted, "Momma, make sure you watch us!"

Lindstrom gave a thumbs-up, and then started paddling her arms to get to the edge of the lazy river, so she could climb out and have a better view as they came out of the waterslide.

"Hey, wait for me!"

400

Lindstrom looked behind her, and saw Bree, walking quickly to the stairs, grabbing an innertube for herself. Lindstrom smiled, watching her daughter, her youngest son, and her husband climb almost five stories worth of stairs to get to the waterslides. As she craned her neck up, she saw Trevor already at the top, patiently waiting for Mark, Ryan, and Bree. From where Lindstrom was standing, she couldn't see the four of them, although she could make out their shadows as they climbed into the starting point of the yellow-colored waterslide. A few seconds later, and the shadows started down the enclosed waterslide, which looked like a giant yellow gummy worm, with various twists and turns, curving all the way down until it emptied into a common pool that four other waterslides emptied into.

Lindstrom smiled. She was happy, happier than she had been in a long, long time. Her family was together again, and everyone was having a great time. She followed the shadows down through the yellow tube, but, as they came closer to the ground, the shadows faded. Maybe it was because the sun wasn't shining on the lower parts of the waterslide, she thought. It doesn't matter, Lindstrom thought, focusing on the exit to the yellow tube. In a few seconds, they would shoot out into the pool, laughing and smiling and having a grand time.

A few seconds turned into ten, twenty, thirty, then sixty seconds. Lindstrom looked up at the yellow tube, and then back at the exit. Where were they? Lindstrom's eyes went to the start of the waterslide and followed its path all the way down. Still, no one came out of the exit. More precious seconds passed, and Lindstrom's mind went from confusion to panic.

"MARK! KIDS! WHERE ARE YOU?" Lindstrom was now yelling from the edge of the common pool, struggling to be heard over the rush of water. "SOMEONE, HELP ME!" She looked around, searching for a life guard or attendant or any customer that could help, but no one was there. Her eyes searched frantically around her. Where was everyone? Where had they all gone? Had they been in the waterpark alone this whole time?

Suddenly, the water stopped rushing out of the multiple waterslides, and the high glass ceiling grew dark. The sun was now blocked by clouds, and the clouds turned from white to silver to gray, growing darker by the second. The sky above her was now a foreboding black, with streaks of lightning shooting through. Lindstrom turned back to the pool and jumped into the water. It was only deep enough to go up to her waist, but as she tried to half-walk, half-jump her way to the yellow tube's exit, it felt like the water was fighting her, resisting her attempts to get to her family. After what seemed like an age, Lindstrom's hands grasped the end of the yellow tube, and she pulled herself to it.

"MARK! TREVOR! ANSWER ME! BREE! RYAN! WHAT'S WRONG? WHERE ARE YOU?" There was no sound, no cry for help. The entire waterpark had fallen into a deathly silence. Lindstrom tried to swing her legs onto the exit, but the water held her down, encasing her like cement. The pool was no longer a few feet deep, as she was being sucked down, the pull of the water fighting her grip on the slide. She refused to look down, keeping her eyes on the darkness from inside the yellow tube, hoping to see her family emerge, safe and sound. As she struggled to pull herself up, the water creeped up her body, like a mouth slowly inching over a large piece of food. Lindstrom felt like the water was trying to consume her, but she fought it. Her family was in danger, and she would fight with every last ounce of strength and courage until she knew they were safe.

Lindstrom's muscles ached, her fingers somehow digging into the plastic of the waterslide, and she was able to pull herself up to see inside the tube. Without warning, the water came on again, blasting her in the face, startling her and causing her to release her hold. She was now being pummeled by the water from every direction, being sucked lower and lower into the seemingly-unending pool. She looked up to the surface, the darkened sky now descending down through the glass ceiling into the waterpark. The inky black clouds merged into the water around Lindstrom, surrounding her, enveloping her. As she struggled against the water and the darkness, the lightning shot out from the clouds, and the inky blackness exploded, erupting into electric patterns inside her eyes. She was afraid to breathe, but she had to. Don't take a breath, and you die. Take a breath, invite the water into your lungs, and die. She fought against the natural impulse as she tried to kick herself upward, using her arms to climb through the water and darkness above her. It was no use. Either way, she was done for. Lindstrom closed her eyes tight, opened her mouth wide, and inhaled, as deep as she had ever inhaled before. Instead of water and darkness, a flood of oxygen, unlike any she had ever had, filled every part of her lungs. Her eyes shot open, and the darkness surrounding her detonated away.

Lindstrom's eyes tried to focus, but all she could see was white, her vision impaired with stars. She flailed, but she found that she was being held down. She blinked and squinted repeatedly, trying to shake her eyes free of the glare around her. She looked down and was able to see her wrists and ankles were secured to a bed. She tried to sit up, but there were more restraints in place against her thighs, hips, abdomen, and torso. She couldn't see them, but she felt restraints against her neck and forehead, as well.

"My dear Detective, whatever could cause you such distress?"

The voice, it was familiar to Lindstrom. Her vision slowly returned, but still, there was only white, white everywhere. Where was she? And where had the voice come from? She tried to speak, but her mouth was dry, her lips parched, and she started to cough. As she coughed, she felt herself being moved upward. Lindstrom realized that she must be on a bed, and it was being raised so she would be in a sitting position. Once the movement stopped, she saw a hand move across her field of vision. She felt her lips being parted, and something was put inside her mouth.

"Go ahead, Detective. I imagine you must be thirsty. Take a drink. In fact, take as much as you need."

The voice, why did Lindstrom recognize it? She puckered her lips, and she felt the cool tingle of water rushing over her teeth, her tongue, and down her throat. She felt as if she had crossed the desert, and this was her first drink. She didn't know how long she sucked the water through the straw, or how much she drank. She only stopped when there was nothing left, when the annoying sound of slurping a straw in an empty glass was all that remained. The straw was removed, and Lindstrom was able to lick her lips, but barely. The restraints against her made any kind of movement difficult. The hand appeared again, and she felt something cool moving over her lips. Was it lip balm, she thought?

"My, my, my, Detective. You were thirsty, weren't you? Well, hopefully that will help you in your present condition." Lindstrom still couldn't tell where the voice was coming from, only that she knew it, somehow, from somewhere.

"Where am I?" Lindstrom tried to speak, but the sound came out muffled, with no articulation, as if she was performing a bad ventriloquist act.

"Oh, dear me, Detective. I can't understand a word you just said. Tell you what, I will loosen your shackle a little. However, I want MY question answered first. If you don't answer my question, I will re-engage the shackle, and I will not answer your question. If you understand, blink your eyes twice."

Even in her current state, the confusion hovering over her brain was subsiding, and she knew she needed to play by the rules, at least for now. She blinked twice, slowly.

"Excellent!"

Lindstrom heard a soft click, and the pressure against her jaw and cheek lessened.

"Now, my dear Detective, back to my original question. What were you in such distress about? Were you dreaming? I fancy dreams, especially when they occur in a state like the one you are currently in. So, yes or no, were you dreaming? If so, what were you dreaming about?"

The details were fuzzy, yet the overall arc of what Lindstrom had experienced was coming back to her. She thought about lying, maybe cracking wise, or even embellishing the truth a little bit. She didn't want to give in to the question. However, some part of her knew it would be pointless. She wasn't in any position of power or authority. Improvising a lie could have terrible repercussions, so it was best to play along until she could get her bearings.

"I was at a waterpark with my family, and we were having a wonderful time, until they disappeared. And I jumped into the water to save them, but I couldn't. Now I'm here."

"Detective, I must say, you surprise me. From what I have read, what I have heard, what I have observed, you strike me as an amazing woman. It is unfortunate that our paths had to cross in this way, but, as you know, life doesn't always work out the way you had planned or intended." The voice stopped, and Lindstrom could hear a soft sigh. The silence moved over her, and a sense of dread took hold. She started to shiver, but she didn't know why.

"Oh, please, Detective, I'm sorry. I didn't mean to scare you. Allow me to help." Through the glaring whiteness in front of her, Lindstrom saw movement, a white-on-white silhouette moving toward her. She looked down, and saw a blanket being put over her body, tucked around her. After a few seconds, the shivers stopped, and Lindstrom realized that the blanket was heated. What the hell was happening here? Who was this person? Why was the voice so familiar?

As if on cue, the voice continued, "Yes, yes, yes, you have many questions, Detective. However, I have rules, and one of the most important ones is manners. You must use your manners at all times. Another rule is quid pro quo. You have answered my question, so I shall now answer your question." The white-on-white silhouette came into focus in front of Lindstrom, and her eyes grew wide with shock, excitement, and fear. It was him, the man from the hospital parking garage.

"Ah, I see that you recognize me! I am flattered, Detective." He bowed slightly and continued, "As you may recall, I am Edward Kirkham. And I bid you welcome to this," he spread out his arms, "for this is stage one of Visceral!"

THIRTY-TWO

It had been a long Friday for Brad Engels. He had arrived to work at 7:30am, only to find Lindstrom leaving. After that, there was the revelation that Tisdale had unknowingly been dating someone involved in the case. Next up was the charity function, then the trip to the daycare, followed by multiple meetings with various businesses and community leaders, and, finally, having a late dinner with his wife, Diane. By the time Engels had returned home after 10:30pm, it was straight to bed. Sleep had overtaken him quickly.

When his alarm went off at 8am on the dot, Engels snapped awake, refreshed and ready to tackle the weekend. He normally didn't go into the station on the weekends unless it was an emergency. Today, though, he had told Diane he wasn't going to be there very long. Since he hadn't done any actual work on Friday, he only wanted to check messages and get a quick update from Lindstrom and Tisdale. He was up, showered, dressed, had breakfast with Diane, and was walking into the garage at 9:15am. As he climbed into his car, Diane had made him swear that he would be home by noon, one o'clock at the latest. He swore, put up two fingers signifying "scout's honor", and backed out of the garage. Due to light Saturday morning traffic, he was parked and walking into the police station by 9:50am.

As Engels left the elevator and walked towards his office, his cell phone rang. The caller ID showed Scott, one of his computer forensics experts.

"Scott," Engels said, "happy Saturday to you!" Engels was in a good mood.

"Morning, Chief," Scott replied. "Hate to bother you on your day off, but do you know where Tish is?"

"Well, I'm about to walk into my office, and I don't see her out here among the other officers. Why?"

"You came in today?" Scott must have realized how that sounded, because he quickly added, "I mean, um, what brings you in on a Saturday?"

Engels smiled. "Scott, relax. I had so many things going on yesterday out of the station that I only want to play a little catch up."

Relieved that he hadn't crossed a line and wasn't in trouble, Scott said, "Oh, I get it now. Well, Tish had Officers Gilbride and Adams drop off a broken computer for me to analyze."

"A computer?"

"A laptop, actually."

"Do you know whose computer it is?"

"Judging from the evidence tag, it belongs to Andy Cole, with a note that it was damaged by Heidi Cole."

Oh lord, Engels thought, what had Lindstrom done? "I'm assuming you tried calling her?"

"Yes, Chief, multiple times on both her cell phone and her land line. The land line rings three times and goes to an answering machine, and the cell phone goes straight to voicemail."

"Any response via text message?" Engels had put his briefcase in his office and went to Lindstrom's desk. It seemed in order, with the computer and monitor turned off, no mess to speak of, everything looking organized.

"None. I got in a little after eight, and I tried calling right away. I left messages, and when I didn't hear back by nine, I tried again. Still nothing. I tried at nine-thirty, and then once more before I called you."

Peculiar, Engels thought. It wasn't like Lindstrom not to pick up or return a phone call from a police number. "Have you started working on this broken laptop?"

"For the most part, yes," Scott answered. "It's in bad shape from a physical standpoint. Fortunately, the hard drive is still in one piece. I'm taking it slow, to make sure I don't accidentally fry anything."

Engels stood and looked around the sea of desks and cubicles that comprised this floor of the police station. He didn't see Lindstrom at all, and the other officers were engaged in their own business. He started walking back to his office and said to Scott, "Okay, keep working on that computer. I will try to track down Tish." With that, he ended the call.

Engels sat down at his desk and moved the mouse to bring the computer out of sleep mode. He typed in his password and pulled up the daily duty roster. Officers Gilbride and Adams were already out on patrol. He pulled up their activity log from Friday and saw they had been called to Sanford Hospital as back-up for Lindstrom. A tag attached to the log indicated a report had been filed. Engels clicked on the report and read the summary that both officers had submitted and signed off. Both officers were standing outside the hospital room of Allison Devlin, awaiting instructions. Upon hearing Lindstrom's call for help, they entered and found Heidi Cole attacking her husband, with Lindstrom trying to protect him. Gilbride tasered Heidi with her department-issued stun gun. As Engels read through the brief pieces after that, he saw that the officers had uploaded a video of the entire incident. He turned on the computer's speakers, opened the video, and watched it. When the video was done, Engels sat there in amazement.

Engels always knew that Lindstrom was a great police officer and excellent detective, but this was something else. He was equal parts angry and relieved. He had instructed her to back away from her instincts regarding Heidi Cole. And yet, Lindstrom's intuition about Heidi had proved correct. Of course, how Heidi Cole fit into everything was still in question. He looked at the time. It was almost ten-thirty. Engels grabbed his cell phone and dialed Lindstrom's cell. Right to voicemail. He called her home phone. Three rings, and the answering machine picked up.

"Tish, it's Brad. If you're there, pick up now." He paused five seconds, then added, "If I don't hear from you in five minutes, I'm sending one of the local officers over to check on you." Engels ended the call. While he waited, he called down to the dispatch and call center that dealt with 911 calls.

"Dispatch, this is Carol."

"Carol, it's Chief Engels. I need you to run a trace and find Detective Lindstrom's cell phone and vehicle."

"Right away, sir, give me one moment." Engels could hear Carol's fingers typing on her keyboard. After a minute or so, he heard her say,

"Um, that can't be right. Let me try again."

"What? What can't be right?" Engels waited on the line, even the brief pause becoming uncomfortable.

"I can't find her cell phone on the network, which means it's either turned off, or the battery is dead. But that's not the problem. The problem is the tracer on her car. It's not pinging."

"You mean, it's turned off, too?" Engels knew every police car had a tracer, which allowed the switchboard operators to track police movements and orchestrate the best response times to accidents, criminal activities, and the like.

"Chief, it's not that simple," Carol replied. "Those tracers are hard-wired into the car, running off the car's battery. The tracer also has a battery of its own. The idea is that it would take something catastrophic to terminate the tracer's signal."

Engels didn't like the sound of that. "Carol, listen to me very carefully. This stays between you and me, for now. I want you to run a search on Lindstrom's cell and car every ten minutes. If you still don't have a response and a location after three tries, in thirty minutes, you call me. Understand?"

"Yes sir," Carol said, and disconnected.

Engels hung up the phone and sat for a moment at his desk, looking out the window. He needed a minute to collect his thoughts and decide on his next step. While it wasn't like Lindstrom to not check in, there was also the very real possibility that, after more than thirty-six hours of work, her body had finally succumbed. Maybe she was in too deep a sleep to be awoken with something as simple as a ringing telephone. Then again, he would have expected her to let someone know, or leave a message, or something to avert any unnecessary worrying.

Engels thought back to only twelve hours ago, when he had returned home. His head hit the pillow, and he was out. He remembered his early days as an officer, trying to shut off the mind and the body after twelve, sixteen, and even twenty-plus hour shifts. They had been rare, but emergencies happened. That's why the police, the fire department, paramedics, basically all emergency services were in place.

Engels shook his head, bringing his thoughts back into focus. What was the best decision here? He knew better than to start an unnecessary panic, especially where Lindstrom was concerned. The last thing he wanted was Tish being embarrassed and holding a grudge against him.

The message that Engels had left on Lindstrom's answering machine told her that she had five minutes to call him back. That was ten minutes ago. He decided to err on the side of caution and give her some more time. He looked at the time. 10:43am. He would give Lindstrom until 11am. He was going to re-open the report from Gilbride and Adams and re-watch the video. If Lindstrom hadn't contacted him by eleven, then Engels would take more action.

Despite movies and television shows that portrayed computer specialists as "amazing hackers" or being able to crack cyber-puzzles in mere seconds by a few simple keystrokes, most computer work was simply tedious. Like any profession, it required patience, knowing what you were looking for, and being able to apply a solution to a problem.

Scott was working on the broken laptop belonging to Andy and Heidi Cole. While the majority of the laptop was unusable now, the three main components, surprisingly, had very little damage. Those three components, the motherboard, the CPU, and the hard drive, came through the carnage virtually unscathed. He had carefully tested the functionality of the parts, making sure that power could be applied correctly, and the components would function. Of course, all Scott needed was enough time to copy the entire hard drive. After that, the laptop could be junked out and used as evidence.

Scott figured it would take some time, since he didn't know how much information was on the hard drive. When he had borrowed the laptop under the pretense of using it as a charger, he had no intention of using it like that. He had gone back into Nathan Devlin's room and set up the laptop so that Nathan couldn't see the screen. He powered on the laptop, hoping that it wasn't password protected, which, thankfully, it wasn't. Scott had put a flash drive into an open USB port, and the ghost program that was already preloaded on the flash drive automatically copied the hard drive's entire contents into a compressed zip file. While it was copying, Scott had worked with Nathan on the digital adjustments for Olivia Sherman's face. About halfway through, an LED light on the flash drive signaled that the program was done. If Andy or Heidi or some tech guy ever looked at a keystroke log, there was nothing to find on the laptop, as

410

the program was self-executing. However, being slightly paranoid, as most computer geeks were prone to be, Scott had quickly grabbed a second flash drive, pulled out the completed one, and started the process over. Better safe than sorry when it came to information on a computer. After all, Scott had the contents of his computers at home backed up on two different storage devices while also using two different cloud services.

Scott had given Lindstrom one of the flash drives, but he had kept the other one for himself. Now, on the off-chance that something bad had happened to Lindstrom, he still had a copy of the laptop's hard drive. He had not accessed any of the information, hoping that he wouldn't have to. Sure, what he had done wasn't legal. Moreover, if word of what he had done ever made it to Engels or Internal Affairs, his career in law enforcement would effectively be done. Still, he did what he did. Justice had to be served, no matter the cost. As long as he didn't get caught, and as long as Lindstrom didn't get caught, Scott was okay with the occasional rule break if the bad guys lost at the end of the day.

Scott's focus returned to the broken laptop. In the event some of the data on the hard drive was corrupted, he could use the copy as a map and fill in any missing data. Scott looked over the connections again, and everything seemed to be in order. He booted up the laptop, watching the startup sequence on a monitor he had attached to the external video port. He stopped the computer from opening the Microsoft Windows operating system, and, instead, started the process of copying the hard drive's information over to a virtual hard drive on one of his forensic computers. A progress bar opened, and it took twelve minutes for the progress bar to move from zero percent to one percent. Scott looked at the hard drive from the laptop, and the label said it was a 3TB hard drive, meaning it had a maximum capacity of holding three terabytes worth of information. Since he was copying over the hard drive in its entirety, rather than compressing it, and also depending on how much actual information was on the hard drive as opposed to unused space, it was going to be a long time to get everything copied over.

Since the entire contents of the hard drive were going to be copied, and to save some time, Scott decided to run a comparison program while the hard drive's contents were being copied to the forensic department's computers on the police network. He took the flash drive that had the hard drive's contents and put it into an empty USB slot on his police computer.

He then opened a utility program, instructing the program to scan the contents of the USB drive and the contents of the hard drive's laptop as they were being copied. Once complete, the results of the program would have an analysis report of any duplicate files, as well as any files that had been modified. He would have run the utility program anyway, but this allowed for it to happen simultaneously to the hard drive copying. When it was all done, he would have all of the same information he needed to examine the hard drive's contents.

Scott looked at the clock. It was almost eleven-thirty. He wondered if Engels had tracked down Lindstrom.

Lindstrom was still missing, and Engels was getting very concerned. Carol had called back after thirty minutes. She still hadn't gotten a tracer signal from Lindstrom's phone or her car. Engels had considered calling the local Brandon police department that was responsible for the small-town Lindstrom lived in, but then thought better of it. That was not an indictment of their department. No, it was merely that he didn't want to raise the alarm if he didn't have to.

Instead, Engels was dialing Dale and Miriam, the retired couple that lived across the street from Lindstrom. He would ask Dale to walk over to the house and see if he got a response from knocking on the door. Dale, who was in his late seventies but still physically fit and sharp as a tack, had answered his cell phone on the second ring.

"Why, as I live and breathe, it's Chief Engels!" Dale was always happy to talk. "What can I do for you?"

"Dale, I hate to bother you on a Saturday morning, but could you take a stroll across the street and see if Tish is home?" Engels quickly added, "We're having some network issues here, and I haven't been able to get in touch with her yet."

"Sure thing, let me throw on my shoes and you can walk over with me." Engels heard mild noises through the phone, and then the soft whistle of wind. "Looks like Trevor's pickup is gone. He must be out working or something. Okay, I'm at the front door." There was a slight pause, and Engels assumed Dale had used the doorbell. "Hmmm, no answer. Let me try again." This time, Engels also heard Dale knocking on the storm door. Several seconds passed, and Dale said, "Still nothing. I see the cat in the front bay window, though, and he seems perturbed. Should I open the garage and go in?"

"Yeah, that's a good idea," Engels said. Lindstrom had given Dale and Miriam the code for the garage door opener, and, while Engels heard the pull of the motor lifting the garage door, he used his computer to log in to Lindstrom's cell phone service. When Lindstrom had joined the force, she had insisted that Engels have access to any means of finding her or her kids, since she was the only officer that was "single" with full custody of her kids. Engels activated the family locator icon in Lindstrom's cell phone account and watched while the cursor turned into a slowly spinning hourglass.

"TISH? KIDS? IT'S DALE, THE OLD GUY FROM ACROSS THE STREET! IS ANYONE HOME?" The only thing Engels could hear was the sound of Blonde's incessant meowing. "LOOK, IF ANYONE IS HOME, DON'T SHOOT AND DON'T BE MAD! I'M GOING TO FEED THE CAT!"

Muffled noises came through the phone, while on the computer screen, two icons appeared on a map of the United States, very close together. Engels zoomed in on the icons and found one in Nebraska and the other in Rapid City. Engels checked the school's website and found a statewide cheerleading competition all weekend long in Rapid City. That would account for Bree. The other icon was located between Wakefield and Laurel, Nebraska, which was where Lindstrom's father's farm was. Engels surmised that Trevor was there and, hopefully, Ryan were there, too. At least the kids were safe. That lifted some of the weight off of Engels' shoulders.

"Tish told me that, because of the four-day school weekend, the kids were off doing their own thing," Engels fibbed to Dale. "Any sign of Tish?"

"Nope, nothing," Dale responded. "Her car wasn't in the garage, and she's nowhere to be found upstairs. I'm walking downstairs right now, so hold on." A longer pause, as Engels could hear doors being opened, and then shut. Three minutes later, Dale said, "Sorry, Brad, but only the cat is home."

"Well, it was worth a shot," Engels said as nonchalantly as he could. "She's probably out having lunch or working the case she's on. Hopefully, our network issues get resolved soon. Thanks for your time, Dale."

"Always happy to help out, Brad! I'll keep an eye out, and if I see anything, I'll let you know. Talk to you soon!" With that, Dale ended the call, and Engels hung up.

The kids were safe. But where was Lindstrom? No cell phone trace, no car trace, and she wasn't at home. If the house had been ransacked, Dale would have said so. He grabbed the phone and dialed Carol again.

"Yes, chief?"

"I want you to send a cruiser to Sanford Hospital. No lights, no sirens, keep it quiet and discreet. Communication between you and the officers in the car should be closed and secure. I want them to search the parking lots, the parking garage, the surrounding streets, the adjacent clinics, anywhere in a two-block radius of Sanford, looking for Lindstrom's car. Let me know what they find."

Engels hung up the phone, and then picked it up, dialing Tisdale's number. After two rings, the line picked up.

"Chief," Tisdale said with more cheer in his voice than he had had the previous day. "What's up?"

"When was the last time you saw or spoke to Tish?", Engels asked.

"Well, I saw her yesterday after we came back from checking out Veronica's old apartment. But I got a text from her this morning."

"What?" Engels was surprised. "When was that?"

"Um, the time stamp says 7:04am. Why? Didn't she send it to you?"

"Obviously not." Engels hadn't meant to snap back at Tisdale, but recovered by asking, "What does the text say?"

"It says, 'You've done good work on the case. I found something in the files, and I'll let you know if you can help.' That's it."

Engels was silent. This wasn't right, not one bit.

"Chief, what is it? What's going on?"

"Get to the station, now. I'll explain when you get here." Engels hung up the phone. He glanced out the window and picked up the phone one more time. He wasn't looking forward to this call.

Two rings later, and a familiar female voice came on the line.

"How did I know that a brief trip to the station would mean you were going to ditch your wife on a beautiful Saturday?" Diane sounded both upset and weary, as if she was mad, yet resigned to the fact that, being married to the Chief of Police, it was going to happen.

"Honey, I can't come home yet. I think Tish has been kidnapped."

414

THIRTY-THREE

Lindstrom sat in the bed, observing Edward Kirkham. He was dressed in white from head to toe. Even his shoes were white. With the walls, floor, and ceiling the same white color, and the brightness of the light reflecting off the white, it gave the illusion that Edward's head was simply floating in place. It was a stunning visual, both in the ridiculousness of it, as well as in the madness of it. Lindstrom's mind was a jumbled mess. She had so many questions, she didn't know where to start. She also realized that a swell of emotions was bubbling inside of her. She was simultaneously scared, angry, happy, paranoid, worried, and euphoric, somehow, all at once.

"Detective," Edward Kirkham said, "I know what you are going through." He moved a few inches forward. "When I first came up with the idea behind Visceral, I laid out my plans very, very carefully. I left nothing to chance. So many hours, so many days, so much thought and planning went into my grand design. Believe it or not, I even endured all of stage one, as you are doing now, to make sure that I understood every nuance of stage one, so that every stage thereafter would proceed smoothly and efficiently."

Lindstrom looked at the head of Edward Kirkham. Her eyes moved up and down where his body should be, but she couldn't make out any details of his clothing, or even see his hands. She surmised that he must be wearing gloves, which, considering the circumstances, must also be white. She tried to focus, to collect her thoughts, but her emotions were making it difficult. Her mind kept drifting back to the dream, of her and her family enjoying a family vacation at a waterpark. She was suddenly gripped by a very real panic, a panic that all mothers have experienced at least once in their lives.

I'M NEVER GOING TO SEE MY FAMILY AGAIN. The thought exploded in her mind. Her brain, which only a few seconds ago was a jumbled mess, immediately became laser-focused on that singular sentence. Her emotions, which had been fluctuating erratically, melted away, until only one remained. Fear. The unbridled fear of losing everything she held so dear in her life.

However, as quickly as the overwhelming terror had gripped her mind, she slammed her eyes shut and forced the thoughts from her. NO, I WILL SEE MY FAMILY AGAIN! KEEP IT TOGETHER! THINK, FOLLOW HIS RULES, LOOK FOR AN ADVANTAGE! She kept her eyes shut tight, so tight that stars started to shoot through the blackness.

"Detective, is everything alright?"

Edward Kirkham's voice, with its old-school inflections meant to disarm and reassure, it was like listening to an older, male version of his daughter, Veronica. The conversations Lindstrom had previously had with Veronica came flooding back to her, with continually changing of moods and tones to fit the situation.

"All the white and bright," Lindstrom lied, "it's a little overwhelming." There were a few seconds of silence, and she assumed Edward Kirkham was trying to decide whether she was lying.

"I do apologize, but it is necessary. Stage one requires a sense of initial disorientation. Now, I am sure that you have a multitude of questions. I will be happy to answer your questions. However, please remember my rules. As I stated earlier, manners must be used at all times, as well as quid pro quo. I will answer a question, but you must answer one of mine. As long as the rules are followed, there won't be any problems between us. Do you agree?"

Lindstrom didn't know what Edward Kirkham was playing at, but she really had no choice. She had no idea of how long she had been unconscious, where she was, or how she was going to get out of this mess. As Mark's father had always been fond of saying, she would have to "play it by ear" and take this whole situation one step at a time.

Lindstrom opened her eyes, hoping that the terror had subsided. She

416

looked at Edward Kirkham and said, "I agree."

"Excellent! As I asked the first question of you, I will let you ask the first question of me."

Lindstrom narrowed her eyes and looked at Edward Kirkham's face. She was trying to process what she had been through, and, more importantly, what she was going through. What was his endgame? Her mind was racing, multiple images and threads from the past flashing inside her brain. It was like a poorly edited movie, bits and pieces in no logical order, being rewound and fast-forwarded all at once.

Why was Edward Kirkham going through such an elaborate ruse? If he wanted her dead, why go through this trouble? Lindstrom looked over Edward Kirkham's facial features, and then surveyed the rest of her surroundings. She closed her eyes, took a deep breath, and tried to access her last memory. She was in the parking garage, with Nurse Isaacson, no, it had been Veronica Kirkham, holding a rag over her mouth. Lindstrom guessed that the rag had been soaked in chloroform or ether, or something that induced unconsciousness. That still left the question of how long she had been knocked out.

"Oh, my dear detective," Edward Kirkham said in a lower tone, "certainly you have at least one question for me."

Lindstrom allowed her gaze to focus back on Edward Kirkham, and then she said, "Sorry. Everything is distorted." She shut her eyes again, took a breath, opened her eyes again, and continued. "I'm still trying to collect my thoughts." She paused for a moment, then said, "While I appreciate you allowing me the next question, I will defer back to you."

A small grin appeared on Edward Kirkham's face, and he replied by saying, "Very well. Tell me, what has been the most difficult part of raising three children as a single parent?"

Lindstrom's eyes grew wide. She was expecting to be questioned about the case, about how much the police knew, but not about her personal life.

"Um, well, I, uh," Lindstrom stammered, trying to put into words a reasonable answer. She locked eyes with Edward Kirkham, who merely stood there, not averting his eyes from her. She began to sense that Edward Kirkham already knew the answer, and that he was simply testing her. If she was going to get out of this, she needed to be truthful.

"I'd say that the most difficult part was managing and budgeting the finances of raising three children. Things were difficult after my ex-husband went to prison, then I married Mark, and things started to turn around. Obviously, after his medical issue, things have been tight, but I've tried my best to raise three happy and healthy children."

"Tried?" Edward Kirkham's face went from a grin to a look of shock. "I would say that you have succeeded! A seventeen-year old, graduating early and going into the Air Force. A soon to be sixteen-year-old that has shown a proclivity for the arts. And a soon to be nine-year-old that has a wonderful role model in his mother to look up to. Forgive me for saying this, but I don't think you have given yourself enough credit. That, my dear detective, is downright shameful on your part."

Lindstrom was stunned that Edward Kirkham knew this, but the amazement quickly faded. He had simply recited what anyone that knew Lindstrom could have found out. As Lindstrom looked at Edward Kirkham, she noticed that his attention had changed, and he was now looking past her. He took a few steps forward, examining something either next to or behind her. Lindstrom tried to turn her head, but the restraints made it virtually impossible to move. She took the brief lull to try to assess her situation.

This man, for whatever reason, had a hidden agenda. Lindstrom wasn't sure what that agenda was, but, considering his question, she figured it was subterfuge, a way for him to keep her off-balance, to discover what he wanted to know without giving away any of his own secrets. She guessed that Edward Kirkham had studied her in some form, and he knew more than he was letting on. Her response to the question was his way of determining whether she could be trusted to provide honest answers. While her mind was still running in multiple directions, she decided that any questions regarding her current situation or his plans for her were off the table. If she asked the wrong questions of him, or she gave the wrong answers to him, the last thing Lindstrom wanted was to put Edward Kirkham in a no-win scenario. She decided to keep things light, for the moment at least.

"Might I ask what you are looking at," Lindstrom inquired.

"Forgive me, but I was merely looking at your bio-monitor, checking your vitals, and making sure the drugs currently in your system aren't doing any kind of damage."

"Drugs?" Lindstrom looked down at her body, which was covered by the blanket. She tried to move her arms, but the restraints prevented it.

She tried to flex her muscles, to try and determine if she could feel a needle in her skin, or even a piece of tape on her skin that was holding an IV in place. If she was being fed drugs by an IV, she couldn't tell.

"Yes, drugs. A special medicinal mixture of my own design. A cocktail, if you will. Don't think about that right now, though. We can discuss that soon enough." Edward Kirkham must have been pleased with what he had seen, as he stepped back and looked at Lindstrom again. "Now, do you have a question for me?"

"Why are you doing this to me?"

"Because I can, my dear detective, and because it is necessary, as you will soon discover." Lindstrom opened her mouth, but Edward Kirkham immediately shot up his left hand, with the index finger pointed up. "Before you respond in anger, remember the rules. Manners, at all time. My next question might seem a bit uncouth, so I will apologize. However, given the circumstances surrounding your ex-husband, the biological father of Trevor and Bree, do you ever have any regrets about your life choices regarding your ex-husband?"

Lindstrom knew what he was insinuating, and a flash of anger surged through her. She fixed him with an intense gaze and said, "If you're asking me if I wished I had never met him and didn't have two children with him, the answer is that I love my children, and don't ever question that again." She kept her eyes staring at Edward Kirkham. It was lucky that she was restrained, otherwise she would have slapped him for even suggesting such a thing.

Edward Kirkham nodded slightly and said, "Again, let me apologize for the question. It is not something that I am happy to ask, but I needed to know. Let us continue, then. What is your next question?"

Lindstrom briefly considered what she had learned about R.T.A., Visceral Medical, First Federated United Trust, Supporting Broken Families Dot Org, hell, pretty much everything regarding the cases. She didn't know how long she had been out since the parking garage at the hospital, but she needed to speed things up.

"Why did you kidnap Nathan Devlin?"

Edward Kirkham bowed his head slightly, a disappointed look coming across his face. "That, detective, was a mistake. A mistake that I have been working to rectify since we discovered it. Mr. Devlin's circumstance should have been properly vetted, and, upon understanding his current situation, he should have been removed as a candidate for Visceral. Unfortunately, an over-anxious underling decided to take it upon himself to mount an unauthorized extraction." Kirkham's gaze wandered from Lindstrom's eyes, to the floor, until finally coming to rest back on her eyes. The look on his face betrayed someone that wanted to be in control yet was ashamed of the current circumstances. Kirkham continued his explanation.

"That extraction was the first domino to fall, which, inevitably, ended with our current situation. You are now here, and I am left to provide the answers, so that everyone involved can move on."

Lindstrom was trying to make sense of what Edward Kirkham had said. A mistake? Properly vetted? A candidate for Visceral? An extraction? One answer in this case kept leading to more questions. She was about to ask for some kind of clarification, but then she remembered "the rules". She simply said, "It's your turn, Mr. Kirkham."

The disappointment on Edward Kirkham's face changed back to a sly grin. "I sense that your questions may be more interesting, so I shall defer back to you. Please, go ahead and ask me another question."

"Why did you have Olivia Sherman killed?"

The question seemed to hit Edward Kirkham, and his face briefly showed genuine anger. However, as quickly as it had appeared, the anger was gone. His eyes narrowed a bit, and he replied, "Detective, I can appreciate that you don't have a clear view of what I am trying to achieve. However, going forward, I highly recommend that you phrase your questions more carefully." Edward Kirkham closed his eyes, took in a deep breath, exhaled, opened his eyes again, and continued.

"Ms. Sherman's death was a result of the over-anxious underling trying to clean up a mess of his own doing. In fairness to you, so that we can move forward, the over-anxious underling in question was Charles Utecht."

Lindstrom's eyes opened a little bit as she tried to fit this new piece of information into what she already knew. Charles Utecht, with the aid of Olivia Sherman and Ronald Vance, had been successful in kidnapping Nathan Devlin. However, Sherman had second thoughts, which resulted in Utecht killing her and trying to make it look like some kind of satanic ritual. Did Utecht then abandon Vance, or did Vance, seeing no way out, kill himself?

420

"Go ahead, detective," Edward Kirkham said, "you may continue with your questions." As he said this, he walked toward the back of the room and retrieved what looked to be an office chair. It was on wheels and, since it was the same white as the walls and Edward Kirkham's clothes, Lindstrom would never have guessed it was there. He positioned the chair where he had previously stood and sat down carefully. Lindstrom couldn't guess at the man's age, but she surmised that the experiences of the past weeks had weighed on him. Considering how he had responded to her last question, she knew that she would need to be careful going forward. She needed to keep him off-balance, but, if she pushed him too hard, well, she didn't want to think about what might happen to her.

"I am sorry if I took the wrong tone with my previous question," Lindstrom began, "but I have spent the last ten days trying to solve a case that began with one dead woman. Now, here I am, ten days later, strapped to a bed, being fed drugs for some reason, God only knows where I am. This is being done by a man that may or may not have sanctioned criminal acts, but this man insists I ask my questions politely." She looked at Edward Kirkham, and the expression on his face didn't change, so she continued. "Very well, I will do my best, but I can't make any promises. If you didn't authorize Nathan Devlin's kidnapping, who did?"

"No one authorized Nathan Devlin's extraction. Charles Utecht acted on his own, enlisting Sherman and Vance to assist him in what they thought was an approved extraction."

The voice came from nowhere and everywhere, and the shock of hearing a new voice in the room frightened Lindstrom. Her eyes moved around, trying to determine who had spoken, but only Edward Kirkham was in her field of vision. For his part, Edward Kirkham seemed mildly upset that the voice had interrupted.

"I thought we agreed that you would stay out of this." Lindstrom looked at Edward Kirkham, who seemed to be talking to no one.

"We don't have time for this," the voice spoke again.

Instead of trying to figure out where the voice was coming from, Lindstrom focused on the voice. There was a kind of distortion to it, but the pattern seemed familiar. As always, she had a hunch, and decided to go with it.

"Veronica, is that you?" Lindstrom wondered aloud, while looking at Edward Kirkham. "I was hoping to get the chance to chat with you about a few things."

"Enough of this, both of you!" Edward Kirkham conveyed an annoyed look on his face, and he cleared his throat as a means to calm himself. "Detective, I have a question for you. Have you decided on how you are planning to spend your fifty-two thousand dollars that you received from R.T.A.?"

Lindstrom looked at Edward Kirkham, with her face twisting into one of annoyance. She thought to herself, why is it this old man is obsessed with asking me questions about my family and personal life?

"I hadn't really had the time to map out a financial plan," Lindstrom began, looking at Edward Kirkham with defiance in her eyes, "but, considering that R.T.A. and Visceral are up to their necks in illegal activity, I will be returning your illicit bribe money to you."

The look on Edward Kirkham's face didn't change. He sat in his chair for a few moments, looking at Lindstrom. He then closed his eyes, shook his softly, while a quiet "tsk-tsk" came from his lips.

"You disappoint me, detective. Then again, maybe it's because you are trying to solve a puzzle without knowing what the finished picture should look like."

Edward Kirkham opened his eyes and looked at Lindstrom with an icy calm that unnerved her in a way that she didn't think was possible. At that moment, Lindstrom realized that there was much more going on with Edward Kirkham than she knew. She had an eerie feeling that she wasn't going to like the answers. Suddenly, she didn't know which she wanted more, to put Edward Kirkham behind bars, or to hold her children again.

THIRTY-FOUR

Engels stood at the window in his office, looking out at the houses, businesses, traffic, and people that were in view. He had been involved in law enforcement since he graduated from high school, beginning with the University of Pennsylvania. From there, he moved through various other academic programs, before he finally became a police officer in Kansas City, Missouri. Engels career continued moving up the ranks in various departments and several different cities across the country, until he finally found, what he considered, the best job as Chief of Detectives in Sioux Falls, South Dakota. Now, all these years later, he was also the Chief of Police. Considering all of the cases he had worked on or been involved with over the course of his career, a layperson would have assumed that nothing would rattle Engels anymore. Shootings, hostage situations, drug deals, traffic accidents, domestic violence, rapes, murders, Amber Alerts, civil unrest, and so many more, the list could go on.

Engels had quietly told himself, on more than one occasion, *"never say you've seen it all"*, because, inevitably, something would happen that was a first. Now, here it was, another first. One of his detectives had been kidnapped while up to her neck in a convoluted murder-kidnapping case that, more than likely, involved multiple linked companies.

Officer Tisdale was standing next to him, not sure what to say or do. He had arrived at the station twenty minutes after he hung up with Engels. He had recounted to Engels the events of the previous day with Lindstrom. Beginning with the car ride, to what had happened at Veronica's apartment, to when they had returned to the station, and how Lindstrom had told him she was going to take a nap upstairs in one of the police station's storage closets.

Tisdale had gone to his desk to try to work, but he was still upset about being used by Veronica. Instead, he had decided to get out of the police station, taking a few hours of vacation, and had headed out to try to clear his mind and decide what to do next. A long workout at the gym, a good meal at Goldie's, and an excellent night's sleep had helped his spirits. The text from Lindstrom that morning had made him feel good. Now, it was entirely possible that someone else had sent him that text.

Engels had brought Tisdale up to speed about what he knew of Lindstrom's activities, and what he had done to try and locate her. After that, Engels had stood up from his desk chair and gone to the window. Tisdale followed suit, and the quiet was only interrupted by the sounds of the two men breathing and any noise coming from the outside.

"Chief," Tisdale said, finally breaking the silence between them. Engels glanced at him out of the corner of his eye. "What's the next move?"

"I have Carol pulling the logs from the tracer in Lindstrom's car. Scott is pulling up Lindstrom's cell phone data. If we can piece together where she was, we can get a timeframe and see what she was working on."

Silence descended again. Engels continued to stand at the window, looking outside. Tisdale, on the other hand, was feeling useless. He felt his muscles twitch, and he wasn't sure what his next course of action should be. He became a police officer to help, to make a difference. Now, here he was, a feeling of impotence overtaking him. His mind was spinning with scenarios. What-ifs, with what could have happened, no, with what should have happened, if he had been here, at the station. He had been selfish, thinking that a workout, a meal, and sleep would help wash the guilt and uselessness away.

"Don't do it, Tisdale."

Tisdale looked at Engels. "What are you talking about?"

"I have been where you are standing right now, thinking what you are thinking. This is not your fault. Whatever we are up against, whoever we are up against, it doesn't matter. Situations go bad, shit goes sideways, it starts raining when the forecast said it was going to be sunny all day." Engels turned away from the window, faced Tisdale, and put a hand on his shoulder. "Lindstrom is a good cop. You are a good cop. Until we know more, we aren't going to assume anything. That goes double and triple for playing out useless revisionist history. Understood?"

Tisdale sighed, looked back out the window, and replied, "I guess."

Engels' face changed. Instead of appearing like a mentor that was trying to help a student understand, Engels features had morphed into a Chief of Police, a direct superior that didn't appreciate the negative attitude that a subordinate had given.

"Tisdale, I asked if you understood!"

Tisdale realized that his nonchalant, melancholy answer had pissed off Engels. He straightened up, turned, and looked his boss directly in the eye.

"Loud and clear, chief," Tisdale said. His face portrayed one of someone that knew he had messed up, was apologetic, and was ready to make amends. Engels, for his part, knew he had gotten through to Tisdale, giving him a smile.

The phone on Engels' desk rang, and he grabbed the receiver before it rang a second time.

"Engels."

"It's Carol."

"Hold on, I'm putting you on speaker." Engels pressed a button on the phone's base, and then put the receiver back. "Okay Carol, go ahead. What do you have?"

"Chief," Carol began, "I, well, I'm not really sure what to make of this."

Engels was leaning over his desk, while Tisdale took up a position standing between the two chairs in front of the desk.

"Carol, start at the beginning."

"I pulled the tracer logs for Lindstrom's car for the past two weeks. Everything is pretty much as it should be, with her car being in the correct locations. Home, the police station, the crime scene, Sanford Hospital, and so on. Then, I get to yesterday's log, and things after two in the afternoon are weird."

"Define weird," Tisdale said, now sitting down in a chair that he pulled closer to the desk.

"The tracer log shows her vehicle leaving the police station, but then it goes blank after two minutes. The log doesn't record another tracer until almost ninety minutes later. At that point, her vehicle appears at the corner of 12th and Kiwanis.   From there, her vehicle is driving through construction and side streets, and finally gets to Sanford Hospital, where it stays for several hours. The vehicle leaves the hospital after six-thirty, comes back to the station for a couple of hours, and then, as the vehicle leaves the station, the log goes blank again. I can't explain it. I've never seen this happen before."

"Carol," Engels spoke aloud, "bring me the tracer logs, starting at ten p.m. on Thursday night to the last log entry."

"Okay," Carol replied, and the line went dead.

Engels straightened and stretched his back. "Think back, Tisdale. Lindstrom didn't say one thing or give you one clue what her plan of action was going to be?"

"Nothing, Chief. We got back from checking out Veronica's old apartment, and she said she was going to grab some lunch and a nap, not necessarily in that order."

Before Engels could speak, Scott knocked on the door and walked in.

"Chief, I had some problems getting the cell phone records for Lindstrom's cell phone," Scott began to explain, "but I think it's cleared up now. I should have everything within the hour."

"Good," Engels said. "In the meantime, have a seat. Carol is bringing us the tracer logs on Lindstrom's car. Maybe you can make sense of them."

"I'll do what I can," Scott replied.

Silence again, with Tisdale going over details of the case in his mind, Engels leaning against his desk while looking out the window, and Scott sitting down in the empty chair. While it might appear that Scott was uncomfortable, he was in his preferred element. He wasn't good at maintaining small talk and was happy with the deafening silence of Engels' office. A few minutes had passed when Carol knocked on the door to the office and walked in.

"Here you go, Chief," Carol said, looking upset as she laid the four pages of logs on Engels' desk.

"Are you alright, Carol?", Tisdale inquired.

"I'm just worried about Tish," came Carol's reply.

"We all are," Engels said, "but let's focus on what we can do to find her." He looked down at the papers, and asked Carol, "Okay, what am I looking at here?"

Pointing at a line of letters and numbers on the first page, Carol began by saying, "This sequence designates the ID for Lindstrom's car. This sequence represents the GPS coordinates of the vehicle, and this sequence is a date and time stamp."

"So, you're able to track police vehicles at all times?", Tisdale asked.

"To an extent, yes," Carol answered. "However, we don't have the system turned on to every car all hours of the day and night."

"What do you mean," Tisdale continued his inquiry.

"Have you ever spent a good chunk of time in dispatch?"

Tisdale looked embarrassed. "I've walked through dispatch, but I can't say that I've stopped and watched. I always thought I'd be in the way."

"Don't worry about it," Engels said. "Dispatchers, like Carol here, are so focused on their duties that they wouldn't notice you. Think of dispatchers as air traffic controllers, trying to safely coordinate the activities of a large amount of people and machinery over an entire city."

Carol smiled. "I never thought of it like that, but the Chief is right. So, if you've walked through dispatch, you've seen the large computer screen that has a satellite map of the city. On the map are various moving icons which represent police cars, fire trucks, SWAT vehicles, and so on. Now, imagine if every icon was represented for every vehicle that we have, not only for the ones in use. The map would be too busy to read. We would have to first decipher who is on duty and who isn't."

Tisdale thought about what Carol had said, and she was right. He remembered thinking that he couldn't make any sense of the activity on the giant screen. The various alphanumeric icons in motion on the map of the city had resembled some massive game of Pacman.

"How do you determine when a vehicle is active and when it is off-duty?" The question from Scott surprised everyone, as he had quietly made his way around the desk and had been surveying the pages.

"Our system has a few different ways to track this. For a standard police cruiser, when the vehicle leaves the garage, an officer can either enter a code at the barrier gate, or, if that system is down, there are underground cables called vehicle detection loops, which automatically catalog vehicle activity into and out of the police garage and parking lot. In the case of a civilian car, like Chief Engels' car, where the transponder had to be built in, the Chief can either enter a logout code from any police computer, or he can enter that code on a small keypad that is mounted discreetly inside the car."

"But," Scott continued, "does that turn off the transponder?"

"Oh no. The transponder is always on unless something catastrophic happens to the unit itself."

Scott continued to look at the pages that Carol had laid out, moving closer, analyzing the data. Engels and Tisdale had moved to the sides of the desk, letting Scott take over the examination of the information that Carol offering.

Scott pointed to the last page and asked, "So, am I correct in assuming you have tried to locate Lindstrom's car via the transponder?"

"Yes. I pinged the unit for activation and location information. Lindstrom has not entered a log out code since she returned home on Thursday night. She logged into the system after midnight on Friday morning, and the transponder has technically been active ever since. Which is why I don't understand these log entries here." Carol pointed at several different lines from Friday and Saturday. "You can see here that the transponder was working fine on Friday morning, then into the afternoon, there is no information until this point, where the transponder began recording again. Then, later, it stops recording again, starts again here, and now has stopped ever since."

Scott placed his thumb and index finger on a section of numbers. He did this to highlight the timeframe that the transponder wasn't working.

"So, the transponder wasn't working, because it didn't record locations and times, but it was working because it was sending information?"

Carol looked at Scott. "Exactly. I have never seen anything like this before."

Before Scott could say anything, his cell phone rang. He grabbed it and answered the call. "This is Scott." He listened to the person on the other end of the call while looking over the transponder information. "Are you sure about that?" Scott looked up and turned toward Engels. Another thirty seconds passed, and Scott asked, "I can guess the answer, but you can't trace it, right?" A pause, and Scott finished the conversation with, "Okay, thanks anyway." Scott ended the call and put away his cell phone.

"Whoever is behind this, he or she or they are good," Scott said. "That was a tech from Lindstrom's and Tisdale's cell phone provider."

"What?" Tisdale was confused.

"Relax. Both of you have the same cell phone provider. Anyway, the text that was sent to Tisdale's phone this morning was not sent from Lindstrom's phone. Lindstrom's phone is not active or on the network. It has either been turned off, had the battery removed, or been destroyed. The last GPS location for the phone was at Sanford, last night, after nine-thirty but before ten."

"Okay," Engels said, "that gives us her last known location. But what about the text Tisdale received this morning?"

"It was sent from a free SMS text website," Scott explained. "Someone registered Lindstrom's cell phone number and used the website to send Tisdale a text. It looks like it's coming from Lindstrom's phone on Tisdale's end."

"Can we petition the owners of the website for the information," Tisdale asked.

Scott shook his head. "The cell phone tech said the text was sent from a site called FreeTxt4Free, which is owned by an offshore banking subsidiary. It would take weeks, maybe even months, to file all of the necessary paperwork to get a look at their files and to track who registered Lindstrom's number, and which ISP was used, and where the computer was located, and on and on." Tisdale was about to speak, when Scott put up a hand. "And before you ask, even if the person had to pay to register Lindstrom's number, the person could have easily used a preloaded bank gift card or prepaid debit or credit card."

Tisdale wasn't ready to accept defeat. "That doesn't mean we shouldn't try."

Engels shook his head. "Time is of the essence. By the time we jumped through every hoop, this case will have gone cold. Let's focus on what we have control over."

"Like what?" Tisdale was starting to look visibly upset.

"We need to focus on you," Scott said, looking directly at Tisdale. Engels and Carol both looked at each other, then at Scott, and then at Tisdale.

"Scott," Engels cautioned, "I don't know where you're going here, but choose your next words very carefully."

Realizing that his words had come out wrong, Scott's face suddenly flushed red with embarrassment. "I'm sorry, it's not exactly what I meant." Scott looked from Tisdale to Engels and back. "What I meant to say was, I understand that you were in a relationship with the female suspect in this case, correct?"

Now it was Tisdale's turn to flush red with embarrassment. "Yes, but what does that,"

Scott cut him off. "Do you have your department issued tablet with you?"

"It's in my backpack at Lindstrom's desk. Why?"

"Wait here!" Scott raced out of Engels' office, leaving Carol, Engels, and Tisdale to exchange confused looks at each other. Two minutes later, Scott was back with the tablet and a USB cord. "Chief, may I use your computer?"

"Go ahead," Engels said. He started to make his way to the keyboard to log in, but Scott had already sat down, connected the tablet to the computer via the USB cord, and entered in a set of login commands.

"Would you mind explaining...", Engels started to ask.

"It's nothing nefarious, Chief," Scott said. "Since I also help with the station's computer systems, I have a separate log in that allows me to access any computer. I'm not looking at anything on your computer, I am simply using your computer to view the tablet's usage." Scott's fingers rained over the keyboard, typing fast and effortlessly, all while scanning lines of code that the other three people had no idea how to read. A few minutes passed with no words being exchanged, with Engels, Carol, and Tisdale not wanting to break Scott's concentration. Suddenly, Scott stopped typing, and he leaned in, reading and re-reading several lines of code. Sighing, he sat back and looked at the others.

"Chief," Scott said quietly, "we have a problem. To put it simply, the police station's computer network has been hacked."

Engels eyed Scott with a mixture of trepidation and doubt. "Scott, I have the utmost respect for your computer abilities. I also know that networks and systems get attacked every day. So, let me be clear. Are you sure about this?"

"Absolutely, Chief," came Scott's immediate reply. As Scott began to explain, he used the keyboard and his fingers to highlight different portions of the computer's screen. "This code here isn't native to the tablet. This code was modified to allow for remote viewing. This shows that a monitoring program was installed onto Tisdale's tablet, and then was uploaded once the tablet connected to our network. But this, this is what worries me. With high-speed internet and today's computers and tablets, tech support is a lot easier. If your computer is on the fritz, you can use an online chat with a support tech, and they can log into your computer and attempt to fix the problem, without you ever having to leave the house."

"You mean," Carol asked, "I could be at home with my computer, and someone in California or Japan or wherever can get into my computer and poke around?"

"Yes," Scott explained, "but, for it to be legal and authorized, you would have to download and install a program that allows a secure connection. Everything is recorded, and, once you close the program, the connection is terminated. Even if you open the program, unless there is someone ready to connect on the other end, it won't do anything. Whoever this woman is that got a hold of Tisdale's tablet, she not only uploaded a monitoring program, but it looks like she cloned his tablet, too. Wherever she is, she can access our network, our files, anything and everything. And, because it looks like Tisdale's tablet from our side, it doesn't raise any red flags as far as an attack on our systems."

"What if I was logged in with my tablet," Tisdale inquired, "and Veronica or whoever did this was also logged in remotely? Wouldn't the system recognize that two of the same computers were logged in simultaneously?"

Scott thought about it, then replied. "I really don't know. I would have to really look into the coding and security software features we have installed. Assuming that specific scenario has actually happened, and we didn't get any kind of warning, then we would have to assume that we have a loophole to close. I would venture a guess that Veronica made sure to stay out of the system while you were logged in."

There was a brief silence, then Carol asked, "So, the transponder is working? Yet, somehow, this person is blocking or deleting the information as it comes in, so we can't see it?"

"Correct. I don't know how extensive the tampering has been, or if anything else has been messed with. I'm going to need some time to figure out how to get around this."

Engels was angry, but he kept his composure. "What do we do in the meantime?"

"Well, I think I can...", Scott started to speak, but was cut off by the computer screen and the tablet's screen going blank.

"What happened," Tisdale almost shouted. "What did you do?"

"I didn't do anything!" Scott exclaimed, furiously typing on the keyboard. Yet, nothing happened. He stopped typing after a minute, trying to figure out what happened, and trying to decide what to do about it.

Suddenly, on the tablet's screen, the volume bar appeared. It was set at fifty percent, but it slowly moved up until it was at one hundred percent. Scott, Engels, Carol, and Tisdale all stared at the tablet's screen, not sure what to make of this development. Then, a high-pitched whistle blared over the tablet's speakers for ten seconds. The sound was piercing, forcing the four of them to plug their ears. When the sound ended, text started to appear on the tablet's screen.

DO I HAVE YOUR ATTENTION?

The four of them looked at each other, not sure what to do.

IF I HAVE YOUR ATTENTION, CHIEF ENGELS, SAY YES.

"Yes, you have my attention," Engels said.

Scott sensed that the tablet's camera and microphone were being used to see the room. He slowly started to move his hand when more text appeared.

DON'T BLOCK THE CAMERA, OR I WILL CRASH YOUR ENTIRE POLICE SYSTEM.

Scott stopped moving, frozen in place.

I HAVE NO DESIRE TO HURT DETECTIVE LINDSTROM, BUT I WILL IF YOU FORCE MY HAND.

"What do you want?" This was another first for Engels, communicating with the kidnapper of a police detective via a hacked police computer.

THE WOMAN, CAROL, CAN RETURN TO HER DUTIES.
TISDALE CAN GO HOME.
YOU AND THE TECH, SCOTT, WILL STAY SEATED IN YOUR OFFICE WHERE I CAN SEE AND HEAR YOU.
ONCE I KNOW THAT I AM NO LONGER IN DANGER OF BEING DISCOVERED, I WILL SEND YOU DETECTIVE LINDSTROM'S LOCATION. I WILL ALSO TERMINATE MY PROGRAM THAT HAS ALLOWED ME TO ACCESS YOUR NETWORK AND YOUR SYSTEMS.

432

"How do I know you're telling the truth?"

The text disappeared, and a picture of an unconscious Lindstrom, tied to a bed, appeared. Carol gasped. Just as quickly as the picture was on the screen, it was gone.

"VERONICA, IF YOU HURT ONE HAIR...", Tisdale started to shout, but more text appeared.

SHUT UP! YOU HONESTLY BELIEVE THAT VERONICA IS CAPABLE OF ANY OF THIS? I HAD HER PLAYING YOU WHILE I PLAYED HER!

"I DON'T BELIEVE YOU!" Tisdale was shouting, making the other three in the room uncomfortable. Engels put a hand on Tisdale's shoulder, in effort to calm him down. Turning to his boss, Tisdale ranted, "CHIEF, WE CAN'T LET HER GET AWAY WITH THIS!"

YOU ARE IN NO POSITION TO ARGUE, DEMAND, OR THREATEN! LET YOUR TECH BOY HAVE A LOOK AT THIS...

About thirty lines of code appeared, and Scott quickly scanned through it. He turned to Engels.

"It looks like a kill command, designed to search out and destroy very specific pieces of code and programs."

VERY GOOD.

THE WOMAN LEAVES NOW, TISDALE LEAVES NOW. NO FUSS, NO RELAYING OF HIDDEN MESSAGES. I AM WATCHING. AND TO MAKE SURE YOU APPRECIATE WHAT I CAN DO, WATCH THE COMPUTER'S SCREEN.

All eyes focused on the computer screen of Engels' desktop. The blank screen was replaced with the standard log in. A blocked-out password appeared, revealing Engels' computer's main page. A file folder opened, showing an icon that was titled BOOM.EXE. A pointer appeared over the icon, and the pointer activated the icon. Suddenly, what appeared to be a digitized nuclear explosion appeared on the screen, rendered in an older, 64-bit color scheme. Thirty seconds later, the computer's screen went blank, save for a blinking insertion point in the upper left-hand corner.

TECH BOY, HAVE I ERASED HIS COMPUTER?

Scott looked at Engels, who nodded. Scott put his hands on the keyboard and tried typing commands that should have brought up any files, a Windows desktop, anything. Nothing happened, though. Only the blinking insertion point remained on the screen, an invitation for a person to start entering command lines.

"Chief," Scott said, stunned, "your computer has been wiped clean."

Before anyone could react, more text appeared on the tablet's screen.

IMAGINE WHAT I CAN DO TO YOUR ENTIRE NETWORK. IMAGINE WHAT HAPPENS TO YOUR CITY AND ITS CITIZENS IF YOU PUSH ME.

The threat was real and clear.

DO AS YOU'RE TOLD, LEAVE ME ALONE UNTIL I AM SAFE, AND EVERYTHING WILL BE FINE.

The text remained on the screen. No one moved or spoke. A minute passed, then the text on the screen started to flash. Everyone remained frozen in place, no one wanting to be the first to move. The text continued to flash, until a new line appeared underneath it.

WHY AREN'T THEY GONE YET? COUNTDOWN TO BOOM.EXE IN: 30...29...28...27...

"Go, now," Engels said. "Carol, go back to dispatch, and not a word about this. Tisdale, go home, go to the movies, just go. No one tries to be a hero, understood?"

"Understood, Chief," Carol said, her face ashen. She nodded, turned, and walked out of the office.

"Understood," Tisdale mumbled through clenched teeth, clearly furious at this turn of events. He fell into step behind Carol.

Once Carole and Tisdale were out of the office, the countdown stopped, and the text stopped flashing.

"I'm getting a chair," Engels said, assuming he was being watched. He quickly grabbed one of the chairs from the front of his desk, set it next to Scott, and sat down.

"Looks like we're going to be here for a while," Engels said.

Scott sighed. "And I really have to use the bathroom."

THIRTY-FIVE

"First of all," Edward Kirkham began, "that money was NEITHER illicit, nor was it a bribe. Furthermore, it cannot and shall not be returned. That money is now yours. It was owed to you by your ex-husband. I have expended time and effort on my part to collect it for you, for Trevor, and for Bree. That money, including interest, belongs to you and your family." His eyes examined Lindstrom intently, as if he could read her thoughts. "You doubt me, don't you?" Lindstrom saw the right corner of his mouth rise, ever so slightly, as if a grin was starting to creep across his face. "Tell me, detective, do you know how much money your ex-husband was indebted to you?"

Lindstrom heard Kirkham say that word, "indebted". The same word that Veronica had constantly used when discussing R.T.A. She also remembered that either Engels or Tisdale, or maybe both, had asked her that very question last week.

"I honestly don't know," she said. "I stopped keeping track after Mark and I got married. If I had to hazard a guess, maybe ten thousand."

"Fifteen thousand, eight hundred, forty-three dollars and twenty-two cents."

Edward Kirkham let his words and the dollar amount hang in the air. Lindstrom wasn't sure why he was pausing for effect. Was she supposed to be impressed that he knew? Or that it was such a large amount? Or that her check was for more than triple what her ex owed?

"So? Your point being, what, exactly? It doesn't explain the last two weeks, or why I'm shackled to a hospital bed like an out-of-control patient."

Lindstrom paused, her brain suddenly confused. Did her ex still owe her money? Or was the check and letter a way of saying that the ledger, as it were, had been wiped clean? She shut her eyes tight, trying to force out the myriad thoughts in her head. FOCUS, she told herself. DON'T GET CAUGHT UP IN SEMANTICS! FIGURE OUT WHAT THIS IS ABOUT AND GET THE HELL OUT OF HERE! Opening her eyes again, refocusing her attention on her captor, she continued.

"Look, there's no way he had that money laying around under his mattress or in a coffee can. His parents aren't wealthy, either." Lindstrom stopped to take in a breath. "I was young, I thought I was in love, but I can't go back. For that matter, I wouldn't want to go back! I love my children, and I wouldn't trade them for anything!"

Suddenly, a thought crossed her mind. "Wait a minute. Do you know my ex? Is that it? Somehow, he got involved in your little kidnapping game, and he told you to give me that money?"

Edward Kirkham exploded in a fit of laughter. It wasn't the reaction that Lindstrom was expecting, and she immediately realized how stupid her assumption was. Once Edward Kirkham's laughter subsided, Lindstrom decided to try a different approach.

"Mr. Kirkham," she began, speaking softer than before, "I'm sorry for that outburst. It was ludicrous to think that, even if my ex-husband was involved in something, that he would have seen fit to give me even one dime of what he owes the kids and me. Honestly, though, I'm having a difficult time understanding you. Why do you continue to ask questions about my children and my ex-husband? You seem to know the answers before you ask the questions. What is it you want?"

As Lindstrom looked at Edward Kirkham, the look on his face turned from amused at her outburst to a playful, almost devilish grin.

"My dear detective, forgive me, but I feel like you are Dorothy, and I'm the wizard, allowing you to peek behind the curtain."

A cryptic response, that was for certain, and it irritated Lindstrom that he was playing these damn games. CUT THE CRAP, SKIP THE GAMES, AND GET TO THE GODDAMN POINT, ALREADY! Her mind was screaming at Kirkham. It was like watching a James Bond movie with Mark, where the villain would monologue. It always annoyed

436

her, and now, to have it happen in real life, dear god, it was taking all of her willpower to keep her emotions in check and to play by his rules. Unfortunately, she had to continue with his back-and-forth banter. OKAY, CALM DOWN! TAKE A BREATH, FAKE SOME POLITENESS, AND KEEP THINGS GOING! Through a false veneer of pleasantness, Lindstrom spoke again.

"You ask me to play by your rules, remember my manners, and follow quid pro quo. I have answered your questions honestly, and yet you haven't truly answered one of mine."

The grin remained, and Edward Kirkham said,

"Then ask me something important, something that will shape our conversation going forward."

Lindstrom felt like she was going to explode, but she needed to keep it together. Edward Kirkham held all the cards, and knowing that his daughter, Veronica, was nearby, probably watching and listening, Lindstrom had no choice but to play along with the old man. She closed her eyes and tried to relax. She took several deep breaths. She thought about all of the different facets of the case. R.T.A., Visceral, Olivia Sherman, Ronald Vance, Charles Utecht, Veronica Kirkham, the reveal that Veronica had been in some form of a relationship with Tisdale, HealthStar Ambulatory, First Federated United Trust, Supporting Broken Families, Heidi Cole, all of the pieces were there. Suddenly, out of the blue, something came to her. It was crazy, a random thought, a germ that was now, front and center, in her thought process. She wasn't sure if it made sense, but there was only one way to find out.

With her eyes still closed, Lindstrom asked, "You are willing to answer me honestly, about anything, regardless of the topic? I can ask you about R.T.A., Charles Utecht, Olivia Sherman, your daughter's involvement, anything I want? No matter the topic, no matter the subject the matter, you will give me the honest-to-God truth?"

"My dear detective, I believe you are finally catching on. No matter what the question is, yes, I will give you an honest answer."

Lindstrom slowly opened her eyes, letting her vision gradually readjust to the incessant white of the room she was trapped in. She locked onto Edward Kirkham, still sitting in his chair. He hadn't moved, not an inch. Her eyes stared into his eyes, with the stare being returned. Most of her hunches paid out. But this one? This one, she wasn't sure about. The words came out of Lindstrom's mouth, quiet and methodical.

"Where is my ex-husband?"

Engels hadn't moved from the chair in over an hour. When he had felt his leg starting to fall asleep, he had carefully shifted his weight. He hadn't eaten since breakfast with Diane, and his stomach had been growling for the last twenty minutes.

Scott was no better off. He had been moving in his chair, trying to keep his bladder from emptying all over his boss's floor. He was hungry and thirsty, and if he didn't use a bathroom soon, well, it wasn't going to be pretty.

"Chief," Scott said through barely moving lips, like a bad ventriloquist, "I don't know how much longer this can wait."

Engels had been thinking about the situation, and he was hoping he would be right.

"Can Scott have permission to use the restroom," Engels asked, leaning forward a few inches and speaking to Tisdale's table that was propped up on Engels' desk.

I'M NOT A MONSTER. GO AHEAD.
JUST REMEMBER I CAN SEE WITH EVERY CAMERA IN THE BUILDING.
MAKE IT FAST.

Before Engels could give permission, Scott jumped out of the chair and raced out of the office. That left Engels, still sitting in the chair. In the past hour, he had let his eyes wander around the room, looking out the window, at Diane's picture on the desk, or at the walls and ceiling. He had avoided looking at the tablet's camera, but, now that Scott was out of the room, Engels turned his gaze to it. He tried to imagine the person on the other end, staring back at him on a video monitor. Tisdale seemed to think it was his supposed-girlfriend, Veronica. However, Engels wasn't sure. While crime statistics dictate that a particular crime was often committed by a specific gender a certain percentage of the time, Engels made it a point to tell his officers and detectives to keep an open mind. Men could be the victim of a rape as easily as a woman could, a woman could be a cold-blooded killer as easily as a man could, and so on down the line.

DID YOU WANT TO ASK ME SOMETHING, OR ARE YOU TIRED OF LOOKING AROUND THE ROOM?

The change in text broke Engels' train of thought. He wasn't sure how to respond, or even if he should. Considering nothing about this case had ever made any sense, he decided to try and get some conversation going.

"Just wondering if my wife decided to rake the leaves in the backyard without me."

The tablet's screen went blank, and it stayed that way for more than a minute. Another minute passed, followed by another, with no more text showing up on the screen. Engels was starting to worry, when Scott returned to the office, looking incredibly relieved. He sat back down in the chair, and, after seeing no text on the screen, turned to Engels.

"Did I miss anything while I was gone," Scott inquired. Before Engels could respond, more text appeared on the tablet's screen.

AS LONG AS YOU AND TECH BOY AND TISDALE AND CAROL AND LINDSTROM FOLLOW MY INSTRUCTIONS, THE YARD WORK WILL BE WAITING FOR YOU TOMORROW.

The text remained on the screen for a minute, before disappearing.

"No, Scott," Engels said, "you didn't miss anything." Engels leaned back in the chair, put his hands behind his neck, and put his feet on his desk. With nothing else to do, he decided to close his eyes and take a nap. Scott, not sure what to do, chose to look past the desk and stare outside, hoping that everything would work out.

THIRTY-SIX

Edward Kirkham looked at Lindstrom, his head shifting in an odd way, as if he was a dog that didn't understand a command.

"Why would you think I know anything about your ex-husband's whereabouts?" The tone in his voice was odd, almost misleading. Apparently, when it came to voice patterns and expressions, it was "like father, like daughter". Kirkham had changed the inflection of his voice to be a strange mix of hurt, confusion, and playfulness.

Undaunted, Lindstrom decided it was best to ignore his question and the tone with which he had asked it. Instead, her eyes bore down on Edward Kirkham.

"Because," Lindstrom began, "it's the only thing that makes sense about your questions. Like you said, you wanted me to ask a question that would shape our conversation going forward. You have been fixated on how much my ex-husband owes me, what I plan to do with the money, how I have been able to raise three children almost single-handedly, and so on. Three of the people involved in this case, Olivia Sherman, Ronald Vance, and Nathan Devlin, owe child support. Meanwhile, a fourth person, ME, is or was owed child support. You own R.T.A., which somehow distributes child support money. And I'd wager a large chunk of that check you sent me or R.T.A. sent me that you are behind Supporting Broken Families Dot Org."

Edward Kirkham returned Lindstrom's intense gaze, and then, to Lindstrom's surprise, the look on his face turned to sadness. He sighed heavily, and the man that seemed so strong and resolute only moments ago looked defeated. His head dropped a little, his shoulders hunched forward, and he rubbed his hands on his knees.

"Detective," Edward Kirkham said softly, "you may not believe this, but I am not a bad man."

Lindstrom eyed him warily. "Kidnapping and murder?"

Edward Kirkham raised his head again, allowing his eyes to lock onto Lindstrom's. Even though his face and body seemed old, Lindstrom could tell from the fire in Edward Kirkham's eyes that he was still very much alive.

"Detective, I can understand your skepticism. However, to use a phrase most police officers know, I am trying to come clean. Please, exercise patience and restraint before you speak."

"Or else I'll end up like Olivia Sherman?"

Edward Kirkham jumped out of his seat, like he had been shot out of a cannon, pointed a finger at Lindstrom, and hissed, "DO NOT JUDGE ME BY THE ACTIONS OF OTHERS! HAD CHARLES UTECHT NOT ACTED SO RECKLESSLY BEHIND MY BACK, WE WOULD NOT BE HAVING THIS CONVERSATION, NATHAN DEVLIN WOULD HAVE ALREADY RECONCILED WITH HIS WIFE AND FAMILY, AND THREE PEOPLE WOULD STILL BE ALIVE!'

Lindstrom tried to hide her surprise, but she couldn't. She had struck a nerve with Edward Kirkham, and she was now afraid that she had crossed a line. Being the mother of three children and a police officer and detective, she was excellent at determining when someone was lying or telling the truth. The way in which Edward Kirkham had reacted, maybe it was an act, but his eyes were almost slits, penetrating Lindstrom to her very core. At that moment, she realized how truly terrifying her situation was. She was about to speak, when Edward Kirkham put a finger to his lips. Lindstrom remained silent.

Edward Kirkham took a few minutes to compose himself. He smoothed out his clothes, rubbed his temples, neck, and eyes, and then carefully sat back down in the white chair. When he was ready, which felt like an eternity to Lindstrom, he spoke again.

"Once upon a time, I was a successful doctor. One day, while attending a conference, I met a beautiful woman. When I wasn't listening to lectures on the latest advancements in medicine, I was in her arms. I begged her

441

to come with me at the end of the conference, but she couldn't. Or maybe she wouldn't. I was heartbroken, but I understood. I tried to keep in touch. Unfortunately, she responded less and less frequently. Eleven years later, I received a phone call from a lawyer. The lawyer informed me that she had died, and, while going through her belongings, had found several of the letters I had sent her. As I was the closest thing to a living survivor, the lawyer asked if I wanted to file for custody of our daughter.

"Needless to say, I was stunned! A daughter?! I was a father, and I never knew it! This woman, who I only knew for a few days, had my child, but chose not to tell me!" Edward Kirkham let out a sigh. "I don't know why she acted the way she did. She must have had her reasons. However, I refuse to judge her for it. I dropped everything so that I could meet my daughter, Veronica. I didn't know what to expect, and when I first laid eyes on her, I didn't know what to do or say."

Suddenly, Veronica's voice boomed through the room, startling Lindstrom. "Father walked into the conference room in the lawyer's office, and I ran up to him and hugged him. I then said the words that my mother had told me to say if or when I ever met my father. 'You don't know me yet, but my name is Veronica. I am your daughter. I hope you will love me as much as my mother has taught me to love you.' Father burst into tears right there."

Lindstrom wanted to interrupt but realized it would be a mistake. It was better to let this backstory continue.

Wiping a tear from the corner of his eye, Edward Kirkham continued. "With the legal paperwork filed, Veronica came to live with me. Yes, there were ups and downs, as there are in any family, but that's what made the two of us a family. Years passed, and, while Veronica was in her third year of college, she met someone. She became pregnant, yet the father refused to acknowledge his responsibility to his own child. Veronica had to fight, tooth and nail, racking up legal fees while trying to support herself and my grandson. Can you imagine? I loved Veronica's mother, and I love my daughter. On the other end of the spectrum, this man, this cretin, denied everything towards his own offspring. No sentiment, no support, nothing. Then, when little Sebastian, my grandson, was three years old..." Edward Kirkham's voice trailed off. His eyes were watery, and he struggled to fight back the emotions he was feeling.

Lindstrom could only watch, not daring to say a word.

"The details aren't important. What is important is that Veronica never once asked for my help financially. She reasoned that it was important for Sebastian's father to take responsibility and provide his fair share for Sebastian. Even after Sebastian's death, the father continued to fight Veronica, claiming she had slept around, that the paternity test had been falsified, anything he could to not only deny his role in bringing Sebastian into this world, but to drag Veronica through hell. I tried to help, to offer encouragement and assistance. I constantly reminded Veronica that I could pay her attorney fees, her court costs, the funeral expenses, anything and everything, but she refused. She constantly told me that Sebastian's father had to be held accountable, in every way, for his part. Two years after Sebastian's death, and the bastard still refused to acknowledge his son. He pulled out every legal trick, every loophole, anything that he could think of, to try and flee from his responsibility as a father." He paused, then, "Fortunately, the universe has a way of balancing itself out."

Edward Kirkham paused again, seemingly to catch his breath. No, Lindstrom thought to herself, he was pausing for effect, to let the situation sink in. The last sentence, though, stuck in Lindstrom's head. She thought back to how the case had started, with Olivia Sherman's mutilated body, and then Nathan Devlin's disappearance, and how her hunch that the two cases were connected had turned out to be true. *"Balance, it's all about balance"*, Lindstrom and Engels had said to each other.

"Even though I had a successful practice," Edward Kirkham continued, "I still found time to help out with other area clinics and hospitals. I happened to be working a graveyard shift in an emergency room when the call came in of a one car accident, and the ambulance was on its way. Lo and behold, Sebastian's father had decided to have a little too much to drink, and then drive a little too fast in a rain storm. As a bonus, he had listed himself as an organ donor on his driver's license." A strange look came over Edward Kirkham's face. Lindstrom couldn't get a read on the expression.

"I considered the situation, and I made up my mind to make sure justice was done that night. It was touch and go for about two hours, and I waited with him. Even if he would have survived, the damage that the accident had inflicted meant that his life would be irrevocably altered. When he finally opened his eyes and saw me, standing over him, the look of shock on his face was priceless. I then described his situation as succinctly as I could. *'Even if you survive, your life will never, ever be the same.'* He looked at me with disbelief and fear in his eyes. He must have realized how awful his situation was because he closed his eyes and did the honorable thing. Once he was declared dead, his viable organs were harvested and donated. The next day, I let Veronica know what had happened. His funeral was attended by only four people, not counting Veronica and myself. After that, it was relatively easy for Veronica to get everything that he had owed her. He had died with a decent amount of money stashed away, and with no other living heirs or spouse, well, actually, with no one at all, we worked everything out with the lawyers and the judge. It was after that experience that Veronica started working with other men and women that were in desperate need of help because of deadbeat and delinquent partners. By dying, Sebastian's father was able to not only help my daughter, but he also helped eight total strangers with the gift of his organs."

Edward Kirkham stopped speaking, turning his head upward toward the ceiling. He appeared to be daydreaming. Lindstrom watched him, fascinated by the story she had been told. Of course, that's what it was. A story. It could be fact, it could be fiction, maybe it was a mixture of both. Either way, if his goal was to "come clean" to Lindstrom, so what? Her job was to catch the bad guys, not to prosecute them or to determine their prison sentences.

The pause continued to fill the white room, with Lindstrom growing wary with each passing moment. Edward Kirkham had displayed his range of emotion, with his outburst of anger frightening her. Should she speak? Ask a question? Offer some form of condolence to both of the Kirkhams for the death of Sebastian? As she struggled with her next action, Kirkham quietly rose from his chair. Without looking at Lindstrom, he walked past the head of her bed, standing there for minute or so. From the edge of her field of vision, she could see his arms moving. He must be doing something with the medical equipment that was attached to her. When he was finished, he walked back to his chair. He sat down again, in the same position that he had been in, and looked back to the ceiling. A few more minutes passed before he spoke again.

"Would you like to know some fun facts, detective?" He asked the question whimsically, while still staring at the ceiling. "Did you know that, at any given moment, there are more than one hundred and twenty thousand men, women, and children on the national transplant waiting list? Or that every ten minutes another person is added to that list? Or that twenty-two people die each day while waiting for a transplant?" He paused, eyes fixed on the ceiling, almost like he was looking through the ceiling, towards the sky outside. "Yes, the universe definitely balanced itself by putting Sebastian's father on that road that night." The words came out soft, dreamily, as if he was suffering from some form of hallucination, speaking to things that weren't there.

He paused again, only this time, Edward Kirkham got up and walked to a table or a wall on the opposite side of the room. Lindstrom couldn't tell, because the effect of white on white still made it difficult for her to discern any kind of details in the room they were in.

As Edward Kirkham walked, he said, "I'm sorry, detective. I tend to get long-winded at times, and I have a lot of things up here," he tapped a finger to his temple, "that I enjoy talking about." He stopped, clasped something in his hand, and then appeared to take a drink from a glass. As he drank, Lindstrom was growing more and more perplexed. Was he stalling, and, if so, why? She was basically incapacitated, yet, by his own admission, he kept prattling on and on. His story, involving his daughter and grandson and their experience with a deadbeat parent, was sad and touching, but wasn't any better or worse than any story she had heard from other single parents. Edward Kirkham finished his drink, and, as he walked back to his chair, he asked Lindstrom a question.

"Tell me, detective, do you know how much child support is currently unpaid in this country?"

Lindstrom was frustrated with this supposed "quid pro quo" dialogue, but she had to continue to engage Edward Kirkham. She thought about the question.

"I don't know, but if I had to guess, several million dollars, based on the number of single parents and the number of children born every year. For a round number, I'll say fifteen or twenty million."

The right corner of his mouth and his right eyebrow both curved up, making the expression on his face look like one of a teacher that had been given an incorrect answer.

"Try fifty-three billion." Edward Kirkham paused, and then repeated it louder, emphasizing every syllable. "Fifty-three billion dollars! It boggles the mind, does it not, detective? And that lack of financial support has repercussions throughout social and welfare services, education, health care, law enforcement, and the judicial system! Think about it, if even HALF of the delinquent fathers AND mothers in this country would simply foot their share of the bill for the life and lives that they helped bring into this world, think about all of the good that could come from it!"

Lindstrom thought about the times that she had to skimp on things like food, clothes, school supplies, or activities, all because she didn't have the financial resources. True, there were government programs to help single parents, like her, that were in need. However, she always felt like her situation wasn't as bad as other single parents she had seen, or come in contact with, or read about. Maybe it was pride, or maybe it was some antiquated notion that she was trying to prove to her worthless ex-husband that she could make it and raise two wonderful children without anyone's help. Of course, Mark's predicament had complicated matters. All things considered, though, being a detective with a deadbeat ex-husband, a comatose husband, and three children, Lindstrom figured she had done pretty damn well for her family.

Lindstrom shook her head slightly, as if trying to shoo away a bothersome fly. Edward Kirkham was looking at her, and as she looked back at him, her frustration was reaching its flashpoint. For all of the rules he had laid out about a conversation and quid pro quo, she was no closer to understanding why she was tied to a bed, what Edward Kirkham was up to, or why he was doing this. Lindstrom was fed up, and she couldn't contain her emotions any longer.

"Okay, I get it," Lindstrom snapped, her voice so loud that it reverberated around the room. "You have a sad story about your daughter and your grandson and a lot of interesting facts and statistics about child support and organ donors. But I fail to see how this is relevant to what…"

The words stopped coming. She looked at Edward Kirkham, who was simply sitting there, in his chair, one leg crossed over the other, his hands resting on the bent knee. He was looking at her with those icy eyes, but his face showed no emotion. Her mind began to race. Everything about the cases, the way some pieces didn't seem to fit, things started to come together. But then, like running into a brick wall, her thoughts stopped.

"Yes, detective?" Edward Kirkham asked the question, almost wistfully. "Oh my, I am sorry! I have rambled on long enough." Edward Kirkham once again stood up from his chair, only this time, he walked to the other side of the room. Unfortunately, he walked at an angle, and, after he had walked a few feet and with Lindstrom still in restraints, she couldn't keep track of where he was.

"When I laid out the rules for our time together, I made it very clear." His words filled the empty air, and, a few seconds later, he was standing next to the bed, holding a large electronic tablet in his hand. "I have not yet answered you, have I?" He adjusted the kickstand on the back of the tablet so that it could rest on her lap, yet still be visible.

"I believe you had asked the question of where your ex-husband is," Edward Kirkham said. He tapped an icon on the tablet's screen, and the screen changed. "Here is your answer."

Lindstrom looked down at the tablet on her lap. As she took in the image on the screen, a wave of cold washed over her. She then looked at Edward Kirkham, who looked back at her. His face resembled that of an elderly grandfather, smiling at the sight of young children playing in the yard.

"You see, detective, the universe will always balance itself."

THIRTY-SEVEN

Lindstrom stared at Edward Kirkham. Her mouth was open, but no words came out. The look on his face, it was a paradox. Somehow, it managed to be warm and inviting, while at the same time, it was also chilling and foreboding. She had to look away from him, for fear that she would be his next victim. Or, perhaps worse, that she would fall under his spell. Inside this white prison she was in, confined to this bed, his vision, his evil, his delusion, she didn't want to be swept away into his madness.

Lindstrom forced herself to look back at the tablet screen. She examined the image, trying to make sense of it. It could have been a trick, a ploy by Edward Kirkham to continue this insane tit-for-tat conversation. She looked back at him, searching in his eyes for some answer that wasn't there. His icy eyes simply looked back at her, betraying no emotion.

Lindstrom waited for Edward Kirkham to say, "Gotcha!", and to start laughing, but it didn't happen. He simply nodded at her, then nodded at the tablet. She turned her attention back to the tablet. After what seemed like an eternity, she licked her lips, swallowed several times to regain moisture in her mouth, and was able to put together a semblance of a sentence.

"What have you done?" The words were spoken, softly, slowly. They were overly simplistic, yet it was the only thing that made sense to her.

"My dear detective, I know exactly what I have done." His response was aloof, no hint of remorse, no twinge of sadness.

Lindstrom continued to stare at the tablet's screen, adding the image

448

being displayed to what she had learned while investigating the cases. She was completing a puzzle in her mind, and with each piece that fell into place, she became more horrified of the man standing next to her. The problem was that, even if she put the puzzle together, without evidence or a confession, the case against Edward Kirkham and his daughter, Veronica, would never hold up in a court of law. She had to tread carefully, knowing what this man was capable of. Lindstrom couldn't bring herself to look at Edward Kirkham, choosing instead to stare at the tablet's screen while trying to restart a dialogue with him.

"I'm not sure where to start."

"Detective, please. I think we have moved beyond subtlety. Ask, and I will answer."

"Very well. Who is Olivia Sherman?"

"Ms. Sherman was my Mata Hari, my seductress, my praying mantis."

"And Ronald Vance?"

"Mr. Vance was muscle, a jack-of-all-trades that could get a job done. Best of all, Mr. Vance knew how to keep his mouth shut and do what he was told."

"And Charles Utecht? Who was he?"

"Mr. Utecht was a career criminal. It pains me that I had to associate with his kind, but it was necessary to have someone that knew their way around certain legalities."

"And where is Utecht now?"

Edward Kirkham smiled, leaned forward, and, using one of his fingers, touched the tablet's screen and swiped the screen from left to right. The image that had been displayed was now replaced by a new image. Lindstrom looked at the new image, realizing it was similar to the previous picture, yet also different. She shook her head slightly.

Lindstrom had continued to stare at the tablet's screen while asking her questions. Now, as events were crystalizing, she laid her head back and closed her eyes. She took a deep breath, going over all of the evidence in her mind. She wanted to confront Edward Kirkham, to question his motives and actions. She wanted answers, how this man could have done these horrible things. In the end, though, Lindstrom knew it would be pointless. She couldn't get into an argument with him, lest he unleash his anger on her. She also realized a debate was pointless, as men like Edward Kirkham would twist words and actions until it suited them.

Lindstrom suddenly felt very tired, deciding it would be better to let him do all the work. She continued to lay there, her eyes closed. She heard movement but didn't open her eyes. She didn't dare to. She was terrified. She had felt scared before in her life. For a mother, it was a natural emotion at times. For a cop, it could be suppressed in the heat of the moment, a surge of adrenaline that took over, allowing training to become reflex. Even on that fateful night, when she had stood up to her ex, the adrenaline that coursed through her, coupled with the very real anger she had felt when he had threatened her life and the lives of her children, all of it had outweighed her fright, and it had driven her to a positive outcome. This situation, this emotion, this was new ground for her. When she heard that the movement had stopped, she merely assumed that Edward Kirkham had walked back to his chair. Lindstrom continued her questions, her eyes closed.

"When did you start this operation?"

"After Sebastian's father died, while Veronica worked with the lawyers and judge to settle the estate. When Veronica began working with social service programs to try and help other parents and children in need, I applauded her for her efforts. Unfortunately, it only took seven months for her outlook to change. Don't get me wrong, Veronica was still positive and tried to make a difference. However, the realities of the family court system, the bureaucracies, and the worst in human behavior, these things changed her outlook on what she was trying to accomplish. During those seven months, I carefully laid out my thoughts and my plans.

"Then, on a Friday evening, while we were having dinner, I asked Veronica how things were going with her work. She immediately broke down in tears, telling me of a number of different cases that she was working on. Mothers and fathers that had been abandoned by their partners, leaving them with children that they couldn't support alone. Children of these so-called parents, malnourished, no clean clothes, no chance to receive even a modest education, living in shelters or worse. After listening to Veronica, I opened up to her, discussing my plan, laying out my alternative. She thought about it, but she told me she couldn't. She needed to exhaust her way, and I respected her decision."

As Lindstrom listened to Edward Kirkham tell his story, the sound of movements started again, small noises, little clicks and scrapes. She remained focused on the sound of Edward Kirkham's voice, keeping her eyes shut, not wanting to look at the man, not wanting to miss any details.

"The following Monday afternoon, Veronica called me. A mother of three that she had been working with was in the hospital. Upon learning that the family judge in her case had ordered the father's child support payments to be raised, the father had gone to the apartment and beaten the mother in front of their children. The oldest child, a mere nine years old, had told the police that his father had screamed that he would rather go to jail than give her or the kids a single penny. The father had even gone so far as to assault all three of his children. That night was the beginning. The journey began, the path to the vision and the goal laid out. The creation of Visceral Medical Supplies, Supporting Broken Families, and R.T.A."

Edward Kirkham paused, the silence of the room only broken by the sound of Lindstrom's breathing and the little clicks and scrapes. With her eyes still shut to avoid looking at him, she continued her inquisition.

"Please explain how a normal, what did you call it? An extraction? How would a normal extraction work?"

"Veronica and I would identify an indebted individual. The individual in question would need to fit all of our established criteria, such as health, habits, family size, outstanding debt, circle of friends, criminal history, and so on. Once we vetted the individual thoroughly, we would decide on the simplest extraction possible. Fortunately, when it comes to the fathers that we have extracted, it was easy to send in a pretty face and spike a drink. Deadbeat mothers were more difficult, but the teams were always able to pull off successful extractions."

"Explain Nathan Devlin, then."

Edward Kirkham sighed heavily. "I regret what happened to Mr. Devlin. He should have been rejected in our vetting process. Unfortunately, as times have changed, Veronica and I have had to make changes to our operation. That involves a stronger reliance on computers." He waited, as if unsure of what to say next. "Almost all of our extractions have been successful, like what you are experiencing now. I could count on one hand the number of extractions that had something not work out. If there was an error with an extraction, it was because of some bad luck or bad timing. Regarding Mr. Devlin, unfortunately, that is all on Mr. Utecht. He gained access to Visceral's and R.T.A.'s computer network. Not understanding what we actually do, he put in motion plans for an unauthorized extraction." A brief pause, and then, "Obviously, it did not work out."

Lindstrom's head was swimming. "You're telling me that you hired Charles Utecht to kidnap deadbeat parents, then he hacked your computers, and tried to run a kidnap and ransom with his team of Olivia Sherman and Ronald Vance? It doesn't make any sense."

"That's right, detective, because the teams never knew why they were performing extractions. The teams that Veronica and I have hired were only told that they need to extract certain individuals. They were never told why or what happened after the individual was extracted. Need to know, if you will. And each team was always compensated well."

Lindstrom finally opened her eyes. It took a few seconds for her vision to, once again, adjust to the brightness of the white-on-white, but she quickly locked on to Edward Kirkham. He was sitting in the chair, but he had moved it to the foot of the bed.

"Teams," Lindstrom questioned. "As in multiple, as in plural?" She paused momentarily, and then, "My God, how long have you and your daughter been doing this?"

"Over twenty years, detective." Edward Kirkham's face broke out into a proud smile. The smug, self-righteous way he had declared, like he was proud of such a grand achievement, it made Lindstrom want to vomit. "My daughter and I have improved many, many lives in that time."

The man's arrogance was grating on Lindstrom. "Tell that to Olivia Sherman and Ronald Vance," she snapped at Edward Kirkham.

"Tsk, tsk, detective. You aren't looking at the big picture."

"Big picture? Tell me, how many people have you killed? No, wait, let me correct that. How many mothers and fathers have you killed, and how many families have you destroyed, with this altruistic garbage?"

Edward Kirkham's eyes narrowed slightly, as if he was examining Lindstrom for the first time. "Tell me, detective, was your family destroyed before, during, or after your time with your ex-husband?"

"My ex-husband has nothing to do with this. You kidnapped and murdered him and expected to slip me the profits on the nightstand, like a john leaving his hooker in a run-down motel room."

Edward Kirkham genuinely looked hurt. "Detective, I really think you need to take a closer look at that tablet. Take a good, long, hard look at it. Tell me what you see."

Without looking at the tablet again, Lindstrom shouted, "I asked you where my ex-husband is, and you show me a map of the United States with ten pinpoints scattered throughout the country. What am I missing?"

"My dear detective, you make me sad. After the team extracted…"

"Kidnapped," Lindstrom interrupted.

"Fine, if it makes you feel better. After the team," Edward Kirkham made the quotation mark gesture in the air, "'kidnapped' your ex-husband, he was brought to me in a room like this. He was strapped to a bed, much like the one you are currently in. I gave him a thorough examination, making sure that our vetting process hadn't missed anything. If it had, my team would have returned him, and he would have assumed he had passed out drunk. However, his tests came back positive. At that point, he was moved from Stage One to Stage Two. Each pinpoint on that map represents a life that your ex-husband improved. Of course, those pinpoints only account for donated organs. His blood, platelets, and various tissues aren't accounted for on that map, nor is a pinpoint on the map for the financial restitution that was given to you. One life saved ten lives, not counting making your life and the lives of your children better."

Lindstrom was becoming incensed. "And you think ten or twenty thousand dollars is enough to make the lives of those children better? What happens if the children try to reconnect with the deadbeat parent?"

Edward Kirkham smiled. "When the family receives their funds, we also send a letter to the children. The letter is written as an apology. The letter attempts to make amends, while also asking the children not to find the wayward parent. The children are better off without the deadbeat parent in the children's lives." He paused for affect. "You see, detective? I have considered all avenues, all contingencies. I am trying to help as many people, as many families as I can. One life for many. It is for the greater good."

"Really? How can you justify this level of murder? Besides, what happens to a person that needs a heart, but can't pay your price, or the price of what the deadbeat owes his or her family? What happens then? You hold a little auction, maybe drive up the price to get a few extra dollars out of someone that needs a lung?"

The shock that registered on Edward Kirkham's face was unlike anything Lindstrom had witnessed yet.

"How dare you! HOW DARE YOU! I am trying to make the world a better place, and you think that I would ask for a dime from someone that is on a waiting list for an organ donation?" He jabbed a finger at her, pointing at the tablet on her lap. "Do you truly not see what is right in front of you, detective? You see, yet you don't understand?" The tone of his voice was filled with exasperation, as if he was reprimanding a small child that continually misbehaved. "Have you not put two and two together yet, detective? What do you think Visceral Medical, R.T.A., and Supporting Broken Families Dot Com are all about?"

Lindstrom wanted to speak yet struggled to find the words. She hadn't expected this. "What are you saying? Where does the money come from?"

"Doctors, detective." Edward Kirkham relaxed, sitting back in his chair, his hands once again resting on his bent knee. "While there are a great many doctors in this country and around the world that will take a patient for every last cent, there are those doctors that believe in the greater good, a better world, and that do everything in their power, and more, to help their patients." He extended his right hand, palm up, in a small sweeping motion. "Like you, detective. For every good police officer, like you, there is probably one bad one, somewhere. That policeman or policewoman is out there right now, planting evidence or accepting bribes or using excessive force." He paused again, another sigh escaping from his lips, before continuing.

"In my many, many years practicing medicine, I have been able to put together a network of doctors. I investigated these men and women who shared my desire to do right by our position as physicians. They were, and are, willing to pay out of their own pocket to help a patient, knowing that the money is going to a family that is in desperate need of it. In fact, let's make sure your heart and mind are at ease. You had mentioned Ms. Sherman and Mr. Vance. As you have discovered during your investigations, they were both in arrears to their respective partners and children. Upon their death, checks were sent to the guardians of the children, wiping out the outstanding debts while also giving the children more than enough compensation to last until the children attain legal age."

Lindstrom sat there, mesmerized by what Edward Kirkham was telling her.

"Although Mr. Utecht had no family to speak of, I made sure his disobedience and the manner in which he took Ms. Sherman's life was dealt with. I harvested his viable organs. His heart, liver, and one kidney have already been successfully transplanted into patients across the country. The other kidney, both lungs, and a cornea are currently in route to patients in Canada, Brazil, and the U.K. Think about it, detective. One life has helped three lives already, and very soon, four more lives will have been saved!"

Lindstrom had been stunned into complete and utter silence. She looked down at the tablet on her lap, the screen still showing the United States map and ten distinct pinpoints. Her ex-husband had been kidnapped, or extracted, or whatever Edward Kirkham wanted to call it. He had been killed and his body parts had been sold off, resulting in almost fifty-two thousand dollars sitting in her checking account. She didn't know what to think or how to feel about it. Was she sad that he was dead? In some ways, it made her life, as well as Trevor's and Bree's lives, easier. At different and separate points, Trevor and Bree had asked about their biological father. Each time, Lindstrom had been honest about his actions, his lack of contact, his disregard for them, and why it wasn't good to hold out hope for his return. She had also reaffirmed that, in every way except DNA, Mark was their father. Not stepfather, no more than little Ryan was a half-brother. Altogether, they were a family, and that was all that mattered.

Still, this, lord almighty, this was something else.

Knowing where the money came from, how could she accept it? How could she, in good conscience, spend any of it, knowing that it had come at the cost of a life? Yet, that same life had assaulted her and threatened to assault his children. He had gone on to commit other crimes. His life versus the ten lives on this map, ten lives that were living and breathing and, hopefully, making the world a better place? How could she justify this?

Lindstrom's eyes were tearing up. This was too much to take. She only wanted to go home, to see her children, to hold them tight, and to repeat that same sequence every day. She was a police officer, to protect and serve. She was part of the good guys. Her job was to catch the bad guys. A police investigation shouldn't be an examination in the duality of man. Social injustice, the inaction of the courts and politicians to help the helpless, these were concepts that didn't occur to her during the daily course of her duties. The tears were rolling down her cheeks now.

"Detective?" Edward Kirkham's voice was soft, like a father's wondering why his daughter was crying alone in her room. "Whatever is the matter?"

So many emotions were flooding through her, and her mind was in overdrive. Nathan and Allison Devlin, Andy and Heidi Cole, Edward and Veronica Kirkham, her children Trevor, Bree, and Ryan, her husband Mark, Brad Engels and his wife Diane, Kara Reed, Jason Iverson, Visceral Medical Supplies, Ben McKinley, Cassie Butler, R.T.A., Supporting Broken Families, First Federated United Trust, Charles Utecht, Olivia Sherman, Ronald Vance. With everyone that she had come into contact with over the past two weeks, and with everything that had happened over that same time period, she now had the puzzle put together. Lindstrom tried to blink away the tears, since she was still being restrained. She looked at Edward Kirkham and asked the only question that mattered at that point.

"Are you going to kill me?"

THIRTY-EIGHT

Edward Kirkham looked at Lindstrom, heartbreak showing on his aged and weathered face.

"My dear detective, once again, I believe you have misunderstood my intentions."

Throughout their interaction, Edward Kirkham had alternated between a fit-looking sixty-year old to an angry thirty-year old to an elderly looking eighty-year old. Lindstrom had figured he had to be in his late sixties or early seventies. It was so hard to tell, though. He displayed such a youthful passion yet mixed with a world weariness. Plus, being in this all-white room did nothing to hide or accentuate the man's physical features. Now, as he stood up from his chair, he put his hands against the foot of the bed, steadying himself, as if he had used his last ounce of strength. Edward Kirkham looked Lindstrom in her eyes, the iciness that had been there now replaced by emptiness.

"I told you earlier, that whether you believe me or not, I am a good man." As he spoke, Edward Kirkham walked to the side of the bed and removed the tablet from Lindstrom's lap. "All of this, over the past two weeks, this was all by my arrogance." He walked to the foot of the bed and laid the tablet on the chair. "I should have taken a much closer look at Charles Utecht. The red flags were there, but I ignored them. Every team that Veronica and I had put together in the past had been exceptional, and the members were rewarded. They never spoke a word, and each settled into a new life that I provided for them." He had walked back to the side of the bed.

"What are you," Lindstrom started to ask, but she was cut-off mid-sentence.

"My hubris created this catastrophe over the past two weeks. If I had never hired Charles Utecht, our paths never would have crossed. You, my dear detective, would have received your check from R.T.A., none the wiser of our greater mission. The universe craves balance, it struggles for it, and even I, I can't escape it. Maybe the universe feels that I have accomplished enough. Or, maybe that I've done too much. Perhaps, I haven't done enough. Whatever the case may be, our time together tonight was to afford you the answers you deserved. You have been my priest on this night, I have been your penitent. My world was ripped asunder. Your investigations were meant to ameliorate the many situations that came about. And I, on this night, have been the apologist, seeking neither acceptance nor absolution. To answer your question, my dear detective, no, I am not going to kill you. In fact, you are free to go."

Lindstrom had been watching Edward Kirkham's face and body language during his soliloquy. She was strangely fascinated, not only by what he was saying, but how he was saying it. If nothing else, he was damn charismatic. Now, at the end, he drops the biggest bombshell yet. Had she heard him correctly? Or were the drugs in her system still impeding her physically and mentally? He was telling her she could up and leave?

"I'm sorry, but what did you say?"

"You heard me correctly. You are free to go." A warm, inviting smile washed over his face. While the intent was to reassure her, after everything that she had been through, Lindstrom was finding his smile eerie, almost repugnant.

"I don't believe you, Mr. Kirkham."

"See for yourself." Edward Kirkham moved backward several steps from the bed. Once he stopped moving, he motioned with his hands to Lindstrom. "Take a look, detective."

Lindstrom's eyes had been locked on Edward Kirkham. Slowly, hesitantly, she moved her gaze off her captor and looked down at her body. She couldn't believe what she saw. The blanket that he had put over her to help with her shivering had been removed and was folded neatly at her feet. She was no longer in restraints, either. She had kept her eyes closed for so long that Edward Kirkham must have been able to remove them without her knowledge. That might have explained the strange noises she had heard. She was wearing the same clothes that she had worn all day Friday, although her shoes weren't on her feet. She tried to move, to sit up, to change her position, but she couldn't.

"Why can't I move?"

"Ah, my apologies, detective. As I told you earlier, I went through Stage One of Visceral, so that I could fully understand its affects. I put you through Stage One as well, so that you could understand. Stage One is where a special mixture of drugs is administered into the body. These drugs include an antibiotic, a synthetic adrenaline, an enhanced vitamin panel, and a paralytic, to name only a few. The purpose of this mixture is to keep the body healthy and viable during organ harvesting. The reason why you can't move is because the paralytic is still wearing off. I adjusted your IV several minutes ago. You are currently receiving another special mixture of my own design. This mixture breaks down the harder of the drugs, like the paralytic, while also providing essential fluids and nutrients to keep the body healthy and balanced."

All the while, his smile remained. He was happy, almost giddy, to tell Lindstrom about his ingenuity. Like a child showing off for a parent. It was maddening to her. Then she started processing what he had revealed to her.

Lindstrom thought back to what Dr. Preston had said regarding his initial tests on Nathan Devlin. She guessed that Edward Kirkham wanted to clean up Utecht's mistake as quickly as possible but hadn't given the clean-up mixture enough time to get everything completely flushed out of Devlin's system.

"How long until I can feel and move again?"

"Every human body is different and unique, but I would say that you should have limited movements in about ten minutes. If you've ever had a shot of Novocain for a dental procedure, you will slowly start to regain feeling in your muscles." Edward Kirkham started moving toward his chair again. As he did, he picked up the tablet he only moments ago set down, and he said, "While we wait, please feel free to ask me any more questions you feel the need to ask."

Lindstrom took a breath. "Very well. Why did you choose 'Visceral' as your company's name?"

Edward Kirkham's eyebrow went up, his expression changing from one smiling at her to one of curiosity. "My heavens, detective. I didn't think it possible that you would surprise this evening! You may find this hard to believe. However, I assure you, like everything else I've told you tonight, and everything else I'm going to tell you, this is the truth. The most difficult part of building this operation wasn't the money, or the equipment, or the people. It was finding the right name. Veronica and I tried finding clever acronyms, witty titles, anything that would be slightly intriguing yet wholly dismissible. 'Visceral' is an adjective, derived from the Latin word 'viscera', which means pertaining to organs in the cavities of the body. Yes, I know, it sounds corny, but I needed a name for my enterprise."

"I believe it also means acting on instinct, instead of acting on intelligence."

"Very good, detective. I would caution you again, though, not to dip your feet into waters that you know nothing about."

Lindstrom received the implication, loud and clear. He had told her she was free, yet he could quickly and easily change his mind. Would he, though? If she pressed him hard enough, perhaps asking the right question with the right tone, could she catch him in a trap? Would it be enough to get him to reveal himself as a liar? It was possible, equally as possible that he would go in the opposite direction. Perhaps he would decide that keeping her alive wasn't worth it. She would die here, never seeing Mark or the kids again. No, she knew better than to risk everything on such an unstable outcome. Instead, she decided to move on.

"How are you able to get these indebted individuals out of jail in the first place?"

"Oh, that?" A devilish grin creeped across Edward Kirkham's face. "That was more of a diversion, a distraction, a red herring, as the saying goes. It was a way to obfuscate your investigation, to leave you with more questions. After watching the machinations of family court play out with Veronica and Sebastian, I would never dream of becoming involved with the authorities. No, every biological parent that my teams extracted were always taken, very much, in the same way that Mr. Devlin was taken. One day they were there, the next day, they were gone. Considering what most of them had done in their lives, I would be shocked if more than one or two people actually missed them. Once again, it's all about the greater

460

good, my dear detective."

Lindstrom was stunned with the utter indifference he seemed to have. A doctor, no less, that took an oath to do no harm, casually discussing the abduction and murder of these people, it was turning her stomach. Still, she needed to keep him talking while these drugs wore off, so she continued.

"How many doctors are in your clandestine group?"

"Tsk, tsk, detective. Please limit your questions to what you REALLY need to know."

Edward Kirkham's answer irritated Lindstrom. She had been looking around the room. She wanted the layout of the area so that, when she did regain the ability to sit up and walk, she would be ready. After his answer, Lindstrom's focus returned to Edward Kirkham.

"I really, really don't understand." Lindstrom's voice came out annoyed and confused. "You went through all the trouble of kidnapping me. We did this dog-and-pony show of an interrogation. You have basically confessed to mass kidnapping and mass murder, not to mention whatever illegalities you committed on the medical and financial side, to keep Visceral up and running. After all of that, now you expect me to believe that you are going to let me walk out of here?"

Edward Kirkham stared intently at Lindstrom. "Absolutely, detective! Must I remind you, again, that I am not a monster? Do you really believe, for one second, with everything that I have told you about me, my motivations, my actions, the greater good that I am working toward, that I would take your life and deprive your three children of their only remaining parent?" He looked aghast, as if Lindstrom had insulted at a level so deep and personal that it could never be forgiven.

"Forgive me, then, but what happens when I can move again?"

"You will have a decision to make. You can arrest me, of course. However, on what charge would the arrest be made? Everything that I have told you is inadmissible in court. Hearsay, Miranda, I'm sure you have heard of those. Will you arrest me on some charge relating to Visceral Medical, R.T.A., or First Federated United Trust?" Lindstrom was surprised to hear Edward Kirkham drop the name of the bank, but kept her surprise hidden. "If you were to look deeper into those entities, you will find that no records can be traced back to me, if you could find any records to begin with. Even in a post 9/11 world, there are cities, states, countries, even individuals, that are willing to bend the rules for select clients."

Lindstrom was racking her brain. She needed leverage, something that would stick and make him uneasy. He must have sensed what she was doing, because Edward Kirkham spoke again.

"False termination of Ms. Butler or Mr. Jacobs? They have been well-compensated, so they won't be pressing charges against me. Tax evasion for this building we are currently in? Oh, the taxes have been paid in full for another two years. I could go on, but I think you see my point. I have thought of every contingency, every possible avenue that you might pursue me down. Besides, as crazy as the world has become, with truthers questioning every act committed by every government and every big business venture, with people in our modern day and age believing that the world is flat or hollow, you could try to convince someone that I have created a secret cabal of doctors and we are running around plucking organs out of people, but only the crazies would believe you. How reliable of a case could you build against me when your only 'believers' are the ones wearing foil hats and searching for anything that is counter-intuitive towards modern science and technology?"

Lindstrom didn't know which was more infuriating, that he was right, or the simple calm that he was using. That calm, flowing out of him, all while sitting in that chair, not moving, speaking with serenity, as if nothing could touch him, let alone hurt him.

"Detective, I am going to make this easy for you." Edward Kirkham took in a long, deep breath, and, as he exhaled, he seemed to age another fifteen years. "I really don't care how you see me, whether you think that I am good or evil, or what I have done is right or wrong. The only thing that matters to me, right now in this very moment and every moment going into the future, is my daughter. I am willing to confess to the kidnapping and murder of Charles Utecht, with the only caveat being that you will never pursue Veronica." He looked towards the ceiling again, lost in thought as he spoke. "It is a parent's prerogative to make sure that the child is safe from harm, no matter the cost. Surely you, a mother of three blessed children, can understand the innate desire to protect our children."

Lindstrom was in a no-win situation. She didn't know what to believe about Edward Kirkham. Even if she had weeks or months to go through his life, every single action that he perpetrated or set in motion, if, by some miracle, she brought him in front of a judge and jury, all it would take is one person to buy into his philanthropic vision, and he would walk. At least by agreeing to his deal, he wouldn't be able to continue his warped crusade. With a heavy sigh, Lindstrom conceded.

"Very well, Mr. Kirkham. I agree to your deal. You in exchange for Veronica's freedom."

Edward Kirkham simply smiled and nodded. However, Lindstrom was frowning, looking down at herself. "Detective, what seems to be the problem?"

"I thought I could start moving soon." Lindstrom could roll her head a little bit, but she still lacked any feeling in her extremities. She was trying to move her fingers and toes, but nothing happened.

Edward Kirkham stood up from his chair and looked past Lindstrom. "I don't understand. Based on your body mass and the blood tests I ran on you upon your arrival, you should be able to stand up by now." Looking perplexed, he started walking to the head of the bed, but only managed two steps before a familiar voice called out.

THIRTY-NINE

"Father, you need to stop, right there, right now!"

Both of them turned toward the voice, but only Edward Kirkham could see his daughter speaking. Lindstrom recognized the sound of Veronica Kirkham's voice. However, she couldn't turn enough of her head to see Veronica or where she was standing. The effects of the drugs in her system were still impeding her recovery. Edward Kirkham stood at the foot of Lindstrom's bed, frozen in place. The look on his face was one of shock and betrayal.

"Daughter," Edward Kirkham said softly, "what are you doing?"

"I am saving you," came the reply.

"Saving me? From whom?"

"From yourself, father. I'm saving you from a horrible decision. Our work is too important to let one mistake bring it all to an end." The words were spoken in a tone of resentment.

"The work, our work, was and is important, daughter. However, I am an old man, and if I can insure that you will be safe, that is my choice to make."

"Oh, spare me! Charles Utecht was just as much my fault as yours. We thought we could control him with extra money. It only fed his greed, and people are dead because of it. That doesn't mean we have to end everything because some cop got lucky!"

"I understand how important this is to you, but I will not make orphans out of the detective's children. We are trying to maintain balance in the world, Veronica, not tip the scales into chaos! The murder of Ms. Sherman was balanced by Mr. Utecht's gifts, and Mr. Vance's death allowed his daughter to be taken care of until she reaches adulthood. It is best to end, NOW, before the scales are shifted again."

"We don't NEED to kill her, father! There are other ways!"

Lindstrom had been sitting in the bed, watching Edward Kirkham's face as he was speaking to his daughter. Whatever she thought of his grand plan, or what he had done in the past, he seemed to have a moral compass, and he was intent on following it. His daughter, Veronica, apparently, was another story. Lindstrom didn't know enough about her to ascertain her motivations, her goals, or what made her tick. She was sure that this was a conversation that she shouldn't interrupt, at least until it was necessary.

"What are you doing, Veronica?" Edward Kirkham's words had an air of pleading, the look on his face and in his eyes making Lindstrom nervous. Then, she felt it, the cold barrel of a gun being pressed against her skin. She had felt it before, with an unloaded gun that was used in self-defense class. However, she had never felt it in the line of duty. The sensation, of knowing Veronica Kirkham had a gun pointed at her, point-blank, filled her with emotions that she had never experienced before. Lindstrom was beyond terrified, beyond anything that words could ever express.

"My father may have poured his soul out to you, but you don't know me, TISH." Veronica's gun was pressed against the right side of Lindstrom's face, and there was vitriol in the words as she spoke. So far, they were only words, the only action being the gun pressed against her flesh. For some reason, a thought darted through Lindstrom's brain. If she could see Veronica, look at her face, study her movements, maybe she could develop a plan to counteract this madness. Unfortunately, Veronica stayed out of her line of sight, playing the boogeyman, hiding from detection. Veronica continued speaking, the pressure of the gun against Lindstrom's cheek holding steady.

"I watched you and that dimwit Tisdale go to my old apartment. I watched you jump the fence and walk across private property to check out Visceral's facility. I watched you from the parking lot, talking to Cassie and Noah. I even watched you run around the schoolyard, screaming for Ryan. I don't need to kill you, TISH. I don't need to threaten to kill you, TISH. I wouldn't dirty my hands with you. Your children, though, are another matter. You can't keep Trevor, Bree, and Ryan safe every minute of every day. If you come after my father and I, your children will pay the price, and you will live, knowing it was your fault, TISH."

The terror Lindstrom was experiencing had been replaced by fury, a fury that she hadn't felt since the night her ex-husband had laid hands on her for the last time. She didn't think it was possible to hate someone, anyone, more than she hated her ex-husband, but she was wrong. Veronica had crossed a line that should never be crossed, and Lindstrom vowed to make sure she paid for it.

"Oh, did that upset you, TISH? You think you can keep your kids safe from me? Maybe, maybe not. But how about everyone else in this worthless city?"

Confusion settled into Lindstrom. She tried turning her head to the right, to see Veronica, to ascertain where she was. Unfortunately, the gun held firm, so she spoke instead.

"What the hell does that mean?"

"Typical cop," Veronica chided, "always thinking you're so clever. I uploaded a virus into your police station's network, thanks to that lovestruck idiot Tisdale's police tablet. Right now, your precious chief and that moron of a computer geek are sitting in his office, waiting to see if I'm going to crash the network and wipe every police computer clean of every piece of evidence, every case, the ability to respond to 911 call's, every last byte of data." A slight pause, and then Veronica continued, her words coming out in a muted tone.

"Think about it, TISH. Is trying to stop our work really worth the damage that I can do to this city? No police response, no fire or rescue. Every criminal case wiped clean from every computer and server connected to the police network. Files, evidence, summons, gone, with a simple keystroke. The only crimes that have been committed have been punished. We have dealt with Charles Utecht. Now, you need to decide which is more important to you. The well-being of your children and the city of Sioux Falls? Or trying to stop the wonderful work my father is doing, based on some antiquated sense of morality and justice?"

Lindstrom's fury had changed to bewilderment and awe. Could Veronica really have hacked into the police system? Could she crash everything? While threatening her children was bad enough, threatening the lives of every man, woman, and child in a city of two hundred thousand

466

by attacking the police department was over the top insane. Lindstrom was having trouble wrapping her head around these threats, especially after everything she had learned about Edward Kirkham and his daughter. She was so frustrated, she wanted to punch her fist into something, but she was in no state to, no, wait!

Did that really happen, Lindstrom thought? Without moving her head, she looked down at her left hand. She could move her fingers! What was going on? She looked towards Edward Kirkham, who silently acknowledged what was happening by grinning, ever so slightly, from the right side of his mouth. As quickly as he did, he stopped so he could address his daughter.

"Veronica," his words were measured, thoughtful, and soft, trying to offer some sense of reassurance. "This is wrong, and we both know it. I never agreed to the computer virus, and you told me that you respected my decision and stopped working on it. Now, you have threatened the lives of the good detective's children, and you have made a terrorist threat against the population of an entire city. I will not allow this to happen!" Edward Kirkham started walking toward the head of Lindstrom's bed again. "I am going to see what is wrong with the detective's IV dispenser, and then I will be walking out of Visceral in her custody."

"Father, I told you, you need to stop!"

Lindstrom no longer felt the gun against her skin, which was a relief. An even bigger relief was that she was beginning to regain sensations in other parts of her body. Surreptitiously, she moved her fingers and toes, but only a tiny bit. She didn't need Veronica to see that she was recovering from whatever Stage One drugs had been put inside her.

"Or else…what? My dearest daughter, we have been through so much. The death of your mother, our getting to know each other, Sebastian, and more than twenty years of our plan. Do you honestly expect me to believe you are going to shoot me?"

"Father, please, you aren't leaving me any other choice!" Veronica's voice had changed, like it had changed so many times when Lindstrom had talked to her on the phone. This time, though, it was different. An earnest pleading, as if time was against her. Everything in her life had led her to this moment, and she was afraid of failing, now, when it meant so much.

Edward Kirkham had continued to walk, and now was past Lindstrom's field of vision. She didn't dare to turn and look, because Veronica would know she was regaining control over her muscles. With both Kirkhams out of her line of sight, and preoccupied with each other, Lindstrom tried flexing different muscle groups. Her right arm and left leg weren't as responsive as her left arm, but her right leg didn't seem to be responding at all. She had to give the old man credit. He had designed a drug to paralyze a person, but that left breathing, blinking, and higher brain functions untouched.

Edward Kirkham's voice spoke again. "There is a choice. There is always a choice. The difficulty is in making sure it is the RIGHT choice. Veronica, my lovely daughter, please, don't cry. This is for the best. I want you safe, and I am willing to sacrifice what little time I have left so that you can..."

"NO!" Veronica's sudden scream surprised Lindstrom, but not as much as the sounds of a scuffle. Lindstrom listened to the Kirkhams struggle, grunts and shouts, she heard things knocking over and the sound of glass breaking, and then came a smell of chemicals hitting the open air. She felt the force of bodies slamming against her bed. The collision pushed her bed forward, and the IV that was inserted into her left arm pulled free, ripping the needle out the vein.

"AAARRRGHH!"

Lindstrom bellowed out in pain. She flexed her left arm closed on instinct, looking down at the damage. Some skin had torn off, and there was some blood flowing, but nothing too serious. The cacophony behind her continued. Should she turn around? Did she dare to try and stand up, not knowing how her entry into the melee would affect...

BANG! BANG! BANG! BANG! BANG!

The gunshots were so loud, echoing through the white room. Lindstrom was about to turn around, when an explosion ripped through the back wall, sending her bed forward and then toppling over, throwing her to the ground. There was no choice now. Lindstrom struggled to get her feet under her, as she felt the air in the room start to burn. She looked to her right, surveying where her bed had been. The wall was engulfed in flames. A body was laying on the floor, tall, with a pool of blood forming underneath it. She tried to make out more details, but the backdrop of the fiery wall made it difficult. Instead, she focused on the figure that was stumbling towards her. It was Edward Kirkham. His white clothes were streaked with yellow and red and black. He reached out his right hand and helped pull her off the floor. Her legs still weren't at her full disposal, but she had no choice but to make it work.

"What the hell happened?" It was a stupidly obvious question, but Lindstrom needed to know what kind of danger they were in.

"One of the bullets hit the IV controlling station, which ignited the fluid inside. I think another bullet hit the oxygen line. We need to hurry. If we aren't clear before the fire reaches the storage room, your children will be returning home to their mother's funeral."

That was all the prompting Lindstrom needed. Edward Kirkham put her arm around his neck, and they staggered forward. Lindstrom wasn't sure where they were going, but she had no choice, except to trust him. They reached the far wall, the fire growing in intensity behind them, the room filling with smoke. He reached his hand out and placed his palm against a reflective panel. Instantly, a door slid open, but jammed halfway in the track. Edward Kirkham shifted his weight to push Lindstrom through first.

Lindstrom quickly looked around. They were standing in a control room. Several computer monitors displayed various readings, video feeds, or screen savers. There was another door on the other side of the room. As she looked around, he had placed his hand on another reflective pad. The door began to close, but didn't seal all the way, maybe a half of an inch gap allowing the rooms to stay open to each other.

Lindstrom took a step, but Edward Kirkham's arm tightened around her. She stopped moving and looked at him.

"We have to move!"

"We can't leave yet, detective! I'm afraid Veronica wasn't bluffing." He nodded his head to a dual-screen monitor. On one part of the screen, big as life, was a live feed showing Scott and Engels, sitting in Engels' office. Scott wasn't moving, as if he was carved out of marble, while Engels appeared to be napping, arms folded across his chest, his feet on his desk. On the other part of the screen, several lines of code were displayed, with a command prompt flashing at the end. Lindstrom and Edward Kirkham detoured to the monitor in question. They looked at the flashing command prompt:

TO ENGAGE TEXT,
TYPE AND PRESS ENTER

TO EXECUTE TERMINAL FUNCTION, ENTER LOG-IN CREDENTIALS TO EVAPORATE WITH KILL CODE, ENTER PASSWORD

"You know what this is all about?" Lindstrom knew this was no time to guess.

"Veronica explained the basics to me when she proposed the idea of hacking into the police network of the city we were working out of years ago." Edward Kirkham coughed, and a small amount of blood splattered onto the monitor. Lindstrom looked at him, concern growing in her eyes, but he merely shook his head. "No time for a medical evaluation, detective. Right now, this computer is connected to that one in your chief's office. Quickly, let them know that you are stopping the virus." He bent his knees, lowering her into the chair. Lindstrom put her hands to the keyboard and started typing.

When Engels had put his feet up and his head down, he didn't know whether he would be able to nap or not. The uncertainty of Lindstrom's fate, coupled with the impotence that he felt regarding a computer hacking that could destroy his police department's ability to serve the city, had left him in a state that he had never experienced before. Since he couldn't do anything, he tried to save his strength, hoping he would be ready when the time came to act. He was able to doze off and on, allowing the minutes to turn into hours. He realized that time was creeping by, as the sunlight coming in through his office window had slowly moved across the room. Now, night was nearly upon them, dusk slowly giving way to dark, another day ending with this case never wanting to end.

Engels had been looking out the window, when Scott whispered to him, "Chief!"

Engels turned his head and saw that the tablet's screen had come to life again.

BOSS, ARE YOU THERE?

Engels was happy that Lindstrom was still alive, but nervous as hell. Lindstrom didn't know that whoever was on the other side of the tablet was holding the police station hostage. In fact, only Engels and Scott knew

470

how horrible the threat was, although Carol and Tisdale had an idea. He took his feet off his desk and spoke towards the tablet's camera.

"Tish? Is that you? What's happening? Are you alright?" A few agonizing seconds went by, and then more text appeared.

SORRY I'M SUCH A PAIN IN THE ASS! STAND BY, I'M ABOUT TO GET RID OF YOUR VIRUS WITH A KILL CODE.

"BE CAREFUL!", Scott shouted at the computer's screen.

"Okay, they've been warned." Lindstrom coughed, but no blood came up. Her cough was because of the smoke now trickling in from the white room. "How do I get rid of the virus?" She looked to Edward Kirkham, who was leaning against the desk, eyes groggy.

"EDWARD", Lindstrom shouted as she reached out and slapped his leg. He was startled, and looked around, trying to regain his bearings.

"Yes, detective. Enter the password."

"What's the damn password?!"

Edward Kirkham's eyes began to tear up, and he whispered the password, as if it would be the last time he ever said it.

"Sebastian."

Lindstrom typed in the password and hit enter. Instantly, all of the code on the screen started to disappear, as if someone was holding down the backspace key.

As Engels and Scott watched, a line of computer code appeared on the tablet's screen. As soon as it appeared, though, it was deleted. Another line of code appeared, and it, too, was deleted. This process continued for at least five minutes, all while the two men watched.

"Do you understand what's happening," Engels asked Scott.

"I'm guessing that, whatever Tish did, it is removing the virus and all of its components from the network."

They continued to watch the tablet's screen, as line after line of computer code appeared, and then was deleted. As the codes were deleted, the process gained speed, performing the operation faster and faster. Engels tried to understand what was happening, but he was at a loss, instead hoping that this little process would rid the station's computer systems of this threat.

"What the hell?" Scott's words surprised Engels. He turned and looked at the computer tech, who's eyes remained glued to the code showing up on the screen.

"What is it? What's wrong?"

"I'm not a hundred percent sure, yet, but whoever wrote this code and virus is absolutely amazing."

Engels was stumped. "Okay, can you enlighten your boss, just a little bit?"

Before Scott could answer, the code stopped appearing, leaving a blank screen. Five seconds later, a new line of text appeared.

VIRUS PROGRAM EVAPORATED. NO TRACE REMAINS. REMOVING MIRAGE FROM SUB-HOST SYSTEM.

The text flashed slowly. Suddenly, on the monitor for Engels' desktop computer, the final image of the nuclear explosion that had displayed when his computer had been erased, appeared again. The image then reversed, as if someone had hit the rewind button. Engels and Scott watched as the image of the explosion played backwards, until the screen went blank. Just as quickly as it went blank, the original desktop was back, with all of the icons and folders and the background intact. Before either man could speak, more text appeared on the tablet's screen.

MIRAGE DISENGAGED. ALL INFECTED SYSTEMS AND NETWORKS CLEAN. COMMUNICATION LOGS HAVE BEEN ERASED. CONNECTION TO HOST WILL NOW SEVER. SINCEREST APOLOGIES FOR THE DECEPTION. HAVE A NICE DAY!

Another five seconds later, the text disappeared, leaving Scott and Engels to look at each other, then at the tablet's screen, and then at Engels' computer monitor. They sat there for a minute, unsure of what to do.

"Well," Engels began, nudging Scott in the back with his elbow, "your guess is as good as mine. Do something."

Scott reached out and unplugged the tablet from the computer. He powered it down and back up again, but nothing happened. The screen remained black. Scott turned his attention to Engels' computer, gently moving the mouse, opening programs and folders. Feeling more confident, he started typing, opening various windows and folders. His fingers were flying, gaining speed and bravado, the windows opening and closing on the monitor, seemingly at will. Engels knew better than to interrupt. Let the man work, and he would explain in due time. Almost nine minutes later, Scott sat back in the chair and whistled softly.

"I take it you are ready to let your boss in on what happened?"

"Whoever was behind this is extremely smart, incredibly clever, overly polite, and immensely apologetic." Scott stared at the window, smiling at the information that was being displayed. Engels looked from Scott to the screen and back again.

"I'm still waiting for an answer, Scott."

Scott didn't want to stop admiring what he was seeing on the monitor but forced himself to look at his boss. "Well, it's going to take some time to explain."

"You can give me the abridged version later. Do you have any idea where Lindstrom is?"

"Is that it? Can we get out of here now?" Lindstrom wasn't panicking, though she knew the situation was escalating quickly. Time wasn't on their side.

"Yes and no, detective." Edward Kirkham looked at Lindstrom and slid from the desk, dropping onto his knees. He was holding his side, which was stained red. More of the white shirt he was wearing was becoming red. "The kill code has been activated, but I won't be able to fulfill my part of our deal." Lindstrom remained in the chair and put a hand on the old man's shoulder.

"There has to be a way, Mr. Kirkham." Lindstrom was searching the old man's eyes and face, trying in vain to figure a way out for both of them.

"I am sorry. It isn't to be." Edward Kirkham raised his right arm and pointed to another door on the opposite side of the room. "That is your way out, detective. Beyond that door is the parking garage. At the far end you will see stairs. Take the stairs up two flights, take the door on the left. You'll find yourself in an office area with many cubicles. Look straight ahead, and you will see a door marked "Front Entrance". Go through that door, and you'll find the way out." He coughed again, and more blood came up, spraying on the ground. "You have to go, now. Be the best mother you can be to all three of your wonderful..." His eyes clouded over, and he slumped forward on the ground.

Before Lindstrom could say anything, another explosion rocked the building. She gathered herself to her feet and, using the desks for support, stumbled to the door. She opened it, and then looked back at the body of Edward Kirkham, motionless on the floor. She said nothing, turned, and ran as fast as her body could. The surge of adrenaline to get out of the building in one piece was counteracting the remaining effects of the paralytic in her body. She immediately spotted the stairs across the large parking garage. As she ran, she counted four black delivery vans, and three ambulances marked with the HealthStar Ambulatory Services logo and lettering. She also saw what appeared to be the van that Edward Kirkham had used as Lindstrom's trap back at Sanford Hospital. And there was her car. She slowed briefly, weighing the chance of using her car to get out. As she was about to stop, another explosion sounded, and the darkness of the parking garage gave way to the light of the fire coming from behind her. Without looking back, she started running again, getting to the stairs and taking them two at a time.

She followed the old man's directions, reaching the top of the second flight and opening the door on the left. In front of her was an abandoned office. As Edward Kirkham had said, there were cubicles everywhere. The overhead lights were flickering, undoubtedly from the affects the fire was having on the electrical system. Lindstrom spotted the door with the words "Front Entrance" on them and started to run again. As she ran, she glanced at the cubicles on either side of her. They seemed abandoned, chairs overturned, loose papers on the desks, even a faded picture here and there attached to a cubicle wall. On the perimeter, open doors led into various offices. Her detective instincts wanted to detour, to investigate and see if there was anything worth pursuing.

Fortunately, her motherly instincts had taken over, commanding her legs to run, run harder, run faster! She reached the door, pushing it open hard. She skidded to a stop on a tile floor, as she found herself in an open atrium, a front reception area in front of windows showing the outside world. An empty parking lot lay only a few feet beyond the windows. A fire alarm was sounding from somewhere. At that moment, she realized that she must be alone in the building. There were no other people running about, no screaming, no chaos for a building being destroyed from within.

Lindstrom ran to the door, as another explosion rumbled from below her feet. The explosion made her lose her footing, and she crashed into the glass door. However, the glass didn't break, and the door didn't open. She regained her footing and pushed hard on the door's panic bar, but it didn't budge. She frantically searched for the locking mechanism but couldn't find one. Another explosion, and now smoke was beginning to roll into the atrium. Lindstrom glanced around the atrium, finding some furniture stacked against the far wall. She sprinted over to the stacks and grabbed a standing floor lamp. She was in luck, as it was metal and heavy. She dragged it back to the door, lifted it as best she could, and rammed the base of it against the glass door. The glass cracked, so she hit it again. More cracking, so she tried a third time. The glass cracked even more, but the lamp broke into pieces. Lindstrom picked up the base of it, held it like a hammer, and hit the glass a fourth time. This time the glass erupted outward. She quickly knocked out a few more pieces, not wanting to cut herself. As she crouched down to squeeze through, three more explosions shook the building. She lost her balance, hitting her head against the door and cutting her left arm on broken glass on the floor. The area outside was brighter than it had been a minute ago, which meant the fire was spreading fast.

Lindstrom regained her footing, crouching and stepping through the hole she had made in the door. Once outside of the building, she quickly surveyed her surroundings, recognizing that she was in the parking lot that she had viewed from a distance on Friday, when she had trespassed. The parking lot was completely devoid of any vehicles, and fire was shooting out from various parts of the building. She ran straight ahead, across the parking lot, into the field. As her feet hit the grass, though, multiple explosions tore through the building. The force of the blasts propelled Lindstrom forward, causing her to stumble and roll through the grass. She laid in the grass for a few seconds, thinking she might be safe. She figured she was at least sixty yards from the building, but the heat from the fire was intense, too intense to be the result of a standard fire. Lindstrom guessed that, whatever chemicals Edward Kirkham had stored and used in Visceral's building was causing the fire to burn hotter and stronger than a regular fire would. The intensity of the fire was affecting the surrounding area, too. Even in this cool November evening, she was finding it difficult to breathe, as the fire seemed to be igniting the air around her.

Lindstrom made her way to her feet and turned away from the inferno. She only made it a few steps before one final explosion ripped the building apart. The blast wave knocked her off her feet and threw her forward. Upon landing this time, her head grazed a rock as she rolled down a small embankment. She looked up, the night sky now an eerily bright orange and yellow. Stars encroached the edge of her vision, and she blinked multiple times to try to stave off unconsciousness. She crawled up the embankment, staring at the burning complex. The heat from the fire was too much, though, even from this distance. She ducked her head down, and the sudden movement caused a wave of nausea to overcome her. A concussion was a very real possibility, trying to resist her body's urge to pass out. Racked with exhaustion, the adrenaline of her escape gone, and the last effects of the drugs that Edward Kirkham had pumped into her body now seemingly gone, Lindstrom succumbed to the darkness. Her body limp, she rolled back down the embankment. The last thing that went through Lindstrom's mind was a prayer she would see her children and husband again.

FORTY

THE AFTERMATH

Engels stood at the edge of the police cordon, surveying the remnants of the Visceral Medical Supplies, a folder in one hand. Two firetrucks were still on hand, along with four tanker trucks filled with water. Construction equipment, including a crane, bulldozer, and forklift, was due to arrive tomorrow to start the process of sifting through the smoldering debris. Assuming, of course, that they would be given the green light to start the cleanup.

The fire marshal and the arson investigator had met with Engels and the mayor yesterday, and it wasn't good news. The extreme heat from the fire had, for lack of a better term, melted the building. The chemicals that had either been stored inside the building, or that had been in use, must have had a high flammability rating, as well as a high reactivity rating.

"I've seen and studied all manner of fires, bombs, ignition points and triggers, what have you," the arson investigator had said, "but I'll be goddamned if I could guess what the hell happened here." The fire marshal concurred, noting that it was one hell of a mess to cool down, and it was going to take a long time to start cleaning it up.

When the firetrucks had arrived the previous Saturday night, they couldn't get close enough to even begin to spray the building. After thirty minutes, with no end in sight, the decision had been made to contain the fire to the building, and let the fire burn itself out. *"Keep the fire from igniting any dry grass and trees,"* were the orders that night. Autumn was upon them, and a wildfire was the last thing the fire crews needed.

"BOSS!"

Engels turned around. Lindstrom shut the door to her rental car and walked up to him. Considering everything she had been through only a week ago, she appeared to be recovering well.

"I thought I gave you the weekend off."

Joining Engels at the cordon line, she said, "You didn't let me know how your meeting with the mayor went."

"Tish, it's a Saturday," Engels replied, exasperation in his voice. "You're a week removed from being kidnapped, drugged, and almost dying in that." Engels pointed to the remains of the building.

"Boss, I feel fine. The kids are okay. In fact, since you went behind my back and insisted on my sister staying with us, I needed some alone time. Everyone is at the new indoor aquatic center, and I told them I would be there after I stopped and talked to you. So, enough stalling already. The mayor's visit?" Lindstrom was desperate to know what decisions had been made about her boss's future.

Engels sighed. It was a pleasant fall day. He was trying to wrap his head around the last three weeks. One dead body had turned out to be much, much more.

"In a minute, Tish. What are we doing out here?"

Engels was perturbed that Lindstrom had insisted on wrapping up all the loose ends, and so soon after her ordeal. He felt she should be home with her family and recuperating, not pushing herself like this. Lindstrom started to walk the cordon line, slowly. Realizing he didn't really have a choice, Engels fell in step next to her.

"I'm trying to figure out one thing that still doesn't make sense."

Engels looked at Lindstrom with a quizzical expression. "Really? One thing?"

"Pretty funny coming from someone that sat in front of a blank computer screen for an entire afternoon."

"If I would have known, Tish." Engels started to say, but she held up a hand and smiled.

"Sorry boss."

They continued to walk in silence, until Lindstrom stopped. She held out her hand, and Engels gave her a picture from the folder he was

478

carrying. She faced the smoldering debris and held up a picture of the front of the Visceral building, mimicking where the building had once stood. She looked behind her, and looked back at the building, and then behind her again.

"Care to enlighten me?"

"In a minute." Lindstrom looked at Engels. A silent acknowledgement hung in the air between them. She paused for a few moments, then added, "I know you don't like the way things turned out. I don't, either. But I think what we came up with will serve everyone's best interests."

"I know," Engels said, his voice low, afraid his words would travel, and their secret pact would be exposed.

The fire had been reported a few minutes after seven on Saturday night. Emergency crews were on the scene within fifteen minutes. It wasn't until almost ninety minutes later that two firemen found Lindstrom's body. She was transported to Sanford Hospital and didn't regain consciousness until after six on Sunday night. As fate would have it, Dr. Preston was her attending physician. Sunday became Monday, by which time Engels had called Lindstrom's sister, who drove an hour from her home in Sergeant Bluff, Iowa, to stay with the kids. Trevor and Ryan were driving back from their grandfather's farm on Monday afternoon when their aunt called and told Trevor to come to Sanford Hospital. Bree wouldn't be home from the cheerleading meet until the early evening, but Engels would have Officer Williams ready at the high school to bring Bree to her mother.

Monday became Tuesday, and finally, on Wednesday, Dr. Preston gave his permission to allow Lindstrom visitors that weren't immediate family. However, against the advice of Dr. Preston, Lindstrom checked herself out on Wednesday morning. "If I'm healthy enough for everybody, I'm healthy enough to walk out of here, doc." She promised to come back for check-ups on Thursday and Friday. Lindstrom spent the majority of Wednesday afternoon and almost the entire day Thursday working with Engels. Her memories were still foggy. Fortunately, she was able to recall the important pieces of her contact with Edward Kirkham. Once everything was put in place, they worked together to come up with viable solutions to the case.

After a private discussion with Nathan and Allison Devlin, they decided not to pursue criminal charges against Heidi Cole regarding her role in Nathan's abduction. The Devlin's wanted to move past it and work on repairing their family. Lindstrom refrained from discussing Visceral Medical or R.T.A.

Andy Cole was recovering from Heidi's attack. With their children present, Andy and Heidi agreed to go through family counseling. In lieu of criminal charges for Heidi, she reluctantly agreed to psychiatric help, as well as any medications or treatments that the doctors deemed necessary. Even though no formal charges were brought against Heidi, a case would be brought to family court. All facts of the case would remain under seal for a minimum of five years, or until the courts felt she was rehabilitated. If Heidi followed through on all counseling and treatments, the case would be expunged.

The destruction of the Visceral Medical Supplies building, as well as the apparent deaths of Edward and Veronica Kirkham, made an investigation virtually impossible. The bank that Edward Kirkham had established, First Federated United Trust, was no longer in active service. Engels made a quiet request of the American consulate in the Cayman Islands for any information regarding the bank and was told the post office box listed for the bank had been deactivated six months previously, and the physical address for the bank was actually an empty lot.

"There has to be a way to track down Kirkham's victims," Engels said to Lindstrom during their Thursday meeting.

"They are only victims if they are missed, Boss." She handed Engels a letter she received in the mail on Wednesday. No return address was listed on the envelope, and the postmark was local. Engels removed the letter and read it silently to himself.

Dear Trevor and Dear Bree,

I can't begin to apologize for all of the pain and suffering I have put the two of you and your mother through. I am not about to make excuses. I made terrible choices, and everyone around me shared the burden of my actions and inactions. I have had a lot of time to reflect, and it is time for me to make changes. One of those changes is the repayment of the financial debt I owe your mother and the two of you. I hope that the money will be put to good use.

However, I realize that money can't undo any of the bad things I have done. I have decided to re-focus my energies and goals and try to help others. Maybe, just maybe, my example can help others that have made terrible choices.

The two of you were my greatest gift to the world. Please, live good and enriching lives, not only for yourselves, but for the world and for the people around you. I ask only one thing. Please, don't try to find me. I don't deserve to be a part of your lives. My apology and my hopes for your futures are what's important.

Sincerely,

Your father

Engels re-read the letter several times before handing the letter back to Lindstrom.

"Edward Kirkham thought of everything, didn't he?"

Lindstrom nodded in agreement. "Without a doubt. He was able to kidnap countless men and women and kill them. Then, he harvested their organs and sold those organs to doctors who had patients that needed those organs. Finally, he gave the money to the families that those murdered men and women had abandoned. By sending a letter like this, it offered a measure of closure. And, if a family member ever reached out to R.T.A., asking for more money or for contact information, I'm sure they had a procedure in place to deal with it. No one says you're missing if you ask them not to look for you."

Other issues regarding the case were discussed between Lindstrom and Engels, too. There was no way to know what had happened at the now-destroyed Visceral Medical Supplies building. Edward Kirkham told the truth, that the taxes were fully paid on the building and land for another two years. When All Things Medical had partnered with the Kirkham's, they had purchased the land and building at the same time. There were many questions, though. Was it merely a transport site? Or could it have been the place where the "indebted individuals" had been brought, quite possibly from all areas of the country? Because Edward Kirkham had several vehicles at his disposal, including the black delivery vans and the ambulances, it was likely that the Visceral building had been used in multiple ways to carry out the Kirkham's operation.

Lindstrom and Engels also discussed calling other jurisdictions regarding any missing persons that owed child support. However, even if the investigation found a person that had been reported missing, and it was found that the person's family had received money from R.T.A., there would be no crime to arrest anyone for. The family that had received the money would not have known that the missing person was dead, as they would have been given a letter similar to what Lindstrom had received.

"What about these other supposed-extraction teams that Kirkham mentioned?", Engels had asked, even though he already knew the answer.

"Once again, chief," Lindstrom replied, "there's no crime to investigate. We have no witnesses, no one to come forward and say they were a part of the Kirkham's operation. We can't put out an advertisement for criminals, active or retired, that helped kidnap deadbeat parents." Lindstrom shook her head in frustration. "Edward was right. If he hadn't hired Charles Utecht, none of this would have ever come to light."

"How about medical technicians? Surely the Kirkham's couldn't have harvested multiple organs from these people without a trained surgical staff."

"It's a non-starter, chief. We have no one to look for, no fingerprints at the burning crime scene. Somehow, Edward Kirkham made it work. He kept his operation low-key and hush-hush."

Now, here they were, late on a Saturday morning, in front of the last tangible link to the case. Engels and Lindstrom had decided to spin the case as a disgruntled ex-employee, Charles Utecht, who had gone insane. He kidnapped Nathan Devlin in a bid to impress Olivia Sherman. When she spurned him, Utecht killed her, then left his friend, Ronald Vance, to twist in the wind. Lindstrom had tracked Utecht to his previous employer at Visceral and walked in on him attempting to cover up his murder of Edward and Veronica Kirkham. Utecht died in the fire. Of course, they never had Utecht's body to begin with, but Lindstrom doubted there was a body left to find. She figured that Utecht's organs were now implanted in people that needed them.

"Waste not, want not, I guess." The gallows humor from Engels provided a strange sense of levity to their examination of the facts of the case. Both Lindstrom and Engels despised the idea of a cover-up, but it was in everyone's best interest. With the Kirkhams dead and no other leads to explore, it was important to bring everything to a close and move on.

Engels asked Lindstrom, "Did you talk to Scott about the virus?"

"Yes, I did. It was frightening when Veronica told me what she planned to do if we didn't cooperate, even if it turned out to be a bluff."

482

Scott and the other IT guys did a complete system check of the police networks and computers, looking for any anomalies. As it turned out, the computer virus completely destroyed itself, leaving no trace of code behind. However, whoever designed the virus and had been monitoring the police computers had left behind a tracking report. The virus allowed for remote viewing and manipulation of tracking data. That was the reason why the tracking program didn't show the location of Lindstrom's car. The information was sent, but Veronica's program deleted it automatically. As for Engels' computer, it was never erased. Veronica had used another virus to conceal his computer from view, essentially installing a blank computer "mirage", so that it only appeared that Engels' computer had been erased. Finally, the tracking report listed five potentially vulnerable points in the police network and computer systems that could be easily exploited by hackers. Upon inspection, Scott and the IT department found and repaired those points.

"It was never the Kirkhams' plan to destroy the network," Lindstrom said. "Edward needed time to explain his motivations to me and attempt a peaceful surrender. Unfortunately, he never anticipated Veronica's reaction."

Once the computer virus had deleted itself, the tracer on her car had shown her car's location. However, since no one was actively looking for her at that moment, the car's location didn't display on the city map until the fire had been reported. Lindstrom knew that her car, along with the HealthStar ambulances and the black delivery vans, were buried underneath the smoldering rubble. She remembered that Edward Kirkham had said he never agreed to the use of the computer virus. If that was true, he must have guessed it would be safer to keep a close eye on Veronica. Maybe he had hired someone to check on Veronica's computer work? Perhaps the virus program was altered so it didn't work as Veronica wanted it to, or a fail-safe was built in, as an emergency precaution?

"How about the websites?", Lindstrom asked Engels. "Has Scott made any progress with them?"

"All three are offline," came Engels response. "R.T.A., Visceral Medical Supplies, and Support Broken Families are no longer active in any capacity, apparently. I watched Scott try to visit all three websites. For R.T.A., you are prompted to a blank webpage with an email address for the site's webmaster. If you try to send an email to that address, it is immediately sent back as non-deliverable. The Visceral website comes back with an error code. As for Supporting Broken Families, the webpage asks you to contact your local department of social services. Scott said he can monitor them for any kind of reactivation or change."

"I guess it won't hurt if Scott checks it out once a week," Lindstrom agreed. "I highly doubt that anything will come of it, though."

As for Scott, once word began to circulate regarding Lindstrom's captivity and escape, he sat in his office in the police station. After much soul-searching, he stopped the utility program that was comparing the hard drive from Andy Cole's laptop and the USB flash drive that he had used to copy the hard drive. He then removed the flash drive from its port, pried it apart with a screwdriver, and smashed the pieces with a hammer. Once he was satisfied that all of the pieces were destroyed, he took the remnants of the flash drive in his hand and walked around the police station. He started throwing the pieces in garbage cans all over the station. Although it wasn't eco-friendly, he even flushed some parts done a toilet in one of the restrooms. Once Lindstrom returned to work, Scott asked about the drive he had given her.

"It's in my lockbox, under the driver's seat of my car, which is under all that burning rubble." That made Scott happy. He apologized to Lindstrom for his reckless actions and vowed to never attempt a stupid stunt like that on another case, ever again. "I'm going to hold you to that," Lindstrom had replied with a smile, and that would be the end of that.

Engels continued to stand next to Lindstrom, while she continued to look at the surrounding area outside of the police cordon. He eyed the charred ruins of the building, wisps of smoke still rising from multiple points. He had asked the fire marshal to pull the blueprints for the building. It had been built in 1972, being used primarily by a rural equipment company to provide seed, fertilizer, and other agricultural supplies. When the business went bankrupt in 1984, the building sat vacant until the Kirkham's had purchased it. The building had been partially built into hill, which allowed for a parking garage and a shipping and receiving station on the other side of the building from the main entrance and atrium. Essentially, any vehicles could be parked inside the building. This allowed the building to look abandoned, which was the point. Lindstrom admitted to Engels that she had trespassed the front of the property on Friday afternoon. Because she approached from the front

484

of the building, her vantage point prevented her from seeing the full design of the building.

"On a somewhat related topic," Engels began, "I have also talked to the city's bean counters, as well as the police department's union representatives, regarding your insurance and restitution. There shouldn't be any issues when you decide on your new car. They did ask that you don't go nuts. In other words, no buying a Jag or a Porsche. Got it?"

Lindstrom laughed. Buying a new vehicle was the last thing on her mind. The only thing she regretted about losing her car was all of the minor details she had to deal with. A new driver's license, getting in touch with her bank and the few credit card companies she had accounts with to put holds on her accounts and order new cards, the little details that people take for granted. Most of all, she was going to miss her cellphone. True, all of her music and pictures were automatically saved in her Google Drive account. No, it was the phone itself. Trevor had purchased it for her, a birthday present from earlier in the year. Oh well, she thought to herself, it was better than being buried with the phone.

Lindstrom had stopped laughing, and was still surveying the area, looking at the picture of the Visceral building, the burned-out remnants lying on the ground in front of her, and then turning to examine the area behind her. Engels had no idea what she was looking at, or looking for, but he needed to finish discussing a few things.

"To answer your earlier question, the mayor and I worked everything out. I will stay on and assume the full title of Chief of Police."

"Good! Don't give up doing what you were born to do, what you are good at!"

"The mayor also agrees that the department needs to have a Chief of Detectives, though. We are going to have a job posting for it. I expect you to apply."

Lindstrom stopped what she was doing and looked at Engels in utter disbelief. "You want me to, wait, you can't be serious. Look, I'm only..."

Engels held up a hand and stopped her. "Tish, cut the crap. You are a good officer and a good detective. Everyone in the department thinks the world of you. And, after what you've been through, I think it would be easier on your family to step out of harm's way. The pay is better, and it's not like you wouldn't be working cases. You would be working ALL of the cases."

Lindstrom was floored by the suggestion of a promotion. "Look, I'm flattered, but I really think…"

"This is NOT a done deal, Tish. I expect you to APPLY for the position when it posts. Go through the interview process and see what happens. Understood?"

"Understood, boss." Lindstrom quickly changed the subject. "What did the fire marshal and the arson investigator say about this mess?"

"It's going to take weeks, maybe even months, to sift through everything. The fire was unlike anything either of them had ever seen. Look at it. Even a week later and thousands of gallons of water, it's still smoking. They have to tread lightly, otherwise the fire might reignite or another explosion could go off. On top of that, there is snow in the forecast next week. My guess is we won't be pulling out the Kirkham's bodies anytime soon. Assuming, of course, that the bodies weren't burnt to ash. And, if the inferno burned hot enough to completely incinerate the Kirkham's bodies, the chance of recovering any evidence of any kind is probably zero, too."

Lindstrom eyed the trails of vapor that continued to escape from rubble. Without looking at Engels, she asked, "Anything else on your mind?"

"You heard about Tisdale?"

"Yes." Lindstrom shook her head solemnly. "What a waste. He was a good cop and could have done a lot of good. Did he give any reason when he turned in his badge and gun?"

Engels replied, "He said that he felt betrayed. He rambled a bit, saying something like, if he couldn't protect a fellow officer, how could he serve and protect others. I tried to talk him out of it, but he didn't stay long enough. Badge, gun, his resignation, and some other forms he had already gotten from human resources, all on my desk. Less than five minutes in and out."

"Do you think it would be worth it to go and talk to him?"

"I doubt it. I would leave Tisdale be, at least for now. He needs some time to sort through his feelings. Who knows? Maybe he will change his mind and decide he can make a difference as a cop, after all. The last thing he said was, 'I need to find something that I know will make a difference'." He paused briefly, coughed lightly, and then added, "And speaking of making a difference, have you decided what you are going to do with your money?"

486

Lindstrom had been thinking about that a lot over the last several days.

"Honestly, Brad," Lindstrom started to say, which got Engels attention. She had always deferred to him as "boss" or "chief", even though they had become friends. To hear her say his first name meant that it was important. "I really don't know what to do. There are so many pros and cons, I just don't know."

"Tish, I remember you told Diane and I one time over dinner that you wished you could have gotten a life insurance policy taken out on your ex-husband. If you had that policy on him, and he would have died under most normal circumstances, you would have collected that money, and you wouldn't have given it a second thought. You have gone all these years not even thinking about him. Now he's truly out of the picture. And, as Edward Kirkham told you, he was able to unwittingly help ten other people, not counting you and the kids."

"So, what are you trying to tell me?"

"He owed you money, and now you have that money. Don't make any rash decisions. You never know what's going to happen tomorrow."

Lindstrom nodded, and then returned to her surveying. They had been out here for an hour, and Engels was still no closer to figuring out what she was up to. He wanted to wrap this up and get home to Diane. Growing restless, he decided to skip to the end.

"Tish, come on, why are you out here, instead of with your family? What are you looking for?"

Lindstrom looked from the building to the picture and to the area behind one more time. She looked at Engels and frowned.

"Where did the firemen find me?"

Engels opened the folder, flipped through some pages, and found their statements that had been typed. He pulled out the statement and read it aloud. "The unconscious female, later identified as police detective Patricia Lindstrom, was found approximately three hundred yards from the building while the firemen were securing the surrounding area, preventing any possible chance of the fire spreading to nearby vegetation." He stopped reading, and Lindstrom turned and walked a short distance, descending a small embankment. Engels followed her, nearly tripping on the slope. Lindstrom laid down in the grass on her stomach, and looked up at Engels, motioning him to join her. He had an infuriated look but decided to humor her and got on the ground, too.

"Alright, now what?"

"I remember hearing the last few explosions as I was running, and the shockwave threw me forward. I hit my head, but I remember crawling up this ditch. I tried to look at the building, but the heat from the fire was too much. The last I remember is starting to black out and rolling down this little hill."

"Okay, so what am I missing?"

"So, stand up and look at the building."

Engels did as he was told. "Well, it's still burned down, in case you were wondering."

"Cute, boss, but that's not the problem. How far away is the building?"

"I'd guess maybe eighty to one hundred yards, give or take a..." His words trailed off. Engels looked at the ground, and slowly moved his gaze from where he was standing to the building. It wasn't a full football field away, but it was close enough. He looked down at Lindstrom, who was now staring at the area behind her.

"If I blacked out here," Lindstrom said, and then pointed off into the distance, "how did I get another two hundred yards out there?"

FORTY-ONE

The motorhome was brand new, having been purchased two weeks ago. It was top of the line, with all the fancy amenities, like big screen televisions, multiple bathrooms and bedrooms, integrated entertainment systems, mobile WIFI hotspot, plus more. Of course, the buyer would expect nothing less, considering that it cost well over seven hundred-fifty thousand dollars. Not bad for three quarters of a million. More importantly, though, everything of necessity was packed and ready to go.

The old man sat at the U-bench dinette, located behind the passenger seat. He read that day's newspaper, skimming through various articles. The headline, about a fire at a local medical warehouse a week ago, didn't interest him. He sipped his special blend of tea, casually waiting and biding his time until his traveling companion arrived. As if on cue, the passenger door opened, and a tall, physically fit woman climbed in. The morning light gently reflected off the minor highlights she had added to her recently cut hair. She decided to forego her customary contacts, at least for the time being. In their place, a new set of contacts, changing her eyes from their original pale blue to a soft brown. A newly purchased pair of designer sunglasses rested atop her head.

"Is everything set?", the old man asked of his female compatriot.

"Almost."

The old man expressed trepidation. "Are you sure about this?"

The woman looked the old man in his icy eyes and replied. "Look, we both admit that we made a colossal mistake with our last team leader. If we are going to be successful going forward, I think it is necessary to bring someone into our level. It is worth the risk. Besides," she paused briefly, a look of sorrow coming across her face, "you might not be around for much longer."

The old man stood up, holding out his arms. She walked to him, and they embraced. Even though she was a few inches taller than him, he gently patted the back of her head.

"You may be right," he said. He pulled away, cupped her head in his hands, pulling her down so he could kiss her lightly on the forehead. He let her go and sat back down, turning his attention to the paper once again.

"Are you sure about the letter and the thank you, though?" It was now her turn to express her own misgivings.

He looked at her with rock solid determination. "I am trusting you with a new course of action for us, so you need to trust me. Believe me, it is for the best."

"You know, sometimes I think you are too brilliant to be involved in all this. There are so many more people you could be helping."

"Now, now, we've been over this before. I may be brilliant, but I refuse to be tied down by bureaucracy, rules, and medical and government oversight. Think of all the people we've helped in the past, and how many more people out there we are going to help in the future."

They both smiled. She started to turn towards the cupboard to get a glass when there was a knock on the motorhome's metal door. She walked back, bent down, and opened the door. She stepped back, and a young man, medium height and good build, walked into the motorhome.

"Hi, sweetheart!"

She wasn't known for outright displays of affection, but she put an arm lightly around his shoulder and gave him a quick kiss on the cheek. Their relationship had progressed slowly, at her request, and that organic patience had been rewarding for both of them. Physical love would happen, in time. For now, patience was of the utmost importance.

The young man smiled at the kiss, and then looked at the old man. He stepped forward, holding out his hand. The old man stood up, looked him up and down and, smiling with approval, took the young man's hand in his and shook it.

The young man spoke first. "It is an honor to finally meet you."

The old man let go of the young man's hand and waved away the words. "Please, Paul, let's have none of that. First of all, I was beginning to think my daughter would never find love. Having said that, please, don't hurt either of us." He sat back down, motioning for the young man to do the same, which he did.

"Secondly, my daughter and I planned our exit very carefully. Unfortunately, when dealing with high explosives, dangerous chemicals, and a rather dramatic production, you have to account for errors. I think the bumps and bruises that were taken helped add to the overall believability of the entire fabrication. Therefore, I would like to commend you on making sure the dear detective was removed to a safe distance.

"Finally, do not refer to us by our old names. My daughter and I have changed identities many times over the last twenty years. In fact, we established the majority of our aliases and falsehoods at the beginning of our mission all those years ago. It makes it much easier to switch from one to another, especially in this day and age." The old man looked at his traveling companions. "Shall we proceed, then?"

"Absolutely, sir," the young man replied.

"Off we go!" The woman stepped down into the driver's well, buckling herself into the seat. She started the engine and made minor adjustments to the seat and mirrors.

"Excellent!" The old man clapped his hands together, rubbing them vigorously. The woman put the vehicle in gear, slowly moving the vehicle onto the road and merging into traffic. Both men settled into their seats at the table.

"Now that we have begun our journey," the old man said, sliding a large manila file folder, at least two inches thick with papers, across the table, "we will discuss building a new team."

"Yes sir," the young man replied, enthusiasm on his face and in his voice. "I'm sure we have a lot of ground to cover and a lot of training to get started."

The old man grinned, delighted with the young man's response. He then slid a large manila envelope across the table. The young man, not sure what to do, took the envelope and opened, peering at the contents inside.

"I don't understand."

Nodding reassuringly, the old man pointed at the envelope. "Today is a new day, a new beginning. Inside that envelope is a fresh start for all three of us." The young man opened the envelope, gently removing the contents and laying them out on the table. As he glanced at the items, the young man's face turned from confusion to comprehension, as a knowing smile formed at the corner of his mouth. The old man continued to speak.

"As such, we need to put the past to rest. From this moment on, we will never again speak the names Edward, Veronica, Kirkham, or Paul Tisdale. Understood?"

EPILOGUE

Lindstrom was standing in the car lot, letting the saleswoman talk to Trevor about gas mileage, tires, and warranties. Bree had been annoyed that they had stopped at the dealership. That is, until her mother had suggested that Bree could maybe, possibly, look for a vehicle, too, as long as she stayed under eight thousand dollars. So, Bree had wandered off, asking Ryan to come along with her and give his opinion.

As she stood there, watching her children, she thought about the past three weeks. Lindstrom's body would heal in time, as would her mind and her soul. She had a lot of thoughts and emotions to process. Of course, the important thing was that she was still alive to process them. She had become a police officer to help others, the way that others had helped her. However, she couldn't deny that the world was changing, and not necessarily for the better. Engels was right, though. She had a family to consider and being the Chief of Detectives would allow her to continue her work while making sure she would still come home in one piece every night.

The sounds of Bree and Ryan laughing with another saleswoman brought a huge smile to Lindstrom's face. She looked at Trevor, and he was smiling also, sitting in the driver's seat of the pickup that he had found on the dealer's website. She thought back to Thursday night, only a few days ago. She had sat down with Trevor and Bree while Ryan played in the backyard with some of the neighbor kids. She had let her children read the "letter from her ex-husband". Being teenagers, they were mostly aloof about the whole thing. Bree had no real recollection of her biological father, and had given her mother a "well, whatever" response, before she asked if she could go back to her room. Trevor had lingered, though, and asked what the letter was supposed to mean.

"I guess," Lindstrom had said, "it means you can move forward with your life, or it means you can choose to accept his apology and honor his wishes and hopes for you." Trevor had thought about it, then stood up and gave his mother a rare hug and kiss, told her he loved her, and went back to his room.

Lindstrom's cell phone rang, and she quickly fumbled for it. She had asked her cell phone provider to try and locate her old cell phone's signal. Unfortunately, the network didn't show any active signal. If her hunch was correct, that phone, the one Trevor had given to her only seven months ago, was probably melted and buried in the bowels of the Visceral building. After parting ways with Engels yesterday and joining her family at the aquatic center, she decided to splurge, taking the kids out to get new cell phones, too. She looked at her new cell phone in her hand. She hadn't yet figured out all of the new settings and apps, and the ringtone was annoying. Fortunately, since her old cell had been linked to cloud storage, Lindstrom was able to keep her old number, and all of her contacts had transferred in to the new phone. "That's why it's a good idea to back-up your phone," the associate had said.

Lindstrom looked at the caller ID and registered a small amount of shock. What the hell was Cassie Butler doing calling her? She swiped the screen to accept the call.

"Detective Lindstrom."

"Hi detective! It's me, Cassie Butler!"

"Hi Cassie. What can I do for you?"

"Actually, this is a little bit weird, but I have a letter for you."

"Oh?" Lindstrom looked around, making sure she could still see her children. "Well, you have me curious. How did you get a letter for me?"

"Well, I'd rather tell you in person when I give you the letter. I stopped by the police station, but a Heather Gordon said it would be okay to call you."

"Are you still at the station?"

"I'm getting into my car. Why?"

"My family and I are at the Billion's car lot, at the corner of 41st and

494

Minnesota. If it's alright with you, why don't you stop over and meet me?"

"No problem!" Cassie Butler ended the call. A few minutes later, Cassie pulled into the car lot and parked next to where Lindstrom was standing by her rental car.

As Cassie got out with an envelope in her hand, Lindstrom said, "Cassie, good to see you!" Cassie smiled, but then looked concerned when she saw some of the cuts on Lindstrom's arms and the bruise on her forehead.

"Wow! Are you alright? I mean, seriously!"

"I'm fine, Cassie, just fine. Feeling better every day." She had no desire to break into the story of her dealings with the Kirkham's, Cassie's former employers. Lindstrom quickly asked, "Now, what's the story with this letter?"

"Well, like I said it's a bit weird." Cassie was holding the envelope, as if she was afraid to give it to Lindstrom. "Last Saturday morning, I was about to leave for the gym when there was a knock on my door. It was Mr. Kirkham. You know, Edward Kirkham? The man who…"

Hearing Kirkham's name shocked Lindstrom, and she held up her hand to stop Cassie. "Yes, I know who he is. Go on, please."

"Well, anyway, he asked me for a favor. He had this envelope in his hands," Cassie held up the envelope, "and asked if I would give it to you. But, he only wanted me to give it to you if neither he or his daughter, Veronica, had talked to me within a week's time. I asked him if everything was okay, and he said it was, but he wanted to make sure you got this letter." Cassie put out her hand, and Lindstrom looked at the envelope warily, before slowly taking it.

"That's it? He didn't say anything else?" Lindstrom didn't really know how to react to this.

"Nope, that was it. He wished me the best with my termination package, encouraged me to use my gifts wisely, and then left. I don't get the paper or watch the news, and I was going to wait until tomorrow, to see if he called, but then I heard about the Visceral building and, well, you know."

"I understand. Thank you so much, Cassie, and do what the man said, okay?"

"Oh, I am, detective! I'm already enrolled in classes for next semester!" Cassie was all smiles now.

"Good for you! I'm going to get back to my kids, so you take care of yourself." Lindstrom put out her hand to shake Cassie's, but Cassie stepped through it and hugged Lindstrom instead. Surprised, she returned the hug, and Cassie got back into her car and drove away.

Lindstrom stood there, looking at the envelope. Good grief, she thought, even from the grave the old man was still in her life. Well, no time like the present. She gently opened the envelope, took out the letter, and read it silently.

My dear Detective Lindstrom, if you are reading this, then, unfortunately, my plan did not work out and I am dead. I have never asked nor cared for acceptance or understanding, but, for you, I am willing to make an exception. I have not yet met you face to face, and we have not yet engaged in conversation.

However, I feel it is necessary for you to know that, no matter what happened between us, no matter how you view me in this world, no matter what you think of my life's work, it really does matter. You strike me as an incredible soul. You have done many things to affect positive change in this world. I admire and commend you for that. It is my sincerest hope and wish that you will continue to affect positive change. Continue to raise and teach your wonderful children to do the same.

Fondest regards,

E.K.

P.S. As I have left this world, I hope I can bestow one final gift upon you and your family.

Lindstrom looked up, eyeing her children, and then turned around, her gaze trying to see if anyone was watching her. She read the letter again, and then a third time. Like everything else, Edward Kirkham had tried to plan everything down to the smallest detail. However, he must have sensed that Veronica would turn on him. If so, this letter was his final way of asking Lindstrom not to judge him. Or maybe it was his final way of...you know what, she thought to herself, what does it matter? He's dead, I'm alive, and I'm happy with my children.

She glanced at the letter one more time, frowning ever so slightly. But what was the "one final gift"? Lindstrom wondered what it could be. Maybe, she had already received it? Had Edward Kirkham made sure someone was monitoring what was going on at the Visceral building that night? She thought about what Engels had asked the previous day, wondering if the Kirkham's had any other staff to assist with medical procedures, transport, or any variety of duties. When things went bad, did Edward instruct this unknown person to make sure she was removed from danger? If so, had this person moved her the extra two hundred yards, making sure she was safe from the fire, and would be easily discovered? If that was the case, should she try and track down this unknown person? But, what good would that do?

To his credit, Engels had played devil's advocate regarding Lindstrom's mysterious movement of two hundred yards. One wouldn't know it to look at him, or at his office in the police station, or even in his home, but Engels was a big sports fan. Football, baseball, basketball, the Olympics, boxing, mixed martial arts, even professional wrestling, there was something about the competition and the athleticism that appealed to Engels. As he had told a new officer several years ago in front of Lindstrom, "I don't have a favorite team or favorite players. I enjoy the games."

As Engels and Lindstrom had walked from the shallow ditch in front of the Visceral building where she could recall her last memory, to the spot nearly two hundred yards away where the two firemen had found her, he had started reciting story after story about various professional athletes that suffered concussions and brain injuries during games. Many of these individuals would claim that they couldn't remember small parts or even large segments of plays and games they had participated in. Most of these tended to be in more violent sports, like football, MMA, boxing, and wrestling, but his point seemed valid. Lindstrom may not remember crawling or walking to where she was discovered, yet that didn't mean it didn't happen. It was easier to accept that, in a situation where she had suffered a concussion, she had amnesia, or some other form of concussion-induced short-term memory loss, instead of wondering if there were underlings lying in wait to lend assistance.

Which one was it? In the end, it didn't matter. There were no leads to pursue, no evidence to examine from the Visceral building. Somehow, Lindstrom had made it an additional two hundred yards to relative safety.

She was starting to get a mild headache from thinking about her experience, trying to replay the events in her mind, when large gaps covered up the whole picture.

Lindstrom closed her eyes and shook her head. Seriously, she thought to herself, it's over. It's got to be over, right? She had joined up with her family after her time with Engels at the Visceral building the previous day, and they had a blast. Lindstrom had even convinced her sister that she could handle things, and her sister had left after a late lunch. She was planning on posting for the Chief of Detectives job the next day, first thing when she got to her desk Monday morning. In the meantime, she wanted to come up with something fun for the whole family to do on Sunday. She sure as hell didn't want to think about Edward Kirkham, Visceral, or anything else related to the case. She eyed her kids again. Trevor was now standing on the truck's back bumper, bouncing up and down, checking its suspension and shocks. Bree and Ryan looked like they were driving while trying to avoid the paparazzi. Or maybe they were driving away from aliens. You never could tell with Ryan's imagination and Bree's flair for the dramatic.

That annoying ringtone startled her again. Lindstrom fumbled again for her phone. First thing when they got home, no, first thing when they got back into the rental car, she was going to have Trevor change the damn ringtone! She looked at the caller ID. First Cassie Butler, now why was Kara Reed calling her? She considered letting the voicemail take it. No, she thought to herself. The idea is to move forward, with a positive attitude. Accept the call, so you can focus on whatever happens for the rest of the day and night. She swiped her phone active.

"Detective Lindstrom."

"Tish, it's Kara Reed. Um, yeah, I know you've been through a lot, with what's been on the news and stuff, but something's happened."

Lindstrom stood there, listening to Kara Reed's voice. As Kara continued to talk, Lindstrom's legs grew weaker. Before she knew it, Lindstrom was kneeling on the ground.

"Trevor, Bree, Ryan!" She called their names, but they hadn't heard. "TREVOR! BREE! RYAN!" She called again, louder, with more urgency.

Trevor heard his mother shout his name, and from his vantage point on the back of the truck, he saw she was on the ground. Afraid something

498

bad had happened, he jumped down and yelled at the saleswoman, "Go get my sister and brother, now!!" Trevor ran to his mother's side and squatted down next to her, putting a hand on her shoulder. "Mom, what's wrong?"

"MOMMA!" Ryan yelled, running up to Lindstrom. "What happened?"

Bree, not known for her concern, looked scared but didn't say anything.

Lindstrom remained motionless, as both saleswomen were now standing by them. "Ma'am, are you alright?", the older of the two saleswomen asked. "Do you need medical attention?"

The younger saleswoman was digging for her cell phone. "Should I call an ambulance?"

She looked at Trevor and said to her oldest son, "Get everyone in the car. You're driving. We have to go, now." Trevor did as he was told, putting his mother in the backseat. Ryan climbed into the back and buckled his seatbelt, but he laid down across the seat, his head resting on his mother's leg while he held onto her right thigh.

Once everyone was in the rental car and buckled, Trevor started the engine and looked back at his mother.

"Mom, what's wrong? Where are we going?"

Lindstrom, an expression of absolute shock on her face, started to cry. Tears streamed from her eyes, flowing down her cheek. She gently caressed Ryan's head. Bree had turned around in her seat, too, and the look of concern had changed to one of fright.

"Mom? Please, what's happened?" Bree was begging to hear her mother speak.

Lindstrom, through her tears, reached out with her other hand and squeezed Bree's shoulder, and then patted Trevor on his elbow.

"Drive us to the hospice center."

Trevor's eyes went wide. He stared at his mother. Her tears were still coming, but the look on her face morphed into one of sheer joy.

"It's Mark," Lindstrom said to everyone. "It's your father! Ryan, it's your Daddy! He's awake!"

ACKNOWLEDGEMENTS

For the record, there are always many people involved in the creation of a book, both directly and indirectly. To try to narrow the list down to a bite-size list is a herculean task, especially when the author wishes to be thoughtful, authentic, magnanimous, and, above all, concise. Having said that, if I left you out, it is not a slight against you. This list is in no particular order, as I am not trying to make a countdown or "best of" list. Therefore, I would like to take this opportunity to thank some of the people that made this book possible.

To my parents, whom I miss every day. You started me on this path, and I thank you for that.

To my sister. We've had our ups and downs, but you are still my sister and I love you.

To my uncle, for giving me my first exposure to the arts and literature.

To Toby, my best friend. 'Nuff said!

To Matt, a good friend and excellent photographer, who designed the cover of this novel.

To Eric, a good friend and lover of books, who wasn't afraid to read my book and hurt my feelings.

To Derek, a good friend, who helped introduce me to the South

Dakota Writes community.

To Jason, founder of South Dakota Writes, who helped give me advice and direction.

To Sion, my editor, whose helpful words and honest critiques were very much appreciated.

To Jenny, a former co-worker and fellow author, for your insight and support.

To the men and women of the Brandon Police Department and the Sioux Falls Police Department, for your help and advice.

To Steve Roach, Jean Michel Jarre, Mars Lasar, Joe Satriani, and Tangerine Dream. You didn't know it, but your music gave me focus and clarity during the writing process.

To family and friends, for your support and questions.

To my co-workers, the Lunch Lady posse. You make every day at work an adventure, and that is said with heartfelt admiration.

To my high school English, creative writing, and drama teachers, for continually guiding and challenging me.

DISCLAIMERS

This book is a work of fiction. The characters and events portrayed in this book are fictitious; however, many of the locations are real. I have tried to be as authentic as possible when it comes to the locales of the cities of Sioux Falls and Brandon, South Dakota. However, for reasons involving story structure or dramatic effect, certain areas have been embellished or adjusted to enhance the overall experience.

When I first conceived of the premise of this book, during my original research phase, I was awestruck with some of the raw statistical data I found. The numbers are based on reports that were published in 2013. As such, I have massaged the numbers to reflect a number that, I feel, closely resembles what those numbers would have been in 2016, when the events of this book take place. While the numbers may not be entirely accurate in a book of fiction, the data is incredibly close.

As a reader, it is vital to understand the difference between fact and fiction, between inspiration and reality, between truth and falsehoods. The most difficult struggle I had in writing this book was portraying my characters, without betraying the locations and surroundings. The real surroundings, like Sandford Health, Avera Health, the Sioux Falls Police Department, Lewis Drug, Billion

Auto, the Washington Pavilion, etc., all exist in the daily lives of many, many individuals. The actions and inactions of my characters could easily take place in fictional hospitals, fictional police departments, fictional stores, etc., in other cities.

What this means is that there should be no judgement made against these locations and organizations. Once again, this is a work of fiction. The hardworking women and men of these organizations should never be judged by what one humble author cooked up inside of his imagination.

AUTHOR BIO

In an alternate timeline in a parallel universe, Daniel Van Deest rose to power by unifying thousands of warring planetoid factions into one Galactic Amalgamation. While the peace and prosperity he helped foster lasted for a thousand millennium, Daniel was always humble, always refusing statues and tributes. Rather, he wanted the populace to better each other and themselves.

Meanwhile, in our current timeline in our universe, Daniel lives with his wife and children. If you bump into him on the street and want to chat, start talking to him about the NFL or fantasy football.

26902592R10309

Made in the USA
Columbia, SC
20 September 2018